SERIES 1 · THE · BOOKS 4-6

DARKSLAYER

SPECIAL EDITION

Danger and the Druid
Outrage in the Outlands
Chaos at the Castle

CRAIG HALLORAN

THE DARKSLAYER
Special Edtion Series 1 Books 4-6
By Craig Halloran

Copyright © 2016 by Craig Halloran
Print Edition

TWO-TEN BOOK PRESS
P.O. Box 4215, Charleston, WV 25364

ISBN eBook: 978-1-941-208-87-8
ISBN Paperback: 978-1-941-208-88-5

THE DARKSLAYER is a registered trademark, #77670850
http://www.thedarkslayer.net

Cover by EamonArt.com
Map By Gillis Bjork

THE DARKSLAYER: Danger and the Druid Copyright © 2013 by Craig Halloran
THE DARKSLAYER: Outrage in the Outlands Copyright © 2013 by Craig Halloran
THE DARKSLAYER: Chaos at the Castle Copyright © 2013 by Craig Halloran

Publisher's Note
This book is a work of fiction. Names, characters, places, and incidents either are the product of the author's imagination or are used fictitiously, and any resemblance to actual persons, living or dead, events, or locales is entirely coincidental.

THE WORLD OF BISH
KEY LOCATION GUIDE

Hohm City

City of Three

The Mist

Hohm Marsh

Dwarven Hole

City of Bone

Red Clay Forest

The Warfield

Great Forest
of Bish

Two-Ten City

Nameless Mountains

Outpost
Thirty-One

Outlaw's Hide

Caves
of the
Underland

Lush Lakes

Outer Outlands

The Mist

N
W E
S

TABLE OF CONTENTS

SERIES 1 • THE • BOOK 4

DARKSLAYER

· FIGHT OR DIE ·

Danger and the Druid

CRAIG HALLORAN

Chapter 1

Venir's fingers ached with every step. The imp had left his mark, a painful one at that. Despite the healing provided by the armament during his battle with the giant, the remaining stubs below his missing fingertips were misshapen and dark, like the wounds he suffered at the hands of the Vicious he battled at the Warfield. Those memories seemed like a lifetime ago, a hundred years. He thought of Georgio, the boy who could heal from such things. He hoped the boy was safe.

He sat down at the edge of the river, facing forward, or at least where he thought was forward. He dipped his blackened fingers in the cool water while he stared across the expanse. There was little to note: blue-gray water as far as the eye could see and a rolling fog floating over the top of the waters. The view across the river was much better than that he was surrounded by: Mist. It surrounded him just like before. His wet hand was shaking as he rubbed his face.

"Bone."

How much farther did he have to go to get back to Bish? The farther he walked, the more time escaped from him. Doubt assailed his mind. Boon the Wizard had told him how much the giants lied, tricking men as men tricked them. Had the giant lied, leading him down a path of death through starvation or exhaustion? He scooped up a mouthful of water, catching a glimpse of himself. His face was haggard, his hair wild and his beard almost reached his chest. He punched his fist into the water and spit.

"What manner of madness is this?"

WHUMP! WHUMP! WHUMP! SNORT!

Every fiber of his body stiffened. The sound had been ongoing since he followed himself into the mist. The image of the black dragon invaded his mind. He pictured rows of giant razor sharp teeth outlining a gaping red maw with an orange furnace burning down its throat. His entire body began to warm as the battle heat spread out to every fiber of hair. He reached over, clutching his leather sack, and craned his neck. Nothing. He sat, the sound of his labored breath filling his ears as he cupped his battered hand behind one ear. He remained still for another hour or minute, he did not know. The flapping of wings had been coming and going. Bedeviling. He remembered fangs as big as his forearm and fire as hot as anything he'd known. He splashed more water on his face. Sometimes it sounded like one massive beast, other times one hundred. The sounds came and faded, leaving him to wonder if they were real or just more tricks of his imagination.

"Come and get me then!" He reached into the sack and withdrew Brool. The axe was warm in his grip, tingling what remained of his fingers, taking the bite from the mangled flesh. He rose back to his feet. "We got to get out of here." He could have sworn the axe replied … *Indeed*.

Again, like so many times before, he donned his helm and shield and walked, one foot splashing on the edge of the water, the other on the soft bar of sand. The helm did little to amplify the sounds of the waters, and his vision was just as obscured as before by a field of feathery cotton that remained in his path, never ending. Venir had walked another mile or two when he began to stomp and rave. Madness was creeping into his thoughts, mixed with festering anger, frustration and rage. He swung and screamed, growled and howled. Not even an echo greeted him.

Onward, forward, unrelenting he walked, jogged and ran. His legs were heavy, and his weakening body begged for rest, sleep. He lay down with his legs in the water, and in a moment he was dreaming of walking along the endless river in the mist.

He snored.

SNORT!

He jerked up, wiping his nose, just as exhausted and weary as before. *Was that me?* The sounds of dragons came again. He replaced the armament into the sack, only to don it again and again. His mutterings and ramblings became more frequent as he conversed with the living and the dead. He laughed, cried, sobbed, lied, thirsted, drifted and starved. Yet somehow he was sustained.

"HELP ME!" he begged and pleaded.

"FIGHT ME!" he raged.

"KILL ME!" he dared.

None replied.

The water that sustained him never quenched his thirst, and the tiny minnows did not fill him. *Kam?* Who was she? *Bone?* Where was he? Venir was losing. Bish's ultimate survivor was being whittled away by forces he could not smell, touch or see. A fighter through and through, Venir moved on without day, night or hope, only instinct. His aching legs carried him on, step by step, mile after mile, league after league.

Plop.

He stopped, head whipping around. His mind muttered. *What was that?* Nothing. He grumbled and continued on.

Plop.

"Huh …" Venir clutched at the stringy hairs in his beard. The sound was nothing like anything he'd experienced before in the Mist, foreign to his mind and senses.

Plop.

Whatever it was, it was ahead of him. A vision formed in his mind of a smooth stone being dropped from a pier into a lake, and then the vision became a drop of rain water dripping from a rooftop into a puddle of mud. Something was going on in the Mist somewhere; it had to be. The tricks his mind had been playing on him were getting old, and his maddening visions must come to an end. *Move or die.* Someone had told him that once.

Plop.

The sound might as well have been a war-hammer smiting him in the ear as the clarity bore into his brain, screaming, maybe warning him that something was out there. He leaned forward, creeping alongside the wet bank, his foot no longer splashing in the water, angling for the next sound. Another twenty steps … *plop* … thirty steps … *plop* … ten steps … *plop plop* … his heart raced … five steps … fifteen steps … thirty steps … nothing. A hundred steps more he counted … nothing. Had he missed it or passed it? He did not know. He punched himself in the head and fell to his knees. He punched himself again and rushed into the river.

"This is hopeless!" He screamed at the top of his lungs.

Venir's feeble mind was breaking. He clutched the sack inside filthy and once powerful hands. He had once been a cunning and crafty warrior so long ago, before the sack. The armament within changed his life forever. The power within changed him, hardened him like stone, not so much as a man but as a minion, a killing machine, a menace to evil. He didn't ask for it, but he had it and hungered for it. He exacted vengeance with it a thousand times, but his hunger was never satisfied.

Underlings. There was a time in his life when for every ten he killed he wanted to kill a hundred more. That fire and fury was no longer there. All purpose was gone.

Plop.

He turned back towards the bank. Venir swore the sound was only thirty feet away in the mist.

Plop.

Head down, he dragged his dripping wet body onto the bank, hauling the sack out of the water behind him. The plopping sound was steady now, so close he felt like he could touch it. There had to be something, anything out there making that noise. He had to find its source. He left the river on foot, the giant's words still lingering in his mind. *Follow the river.* He had done that. The giant must have lied to him, and there must be another way out.

Plop.

The river was his only friend and ally, and he had left it. He looked back one last time, watching its silent waters flow, realizing he would never see it again. He realized something else: he hated the giants.

Plop.

Without fear or hope he wandered back into the mist.

CHAPTER 2

I T WAS PITCH BLACK BEHIND Castle Almen. A delivery depot stood in the view of a shadow pressed into the gloom. A glimmer of pale moonlight reflected in a puddle in the cobblestoned road a few feet beyond Detective Melegal's nose with drizzling rain shimmering the image. For months, on and off, he had crouched in this very spot, alert to the comings and goings of the castle. At his back was the encompassing wall of the City of Bone, nearly five stories high, a monolith of rock, imprisonment and safe-haven.

His mind gave an inward sigh as his skinny knees began to ache. More than thirty yards ahead of him, a secured wagon rumbled over the road, making its way downward into the dock below the castle. He saw hapless faces, small and dark, pressed against the bars of the windows: urchins, some with talent, others without, all scraped off the streets to serve the unforgiving Royals. His heart didn't skip a beat at the thought of what awaited them, knowing full well he had little more advantage than them. He now—the mighty Detective of the Royal Almens— was little more than a slave himself.

He rubbed his knee. *I'm not old enough to ache.* Yet he did. The memory of himself as an urchin—kneeling in silence, hour after hour, inside the castle, either holding a goblet of wine or a candlestick during another one of their pompous and overbearing ceremonies—swelled the anger within him. The fate of those children would be no worse or no less, but he no longer cared. Without him realizing it, every ounce of compassion had been almost entirely driven from him by none other than Lord Almen, complimented by his Lorda.

A pair of rats crept over his toes where he hunched inside a nook within the city's giant wall. Each sniffed the cuff on his pants. *Looking for a crumb, are we?* Melegal's steely gaze scanned the backside of the castle's reinforcements, noting three heavily armed sentries with halberds dragging in the urchins while another half dozen stood watching from a stone balcony, wearing steel helmets and clutching small crossbows to their chests. All eyes were on the wagon when he made his move.

Jab. Jab.

Two dead rats were skewered on the end of his razor thin dagger's blade. A thin smile formed on his tight lips as he slipped up into a standing position along the way. *I still got it.* Indeed he did. There was little room for error working for Lord Almen, and his training—something forced upon himself, by himself—came from fear and necessity. He studied the two rodents for a moment before flicking them away. *The Rat.* His deceased mentor McKnight had called him that, many times. The image of McKnight's face was permanently etched in his mind when he drove his double hilted dagger in one side and out the other. He had figured life would get much easier in Bone for him after that, but it had only become more complicated. Vastly so.

He stood in the solitude of the drizzling rain, careful to look away from the castle lantern's glow, pondering his demanding charges. Lord Almen wanted results every week when it came to tracking down the Slergs and any others that crossed his path. Every week, death and torture had been led by Melegal's hand. He'd never had much taste for blood, considering it nothing more than leaky filth that would stain your garments. Now, drawing it had become routine and numbing.

Results. Results. Results! Lord Almen demanded them, and the tall powerful man would have them. Not in all of his life had Melegal been intimidated by another man, but Lord Almen had managed to shake his core.

As the wagon disappeared beneath the castle, another one emerged, driven by a slouched over silhouette of a single man, drawn by a single work horse, filled with barrels, crates, sacks and other misshapen things. No sentries escorted them out. *Same time every week.* Melegal craned his neck. He could hear the murmured greetings of the sentries on the upper balconies changing shift with their fellow guardsmen. This was what he had been waiting for. *Tonight's the night.* He tucked his dagger away as he pulled his cloak tighter around him and slipped along the shadows of the wall.

The wagon, unlike many this time of night, did not have the glow of a lantern on its backside. The sound of the hard wheels rolling and the drizzling rain comforted Melegal on his trek through the darkness. The driver led the wagon another fifty yards past the lower wall courtyard and into a wide alley that ran between the walls of Castle Almen and Castle Kling.

The area between the two was vast, large enough for three wagons, but not heavily guarded. It was unlikely that any rogue or rebel would attempt to traverse into the private outer corridors of the castles. Many heads had been spiked, and many necks had been stretched for even the mildest of trespasses. And the last city-wide rebellion had resulted in live bodies being catapulted, on fire, over the walls. Melegal was still a boy when he witnessed that. He remembered it being one of those rare moments when he and his fellow urchins were laughing. The lashings were worth it for some sick reason that day.

His fingertips were tingling. He watched and waited for his chance to dart from the wall and into the alley. If the Kling or Almen sentries saw him, crossbow bolts would pin him like a cushion. As his keen eyes scanned the ledges of the upper balconies, his keen ears listened for any artillery sounds. The wagon was rolling deeper into the alley, loud and lonely in the night. Usually a head or two would peek out from above. Melegal waited as the wagon disappeared from his sight. *Move.*

His black shadow dashed over the cobblestones, through the moonlight and into the alley. He waited for his heart to stop pounding in his ears and then moved on. It was another fifty yards to the end of the alley, where the wagon had stopped. Before Melegal caught up, it had lurched forward again. From the darkness he watched as the sentries, one from the Klings and another from the Almens, exchanged words before returning to their posts. The lanterns on the guard shacks and on the main street offered ample light to the corridor. No chance he'd slip by unnoticed there. He had to move quicker. He focused as he crept to the end of the alley and peered around the corner.

Look up. Look up. Look up.

His mind illuminated, and his hair tingled. He slipped behind the Kling guard shack stationed on the corner of the castle wall and rounded to the other side. The sentry was staring straight into the sky as he spun around slowly on his heels. *Perfect.* The wagon with its cargo was heading into the bowels of the upper city districts, passing underneath the colorful district banners that sagged down towards the ground. It wasn't the only traffic, either. The roads, though not as busy as daytime, still thrived with workers and commerce. Melegal walked backward into the road looking upward, and it wasn't long before he, the sentries and small passing groups of people were doing the same. *Fools and followers.*

"Heh-heh …" he said, rubbing his cap, before turning back after the wagon.

Block after block, turn after turn, he kept his eyes glued on the wagon. A full hour must have passed before it stopped. Something was moving. Melegal crouched along the wall. *Yes. Finally.*

Tonight is the night. The silhouette of a robed man emerged from under a heavy canvas. The person rolled off the back and fell onto the street as the wagon rolled forward. *Hah.* Melegal smiled as the figure rose to its feet with a groan and rambled forward. He followed, closing in on the lumbering figure block after block, turn after turn. The smell of fish oil wafted into his nostrils, the sounds of wheezing filled his ears, and vengeance filled his heart as his hand clutched around the hilt of his dagger. The feverish eyes of Sefron the cleric peered back over his hunched shoulder from time to time, but Melegal kept himself concealed in the shadows. *Where are you going, Fatty? I've got a surprise for you.*

The man he hated, Sefron, was little more than twenty steps away, and the urge to slip his dagger into his neck consumed him. He had more disdain for Sefron than he had for McKnight and Lord Almen put together. He respected them as much as he hated them. The creepy cleric, filled with sickness, driven by defiling, had nothing redeemable to offer anyone as far as he was concerned. Lord Almen felt otherwise, but Melegal was determined to prove him wrong.

Don't lose him. Focus.

Another hour of cat and mouse was played in the drizzling rain until Sefron cast one final glance over his sagging shoulders and ducked into another alley. Four seconds hadn't passed when Melegal crept around the corner and found himself staring down a long and empty corridor filled with an overwhelming smell of excrement and fish oil. *He has to be here.* He pushed his cloak up to his nose and followed the alley to a dead end. No doors, no ladders, no windows and no Sefron. The cleric had disappeared ... again.

"*Sunuvabish,*" he exclaimed under his breath.

An eerie voice from behind him replied, "No, son of a whore is more like it."

Melegal ducked and rolled as a long blade ripped through his cloak.

Chapter 3

S NOW AND ICE.

"Rah-OOOR!"

A wooden club slammed into the ground where Fogle Boon's mirage had stood. The image shimmered and faded as an ogre, covered in furs, with hairy white arms and an unforgettably ugly face, grunted in alarm. It raised its club high once again before bringing it down in the same spot, sending shards of ice along the icy path. Fogle Boon's teeth were chattering as he fought to form the words of power for his spell. *Blasted cold! Where is Mood?*

The ogre—a full eight feet of bulging brawn and belly—snorted the air. Its yellow eyes widened on a head as big as a barrel of ale, which turned his direction. Fogle Boon felt so cold on the inside, and now his veins turned to ice as the ogre stormed his way, heavy steps thundering into the ground.

Fogle fanned his frozen fingers outward as he shouted, "KRYZAK-SHO!"

The power warmed inside him. Four radiant darts of energy slammed into the ogre's chest, drawing a howl of agony. *Not good.* The angry ogre was still coming. His spell had misfired. A single syllable from his chattering teeth had slipped, and a barrage of needles designed to enter the face and pierce the brain had simply bored into the thickset muscle and bone of the massive humanoid. The effect would do little more than leave a scar on the monster's smelly hide, but Fogle didn't have time to worry about that now. *DUCK!*

The ogre swung over his head as Fogle rolled through the snow, fumbling inside the pockets of his robes. He grabbed a small rod of steel and thrust it before him, catching the next blow that glanced off a field of energy of bluish hue. Fogle's fragile arms shook under the force, loosening his numb fingers along the rod. *Focus, mage! FOCUS!*

He clutched the rod in two shaking hands now as the ogre pounded away. His body shook to the core. It gave him some idea of what actual fighters went through. He had previously only heard them discuss melee. The spell within the rod only had so much it could take. The transparent field of magic was chipping and cracking like the shell of an egg. He caught his first close-up view of the ogre as it snarled in his face. His razor sharp mind noted the large canine-like teeth, jutting chin and protruding brow. Its expression was evil, cruel and without compassion. The smell of salt and manure didn't mix well with the pure cold air he was growing accustomed to. The smell was pungent and unrelenting, and his eyes watered. The humanoid continued to pound away, not a mindless beast, but a cunning creature that was going punish him before it ripped him apart and ate him. Fogle screamed.

"MOOD!"

His shield was fading, the fragments falling and dissipating in the air like blue crystals. There was nothing he could do at this point to save himself except cry out for help. His arms began to sag because his joints ached. *I don't want to be an adventurer anymore!* He wanted to say it, but he didn't have the wind to say something that long.

"Mood!" he managed, as the next blow punched him deeper into the snow, wracking every joint in his bony body.

Futility. Fatality. He was going to die. Any second now, the next blow was bound to smash through and crush his skull. It made him more mad than fearful. A stupid beast was about to crush his brilliant mind. Even worse, he would die a virgin. He seethed.

"MOOD!"

It was too late. He never thought about his own family until this very moment, and all of those years of studying, ignoring the social pleasantries of his kind. The fun oh-so-many had and bragged about, he'd passed on for knowledge and power. And all for what? To be squashed like a bug without his own seed ever sown or spilled.

"MOOD!" *BONE!*

The ogre raised up its stubbed club one last time as the last shards of magic faded away from Fogle's shield. The ogre showed a growing leer of triumph. Anger and shame swelled inside Fogle, raced from his mind and into his booted leg. *If I can't procreate – this mindless bastard shall not either!* He launched the heel of his boot into the beast's harry crotch, drawing a howl of alarm. Fogle fell back in the snow, exhausted, laughing and muttering.

"No celebrating with your ugly counterpart tonight!"

The ogre snarled with rage as it raised its club once more. Fogle's eyes widened as the club reached its zenith and began its downward arc. *Well, if you can crack my skull you can crack anything.*

Slice! Somewhere a hand axe began to sing.

Howling, the ogre reeled backward.

Slice! Slice! Slice!

A streak of blood splattered across Fogle's face and robes. He noted the warm syrupy feeling and the smell of boar's blood. He'd seen Mood gut one back in Dwarven Hole. There was a sickening sound, like an axe chopping into a rotting log, as he managed to force himself up on his elbows.

There was Mood, standing over the dead ogre, ripping his axes from its skull. The Blood Ranger was coated in dark blood, unlike that of his hair and beard. He was big and grizzly, his emerald eyes blazing like fire underneath his bushy brows. His head shifted left and right above his thick shoulders, wild and frightening. Fogle still wasn't used to it, the Blood Ranger's odd way. But, the King of the Dwarves was the only friend he had. Fogle let out a trembling sigh, and his warm breath fogged, reminding him of how cold he was.

"Yer going ta need a bath, Ogre Bait," Mood said, slinging the blood from his blades into the snow.

He managed to sit all the way up, happy that his cold arse was still a part of his living body, and to say, "Me? Look at you, Ogre Slat."

Mood glanced over his shoulder, checked the blood on his clothes and laughed. The dwarf was coated in blood from head to toe. "Hah!" The husky dwarf walked over and pulled him up off the ground like a child. "Never seen that before."

"What? Ogres? That's the seventh one we've fought since we've—"

"Tenth!"

Fogle gave a quick nod of his head. "I see, so the tenth since we've been wandering these mountains. What are you talking about? 'Never seen that before'?"

"Never seen no wizard kick an ogre in the family jewels before!"

"Is that so?" he replied, rubbing his hands feverishly together. *I hate this cold.*

"Aye," Mood replied, "saved your life, it did. I's coming over ta bank, too late, certain ye was gone."

"Where were you anyway?"

"Killing ogres, Wizard. I thought you could handle them by now."

"I thought I had back-up!"

"Ye did, er ye'd be dead," Mood stated. "Ho! Ho!"

Fogle's teeth were chattering again.

"What are you so ho-ho about?"

Mood lit up a cigar and said, "Ye did good. Saved yerself. Fought till the end. Venir'd a liked to have seen that. I like it. Glad you still be."

The ancient Blood Ranger's words warmed him, leaving him with a sense of pride, unlike his old kind, but the new kind, something good. He reached out his two quivering fingers.

Mood smiled and said, "A smoke, eh? … Well, ye've earned one this day."

"How about a fire, too?"

The fire was warm, but Fogle was still cold and miserable as his victory, albeit a small one, did little to warm his spirits. Now here he was, traversing icy mountains filled with avalanches and monsters, all to help find a man that he hardly knew. Mood had led him on ice cold feet in and out of crevasses, caves and over the tops of mountains for weeks on end. Every step was just as treacherous as the last, and if Mood saved him once on this trek, he'd saved him over a dozen times.

He shivered as he rubbed his hands over the fire and said, "Mood, tell me more about your dwarven women."

Mood's bushy red brow perched in the firelight as he asked, "Whatcha want to know?"

He didn't want to ask any questions at all. He had always assumed he knew everything he needed to know, but when it came to women, the subject was as foreign to him as the Nameless Mountains.

He pulled a thick woolen hood over his head and blew out a long puff of white breath.

"I was just reflecting on the colorful stories that Mikkel and Billip shared. I was wondering if what I heard was true, or if it was more of the same ole' orc's slat men like to tout."

"Hmmm …," Mood tugged at his beard, "I see. Yer sounding more like an adventurer now. Ho! Ho! That's grand. Almost dyin' gets many men thinking about women, children and such."

Fogle glowered at the Blood Ranger. *Answer my question.*

After a long moment Mood sat up saying, "Oh. Ah, well, dwarven women are frisky sorts, so I'd say what ye heard was true. But, don't be disrespectful of them. They'll get you back. Kin of mine once woke up hanging naked by his beard over top a pile of hot coals."

Fogle cringed as the image formed in his mind.

"And another kin with his—"

"That's enough. I get the picture. Be nice and courteous. I got it. Ah … Just forget it."

Fogle stood back up and headed for his tent.

"Don't worry, Wizard. I'll have my wives take care of your needs when we get back," Mood rumbled.

The offer, as generous as it sounded, didn't seem quite right. Fogle turned and said, "Would there be any unmarried ones available instead?"

Mood slapped his knee and said, "Ho! Yer a funny one. An unmarried dwarf! That's silly."

Fogle pulled the flap of his tent open.

"See ya in the mornin'."

He entered, sat inside the darkness and muttered a spell. The canvas of the small tent began to warm and glimmer. *Ah, that's better.* It was a small cantrip, not powerful but effective. He'd been using it on and off, trying to get used to the cold, but the icy air was barely tolerable. *Inhospitable!* Mood told him he'd need to toughen up, but he wasn't Mood. He was a scrawny man with frozen toes. He sneezed, pulled out a cloth handkerchief and blew his nose, remembering something he needed to ask Mood. Reluctantly, he peeked his head outside in the cold saying, "Mood, do you really still think we'll find a druid up here? I've almost lost track of the weeks."

Mood was gone, the fire was out and only the petite figure of an alabaster woman clothed in a snow white fur toga remained. Behind her was a pack of large wolves, shoulder height, with saliva dripping from growling teeth. *Not possible!* Fogle rubbed his eyes as she turned to face him. Two pink eyes, buckled in anger, ran over Fogle as a sudden chill raced through his spine. She was the most beautiful thing he'd ever seen, and she scared him.

Her voice was haunting and powerful as she spoke:

"You killed my ogres ... now you will die."

Chapter 4

Two babies cooed in the nooks of the underling Lord Verbard's arms: one with emerald green eyes like his mother, the other with golden eyes like his uncle. Verbard snorted lightly through his nose, and the two underling babes clutched at his chin with their sharp little fingernails and sneered.

A seductive voice from behind him breathed in his ear.

"Glad to be back among your family, I see. Aren't your babies so adorable, Verbard? Were they not worth the all the suffering I put you through?"

The green-eyed one was tugging at his finger when he cleared his throat and said, "Dearest, I'd rather walk barefoot on the sun-scorched land above for another year than spend another single moment with your over-pregnated hide."

Her fingernails tugged into his shoulders as she squeezed them and replied, "That's my Lord. A heart like a rock and a tongue like a forge. Oh … how I missed it." She snickered as she came around him and scooped up the babies, draped in midnight-colored cloth. "Now, now, little ones, we can't have you getting too attached to your father. That would make you soft and weak, like humans."

Verbard's silver eyes glimmered under his mate's playful and penetrating smile. Her rose colored eyes, long silky white and black hair and gossamer slip stirred the blood within him. Her figure weeks earlier was a monstrous thing unworthy of an ogre. *Ghastly.* He shuddered at the thought, for he'd never be able to shed the horrific image from his mind. His passion didn't come as easily as before, but in a few decades he was certain he would overcome that. His mate, now back in her prime, was hungry and lonely, but his new duties from Master Sinway kept him on the move, much to his relief.

Two underling women entered his den and took the children away. *Not what I had in mind.* His mate wrapped her arms around his neck as she slid her lithe frame onto his lap. *Not again.*

"Lord Verbard, there is one way to escape me: you only need to impregnate me."

He groaned and hissed under his breath.

"Your urgings are getting thin. Perhaps it is not me you long for, perhaps it is my brother that you miss."

He studied her eyes, hypnotic and unmoving, capable of hiding the darkest secrets about any mental inquisition. No, she would never reveal what he suspected, not that he cared, but somewhere within he did. He shoved her from his lap and floated away, robes dragging across the black marble floor.

"I've responsibility."

Her hiss was cut off as he flicked his palm, slamming the doors shut behind him.

Things had changed for Verbard in the Underland. His kin—brothers and sisters one and all— treated him differently than before. He and his brother Catten were of the highest order, well regarded and feared, but it had been his brother, the more astute politician, that garnered the majority of their admiration. Now that had changed. Verbard was not only feared, but now admired as well. He liked it and all of the additional pleasantries that came with it. After all, it was he who had rid his people of the pesky but formidable menace, The Darkslayer.

Everyone bowed or nodded as he passed them on the streets of the city. The underlings traveled on foot, along narrow black roads that led up and down the caves and around the spires in the bowels of Bish that hung up and pointed down in cones. Commerce: fruit, meat, some cooked and some raw, were skewered on sticks. The smell would rot an urchin's nose, but to the underling pallet it was quite salivating.

Verbard paid his greeters little mind as he made his way to Master Sinway's Castle, which overlooked the Underland City. There was no need for a road to get there, but there was one. A crossing of sorts. It turned around the hard rock like a coiling snake, defying the odds of engineering, instead consisting of magic entwined with minerals and glowing with the bluish hue of the underlight. Verbard had no need for roads, unlike most underlings, as he sailed upward to the mouth of the cave castle entrance and proceeded through a portal over thirty feet in height.

There were guards, at least a hundred, if not a thousand, how many he did not know, but he often wondered. No challenges came—though his heart did beat a little faster—as only a fool would challenge the Master inside his own castle. He knew where to go. *Through the iron doors to the iron throne.* He hated iron. It was such an ugly color and a tasteless metal. The rat-like fur on his arms began to rise as he proceeded, remembering that last time Master Sinway's iron-irises almost bore out his mind. He saw no need to challenge Sinway any more, not without Catten. Besides, he had done it more to piss off his brother then to challenge the master. *Ah Catten, tis not the same without you.*

He floated by the humongous iron doors, landed at the empty throne and kneeled. He hated this part most of all: being there at the appointed time and waiting. He was careful to shield his resentful thoughts. He thought of death instead, death of mankind above. His body began to relax.

Little more than an hour had passed when the air began to shimmer around him. Verbard opened his eyes and fixed them on the floor at the sound of cave dog nails clicking over to the sides of the throne. The cave dogs weren't alone; another strong presence was there. *The Vicious?* He had not seen one in months, but he did care. The mystic bodyguards of Master Sinway were not something he was comfortable around. It wasn't a fear of them, but rather his lack of command over their power.

"Rise, Verbard," a voice as ancient as the ore of Bish spoke.

He rose to his feet and found himself face to face with a Vicious: smooth black skin wrapped over a body of corded muscle, sharp teeth bared in a grin over crossed arms. *What is this?* His underling heart, as black and fearless as it might be, began to pump quicker in his chest. Its black eyes with white pupils met his, boring into him as if he were some kind of meal. It leaned a little closer, almost touching his chin. Verbard didn't like it, but as he brought up the energy to defend himself against it, it backed away, stepping alongside the arm of the throne.

Sinway looked to be smiling within his deep black robes, iron colored eyes gleaming in the dark, fingers needling his chin. The cave dogs, four in all, grey with matted hair, sat four feet high, to the tops of their heads. The fearsome beasts looked ready to tear him apart at a single command. His heart pumped faster still. *Let them try and eat me. They'll be worm food in an instant.*

Master Sinway's voice echoed softly as he spoke.

"I know it isn't customary of me, Verbard, but relax. I didn't bring you here for slaughter, instead for celebration," he said, snapping his fingers.

Verbard's heart flinched as his ears popped. A fine table of hardened wood appeared, encircled by chairs wrought in gold and silver. A vat of wine and pewter goblets were the centerpiece. His silver eyes flitted between the display and his master. *What is he up to?* He stepped back, bowing, as Master Sinway eased his way over to the table and sat.

"Underling Port, isn't it?

"Yes, Master Sinway."

Suddenly, Verbard felt like a boy, helpless before his father, or grandfather, both of which had creative ways of initiating punishment. He swallowed hard and hoped his robes hid it.

"Sit and drink with me," Sinway said. "We've much to talk about."

He moved to the table, sat and picked the goblet up in his hand. He could smell the port, full and rich, salivating to say the least, and if he ever needed a drink to ease his tensions it was now. He was in uncharted waters with the most powerful underling of all.

Sinway cracked a smile as he hoisted his glass and said, "Drink Verbard, vanquisher of The Darkslayer. Drink and be fulfilled."

The Vicious, lone and dominating, had slipped behind his chair as the cave dogs surrounded the table.

You first, he wanted to say as he brought the cold rim of the metal goblet to his black lips. *Poison is such a cowardly way to kill me. He could at least tell me what I fouled up this time. Bottoms up, then.* He drank. Sinway let out an unsettling chuckle as his world was turned inside out.

Chapter 5

CLONK!

C White spots burst into his eyes, and pain lanced back into his brain. Georgio's legs wobbled as he fell hard onto his butt. He clutched his stomach and head, fighting the urge to retch, fuming at the giggling sounds of halflings followed by Mikkel roaring in his ear.

"BOY! If you don't cut that out, I'm gonna skin you!" the large black man said, jerking him back to his feet. "That's not what I meant by using your head, Stupid!"

The little giggles ensued.

Georgio tried to shove Mikkel away, saying, "Get off me." He turned and faced off with his opponent, a mintaur, ram-faced and horned, and a full five feet of fight. He stood taller than the hooved creature and sneered down at him.

"Get him, Georgio," Lefty cried, sitting on top of a wall nearby, eating an orange pear.

The halfling wasn't alone. A small brood of halfling children, all barely two-feet tall, were scrambling around with sticks, attacking one another in joy, screaming aloud and laughing. It had been like this all day, hot and annoying.

"Wrestle, Boy!" Mikkel said, shoving him forward.

The mintaur charged, rounded horns catching him under his chin and driving him onto his back. He wrapped his arms around the mintaur's waist and fought to regain his feet.

Mikkel huffed in his ear.

"No! No! No! That's not what I taught you. Get up! Escape!"

He grunted, twisted and forced himself upright only to be slammed into the dusty ground again.

"Oooooh!" the audience exclaimed.

Georgio fought to suck the air in through his teeth. His lungs were thinning, and his own sweat was stinging his eyes.

"COME ON! GET UP!"

He clawed at the dirt and screamed in frustration. The mintaur was tying his legs in a knot, and the pressure was beginning to hurt.

"Are you just going to sit there and let him break your legs? Huh? Do something or die, Georgio!"

It wasn't fair. He was a boy, or a teenager, but the mintaur was a man, older, smarter and more experienced. He wasn't ready to fight. He'd been training all morning, and he didn't want to any more.

"Come on, Georgio," Lefty cried again, "you can do it!"

"Aye, Boy, ye' can do it."

Gillem!

Ever since the older halfling had arrived, Lefty had never been the same. Georgio hated Gillem. Something inside him began to boil over, and his ears began to steam. He cast an angry glance at the little cheerful pie-faced man, sat up and began wailing on the surprised mintaur's face.

"Stop it, Georgio! You'll break your hands!" Mikkel warned.

They didn't break. They hurt, but he didn't care.

Whap! Whap! Whap! Twist!

As the creature loosened its grip, Georgio seized it by the horns and twisted. The mintaur's neck was like iron, not meant to be broken, but it happened. The creature cried out like a sheep, thrashing left and right. Georgio held onto the mintaur, his stare never leaving Gillem.

"RRRRAAAAAH!!!"

He hoisted the mintaur over his head and tossed it to the ground at Gillem's leaping feet, scattering the tiny children like flies.

Georgio was heaving in the silence as all eyes, man, halfling and mintaur, looked on him as if he had gone berserk. The mintaur snorted, breaking the awkward silence, shaking its head as it regained its feet. Lefty was pale. Mikkel held his hand on his head, mouth agape, while Gillem dusted off his boots and lit his pipe with a nod. Georgio wanted to shove that pipe down the man's throat.

"Very impressive, my boy," Gillem said with elegant cheer. "Did you children see that? Georgio the strong one!"

The little halflings looked at him wide-eyed, then burst into applause and cheers.

Georgio shook as his eyes began to water. He covered his face and ran.

Mikkel slapped the mintaur on the shoulder and said, "Sorry about that."

The ram-faced man patted the big man on the back, nodded, gathered his gear, and departed.

"Same time tomorrow then?" The mintaur waved.

Lefty was numb: smiling outwardly, but in turmoil inwardly. He'd never seen such fury on Georgio's face before. It was frightening to see his once cheerful friend so grim. He felt responsible. He didn't know why, but he felt responsible somehow. He looked over at Gillem, who was handing each of the children a copper talon to spend in the markets. In a moment their existence in the small proving grounds was vacant, leaving only Lefty, Gillem and Mikkel.

"Think I'm pushing him too hard?" Mikkel asked of Gillem.

"Never."

Mikkel's smile broadened.

"Maybe I'm going too easy on him."

"Seems likely," Gillem winked. "Very well then, I'll see you two later on I assume, but if you don't mind, try to stay away for a few days. Georgio loses his focus with all of you halflings running around."

"You're the boss, Master Mikkel."

Lefty was silent as Mikkel walked away. He was sad, too. He didn't see enough of Georgio as it was with all of the demands of Gillem and the guild. His own thief training was intense, even rigorous at times, but he liked it. He liked Gillem, too.

"Don't worry about yer friend, Lefty." Gillem said, stroking his long fingers across his back. "He's getting to the age of puberty. Young men start acting strange, is all."

"What's *puberty*?"

"Er ... nothing you need to worry about for another decade er so. Now follow me."

"Where are we going?" Lefty said, hopping from the wall.

"First, we have some stealing to do. Then, it's time to pay Palos his dues."

Lefty's chin dipped as Gillem passed him by.

"Georgio, slow down," Kam ordered.

The teenager stomped through the kitchen, his face turned away.

"Don't you dare walk through my tavern looking like that: a frowning, sweaty little dirtball—get back here."

He stopped with his back still towards her. Kam wasn't in the mood for another of Georgio's fits. She couldn't relate. She looked over to Joline, her confidante and full-time "boys growing up too fast" sitter. Joline's pleasant face mouthed the words, *Be nice.*

"Hungry?" She asked.

Georgio turned and gave her a sheepish look.

"Yeah."

When wasn't he hungry? Georgio was a big boy going on big man. She was taller than most women, but now Georgio's head was up past her chin, and that was big for a fourteen or fifteen year old. At least, that's how old she thought he was. Joline put a steamy bowl of soup and half a loaf of barley baked bread on the table before him.

"Thanks," he mumbled before shoving in a mouthful from the loaf.

She pulled a stool beside him, grabbed his chin and lifted his eyes to meet hers. She loved his big brown eyes and his thick mop of brown hair. He'd be a handsome man one day, any day now at the rate things were going. Some of the waitresses had already expressed keen interest in him, batting their eyelashes, brushing against him, everything but removing their amply-filled blouses before his innocent eyes. She shook her head.

"What?" he asked, frowning.

"Oh nothing. You know, I'm starting to miss those chubby cheeks of yours. Are you sure you're getting enough to eat? Joline, bring him some more food: cheese and milk, lots of it."

"Huh?" both boy and woman replied.

"Eat, it's good to have a belly full for your nap."

Georgio gave her a funny look and said, "Are you right in the head, Kam? You're acting strange."

It was a fair question. For the most part she was feeling as good as ever, strong and fearless, but busy. Deep down she had come to accept that Venir was gone. He was hard to forget, but without Georgio and Lefty around so much, it was getting a little easier. She wiped his mouth off with her apron.

A waitress came inside the kitchen: a few years older than Georgio, long legged and pretty, her bright eyes attaching themselves to him.

"Pardon me," she said, smiling. "Need some frupp steaks, onion skins and deer broth, Joline. Hi Georgio."

Georgio stopped chewing, grinning from ear to ear. "Uh ... hello ..."

"Get your arse out there and wait tables!" Kam blustered.

The girl's face turned ashen as she said, "Sorry Kam," and scurried out the door.

Kam squeezed his face in her hands and said, "Don't be anywhere alone ever with my girls. Do you understand me? Not ever!"

"Sure, Kam. But what's the harm in it and all?"

She summoned up her energy; the rims of her green eyes began to glow.

"Never."

Georgio had a bewildered look as he shook his head.

"I … Said … Never!"

He nodded over and over.

"Good. Now, tell me what is wrong, and don't lie. Be honest; I need to know. Is Mikkel being too hard on you?"

"No."

"Are you still mad at Lefty?"

"No."

His eyes flitted, though. Even she had a hard time with Lefty. Her sickness, so sudden and strange, by all account might have killed her. Little Lefty, for some reason, seemed to know more than he let on. Call it women's intuition, but something was no longer right. Not after that encounter with Palos, the prince of thieves. She was certain that their encounter was far from over, but what that had to do with Lefty, she didn't know. She kept her eyes open. Billip and Mikkel were very helpful look-outs.

"Is it one of my waitresses? Do you … uh … have feelings for one of them in particular?"

"No Kam! Can I just eat and go? I mean, thanks and all, but I'm not hungry any more. Can I please go? I've got chores to do."

"Just tell me what's bothering you. Don't be hard headed. I don't want you stomping around here anymore, so let's fix this and be done with it. Tell me, Georgio!"

"NO!" he yelled, jumping out of his stool.

As Kam drew her hand back, Joline wrapped her arms around her with a hug and said, "Georgio, go and do what you have to do, but don't you ever do that again."

"Pah!" he said, storming away.

Kam was shaking. "Did he just yell at me? At me? I'm gonna kill him!"

Joline squeezed her even harder. "You'll do no such thing, Kam. The boy's growing up and missing his friends something terrible. You don't see it so much as I do, being so busy with little Erin and all. Now take a deep breath."

She inhaled and exhaled deeply.

"Oh my," Joline said.

"What?"

"Looks like you've got a hungry baby to feed," Joline said, glancing down at her chest.

Kam's breasts were soaking through her blouse.

"Aw, I hope Georgio didn't see that."

"I'm thinking he did," Joline giggled. "No hiding those things. Now get up there and feed that baby."

Kam muttered a spell—concealing her clothes—before she cut through the tavern and made it up the stairs. Her chest was aching. *Someone's awfully hungry.* As soon as she opened the door there was the awfullest scream. *Oh my!*

Chapter 6

(The Past: 5 years earlier, after Venir escapes the Brigand Queen)

THE COLORFUL BANNERS OF THE Royal houses of Bish flapped above the massive wooden walls of an ancient fort. Outpost Thirty-One was one of a kind, the only structure in Bish built from the massive trees of the Great Forest. Yet these trees had not been cut down. Their hard dark woods were rare, fallen specimens, carried by giants long ago. They had been gifts to the good men of that time.

Such was the story passed down over the centuries. None knew if it was true, but none cared, for such was the way of most men: self-centered, cold, and focused only on the present. The fort complex sat high on a forested hilltop in the southern lands of Bish. It was a perfect square, with outer walls twenty feet high. The gates in the opposite corners of each wall faced north, south, east, and west, from which straight, gravel-filled roads ran. They were busy roads, which made Outpost Thirty-One a strategic foothold that maintained order and protected key commercial trade routes in this region. All of the subordinate forts scattered throughout the south were commanded from here.

In the burning midday haze the fort appeared like a majestic castle, blending in with its surroundings among the distant hilltops that gazed upon it. Many unwanted eyes now stared at Outpost Thirty-One, for the outpost was the subject of their siege. The underlings and the brigand army had cut off all the roads and laid waste for miles around. All human communication throughout the southern lands of Bish was halted. Many would have agreed that the Royals had it coming, but when it came to defending against an underling assault on the upper world, the proclaimed Royal superiors of the selfish human race were Bish's one and only hope.

Jarla's brigand army was busy taunting the confined Royal soldiers, sending kobolds close to the southern gate to deposit the mutilated torsos, heads, arms and legs of the fallen. The tiny horned humanoids cowered behind small wooden shields, but occasionally an arrow from a vengeful archer would pierce their small bodies, adding to the stinking heap of flesh and flies that lay baking in the suns.

Deeper south in the forest was the large beige tent that quartered Jarla, the Brigand Queen. Alone inside, she was studying maps and battlefield notes. Her beautiful face—now scarred and twisted from a fate she'd been unprepared for—was drawn in a tight frown. Unlike most women on Bish, she was a born warrior. She stood taller than most men, with strong shoulders and arms that were sinewy from years of battle. Her jet black hair was tied back, revealing deep blue eyes over her tanned face and scarred cheekbones. She took a deep breath and exhaled, bit her thin red lips, and flung the table over. Everything she had planned for years was about to unfold, yet everything was wrong. She cursed, spat, and drained a glass of wine. *Venir!*

Not only had he stolen her magic armament, but he had also embarrassed her by escaping her camp, slaughtering her commanders, and evading the underlings' bounty on him. Her alliance with the underlings had never been on solid ground; now it was falling apart. She wanted to break the alliance and disappear. She had even felt her grip on her army loosening not long after the young warrior slipped from her side. She spat at the thought of his cocky grin. But, the worst was he had taken her precious, powerful weapons, or they had taken him? For the first time in years she felt vulnerable, rather than invincible.

Nevertheless, she was not ready to abandon her loyal brigand army, who had taken her in when others would not. As for the underlings, they were her best vehicle to take revenge on the Royals who had ripped her life asunder. She had once been one of them, a Royal household member and a rare soldier, rising to become a trusted leader. She clenched her teeth; how naïve she had been not to see it coming. Men were men, after all, and Royal men were the worst. They took what they wanted, willing or not, and made it their own. She, too had been taken, against her will, and she had never been the same. She wiped her dry eyes and sneered. Her hatred burned like a hot iron. It would have to do.

She was on the cusp of extracting her revenge. Outpost Thirty-One would fall. But then what? She sensed in her gut that Venir would come for her. With the mystic arsenal in his grip there wasn't much she could do to stop him. She only hoped she would live long enough to see the outpost destroyed. She was almost certain the underlings would ensure that.

Stepping outside into the light of the two burning suns, she walked up a rocky hill and grabbed a spy glass from a kneeling orcen sentry. She peered at the great outpost, taking mental note of the defense arrangements underway. The outpost should have been taken by now. She knew Venir was in there, and it left her uneasy. They had tried to catch the man, but could not. He and his comrades were far fleeter than her cumbersome army.

She slung the spyglass at the orc, returned inside her tent and called for her commanders. They discussed how the siege might take weeks or months now, thanks to Venir's warning. She had to remind them that she had people on the inside of the outpost as well. They snickered. The day of her reckoning had come.

A small group of scouts were still outside the walls of Outpost Thirty-One. The three men were outlanders of repute, even among the Royal soldiers that had dealt with them over the years. It was no coincidence that they had been the ones who had given the troublesome news of the underling invasion.

Dusk had settled over the thick green forest that surrounded the outpost. All around the fort were steep ravines that served to drain the heavy rains. They also created vulnerable points where foes could creep undetected right up to the complex. Deep within a ravine, the three men crouched with eyes and ears intent on finding any comers. Skirmishes had been breaking out day and night. Shouts of pain and terror, blended with the sound of battle, came and went as the thick foliage muffled the noise. It was difficult to tell who was winning, but the trio sensed that it was only a matter of time before the fort was stormed.

They had already encountered three underlings earlier and five the night before, but the foul creatures had been no match for Billip's deadly arrows. He possessed a special short bow and arrows that were a gift from an old Royal soldier in the fort. The man's son, who was to inherit them, perished at the hands of the brigand army. It was clear to Venir that Billip relished the rare quality of this bow. The archer made good use of the power and accuracy, grinning each time he dropped an underling with an arrow straight between the eyes or clean through the heart. His comments to the archer irked Mikkel, who cared little for his friend's success. The big man wanted the first crack at the underlings himself.

"Come on, Vee," urged Mikkel in his deep voice, loading his heavy crossbow. "Let me take the first shot. He can't shoot better than me and Bolt Thrower."

Venir had witnessed Mikkel's long bolts impaling two underlings at a time. The problem was that once they were fired, there was no time to reload. Mikkel would charge like a bull into the fray with the massive studded club he called Skull Basher. Mikkel was the only man with less patience than him when it came to fighting.

The archer cracked his knuckles and chuckled, always calm amid chaos. Indeed, the only one cooler was Melegal, but the thief cared little for venturing in the Outlands too long. That man was more disposed to the comforts of the city.

Smaller than his comrades, but hardy and weathered, Billip twisted his goatee with calloused fingers.

"You can't hit one to my five, Mikkel—you know that." "I don't need to!" the man jumped in his face, club high. "I fight like a man. Skull Basher will take ten to your five any day—you know it!"

"Yer an idiot," Billip retorted.

Venir stepped between them.

"Do we have to do this every time?"

"Yes!" they both insisted.

Venir shook his head.

"Mikkel, you know the drill. Billip sets them up, we flank them."

"And if he misses? I get hit with one of his arrows!"

"That's never happened," Billip replied in irritation.

"It almost did."

Billip jumped in his face.

"It almost didn't! It wasn't my arrow, and you didn't get hit! That was three years ago! Let it go!"

Mikkel kissed his club and pointed his sausage-sized finger at the much smaller man. "It better not happen. If it does, you better hope it kills us … or Skull Basher and me are gonna smash you."

Billip rolled his eyes and walked away.

Their bickering was part of the preparation for combat. The competition between them kept them focused. It was what Venir wanted. The two racked up body counts faster as a team than alone, though neither would ever admit it. He loved their spirit and looked to them as older brothers, but they were comfortable with his lead because he had instincts they lacked. The fearsome threesome had become a force to reckon with over the years, but their notoriety was not always well received. They were sometimes considered common bandits as each had his own needs to satisfy.

The men had exited the storm drain, and were once again headed down into the plunging gulch. They navigated the rugged terrain like mountain cats. No leaf rustled in the inert heat. Sweat stinging their eyes, they tried to suppress the sound of their own breathing. Even the panting of Venir's little dog Chongo was undetectable.

Venir watched Billip and Chongo break off toward the far side of the ravine, communicating with hand signals and soft tapping on leather chest plates. The dog's ears perked up at the sound of those signals, and he responded in accord. They took their positions, waiting minute after minute in the thickets. Venir would glance back from time to time, only to see heavy sweat dripping from Mikkel's silent face. He contacted Billip.

Nothing, the archer's white hands signaled back.

Venir's gut told him they needed another accurate volley tonight. Things were just too quiet this time out. His mind began to wander as he wiped the sweat from his brow.

He felt an urgent tap on his shoulder. He looked forward. In the dimness he almost didn't notice the bowman's urgent signaling. Underlings were coming. Billip was trying to make out how many.

"What's up, Vee?" a deep voice asked behind his ear.

"We have company."

A white grin flashed in the darkness.

"How many?"

Venir shrugged his heavy shoulders. The blood of battle began to pump through his veins. His stomach started to knot, and his mouth became dry. He clutched Brool, his war axe, and waited.

Five, was signaled.

He acknowledged and readied himself. Mikkel leaned his club against a tree, taking up position with his heavy crossbow. Venir checked the buckles on his chainmail shirt and lifted his newly acquired shield. He was amazed at its lightness, despite the heavy metal banding and engraving. He studied his great axe and smiled. Its oak shaft was warm in his hand, almost living.

Only a few days ago he had wrangled the magic weapon. He had given little thought to how it now came to be in his hands. The large leather sack it came in was a mystery. When Jarla reached into the sack it contained two smaller axes, a lighter helmet, and metal arm bracers. Yet, for him it had yielded the large helm, shield, and a war axe unlike anything he ever imagined. He remembered the moment she was about to kill him. He smiled a tad. The shock and fury he saw on her face when the mystic arsenal came to his aid had been glorious. Grasping the weapon and feeling the power surge through his hands almost made him laugh, it was so delightful.

Someone tapped him again, snapping him out of his thoughts. The count was now ten.

"Better put on your helmet," Mikkel said, putting on his own metal skullcap that sloped down the back of his neck.

The warriors didn't like to wear armor unless they anticipated a skirmish—or full battle, as in this case—and even then they still opted for lighter armor than most of the Royals around the fort. Venir hadn't yet bothered to extract his helm from the sack. He felt no need for it and feared it would obstruct his vision. And so far the situation hadn't been too risky.

Twenty underlings!

The archer's fingers and elbows were frantic.

Fifty paces. Moving fast. Now what?

The sudden change of circumstances demanded a decision. Venir had been setting up ambushes by letting small underling squads move between them, but this was no small group. It seemed that the underlings had become privy to their tricks and that larger numbers now made those impossible. That tactic would cut Billip off, leaving the archer overwhelmed without an escape route. Indecision began to churn in Venir's belly. He had to decide whether they should retreat while there was time. They could make time to alert the rest of the fort as well, or fight. He wanted to fight, but wisdom prevailed.

Run, Venir signaled Billip.

Hit and run? Billip returned.

When facing a larger force, scouts needing to buy time would drop the point men of the enemy's front line with bolts or arrows. This slowed the enemy and made them more cautious until they could ascertain the strength of their assailants. It also provided critical extra time for a hasty retreat. But twenty was a large group of underlings. Venir didn't want to alert them to their presence. There could be still more underlings as well.

His keen eyes detected several dark silhouettes in the distance. Billip was signaling again for a reply. The underlings were armed with small round shields and curved swords, similar to the bulkier tulwar swords of men. It was a heavier force, and judging by their additional weapons and armor, a full-scale assault was underway. The axe burned in his grasp as the underlings approached, but he made his decision and signaled back.

Run!

Venir could make out the shape of Billip and the smaller shape of Chongo creeping back up the ravine. The archer's arrow was nocked along the shaft of his new bow.

Clatch—Zoop—Thunk!

Mikkel's heavy bolt ripped through the air, clean through the neck of an underling and imbedding into the chest of another. "What are you doing?" Venir said, shoving Mikkel's crossbow down. "I said *run!*"

"Sorry, Vee. I must have missed that," Mikkel shrugged. "I thought it was *hit* and run."

Venir knew better. Mikkel wanted the first kill, and Billip was moments from releasing a few arrows as well. The pair couldn't have cared less about the risk. Their passion to kill underlings took over reason. All three were guilty of this affliction.

Billip began his own onslaught. Two more underlings found their throats punctured with feathered shafts, their warnings gurgling in dark blood. He watched as their hit proved to be a mistake. The underlings scrambled up the ravine like hungry wolves, and thick webs began to form, spreading over the trees, surrounding them from behind and cutting off their escape. In an instant they were trapped.

"Helmet on," Mikkel reminded Venir, picking up his studded club.

Venir felt foolish for a moment. The webs had grown further up the edges of the ravine, trapping the archer and his dog below. He groaned. The underlings had the jump on them.

Venir opened the leather sack and pulled out his helm. Its eyelets had an eerie glow that unsettled his stomach. How would they make it out of this jam? The odds were against them. A superior force approached, and they had nowhere to run or hide. He had a single burning thought: *kill all you can before they kill you.* Oddly, when he pulled the spiked helm over his blue eyes for the second time in days the odds of survival seemed to shift back in his favor.

As he strapped the thick leather chin strap under his grizzled jaw, he felt a heightened sense of awareness he hadn't noticed before. His mind became razor sharp, intent on the task at hand: to find and decimate the underlings. He felt he could handle the score of them alone. Excitement rushed through his body, tingling from fingertip to toenail. Better yet, his vision, far from being obstructed as he had feared, was enhanced. Not only could he see the underlings, he could feel their presence … it was awesome.

Dusk had passed, and the thick forest was almost pitch black, which made battling the creeping underling warriors more difficult. The cave-dwelling creatures could see as well at night as in daylight, an advantage shared by only a few other races. But the men on Bish had no such ability, except now for one man.

Venir's head peered around, and he could make out the details of the landscape before him. *This is good!* He noticed the warmth of the bodies of Billip and Chongo not too far in the distance, and then he saw Mikkel's worried look.

"Vee," the man whispered, "what are we gonna do now? I hate this dark. Can you see them?"

"*Yes,*" he said in an unfamiliar voice.

Mikkel fell silent for a moment.

"You better be able to see them, 'cause I'm following you."

Venir tapped his helm.

"Trust me, then. It's time to take them head on, no choice."

"Sounds good."

"Stay close, and watch out for those webs."

Quiet as shadows, the two slipped deeper into the ravine. In his hunger for battle, he moved faster than normal, and a big hand had to nudge him back. The underlings were holding their positions less than thirty paces away, but the thick vegetation kept the pair out of sight. Concealed on the ridge of the ravine, Billip waited, not moving a muscle, his bow aimed on his next approaching target, his brow and hands slick with sweat. Venir knew the archer's fire would offer them scant protection once combat began. It would have to be enough.

He motioned for Mikkel to stay put, then crept alone toward the underlings. He heard the man mumble in protest, clutching his club from behind. Like an iron panther, he crossed the forest floor. He came within ten paces of the oncoming underlings. He squatted before them like a tree trunk as they came, slow and quiet. Hadn't they seen him? His blood rushed in his ears. He could see, hear and smell every sickening aspect of them. Now they were five paces away. He didn't budge, legs tense, ready to spring. He almost gasped as the underlings passed by. They hadn't even noticed him. The underlings' colorful eyes were dim sparkles in the dark as they glanced back at him and moved on. He couldn't believe it. He couldn't resist their exposed backs, either. His hatred overcame all reason.

There was a flash and a whistle in the air as Brool ripped out the backs of two underlings in one swipe. They dropped lifeless to the ground as the third underling whirled to attack. A whizzing arrow struck the back of the underling's head, pitching it forward. He could see Mikkel's white teeth coming his way as the battler charged along his side.

"Let's do it, Vee!"

He felt the underlings swarming from all directions, chittering loudly, shields low and curved blades high. It raised his fervor more. Underlings surrounded him and Mikkel; their slashing blades were quick and deadly. He parried in broad sweeps, holding the smaller race at bay. The underling blades slashed and licked at his skin like razors.

"Hit 'em Mikk!"

"Bashing time!"

Mikkel burst into assault, his first overhead blow smashing an underling's shield and arm. As the fiend howled in pain, Skull Basher's studs caught another's nose with a sickening smack. Mikkel whirled to block the third one's slash, but too late. The underling punched a hole deep in his thigh, sending him down with a groan. The black warrior's blood flowed, but the man responded by bringing his club down hard and fast, pulverizing the underling's skull like a ceramic vase.

Venir heard his friend scream. He dodged as he jabbed his spike deep into the leg of a charging underling, ripping muscle from bone. He eyed the two other underlings that flanked him, and slammed his shield edge into one's chittering mouth, slicing through the neck of the other. Venir charged the other two hobbled underlings and hacked them down like saplings. As he turned, he saw Mikkel break the other arm of his first victim, then bust its ribcage like a crate of melons. Six underlings were dead now, but more were coming. *Let them come*, he thought.

"You all right?"

Mikkel grimaced as he tied a cloth around his bloody wound.

"Leg's bad, but I can fight fine. No running away from this."

"Stay low while I check what's coming. We need to get out of here," Venir said.

"Don't go far," the bleeding man said, but he didn't even hear it.

Billip had his hands full. Several underlings were closing in on his superior position. He pressed back into the brush. The high ground was an advantage, but the thick vegetation made it hard to track their small, dark bodies. If not for the occasional glint of their colorful eyes he would have lost them. He relied on his excellent hearing to help pinpoint their whereabouts. He fired away. Their howls of pain and anger gave him relief.

Focus. That ain't all.

His eyes strained in the darkness.

Three maybe?

He had killed one, maybe two, but more still bore down on his position. He heard a painful bellow from Mikkel, but the sounds became muted. Would he have to start swinging steel soon as well? He edged farther up the bank. Dreading the thought of melee, despair crept over him. He knew he was trapped. With nowhere to go, he dug in.

He watched the dark figures continue to press upward through the brush.

One more shot.

He had to make it count. He nocked two arrows this time and drew them back. It was a trick shot he often used to infuriate Mikkel and gamble against Melegal. He had never before considered using it in combat, but now it seemed his life might depend on it.

He took a quick breath and held it, watching two underlings, side by side, moving fast up the hill, shields raised for cover.

Bish! Too far apart!

The shot was difficult. The underlings were tacticians of terror in confined spaces, and darkness was their forte. He knew they thrived in it. Just twenty paces were left between him and his assailants. He had to fire. Sweat dripped from his nose. At least one of them had to go, so he let loose into the nearest one.

His arrows whizzed through the air. One imbedded itself in the raised wooden shield, the other streaked straight and low into the underling's exposed belly, knocking it down the hill.

Yes!

The second underling warrior was closing in fast. He nocked another arrow. The wicked face was upon him and shrieking. Billip raised his bow, blocking the underling's slashing sword, jolting his arms and driving him into the ground.

At close quarters now, the ferocious underling warrior had the advantage, and he had no means to defend himself. He tried to draw his sword as the underling lunged at him. The pommel of the underling's short sword caught him on the head, stunning him, bringing a sharp pain as blood trickled in his eyes.

The underling launched a chop at his head. He ducked just enough to avoid a split skull, but it took a slice off his right shoulder. Gasping in pain, he managed to plunge an arrow into the underling's thigh. It staggered back. Dropping its sword with a hiss, it didn't back down, but beckoned the man for closer combat. He had no desire to wrestle the creature, knowing full well it could tear him to shreds. He'd seen that happen before. Underling fingernails were like steel files. His right shoulder drooped, forcing him to draw his broadsword with his left hand. Billip jabbed at the wounded creature, each futile blow glancing off of its shield. Its leg stopped his upward press as it chattered back in mockery. *More must be coming.* He pressed hard, growling in return, shoving the creature downhill. Chunks of the wooden shield were chipping away, but the skill of the underling was too swift. It taunted and clawed at him in anger.

Reaching the bottom of the ravine, Billip disengaged the creature. His arm felt like lead, and his shoulder burned. He sucked in a deep breath. Exhaustion and frustration beset him as the emerald-eyed underling raised its shield in triumph. A shadow raised behind the unsuspecting creature, drawing a grin on his face. A studded club smashed down on its skull, erasing its wicked grin, shattering all of its teeth. It fell over dead in a pile of its own ooze.

Mikkel was almost laughing as he wiped the gore on the grass.

"It's about time you started fighting like a man, Billip! I didn't even know you had a sword, let alone the strength to use it."

Billip struggled to spit out his words but said, "They're everywhere, and regrouping for another attack. We have to get away. Where's Vee?"

The big man shrugged. Billip could make out the bloody bandage on the man's leg. Their bleeding would hobble them in a further fight.

"Come on," Billip said with a groan, heading back up the hill.

Mikkel grunted and followed.

"If I can get to my bow we can hold them off for a while."

Billip trudged up the bank as fast as he could, pulling Mikkel over the slippery spots. He could hear more chittering nearby. Wherever Venir was, he was on his own now. He wouldn't wait around like a crippled calf to see when he might return. He recovered his bow as they reached a small outcropping of mossy boulders, where they hid.

He could see the walls of web billowing at their backs. He turned cold. *Nasty.* This spot would have to do. But it gave better cover, so for the moment they were safe. He checked his wound. A nasty sliver of meat was taken off of his right shoulder. His leather armor saved it.

Maybe armor isn't so bad.

His jerkin sleeve was soaked to the cuff. The men patched each other's wounds, staunching the bleeding the best that they could. Billip's heart thundered in his temples as he listened for the next wave of comers. As the howl of distant battle reached his ears he wondered if they would see Venir or anyone else ever again.

Venir had forgotten the wounded man he left behind. He was hunting now, and his comrades weren't his concern; his enemies were. Gripping Brool's oak shaft with white knuckles, he felt invincible. The helm heightened his awareness. He had questions ... *Why hadn't they seen him?* ... but that could wait. He moved on with caution, over the creek and through the dense foliage.

He wasn't alone; Chongo had found his side. The pair had tracked underlings together for years, and now they both had heightened senses to serve them. The dog stopped, ears perked up. He hunched down. He saw the silhouettes of underlings coming up the mouth of the ravine. *Keep coming, vermin!*

Bloodlust stirred inside him, and his compulsion to kill them was overwhelming. He could smell their oily stench, almost burning in his nostrils. His hatred of these foul creatures that had destroyed his life so many years ago began to boil over. The helm amplified his senses as the eyelets burned blacker than the night sky. He no longer cared what happened to him, only what happened to them.

Destroy them!

Thought and magic intertwined into a focal point and down the ravine he bounded. Rushing their flank never occurred to him, nor did an ambush. He padded over the wet stones and braced himself along their path.

He counted six underling warriors moving up the gorge. Some of them crept in a staggered column, while the others covered the ravine banks to the left and right. Their faint multi-colored eyes glinted as their heads moved, left and right. He heard their low chittering commands escaping their narrow lips.

In place of physical battle prowess, underlings preferred to trap and outnumber their opponents. Their magic, combined with their cunning and callousness, made them a formidable force, and difficult to kill. Their warriors were as big as an average human woman, bigger and stronger than ordinary underlings. Their bodies were hard from decades of battle that gave them strength that belied their smaller size.

Several footfalls away, the foremost underling stopped and gave a signal. Venir watched them turn still and almost disappear. He could see them clutching their curved blades, waiting to pounce. Like a four-legged ghost, Chongo padded down the path. He followed, like a wraith, watching their gleaming eyes focused on the lone dog. Could they really not see him?

The underling in the front, donned in chain mail, hissed at the growling dog. *It's not even looking my way*, Venir thought. His body was bursting, the axe white hot in his grip. He let out a blood curdling yell.

"*RRRAH!*"

Venir sheared the bewildered lead underling's head from its shoulders. The others stared in astonishment as he appeared from the darkness and descended on them like an angry minotaur. His appetite for blood unsatisfied, he pressed his attack like a steel tornado, deeper into the brood. Yelling like a berserker and chopping like a lumberjack, he came down on the next two underlings, hacking their small shields into splinters and mutilating them with splattering swings. They rushed in. His anger rose. Hurling his shield, he caught one in the ankle. A series of cuts and stabs drew his blood before he battled them away. The iron shod of his great axe shattered an underling's chin, and another fared still worse as he jabbed the long axe tip into its throat. He tore the spike out, ripping its neck open.

He was ready for an entire hoard, his mind one step ahead and his body responding in kind. He watched in slow motion as another underling charged toward him, a curved sword in each hand. He leapt right over the bewildered creature, swinging his axe deep into its gaping maw, splitting its face before he descended to the ground. Blood from his gory axe dripping on the ground, he awaited more attackers. *Where are they?* He could feel them.

He was picking up his shield when he saw one scurry away. He cursed, and then scanned the area. Somewhere nearby he heard his dog yelp. He rushed to its aid, finding the shaggy brown pooch ensnared by forest vegetation. *Underling magic!* He had encountered it before.

He felt the hairs on the nape of his neck rise. As he approached his dog, his boot snagged on the vines, tripping him. He watched smaller roots and grasses reaching upward like tentacles, encircling his legs like serpents.

"Bone!" he yelled, tearing and twisting at them. The foul foliage had engulfed the dog entirely, leaving only a trace of muffled whimpers. His skin crawled with the evil presence he felt bearing down on him.

Two dark-robed underlings, armed with small double-shot crossbows, descended towards him from the ravine bank as if on air. He jerked his shield up as the closest one fired at his chest. The bolt ricocheted away, drawing an angry hiss. He heard murmurs echoing somewhere in his helm. Above him he noticed long fingertips pointed his way, glowing red. He had to free himself.

He sliced at the roots with the edge of his axe. To his surprise, the vines recoiled and began to wither at the blade's touch.

"Chongo!"

The other suspended mage fired another bolt into the foliage where the dog was engulfed. Chongo yelped and fell silent. Venir lost control and charged the airborne assailant. It blasted him with a volley of burning red missiles that bore into his flesh. He cried out in agony. The air filled with the stench of his singed skin. The pain strengthened his rage. He kept going, climbing up the bank, jumping up and catching the cloak of the floating figure. He pulled it to the ground. It chittered, trying to crawl away. Its strength was no match for his weight as he crushed into it, bringing a groan. Pinning the little figure down by the arms, he smashed his helmeted forehead several times into its gnashing face. Its evil countenance burst open like a rotten pumpkin as it died. He fumbled for his axe and turned back toward his dog.

The remaining underling uttered something. The air seemed to be sucked away in the gap. Shock waves blew through the trees, bending the saplings, slamming into his body and down his spine as if he were being pummeled by a hundred hammers. He fell to his knees, face dripping blood, unaware of his surroundings, lost. The pain was something he never recalled. His hands and feet were numb, burning, cold and limp.

Somehow he got up, stumbled towards his pet and fell just close enough to reach the snare with his axe's spike. He could see the bonds disintegrating as the dog lay prone, panting and bleeding.

Rising up on one knee, he found himself between the dog and the lone underling mage, now hovering twenty paces away. He saw its mouth moving, thick black hair covering its head like a shroud. Raising his powerful arms, Venir slung his axe over his head with a scream. Straight as a spear it sailed, the tip crunching deep into the underling mage's chest, driving its floating body to the ground. He staggered over to its crumpled body. The spike was wedged deep into its black heart. Its gemstone green eyes stared blankly at the sky.

He spat the blood from his mouth, wrenched out the axe, and checked for more enemies. He pulled out the wooden bolt from Chongo's hindquarters. He tasted the tip and spat. *No poison.* Unable to feel his legs, but desperate to save Chongo, he lifted the dog in his arms and got a lick in the face as he backtracked up the ravine. The forest was quiet, but he knew underlings were still everywhere. His battered body forged ahead.

Trapped behind a massive rock on the steep hillside, Billip felt his neck hairs prickle. He could see the sweat dripping off Mikkel's body like rain drops as water trickled down the bank. The forest was quiet other than occasional sounds of the skirmish deep in the ravine. His shoulder ached. He craned his neck, but his comrade's ragged breathing hindered his ability to detect approaching assailants. *They could be anywhere.*

He had fought underlings often over the years and knew their tactics well, but it did little to quell his terror. Unlike Venir, whose hatred for underlings blazed as pure as the suns, his was still like all other men on Bish. Billip's hatred for cave dwellers was at times surpassed by his fear of them.

Glancing at Mikkel, he managed to make out the whites of his eyes. The big man was nodding his head. Billip kept his arrow nocked, bowstring straight, resting his shoulder while his friend clutched his club.

Several feet above the forest floor, two cloaked underlings floated undetected in and out among the trees, their clutching hands motioning in the air with intricate patterns. A soft blue glow wavered in their palms.

Where are they? Billip thought.

He scanned what he could, oblivious to the floating figures in the trees. He was certain if he could not see them, they could not see him. Not far from his hiding spot, his ears didn't detect the faint whisper of an underling chanting through its thin black lips. His instincts told him something was going on; he just did not know what.

The low hum of tiny wings caught his ear, and he crouched down as the sound grew. A plague of mosquitoes had found its way among the rocks where they hid. The whining of their buzzing wings increased inside his ears. It seemed as if every mosquito in the ravine began swarming around the men.

What is going on?

The mindless insects consumed the men in a frenzied search for human blood. He could see them, tiny and large, gathered all over Mikkel, who brushed at them in frantic alarm. He could feel them sink their needles into him a hundred times and drink his blood. ***It has to be magic...*** his mind reasoned. He choked down the urge to run. He knew they were being flushed out. *Don't panic.* Tiny welts appeared on his corded forearms as the insects tapped into his veins. Mikkel was covered from head to toe, tormented by the little fiends. Billip tried not to flinch, but his will was tested beyond the limit. He could see Mikkel biting his lip and covering his nose. It was time to act. He mouthed and gestured the words to Mikkel.

Run. Flush them out. Find cover. I've got one shot. Go. The tortured man turned to face down the bank. With Billip readying his bow, the larger man charged out from behind the rock and down the ravine like a maddened bull. Through his swollen eyelids, he caught a flash of light blasting into his powerful friend, who fell down in a scream.

There in the trees.

Down below, he could see the brawler's silhouette engulfed in a mysterious blue flame, drawing forth a sound of searing skin. Mikkel fell to the forest floor, screaming before rolling out of sight.

He wondered which fate was worse, the bugs or the fire. Only Mikkel would know now, but he thought he'd prefer the fire. A smell of charred insect bodies and smoldering hair drifted in his nose. He feared his friend might be finished. Billip heard a throaty laughter below. Mikkel appeared, rising to his feet, only to fall backward as a small crossbow bolt struck his belly. He lay in a singed, motionless heap, Skull Basher still in his hand. Billip couldn't believe it. He scanned the trees; he couldn't let his friend die for nothing.

He replaced the arrow he had nocked, drawing another from his quiver. It was unique with blood-red feathers, a blue-black shaft and a ruby-like arrowhead. The old warrior who had given him the bow assured him he would know when to use it. *That must be now.* He nocked the special arrow with his mosquito-covered hands. He took aim in the trees, scanning back and forth. The arrow tip twinkled as he did so. Maintaining his poise, he searched for any sign. Nothing showed of their concealed assailants. His eyes moved with the arrow, left, right, up and down, but the whining flurry of insects piercing his arms, neck, face, and eyelids was distracting him. As he swept up and across the ruby arrow tip flashed.

He swept it down.

Nothing.

Then back up, and it flashed again.

He lined up the tip so that it glowed steady in light. A silhouette began to form in the tree tops. It was an underling, floating near the upper branches of a willow tree.

Got him! Center mass. An excruciating surge of pain dug into his shoulder when he pulled back the bow string, but he let the shaft fly.

Twing! Zip!

A streak of hot red light punched straight through the sternum of the hovering underling and out of the other side.

Bulls' eye!

The underling still came toward him, chittering with rage. Had he missed? No, he knew he had hit it, yet it came. He fumbled for another arrow, brushing the ravenous insects away. As the underling began descending toward him, a look of horror crossed its features. The underling began to glow, eyes and mouth catching fire from the inside. Suddenly, it exploded in a bright red flash. A cloud of black ash filled the air. Billip crouched back down, noticing the mosquitoes losing interest in him as well. He wiped the creatures away, and gathered his thoughts. *Got to check on Mikkel!*

He ventured down the ravine, bow ready. Another shadowy figure descended on him from above, and he dropped his nocked arrow. He clutched after it as the cloaked underling drifted toward him. Terrified, he watched it touch the ground and crumple in a sagging pile.

Billip inched closer and noticed his red-feathered arrow lodged deep in its brain. Shivering at the sight, he marveled that the arrow had somehow found two targets from his single shot. *Powerful magic, indeed.* Did the same apply to the bow? He reached for the arrow, noticing that the feathers were now blackened and dry, its magic spent.

He slid down the ravine and soon came upon Mikkel on the ground; his breathing was shallow and raspy, lips caked with blood. The man groaned as he sat him up. He put his canteen to Mikkel's lips.

"*How is he?*" an eerie voice said from behind.

He turned and saw a startling figure of muscle and metal splashed with gore. *Vee?*

"Not good. I haven't seen him this pale since his wedding. We need to get him away from here."

The sounds of battle grew louder all around them. A full-scale attack must have begun.

Venir handed Chongo over to Billip and hefted Mikkel over his shoulder.

"Agreed—let's move ... they'll be on us in no time."

The thick webs peeled away as Venir's axe sliced through them. Gasps of pain escaped labored lips from behind him as they treaded back up the ravine. He was exhausted, body wracked with pain. Holes had burned in the mail that covered his belly, singing his flesh to metal. The men reached the bottom outpost wall and entered through the same steel storm drain they had been defending. He locked it down as they headed inside the bowels of the outpost.

Three stout Royal henchmen in scale armor guarded their path, but moved aside with wary glances. Venir could see debris falling from heavy activities above. He led the way upward through the wide tunnel of rock and soil while the sounds of chaos grew. Dim light filtered in at the far end where a steel ladder led twenty feet up through a man-sized hole.

A lanky figure in pale green terrycloth robes and ankle-strap sandals descended the ladder at a brisk pace, hopped off the final five steps and rambled towards them. It was a tall man, near seven feet in height, his narrow face light-skinned and boyish beneath short sandy hair. His voice was soothing, somewhat childlike, his light blue eyes showing a wisdom and compassion that was rare on Bish.

"I knew you would be here."

"No surprise you knew that, Slim." Venir said.

Slim was a man who had answers and seemed to know more than most men, despite his youthful appearance.

"I know you. You never miss a party," Slim said, raising his eyebrows. "Mikkel looks bad." The boyish man began inspecting the brawler with his fingers, motioning his hands downward.

Venir lowered Mikkel to the ground and started to take off his helmet.

"Leave it on," Slim gestured. "You're not out of the woods yet."

The young man noticed the archer's load.

"Ah, it's my favorite pooch ... how sad."

He laid his long slender fingers over Chongo's hip.

"Be still," the man whispered.

Venir could see Slim's face twist in agony for a fleeting moment before returning to normal. He grunted.

"Ah," the cleric said with a smile as Chongo licked his face. "That wasn't so bad, was it, Boy?" Slim then turned back to the man laid out in the tunnel and said, "Now the big man. Hold him still, you two."

Venir pressed down on Mikkel's shoulders and watched the young man work. He couldn't believe their good fortune. Slim always reminded him of a young Melegal, except more friendly, something the thief resented. Billip helped him pin down the listless man's powerful arms and legs. *Here we go.*

The long-limbed man grabbed the shaft of the small bolt lodged in Mikkel's belly. The iron warrior's mouth and chin were covered in spit and blood. Slim's slender lips muttered a fast cadence of words, and as he spoke, power radiated into his glowing and elongating hands. The bolt blazed in his hand like a furnace poker as he extracted it inch by inch. The warrior screamed and writhed. The smell of burning flesh filled the tunnel as the charred bolt turned to ash.

Mikkel groaned, his light eyes flitting open and closed. The cleric placed his hands on the man's hard belly and gashed thigh. Again, Slim's face distorted in anguish, but this time he aged before their widened eyes. The wounds closed, and it was over as fast as it had begun. Slim gasped for air, his now withered face full of hard lines and cracked teeth. Venir thought Slim looked like the oldest man he'd ever seen.

"He'll be all right," the cleric said in a ragged voice. "He should be able to walk in a minute, but he's not up for fighting for a while." Slim stood up, hunched over, and cracked his skinny neck. "Ah ... man, sometimes I hate this." "What's going on up there, Slim?" Venir asked, looking at the shaking ceiling above. "They need to know that the underlings are bringing more forces now."

"Too late; it's over. Outpost Thirty-One is already lost. And if we don't get moving, *we'll* be lost, too."

His and Billip's eyes met as Slim continued.

"You don't want to go up there. It's overrun. I'll fill you in."

Slim stretched out his long arms, and Venir watched the older face slowly regain its youthful vigor. The young man now inspected Venir's wounds and began chatting in the quick.

"Here goes—the brigands stormed the east gate. Three hundred Royal horsemen rode out to battle them, or so we thought, but they just kept on riding, giving the brigands clear access to the outpost. I'm not sure which Royal general it was, but he clearly betrayed the rest. It won't be long before all the gates are compromised and we're up to our elbows in underlings. Now, we've got to go back out that way." Slim pointed his long index finger toward the south grate where they had just entered. "No choice."

Venir saw Billip's dumbfounded look. It was a heck of a story.

Mikkel groaned and sat up.

"Man, my stomach hurts. What did you do, Slim?"

"Saved your life, that's all. The tummy ache's a side effect. It'll go away," Slim said, patting the man's charred head.

"Thanks," Mikkel muttered as the healer helped him onto his feet.

"That's a heck of a haircut, Mikkel!" Billip said with a faint chuckle.

"What?" The warrior reached for his head, feeling the singed remains of his black hair. "It might grow back," Slim said with a shrug, "one day. Let's go."

"Wait," the archer said, tugging the man's robe. "We need a plan. And I can't even pull back a bowstring."

"Man, what did you guys do out there? And what's with all the bug bites? That's gross!" He said it with his face drawn, hands on his chest. "You got whipped by a bunch of little underlings, didn't you?" Slim now ran his ginger fingers over the archer's shoulder, then reached into a pouch and pulled out a small jar and applied a pasty blue salve to the wound.

Billip's face lightened up.

"What's that amazing stuff?"

"Pigeon dung."

Billip's face turned sour.

Slim had a childish grin and said, "Just teasing, it's a little something I whipped up. I haven't named it yet. Good thing your wound was only cosmetic. It's just a little make-up to match your cheeks. You'll be fine."

The chuckles came, but were hollow, none more so than Venir's. He wasn't so sure he could get them safely out of there.

Billip rolled his shoulder, releasing a brief smile, cracking his knuckles. Touching the scar that had already formed over the wound, he said, "It's closed up!"

The healer slapped his tender shoulder, bringing a grimace.

"And don't worry about the scar. Get a nice tattoo over it and the ladies will love it, especially the orcen ones."

The tunnel was silent for a moment as Venir watched all eyes draw on him. Other than Slim, the bunch looked ragged and beaten. He wanted to collapse. His belly burned. His body ached from head to toe. It seemed there was no other way out. One choice, *Fight or flee.*

"Let me take care of you, Big Man. That's a nasty mess in your belly."

Venir's voice was harsh.

"No, let's go."

The cleric stepped out of his way.

Slim tried to convince the sentries at the outer grate to come along, that remaining would be to their immediate peril. They laughed. They were hard and loyal men who would not abandon their duty. The soldiers made it clear they would rather die than run, wished the men good fortune and turned away. Closing the storm drain behind them and then sealing it shut, one yelled out.

"Bish be with you!"

Now the men stood in the forest, listening. Venir could hear the rising crescendo of bloodshed ringing in his ears. He could picture the underlings and the brigand army spilling inside the outpost and blackening its interior. The gates were compromised. The shouts of Royal orders were silenced by magic, missiles and manslaughter. Plumes of fire and smoke filled the sky.

It was clear that the onslaught was overwhelming and no Royal man or beast would survive. A great chunk of evil would follow the valiant soldiers into the bloodied ground, however. That seemed clear judging by the roar of the fighting above, but it would not be enough.

Mikkel was nodding his head.

"What's the plan?"

"The last plan was to get word to the northern cities for assistance," Slim said. "So let's head that way, or else I'll go alone."

Venir said, "No, we go south. They won't be looking as hard there. The northward route will be the most heavily guarded. The underlings will be thick for miles."

"The underlings will be everywhere—period!" Mikkel retorted.

Slim had something to offer.

"I have magic that should conceal us all. But, I don't want to use it until the last possible moment. It won't last long. We're going to have to move like the wind to get clear. I've got other ideas, too. Are you with me?"

Having ventured with Slim before, Venir had some idea of what he had in mind. He wasn't keen, but they had little choice other than to trust his magic. It could do more than heal.

"I'll take the point. For some odd reason they can't see me. The rest of you should be fine. I just hope there's nothing worse than underlings out there looking for us."

Slim tightened the cords on his sandals.

"That's grand, Venir. You just gave me another idea. By the way, nice helmet or whatever that is. It makes you look mean … like Melegal."

Venir barreled down the ravine with Chongo at his side. The others followed not far behind, all thoughts heavy on the downfall of Outpost Thirty-One. Mikkel managed to recover his heavy crossbow as they passed by the ambush site. Venir maneuvered through the thick foliage like a metal apparition, striding through the dark like a bobcat. He could sense underlings were all around, but not close enough to pinpoint. He fought the urge to find them, as the helm's awareness made the battle very compelling. He began to realize that he could lead them all out of harm's way if he could stay focused on fleeing, rather than killing.

Nevertheless, the spiked helm on his brow beckoned him to make contact and destroy the underlings. He had to stop more than once to regain his composure, rather than succumb to the battle lust. His will was strong, but only his loyalty to his friends prevented him from giving in to his reckless desires.

He led them through the forest, minute after minute, stirring little more than a muskrat. His nerves were on edge as every unfamiliar sound seemed amplified. He looked back time and again, but Billip signaled they weren't followed. They were already a full mile down the hill. *Almost free.* He kept them moving.

At this pace the great hill that held Outpost Thirty-One would soon bottom out; they were almost halfway down. He felt something strong ahead and froze.

Slim fidgeted beside Mikkel.

Venir signaled back, *Nothing.*

Venir began moving again. He heard the lanky cleric sigh in relief. Their careful footfalls through the humid, bug-filled forest became agonizing; they had been creeping along for almost an hour.

Again he stopped.

They all went still. *Small underling patrol!* he signaled. *Straight for us. Hide!*

Slim began muttering soft chanting words.

Venir turned to watch. The air around the three men and the dog thickened. Next, all he saw was a small grove of trees where his comrades had stood. The illusion worked.

Venir sunk beneath a thick willow tree. The silhouettes of three underling hunters, armed with light crossbows, stood in a small clearing not far from him, chittering in the quiet.

Venir's bloodlust plagued him like a growing migraine. They were right in his path. He should sheer them like sheep. He quelled the urge with iron will, controlling his burgeoning lust and watching them begin to move on up the ravine his way.

Don't move. Don't breathe.

They passed him and were standing beside the grove of trees that were once men. Venir heard one sniffing the air into its hawkish nose. Venir tightened his grip on Brool.

Here we go.

Another underling shoved its comrade along the way, more intent on the sound of the fracas farther uphill, and they passed onward. The throbbing in Venir's head subsided after another long minute, and he started moving again with more haste. The odd grove of trees followed him. Within the hour they were at the bottom of the hill, safe and facing the open plains to the east.

"Wow!" Slim exclaimed, checking the looks of his tree-like arms and hands. "I can't believe we just waltzed through that nest of evil. Insane!"

They all shook their heads, stretched their limbs, and basked in the red moonlight. Such moments as this didn't often come without consequence. "Now what?" Mikkel said, rubbing his tender thigh.

They all looked at Venir. The outpost had fallen. Good men would die. He wanted to take an army in himself and drive the underlings back into their caves. Mostly, he wanted to find Jarla and make her pay. He swore he would hunt her down and kill her, but now was not the time.

He took off his helm, dropping it into the sack, feeling the warm night air soothe his aching head. He ran his fingers through his thick locks of blond hair.

"Two-Ten City … we'll spread the word as we go."

Chapter 7
(The Present)

Plop.

Louder and closer. Venir was blinded to everything but that steady sound. A beacon of death or a beacon of hope, which he did not know, nor did he care. *Move or die.* So be it.

The ground beneath his feet had turned to blackened shale as he treaded steep inclines only to slide downward again. His despair was replaced by anger only to turn back to despair again, but the sound kept coming.

Plop.

What was that sound? It seemed familiar now, like streams that rippled over the rocks where he fished as a child. Those days—singing in the sunlight, sucking down fish eggs and washing in the streams—seemed ancient and impossible now. Blood and body parts littered the water like rotting logs, and his days had been darker ever since, no recourse, no choice. *Fight or Die.*

"URK!" he gasped as his body pitched forward, and then he tumbled downward over the shale, each tiny rock cutting under his skin like broken glass under the force of his momentum. His fingers clawed into the ground. His feet kicked, but he did not slow. He slipped off the edge of something. The wind whistled through his ears as he fell.

SPLASH!

The water was cold, dark and unfriendly. The weight of his helm and axe was pulling him downward as his feet paddled for the top, but he had no idea which direction that was. In the back of his mind he figured he was back in the river and just needed to find the bottom. How deep could it be? He could walk back ashore. He sank. His body began to labor for air, twitching and jerking in the murk. Brool glimmered with life as his lungs began to collapse with death. Drowning, what a pitiful way to go. *Bloody lying giants!* Then again, maybe he should have taken the advice he was told.

He closed his eyes, letting the icing waters slow his struggles, and thought his final thoughts of Kam, underlings and grog. *Ah, but to have at them all once more.* Something burst through the water, wrapped around his body and yanked him out. He gasped for air, writhing against the grip that had his arms pinned to his sides. As the icy water cleared his eyes and ran down the rivulets of his helm, he found himself face to face with another foe. A giant with a boyish face, bald and one-eyed, held him like a child's doll in its mighty grip. The face was pitiful and scary at the same time. Its skull, as big as a boulder, was misshapen at the top, one ear sticking out and the other looking melted on the side. Its breath of seaweed and fish wasn't the most unpleasant he'd encountered, but the split blue-green tongue rolling in its mouth might've been the ugliest. Venir was certain he was about to be eaten.

It screamed in Venir's face.

An army of orcs couldn't have been any louder.

Venir screamed back.

It screamed again, louder than the last, shifting his helm on his brow.

Its grip loosened, and Venir took in a full swallow of air.

"RRAAAWWWW!"

Its brown uni-brow perched above its one good eye.

"Hur-Rah?" it said.

Venir gazed at his foe. A deformed giant with only one working eye was standing knee deep in dark water that was surrounded by a lake shore, encompassed by rocky ridges that jutted from the mist. A cone of mist went up as high as he could see before it stopped again in the clouds. Rocks jutted left and right from the smoky spirals, but near the shores there was green, brown and life. A drop of water, as big as his head, fell in the water beside him.

Plop.

Venir warmed at the thought of the small victory, but it was short lived as One Eye started to carry him away. The one big brown eye stared at him, with admiration it seemed. Venir's head whipped around. *Must escape.* But there was only water, rocks, a mile long shore line, if that, and more mist. If he killed the giant, then where would he go? *Think Venir.*

"Where are you taking me?" he yelled.

Its working eye squinted, and its split tongue rolled as it gave him a curious look and spoke.

"HUNG-GAREE."

Venir gulped as its enormous belly groaned.

CHAPTER 8

A<small>S</small> M<small>ELEGAL</small> <small>SPRANG</small> <small>BACK</small> <small>TO</small> his feet, his short swords, the Sisters, were gleaming in his hands. The leather wrapped around the pommels was reassuring as he crouched and faced his unseen foe. Two small figures, decorated in wooden masks, were blocking his path back into the street.

You can't be serious.

"Coin or death, Whore Bred?" A long steel knife flashed in one urchin's hand as the other flanked him with a notched and rusty longsword. Melegal was in no mood to laugh as the renegade urchins adorned in ruddy red robes and bare feet closed in. They were members of the guild, one of many that bred thieves, liars and whores. *You can't be serious.* This bunch in particular called themselves the Wastrels of the Rose, he recalled, a peasant lot of cutpurses at best. They leaped back as he made a quick lunge at them.

"Come now, children. Run, before I have to skewer you," he warned.

Each masked face turned toward the other before returning their weird little gaze back to him. *I should kill them. Stupidity is a crime, in some cases. How did they sneak up on me, though?* Melegal shouldn't have been surprised, ever, but his focus on Sefron had almost proved to be his undoing. A more formidable stalker might have been successful in putting his life to an end. He'd have to be more careful.

"Coin or death—"

Melegal swatted the flat of his blade on the front of the boy's mask.

"Yes, I know—Whore Bred. Is that the line your guild master has you using when you rob the honest and stupid folk?"

"Yaaaaar!" the other one lunched.

Clang! Melegal smacked the boy's blade from his hands.

The other charged. *Really?* Melegal cracked the flat of his blade on the other urchin's mask, knocking it clear off. The Sisters became a blur of steel in the twilight.

Whap! Whap! Whap! Whap! Whap! Whap!

The pair, one boy, one girl, both ugly and pitiful, fell to the ground clutching their heads as they tried to crawl away. Melegal's booted feet pinned their robes to the ground as he warned them, "Keep moving. Start crying or screaming and the next strikes will be with the edges of my blades. Got it?"

They nodded as their elbows scraped over the pavement.

"Mercy!"

Tears of pain and fear dropped onto the stones below them. It was uncharacteristic for these little thieves to try and take a full grown man like Melegal. They tended to work in small groups, strike fast and bully younger or elderly people, but times were as desperate in Bone as they had ever been. There was a clamor coming from the other side of Bone's massive walls that the underlings were coming, coming to kill them all. Of course, it might have been rumors alone, but there were more desperate people being taken in than ever before. However, Melegal had other things to worry about.

"Tell me something, urchlings. Are more of you nearby? Cause if there are, I'm going to carve a hole in you both this big," he said, making a large circle in the air with his blade.

They both shook their heads.

"Good, so tell me this: how long have you been following me?"

It was the girl who spoke.

"Just a few corners, M-m-master."

That's more like it. Maybe I should keep them around.

"Ah ... I see," he said, slowly strolling around them. "Tell me, did you see a man enter this alley before me?"

They both shook their heads.

He kicked the boy in the head. "Don't lie to me! Did you not see a man shuffling like a snail over the ground, a mere twenty paces ahead of me?"

"No Master, I swear!"

"No, no such man. Only you!"

He wanted to kill something, anything or anyone. He touched the tips of his blades into their empty bellies, drawing blood as he grimaced with rage.

"Don't lie to me! Where is the man you saw before me?" He looked down the alley, a dead end one way, a street up the other. He didn't miss anything, not one single detail. Studied the walls, not so much as a portal, ladders, or ledges to climb along, not Sefron anyway.

"P-Please don't kill us, Master. Mercy!"

Melegal's voice was cold as ice when he said, "Why not? You've nothing to live for."

"We don't want to die," the girl said. "We want to live to see the morrow. Please don't kill us. We'll help you find the one you lost."

Stupid urchins.

Melegal sheathed his blades. He knew the difference between a lie and the truth when he heard it, and these pathetic waifs had not lied. But, he was still certain they'd be better off dead. "Pah! Go rodents, and remember: if you cherish the morrow so much, make sure I never see you again." He stomped their wooden masks to splinters. "I'll not forget your faces, not now nor twenty years from now."

He could hear their scampering feet as he headed toward the dead end of the alley and began his search. He was seething inside. Sefron had slipped him again, it seemed. He ran his delicate fingers over every niche he could find. Nothing. That left only one other option, and the thought left him uneasy. *Magic, and maybe he was on to me.* Melegal stuffed his hands in his pockets and began the long walk home. *I guess I'm gonna have to kill him in the castle.*

Sefron took one feverish glance over his shoulder after another as he lumbered down a steep series of narrow steps. He labored for breath and wheezed through his nose as he stopped and looked back over his shoulder. Paranoid. He waited a few more moments, confident his spell worked, before he continued his descent. *Good. Good.*

He was oblivious to the fact that Detective Melegal had been following him, but that didn't mean he didn't take precautions whenever he slipped outside the castle walls. For over a decade, almost two, he had been avoiding the prying eyes of the Royals. A spell he had mastered, an apparition of himself, had unloaded itself from the wagon, hours earlier, and in his guise wandered the streets until it expired. Not just one, but two shades were out there before he made his own secretive trek. If someone had indeed been following him, he would not have known, but that didn't matter. What did matter was that no one, especially not the Almens, knew where he was going or who he was about to see. He peeked over his shoulder again. As much as he enjoyed watching others being tortured, he had nightmares of it happening to himself. A betrayed Almen was as merciless as merciless could be. *Hate 'em. Hate them all!*

As the light faded above him he muttered a quick incantation.

Shazal-ong.

A copper ring on his middle finger came to life with a soft glow as he stood on a landing barricaded by an ancient door covered in rust and grit. A new sense of security washed over him as a pair of rats scurried over his feet. He pushed his way through. A cool damp breeze cut though his clothes and raised bumps over the clammy skin on his neck. He swallowed hard. *Slow and easy.* His frail legs ached. His lungs wheezed. It took another twenty minutes for him to reach the bottom of the slick rock stairs that bottomed out in what looked to be an unfinished room that opened into a cave.

The light from his ring did very little to expose his surroundings, and anyhow, the curiosity that bred a need for exploration evaded his being. What lay beneath the City of Bone was of little concern to him. Humans feared what was beneath the ground, always assuming it was filled with ghouls, trolls or underlings, at least at the subterranean levels. The sewers, almost another two hundred feet above, were another matter, but even those desperate enough to try the sewers never crossed to the deep levels, and they hoped whatever lived in the ground never crossed them. Yet it happened. There were monsters that wandered below. Sometimes they reached the sewer levels, and rarely one would creep into the city, but most witnesses never lived to tell about it.

Sefron wiped the sweat from his forehead with a handkerchief as he waited and waited. The sounds of dripping water echoed from everywhere. He began to pace back and forth on his aching and shaking legs, his wheezing just as heavy as ever. He knew he wasn't late. He never had been, not once over the years. He was in the same place as the last time, a place no one would ever think to look: cool, damp, deep, dark and dangerous.

With a raspy sigh he sat down, allowing his lids to close over his bulging eyes. This trek took a lot out of him, and he was grateful that he only did it once a year. His thoughts drifted to the castle's serving girls. *They'll have much work to do, massaging my sagging old muscles.* His dry mouth began to water.

"Taking a nap, are we?" A sinister voice cut through his thoughts.

Sefron shouted out in terror at the sight of the horrifying face before him. It was an abomination of cat and man: black, twisted and cunning, layered with muscles from its toes to its shoulders. It hoisted him off the ground by the neck with a single hand. Sefron could feel its steel file-like claws digging into his neck as it choked him. The smell of piss wafted in the air as he soaked his robes. The monster, unlike anything he ever imagined, sneered at him with fiendish eyes.

Sefron's legs twitched. His eyes bulged like boiled eggs as his slimy tongue writhed inside his mouth. He watched in horror as the creature opened its large mouth, revealing fangs and rows of razor sharp teeth. He must have failed his master. His time had come, his efforts undone. But he wasn't going to die without some kind of fight. He stared into the eyes of the monster, channeled his thoughts and energy. *Let me go. Let me go,* he commanded. The monster's gaze filled his gut with despair as its grip tightened around his throat. *No! It's not working!* Laughter echoed and began to fade.

Chapter 9

Underneath an ancient snow covered pine, Fogle Boon's knees shook beneath the ropes of ice that bound him. He had been there for hours, his shivering beyond control, without so much as a sound or visit from his gorgeous captor or her pack of wolves. He strained to hear something, anything, but he could only feel the icicles growing on his earlobes as the howling wind continued to rip through him to the bone. He had been miserable before, but nothing compared to this. *I can't go like this. Not without a fight.* Yet, he still felt his chances for survival dwindling away.

Nearby was Mood, frozen up to his neck in a single block of ice, head down, unmoving. Fogle tried to imagine which was worse, his situation or the Blood Ranger's. *He's probably enjoying this. Bloody dwarf!*

He tried to focus on what magic he had left within him, probing his superior intellect to see if there was anything he could use. His hands were bound, and his mouth was gagged with a dirty piece of cloth that tasted like sweat. He was all alone with his only remaining weapon: his mind. Yet she, whoever she was, some strange guardian of ogres and wolves, was careful not to catch his eyes. Instead, two men as tall as small pines, bearded like dwarves and armed with picks, had bound and hauled him away. Two ogres shoved along the block of ice that kept Mood imprisoned.

It was a long trip that led them deep inside a cavern, a veritable garden where vibrant plant life of many colors was bursting through the ice and snow. Flowers, trees and streams filled with jumping fish were abundant in his field of vision. As spectacular as it was, Fogle was far from impressed. It was still cold, colder than a lich's tit, and all he wanted more than anything was fire and a blanket. He groaned a pitiful sound as his teeth clattered together. He was certain they were about to break like ice tablets at any moment.

Another sliver of fear raced down his spine as the pack of wolves appeared from behind him. Their coats brushed along his knees as they growled and barked in low puffs. He watched the saliva drip from their fanged mouths. *What a wonderful coat you would make.* A fearsome sight, the wolves, each one's back stood almost four feet at the shoulder. He thought of Chongo and wondered if the giant two-headed dog could make quick work of them, or if they would tear him to pieces. Chongo, the reason he was here and freezing in the snow.

As the dogs sat, the two tall men reappeared, one carrying a short log as thick as a man on his shoulder, the other a heavy blanket. Gently the man set it on the snow in front of him, and the other laid the blanket on top of it. They both then stood on either side of the log, arms crossed over broad bearded chests, unmoving. *Nice blanket.* Fogle would have fought them both bare handed for it. He looked up at them, each standing taller than even Venir, eyes straight forward, hairy and scary. That's when Fogle noticed the heavy blades with long hilts on their hips. Bastard swords. The heavy picks they had earlier seemed more adequate to the conditions, the swords more out of place because the roughhewn mountain men looked more like executioners. He swallowed a frozen glob of snot. That's when she came. *Oh my Bish!*

She was back, her pink eyes almost glowing in contrast to her soft skin and snow white hair.

A tiara of twigs and small flowers adorned her hair while her toga flapped loosely in the air. She eased her rear end onto the blanket, and without a word the two men lifted her from the ground, holding her a head's height above Fogle's frozen face.

She pulled the rag from his mouth. "Tell me, Wizard, why did you kill my ogres?" Her powerful voice was not as threatening as it was before.

Fogle searched for her eyes, but he could not find them. They looked out above him as if he wasn't there. Deep inside of him a pot of anger stirred. It was one of the stupidest questions he had ever heard. He wanted to tell her that, and less than a year ago he certainly would have, but now things were different. Still …

"Cah-ca-cause they were trying to kill us," he somehow managed to sputter out.

She looked around, making an eerie sound as she did so, before she made her reply.

"My ogres protect me, my brethren, my haven," her voice rose, "they are sweet creatures to be cherished, not slaughtered."

Sweet and ogres didn't mix, not since the dawn of any timeline. Any fool knew that. This witch, or whatever she was, was crazy. *Be wary of the crazy ones,* Venir had told him once.

"Not in this world. Anyone knows ogres are every bit as evil as their armpits are smelly. What I can't understand is—"

"SILENCE!" she yelled. Her wolves began to snap and pounce. She lowered her palms, and they all sat. "Tell me then, why have you come here? What is it that you hunt?"

"I hunt nothing. We've come to help a fah-fah-fah-friend. We need to find a druid."

Fogle thought he saw her eyebrows perch for a moment and noticed her shifting a little on the log. He started to continue, but she cut him off.

"Liar! Men have no use for druids. I have no use for liars," she said, slipping from the log, her feet landing softly on the snow. As she started to walk away, she made an order. "Chop off his head, and feed him to the wolves. Stab that Blood Ranger in the brain."

The thought of losing his head at the swing of icy steel made his teeth ache. He always figured he'd have a peaceful death in bed. His head was cast down in failure as he murmured his final words, "I guess I'll be dying a virgin after all." Fogle cringed as cold steel was scraped from sheaths. *Freeze and die.*

CHAPTER 10

THE INSIDE OF VERBARD'S HEAD twisted inside out. *Poison!* He was certain it was in control. Before him, Master Sinway's image stretched, contorted, swirled into a pinwheel and exploded. The urge to vomit came, but it never played out. Instead, something else happened, very unexpected. Everything came to a halt: his heart, his brain and his breath as he took in his new surroundings. He was back underneath the blazing suns of Bish. He was mortified. *Banished!*

"My, my, Verbard, you almost look as pale as a human," Master Sinway said, standing at his side. "Feeling a tad uneasy, are we?"

Verbard turned his back to the suns, clutched at his sides, and retched, but nothing came out.

"Pah, Verbard, you are not in your body; you cannot vomit. My, Catten would be ashamed. An underling mage vomiting from a dimensional spell. Well, I suppose powerful magic is not for everyone."

Master Sinway floated away, tall and foreboding, but in a different light now. The bright suns brought out features of the underling, who looked like part man, part wraith in his fathomless black robes. Verbard went after him, trying to acquire his senses. He felt nothing: no heat, no air and worst of all, no magic. *I live.*

Master Sinway stopped and turned. His ancient face was magnified in the sunlight: intelligent, cunning and omnipotent. His iron eyes were deeper than a mineshaft, his shoulders broad and his hands gave Verbard the impression his master had broken necks before. His master wasn't one to hide from the suns or the moons or anything above. Verbard had the feeling that—if anything—they should hide from him. Master Sinway's evil countenance seemed invigorated, almost cheerful.

"Have you adjusted?"

Verbard nodded.

"Good then. Try to keep up; I've much to show you and little time."

They seemed to move as fast as thought, in a fashion that reminded Verbard of Eep's eye, but this included more sights and sounds. This spell was powerful, dangerously so, something he'd never imagined Sinway had control of. He felt small. Then, Verbard wondered if Master Sinway was defenseless in his home now. *Who's protecting him? Can he be in two places at once?* His idea was fleeting, as his respect for Master Sinway grew. He looked down as they soared through the sky where a plume of heavy white smoke was building. Dark ranks of creatures became more distinct as they fell closer. He gasped. *How glorious!* Judging by the terrain, Verbard was certain of exactly where they were, but this was south of the Great Forest of Bish, somewhere between there and the jungles. Crops, miles of them, had caught fire, but that wasn't all. An army of underlings, a thousand or more strong, were killing men, women and children like sheep.

He and Sinway stood in the center of a village now as underlings on spiders and on foot decimated human flesh like fresh poultry. A woman's head was tossed through his ghost-like form, and that brought forth a chuckle from Master Sinway.

"When, Master? I beg of you, why was I unaware?" He was very careful of his tone.

A man wielding a pitchfork tried to defend himself from the attack of one underling only to have a crossbow bolt shot point blank into the back of his head by an armorless underling. It was strange, euphoric, being in the center of the melee as all sorts of creatures passed through their forms, screaming in terror and glee. Verbard was enthralled, but he needed his questions answered, too.

"Come," Master Sinway said.

In a single step they moved miles. In a field he stood, once vibrant with full crops, now burned to the ground and converted into a graveyard of sorts. Pairs of legs were sticking from the ground, some clammy, some bloody, some twitching as far as his silver eyes could see. Underlings, diggers they called them, were dragging living corpses from all directions, leaving smears of blood over the green and blackened grasses. Verbard began counting. It was unlike anything he imagined. *Simply beautiful.*

He looked over at his master and said, "There's over a thousand, practically an army of men dead. How? When?"

"Ah, that's the best part, less than a couple of months, not a day more. Consider it a tribute for what you have done, Verbard. With the Darkslayer gone, the small towns and villages are so much easier to burn." Master Sinway whirled slowly over the muddied ground then let his eyes rest back on Verbard. "I assume you have a question? Your eyes do not show the glee I anticipated."

Verbard took in a sharp breath as his chin dipped.

"Master, am I to understand the Darkslayer prevented such carnage all alone? He was one man. It seems unlikely that he could have stopped an entire army. There has to be something more to this force than just the Darkslayer's demise." He hated to say the next line. "I could not be the one to take all the credit. Surely your hand is in all of this." When he looked up again, Master Sinway's broad back faced him.

"Heh … is that humility I hear? From my most impudent and challenging servant of all?"

Verbard began to speak but was cut off.

"Don't pretend to think you are undeserving, even when that's the case. Humility is not your way, Verbard. My, without your brother you've become uninteresting. I don't like it."

The sharp words somehow stung his black heart. Sinway continued:

"Now, come alongside me."

"Certainly."

"Hmmm …" Sinway glanced at him, rubbing his chin, then looked away. "You'll figure it out. Now, as for you observations, yes, you are right, this isn't all because of the fall of our foe. But, it did play a key part. These wretched humans lack the will without his presence being totted. The Royals, our greatest enemy of all, squabble amongst one another and let their world fall to ruin. Without man helping man, well, you see the result."

"So, we burn their crops, kill their people and little more than a few hundred soldiers have been sent to stop us. All dead." He fanned his hands over the crops. "The orcs, dwarves and ogres are naught to be heard from. We've hardly been challenged. Our treks of terror began in the twilight, just to see if your words were true. Just to see if the man would come. He did not. Now, we press into the day and strengthen our grip on the South. In a few more months, everything below the Great Forest will be ours. By the time the Royals make a show of force, it will be over."

Following Sinway over forests, jungles and cities large and small, Verbard could see people in large caravans heading north and other humanoid races moving south. He could see fear, worry and starvation on their ugly faces, and his hatred fed on their destruction. He felt stronger.

"What are your thoughts, Verbard? You've been so quiet. It's unlike you," Sinway said with a twinge of annoyance.

"How many of our kind roam the lands?"

"Five thousand."

"That's a huge force for us. The humans can summon armies as big as ten thousand on a moment's notice. We could be slaughtered," he said matter-of-factly.

Sinway hissed.

"But they have not! They sit, whine and wallow in riches, fighting over the next bauble or glimmer of power. It's an opportunity like none from ever before."

Verbard wasn't so certain. The death of thousands of humans was always a good thing, but the way it came about seemed unnatural. Century after century, underlings and humans chipping away at one another had become a ritual. What he saw now was a slaughter. He liked it, but it seemed too easy.

"Oh so many months ago, Verbard, did you not feel a shift in your powers? A quake, a shimmer, an ebb? It was like the entire world of magic we know wobbled and flipped."

He had, several times, and it terrified him. Had it jolted his master as well?

"Indeed, it almost cost me my life more than once. But, it filled me with power so great I sometimes could barely contain it. Like a rich well of energy deeper than our caves. That feeling was indescribable, but the feeling is still with me, just more faint."

"And you brother felt this as well, did he not?"

"He did."

They were hovering over the mirages of the Warfield now, the place of fight and die. Far below, from the ledge of a giant hill, two pairs of unseeing eyes were watching them: the Nameless Two. From within their cave they could see all coming and going, no matter the dimension. Verbard could not contain his grimace as his clawed hand rubbed the heavy scar on his chest. It ached as the agony of dying settled in. In that moment in the cave, when he and his brother felt so invincible, he'd been quickly humbled by the single thrust of a blade. He winced again.

"Problem, Verbard?" Sinway said. "You almost look pale."

"No, Master." *Just you.*

"Then keep up," Sinway almost spat. "We've little time left."

His master sounded stressed. Perhaps the spell was fading; he could only assume.

In merely a few more moments they were hovering just outside the City of Bone. Verbard had last seen it months ago, a fleeting moment in Eep's eye, but his memory didn't serve it justice. The city of Bone was enormous, black against the shades of the suns, spires and lookouts almost ten stories tall. The miserable place was filled with humans, and all Verbard could think was how much he wanted to see them all burn alive. *That would be grand.*

It was strange though, being so close to his enemies, inside the former home of the Darkslayer. His little black heart began to pound even faster. Why were they here? As they floated closer, the multitudes of people on the outer walls began to thicken. They were coming from the Outlands, in droves, crowding the walls and fighting among themselves.

"Master," he hissed with a twinge of joy, "the exodus is, well ... masterful!"

"Indeed, Verbard, indeed. They fled the south like drowning rats, causing their own disorder. The soldiers within can barely depart without trampling their own kind like rodents. They are weak, weary, broken, sick and starving. All coming to seek refuge in the great City of Bone. Hah! They can't even bring in rations." Master Sinway's iron eyes glimmered with glee. "They have themselves under siege without even the necessity of our presence."

"How long do you think their reserves will hold them, Master?"

"Ah, well, they are prepared, but less than a year; I am certain. Hardly a blink for us, but long enough to kill off thousands more of the humans. In a few more weeks they'll be eating their dead."

Elation filled Verbard, and even Master Sinway's satisfaction was abundant on his hardened face. Verbard sensed that his master had been waiting on this for a long time. He pulled his shoulders back, lifted his chin beside his master and observed the deteriorating throng of people. Deep down he felt satisfaction that he had something to do with this. Not his brother, not Sinway nor any other underling. Him. *I rule!*

Sinway turned to him, almost with a smile on his face, his flattened teeth bared. "I've not brought you here just to bask in glory, Verbard. We both know how quickly things can change, so we are seizing the moment. I wanted to share something else with you about this grand city that you don't know."

Sinway gazed down on the city, shook his head and pointed.

"The City of Bone, as men would call it, was not always so," Sinway said, lowering his ethereal self to the ground.

Ugh, Verbard thought as the filthy people passed through him with pitiful looks and wallowed around with screaming babies. Verbard looked up the rock walls, so tall and formidable up close. *Impenetrable.* He wondered who had moved such massive rocks and was certain it was the giants or the dwarves. If Sinway was contemplating attacking it, then they would need many siege machines, a full army of soldiers and all the magic powers at their disposal. Outpost Thirty-One was one thing, but the City of Bone was quite another.

"When I was young, Verbard, the City of Bone was what the underlings called home."

Verbard silently mouthed the words, "What?"

But Sinway wasn't finished.

"The time has come to take it back, and I'm placing you in charge of that."

Verbard tried not to stammer as his nails dug into his palms. *This is my reward. I'd rather eat urchling slat first. Slat on that.*

"It would be a great honor," he bowed, "Master Sinway."

CHAPTER 11

KAM RUSHED THROUGH THE DOOR, her nerves jangling with danger at the sound of her baby's screams. A man was in the room, stout and wiry, his face aghast, her baby in his corded arms. The man was patting the baby's back, while bouncing the baby on his knees, his face distraught. It appeared nothing was working to shut off the baby's screams.

The little baby's face was red, its small mouth widening into a gaping hole. Kam's moment of panic subsided as she eased the baby into her arms and allowed the little one to latch onto her breast.

"Ssssh. Sssssh. Sssssh. Your mommy's here, you hungry little thing," she said, taking a seat on the couch. She winced. "My! Easy now, Little Girl, I'm not a cow."

Kam gently rocked her baby girl, Erin, back and forth. She felt Billip's heated gaze on her and looked up only to see his eyes quickly flit away. He was a nice enough looking fellow for such a hardened man, shifty and nervous at times, but she still caught an ornery look in his eyes now and again. He popped his knuckles, looked down in her eyes, then lower and away again. Her cheeks turned a little rosy, which was odd because over the years she'd become calloused to men's wanton eyes caressing her features.

"Eh … Kam, I'm sorry about little Erin getting so excited. One second she was fine, then the next she sounded away like a banshee." Billip twisted his black goatee and added, "Can I get you or the baby anything? Milk … er, I mean tea or some plum juice? I'd be happy to fetch you some."

"No thank you, Billip. I can take things from here, and I apologize. I should have come up sooner. I just got caught up with things down there," she said, shifting away from him.

Billip had been a great help since day one, but she had let herself get to a point where she relied on him, as well as Mikkel, too much. It didn't help that both men, each with his own rugged brand of attractiveness, had been more than willing to cater to her every whim. It was nice, though, having two men that appreciated her in a different way than the City of Three's more scholarly types did.

"Perhaps I should head on downstairs, "he said. "I'm sure Joline could use the help. It's been busier than a hive of flying toads these past few weeks. Good for business, but maybe not so much for babies. Poor little gal missed her momma something awful, even if it was for just a few hours. She's a light sleeper, that one."

Billip gave her a quick bow and turned to walk out.

"Billip, what do you make of these crowds? Do you think the rumors are true, that the underlings are taking over the south?"

A nervous look was in his eyes as he said, "There's something going on; I'm certain. Mikkel and I talk about it much, and we've been hearing lots of things, nothing like we haven't heard before, but up here in the North, well it's unheard of. Mikkel's worried—er—"

"Worried? About what?" she demanded, rising to her feet. There was something in Billip's voice that worried her.

"Er, nothing you need to concern yourself with."

"Tell me, Billip. Tell me!" she urged.

He rubbed the back of his neck and said, "I'd rather not; it's personal and all. Mikkel would kill me. Man's honor."

Now it would drive her crazy, not knowing what was being spoken about. She couldn't stand it, but she was certain she couldn't force the man to give in to her every whimsy. Or could she? As Billip stood there, eyes shifting back and forth, she shifted Erin from one breast to the other, taking her time in doing so.

"Billip," she said, parting her perfect full lips, "tell me what is on Mikkel's mind."

He blushed.

"All right! But promise you won't say anything."

"I won't," she assured him, recovering herself.

"He's worried about his boy, Nikkel."

"I didn't know he had a boy. Where is he?"

"Two-Ten City."

Kam felt a mix of anger and shame. Too many people were protecting her for her own good and not protecting themselves.

"How old is Nikkel?"

"About the same age as Georgio."

She wanted to slap somebody.

"Is there anything else I should know? Is the boy with his mother? Are there more children? And what about you, Billip? Certainly you have some children of your own."

He sucked in his breath and said, "None that have claimed me as of yet."

"Why doesn't he just go? Both of you? You don't need to stay around here. Go get Mikkel's boy and bring him back here where it's safe."

"I've tried to tell him it would be well, but we promised Venir."

Kam frowned, and her eyes began to water.

Billip cleared his throat and said, "I'm sorry, I didn't mean to say—"

"It's … it's fine, Billip."

But it wasn't. The mere mention of his name sent shivers through her. Sometimes, down in the tavern, she thought she heard his voice or laughter among the crowd, only to be left with a hollow feeling a moment later. That's why she liked to stay down in the tavern as much as she could, hoping he might swing back in the door, but she'd never admit that to herself.

"You all right?" he asked. She didn't even notice that he was sitting beside her with a hand on her knee.

"Billip, I know what you promised Venir, but the boys will be fine. Don't you think he'd understand?"

"Well, he always was pretty understanding. But, what about you, Kam? And baby Erin."

"Your promise was to take care of the boys. You've done that. Besides, seeing how I am the mother of his child, I think it's fair for me to reserve the right to speak for him in his absence. Don't you think?"

Billip tilted his head as he stroked the long hairs of his mustache

"I suppose, but—"

"Good. Now, I'll bring it up to Mikkel later—"

"No, you can't!" Billip stammered.

"Don't worry, Billip. I'll let him convince himself it was his idea. I'll fool him into asking me."

"Now, that's my kind of thinking. Cunning like a fox you are! Very well, then." Billip got up with a squeeze on her knee. "I'll be downstairs, then."

As he closed the door, Kam let out a heavy sob. She grabbed a handkerchief and blew her nose. Her life had been so much simpler before Venir had come and turned it inside out. Even though she had Erin, she still didn't know whether she was happy or sad.

"Ah, finally," she said, pulling the drowsy looking little girl away from her chest. "I see all of that screaming took a toll on you, you sweet little thing." Baby Erin cooed at the sound.

The little baby girl was sweet, with a thick mop of dark brown hair and light eyes that were opening and closing. Unlike Kam's little nose, Erin's was more broad like her father's, but the rest of her was petite, with little hands and feet topped off by a pink ribbon tied into a long braided lock of hair.

She hoisted Erin up in the air.

"Whee!"

Erin's eyes widened before she let out a sweet little giggle on the way back down.

Kam felt all of her problems leave her in the moment as she stared into her daughter's bright little eyes. She was in control. Erin was happy. She was happy, but why couldn't she stay happy? She ran through the list.

Venir, Lefty, Georgio, Fogle, Billip, Mikkel ... all men.

She nuzzled her baby's warm little body into her chest, patted her rear end and said, "I hope you fall for a much simpler kind of man that me, Erin because I don't want that little heart of yours breaking. They're hard to put back together."

Over by the windows she took notice of a rocking chair that had been a gift from Lefty and Master Gillem. The wood craftsmanship was worthy of the interiors of Royal castles, simple yet distinct. She hadn't used it yet, but the others had, from Billip to Joline. Master Gillem had been nothing but the perfect help in mentoring Lefty, and therein lay the problem: too perfect.

She patted Erin on the back, bringing forth a hearty burp.

"That's my girl." She hadn't lost her soft spot for Lefty, the tiny fair-haired halfling boy, but his not-so-innocent charms had not eluded her. He was hiding something, but it didn't bother her so much as it did Georgio. She kept telling herself they were teenage boys and that teens make mistakes, but that justification was a poor excuse on her behalf, and deep down, she knew it. Some days it was better not to try and resolve any problems at all than to bother with any of them. Some things have to work out on their own. So she told herself.

Outside, she could hear the carriages rolling over the cobblestones along with the usual greetings and pleasantries. Below the window sill was the entrance to the Magi Roost, and she recognized many patrons' voices sauntering in from a day of work in the magical city. Erin had gotten used to those sounds, and before long she was fast asleep. Kam laid her head back, closed her eyes and meditated.

She opened her eyes feeling at rest, with baby Erin still sound asleep on her chest.

Coffee.

Raising her arms up over her head and extending her fingers, she mouthed a silent incantation.

Snap-Snap.

The coals inside the stove fired with life, and the metal canister began to percolate. Two minutes later the aroma invigorated her as she laid Erin down inside her purple and olive colored cradle. She muttered another incantation, and the cradle began to rock and hum a soothing ancient tune.

"Nothing's quite like an invisible baby sitter," she said as she walked over and filled her ceramic mug. "You can thank your grandmother for that. Hmph. She even said it was the same one that I used to fall asleep to, but that was awfully long ago."

She stood near the cradle, sipping her coffee and looking out into the street. *Where is he?* All of the murmurings about the underlings had gotten to her, and the stories she overheard Billip and Mikkel telling Georgio disturbed her. She was convinced that Venir being missing had something to do with all this. *Only he could manage to piss off an entire host of underlings.* She let out a short giggle before she reached down and put her warm hand on his daughter's face. She wanted to Erin to know her father. She wanted him to come home and hold her in his arms. She wanted to kill him before anyone else did. She kept assuring herself that he wasn't dead, but every day made it seem more likely he was. Even Billip and Mikkel seemed to have resolved as much, judging by their subtle advances.

At some point you are going to have to let him go, Joline had begun to say.

But for Erin's sake she couldn't do that yet, and another thing bothered her as well: Where on Bish was Fogle Boon?

Chapter 12

Strapped to a tree like a frozen log, Fogle Boon awaited his inevitable death shivering his last moments of life away in utter misery. He didn't even bother to look up into the eyes of the mountain man coming his way gripping a gleaming bastard sword in his hairy hands. Deep down he felt shame, realizing his only friend left in the world was about to die as well. He couldn't, he wouldn't, watch his friend die first. Instead he was ready to go.

Keep your chin up before you die, Venir had said someone told him once.

"Bish!" he managed. His head felt like a block of ice as he raised it. At least he could try to volunteer his life first and maybe give Mood more time. He opened his mouth to speak, one last time, as the blade rose over his head.

"Did you say, '*I guess I'll be dying a virgin after all*'?"

The woman stood there, beautiful and cold, pink eyes filled with curiosity.

"I suppose," he said, then sneezed. "Aw … even that hurts."

Her next question caused his brilliant mind to thaw.

"So, you came up here to lose your virginity … to a druid?"

Fogle took a moment to reassure himself that she had said what she said she had. Lying wasn't his thing; he'd never needed it until now.

"Y—y-yes," he managed.

"Get me my log!" she ordered.

The big men looked at one another.

"NOW!"

Snow fell from the tree, coating Fogle as the big men burst into action. In a moment they had her propped back up before them.

She folded her arms below her ample and pleasing breasts and said, "So, why am I to believe that you—unlike every pig of a man in this world—have not been sleeping with harlots and treating uncommonly good women like whores?"

What a highly uncommon question! Fogle felt some of his inner strength return, and he was going to need every bit of it to pull off the rest of the lie. He was no story teller, but he was going to have to spin one if he wanted to make it through the day.

Here we go.

"I'm not so certain that it is possible to prove whether or not I am still a virgin, but I am, not that it matters at this point."

She kept her eyes away from his as she seemed to ponder his words.

"So, you seek to lose your virginity to a druid? Why? Certainly a common woman would do. What man travels so far to lose his innocence, a man of your age at that?"

Fogle felt his mind begin to smile from one side of his brain to the other. *She's a dolt? Is this possible? Go along with it.*

A woman beautiful, formidable and exotic sat before him, as picturesque as the great falls in the City of Three, and he had her undivided attention. The trick was keeping it.

"As you know, I am a mage of sorts, and I've been told that magic runs strongest in the veins of druids because they are the purest magic users of mankind. I want my legacy to be pure and strong." He bragged. "My mentors shielded me from my physical needs and desires until my time had come. My time is now they said, to find a druid woman, a gift of nature, and offer myself to her. If my seed is strong and she wishes to bear my child, then it shall be a strong, formidable force that even the underlings would fear to reckon with. It's—"

"Shut up! That is the most ridiculous thing I have ever heard. You are a lousy liar, but I still, for some reason, "her eyes twinkled, "suspect you are a virgin." She rubbed his delicate chin. "Hmmm. Now, tell me, really, why you have sought me out, or I'll have my men pierce your eyes with an icicle."

So much for that, but at least she admits she is a druid.

"Any chance of being warm one last time before I die?"

She reached over and cupped his face in her ginger hands. A feeling of warmth slowly made its way through his face and down to his toes. Her breath was hot steam on his face, and it had the sweet scent of honey. Feeling the urge to kiss her pale lips, he leaned forward.

Slap!

"Seems you want more than you asked for, Virgin," she said, but her tone was not one of anger. "I'm waiting."

"I'm a virgin, but that's not why we are in these, or rather, your mountains. We have a dog, a giant one with two heads, named Chongo. He's sick, and Mood," he caught her eyebrows perching as she took a quick glance over her shoulder. Maybe he said too much. "…said only a druid might be able to heal him."

Slap!

She could have slapped him a hundred times, and he wouldn't have minded. He was still warm. *She's amazing.* He smiled.

"Why are you smiling and lying?" she demanded.

"I'm smiling because I can feel my toes again and because this is the only foreplay I've ever had," he said, offering a grin.

The fingers on her hand transformed into an array of long sharp sticks that reached over and dug into his shoulder.

"Is this foreplay amusing to you, Virgin Liar? Shall I dig a little deeper into your heart's desires?" she said, squeezing.

"Gah!" he blurted out as the wooden finger punctured through his robes into his skin and began to burn. "No, I swear it! There is such a dog, and that is why we are here: to heal it!" He was getting angry now. "Kill me if you must, but know that you are killing an innocent man! Your ogres, every smelly arsed one of them, needed to die! Oh, why does a woman as glorious as you consort with the likes of them?"

She released him.

"Druids don't pick and choose between the races. We each have our purpose. The ogres are no more good or evil than men."

"That's a bunch of slat! Does the same go for underlings as well? How is your consorting with them treating you? It seems to me that you are about as far away from them as anyone could be!"

She made no reply.

He didn't notice one of the mountain men whispering something in her ear. Fogle just stared into the ground.

"Humph," she said to the mountain man. "Are you certain?"

He gave a quick nod.

Once more, she addressed Fogle, "Describe this dog, then."

Fogle spilled out every little detail, from Chongo's two whipping tails to his large dangling tongues. He told her about the albino urchlings and the wounds they had caused. The druid hung on his every word with a growing look of concern on her captivating face.

"What is your name?" she asked.

"Fogle ... Fogle Boon. And yours is?"

"Cass," She replied. "Virgin Fogle, did anyone ever tell you that you are a strange looking man?"

"Not to my face. Did anyone ever tell you that you are the most perfect thing they ever saw?"

"Flattery. Hah, you're as good at that as you are at lying. Cover his face and bind his hands," she ordered, turning away.

"But—"

She was gone. He was gagged, and a smelly sack now covered his face.

I'm not very good at this woman thing.

Chapter 13

The more Venir struggled, the more the ghastly one-eyed giant squeezed, pinching his ribs to the verge of cracking.

"S....top it!" The creature slurred out of deformed lips.

Venir would have none of that; he wasn't about to be a meal if there was anything that he could do about it. The monster, waist deep in the water, traversed from one side of the lake to the other. Ahead, Venir noticed the mouth of a cave. A black cavern over a hundred feet high loomed. *Not good.* Perhaps One Eye was planning to feed him to something else, or roast his skin in there.

Brool was still wrapped in his tight grip, the shaft warm to the touch, and if he'd get enough wiggle room he promised himself he would slice the giant's fingers off. *Wait and fight.* He let his taut muscles begin to slacken, but the grip that held him did little to subside as they entered the dark mouth of the cave.

The light of the mist disappeared as One Eye sloshed deeper into the darkness. Venir looked back for the glow of the mist, his memory flickering as to what illuminated the mist to begin with. Reason told him the mist should have blocked out the light, yet it provided it.

His eyes strained in the black behind the eyelets of his helm, but wherever he was, it was devoid of walls. How did the giant see in the black, with only one good eye no less? Something began to hum a tune, throaty and strange. It was his captor, whose belly continued to groan like an enormous bullfrog.

There was a loud slosh of water, followed by another that jolted Venir. Wet steps slapped on slick rocks he was certain he was hearing.

"Mmmmm-mah ... almost time to eat," it said.

Venir's own stomach growled.

"Great Bish ..."

"What you say, Little Giant?"

"I say," Venir yelled, "I'm gonna make your belly sour."

He bit his lip, drawing blood, as the giant shook him like a rattle. Miserable, maniacal and mortified at the thought of being eaten, Venir fought against letting his efforts subside. *Patience.* He glanced up one last time into the hot, rotten breath of the giant that was now shadowed from an unknown source of light. As he twisted around, his eyes beheld something he never would have imagined: a forest, filled with an odd assortment of strange vegetation. Green, purple and white leaves hung from branches of trees that stood taller than the giant. The ground was a familiar red, red clay.

It could not be.

No, it was not the Red Clay Forest, but it could have been, aside from the fact that it was inside of a cave and illuminated by a million speckles of yellow and orange lights that littered the sky. There was fruit hanging in abundance: green apples, purple pears and deep red cherries the size of his hand. The deformed giant stuffed him into the high branches of one of the trees. His big ugly face had a smile as he patted his big belly.

"Hungry, little giant must eat?"

Venir fought the urge to stick his axe spike into its other eye, opting to stick it into the knotted grey branch instead. He crunched into the first fruit that he could grab. It was succulent and filling. *Delicious.* Three bites into it and the only thing left was the core. He climbed down along the trunk and plucked another apple from the branches. Nearby, the giant was stuffing handfuls of the tiny fruit into his big jaws. Venir kept his distance as he ate, Brool gripped at his side. He looked around the wondrous cave and felt just as lost as ever.

"Good? Belly full?" One Eye said, with a throaty child-like voice.

Venir nodded.

"Now we play?"

Venir's mind began its trek back into reality. As his ravenous hunger and thirst were quenched, his strength and sanity began to return. He had a choice: chop the scary looking giant down like rotting timber or let his insane journey in the Under Bish play out. He ran his thumb along Brool's keen edge, drawing blood. *Must be real.*

He scanned his surroundings: trees as far as he could see, the ground covered with soft mosses, thick grasses and beds of flowers. It all had a dim hue, unnatural but not foreboding. He had the feeling he could live here for a while, in peace, not harming himself or anyone. He looked at his twelve foot tall captor and thought of Georgio, Kam, Lefty and even Melegal. He took another bite of fruit.

"What kind of game do you want to play?"

The giant stood up, big eye blinking and hands clapping.

"Name game," he said, rubbing his belly.

"All right, what is your name?" Venir asked.

"No, no, we don't play like that. You have to guess my name. I have to guess your name. See? Fun. Fun like that."

Stupid like that.

"Well then," Venir said as he swung Brool onto his shoulder and began to walk around. "If I guess your name, what do I win?"

"You get to play another game with me."

"No, that's not good." Venir rubbed his aching ribs and sighed. "I'll need something better than that."

"Like what?"

"I need to go home. To Bish, the world above this. Can you take me there if I win?"

"The river will take you there, but it's a bad place. Don't go there."

Venir gawped. The other giant hadn't lied. All he had to do was follow the river after all.

"BONE!" he swung his axe into a tree.

"Hey, don't do that!" The giant warned him, storming over. "No hurt the tree."

Venir ripped the axe out. His patience was lost as he bore down on the giant and stabbed it in the foot.

"OW!" It yelped, jumping up and down. "Why you hurting me?"

Pity and remorse for his action fled Venir as he looked upon the distraught giant's ugly face.

"I need to get back to BISH now! Can you take me there? And remember, if you lie, I'll cut your tongue out."

Leaves and fruit fell from the trees, the giant's ghastly scream was so loud. Venir covered his ears, but now was not the time for mercy. He would have his answers.

"I feed you, Little Giant, and you stab me. You don't play nice."

"Can you take me to Bish or not?"

"Not if you don't play with me first," the giant said, holding his bleeding foot.

One Eye cringed as Venir hoisted his axe over his head.

"S......top it! S...top it! Mean little giant!"

"You'll live, you big one-eyed baby." Venir poked him in the leg with Brool. "And no tricks."

"I take you, you play with me."

"NO! You take me and I promise I'll find you someone to play with. I've got things to do."

"Let me guess your name first."

"It's Venir."

"No! Don't tell me! Drat. You stink, Venir. You worse than the giants that don't play with me 'cause I ugly."

"Are you a runaway?"

"NO!"

Venir shook his head. He didn't have time to deal with this nonsense. He wanted to go home.

"Just take me out of here." One Eye pulled his knees up to his chest and buried his face.

Venir sighed. Perhaps he needed another approach, and seeing how he wasn't starving to death he could exercise a little more patience. He grabbed a purple pear that filled his hand and took a hearty bite. Fruit wasn't ever a steady part of his diet, just an occasional substitute for meat and bread when he was out on the hunt. It was tasty, not juicy like a steak of venison, but just as satisfying.

As his aggravations began to subside, the taut muscles in his broad shoulders began to soften. He stuck his axe in the ground.

"So, Giant, what is your name?"

The big bald head waddled back and forth.

"Nothing."

"Is it Big Baldie?"

The giant grumbled a no.

"How about Dragon Rider?"

His head popped up, his big eye glimmering.

"No like that!"

"Ah … Dragon Crusher, then?"

One Eye rose up from the ground to his full height, arms raised over twenty feet in the air, fists clenched. Venir grabbed Brool and stepped back into the trees. *Oh no.*

"Barton like that!" he bellowed, pounding his chest.

Yes! I've got his name.

"Ah …then it's Barton the Dragon Crusher!" Venir yelled.

"Barton hate the dragons!"

"What about the one called Blackie?"

Barton's eye widened beneath his uni-brow as he flopped to the ground and faced Venir.

"You know Blackie?"

"Yes. As a matter of fact, I clipped his wing with my axe after he tried to scorch my flesh from my bones. I sent him wailing into the mist yelping like a wounded dog."

Barton poked his log sized finger into Venir's chest.

"You not lie?"

"No."

"Baron hate Blackie. Blackie always bring Barton home. That's why I hide in this cave. Blackie no come in here and take me away. Barton safe."

"Barton," Venir said, "you also told me your name."

"Huh … ah, stupid me!" he slapped his head.

"You have to take me back to Bish now, Barton. I won the game."

"No," Barton huffed.

"Barton, do the giants break their word to you?"

It frowned and said, "Yes."

"Does it make you mad when they lie?"

"Yes."

"Well, you're doing the same thing to me. You don't want to be like them, do you?"

Barton got up, scratching his chest, big eye blinking. Venir searched the eye of the giant. It was an odd creature, humanoid, scarred and misshapen, that moved more like a child than a man. Venir felt some sorrow for it, but now was not the time for compassion. Now was the time to find freedom. *Come on, you lout, be honest this once. I don't give a slat for the rest of the time.*

"Barton, you get me out of here and I'll tell you where to find a friend."

It'd be pretty hard to sneak up on underlings with you around.

"You be my friend. I stay on Bish with you."

"Sorry Barton, but I've got things to do there. I can't take you where I'm going. All I can offer is a friend, here, that you can count on. He can take care of you, assuming he's still alive." He lied. Boon the wizard was dead in his mind by all accounts. He'd seen the giants swat him on the wall, and he figured if anything, he'd splattered like a bug. Of course, there was the were-rat too, a sly female of silky gray fur. The question was, had any of it at all been real? Barton seemed to confirm that. But, was Barton real? For all Venir knew, he was still walking along the river. Maybe he was even dead or imprisoned somewhere, for that matter.

"What? You try to give me a dead friend. What kind of friend is that? I'm not stupid!"

Yes you are.

"Either way," Venir placed his fists on his hips, "you still have to take me home."

Barton pounded his chest with his meaty hand, shaking his belly and saying, "I have honor." A large tear dripped from his eye and splashed onto the ground. "I take you home, Venir, little giant."

"Why do you call me that, little giant?"

"Hmmm," Baron rubbed his chin and said, "maybe tiny giant better. You smell like a giant."

Ew.

"I hope not."

Venir didn't understand the entire giant thing. It wasn't the first time he had heard that, and he couldn't help but think there was something to it.

"Hee hee, you funny, Venir. Mean, but funny." Barton had a devious look in his eye. "Uh … Venir, I can't take you with your stuff. Giant magic not like metal. You must leave it behind."

The hairs stood up all over his body.

"*I can't do that,*" he exclaimed.

"Then you have to stay," Barton said, eyeing his axe with a keen interest.

Venir had the feeling the giant was lying and wanted the armament for himself. *Toys to play with for an under grown man.* Not so stupid after all, Barton had shown he had another card to play. What choice did Venir have but to believe him? *Think.* He had an idea.

"Tell you what, Barton: since you are helping me I'll leave it all as a gift, to remember me by."

"Really?"

"Yes, but first, one last game, for fun. I'm going to hide them in the forest here, so they'll be safe. When you get back, you can have some fun finding them."

"That does sound like fun. But don't hide them too hard. Barton has trouble seeing sometimes."

"All right, well can you turn around while I go and hide them? And no peeking."

"Hee hee, this is fun. I'll even count," he said, turning his back to Venir. "One ... Two ..."

As Venir clutched his axe, he had the feeling now would be the best time to brain the brute. Maybe he didn't need Barton after all. *Gonna have to trust him.*

Venir dropped the armament into the sack along with several fruit. *Why not.* He folded the sack and stuffed it beneath his shirt.

"Well enough, I'm finished."

Barton whirled around, dumbstruck.

"Already?"

"Yep, I made it easy," Venir said, arms folded across his chest. "Can we go now?"

Barton pushed up some branches as he peered deeper into the grove of trees and said, "This will be easy." He looked over at Venir, stroked his hair and added, "You look much better now. You have pretty hair like a girl, but you still make an ugly girl."

Venir bit his tongue. *You still make an ugly giant.*

Barton extended his hand and said, "All right, it's time to go. Hang on tight. I'm not very good at this."

Venir grabbed the giant around the wrist and held on for dear life as he felt his body turn inside out.

Chapter 14

"**M**UST YOU STILL BE HERE?**"** Melegal slung his cap onto the mantle where a small fire blazed from underneath.

"You keep saying you'll change the locks, but you never do," Haze picked up his cap from the mantle and dusted it off before hanging it on a small nail beside the fire.

He sneered as he pulled off his boots and sat down in a pillowed high-back chair that sat in the corner near the fire. He didn't give Haze a single glance as she pushed a stool beneath his feet. He laid his head back and closed his eyes, tracking every movement of Sefron in his mind. *Magic.* The sloppy cleric had foiled him again, and his head ached for it.

As he ran his bony fingers through his salt and pepper hair he could hear Haze creeping through Detective McKnight's former apartment that he now called his own. A smell of spiced soup was in the air, and he heard a cork being pulled from a wine bottle. His face allowed the ever slightest smile while the fire began roasting his toes.

Haze sat beside him on a much smaller chair, holding out a bowl of soup and a goblet.

"I tell you to leave, threaten your paltry life and there you sit like an urchin offering me more piss porridge. I'm beginning to think your sisters are the brightest of the three nitwits."

He sat up in the chair and sniffed the air.

"They haven't been in here, have they? It smells like the fat one's sweat and armpits."

Haze sat there, plain and serene, quite content among his insults. She'd been like this since the day he diddled her like a trollop: fawning and obedient, like he was a Royal of sorts. Despite his reminders that she was of as little worth to him as a field mouse in a cat house, she stuck around like a stubborn child that wouldn't go home. She had even painted her nails, combed her hair and worn more revealing clothes that offered little more than a pair of skinny legs below a tight little rump. She even smelled good.

"You look tired," she remarked.

Melegal swiped the goblet from her hand, swished it around his mouth and spat it into the fire, bringing a sizzle. Octopus rumbled from his spot on the hearth, his back muscles rippling beneath his black coat before lowering.

"Are you trying to poison me, Woman?" he exclaimed, pulling the bowl from her hands.

She blanched. "I thought you might like something different. I'm sorry. I'll get your usual."

She scampered away to grab another goblet, a look of worry in her grey eyes.

He sipped the soup. It was good, not Royal good, but better than his usual fare. He hated to admit it, but she was pretty good at making soup and some other things, too. He grunted.

"Wine please," he said, handing her the bowl.

"Ah," he sipped and swished, "so much better. What was that drivel you gave me?"

"It's called port. I heard many people talking of it in the city. I thought you would—"

"Please don't think on my behalf, understand?"

"Yes Melegal. I'm sorry. I'll pour it out."

He waved her off and said, "Nay, perhaps I'll serve it to my enemies one day. Port, you say?"

She nodded, a half-smile cracked over his thin pale red lips.

"Never heard of it," he lied.

Haze reached over and touched his feet. Her touch was light as a feather, almost soft enough to tickle.

He sighed.

"Must you maintain this obsession with my glorious feet? Do you miss those days beneath the castles, rubbing the feet and arses of the self-glorifying and vain?"

Without saying a word, she twisted and rubbed, while he drank, frowned and enjoyed.

As much as he wanted to give in to the moment, his mind began running over his checklist.

Kill Sefron. Find the Slergs and have them killed. Do what Lord Almen says. Do what Lorda Almen says. Don't get yourself killed. Kill Sefron. Uncover threats to Castle Almen. Find valuable information and deliver it to Lord Almen. Avoid the Castle. Avoid the Almens. Drink more wine. Sample more port.

"Ah! Easy now, I'm not one of your hooved sisters."

She rolled up his pants legs and rubbed his calves.

"So, Melegal, have you found what you're looking for?"

"No."

Without looking at him she said, "I can help."

"No, you can't help, and quit asking."

"But I found some Slergs," she reminded him.

She actually had helped. He hated that.

He pushed is pants leg down and said, "Yes, but I could have paid any urchin a silver booger and that would have yielded the same results."

"I'm not finished," she said as he stood up.

"My feet are fine," he said, removing his vest and shirt.

She grabbed his arm and pulled him back.

"I'm not talking about rubbing your bloody feet!"

In a single motion he had her wrist twisted behind her back. He made a throaty whisper in her jeweled ear saying, "What are you talking about?"

She pushed her hips back into his and said, "I think I know where the rest of the Slergs are."

He twisted her wrist a little harder and whispered, "You lie!"

He felt her chest begin to heave.

"No, I can prove it!" she squealed.

With his other hand he grabbed the back of her hair and began to pull.

He didn't know whether to believe her or not, but it didn't matter. His blood began to run hot as she let out a soft moan.

"Tell me everything you know, Haze, or I'll take my belt to you."

He saw the goose bumps rise on her neck as she shuddered.

"There is a price, Rogue. Either pay it or kill me," she panted.

"You better hope I don't do both," he said as he pulled her into a small candlelit bedroom and slammed the door closed with his foot.

CHAPTER 15

A SMALL GROUP OF RAGGED MEN carrying small torches traversed the tunnels beneath the City of Bone. Each was wrapped from head to toe in torn and tattered clothes, their faces covered in dirty cowls, some feet bare, the others sandaled. Their soft steps and breathing could barely be heard except for one in the rear, a large one that seemed able to plug the narrow corridor with his bulk. He was bigger, significantly so, his breathing heavy, his footsteps loud. He was drawing the ire of another who continued his complaints from the front.

"Leezir, your giant urchin continues to slow us," Hagerdon said with a sneer in his voice. "It's time to cut bait and run."

"Must you be so dramatic, Fool?" Leezir replied, pushing his way through a massive water pipe that was as dry as a bone. "Can you even count, you moron? How many heads do you see?"

Hagerdon pulled his cowl down, revealing a shaven head in the dim torchlight as he hurried along. They all were shaved now; it was the best way to conceal their identities from the searching eyes above, as well as those below. Hagerdon hated it. He loved his thick locks of glorious hair, and he missed the feeling of painted finger tips running through it. All his leader Leezir could offer him was that he wouldn't have to worry about lice, or dandruff for that matter. He scoffed; he'd never had a flake in his life.

"I know, eight Slergs, but we have an army of man-urchins at our disposal," he said, now crawling over a patch of wet and sticky muck on his knees and elbows. Even worse were the comings and goings of abhorrent stench, but he'd managed to get accustomed to them.

Leezir shook his white cudgel in Hagerdon's face.

"You are such a fool, Nephew! Two weeks ago there were fifteen of us. The man-urchins have suffered even greater losses taking bribes for our cause, and now you, still impudent and young, want to abandon a fighting man who is three in one? Was he not the one who pulled you from your grave a mere week ago when the City Watch had us by the balls? And now you want to cut loose the only redeemable man, er boy, er whatever from us?"

Hagerdon was adamant.

"Yes."

He could see Leezir's eyes blaze like fire underneath his black cowl as he swallowed hard and stepped back. When the cudgel began to glow there was a gasp from behind.

The last few months had been hard. The once mighty Slerg House was being dwindled away. Not one Royal house, not even the lowest on the tier, would give them audience. If anything, they gave them away. Lord Almen would not end his hunt until he was certain every single threat was gone.

Leezir added as he turned around, "It's days like this that I wish it was you who died and not your brother Creighton. He was sensible."

His hand clutched the pommel of his sword, but Leezir was already hurrying down the dingy corridor.

"SLAT!" Leezir screamed from up ahead.

Hagerdon and the rest caught up and groaned at the source of their leader's aggravation. A five foot iron grate barred their path, its iron bars eroding but thick.

Leezir kicked. Hagerdon pulled.

"We're just going to have to go back up top," Hagerdon said.

"Is that so?" Leezir walked up on his toes. "Then you go back and lead the hounds from our trails. I'm sure they won't devour your scent." He smacked his cudgel into the stone walls. "Does anyone else want to go back and face the City Watch or suffer an inquisition of Detective Melegal and his brood of Almen thugs?"

No one said a word, until Hagerdon broke the silence.

"It seems we have no choice but to go another way. Certainly we can double back and find another course or wait until night and take our chances on the streets. Leezir, we can't hide forever down here."

Month after month they had stayed down below, stealing from above like common orphans. The man-urchins did most of the work, but the results were paltry. Hagerdon had his fill of the stink, rot and filth that was now his life. Just one more time he wanted to take a shower, adorn clean clothes and swing his steel in one last battle to the death. There was nothing dignified in living like a rodent, but Leezir, in his obsession to avenge himself on the Almens, insisted on this course. And being somewhat of a coward, Hagerdon followed those orders. Life is preferable to death after all, no matter how slatty it gets.

Leezir let out a long drawn out sigh. His shoulders slouched as he slid down the wall onto his haunches. The others followed suit except Brak, who stood like a golem at the end.

"Perhaps, brothers, Hagerdon is right. Our time may have run its course. Jubilee, dear, have we been followed? And please say your pepper left the dogs from our trail."

A small figure crept forward, naked feet pushing through the grime before taking Leezir's hand.

"Aye Grandfather, I've lost the dogs, ten tunnels since. But my pepper is low. I'm sorry."

He patted her ragged head and said, "Well enough, dear one. And, Taggert, are we still on course to the northern most corner of the city?"

"Aye, Leezir. Direction's good. I'm certain."

"Hmmm … I believe my ears have detected something disturbing," Leezir said.

Hagerdon frowned as he heard something, too.

A sound of barking dogs was echoing down the corridor.

The little girl's eyes widened.

Hagerdon's swords sang from their sheaths.

Rising to his feet, Leezir's cudgel burst aglow.

"This is it, Slergs! We will survive this, not all but some. Brak, today you live or die a Slerg."

Brak was coming their way.

"Brak," Hagerdon said, barring his path, "you oaf, what are you doing? Get in front and protect us!"

Everyone cleared out as Brak waded past them as if they weren't there. There was nothing but stark determination in his close-set eyes when he wrapped his big meaty hands around the iron bars.

"You idiot! Get back there and fight, Coward. There's no doorway to run though there."

Brak's short powerful arms began to pull.

"Heave Brak!" Leezir prompted in his ear.

The massive man-boy squatted down, putting his arms and legs into it.

"*Hurk!*"

Hagerdon couldn't hide his amazement as the metal began to groan.

The yelping of the hounds became louder.

"Pull, Man! Pull and I'll roast you the fattest sow you ever saw!" Hagerdon promised.

Sweat was rolling down Brak's forehead as his big face began to turn red and purple under the torch glow. The bars began to bend, the ever slightest.

One of the Slergs said with astonishment, "It's bending! Bend it, Brak!"

Brak dug his heels into the lip of the grate and tugged. The iron groaned in defiance before giving in to living muscle which had turned to steel. The first bar rolled upward.

"I can't believe it!"

Brak grabbed the next bar and pulled.

"Hurry, Brak!" Jubilee cheered.

The bar groaned and gave way. The hounds became louder in the distance, intertwined with the shouting voices of the City Watch.

Leezir shoved Jubilee through the gap.

"Quick everyone, go through!"

There was little more than two feet of space to squeeze through the bars, but none hesitated. One by one they crawled through, tearing clothes and skin, scraping sides. Hagerdon was the last to go.

"Come on, Brak! Bend one more and join us. The roasted sow is waiting!" he said, his green eyes glinting in the torch light.

Brak reached down and bent the first bar downward.

"What are you doing, you buffoon? You'll get yourself killed! Get over here!"

Brak bent the second bar back down and slumped against the wall, chest heaving.

"No!" Jubilee cried. "Brak, no!"

"Go," Brak gasped. "I'm only slowing you down. Goodbye, Jubilee." He reached through the bars, wiping the tear from her cheek. "Slat on the rest of you."

Leezir stood there, face pressed against the bars, his wizened face bewildered. He shook his head.

"Come on, Jubilee. He's bought us time, no reason to stand around and watch his slaughter. Move with haste now; the Watch may have magic afoot, too."

Jubilee sobbed as they scurried away, her eyes drifting back then out of sight, but Hagerdon remained.

"Here," he said, tossing a knife at Brak's feet. "You'll need that in close quarters, you lout. Stupid like your father, I see. Giving your life for others." Hagerdon added a quick salute. "Maybe what I taught you will give you an extra minute to realize how stupid you are."

Brak sat with a glum look on his face, watching him go.

The barking dogs were echoing with loud ferocity now as Hagerdon bolted down the tunnel, happy to know that Brak, the son of Venir, was about to be eaten alive. *At least I gave him a fighting chance before he becomes dog food.*

"More sow for me."

Chapter 16

FOGLE AWOKE IN DARKNESS, HEAD aching and unable to move. *Where am I?* He tried to choke down his panic as he struggled with his bonds. He found comfort in the fact that his fingertips were no longer frozen, or the rest of him for that matter. Wherever he was, he was upright, sitting on soft ground of an unfamiliar texture. *Mood.* Was his lone protector with him or dead? Mood had told him there would be days like this when you adventured outside your home, and he needed every detail he could find of his surroundings if he was going to formulate a plan … to escape.

Mood's advice had seemed silly at the time, weeks ago, but the Blood Rangers' wisdom seemed crystal clear. *If you don't have your eyes, use your ears.* He listened. There was a soft rustling nearby, and the wind was rolling over a canvas, like a flag. *A tent.* He balled up into a knot as something growled, hungry and horrible. A picture of the big wolves with those rows of pointed, saliva-dripping canine teeth appeared in his mind. Hadn't Cass said she would feed him to them?

Use your nose, Mood had told him.

"It smells like dogs," he said out loud. He tightened his lips as something padded by him, brushing fur across the bridge of his nose. He took a deep draw through his nose. "And scented candles?"

Skin, he thought.

It was warmer, much more so, as if a fire was nearby, but the sound of crackling wood was not there. As happy as he was to be able to feel himself again, he could only imagine his situation had gotten worse. The woman, Cass, seemed a little touched in the head. Her voice was eerie, and her pink eyes were shifty. Mood had said druids were tricky, and with this one he was certain she was everything a druid could be: strange, sneaky and magnificent. He thought he could smell her breath.

"Aaaaa-CHOO!" he sneezed.

The wolves barked and growled. He could feel them nipping at his face.

"HEEL!" a strong feminine voice commanded. *Cass?*

"Don't make another sound, Virgin Fogle, or my wolves will devour you," she said, her voice dark, ugly, dangerous.

He didn't care.

"If I'm going to—"

A pair of jaws snapped at his face.

"Egad!" he cried. His body began to shiver at the thought of the canines crunching his bones. *Make a plea.*

He cleared his throat.

"Can I at least glance at you on last time, Cass? At least I can dream I'm no longer a virgin in my last moments."

She made a funny sound. Next, he heard footsteps, like petals coming his way. All of the most wonderful fragrances of nature filled his nose as something soft and plentiful brushed into his face.

He swallowed as he felt two petite hands working the knot behind his head and slowly removing his blindfold.

"Happy, Virgin Fogle?" Cass's chest was inches from his nose. A pink gossamer robe adorned her exotic figure. Her skin was perfect: translucent and soft, and her white hair seemed impossibly curly and long. Another wave of feeling washed over him, not the kind he expected to have when he was about to die, but something else quite unexpected … Lust.

"Hmmm …" she purred as she got down on her knees and began loosening the bonds around his ankles.

Fogle didn't want to take his eyes off of a single inch of her figure, but he fought to do so. His eyes flitted over his surroundings. A tent surrounded them over the top of a bed of green grass. Six large timber wolves had them both surrounded, sitting, licking their chops and other parts as well. Forty one candles of all shapes and sizes were in the room, eleven lit, flames wavering from a draft. Incense sticks burned from a small mantle made of trees. He never imagined he'd experience that again. Three sheep skin rugs. Fifteen pelts of fur. And in the middle, laying over most of the grass, was the pelt of a silverback grizzly bear. He knew, because Mood had killed one weeks earlier. His eyes went back to Cass. His mouth was watering, no longer dry as he began to thirst like he never thirsted before.

"Virgin Fogle," she whispered in his ear, "you are here for a reason. It can only be, because I too am a virgin."

He tried to find the words to speak but could not as she pressed her finger to his lips.

"I've rejected the world of men, Fogle. They can't be trusted, but I know your words are true." His legs trembled as she pulled him up from his chair. "I want to help you, and I want you to help me. I've waited so long for this."

Oh my!

He searched for her eyes, but he could not find them as she pulled him down onto the grizzly pelt. As his heart thundered throughout this body his brilliant mind fought one last time to regain control. *Druids can't be trusted,* Mood had warned.

"Take me, Fogle," she said, pressing her full body into his.

All of the passion buried inside him exploded as he kissed her.

She tugged at his hair, pulling him down on top of her. He glanced at the wolves one last time and said, "This isn't how I imagined it."

"Me either," she added, pulling off her robe. "Disappointed?"

His smile was as broad as a rainbow.

"No, it's an adventurer's life for me." Her chuckle was low and wicked, but he didn't hear a thing.

Outside the tent, Mood awakened inside his icy cocoon. Nearby, two mountain men were sharpening their blades and chatting. One said to the other, "Shame he won't even have time to enjoy it."

CHAPTER 17

FOR THE FIRST TIME IN his life, Sefron saw pure evil. It lurked behind the black eyes of the Vicious that squeezed his life from his throat. He managed a sickening gag as his tongue rolled inside his mouth like a salted slug. His mental pleas to be released quickly gave way to despair as he began to slat on himself.

"Release him," a cool voice said from somewhere.

Sefron fell hard to the ground, both knees cracking on the stone as he fought for a breath of air. He hacked, wheezed and sat confused for over a minute before he managed to compose himself. He pulled his skinned up knees to his chest and looked up.

The black creature, inhuman, cat-faced, a monstrous hulk, was now standing behind a much lither figure. An underling stood tall in his black chain mail, a pair of sheathless swords hung criss-crossed on its back, their gleaming edges keener than the sharpest razor. A bandolier of knives was wrapped around its chest. Its eyes were like copper ore, its hair short, almost shaven to its head. The underling was known to Sefron as Kierway, a black ranger of his kind, he had boasted, and the finest swordsman of his craft. The underling man seemed every bit as formidable as the newcomer, but in a different sort of way.

Kierway had his hands on his hips as he said, "Do you have it, Human?"

"Nay, Master," Sefron said, falling to his knees, "but I am close."

Something flashed through the air, and Sefron wailed in misery. A small throwing knife now protruded from his knee.

"Human, I have ten more of these, you know, some poisoned, others not," Kierway said, juggling three in one hand. "I'm beginning to question your loyalty. Perhaps your needs are being fulfilled above, and you no longer desire what I have offered."

Sefron's arm shot out despite his agony.

"No Master Kierway! I am close. Oh so close. The key shall soon be yours. I know where it is, but I don't have the skills to acquire—YEE-OUCH!"

Another knife buried itself deep in his shoulder.

A cave moth fluttered in the dank air only to be cut down by Kierway's longsword in one fluid motion.

Sefron blinked hard.

"Did you see that, Human? Fast, wasn't it?" Kierway began to saunter around. "My, it's been a long journey, only to wind up here and find out that you have been an utter failure. Hmmm … I can't help but wonder how long it would take me to cut your leg into twenty pieces."

Sefron's blood went cold as he watched in helpless horror as Kierway's swords buzzed in the air like humming bird wings. He had to survive. He would survive. He would have vengeance on all of those Royals who had used him for decades. The City of Bone would be run over by underlings, and he was promised a castle and all the human slaves he wanted of his own. All he needed was the key.

"Y-yes, Master Kierway. May I beg of you, this key, will you share with me what it does?"

"NO!" Kierway said, plucking his blades from Sefron's wounds.

"Ah …," he stammered and groaned as he tried to speak, "But …"

"Time is running out, Human," Kierway said as he and the Vicious walked back into the darkness. "When you get it, we will know. Get it soon, or I shall find someone else to gain the prize."

NO!

Sefron stiffened as he sat up. Grimacing, he pulled out a small jar and applied ointment to his wounds. It burned, sealing the wound shut, but he was used to it. Kierway had stabbed him many times over the years, just not this many times at once. Sefron fought his way back to his feet and began the painful walk back up the stairs. He thought he knew where the key was, but he would need help trying to get it. Who would he have to fool to get it? *Maybe Detective Melegal can be useful after all.*

CHAPTER 18

IT WAS A GRUESOME SCENE, a man and woman, neither more than a day over thirty, torn and broken in broad daylight. The City Watch, decorated in their brown and gray, mired with hate and grime, remained casual about their business. They had seen death in the streets of Bone before, although this situation was a little more unique than the rest. The dead man, a well-known labor boss of the 14th District, lay in a pool of blood, his head missing.

"I'm telling you, I saw the man twist his head from his shoulders and toss it up on the roof."

"Hrmph," the watch sergeant said, "and what about the woman? How come she's still got her head?"

The residents murmured. They didn't normally fool with the Watch, and answering questions usually got you into more trouble than it was worth, but this time things were different. This time, they were under attack and needed protection, of some sort, anyway.

"The monster hit her so hard with its fist I heard her neck snap like a busted pallet. The man pulled his sword and lunged, but the murderer was much faster. Grabbed him by the neck by one hand he did, lifted him from the ground and squeezed."

Another chimed in.

"The man, the dead one, he was big, too, and the other, picked him up like a child, rattled him in the air, then twisted his head off."

The watch sergeant spit brown juice on the ground and wiped the sweat from his brow on his sleeve.

"No man twisted his head off! That's impossible. That's a cut! Idiots!"

"Did too!"

The sergeant nodded his head saying, "Well, did any one of you get a closer look at this big monster of a man? I'm hearing lots of stories, but not many descriptions. And by the way, where is the man's sword that he drew? Which one of you stole it?"

"The monster stole it, not us!"

The watch sergeant grabbed the uppity man by his shirt collar and said, "Don't talk to me like that."

"I pay my fees, I'll say what I—*oomph!*"

The man crumpled in a heap under the force of the Watchman's punch.

"Any more of you want to discuss your fees?"

The small group backed away, but one remained. An older woman, heavy set with deep wrinkles in her forehead, jutted her hip out and said, "That's ten murders in the past few months, and they not so much as stopped yet. And I hear the other districts got murders, too." She spat juice on the road. "What's you gonna do about that?"

He slid his watch stick from behind his belt and began to slap it into his hand.

"Heads up!" a voice yelled from above.

Clonk.

A man's head bounced off the cobble stones and rolled at his feet. It was the labor boss, his long yellow hair matted with blood.

The woman said, "He kinda looks like you, Blondie. Seems the monster-man doesn't like pretty hair like yours. Ain't it true, all them dead men had straw colored hair? Big fellows, too, same as you, except I think your belly's a bit fuller."

The Watchman gawped a bit, his Adams apple rolling under his chin.

The feisty woman began twisting her fingers in her blonde hair and added. "What about that other man, two roads over, everything chopped up from his neck down to his toes? Wasn't he one of yours?" She cackled, but she wasn't alone. It wasn't often that the citizens got a chance to poke at the City Watch. "It's a shame you all aren't yellow headed, then that monster would be a hero."

The lead Watchman looked up on the rooftop and yelled, "Get down here, Clovis. The rest of you," there were four watchmen in all, "get a cart and take them to the morgue, and we'll give the family a day to claim them." He straightened himself up and said, "You fine citizens of Bone better get your stories straight. Whoever is doing this is a man, not a wight, underling or ghoul. It's just some crazy bastard with a sword that is touched in the head. Lock your doors, don't go fooling around at night. As of now there's a curfew."

They groaned.

"And it starts now. Whoever it was must be close; this just happened less than an hour ago. If you see anyone strange, just whistle. In the meantime—"

Somebody whistled.

"Fine, I was being kind, but if yer going to be a bunch of pigs arses—"

Clovis shouted from the roof top.

"Hey! It was me! Look," he said, pointing down the roadway.

A man stood tall and broad a little ways down the road. A bastard sword stained in blood was gripped in his hands. His armor, partial plate, had the insignia of a Royal, and the rest of his body was draped with a dark cloak with a cowl wrapped over his head.

Most of the crowd gasped, but the woman screamed.

The sergeant drew his sword and yelled, "You're under arrest!" The other watchmen followed suit, swords in shaking hands. Clovis watched unblinking from above.

"VEE-MAN!" the man in the road cried.

"Get him!" the leader ordered. The City Watch charged.

CHOP! One Watchman's head was split in twain.

CLANG!

SWIPE! Another fell, writhing in his blood, screaming for mercy as his entrails were spilled.

CHOP! The third turned to run a split second too late.

The leader fell back on his footsteps, gawping in horror.

Fear managed to pull his tongue from the roof of his mouth as he screamed, "Someone go for reinforcements!"

Only the sound of running feet and doors slamming shut greeted him, then he stood there all alone.

"VEE-MAN!" He slipped and fell as he turned to run. The man snorted a laugh, coming his way on heavy legs with armor and weapons creaking and clanking.

Tonio saw a big man with straw colored hair falling to the ground and screaming something at him.

What the man was saying didn't matter, as he assumed they could only be more insults from Venir. He thought he'd killed his adversary, if not once, a dozen or more times, only to see him back on the streets again, gloating and mocking him. His broad face and yellow hair was always mocking and taunting him.

He swung into the man's leg and watched it skitter a bloody trail across the road. He followed up with a deep swing into the man's heaving chest, oblivious to the blade that was thrust into his side. It was a pinch at worst in his deranged mind as he swiped the blood from his mouth, knocked the man's cap from his head, pulled him up by the hair and chopped off his head. Somewhere nearby a man screamed, and he peered up on the roof and gazed at a man covering his mouth, tears filling his eyes.

He looked at the face of his vanquished foe, Venir, or so he wanted to believe, and hurled the head through a window.

"Vee-man!"

Bloody sword in hand, Tonio departed from the scene, still hungry for vengeance. He would kill them all if he had to, and make his mother proud. The once empty streets began to fill as he went, and not one person crossed his path. The whispers of horror and sounds of pursuit became loud in his ears as he disappeared into the tunnels beneath the City of Bone. How many more times would he have to kill Venir before Tonio could return home to Castle Almen?

In the darkness he huddled inside a small cell, a former home of other miscreants that all now were dead and washed away in the sewers. He pulled at his hair and mumbled. He knew he didn't always used to be this way, that he had a home, a mother and father. He had eaten at the finest tables, and beautiful women had filled his bed. Everything was confusing though, distorted, blurry, vague and twisted. He snatched a rat and bit into it.

Where was McKnight? That man could help him, give him guidance to something, but without direction all he had was vengeance on his mind, and he would enact it over and over again until the last Venir was gone.

Bish have mercy on the fair-haired citizens of Bone.

CHAPTER 19

"T HE BLACK FIENDS FROM THE Underland have come!" a warrior, fortyish, with a beard touched by grey clamored.

Mikkel and Billip had the man pinned up against the wall near one of the corner fire places in the Magi Roost. The warrior wasn't any slouch, either. His arms were like hammered iron, and his wounds were fresh, but dried. His eyes were darting back and forth, his cracked lips yearning to speak more, but Mikkel kept his forearm shoved in his throat.

"This isn't the place for spreading rumors," Billip warned. "You'll be moving your bad news elsewhere, or you'll be dead or in the hole."

The Magi Roost was in full swing, and the scholars as well as the racial variety of merchant had gathered a keen interest. The serving girls began refilling goblets, batting eyes and swinging their hips, drawing away the customers' attention. But not all the girls could hide the nervous look in their painted eyes. This wasn't the first time a dark tale of underling hordes found its way behind the walls of the tavern. It was just another one of what had become many over the passing weeks.

"Let me go," the man managed. "I'm a warrior, such as you both, and you know my words ring true. I must tell these people what is going on." The warrior's voice was strong and convincing. "The Royals sit in their towers and castles doing nothing while we sit here like sheep waiting to be slaughtered."

Mikkel and Billip eyed one another. They both knew what the underlings did to men. It didn't help that most of the stories that were spreading around the city were for the most part, accurate. Mikkel lowered his arm from the man's neck and said, "Keep it low, Man, and sit. I want to hear more."

Billip raised his eyes in objection, then directed the man to a table tucked behind the bar in the front. As they sat, Mikkel sat down with a pitcher of ale and one of the waitresses brought over a half loaf of bread and cheese.

"Thank you, men," the warrior said. "I've not had real food in a month, and three days travel to here seemed like an eternity." The warrior said it while stuffing his mouth with bread and washing it down with ale. "Sweet Bish, I swore I'd perish before I ever tasted this nectar again."

Mikkel filled his own mug and said, "Tell us more, and keep it down. There's nothing but magi with big ears in here."

"Maybe underling spies, too," the warrior offered.

"No, couldn't be," Billip disagreed, craning his neck and popping his knuckles.

The warrior shrugged. "I'm crossing over from Hohm, part of a heavily guarded merchant train, not a day any different than before. Over twenty well-armed men bringing in the goods, wagons full of spices, seeds, grain, gold and other things. My face is known here, my comrades as well; you can check."

Mikkel rolled his wrist before leaning back and crossing his arms over his chest.

"It was hot, the landscape full of mirages, and tricks began to play on our minds as the first dusk began. We were setting up camp when the horses began acting funny, snapping and stomping men and one another. I don't know about you, but I've never seen horses bite one another like that before. Then the wind came, a crying howl, like a woman in pain, stirring the dirt and blinding us from seeing anything."

The warrior finished his first mug with a loud gulp and whipped his sleeve across his mouth.

"Ah! So, a storm was all, and we'd been through over a dozen land squalls like that before, so we hitched down what we could and prepared to ride it out. As suddenly as it started, it stopped, and that's when the screams began."

Billip re-filled all of their mugs, itchy fingers twisting at his goatee.

"The second dusk had settled, and our camp was swarmed with dark figures, at least two to our one. Some of them rode spiders. Others walked in the air, like living nightmares. I never could have imagined something so terrible if I had not seen it for myself. The underlings, thick furry little faces and bright gemstone eyes, chittered in elation as they began to chop us down. Webs sprung up in the air, taking my men down like helpless flies only to see their throats cut."

Billip interrupted saying, "So did you stand there and watch, or did you fight?"

The man's eyes narrowed.

"I don't know you, Man, and you don't know me, but I didn't stand around with my sword up my arse. I split the skin and bone of two or more. Either of you two waiters ever seen an underling before?"

Mikkel and Billip nodded.

The old warrior placed a folded up piece of cloth, stained in dark blood, on the table.

"Perhaps you'll recognize this, then," he said, unwrapping it.

Two small bolts of a crossbow lay there, the tips a dark metal and the shafts stained black.

"And that isn't all."

The warrior produced a knife and slid it over on the table. It had two sets of blades and forked edges around the pommel.

Mikkel knew underling steel when he saw it. He tossed a dish rag over all of it. Immediately his thoughts went to his son Nikkel, hoping that Two-Ten City hadn't been over run and his boy slaughtered.

Billip pressed on with more questions.

"So I merit that you killed all of the underlings before you managed your return?"

"Why are you mocking me? Of course I didn't kill them all. I gathered a horse and escaped. Those bolts were in my armor—see—here are the holes." The warrior stuck his fingers in the pierced leather shoulder. "Then, I grabbed that blade from a dead one's grip when I lost my own knife." The warrior rapped his fist on the table and got up. "Pah ... you two dimwits wouldn't know an underling if you saw one, but I've warned you." He grabbed the underling weapons and tucked them away. As the warrior reached for the bread, Billip pinned down his wrist.

"You've had your fill here. Now, we've been good enough hosts, so if you want to spread more of your stories, do it elsewhere, Scavenger."

"What? I'm no bloody scavenger. I ought to cut your throat," he said as his hand fell to the pommel of his sword.

Billip rolled his eyes, but Mikkel got up and looked down on the warrior.

"Time to go," he said, taking another step towards the man, "quietly."

"So be it," the warrior said, turning and marching through the door.

Returning to his seat, Mikkel rubbed the back of his head and watched the man go.

"Billip, this isn't good, not good at all."

The archer sat with a glum look on his face, cracking his knuckles.

"Our time has come, Mikkel," Billip said.

"What do you mean?"

"You know what I mean. We need to head back home to Two-Ten City and check on Nikkel."

Mikkel slumped over his big forearms on the table. "Ah … I'm sure he's fine."

He didn't believe that, though. He was worried, and every day got longer and longer as the swirl of rumors of the underlings in the South added more fuel to his concerns. "Besides, we gave Venir our word to keep check on these boys and such. And Kam … she needs our help."

Billip said, "Mikkel, it's time to assume that Venir's gone."

Mikkel frowned. It was too sad to even consider, but it tugged at him anyway.

"Besides, the boys are in good shape here with Kam and Gillem. You've got your own to look after. You know Venir would understand, and you know we can't sit around on our butts when underlings are starting to crawl all over." Billip pushed away his mug. "We're fighters, you and I, and we aren't meant to sit around and watch babies grow. Tell Kam about your boy, and we can both go."

Mikkel sighed. Billip was right. There wasn't a whole lot left that he could do here, and he couldn't sit around and feel guilty all the time. He needed to get his son and bring him back to the City of Three, if need be.

"It's going to be a long ride, Brother," he said, taking a drink. "And the bountiful women will be pretty scarce on the trail." He allowed himself a broad smile.

"Agreed," Billip hoisted his mug of ale, "and there won't be much strong drink to take with us, either, so I suggest we round up a cask and head to the nearest brothel."

He clonked his mug on Billip's.

"Ssshh," he grinned, "Don't be so loud. You don't want Kam and Joline to hear. All of these women have big ears," Mikkel said, looking over his shoulder.

Billip hoisted his brows and added.

"And bigger breasts to boot."

From a balcony above, Kam heard every word. A tear ran down her cheek. She wiped it from her rosy cheek and blew her nose in a handkerchief. Her simple suggestion spell was powerful, a bit risky, but it had worked. She'd managed to have Billip do all the dirty work, and he hadn't even known it.

Before he'd left her room, she had already planted the question to ask Mikkel in his mind. That part had been easy, very unobtrusive. The next part had been a little more difficult, opening Mikkel's stubborn mind to the suggestion. His mug of ale, mixed with a part of hers and a part of his, entwined with magic, had done the rest with a little mental prodding.

The whole process left her exhausted, sad and even worse … lonely. Her fingernails dug into the rail, and her heart began to race as she looked down on the two impressive men. *A brothel. I could show them a better time than that.* She almost felt possessed as she pulled back her shoulders and headed down the stairs. She needed companionship as much as they, and if she went another day longer she might explode. *Why not. It's the least I could do.*

As she made her way to the bottom floor, a loud commotion began to stir among the patrons. Shouts and screaming were coming from outside as she watched Billip and Mikkel bolt from the table and head out the tavern's door. Without even realizing it she was running, squeezing through the patrons as she pushed her way outside.

People were running and screaming from all directions like they were being chased by a swarm of bees. Amid the throng of panic stricken faces she searched for Mikkel and Billip, and that's when she saw them, up the road, facing a small force of unlikely assailants. Her blood ran cold as she cried out their names, but her voice failed to rise above the sounds of chaos.

"NO!" She shouted when a group of patrons began pulling her back inside the tavern.

She saw Billip and Mikkel and a few others one last time, squaring off against the dark skinned and black clad brood of underlings.

Chapter 20

Verbard felt like his stomach was in his chest as he rubbed his aching head and his silvery eyes. Across from him sat Master Sinway, broad and serene in his chair, and beside him stood a Vicious, its long clawed hands clutching open and closed beside his throat. Apparently, Master Sinway wasn't taking any chances on their little journey. Master Sinway was exposed, or was he?

As Verbard collected his thoughts, Master Sinway stood up and smoothed over his robes. He didn't ever recall seeing his Master act this way in all of his years, relaxed and poised. Master Sinway's fearsome disposition was gone, but the edge of his iron will was still there. He made a quick chit sound. The Vicious returned back to his master's side, and the cave dogs sat up and padded his way as well.

"Take it all in, Verbard. The charge I have given you is a big one indeed, but all the forces you need are at your disposal. Your time for greater glory has come. You can help us take back the surface world," Sinway said, almost smiling.

He groaned inside. His stomach was still a knot of writhing worms as he fought back the bile building in his throat. He forced himself upright in his chair and tried to assess how much power Master Sinway had. The trip, as marvelous as it was, had left him dumbfounded at Sinway's power. He and his brother combined couldn't possibly have achieved such a feat. He wanted that power.

"Perhaps, Master, I can finish this port? It should help me conjure a plan."

"Have all you want; it induces creativity."

"And you?"

Sinway waved his hand and said, "I haven't the craving. So ... Verbard, I'll offer you my wisdom at the moment if you wish. You have questions ... ask, or else I'll go."

Verbard took a swallow and felt his tongue begin to melt in delight. The underling port was unlike anything he could have ever imagined. *I could sit and drink this all year, but instead, I have to evict an entire city of humans.*

"I would ask how you would have me go about it, Master. And please forgive me, my knowledge of human settlements is somewhat vague." He hated to admit that, but placing a siege on a human empire wasn't something he would consider to be his forte. His silver eyes went from Sinway's chest to his back, as the Master of Underlings paced the floor like a man, robed arms crossed behind him.

"So long ago it was, Verbard, like a dream, when I lived within the city. The stone walls were not there, nor the spires and towers, nothing but the ground and the waters below, an oasis in the Outlands. Underling Lord Master Sidebor was the Master then, my mentor ..."

Verbard let out a short cough at the mention of Master Sidebor's name, the one considered to be the greatest of all underlings. Master Sidebor had vanished at some point in time, no one really knew when for sure, as the new Underling Master kept his matters very private and exclusive. The only remaining trace of Sidebor—so the underling sages said—was the robe that Master Sinway wore. It seemed strange that Sinway chose this moment in time to bring it up at all.

"... who led us below ground. Mankind has driven us from our home, our caves, our water, our structures. They—with the help of wizards, giants and dwarves—drove us from that land. They sealed off the waters and choked the ground, which was once fertile, but is now what they call the Outlands: barren, wasted and dreadful."

It seemed unlikely to Verbard that any of this was true. The lands of Bish always had been and always would be what they currently were. The underlings lived in caves and not dwellings above the ground, as they found the heat and bright light uncomfortable.

"So you ask how I would take the city? By siege? By deceit? Magic? Alchemy? Mayhem?" Sinway goaded.

With his stomach settled, Verbard rose from his chair. "I like the sound of them all. Chronic attrition?"

Sinway gave a little snort.

"Yes, you have observed what we are doing on the outside, Verbard, but we need to begin the pressure on the inside as well."

The pressure in between Verbard's eyes was rebuilding. *Please don't tell me you want me to go inside there.*

"Verbard, I want you …"

He felt his black heart stop for an instant as be began missing his quest for The Darkslayer.

"… to work with my son, Kierway, on this."

I'd rather play in cave dog dung.

"It would be an honor."

"I thought so," Sinway sniffed. "Kierway has intimate knowledge of the City of Bone, as did Oran the outcast. You see, despite our hatred for humans and the human hatred for us, we have many allies out there."

"Certainly, Master, hence the demise of Outpost Thirty-One."

"Yes," Sinway began to smirk, "and being such, we know that men can be manipulated just as easily from the inside as the out. There is a key, a magic relic, something Master Sidebor left behind in his failures when he forced us to abandon our city." Sinway's face formed a deep frown. "I believe it was done purposely. That key possesses many secrets to the city and all of its long buried wonders. Kierway has worked dutifully for generations in trying to re-acquire it."

He began to simmer inside. How many things were going on that he didn't know about? He was one of the most powerful underlings in the Underland, but it seemed he was naive when it came to his kin's plans in regards to the domination of mankind. He couldn't help but wonder how much his brother had known that he didn't. There had always been something between Catten and Sinway that he never understood, until now.

Sinway continued.

"And I'd have you rendezvous with Kierway and help him acquire it, but if you feel there is a better way, then before you move on, I would like to hear it."

Patience. It was the underling way, but the tone in Master Sinway's voice was beginning to shift, reverting to his normal demeanor and demanding self. Verbard was beginning to suspect that it wouldn't be up to him after all on how to take the City of Bone, that once again, he'd be another instrument of his master. He hated that.

"Shall I meet with Kierway first, or shall I begin this conquest on my own … Master?"

Master Sinway removed something from within his robes that Verbard had never seen before: a brass amulet, intricate in its works, with a clear crystal as big as the palm of his hand in the middle. Sinway said, "Take this. You can use it daily, if need be, and keep me apprised of your situation.

Keep your reports short and accurate, that's all I require," Sinway finished, setting it on the table. "Now, your time to depart from me is here, and your time for greater glory has come. Follow."

They floated through the castle cave of rock and stone back outside to a ledge overlooking the Underland city. Ranks of underlings stood in formation on a stone plateau below. Soldiers stood, solemn and striking with polished steel spear tips pointed skyward. Some were adorned in armor, others cloaks, crossbows and steels. Albino urchlings were mixed in there with cave dogs, giant spiders and lesser magi conjurers. Badoon underlings headed the ranks, well over a hundred strong, some bald and barren, the others covered in leather, mail and chain. In all, the host looked to be over five hundred underlings strong. It was an army that would bring a new meaning of terror to the world above.

Is this all I get to take over the largest city in the world?

"Your army awaits your orders, Lord Commander Verbard," Master Sinway said in his ear. "See to it that they do not perish, and do not return until the City of Bone is ours once again." Master Sinway departed, leaving him alone on the ledge, staring at his new army. *I'm a fool.* He'd just been handed an army to destroy humans and wipe them from the world, but it didn't seem right. If Verbard ever missed his brother, Catten, he missed him now, as he floated down to greet his commanders. *How did I get myself into this? I don't even have the Vicious. I'm going to have to find an easier way.* But he knew in his black heart there wasn't one.

Chapter 21

Lefty and Gillem stood beneath the City of Three's spires. Long and ornate, the clay shingled towers twisted upward towards the sky. Lefty marveled, as always. Gillem was at his side, guiding him through the streets, a satchel of flowers strapped to his back. Again Lefty peered upward, gaping at the smooth surface and long length of the tower, which was part of a different type of castle system than that which held the Royals, much more elaborate and sophisticated than the rough cut rock of Bone. *I've got to get in there.*

"Come, Lad," Gillem said, "stare too long and the magi will come after you."

Lefty followed along Gillem's side, still looking back and up over his shoulder.

"Do you really think they know we are watching?" He asked. "I mean, I've never seen anyone come and go from one of them. How do you know they are even in there?"

Gillem bumped into a woman carrying a package wrapped in decorative ribbon. She snorted.

"Watch it, Halfling," she said, sneering down at him.

He produced a purple carnation with a long blue stem and bowed saying, "Apologies, Miss."

"Oh … well, there's no need," she remarked, reluctantly taking the flower from his hand.

Lefty sauntered along Gillem's side, smiling.

"And some baby's breath to go with that, young lady."

"I, uh, very well. Thank you, little halflings, but be more careful. I wouldn't want anyone to call the City Watch, which I was about to do."

Lefty sneezed as she grabbed the flowers.

"Goodness!" she said.

"Pardon me, Miss … uh, you were saying?"

She took the baby's breath, combined it with the carnation, and said, "Oh, be careful of the Watch. People don't like how halflings always pester us, but in your case, you've been nothing but pleasant."

Gillem added, "And you are as forgiving as you are lovely, and me and my boy, we promise to be more careful."

Both Lefty and Gillem bowed as the woman smiled before she turned and walked away with a spring in her step.

Lefty felt Gillem Longfingers massaging the top of his head.

"So, Lefty, what is it I've acquired?"

"I must admit, you were quick, but not quick enough. All you got was a silver talent from her pocket."

Gillem led the way, flipping the coin and saying, "Is that all you saw?"

He and Gillem Longfingers had been hard at it the past few days, roaming the streets, selling cheap flowers and gifts while picking pockets and running small skims. Lefty liked what he learned, but he was becoming bored with it all and lonely, too. Georgio would hardly speak to him, and Kam didn't seem to like him anymore. He missed learning magic from her, but with the new baby,

Erin, she was too busy. Of course, Gillem saw to it he was busy, too. He just wanted things to go back to the way they were, before he and Georgio met Gillem and Palos.

"Yes," he said, "Is that all you saw?"

Gillem stopped and looked down on him and asked, "What do you mean?"

Lefty dangled a small golden bracelet in front of Gillem's puffy eyes that grew like saucers.

Gillem snatched it from his hand and stuffed it inside his coat in one fluid motion.

"Too many eyes, Boy … but impressive all the same." Gillem shook his head. "My, you are picking up on this stealing too quickly. Ho! The sneeze, that's brilliant, never thought to use that. Come on now, we've got enough booty to report back to the Nest. Prince Palos will be expecting us."

Lefty tried not to slump as he followed Gillem through the busy midday streets, still trading and selling flowers and carrying on. He hated Palos. The man was pushy, demanding, demeaning and cruel. Palos talked to Gillem like a dog and treated Lefty like an infant. The Nest however, was a little more to his liking, as it reminded him of Bone, but with dwarves and even a few halflings. He thought of Melegal often and wondered how he was doing. He wondered what Melegal would do if he had to deal with the likes of Palos and Gillem.

By the time they made it back to Gillem's flower shop Lefty was droopy-eyed. They gathered their hoard of about six pounds of coins and trinkets of gold, silver and tiny gem stones and slipped through the streets, down the alley and into another underground dock where the gondola waited. He rubbed his eyes as he lit the tiny lantern.

"You've not spoke much today Lefty," Gillem said as Lefty rowed. His shoulders were already aching, but not so much as his heart. Things just weren't right.

"I'm in good order, Gillem. No worries."

Gillem lit his pipe and puffed away.

"Now, no sense in lying to me. Just come out with it, Lefty. You and I, well, our kind need to stick together. The thief's life may not be honorable, but you'll still have to trust one of us in order to survive. That might as well be me. Who else do you have down here?"

Lefty felt himself begin to shrink. *No one.* He wiped his eyes on his sleeve and continued to row, the oars splashing into the dim waters. The trip to the Nest was never as pleasant and soothing as when leaving it, but he had gotten accustomed to the quiet and the calming effects of the surrounding waters. Today however, he wished the trip was already going the other way, for there was no telling what deed Palos would have lined up for them next.

"Gillem, have you ever thought about doing something … elsewhere?"

He could see a frown form on Gillem's abnormally cheerful face before he replied with the usual zeal in his voice gone.

The elder halfling sighed. "I gave up such thoughts long ago, Lefty. You would be wise to do so as well, and let me warn you, Boy: Palos will decide when it's time for you to go, and he'll have a new home waiting for you."

As they made their way through the final passages, Lefty took a look over his shoulder at the smoldering lit windows of the underground city. His little heart began to beat faster as the smell of decay became stronger.

"Take us over that way, on the other side of the docks. I want to show you something."

The little muscles in Lefty's back bemoaned the effort as he realized he had to paddle farther than he normally would. After a few dozen more strokes, Gillem held his hand up.

"This is good, Lefty," Gillem said, puffing his pipe.

He rubbed his aching shoulders and back. *Thank goodness.*

Gillem motioned at the small lantern hanging behind him.

Lefty grabbed it and held it in front of Gillem.

"These lanterns, did you know they work in water? A little something we acquired from our favorite customers, the magi. Of course, the light is not so bright, and they don't last so long." Gillem peered over the bow and motioned Lefty closer. "Now, go ahead, drop it in the water."

Lefty gave Gillem a funny look and said, "It seems like a—"

"Drop it!" Gillem ordered.

Splash.

"Now watch." Gillem's voice was dead and hollow, smoky eyes obscuring in the darkness.

Lefty got a funny feeling in his feet.

As the green glow of the lantern drifted downward, strange shapes began to take from: bloated men, tethered by chains, hands crossed behind their backs, mouths gaping open as their flesh was separating from the bone.

Lefty gasped and turned away. *How horrible!*

Two strong hands gripped his tiny face and forced him to look downward again.

"It is the Nest or this watery grave that Prince Palos has to offer, Boy! Nothing more, nothing less! Look!"

Terror filled his heart as his eyes remained affixed and frozen open. It wasn't just men, but women, boys and girls, halfling, mintaur and dwarf. He began to shake, but he did not cry as the lantern continued its slow decent into the murk and the illumination of horror expired.

"Take us to the dock," Gillem said as puffed on his pipe.

Like a zombie Lefty moved, his heart pounding, his thoughts frozen. He didn't even realize he was rowing until they pulled alongside the dock. *I'm going to die here.* He looked upward for a sun ray of hope, but of course there was none way down here.

The usual greetings from the inhabitants of the Nest were null. Gillem seemed to be shoving him over the planks as he walked along on numb legs, head hanging down. He felt the others staring at him as if this were his funeral procession. No more games, no more illusions. They all knew his secret and he knew theirs. Palos was the prince and executioner of every man and woman of the Nest. Where were Melegal and Venir when you needed them?

CHAPTER 22

H E WAS ON HIS HANDS and knees, eyes squeezed shut, head reeling, trying to figure out how his body had been turned inside out. It was an awful moment, wrought with despair as he vomited all over the ground. Venir could smell the bile, and as malodorous as it was, it was relieving.

"Ha! Ha!" A booming voice laughed. "You are barfing, Venir. Do it again; it's funny."

Venir groaned out loud, wiping the milky saliva from his chin. Slowly he rose to his feet, searching for Barton's voice. There was nothing but white cottony mist.

"Blast."

And no sign of the giant. Another trick perhaps.

"Where are you, Barton? We have a deal," he said, not holding back the anger in his tone.

He felt a pair of hands wrap around his chest and lift him from the ground.

"I've got you, Venir."

The mist was wispy around Barton's big nose, his face fading in and out of his field of vision. Venir could still make out the eyes, one eye as big as his head, brown and dull, the other sealed shut. He tried to wriggle free, but Barton's fingers were like hammered iron.

"You promised to take me from the Mist, Giant! What treachery is this? I'm no farther than where I started.

"You are almost out. I can see your world, Venir. But first you promised me a friend. You tell me where that friend is right now, or Barton will crush you."

Venir's eyes bulged as Barton squeezed. He let out a dry gagging sound, and something snapped, somewhere inside him, piercing his lung with pain. Another rib, he supposed. How many of those could break, anyway?

"Ease up," he managed to croak out, "so I can speak."

Barton's fingers eased around him, but his prison of flesh and bone was still secure. Barton said, "Now tell me, Venir. Barton needs a friend."

Now was the moment of truth. He suspected Boon was dead, but that was the lie he had told Barton: that he knew of a friend who still lived within the giants' stronghold. But what if Barton already knew about Boon and his demise? He was certain Barton would crush his body like a yellow tomato and stomp his bones like glass. There was another option he had not considered.

"Barton, do you know what a Lycan is?"

Barton responded with a fierce shake, cracking his teeth.

"DON'T PLAY GAMES. NO LIKE THOSE PEOPLE."

Bad idea.

"Do you know about a wizard, like me, who lives with the giants and does tricks?"

Barton tilted his head.

"No … but I like tricks. Tell me more about this wizard."

"His name is Boon."

Venir waited for a throttling but nothing happened.

"Can he do tricks for me?" Barton asked, curious.

"Well, he made me as big as you."

"He did?"

Barton set Venir on the ground.

"Do you think he can make Barton small like you? Hmmm?"

"Well, yes, or even bigger if you wanted. Twice as big. Think what you could do to Blackie the next time he came for you. You could break his neck."

Barton began clapping and stomping all around.

"Yes! Yes! Yes!"

The ground was shaking beneath his feet, and his eyes began to pop with every loud clap. "Where is he? Where is he?" Barton demanded, picking up Venir and swinging him through the mist.

Venir felt himself turning green.

"Stop! Stop!" he yelled. "Let me down, I'm going to—*blecht*!"

Barton fell down laughing.

Venir had to fight the urge to pull out Brool and begin whittling the giant down to bits. Instead, he fumbled through the mist, found Barton and jammed his heel into his groin.

"Ow! What did you do that for?"

"Do you want the find the wizard or not?"

"Yes. Yes, Venir. Tell Barton now!"

Venir clutched at his aching ribs and said, "His name is Boon. He is in the castle with the maze. He guards the prisoners that fight in the labyrinth."

Barton sounded elated.

"I know where that is. I go get him now."

Venir tackled Barton's legs and hung on saying, "No! Wait!"

Barton began peeling him off.

Venir said, "Your end of the deal, Barton! Send me back to Bish."

Barton laughed as he picked Venir up by the ankles and dangled him before his eyes.

"You are right, Venir. Barton send you back to your Bish now."

The giant flipped Venir over his back like a pack and began running, jostling Venir all over the place.

"Good-Bye, Venir! And in case you lied, I want you to know I'll come for you and you will never leave the mist again."

"*URK*!"

Venir's neck snapped forward as he flipped head over heels through the mist. He swore he kept going higher and higher as the sound of giant laughter began to fade away. As the icy wind whistled and nipped his ears the snow white mist turned to black. His time careening in the air came to a brief stop. *Oh slat!* The wind whistled through his ears as he plunged into the darkness. He braced his body for what he knew would be a mighty long fall.

Chapter 23

"WHICH ONE DO YOU WANT, the man or the dwarf?" One Mountain Man asked the other.

The other, with a long face and yellow beard full of frost, snickered. "I'll be killing the Blood Ranger; not many men live to tell about such a feat."

The other one, hefty and surly, covered in pelts, frowned as he said, "Nay, I saw him first, so I get to kill him. Or … we both say we both killed him."

Mood, still warm within his icy cocoon, kept his bushy eyes closed.

"So, if we kill him, do you think the other Rangers will come after us?" The taller one said as he tested the edge of his bastard sword.

"They'll never know what happened to him up in these mountains. We'll bury him in the lake of ice. Not even the best trackers could find him there."

The one with the brown beard had a worried look as he said, "I don't think it's a good idea, killing him in cold blood. The Blood Rangers will find out. They say they know anything and everything, that they can find a needle in a snow storm."

"Har!" the other one laughed. "Those are just stories. This one here, Mood, is the King they say, and he couldn't even find a druid. She found him. Blood Rangers, pah. I'd be surprised if he wasn't the only of all of them. Look, he's just a big man is all. There ain't no such thing as a dwarf that tall."

The mountain man nodded his head, a look of satisfaction enlightening his cross face.

It was true; not many men had even seen the Blood Rangers, and if they did, it was most likely only one, in passing. The Blood Rangers came to the aid of man from time to time, but for the most part they kept to themselves in Dwarven Hole. Only for the most treacherous of events in the world did they venture out.

Mood began to feel the icy block biting into his fingertips. *Need to move.* His skin, thick and protective like wool, was turning cold. Not a thing on him was ever cold, not even his nose that usually snorted the air, until today. It was time. *Move or die.*

"Have ye ladies decided whose gonna kill me yet," he rumbled, "because I'm getting tired of ye squabblin'."

The two mountain men whirled, their faces aghast. The brown-haired one's sword slipped from his grip. The men looked at one another, then back at Mood. He could smell their fear. It strengthened him. He let his inner power go.

Both men stepped backward as Mood's fists began to gleam red hot from within the ice. Their jaws dropped as he spoke.

"Fools. Did ya' really think I couldn't find you or your wily leader? I wasn't slaughtering the ogres for fun, even though I enjoyed every bit of it. No, I was drawing you fools out, and now I have you! Ho! Ho!"

The bewildered men raised their swords and charged.

Mood's muscles thickened and bulged inside the block of melting ice. There was a popping sound as shards of ice broke free. With a fierce growl he pulled his shoulders back.

Crack!

Chunks of ice fell to the ground as he shivered and shook his shoulders. In one hand a razor sharp hand axe was free; the other hand was still a block of ice. As the two wary Mountain Men came on, Mood tried to lift his feet and return their charge.

"Huh?"

His feet were still frozen in a solid block of ice when he looked down.

"Ah … who needs 'em anyway. Come on, Fools!"

He failed to notice the Ogre's club rising above his back as a black shadow fell over him and the Mountain Men's yellowish eyes gleamed in relief.

Elation. Euphoria. Exhaustion. Fogle Boon never imagined anything could have been as exhilarating as this. His skinny chest heaved in and out. Her fingernails ran down his spine, raising goose bumps from his toes to his eyelids.

"Everything you imagined it would be?" Cass said, her voice a silky purr.

He was shaking as he nodded, ashamed for doing so, but he resisted the urge to pull away when she hugged him from behind, wrapping her legs behind his waist. It was the warmest and most magnificent feeling he had ever felt: hot flesh, soft and firm in all the right places like a blanket that had so much more to offer.

She nibbled at his ear and said, "I thought you were wonderful. You were so, oh, how should I put it … creative."

He perched his eye brows as he managed to say, "Well, I have given it a moderate amount of thought over the years. Of course, there were never any wolves in my fantasies … or any other creatures, for that matter."

"Not even another woman?" she said, twirling her finger in his hair.

"Hah … well, no I suppose."

Woof!

The timber wolves' ears perched up as they growled and stammered on their paws, the thick fur rising on their backs. There was a commotion coming from right outside. He felt Cass unwrap her body from his and watched her wriggle back into her robes. She made a funny sound, her pink eyes leering at the four massive dogs, and Fogle found himself surrounded again.

"What is that?" he asked, rising to his feet, gathering his nearby robes.

But the druid was gone, the tent flap closed.

"Great!"

One of the wolves, black and dark grey, barked and snapped in his face. That's when he heard Mood's thunderous bellow smashing through the canvas. "HUZZAH!"

Something that sounded like a battering ram slamming into ice rocked the air, followed by the sound of silence. Fogle's gut began to churn. Something was wrong. He had to do something and help out his friend. He'd failed him once, and he couldn't let that happen again, but how was he going to get past the wolves without being eaten alive?

"Blast it!"

The wolf snapped in his face again.

He closed his eyes, letting his mind peel away the layers of mystic energy that were lying dormant within him. No longer was his mind numb, but rather rejuvenated. Every wizard had power within that didn't require components, wands or scrolls to activate, but just a disciplined and powerful mind that could tap the mystic energies of the world without losing his sanity.

He put his fingers to his lips and whistled.

The wolves barked and snapped, coming closer and closer. He could feel their hot breath as their snouts nipped at his robes.

Just enhance the sound.

He opened the gate inside his mind and let out his reserves.

The whistle went from a feathery twill to high pitched shrill.

The wolves howled upward.

It's working.

Fogle blew harder.

The wolves' ears flattened; their howls looked to be cries of pain.

He could feel the energy within begin to grow into a monster of a force, as the high pitch twisted into the roaring forces of a storm. The sound waves were twirling around him, slinging the pelts through the air, grinding the grasses to the ground. It felt good, cutting it loose like that. He saw the wolves' feet lift from the ground, their bodies twisting in the air. Then the canvas walls of the tent buckled and rose, the stakes that held it ripped from the ground as the final ear shattering sound came.

BOOM!

Fogle's knees sagged, his energy spent, and then he fell to the ground.

Mood heaved himself forward a split second before the ogre's club came down.

Crack!

The blow smashed into the frozen block of ice that imprisoned his feet.

"Thanks, Stupid," Mood said, swinging his giant axe into the ogre's exposed skull. Blood spurted up as the heavy blade penetrated bone and punctured brain. The ogre twitched, sprawled out and stopped moving.

He wrenched his axe free and rolled left.

Swish! A long blade almost severed his leg. He rolled right as the other Mountain Man stabbed at his belly, clipping the outer edge of his gut. His frozen axe crashed into the towering man's legs, sweeping his legs from beneath him.

Chop! The big man howled in alarm, his foot detached, his leg stump gushing blood.

"Curse you, Ranger!"

Quickly, Mood rose to his feet and squared off with the lone standing Mountain Man.

"Yer a fool to trifle with me, Mood, King of the Blood Rangers!" he snorted. "HUZZAH!"

The Mountain Man let out his own cry and charged. High and low his sword point stabbed.

Mood parried.

Clang.

Another thrust clipped the hairs at his neck.

Clang.

He knocked it away.

"Ha, working up a sweat before you die I see."

"The Bone with you, Dwarf!" the man yelled, swiping at Mood's side.

The sword and axe crashed with a terrible sound of grinding metal. The bigger man leaned into him, pressing him downward, eyes blazing with battle. Mood rammed his head underneath the man's chin, rocking his head back.

"I bet that hurt, but don't ye worry, yer not be feeling the pain for long!"

Mood clubbed the man over the head with his half-frozen hand, breaking what was left of the ice block that froze his axe to his wrist. Blood began to spurt from the busted nose on the man's face as he howled in pain.

With both hands free, Mood stepped in for the kill.

"Gah!"

Something seized hold of his feet. He looked down, thinking to brain the man with the missing foot, but instead he watched the ice begin to crystallize and grow up and around his feet.

"Ah, not this again," he said, launching his hand axe into the chest of the last mountain man. The man fell backward, dead.

He chopped at the ice that was up to his knees now.

"Save your energy, Dwarf," the druid woman said, "and perhaps I'll show mercy on your friend. As for you, however, I think you'll make a nice frozen ornament for me—what in Bish?"

A shrill sound erupted from inside the tent. The druid woman pressed her hands over her ears. She wasn't screaming, but whatever it was, Mood could not hear. He chopped into the ice, trying to block out the foul noise. From the corner of his eye he watched the tent rip free from its tethers and blow away with the force of a gale. Pelts and wolves were flying in the air.

BOOM!

Mood felt like a giant just smashed him in the head. He fell to his hands and knees, struggling to regain his feet. All around him was some form of devastation. The snow was gone from the leaves of the trees; smaller growth was ripped from the ground, and the druid woman lay quivering on the ground, clutching her head. Where the tent once was a man now stood, his big bearded face pale, his bright green eyes exhausted.

"Yer just full of surprises, aren't ya Wizard?" Mood said.

Fogle raked his brown hair back from his face and said, "As impossible as it seems, sometimes I surprise myself."

Mood gathered his other axe from the Mountain Man's bloody chest and said, "So, I take it you're a full-fledged adventurer now?

Fogle smiled as he looked over at Cass's voluptuous form.

"I guess you could say that."

Mood snorted, pulled a cord of thin rope from his pouch, and tossed it as Fogle's feet.

"Bind her hands, then. It's time to go." Cass mumbled something, but didn't resist his binding.

"Should I gag her?" Fogle asked. "And what makes you think she'll help us?"

Mood procured a cigar and lit it up, saying, "Wizard, ye've whipped her. She'll not be crossing you again. At least not until this deed is done. After that, anything goes I suppose."

As Fogle pulled her up from her knees she spoke.

"My word, Fogle and Ranger, I'll carry out this quest, just don't release that awful sound again. If I had pants I swear I would have pissed them. So take me to Dwarven Hole to see this two-headed dog. I promise I'll do what I can."

It didn't seem right, marching a woman he had just bedded hours earlier through the dangerous mountains like a prisoner. Still, Fogle had been warned by Mood several times already, *Ye can never trust a druid.* He couldn't help but wonder if they all looked as incredible as her.

Mood led the way, dragging a small sled that secured their gear. The Blood Ranger was a determined juggernaut, his thick back and heavy set shoulders unusually broad, with his blood stained axes criss-crossed on his back. Fogle couldn't help but wonder if he saved Mood, or if Mood saved him ... again. And where had all that magic and power come from, which had leveled the druid's fragile home?

He looked over his shoulder. To the right and left, a pack of humbled timber wolves followed. For whatever reason, he was glad they were there. The journey home, Mood promised, wouldn't be any easier than the journey there.

He guided Cass forward, his hand pressing into the small of her back.

"Feeling frisky again are we, Fogle?" she said, stopping and somehow grabbing his hands in hers. "Unbind me and I'll make this trip ... more interesting." Her pink eyes looked deep into his. "Or just take me as I am."

A flush of red washed over his normally pale face. One thing was for sure, the journey back seemed much warmer than the journey there. Still, a question hung in his mind.

"Are you sure you were a virgin?" he asked.

Mood's gruff voice cut in.

"Of course she weren't no virgin, Wizard. What do ya think she kept those two brutes up there for, protection? Now pull your brains out of your groin and get moving. Storm's coming!"

Cass giggled as he pushed her away and frowned, thinking of the two brutish men that both lay dead, frozen blood mixed with snow. She had not even mourned their loss.

"Ah, don't believe the dwarf. He's just jealous. Of course you are the only one to lay with me, my defiler ... er ... deflowerer," she said with a hint of discontent.

Fogle just shook his head and moved along. The sky was darkening with his attitude. He wanted to believe one thing, but he knew the truth was another. Was Cass just a common slut, the kind his mother warned him about? Some men could make the most of that, but he was pretty certain that he could not.

Chapter 24

"**D**ETECTIVE! DETECTIVE!"

Melegal had been driving the City Watch beneath the City of Bone for hours, closing in on his prey, all thanks to a skinny little bird whispering the Slerg whereabouts, among other things, in his ear. And now, after preaching and disciplining the men of the Watch, all Bone had broken loose. The dogs, loud and slobbery, had gone into a frenzy when a family of sewer cats crossed through the tunnels.

"Shut up! Shut these mangy mutts up before I slit their throats, you buffoons," he ordered, shoving one unsuspecting Watchman from his path. He sucked in some air through his teeth, resisting the urge to kick a dog—choked tight on his short leash—in the throat. He had come to hate dogs, all except one, he supposed, giving the fleetest of thought to the two-headed Chongo.

The men pressed along the slopes of the dank tunnel walls, heads down, eyes averted. A City Watch sergeant straddled his long legs on both sides of the tunnel, peering through a portal that was a little over two feet in diameter. The sergeant was long and stringy, too tall to enter a common door, now bent over almost unnaturally, seeming to be quite uncomfortable. Sweat was dripping from the man's long slender nose as he sucked in his raspy breath to speak.

"I sent my hound, Oggie, in there. He made it back thirty feet or so, let out a bark and yelped." The man shuddered a sob. "That was it. I think something got him. I never heard him yelp like that. It must be those Slergs, I tell you. They better not've killed my Oggie."

Good, one less noisemaker the better. Hmmm. This might work out well for me.

"Well, what are you waiting for? Send in the rest of your hounds. Avenge your beast!"

"But Sir," the sergeant started to speak, but stopped. "*Ulp.*"

Melegal stuck his dagger half an inch up the man's nose.

"This isn't a booger picker, Dolt. Now, shall I give the order again? Am I so low as you that I must order dogs and not men?"

"Apologies, Detective! Apologies!" the sergeant blinked rather than nod.

Melegal withdrew his blade and said, "Shut up and do your job."

The man looked confused.

Melegal warned him, saying, "I'm going to kill you, Fool. Now speak and do your job."

The lanky man nodded his head, turned and yelled down the tunnel.

Don't yell!

"You heard 'em men—Release the hounds!"

Brak loved dogs. He had played with them all his life, all kinds, big and small. Some were herders and others hunters, and now one lay unmoving at his feet, a herder and scout. He could tell by its calico coat. He wanted to cry, but there was no time for that. At least three more were coming, and they sounded different than the last: ferocious and hungry for flesh. He didn't want to hurt any more of them, not innocent animals, anyway.

"I surrender!" he yelled. "I SURRENDER!"

There was a series of sharp whistles, and the dogs came to a halt.

Someone in the background was saying, "Did you hear that? That ain't human."

"Shut up, Fool!" a hateful voice sounded. "Unarm yourself, then, and come forth so we can see you."

Brak lumbered down the tunnel and let out a loud sigh. The dogs, four in all, growled at his side. "Easy boys," he mumbled.

"Any sudden moves and those dogs will tear you to bits."

"I'm not going to do anything," Brak said.

"He's coming. Be ready; it might be a trick."

"Shut up already!" the hateful voice came again.

"I'm tossing out my weapons," Brak said. One knife and two swords, one his, the other his dead mother, Vorla's. He wished she was still here, caring for him. He dreamed of her often, and it was of very little comfort, but it was something.

Slowly, he began to squeeze back through the portal, into the torchlight, where many men with swords and torches waited. He wondered if he would be heading into the furnace to join his mother and so many others. So sad, he had failed in his quest to find his father, Venir.

"Sweet Mother of Bish. Look at the size of his head," the sergeant exclaimed.

In his life, Melegal had been surprised a few times, but even he could never have anticipated Brak's big droopy face popping out into the torchlight. He was at a loss for words.

"Do we kill him?" someone asked.

Everyone moved backward as Brak's form began to slowly fill the tunnel.

"How'd he fit in here?"

"I'm not carrying him out. We'll have to cut him in pieces."

"What do we do?"

Brak's lazy face showed no emotion or expression as he stooped inside the unyielding confines of the corridor. Melegal's thoughts raced to Venir, the Drunken Octopus, Chongo, Lefty and Georgio. Everything good he remembered washed over him as he felt compelled to grab Brak and run. *This is not good for the boy, er man.*

"Detective, shall we gut him?" the sergeant said. "We've still got more pursuit. They've left this one to slow us."

Slap!

It stung Melegal's hand as much as the man's pock-marked cheek, but it felt good.

"Are you doing my thinking for me now? Is your tongue privy to things that I am not? Are you the detective or am I?"

Slap! Slap! Slap!

"Who is making the decisions here?" Melegal demanded.

The truth was, he enjoyed tormenting the City Watch. It was one of the few perks left of his job, better yet he could see to their demise from time to time. The City Watch were not of the Royal families' fabled sentries. They were chattel, nothing more. He liked their disposability.

"Y-you are Detective, Melegal, Sir. Apolo—"

"Piss on your apologies, and shut your ignorant hole. Now …" Melegal gestured to the nearest

Watchman, "you two pissants crawl through the hole and see what lies ahead, and take your stupid little dung eating pets, too."

He felt Brak's heavy eyes on him, but he ignored his gaze. *Maybe the young dolt won't remember me. Pah. I better gag him … and blindfold him, before it's too late.*

"You—Wart-face! Blindfold and gag him. Gag him first."

"Y-yes, Detective."

Melegal looked through the portal now, satisfied Brak was well under control. If this man was truly Venir's son, then he had to be careful. Such knowledge would be valuable because Venir was still, for all purposes, a wanted man by the Royals, regardless of Tonio's involvement. He'd watched over Venir before in his own kind of way, and he didn't take much comfort in taking his son in. *It can't be his son. It just can't be.*

A voice shouted from up ahead.

"Detective, there's a grate here, bars, no way through."

There was a lot of barking going on, too.

"Shut those beasts up! I can't hear you, Fool! What's this about bars?"

There was a yelp followed by the man's voice resounding off the rock walls.

"The bars on the grate … er … well they look bent, but there's no room for someone to crawl through, not even a pooch."

As Melegal made his way through the portal, he poked the lone remaining Watchman in the chest with his dagger and said, "Don't lose my prisoner. Fail at your peril."

"Aye, Detective."

That's the same dolt that lost the last one. Run man-child, Run.

Making his way to the men, he ran his slender fingers along the stone corridor. His keen eyes searched for any disparities in the architecture of the walls. He noted none.

"Well," he said, folding his arms across his chest, "step aside, torch bearers, so I can investigate your brilliant discovery."

The men shuffled away, eyes nervous and averted.

"My, well look at this. You've indeed found a grate. A barrier of some sort, agreed?"

They nodded.

"I tell you, it takes more than the brain of a gnat to make such a discovery. I'll be sure to report this to your superiors."

Melegal swooped his cloak around his back and over his knee as he squatted in front of the bars.

"A little more light, please," he beckoned with is hand and pointed.

As the Watchman lowered his torch along the rim, he made a startling discovery. The wrought iron, thick and ancient, had been bent. *Fresh debris. Interesting.* Small chips of stone lay along the edge of the grate's metal rim, but worst of all were the markings. The scratches in the iron were fresh, and he could feel the tiny jagged edges around the bottom bars where something had pulled them out and pushed them back again. He looked back down the tunnel. Through the portal he could see Brak's bulk dimming the torchlight from the other side.

One of the Watchmen cleared his throat and said, "How'd they get through there?"

"Huh," Melegal sort of laughed, rising back to his feet. He'd seen Venir bend bars as thick as these before, but he never saw him bother to bend them back. *Wouldn't that take more energy? My, what a seed he has sown!*

He shifted his hat on his head and motioned for the men with torches to step away from the bars. *Look. Listen.* He closed his eyes and opened his mind to the magic with his cap. It was something he'd been practicing which he was becoming quite fond of. Winding through the darkness of the endless corridors were footsteps, confusion and something else unexpected. Something breathed, evil and luminous, beckoning to him and picking at his mind. Something dormant was now awakened, and it was hungry. *Slat!*

Melegal flattened himself on the ground.

Clatch. Clatch. Clatch. Zip. Zip. Zing.

He was running.

Son of a Bish!

Ignoring the impaled faces of the City Watchmen, Melegal dashed down the tunnel and leapt through the portal. In the next instant, one dog after the other was piling on top of him and yelping in a frenzy.

"Get off me, hounds!"

"What was it?" The alarmed sergeant cried out, ducking along the wall.

Melegal was wiggling his finger through the hole inside the hood of his cloak.

"Just cornered Slergs, is all. It seems they can't find a way out."

The sergeant scratched his head, pushing his back to the wall, while peeking back and forth through the portal.

"Your charming friends are dead, but they died valiantly, discovering a murderous sewer grate. Now, take our prisoner to interrogation. You, Dear Sergeant, will get the glory of continuing this pursuit from the other end."

"Y-yes, Detective."

Melegal tried to contain his inner shivers as he made his way out of the tunnels. He couldn't find the moonlight fast enough. Something was down there: evil, insidious and powerful, and he had no desire to find out what that was. He'd heard stories about hoards of ghouls and other monsters that lived within the catacombs of the ancient ruins of Bone. Now he had an overwhelming fear that he had just awakened something that didn't want to be woken. *I am already having enough trouble sleeping.*

Brak didn't know what interrogation meant, and he didn't care now that he could smell the clean air above the ground for the first time in days. Maybe, just maybe, without anyone's help, he could escape. Maybe the skinny man called Detective might help. He could dream, dream of many things vast, unnatural and wild, but those dreams had not come lately. The dreams of his father were gone.

Chapter 25

"**B**ish!" Mikkel cried out as the multi-bladed knife of the underling clipped his nose. He ducked and dodged, shaking off the rust, back pedaling back and forth between the two underlings as he parried with his club. It was the fighter's instinct that rushed him back into the battle against man's most ancient of foes. He wanted to retreat, his mind recoiling, the frightening countenances of the underlings boring into his flesh: fearless, merciless and cruel. They came at him, one striking high, the other low.

Get it together, Man!

Clumsily he batted their blows away. How long had it been since he'd been in a fight, anyway? Perhaps it was the old warrior, the man they turned away, who cried out the first warning and charged into the fray. The weathered warrior now lay in a pool of his own blood, face split in half like something had just hatched from his skull. Mikkel couldn't shake the sadness that crept though his skin and chilled his bones.

Bang!

Clank!

Whomp!

Bang!

People were screaming, running in all directions, falling prey to the fearless little hoard that invaded their sanctuary. There were at least ten of them, but Mikkel wasn't making a count. He found himself pinned up against a wagon. The underlings chittered, their rat-furred faces and beady emerald eyes unblinking, cold and bright as they began to whittle him down.

Smack!

Billip caught one of them on the wrist, drawing an angry howl.

That's more like it! Now fight like a man!

The underlings weren't any different than any he'd faced before. Small like women, hairy grayish skin corded in knots, fluid in motion, confident in gait, evil in intent, their jagged blades—cruel tortuous devices—licked in and out like striking snakes. Bandoliers of knives and darts and small swords made an eerie jangle on their hips, and even without that armament the rest of them was just as scary. Sharp teeth that could rend flesh like a wild animal and claws that could shave the bark from a tree allowed the minions of the Underland to kill and hunt at all times.

Out of the corner of his eye he noticed a young woman and her boy trapped beneath a carriage. Two other underlings, blood dripping from the blades in their hands, screeched, rushing towards the helpless prey.

Nikkel!

The reminder of his own son's life and safety tore away his fears, unleashing his dormant fury. Mikkel roared. The sluggishness of his long powerful limbs had burned off, turning his defensive actions into a bludgeoning fury. His club, long, studded and heavy, twirled high in the air a split second before he brought it down with a skull-cracking blow. Parts of the underling's brain oozed from its nose as it fell over, leaving the other's serrated maw of teeth agape as it turned to escape the black warrior's fury.

"Where do you think you're going!" Mikkel yelled, giving chase, twisting back away at the sound of the woman and boy screaming. "Bish!"

There was a thrashing of blood spilling out from underneath the wagon. The underlings were a tangled mass of black flesh and leathers, claws clutching as the woman and boy kicked and flailed. Mikkel caught one underling by the foot and yanked it squealing from under the carriages.

"No you don't!" he said, dropping his club and pulling the underling away.

Dark black finger nails dug into his wrists. Mikkel cried out in pain, releasing the fowl underling that scurried away.

He looked under the wagon. "Bone!" The woman and boy lay dead, throats torn open and eyes gouged out. A swell of emotion formed in his light watery eyes. "BLAST THEM ALL!"

Mikkel whirled around at the growing sounds of chittering underlings. His club, Skull Basher, was nowhere in sight. The cobblestone road he defended was smeared in blood where Billip stood, coated in black blood, brandishing a blood-soaked broadsword. He wasn't alone: a dwarven fighter, stout as a stump of oak, black bearded to his knees, grasped a blacksmith's hammer in his hand. Beside him, another dwarf was on his knees, choking up blood and fighting for his breath.

"How are you holding up, Billip?" Mikkel asked, rushing to his comrade's side.

Billip swayed where he stood; a jagged gash in his pants was soaked in blood.

"I'd be better if I had my bow in my hand. This melee's exhausting. Bloody underlings!"

"Aye man!" The dwarf interrupted. "You'd be better fighting from afar, bow or sword. I've seen one-armed halflings swing better steel than that," the dwarf gloated, "but at least, being a man and all, you tried."

Billip said to Mikkel, "This must be a friend of yours."

Mikkel said, "No, never seen him before, but he seems to know you pretty well."

But the time for jokes was over. The streets were cleared, all of the fighting men were dead as far as they could tell, and the underlings, with superior weapons, armor and numbers, had them surrounded. A dark cloud had descended on the City of Three.

"So, you going to go down barehanded?" Billip commented, wiping the blood dripping in his eyes on his sleeve.

"Just like the day I was born, I guess."

"We dwarves are born with hammers for hands. Here, soft black man, take this," the dwarf growled, tossing his hammer to Mikkel. "You'll be needing it more than me. Now, by Mood's blood red beard, who wants to pummel these underlings!"

"Come on, Dogs!" Mikkel yelled.

Billip remained silent, sword up, eyes forward.

"It's time to crush some skulls!"

The underlings chittered with mockery, small crossbows aimed and ready. Mikkel could see the wet dew of poison reflecting on the bolt's tip. There were many men on Bish that could dodge a crossbow bolt, but he wasn't one of them. All he could do was hope he got one last swing.

Billip muttered at his side, "It wouldn't be so bad if I had my bow in my hand."

"You two ladies run, I'll cover you," the dwarf said. "Those little bolts won't hurt—"

Clatch-zip.

The bearded dwarf caught a slender six-inch dart in his burly arm and fell over dead.

"Slat!"

Every underling bolt in Bish looked to be pointed their way.

Clatch-zip.

Clatch-zip.

Clatch-zip.

Clatch-zip.

Clatch-zip.

Clatch-zip.

Everything seemed to be moving in very slow motion. The bolts, each and every one of them, he swore he could count. Three were bearing down on him, agonizingly slow, all center mass, one left, one middle, one right. If he twisted and turned either way it wouldn't matter. He was flat footed and ready to die. He glanced over at Billip, and to his surprise Billip was glancing at him, eyes wide as saucers. He turned back to look at the deadly missiles, each and every one twice as close as it had been before. *Huh?* Then he heard a familiar voice bellow.

"MOVE, YOU TWO IDIOTS!"

Mikkel dove to the left, Billip to the right.

Whap. Whap. Whap. Whap. Whap. Whap.

The bolts juttered as they embedded themselves in the cart behind him. The underlings howled with outrage, their bewildered faces searching the ground and sky.

"What in the—"

"TAKE COVER!" A woman said it in a convincing and powerful voice. She was gorgeous, radiant, and dangerous all at the same time. Her wavy tussles of auburn hair billowed in the sky. She was no ordinary woman, rather an extraordinary creature, an angry mother whose nest had been disturbed. Mikkel sucked in his breath as he caught a glimpse of her warm glowing face.

"Kam!" he exclaimed.

And she wasn't the only one.

Two men, one robed in pure white, the other robed in a color of blue he had never seen before, dropped down behind the pack of underlings. The one in white, older, hair yellow as a bale of straw, held out a slender long black staff, inches from the nose of an underling. The creature grasped the staff in both hands and tried to yank it away. Mikkel gawped. The underling turned white from head to toe and then its body collapsed in on itself.

"Sweet Mother of Bish!"

The blue wizard scattered a cloud of silver and dark purple dust in the air. The agitated underlings began to snort and wheeze. Mikkel almost laughed as they fell to the ground in writhing spasms, kicking clawed feet over the cobble stones in agony, twitching and lurching like fish out of water until they moved no more.

That's when Kam came. Her wrists were entwined with ropes of white lightening as she unleashed her tendrils of energy. The remaining underlings clutched at the burning energy that wrapped itself like a snake around their necks. The mystic snake slithered inside one underling's mouth. It disappeared for an instant, then the underling's eyes flared with white hot light. Slowly at first, Mikkel watched in astonishment as the energy passed through one ear and out the other. Again it raced, passing in one underling and out the other underlings, boring new holes, faster, gaining blinding speed and fury.

Mikkel shielded his eyes as the brilliant light continued to grow.

FOOMPH!

When he turned to look, nothing remained of the underlings but several piles of black ash. The three wizards, Kam, the White and Blue ones, methodically gathered up the dead underling bodies, hoisting them with unseen hands, guiding them through the air and piling them all together. A crowd of citizens now gathered, murmuring in amazement. The blue wizard, his features ageless, handsome and dark, muttered something unintelligible to the common man. The pyre of black underlings blazed to life and burned green with black smoke rising to the sky.

Mikkel covered his nose, eyes squinting when he noticed Billip standing beside him. They both shrugged as they returned their gazes back to Kam.

A cry rose up from behind the crowd, and each of the wizards faces turned. Someone was pushing their way through the crowd with a dead underling hoisted over their shoulder. A pair of underling blades was jammed in its black-haired skull. As he tossed the underling into the fire, Mikkel could hear the young warrior say, "You missed one."

Mikkel couldn't contain his smile.

It was Georgio.

Someone screamed from a nearby window.

CHAPTER 26

HOHM CITY WAS CONSIDERED TO be the most dreary city of all. Tucked in the northwestern most corner of the word, Hohm remained in chronic seclusion from the sunlight. A thin veil of fog rolled over the city and through the streets, bending over window sills and corners, a constant companion of those who preferred the seclusion.

The marsh itself, leagues long as it was wide, kept any curious people or invaders away. The willow tree roots were sunk deep in the mud, but their height rose over a hundred feet in some places. Black backed crocodiles rested on massive lily pads, and swamp toads were as big as a man's head. Every crawling, climbing, murk dwelling creature was ten times bigger than anything you'd ever known. So the people of the City of Hohm said.

Morley Sickle, a man of age, long forgotten by his neighbors, had lived in the City of Hohm all of his life, with no desire to go elsewhere … until now. He had come across a stranger of the most amazing character, weird and undeniable, when taking his wares, a very potent homemade wine he called Jig, to sell in the general store. The stranger, handsome beyond reason, asked to sample his Jig, and they'd been talking almost incessantly ever since. This all started months ago, and it had its benefits … at first.

"Morley," the newcomer said, his tone pleasing and demanding, "tell me, how many pickles do you think are in that jar?"

Morley, pinching the upper bridge of his nose, eyes squinted, tried not to think about it. *I don't give a slat!*

"That's not a number," the man said, raking his fingers back through his long locks of blond hair. "Really Morley, you need to do better than that."

Morley scooted towards the burning hearth in front of the tavern fire, trying his best not to think. If he could stop breathing, he would. He rubbed his bejeweled fingers as he stared at the brilliant gold and precious gems that adorned his hand. They were worth a hundred times more than anything he ever wanted. A thousand times if that. He groaned. What good were they when he was under the steady watch of his unavoidable new companion?

"Guess, Morley. Guess, I say!"

Morley lurched up in his seat.

"One hundred twenty, Scorch! One hundred twenty!"

Scorch grabbed him by the face, perfect hands squeezing his saggy cheeks up on his fear filled face, shaking his head.

His heart was thumping like a drum behind his ears, and a drop of water slipped from his eye duct and ran down along his nose.

"Hah! Morley, there's only fifty one. Fifty one pickles in that jar. But, after you go fetch me four of them, then there will be just …"

Morley swallowed a glob of spit and said, "Forty seven?"

Scorch released him, sat back and slapped his crocodile boots up on the table.

"Of course, you dullard. Now, fetch more jig while you're after it." Scorch snapped his fingers, popping Morley's ears, "and some more of that mossy cheese, too. I love the smell. I don't know why I love the smell of cheese, but I do. Ah yes … cheese, pickles, and jig. Mmmmmm. …"

Morley shuffled away, taking his time as his feet creaked over the floor boards. Every day had been like this, one nonchalant meaningless task or question after the other. But, he dared not think that. *I need to die.* If there were only a way to kill himself without thinking.

"Morley," Scorch chimed, "I don't like what you're thinking. And no, you can't make me angry enough to kill you, either. As a matter of fact, I don't think I can even become angry, but I think I can become drunk."

Scorch hoisted his strong chin up towards the rafters, closed his eyes and slowly brought each of his index fingers to the very tip of his perfect nose.

"Er, well, I think I can be drunk, but still very formidable all the same, unlike your kinfolk. A bunch of sots they are, except the dwarves; now they are good for mixing."

Get the pickles. Get the wine. Get the cheese. He repeated over and over in his mind, casting his glances at the empty tables and chairs of what used to be one of the liveliest places in Hohm. The most colorful men and women thrived in Hohm despite the dullness of its gray atmosphere. The strange fog from the marsh softened the tones and features of everything procured or living. It gave people a permanent sense of privacy, and the Royals, with their own dark and mysterious ways, didn't seem inclined to interfere so long as the people behaved themselves and paid taxes on time.

A man, head shaven, tall and brooding with a jagged scar between his lips, twisted the top from the large jar of pickles and handed him a wooden tong.

"I like the big ones, Morley, much juicer, and don't forget the cheese or the jig."

The sound of the man's perfectly strong and tranquil voice had the effect of a tack hammer tapping on his head. The barkeep returned with a rather large block of greenish and yellow cheese on a plate with a thin layer of white fuzz coating it.

"Ah, it smells wonderful," Scorch continued, tapping his fingernail on the table.

Morley flinched. The sound of Scorch's voice did that. He couldn't control it.

"Thanks, Sam," he muttered, returning back to his table with a plate full of rank smelling cheese, tongue assaulting wine and big bumpy green-blue pickles.

Scorch licked his lips as he tucked a handkerchief under his chin.

"Care for some?"

Morley shook his head.

Scorch carved off a chunk of moldy cheese and stabbed it onto a pickle. Stuffing it into his mouth, he said, "Where is everyone?"

"It's after curfew, the dark of night time. No one can leave their homes during this season. The marsh gets edgy. Dangerous," he said, hiding his trembling hand under the table.

Scorch pointed his fork in his face and said, "Are you certain it's the marsh and that they're not just terrified of me?"

"No," Morley admitted.

"But Morley, explain: why would these people be frightened of me? Am I not as handsome and charming as a man can be? Do I not fight like ten men in one? Did I not vanquish that horrible creature, er … what was it called?"

"A slog dragon."

"Yes, that ugly thing. Big as a pair of ogres it was. Breath like a sewer. Did that not bring comfort among your citizens?"

If Morley could've bitten his tongue off he would've, but he hated pain and blood, and tongues for that matter. He stammered as he said, "No."

Scorch rapped his fist on the table.

Morley banged his knee on the table.

"Why don't they like me, then?" Scorch said, stuffing an entire pickle in his mouth.

"Because you challenged so many people," he said, thinking *pickles*.

"Such contests are considered enjoyment and profitable by your kind, are they not?"

"Yes." *Pickles. Pickles. Pickles.*

"So what happened?" Scorch said, washing down the remaining cheese with a tankard of jig.

"You won the contest."

"So I did, and that's a good thing."

"But they all died ..."

Scorch frowned as he rubbed Morley's shoulder. "So they did." Scorch then smiled. "But only because I am so ... oh what is the word?"

"Marvelous?"

"Yes! Marvelous. I like that word," Scorch said, standing up from his seat. "Now, let's take a walk in this marsh, shall we? I can't have anything more dangerous than me running around out there."

Pickles. Pickles. Pickles.

It was all Morley thought as he dragged himself along behind the most powerful man on Bish.

CHAPTER 27

D ISTRICT TWENTY SEVEN IN THE City of Bone wasn't the same as it used to be. Tucked behind the enormous wall of the north-eastern most hemisphere, it was known as the lost city within the city. Vagabonds and murderers ran the streets, along with the most indecent and dangerous of guilds. The Royals, whose City Watch patrols maintained a presence just about everywhere to some degree, had avoided this place entirely. It was foul, abandoned, the streets broken, store fronts rotting, every other piece of glass shattered and every corner a harbor for violence or deceit to some degree. It was the place where people went when they had given up, the most desperate of all people, which was rare, because quitting was not part of the make-up of the people in the City of Bone or in all of Bish, for that matter. Trinos had made it that way, but things had changed and she didn't like it.

Trinos stood in the street like a magnificent piece of china displayed in a butcher shop. Her platinum hair cascaded over her elegant shoulders. Her deep luminous eyes were probing and curious, her clothes of the common sort in design but woven with materials one could not discern or describe. When she spoke, everything moving or crawling stopped to listen, for when her lips moved it was like watching red porcelain lips pouring wine.

"This is not good," she said, shaking her perfect chin. "I need more able people to continue this work."

A large group of men surrounded her, bowing and nodding in acknowledgment. They might as well have been hairy ogres among a new born child, each as rough in feature and texture as a man could come. Their clothes were little more than rags, but every button was buttoned and every stitch had been stitched. They bore scars, marks, burns and some were even missing one of their murderous eyes, but something was different among them beyond the appearance of their character. They moved with purpose.

Trinos lifted her hand and said, "Find me twenty more able men."

A man with a bent nose and wavy black hair that was combed to one side of his head, his calloused fingers fidgeting with the mismatched buttons on his shirt lifted his head to speak.

"Trinos, all of the men we have are rebuilding the castle. All the rest are our sworn enemies. We've betrayed our own to follow you," he swallowed hard, "and our pleas of compassion have gained nothing more than open hostility. Falcrum died by his brother's own hand, and Valcor was poisoned by his own mother's hand." She had brought food, built shelters, bathed children, and yet still the hostility remained. She had even parlayed with Royals only to be rejected with open mockery and disgust as she petitioned for them to take better care of their citizens. Most of them had laughed in her face while others just gaped at her in fascination. The men, their minds as vile as snakes, had peeled off her clothes before her first toe crossed the door's threshold. When she departed, for the first time in her infinite existence she had been concerned for her safety.

She nodded in a graceful motion.

"I just said find me twenty men, and I shall take care of the rest."

"But where?"

"Anywhere you think you can find them. Now go," she commanded.

District 27 was changing. The old was being used to rebuild the new. The citizens, the most pitiful lot in the entire city, smiled on occasion at the sound of the troubadour that played a small gold-painted harp and sang. The ramshackle storefronts displayed a vase of flowers or two. She liked flowers. And fresh food was being baked nearby, which was necessary because she had become very fond of pie.

Her toes didn't seem to touch the ground as she walked and settled herself on a bench near a dried up fountain centered in what used to be a very active plaza. She peered up into the sky, filling her lungs with air behind her perfect breasts, and pondered the suns she had created. She wondered if Scorch was experiencing the same resistance she was or if he even cared. She could do just about anything that she wanted with material things in her world, but she didn't have that kind of power over the willful people. It was frustrating.

"Men," she said, addressing a hapless looking crew that was working on the stonework of the fountain, "are the repairs complete?"

A young man with blue bags under his eyes pulled off his cap and replied, "Yes Trinos, but if I may: there is no water in this place. It's not run with water since I was a boy, and even then it ran with very little."

She rubbed her hands on her skirt that covered most of her voluptuous thighs and said, "The water is coming, and this fountain will return to its original vitality for all to enjoy." She smiled.

The man stammered, saying, "But the Royals—you can't steal their water! They'll wipe us out."

All of the workers blanched as Trinos let out a pleasant little laugh and said, "It's not their water, Corrin. It's mine."

CHAPTER 28

THERE WAS DARKNESS, FAMILIAR SOUNDS and pain. Voices, more than one, like shattered crystal, penetrating the recesses of his hazy mind, speaking in a language he swore he understood. There was wheezing and a bubbling sound coming from his busted face, and when he tried to open his mouth to speak it felt like a stake was jabbed in his head. He tasted blood and gravel.

"What now?"

Venir heard that. He strained to open his swollen eyes. One remained shut, heavy as a stone. The other cracked open the ever slightest, catching what he believed to be a moon's blue light. He coughed hard, and his entire body lurched in pain.

"He lives, so let him live," a voice as rough as rusting iron said. "Times like this we need all the help we can get."

"Blast you and your ideas," said another whose voice was full of irritation. "We've no time or supplies to be tending to some stranger, clearly left for dead. He probably has more coming after him, and it's just more trouble for us, as if we don't have enough already."

Venir heard the man spit and curse.

"We take a vote then," a reasonable woman's voice offered. "It's only fair. Look at the man. He's a fighting man; his size is even greater than Baltor's."

Somewhere, a man who sounded as if he had a mouth full of food complained, "What do you mean? Baltor's bigger than that cripple and stronger than any man. Yellow hairs are weak, like women." He sounded stupid, too.

The woman continued.

"Finish your meal, Baltor. I only meant he was almost as big. Your belly and head are far superior."

Baltor made a sound of satisfaction, but a few others laughed quietly and snickered. Venir wanted to laugh himself, but it hurt to even think about it.

"Listen," another man interjected, "I've drug this lout for three days already. He must be three hundred fifty pounds, and I'll not take him a foot farther. My back's killing me. Let the vultures and wolves have him, I say. He'll not be fighting anything but misery for weeks, maybe months. I certainly doubt he'll ever walk again."

Lazy Bastard!

"I'll pull him," the woman said, "and a good bit quicker than you. You might as well ride the stretcher as well. Those stumpy legs of yours aren't worthy of a dwarf."

"What did you say?" The man said with a sneer.

"Maybe you can ride Baltor's shoulders and get some fresh air to fill that big nose of yours, seeing how you've had it shoved up Caralton's arse—"

"Enough!" The voice of the first man who had begun the conversation interjected. "We vote, then. There are seven of us, and I'll break any ties.

"I want to make a plea for the man's life first," the woman decried.

"You've made your case clear Adanna, and we haven't the time to be slowed any longer. We are days away from the nearest Outpost."

Outpost!

Venir's mind was on fire with elation. Men, women, the smell of stew, the taste of Bish's dirt, a hooting owl, the smell of a fire, crackling embers and the metallic pings of a heating metal pot. He was back, back on Bish, and judging by things he was in the south. If he could only speak or pull free of the bonds that had him strapped to a man-made stretcher.

"What about Outlaw's Hide? It's closer," one man said.

"And filled with orcs and gnolls," the woman responded.

"And men just as well. For all we know the Outpost is wiped out. You've seen the fields. The Royals have fled the south, and no word of aid has come," the leader added.

What are they talking about?

"We don't know that!" she disagreed.

"Silence! We'll vote now! Let me see a show of hands of those who think the man should remain in our care and custody."

The voices were coming from behind his head, only adding to the agony that he could not see them. He was propped up at a low angle, leaving him an unfortunate field of vision as well. It was as if he wasn't there, his fate sealed by a council of accusers that he could not face. Venir's dry mouth and swollen tongue were yearning with thirst. *Water.* Maybe that would loosen his jammed up jaw.

"Humph! Only two votes to care for the man, I see."

SLAT!

Venir began to struggle with his bonds, but he could feel little more than his fingertips moving.

"I'm sorry, Adanna. It seems you and your mother have lost out again."

"Father, this is an outrage! That man deserves life. He's a fighter, I tell you. We'll need him."

"Sit down, Girlie," one of the other men chided. "The man will last little more than a day at most. No man can live without taking in water for more than four days, and I'll not be givin' up any more of mine."

"No, Father! At least loose his bonds and leave him to die with whatever he has left."

"Adanna, let go of me. I'll not leave the man, a criminal so far as we know, to be a prone meat basket and be ravaged by coyotes or bugbears."

"More likely underling scouts will take his head and parade it like the rest in their horrible fields."

Underlings!

Venir's hands clenched in and out, pumping more life into his broken body. After all, it had been an underling that cast him in the Mist. Underlings that slaughtered his family. Underlings that slit Georgio's throat. And Underlings that he lived to hunt and kill. He hadn't made it this far and escaped the madness behind the Mist to fail now.

He heard the scrape of a sharp blade coming out of its sheath. His blood surged behind his temples.

"Someone hold his head down while I slip this into his heart. Baltor, start digging a hole. Rogue or not, he deserves a man-made grave.

The sound of sobbing women was drowned out by his instinct to stay alive. Venir summoned every fiber of remaining strength and heaved at his bonds.

Snap! Snap!

He growled in pain like a wounded beast.

There was a sharp gasp behind him when he sat up, half-blind, and began to rise to his feet.

"Great Bish!" someone exclaimed.

Venir winced as he felt a pair of hands wrap around his waist and steady him.

"Someone help the man!" the father commanded.

"But we voted!" One said.

"Yes!" Another agreed.

Venir got a better look at them now, a well-armed but ragged bunch of strangers. Straightening his knees, he pulled back his bullish shoulders and rose to his full height.

"Eek, he's tall, like an oak."

"But can he walk, or follow? He'll slow us down."

Venir grimaced as he stepped forward.

"Easy, Man," the woman said.

He was trying to say, "Let go," but it came out as, "Wetgrowr."

A man, tall and lean, in trousers, bearded and with a strong chin eyed him with suspicion, the short blade in his hand rapping on his pants leg. He, as well as the rest, appeared to be of a better ilk than outlaws or Brigands, but one could never tell for sure. He spoke with more patience in his voice this time.

"Man, can you speak or not? We don't need some mute that can't sound the alarm tagging along."

"Aye," he said, managing a half-hearted smile. He lived, back in Bish, southern Bish to be exact. "Need g-grog."

"Hah, well some water will just have to do. No grog or ale for leagues, Man, just a ragged bunch of mercenaries scurrying along the safety of the Mist. No safer place than the edge of the world right now; the underlings have seen to that."

A moment of panic seized him as his hands fell to his chest. He groaned. His body tamped from head to toe in agony. Something pinched his insides. Busted ribs and splintered bone. *Suck it up!* The sack, once safely tucked in his shirt, was gone. He looked at his fingers, where one appeared to be dislocated. He pulled it back into place with sickening pop. On his other hand, the left, the tips of his outermost fingers remained blackened and gone.

"Sack," he mumbled.

"I have it," the woman said, "but it was quite empty."

"Smother him with it!" someone said. Venir turned away from them all, looking into the mist that was less than a mile distant. He wanted to be as far from it as far could be.

"Get me my sack, and I'll leave you to yourselves," he said, the weariness still heavy as wet canvas. He could barely stand, and walking more than a dozen feet seemed an impossibility at the moment. Pain was something he'd become accustomed to over the years, but being immobile was not.

The woman that was helping him stand up looked up at him. She was a stocky woman, a short-haired red head with round and caring eyes. She said, "Your injuries are too severe, Stranger. You've a busted shoulder and ribs, and your leg seems to be broken."

The leader handed him a canteen of water, eyeing him with concern. "Don't drink it all."

Venir gulped in a mouth full, then another.

"Ah!" he said aloud, his voice rich and robust once more. "Now that's good water, and I'd kill a hundred underlings for more."

"Man, I should cut you where you stand for drinking all of that."

"Kill him! He's a thief!"

"A big, giant, stinking crippled thief."

Venir laughed. My, had he ever missed the insults of people. He said, "You'll do no such thing, my friends. Not without being dragged into the blood and dirt as well."

They all bristled.

"The fool doesn't have a weapon, and now he threatens to kill us all? Kill the lunatic."

"Will you shut up, Lout," she pleaded to Venir. "My father's not one to be trifled with. He's not one for joking; he's moody."

"Ha, your father must have been fed breast milk from an orc when he was a child. A big fat one with three tits and two teeth at that. He misses her, I bet."

No music could have sounded sweeter to his ears than the sound of steel coming unbridled from their beds. In a moment, four men surrounded him as he stood face to face with the leader, but looking down upon him.

The leader said, "Man, your tongue is as twisted as a serpent's tail. My orc mother had four tits, not three!"

Everyone looked at the leader, then Venir, then back to the leader.

Venir knew they were waiting for their leader to spill his blood. He could feel their fear and anger, but the man before him remained calm, eyes giving him closer study.

"Perhaps, Stranger, if you shaved that beard from your face you might not seem so disturbing. You look like a bugbear's nanny. Of course, I can only guess you are trying to hide the ogre portion of your heritage."

"Good for me, but sad for you, clearly being bred of two-legged swine, but your eyes are still quite dashing," Venir said, stretching out his aching limbs, feeling his knotted muscles begin to loosen beneath his skin.

"By Bish," the leader said, "Venir, is that you inside that busted face and elder's beard?"

"Aye, the underlings haven't gnawed the meat from my bones yet, Hogan. I live."

Hogan came over, clasped his hands and looked up in his eyes saying, "Before, you were almost as big as a horse, but now you are, Venir. It's been ten years since we last hunted together, and I thought for certain you were dead, Man."

The rest of the men and women were stupefied. An older woman, Hogan's wife, handed Venir a small loaf of bread and some wine.

"Ah, you were holding out on me," he said to Hogan.

"You asked for grog. But Venir, where have you been, Man? The underlings are over running the entire world these days it seems," he said, guiding him to the fire.

Venir limped over and sat down. The fire's glare seemed to ignite the coals of his blazing blue eyes as he said, "Tell me more about the underlings."

CHAPTER 29

"How do you expect me to defend myself in these treacherous mountains in these bonds, Fogle?" Cass asked, interrupting his thoughts.

The journey back to the hot ground of Bish wasn't any less treacherous than the journey there. Fogle's razor sharp mind had regained its focus with the help of a few feet-warming spells. Still, his head was clogged and draining with snot, and there was little he could do to control that.

"AH-Chooo!"

Cass stopped and turned, saying, "Ah, poor little wizard has a runny nose. Unhitch me and I can help you with that."

"No thanks," he said, avoiding her irresistible gaze.

She was a distraction now. The seductive swagger of her hips drew his gaze when she navigated the snow as if she was part of the snow itself. And every hour or so she had another comment to say: playful, wonderful, tempting, suggestive and even evil. Fogle had defeated her, though. He was the smarter person and stronger as well, but her power was in what she offered him, a want once fulfilled but not fully satisfied. He was curious.

She stood there, waiting for him to catch up, offering a smile.

"Fogle, you have won. I've given my word. There is no need for these bonds," she said, pleading, submissive. "The Blood Ranger knows this. You know this, and if something happens to me, then who will care for your dog? I would hate to see your journey wasted, beyond you losing your virginity, of course. And there is so much more exploring we can offer one another." She smiled the kind of smile that offered many splendors. "After all, it's going to be a long walk." She brushed up against him, looking up into his eyes, the snowflakes falling gently on her beautiful face.

He tore his gaze away, shoved his way past her and trotted up along Mood's side.

"She's witching, isn't she, Wizard?"

"What do you mean?" he answered.

"Ho! I can hear every little word of yer chit chat back there. She's controlling everything from your head to your groin."

"No, that's not the case," he denied. "If anything, I'm controlling her. I'm just letting her think she's getting control. Ah-CHOO!"

A heavy hand slapped him on his back, almost knocking him to the snow-covered ground.

Mood then said, "Keep telling yerself that then, Man, and you'll be in the grave sooner than expected. Remember where you are; this is Bish, yer never in control."

Fogle disagreed. He was always in control.

"No, I have control over my own actions, regardless of the circumstances."

"Is that so, Wizard? Then tell me, were you in control when you slept with her? Was that part of your plan, or hers?"

"That's different. I was trying to seduce her," he said, immediately feeling like a fool after he said it. Cass had caught up and was laughing along with Mood's robust *ho' ho's.*

"Bish on you both!" he cursed. "You outland peoples are impossible."

He walked away, hiding his blushing face and fighting to ignore the soreness of his icy nose.

"She's right, you know," Mood growled back at him.

"About what?" he shot back. He watched Mood slice her bonds apart.

"She has to be able to fend for herself if needed, and we have a long way to go."

Great! Fogle kept on walking over the frozen and rocky tundra. He didn't bother a glance at Cass when she knelt down to nuzzle with the wolves, but he could feel her pink eyes on his back, stirring the memory of her soft lips pressed against his.

"Whoop!" he cried, as his boots slid out from under him and he crashed to the ground. *BONE!* He tried to scramble back to his feet but slipped again, this time jamming his knee into a jagged piece of rock. Pain jabbed into his flesh, and he felt his anger and frustration swelling. Mood's words were loud and clear in his mind for some reason, *Remember where you are; this is Bish, yer never in control.*

A strong pair of arms lifted him back to his feet.

"Thanks, Mood," he said, limping forward.

"Hah," Cass grinned, "is that an insult or a poor attempt at humor?"

Fogle turned to face her, unable to hide his surprise. She locked her fingers around his and held him tight. He tried to pull his hand away, but her firm grip would not give. A moment of panic surged within him. "What are you doing?" he said, "Let go!" He summoned his energy, but her next words subdued his efforts.

"I am your prisoner," she said, kissing his hand.

A lump formed in his throat. His embarrassment at her being stronger than him, physically, began to fade, and he allowed her warm flesh to become one with his.

Mood stood before them with big meaty hands on his hips, a burning cigar hanging out of his mouth.

"Sheesh, just try in' keep up. I'm starting to miss my home already."

But for the time being, Fogle Boon was in no hurry.

Chapter 30

"I'm going, Kam!" Georgio yelled.

Kam shot back, "No, you certainly are not!"

The Magi Roost was empty except for a handful of people including Mikkel, Billip, Joline, Georgio and herself. The madness that consumed the City of Three the prior day had finally come to a close, and now the morning suns of the new day were on the rise. The underlings had brought not only chaos, but fire to the safe harbor of the city. The damage was minimal at worst, but the impact the presence of the underlings had was devastating. For the first time in decades, so far as anyone knew, almost every window and door was locked.

Georgio rose up to his full height, a young man now, but a man nonetheless, and said, "I can do whatever I want. I have family in the south, too, and I want to check on them. I can take care of myself, and I'll have Mikkel and Billip with me. You can't make me stay!" He rapped his first on the bar.

Kam's green eyes were like burning emeralds, and she was shaking with anger and guilt.

"No you won't!"

"Yes I will!" Georgio jumped in her face.

Her eyes fastened on his, blazed with anger, and she began to mumble a spell.

Joline's perspiring face came between the two of them.

"Enough, you two!" Joline stammered, unable to hide the shock on her face. "This isn't the right way to settle this," she said, voice shaking. "Georgio, you are way out of line, talking to Kam that way. She's only done the best by you."

Georgio sulked and turned away, but Joline caught him by his earlobe.

"OW!"

"Sit down, Boy! And don't make me raise my voice again."

Georgio frowned as he plopped down on the nearest chair and brushed his long curly locks from his face.

Mikkel stood up, mouth beginning to fill with words, drawing Kam's glare. He closed his mouth and resumed his seat on the groaning stool.

I can't believe this. She took a deep breath and rubbed her forehead. Her nose was running. Mere hours ago, she had slaughtered a small host of underlings, yet now she was struggling to maintain her wits against the will of an elder boy. She raised her fingers and a half-moon bottle of Muckle Sap floated her way—and was intercepted by Joline.

"Joline," Kam warned, "now is not the time."

As the older woman's lips parted, Kam snatched the bottle from her hand.

"Don't you dare do that again!" Joline fired back. "I can still turn you over my knee!"

Mikkel and Billip's brows perched.

"I'm hungry," Georgio said.

Kam felt her mind unraveling. Things seemed to be happening all at once: underlings had invaded her city; Mikkel and Billip were leaving, and now Georgio wanted to go. Venir was either dead or had abandoned her and his daughter Erin. She tilted the bottle to her lips and drank. *Pull it together.*

"Kam," Joline said with shock, "you aren't some commoner. You're a Royal."

Kam handed her back the jug and said, "And I just killed a hive of underlings, so I think you can give my bad graces a pass." She wrapped her arms around Joline and said, "And I'm very sorry, too."

The brief awkward silence was broken when Billip offered a suggestion, saying, "I think she still deserves a spanking."

Kam let out a little laugh, quiet and pleasant. Joline started to get the giggles. Before she knew what was happening, everyone was laughing, even Georgio chuckled a little. Still laughing, she pulled him up from his chair and said with tears in her eyes, "I'm sorry."

"Me, too," he admitted, hugging her.

Now that the mood had softened in the room, everyone gathered at a big round table by the largest fireplace. Kam was exhausted. Joline looked exhausted, and for the first time since she knew them, Billip and Mikkel's energy seemed drained. Only Georgio remained bright-eyed as he dug a wooden spoon into a large bowl of Joline's stew. Billip and Joline sat beside one another, shoulder to shoulder. It seemed Kam wasn't as aware of things as she'd like to think she was.

"Now, let me be clear," she said to all, but looking at Georgio. "I don't want you to go, but I can't make you stay, any of you, and," she fought back a choking sob, "I don't like it."

"Ah Kam," Mikkel said, "I'll stay."

"No. No, you won't. You have to get your son, and you'll need help. Bish, this is so hard! "She had always figured that things would be simpler once the formidable men parted ways and the boys grew up, but this was painful. Her heart ached. And underlings, ghastly creatures unlike she ever imagined, were waiting out there. She didn't understand how they had the courage to risk their lives going back, knowing full well what was out there.

"Also," she continued, "what about Lefty?"

Georgio looked away, arms crossed over his chest, frowning.

"Don't you want to say good-bye, Georgio? He's your best friend."

Georgio mumbled something.

"What was that?" she said.

"*Was*—I said!"

"You don't mean that," Kam frowned.

"I do mean that. His best friend is the freakish fingered Gillem now. I swear I don't know why all of you like him. He's evil!"

Georgio started to get up, but Mikkel's stern look sat him back down.

For the life of her, Kam hadn't found a single reason to distrust Master Gillem. She'd been paying attention, but maybe not so much as she thought. After all, there had been more than enough distractions lately. As for Gillem being evil, it was absurd, but Georgio was young, and he and his best friend had clearly drifted since Gillem's arrival. Her sudden sickness and the relief Gillem brought did seem a bit too timely.

"Men," she said to Mikkel and Billip, "is there any reason to distrust Gillem? Do you think he's posed a danger to our dear Lefty?"

Mikkel shook his head and said, "No, he's been more than helpful."

"And not overtly so," Billip said, popping his knuckles.

"Stop that," Joline said, wrapping her fingers around Billip's. "Will you ever learn your manners?" The older woman let out a squeal as Billip wiggled his fingers around her waist.

"I think Georgio's just missing his little friend is all," Mikkel continued, rubbing Georgio's head. "But, it's just part of growing up, and halflings are a different race. They have their own ways."

Georgio shoved Mikkel's thick wristed hand away and said through his teeth, "You are an idiot, Mikkel. And so are you, Billip. If Venir were here, he would know better."

Joline gasped, saying, "Georgio!"

Kam slammed her hands onto the table as she rose, saying, "What has gotten into you, Georgio? You're the one acting evil!" She would have done anything to retrieve her words, and if there were such a spell she would have used it. Georgio's handsome round face was now pitiful and sad. His brown eyes watered, and he began to snivel. She reached over to touch him, but he turned his chair away.

"Everyone ease up," Billip suggested. "Georgio's upset and mad, and he's entitled. Besides, it's not like I haven't been called stupid before. Well, at least I don't think I've not been called stupid, so far as I remember."

But no one seemed to be listening to his words, least of all Kam, who felt like dirt. *Venir. Where is that handsome lout who caused all this?* She dabbed her nose with a dish rag and blew. It was an awful sound.

In the meantime, Mikkel reached over, grabbed a handful of Georgio's curly hair, pulled him half out of his seat and said, "You call me an idiot again and I'll bust your fat little arse, Boy."

Georgio's eyes enlarged like moons before Mikkel let him back down.

"Sorry," he managed. "It's just that, I know Venir is out there, and I want to go find him. Maybe he and Chongo are back in Bone—or Two-Ten City? He has to be fighting underlings. Maybe that's why they're leaving the south, because Venir's slaughtering them like he always does."

Kam blew her nose again. She saw Billip and Mikkel give each other hopeless looks. Georgio was a long way from letting Venir go, unlike the rest of them. If anything, the underling assaults were the result of Venir being dead, not alive.

Joline then said, "We can't be parting ways like this, and I can't stay up all night, either. Georgio, I'll keep tabs on Lefty and Master Gillem. I have to say, no man or halfling should be so charming, and he is a bit too nosy for my liking. I love the flowers, and his words, and the way they trickle from his tongue like honey, but ... well ... I'll leave it at that. I think we all need to be more careful ... times are not as they were."

The roasting fire behind Kam did little to warm her spirits. Her friends were leaving, and like Venir and Fogle, she didn't know if she would ever see them again. She scanned the Magi Roost and was overwhelmed with memories. For over a decade it had been her home, and she knew every inch of its fabric from the creaking floorboards to every glass and goblet behind the bar. It was all a part of her. But it had never been so filled with life as it had been these past few months. She looked at the bloodstain on the floor, one table over, where Venir and Fogle had held their legendary Mind Grumble. She whimpered inside. She wanted him back. She wanted them all back to have things like they were before, even if only for one more day.

"Kam," Mikkel's deep voice interrupted her thoughts, "are you well? You look a little lost over there."

"I'm fine. I just realized that, like so many people, I've never been anywhere else before."

Joline kicked her in the leg.

"Do you think you're going to run off and leave your baby? Or me, for that matter?"

"I'll take her with me."

"You set one foot outside of this city with baby Erin … well … neither of you might ever come back again. I can't handle that," Joline got up, flushed, and rushed off to the kitchen.

Kam felt foolish for even suggesting such a thing, and the looks in the men's eyes were ones of grave concern. Georgio had the most worried look of all.

"Clearly I am the only idiot here," she said, standing up. She walked over to Billip and Mikkel, hugged their backs and kissed their heads. Then she did the same to Georgio. She was numb as she walked away and said the rest: "See me before you go. I'll have something for you."

For now, all she wanted to do was crawl in a hole.

CHAPTER 31

THE NEST HAD MANY WONDERS one would never imagine … a secret city beneath the golden thrones above. Not many men, or women for that matter, knew of its existence. Even the highest ranking Royals in the City of Three did not know of the location, nor did they care. But there it was: private, quiet, with as many amenities in its crowded nooks as the world above, except for the burning suns and eerie moons. As a matter of fact, it would be a great place to live, if it wasn't full of thieves.

That bothered Lefty as he hurried alongside Master Gillem with a nervous look in his eye and a rapid little heart pounding behind his breast. The novelty of stealing had begun to wear off. It was one thing to make a few ends meet and quite another having to do it against one's own free will. He rubbed his running nose. Something about the moldy air in the dank city bothered him.

"Gillem," he said, "are we going to see Palos now?"

"Prince Palos," Gillem responded, strutting the streets in a long gait, nodding to all of the cohorts they passed by.

The last few hours had been out of the ordinary. Something was going on, and every crooked spine in the Nest had an urgent gesture about it. Whatever was going on, Lefty wasn't being filled in.

He pulled at the long sleeve of Gillem's cotton white shirt and said, "Will you tell me something? What's going on?"

Gillem rubbed his blond locks with his skinny, man-sized fingers that reminded Lefty of Melegal. "Lefty Lightfoot, now is the time to be silent, follow and listen. Yes, something is going on, but that is no matter to us. We serve the Prince of Thieves, and that is all that matters. He will tell us what we can worry about and what we cannot. Now come along."

Lefty didn't like the sound of that. He rubbed the goose bumps on his arms, but they wouldn't go away, not since he'd seen the trove of bodies in their watery graves. He knew, right then and there, he had to make a change. But how? Palos would kill him, of that much he was certain. The Prince of Thieves had made that perfectly clear on more than one occasion. *What would Melegal do? When will Venir get back?* He had convinced himself he wouldn't need them anymore, but on days like this he was reminded how much he did.

"Come on, Lad. We don't need to make the Prince mad," Gillem said as they entered the tavern home of Palos. Gillem didn't offer a single word to the handful of patrons as they made their way up the steps to the balcony.

There stood Thorn, tall and gruesome, big arms crossed over his broad chest, short swords dangling on his hips, blocking the door to Palos's haphazard throne room. Behind Thorn, leaning on the balcony rail, was the other man, small crossbow in hand, toothpick dangling from his mouth, whose name Lefty did not yet know. The man's mousy eyes fixated on Lefty as he stood up and leveled the crossbow at his chest, winked and turned away. Lefty slid a little farther behind Gillem.

"He summoned us, Thorn," Gillem said with an agitated tone, "so open the door, Cretin."

Thorn let out a little snort as he glared down on them like rodents and pushed the door open, taking his time before he stepped aside. Without hesitation Gillem entered, and Lefty stayed on his heels. A brush of air bristled his hair as Thorn slammed the door closed behind them. Lefty let out a sigh. *Here we are again. How dreadful.* The room was empty of life other than the blazing fire inside a marble mantle made for a Royal, with a great sword hanging over the top.

"Have a seat," Gillem gestured toward the table that was half covered with piles of silver and gold coins among other trinkets and jewelry.

The older halfling pulled out a small sack and dropped it with a clank in front of Palos's chair at the head of the table. Lefty saw Gillem's face bunch up as he drew his long fingers away in slow motion. Two weeks of work was in there, a small fortune, a bag of trinkets and trophies, all gone to where? Lefty couldn't help but wonder where it all went and how Palos could possibly spend it all.

Gillem sat down beside him and poured a goblet of wine.

"Thirsty, Lefty?"

My throat is as dry as a cup of Outland sand.

"No."

"Don't be rude, Lefty. If Palos drinks, you drink."

Lefty crinkled his nose. Wine and ale weren't anything he cared to indulge in, unlike the rest of the populace of the Nest, who took a great deal of pride in swilling wine and telling foul jokes. It was fun at first, until the women came, carousing the tavern and stirring the men into a frenzy of hooting and hollering beasts. Lefty never knew the meaning of the word *appalled* or that such a feeling existed until he came to the Nest. Now he found himself feeling appalled every time he came back. He wondered if Gillem ever felt the same, but the master thief didn't ever seem to be bothered by anything, except by Palos.

Gillem slapped him on the shoulder, causing him to raise his head from the table. The warmth of the fire began to seep into his little bones and fill his head with weariness. Palos's bedroom door creaked open, and there the Prince of Thieves stood in a long flowing black silk bathrobe with a belt tightly wrapped around his rotund belly. Palos had put on a few pounds since the first time they met, but he still moved with grace that belied his girth.

"Little thieves," he said, taking a seat at the table, "literally, and with little purses, I see." Palos snatched up Gillem's sack, tested its heft and tossed it aside with all rest. "Really, Master Gillem, that's hardly a day's work, if that."

Lefty watched Gillem's shoulders draw back. It was double what they turned in two weeks before, if not more, and it had been a prosperous couple of weeks.

"You two wouldn't be holding out on me, would you?" said Palos, like a slithering snake.

Lefty looked into Palos's pale probing eyes that were filled with an unnatural, tireless energy. It was as if the man was too greedy to sleep for fear of a rat snatching a golden crumb of cheese. Gone was the charming man he met above, now permanently replaced by something maniacal and greedy. *I can't do this.*

"Certainly not, Palos," Gillem shot back, his fingers falling to his pockets.

"Oh Master Longfingers, I remember our days when you mentored me. Did we not return with more booty than this little sack?"

"No, we did not," the halfling disagreed.

You tell him, Gillem!

"Huh, it seems you are getting old, Halfling. As I recall, we returned with at least two sacks this size," Palos said, stretching out his arms, fighting a yawn.

"In two months maybe," Gillem said, standing up in his chair. "Lefty and I got this in two weeks. I was a master thief then, I am a master now, and I was a master before you cut your first purse."

Lefty couldn't find his breath. Something was wrong. He had never seen Gillem upset before. He grabbed his mentor by the shirt tail and tried to pull him down, only to be swatted away.

Palos fired back, "Sit down, Gillem! Else I'll have Thorn come in here and skewer you like a fat little pig."

The man meant it, every word; Lefty could tell. He tugged at Gillem again, who to his surprise, sat down with a blank look on his face. It was as if Palos's threat sucked all the life from the vibrant halfling man, as if he was looking at his own grave in the murky waters. Lefty remained still, his little heart the only thing moving, like a frightened bunny, barely breathing.

"Now, Gillem, I'll forgive your little fit this once and even this paltry tithe, but one more outburst like that and you both will die! Understand?"

Lefty nodded along with Gillem.

"Now, Boy, bring me a goblet of wine."

Lefty did as he was told and returned back to his seat. Gillem sat stone faced. Sensing that something was very wrong, Lefty slunk deeper into the confines of his chair.

"So, it seems that our gains are meager, and it's not just the two of you, even though you are the most disappointing." He ran his finger around the rim of his bejeweled goblet. "So you both, at my direction, are going to begin playing a bigger game."

Gillem shifted in his seat, and Lefty sat a little farther up.

"It's called *Ransom*. Lefty, do you know what *ransom* is?"

The word sounded familiar, but he didn't know for sure, and he was too scared to guess. He shook his head.

"Oh … well done, Gillem. What a fine mentor you are, not telling him about one of our favorite challenges."

Gillem gave Lefty a sad look over his shoulder that ran a chill down his spine.

"Ransom, little halfling, has a big payday. Maybe ten years' worth or even a lifetime if you play the game right." Palos's polished and charming tone had returned. "Would you like to learn how it's played?"

Lefty was curious. He nodded his head.

"Good," Palos pulled himself up from his chair and leaned on his forearms, eyes intent on his. "First, you need a target, someone of great wealth and passion. Someone who has compassion and a lot of gold. Like a Royal, for instance."

Lefty nodded.

"You find something of theirs, something very valuable, that they cannot live without. Something that they would die for."

Lefty nodded again. It sounded like a challenge, and his thoughts went to the Wizard Towers whose smooth spires reached into the sky. Something valuable or something worth dying for would have to be in there. Maybe this would be an opportunity, a dangerous one, but something new nonetheless.

"Or someone valuable," Palos continued in a whisper, "like a baby, perhaps."

All signs of life went numb from fingertip to toenail. *Erin! Bish! You can't say Erin!* Lefty wanted to run, to hide, to scream or do anything to avoid hearing what Palos said next.

"Yes, Boy, you are going to steal Kam's baby for me." Palos's eyes flickered with evil, his voice as vengeful as a viper and somewhat deranged. "That witch owes me a favor, and I'll have her groveling on her hands and knees before me, offering me anything and everything I want. I'll shackle her, defile her and make her beg for more." Palos slammed his jeweled fists into the table.

Wham!

"I will have her baby, and she will be my whore!"

Lefty couldn't believe what was happening or why. *No! No! No!* How had skimming led him down this dark path? It was his fault and his alone. Now he was being forced to do the unthinkable. Something bumped against his chair. It was the crooked-nosed Thorn, as tall and dark as a stormy night sky.

"You, Gillem and Thorn shall execute this kidnapping, and mind you, little halfling: fail in this charge and Kam and all the rest of your companions will be strewn across every dark corner in this city by the entire thieves guild."

CHAPTER 32

"**I**MPRESSIVE, DETECTIVE," LORD ALMEN SAID.

It was a compliment; a sincere one that wasn't layered in an accent that suggested anything otherwise would mean death. Instead, Melegal stood tall, not proud, before the Royal Lord's desk beneath the castle kitchens. It had been almost three full weeks since he was last summoned to the hawking man's private study, which gave him great relief and curiosity as well. Lord Almen, an image of strength and power, looked drained. His vulture-like countenance almost sagged, as if recovering from a sudden illness. It wasn't something one would normally notice, but nothing escaped Melegal's notice.

Lord Almen continued as his ring-clad fingers rolled a strange foreign object over his desk. It was one of the items seized during the capture of the Slergs, perhaps the only thing of value at all. The Royal Lord smiled and said, "This is a great prize: a Slerg weapon, very potent. Have you ever seen anything like it before in your life?" Lord Almen held it before his own face, eyes filled with admiration.

"No, Lord Almen. I'm not very familiar with the various forms of weapons, especially one of such a crude make," he said, staring at the white ash cudgel of the one called Leezir, a man he knew from long ago. It looked like nothing more than a club carved from a trunk of wood and shaved down, smooth at the top with a grip carved out for a handle. It had a strange white hue about it.

"Spine Breaker," Lord Almen said, rising from his chair and toying with the hefty weapon. "Tell me about its acquisition. I've heard nothing about this capture of my foes, and I'd like to have some intimate details."

Almen waved the fat end of the cudgel inches from his nose, like a giant rattle. Melegal fought the urge to step back as images of the battle of the Slergs swelled inside the confines of his mind. *Oh, the sick Lord will enjoy this.*

He cleared his throat.

"The short version, Lord Almen?"

"Yes, but don't leave out the interesting parts. I know there must be some," Almen commented while he poured two goblets of wine and handed one to Melegal.

I better make this good, then.

He thought of Venir, the story teller, the man with as much mouth as he had brawn. Venir had his ways, and Melegal had his own, but he'd never been one to entertain men, as opposed to women when it came to using his tongue.

He took a sip, thinking *Oh, that's wonderful,* and began:

"We had them cornered in the catacombs in the sewers beneath the city, between the Northeast passages and the manufacturer's district. I estimated there were only six of them remaining, trapped between the grates with their only way out being up through the storm drains. I ordered the City Watch to drop the smokers in. We had the lone rain portal sealed, twenty Watchmen, swords and watch sticks in hand, ready to dispense your will by my command."

Taking a sip, Lord Almen nodded for him to continue.

"As the smoke billowed from the hole in the street, the first man came out, arms flailing, coughing. An eager Watchmen cut his neck out with a sword, a bit too eager, it seemed. I reminded the dullards we were to take them alive, not dead. So, I had them sheath their swords."

Lord Almen interrupted saying, "Seems risky. They've been a dangerous lot."

"True, Lord Almen, but I needed to interrogate some of them. I had to make sure we had them all," he reassured the Lord. The truth was, he was hoping the City Watch, one or two at least, might be caught off guard. The fewer the Watchmen, the better.

He whet his throat with more wine. *With grapes pressed such as this I could tell stories all day. Man and babe alike. Delicious.*

"The next man burst through the hole in a black cowl, waving that cudgel, which was glowing like the moons. Two watchmen bore down on him, and there was a clap like thunder." He smacked his hands together with a sharp pop. "One man fell to the ground, in a pile of boneless flesh, and the other gawped long enough to have his head cracked open like a nut."

"Excellent," Almen commented, hands caressing the wood.

"About that time another character climbed from the hole, his swords chopping through a small wave of watchmen like they were wheat. He was fast: punching holes in throats and slicing open bellies like a seasoned soldier. Another thunderclap followed. This time it shook the ground, knocking men from their feet. That's when I let loose your snakes."

Melegal opened up his palms. Two coiled pieces of intricate metal shone dully in the lantern light as he set them on the table.

"I'm not a mage, and I had my doubts, but I did as you instructed me. Dropping them to the ground made the things come to life, slithering like sidewinders over the stone and wrapping around the legs of the two formidable Slergs like whips. After that, it was over."

Melegal finished his goblet that Lord Almen refilled.

"Thank you, Lord Almen. At that point, the City Watch overwhelmed them, beating them like a pair of dirty rugs. Really dirty. But the damage had been done. Four of the Watchmen looked like they had just fallen from a cliff and landed on a pile of rocks. Three more were dead from the one Slerg's steels, two others wounded. Blood and guts smeared the road, until the rain came and washed it away. The only ones left of the Slergs were the two and a young girl."

"And wasn't there another, a giant brute of some sort?" Almen asked, hoisting the hefty cudgel on his broad shoulder.

"We'd jailed him earlier. Can't tell if he was kin or not. Seems too big and slow, somewhat mute." Melegal didn't want to say too much. Brak's fate was not in his hands, but if anything, maybe the man could bust rocks for the rest of his life in shackles. *Better than being dead.*

Lord Almen took his seat, dipped a quill in a jar of ink and jotted something down on a piece of parchment. "So, Detective, how confident are you that there are no Slergs left?"

He didn't shift or sigh, despite his resentment of the question—how in Bish was he supposed to know? He had poured over every last bit of information that the torturers had extracted from the men. No man, under thumbscrews or bamboo shoots, was unbreakable, and in the case of the Slergs, they had a weak line of faith. He could only assume they did not lie when they screamed. He had to be right. Of course, it was expected that he would be—after all, he was Castle Almen's Detective—a position he had come to discover offered a degree of reverence, even from the Almen family. *Right or wrong, I'll be dead one day anyway.*

"Certainly, Lord Almen. Every lice-ridden head accounted for. All survivors in uncomfortable and agonizing custody," he said in a reassuring voice.

"Not too agonizing. I have plans for those who remain."

Is that so?

"Lord Almen, may I ask ... Do those plans involve me?"

Lord Almen raked his fingers through his long brown hair, fastened his handsome countenance on Melegal and said, "Of course, Detective. With all the work that you have done, it would seem fitting to let you in on our final farewell to the Slergs. I plan to have you and Sefron work on this little project together, along with my family and other Royal friends of mine."

Melegal could feel the blood curdle in his veins at the mention of Sefron's name. He felt his nostrils flaring like galloping horses, even though they weren't, he still struggled to maintain his accommodating composure. *Great, maybe I'll accidentally kill him.* He had already seen the creepy cleric spill more blood in the castle dungeons than most seasoned soldiers spilled on the battlefield. The sick man enjoyed delivering misery, death and pain.

"Excellent, Lord Almen."

"I think you'll enjoy it. There will be a coming of age ceremony for several fine young Royals. It almost makes me want to laugh, thinking about Sefron's plan for the meddlesome Slergs"

"And that would be, Lord Almen?"

Lord Almen raised a brow and said, "I'm sure you are familiar with the Coming of Age ceremony, Detective?"

"Certainly," he answered. Most urchins that served in the castles were very aware, especially the large and slow ones, like Venir. Melegal's memory of back then was as clear of the details as if it had all happened yesterday. It had been at least two decades since he had seen the last one, the one where Venir had fought the Slerg brothers, Creighton and Hagerdon. Leezir had been there, too. Funny how things happen, he thought. "So, the Slergs will be the contestants against the upcoming youth, I suppose?"

"Yes," Almen said, his face showing mild delight. "It's only for the Almens, and as I mentioned, other friends that lie outside of the constrictions of the Royal Castles. I can't have word getting out of this event, Detective." Lord Almen picked up the cudgel that self-illuminated with pale light. "It wouldn't be viewed favorably among other Royal Castles."

"Understood. Is there anything else?"

Lord Almen hawkish eyes fixated on his.

Please don't ask.

"How are you coming along with the Lorda's investigation of my deranged son ... Tonio?"

Lord Almen hadn't mentioned his son in weeks, and now he was interested again? Melegal had no answers. Except one.

Be bold.

"They say a wild butcher in Royal armament runs the streets. They say he is a ghost or ghoul from below. I say that ghoul is yours, Lord Almen."

Lord Almen gave him a wary look and said, "Is this what you have told the Lorda?"

"She can't be as easily convinced, but yes, I have."

"Can you hunt him down and kill him, if need be?"

"I can on your command." *But I'd rather not. I don't think he can be killed.*

Melegal stood there waiting for the Royal Lord to respond. When his feet began to ache, he asked himself the same old question: *How did that big man sneak up on me?*

Lord Almen continued to jot down more notes.

Melegal waited.

Oh, not this again.

Minute after agonizing minute passed.

"I'll be expecting confirmation of what you believe at some point, Detective. Dismissed."

Melegal backed towards the door and left as quietly as he could. How could he confirm what he believed without bringing Lord Almen proof? *Kill Sefron. Kill Tonio? There has to be a way out of all this.* Up the stairs he went, stride after stride, with the full realization that he wasn't going up, he was going down.

CHAPTER 33

Outlaw's Hide was a place of wary faces. Venir welcomed them all, however, offering greetings and salutations as if they were all long lost friends, not a stranger among them, yet there were many.

"Hello, Pretty One," he said to a chubby half-orcen woman wrapped in tattered robes and carrying a sack of flour.

Adanna, Hogan's daughter, jabbed his ribs with an elbow. "Will you stop that? You draw too much attention upon yourself. And calling that two-legged sow pretty is sickening."

Venir reached over and tickled her ribs, bringing forth a squeal of delight.

"Jealous, I see."

"Hardly," she said, reaching up to pull the clay jar of grog from his lips, "now give me that. You've drank yourself blind."

Venir dangled the jar high over his head. "And before the night's over I'll have drunk myself deaf as well, but not so much that I cannot enjoy your soft lips crying for more." He slapped Adanna on her rump, lifting her to her toes.

"Lout," she said, slapping him away … with a smile.

Outlaw's Hide was little more than a tent city, the heavy canvasses large, small and some even grand enough to house a hundred people, others little more than a stick and a rug. There were buildings, but these were few and rotting like fallen logs in a swamp. It hardly mattered. The inhabitants of Outlaw's Hide didn't often stay for long. The Hide was dangerous: even the deadliest criminals and renegades were at risk within its shadowy clutches. Some came and went quickly, others didn't last through the night. Venir wasn't worried about any of that.

Venir tossed his empty jug into a small tent, busting it with a crash. A cry of alarm went up, and angry voices stepped out, a pair of stout men, one as scarred and calloused from battle as the other, hands gripping the pommels of their swords. Venir was whistling as he walked by, paying neither man any mind.

"You're a dead man!" one said, ripping free his sword, its keen edge glinting in the moon light.

Venir stopped, turned and laughed, his big hands falling onto two broad swords strapped around his waist.

The men were almost a head shorter than Venir, yet taller than most men. Their opposing demeanor was criminal from head to toe as they spread apart, both brandishing steel. The murderous intent in their eyes began to fade as Venir's shadow fell on them.

"Did you jackals say something?" Venir said.

Both men made grumbling sounds, sheathed their swords and returned inside their tent.

"That was strange," Adanna said. "Oh!"

Venir hoisted her over his shoulder and said, "Let's give those pretty little legs of yours a rest, shall we?"

Other than an excited sigh, her warm, supple body offered little resistance if any at all.

Venir jostled through the throngs of orcs, men, gnolls, kobolds, dwarves and even striders and halflings as if they weren't there. He was the most popular man in the Hide, and that wasn't good.

Outlaw's Hide, on the southernmost corner of Bish, once small and secluded, was getting crowded. The races at most times were barely tolerant of one another, but now they were almost amiable. It wasn't uncommon to see men and gnolls playing cards, though the dwarves still were intolerant of the handful of half-ogres. The Hide was a reminder of Venir's time spent with the Brigand Army, another secure location tucked behind the jungles, behind the grasses and atop jutting hillsides.

"Venir, will you please put me down? I'm getting sick," Adanna said.

He set her down and took a long look in the sky.

The moons in the sky, both a dull reddish hue, stirred his blood. Hogan had caught him up on mankind's plight and the onslaught of the underlings. The days he thought he was gone in the Under Bish and Mist had turned out to be months, perhaps longer. No, it seemed Bish was upside down. Something was wrong, very wrong. He could tell.

"Are you a'right? You seem lost," the soft woman said, pulling him into their small but accommodating tent. "You've been a bit aloof these past few days." She pulled his shirt off and began running her fingers over his scars.

The underlings. According to Hogan, they were as thick as weeds in every direction, subjecting their terror on every race with extreme prejudice. But humans, however, seemed to be taking the brunt of the punishment. Venir was happy to be living and breathing among men again, relishing every day of life. He was different, his vitality returned, a spring in every step, and brightness behind every word. He feared nothing. His belly was filled, and other needs satisfied. He was ready to live again, and for now the underlings would have to wait. But something in the back of his mind was beginning to ebb.

Adanna pushed him down onto the blankets, straddled him and began pulling her top off.

He reached for her breasts.

"Venir!" someone shouted from outside his tent.

Adanna dived for her clothes.

"Go away, Hogan! I'm—"

"Shaddup, Man. I know what you and my daughter are doing. There's no time for that. You need to come and come now!"

Venir stepped outside, the hot night air bristling on his scarred and naked chest.

"I see you trimmed your face."

"Actually, I did that," Adanna said, stepping out from behind the tent flap.

Hogan shook his head. It was clear he was perturbed by their relationship. "Baltor is coming." Adanna's father waved his hand in front of his face. "Man, how much have you been drinking? You smell like a half-orcen sot. And now Baltor comes, full of fire, wanting to challenge you for Adanna."

"What!" she interjected. "I'm not some trophy whore. I can choose whom I please."

"No you can't!" Hogan warned. "You agreed to be Baltor's mate, and word bound it. Now you've gone and broke your oath."

"I never made an oath, Father! Baltor was there when I was alone. There's not some pact between us."

"Well, the fool does not care, and he's not alone. Venir, he's dangerous. Stupid, but dangerous as a gnoll. And I'd be lying if I said he didn't worry me."

Venir smiled grimly and said, "Let him come. I've fared pretty well against better."

"At least hide until you can be prepared, Man. You're swaying like a tree about to fall."

"Too late," Venir huffed, rubbing his blurry eyes.

Baltor had arrived, accompanied by a handful of Hogan's men and another troupe of outlaws and renegades. Baltor was big, his muscles solid as if he were carved from the trunk of a tree, unyielding. His head was shaved on both sides. A strange black collar adorned his neck, and his brutish body seemed unnatural beneath the face, with a sinister look lurking behind his wild eyes.

"Adanna, come with me!" Baltor ordered, thumbing his chest.

She stepped forward, mouth opening to speak when her father pulled her back.

Venir crossed his arms over his chest and sighed, saying, "What's the matter, Baltor? Are the hairy hind ends of your orcen sisters too much for you to handle?" *hic*

Out loud chuckles erupted from the growing crowd, gnoll and orc among them.

Baltor rushed up and jabbed his finger in Venir's face.

"I'll kill you!" he said, practically frothing at the lips.

Venir, despite his impairment, could see the glazed look in the man's eyes. Baltor, already mighty of frame, was endowed with something else. Mystic herbs, dark ones, most likely. It was something the black markets from Outlaw's Hide sold. He couldn't remember what it was called, but it was pricy, something that the Royals were more apt to get their hands on as opposed to common men.

"You couldn't beat me if my arm was tied behind my back," Venir said, sneering down on the man. He was getting annoyed. Then he heard Adanna gasp.

"You heard him! One hand tied behind his back! A Challenge!"

A fervor arose in the crowd. Venir's big mouth had landed him a few challenges already. All of his talk of dragons and giants had branded him as a bit of a loon, though his stories did sound quite convincing and even caused the oldest of crones to swoon.

Unlike challenges in the more civilized establishments in the world of Bish, Outlaw's Hide played by very loose rules. Anything that sounded like a challenge could be construed as a challenge, which was a strong reason why most outlaws kept to themselves. The mildest of disagreements could be turned by gossiping mouths into the bloodiest of contests.

Hogan reached over, grabbed him by his arm and said, "Are you a fool! Baltor's an induced bull."

"Hah, more like an induced imbecile. I've fought a minotaur, and if anything, he's a sheep, or a cow." *Hic* "You're a cow, Baltor."

Adanna stood in front of him, her round face looking up at him like he was a complete lunatic. "What have you done, you fool?"

Hic "I'm taking measures so that the next time we lock legs there'll be no interruptions." Venir swept her up in his arm and gave her a hungry kiss. "Hold on to that until this is over."

Adanna gawped and turned away.

Venir was being shoved into a circle that had formed, of bloodthirsty men, orcs, gnolls and striders. The dwarves and halflings stood in the front. As he peered around, a brief thought of Melegal came to mind, as the coins began their clinking journey from hand to hand. Somewhere, a one-armed troubadour with an eye patch played and sang a semi-rousing tune on his lute.

There was a day when the underlings came
And the Darkslayer wasn't there to slay the day …
Instead a loon and bald-headed goon squared off to play a game.
Tis the day when one brute must die.
Bye, bye in Outlaw's Hide

Where the liars and the convicts come to live and die, and
The good ole dwarves mix the grog and the wine, singing
This'll be the place that ye'll die.
Bullslat! Someone interjected.
This'll be the place that ye'll die.

"Right or left handed?" A gruff looking man with a long piece of rope asked. "Ah … it seems you're right handed," the man said, looking at the missing finger tips on his left, then proceeded to tie off his right arm. He tested the bonds and yelled out, "He's secured."

Venir gave his missing fingertips some study as Baltor paced back and forth like a caged animal, drumming his head with his fists. That's when Venir noticed a series of very tall and large figures looming farther behind the ranks of the crowd. He was beginning to think that maybe, just maybe, someone was trying to kill him.

A tall slender man, long haired and wizened, stepped in the middle of the circle, robed in brown clothes from head to toe. Venir had never seen him around before. The man lifted his hands, and the crowd fell silent.

"You, Venir, have made a challenge against Baltor. One-armed you'll fight until one of you begs for mercy or succumbs to death. Is this correct?" the man said, his voice loud and tranquil.

"Aye," Venir said.

"And you, Baltor, you accept?"

"Aye," Baltor said, his sneering face fixated on Venir's as he smashed his fists together.

Venir couldn't ever recall having fought one armed before. How much harder could it be? "ONE!"

The rambunctious crowd gasped into a whisper as every eager eye widened with elation. "TWO!"

CHAPTER 34

EXHAUSTION. THE WORD WASN'T SUFFICIENT. Fogle lay in a bed that was little more than a mattress stuffed with feathers and hay that sat on the floor. It might as well have been one of the finest beds and mattresses in the City of Three as far as he was concerned. He was no longer cold, and that was all that mattered. He yawned, stretched, tossed and turned, but nothing eased his jangled nerves. However, he did find great comfort in the fact that he lived. Even if it was in Dwarven Hole.

"One adventure down … no more to go," he murmured to himself.

At least I'm warm. His room, consisting of the heaviest wooden furniture he'd ever used, was uncomfortable. But, a sense of security filled him, despite all of the commotion that occurred outside. The dwarves, a more melancholy than mirthful race, were active. Hammers striking steel were always echoing from within the Hole, along with the sounds of a roaring furnace being stuffed with coal and stoked.

The underlings. It seemed the dark vicious little race of creatures had begun to crop up everywhere. On his travels back, Mood had apprised Fogle of their bloody presence and wicked deeds. The most horrific things had happened to several villages and farm towns south of Dwarven Hole. A longtime safe haven under the dwarven wings had all but been wiped out.

It was there Fogle Boon witnessed mankind slaughtered. For the first time, Fogle had been filled with horror. The people, many weeks dead, coated in flies, rodents, worms and decay had even been buried head first in the ground. Their swollen, rotting, gnawed on legs were the most repulsive things he'd ever seen. Jackals and other animals that fed on carrion had picked many of the bones clean. That was far from the worst of it all. The heads of men, women, and children sagged on wooden stakes, mouths hanging open, eyes gouged out. It seemed the vulture hawks considered them a delicacy. And the smell, so horrible, foul and rotting, had made him retch. His stomach became queasy at the thought of it.

Sitting up, he rubbed his weary eyes. Three days had passed since he, Mood and Cass had returned, and for three days, two of which he hardly moved from his bed, he had done nothing. Mood was absent and Cass as well, but his dreams of her had kept him company. Now he was bored and lonely. What was his next move? Remain, or return home? Return home, or resume his quest to find Venir? And what had happened to his ebony hawk, Inky, that he'd sent into the Mist after the brutish man?

A soft knocking rapped at the door.

His heart raced. *Cass.*

"Come in," he said, returning to his feet.

The door swung open, revealing two dwarven women, laden with heavy terry cloth towels in their arms.

"Yes?" He said.

They entered, followed by a third, a brown bearded dwarven man pushing a heavy cart that appeared to be filled with a giant tub of water. The dwarven man set two blocks behind the wheels, gave him a gruff look and departed. The two dwarven women remained. One added something to the water that made it sizzle, and a pleasant smoky aroma filled the room. That's when Fogle realized that he hadn't bathed in months, perhaps longer. He felt disgusting when the moment he last bathed hit him. *What would my mother think?*

He rubbed the wiry hairs on his bearded chin and began to wonder if he should shave as he watched the little women get to work. The two stout little figures moved with purpose and grace that seemed odd. Their round little faces were smooth and warm, eyes narrow and inviting underneath thick heads of hair pulled up in buns. They wore tight sleeveless robes of fleshy tones that revealed short muscular arms and well-rounded chests and rears. Fogle swallowed as he recalled the conversation he'd been having with Mood, before they were captured by Cass. It seemed the King of the Blood Rangers remembered. Either that, or he just stunk really bad.

"Eh … I suppose you want me to get in?"

The closet dwarven lady didn't respond. Instead, she reached over and began helping him out of his clothes. His rosy cheeks did little to hide his embarrassment as the two silent women helped him step up into the tub. As his first foot sunk into the steamy bubbling water, he felt his eyes begin to burn. *Oh my, that feels good.* A smile broke out on his face as if the last three years of his life had been returned. There was no shame now; his surroundings were as meaningless as the dust on the floor as he sank down into the water feeling like a king. *Ah … I deserve this,* he thought, letting his heavy lids close. Strong fingers began rubbing the knots out of his shoulders, and the other lady dwarf began scrubbing him into a thick lather. All embarrassment washed away. *I could get used to this.*

"Fogle Man-Whore! What do you think you are doing?"

Water splashed over the lip of the tub as he twisted his body around. There stood Cass, arms crossed over her chest, her bare foot tapping on the floor with a perturbed look on her delicate face.

"I, well," he stammered, "I haven't bathed in months."

"So, I suppose it's been so long that you have forgotten how to do it yourself?"

His mind scrambled to find an adequate excuse. *I don't need one.*

"No, as a matter of fact, I'm lazy. And there's nothing quite like the hands of a strong dwarven woman to rub out the icicles you used to freeze my thews and bone. And who are you to reprimand me on my bathing habits? Aren't druids notorious for bathing in nothing but mountain sludge?"

Cass's jaw clenched on her pale face, and her pink eyes narrowed with a murderous intent.

He didn't care. She had brought him nothing but misery the entire journey back, offering comfort only to pull it back. Maybe it would have been better to have remained a virgin, after all. *Ah, but those pink lips are as delicious as wine.* He slunk deeper into the warm watery confines of the tub. "What is it? Have you come to gawk or to torment me more?"

She shoved his head down under the water and pulled him back up by his hair.

"Fool! I've come about the dog, and your thoughts are of yourself, Man Whore Fogle." Cass turned and left, the door slamming behind her.

"Well fiddly-dee," he said, as the wonderful bath seemed to sizzle through skin, muscle and bone. He felt short fingers rubbing the muscles in his knotted shoulders. *Ah …*

Wham!

A door slammed into the wall.

"FOGLE MAN-WHORE! Get your arse out of the water and follow me!" Cass stood in the doorway again, her eyes like burning roses. "The dog is about to die!"

CHAPTER 35

THEY CAME. LIKE A BLACK snake Lord Verbard's army slithered beneath the world of Bish towards the unsuspecting City of Bone. It was agonizing. Verbard stood in the back of the bow of a barge that hosted over fifty underlings. Moving an army, though a small one by some standards, was like pushing a heavy cart through a trail of mud. The barges, six in all—each hosting Juegen soldiers that controlled Badoon hunter squads that minded the mindless albino urchlings and ravenous cave dogs—crept over the black waters of the Current with agonizing haste. As patient as the underlings were, Lord Verbard had no patience for this.

I haven't the faintest idea where to start in the City of Bone. Does anyone? Or, is this Master Sinway's way of sending me on a suicide mission?

Verbard sharpened the tips of his fingernails with a metal file. Nearby, hunkered between the weapons and supplies, a pair of large mangy cave dogs were ripping troll meat apart. Days ago, his army happened upon a handful of the slimy and brutish race. More or less, the trolls were the ogres of the lands below: rare, unsightly and monstrous. One barge had been tipped over during the surprise attack, the underling bodies either crushed or dragged into the dark. Thirty had been lost, his army already diminished before his battle even started. He had taken precautions to avoid another tipping experience.

I hope Kierway doesn't plan a head count. The brat probably will. Perhaps I can gather the details from him. I shall have him do my work for me.

It was strange. Verbard was an underling with nothing more than pure hatred towards the race of men. His hatred stoked fires within him, sparking imagination of inflicting the cruelest and twisted things. After his battle with the Darkslayer, he had had quite enough, but now he was pressed into delivering a siege on an entire human city.

Men will not be ready. Men will die. But at what expense?

He reached down into an unnaturally deep pocket inside his robes, wrapping his fingers around the dry parchment of an ancient scroll. It gave him comfort. He knew something about the City of Bone. He'd seen glimpses of its interior before. Would it be possible to conjure the imp once more? Could he control it without the help of his brother? He tucked the parchment back inside his robes. *Did I ever even need my brother's help?* Verbard's feet shifted beneath him as the barge came to a complete stop. He made his way to the fore, where two heavily armored Juegen stood, pointing ahead.

As black as it was, there were still faint traces of light to an underling's discerning eyes. Ahead, the wide expanse of the Current's waters began to broaden, but a dam of rock and stone had barricaded their way through the next corridor. Were they stuck? Not that Verbard was in any hurry, but it would take a day or more to clear the way. The other half of the army, he hoped, didn't experience such delays by trekking through the caves. It had seemed better to split his forces than to move them all as one. Perhaps he should have split them into three. It seemed that something was intentionally trying to slow them, and it wasn't men. *Trolls.*

"Protect me," Verbard ordered.

The Juegen, covered in plate armor from head to toe, withdrew their long curved blades. Another set, each with a barbed trident in its grip, gathered near as well. A silent word traveled back from one barge to the other. If the trolls attacked again, they would be ready.

Verbard's silver eyes opened, gleaming with light. He stretched his palms upward toward the cave ceiling. Mystic energy filled him, tingling first around his ankles and spiraling upward around his body, through his neck and into his mind. It was arousing his senses, which began to heighten to another level. Something primitive lurked nearby, dormant, maybe lazy, but strong and formidable. He felt it. It was agitated. But where was it?

The Current, a long series of stagnant rivers that did not flow, ran through enormous lakes and tunnels. At the moment the underling army drifted along the nearest bank. The creature, wherever it may be, could be down in the deep, how far Verbard did not know. He channeled his thoughts, pushing them forward, looking for any formidable life ahead. There were some trolls: stupid and hungry, their tiny minds having little purpose at all, but it was clear they did not like the invasion. Verbard released his spell. It was decision time.

Four albino urchlings appeared at his thought. Small and hulking, with large hollow nostrils and ears, they snorted and awaited his command. With a nod they dove one by one into the water, out of sight, leaving a trail of rippling waves above their path. Verbard watched as they emerged on the barricade of rocks, two crawling over the pile, disappearing over the other side. The others began pushing rocks out of the way.

Verbard let out a little grunt. Something was wrong. The normally quiet Current was even more so at the moment. He couldn't afford to lose any more underlings, either.

"Ready the lanterns of the underlight," he commanded.

Light. It wasn't the enemy of the underlings, but it was of many other subterranean creatures. The underlings and other cavern dwellers tolerated each other because they were mindful of not disturbing one another, but in this case, it seemed, something else had already been disturbed.

A faint blue light warmed from at the bow and stern of the lead barge. The next barge illuminated to life as well, followed by the next and the next and so on. The underlings, each and every one, were staring abroad, their colorful gemstone eyes filled with a degree of uncertainty. The only things Verbard could hear were the cave dogs slobbering quietly on the troll bones. Irritation mixed with worry.

Scanning his surroundings, he got his first look in a lifetime at the ecosystem of the Current. Enormous stalactites jutted from the ceiling like teeth, smooth and round in some places, jagged in others. Verbard became anxious. One single formation falling would capsize a barge, not just one, either, but possibly all. It seemed too perfect not to be a trap.

The albino urchlings were moving the rocks from the corridor ahead, but their efforts would not be enough. Some of the boulders were huge, maybe over a ton, and it was going to take more than muscle to move it quickly. It would take magic, a great deal of it, too.

"Fetch the magi," he commanded.

Suddenly, the barge pitched and rocked over the waters. Verbard watched the lake come to life, waves rolling and splashing into the barge. Something enormous emerged, rising higher and higher, towering twenty feet above the waters. Verbard hissed.

"Ready the harpoons!"

It was like nothing he'd ever seen: grotesque, humanoid, more fish than man, coated in weed and sludge. It stormed through the waters, a mindless juggernaut of fins and scales. Verbard summoned a protective spell. *I hope it's alone,* he thought as the first barrage of bolts, arrows, spears, tridents and harpoons bounced harmlessly away.

Waves of water crashed over the bows, filling the barges, as the creature roared like a dozen trolls gone insane and smashed its arms into the ceiling. A stalactite fell, splintering wood and crushing underlings. Verbard shouted out another warning as more trolls spilled out from the mouths of the caves. They were trapped.

CHAPTER 36

GONE. MIKKEL, BILLIP AND GEORGIO had all departed with all the supplies they could handle in tow, helped by the shaggy pony, Quickster. That had been weeks ago, and Kam had barely been able to contain her emotions since.

She sat in her apartment above the Magi Roost, baby Erin propped up over her shoulder, as she patted the small of the baby girl's back.

"Come on now, little girl, let it all out," she said with a sniff as she rubbed her watering eyes on Erin's pale blue blanket. She kept on patting, every minute seeming longer than the last. Baby Erin wouldn't sleep without a thorough belch, which meant Kam wouldn't get any sleep either, and sleep had been hard to come by since the underling invasion.

"Oh come on, Erin. I need rest; you need rest," she said, patting harder.

Buuu-urp!

"Thank goodness," she said, looking into Erin's twinkling little eyes as she wiped her baby's mouth. "That's a big girl."

Erin smiled with toothless delight, letting out the tiniest of giggles, melting Kam's heart.

She hugged her little girl tight. She had never adored anything like her baby girl. Laying Erin down in her bassinet, she whispered a word and the gentle side to side rocking began. It was late in the day, the time between work and play, those precious moments before all of the worrisome patrons came to spread gossip and rumors.

Kam lay down on her sofa, pulled a blanket over her legs and closed her eyes, now too tired to cry.

KNOCK! KNOCK! KNOCK!

Who dares! She swung her legs to the ground, hoisted herself to her feet and checked on Erin, who was fast asleep. *Thank goodness.* She swore under her breath as she wrapped a blanket around her barren shoulders. *I'm gonna kill someone.* Joline was the only friend she had left, and the older woman never would have bothered to knock, seeing as how she was the only one besides Kam who had a key.

"Who in Bish is it?" She tried not to yell.

A peppy voice from the other side of the heavy oak door responded by saying, "It's just yer favorite halflings, Master Gillem and Lefty Lightfoot."

She slapped her hand to her forehead. Gillem and Lefty had been hanging around more often now that the other men were gone. They were helpful, in an annoying and pestering way, offering to do things one normally wouldn't want done or showing up during the most inappropriate times. Like right now.

"Go away," she ordered them. "I'm taking my nap."

There was an odd silence on the other side. She checked the lock. *Just leave!* Something about Gillem and Lefty was just plain odd.

"Kam," Gillem said, "we don't want to be any trouble, but we wanted to share a concern."

"Blast," she muttered under her breath. They were both full of concerns and suggestions, like two old hags who knew how to do everything but were too old to work. One day the food was served too hot, the next too cold. The flowers needed more water, and then they needed less. Dwarves should have their own section, outside, and men taller than six feet should always have to sit, not stand. She'd had enough.

"I don't care. If you don't like something, just go somewhere else that you do like, if that is at all possible, you two festering ear aches!"

That ought to do it. She leaned towards the door, brushing her hair behind her head as she did. *Now, please go away.*

Of course, insults only seemed to encourage the halflings to do better.

"Eh, Miss," said Gillem, "er Kam, we don't mean any trouble. It's just that … there's a man, a strange looking fellow. He's, well, he's frightening."

Ah yes, he's probably seven feet tall and rides a rabbit the size of an ox. Little idiots.

"Have Joline take care of it. Now go away."

"But, Joline went to the market."

"Not this time of the day," she argued.

"She ran out of onions," Gillem said.

"And 'shrooms," Lefty added.

Kam outstretched both of her arms on the door and fought the urge to slam her head into it.

"Why didn't you go to market for her?" She asked through gritted teeth.

"She insisted," they both replied.

Their voices were as reassuring as a grandfather's hug.

"Just give me a minute."

"Excellent, we'll be right here."

"No, I'll meet you down there."

"But I'd like to watch Baby Erin," Lefty pleaded from the other side.

Kam shook her head. "Send up two of the girls."

"But yer very short handed down stairs, it seems."

"Get them now!" She said, kicking the door.

Lefty felt like a nest of baby snakes were churning in his stomach as he and Gillem headed back down the stairs. The moment had come, despite all of his attempted delays. *How did this happen? Why me?*

Georgio, his best friend, was gone. He didn't even get to say good-bye. Now, his best friend, who he had put up to so many devious tasks, had left him for the Outlands, leaving him with no one to turn to, not even Kam. His head was aching, and his heart was broken. All he had was Gillem.

He felt Gillem's long fingers squeeze his shoulder, and he fought the urge to cringe. He'd suppressed many things, bottling them all up within, turning his core to stone. He was starting to understand that was what they wanted.

"Yer doing fine, Boy," the halfling man said. "It's almost over."

Lefty nodded, but didn't' agree. If anything it was only the beginning of his career as a criminal, a hardened one, slavery without a personal cause. But he had to do it, so he thought, to protect Kam and his friends. Now they were all gone, and it was up to him. The lives of Kam and Erin now were solely in his hands. He wanted to save them, warn them, but visions of his own horrible watery death froze his tongue inside his head.

While making their way down the stairs and into the main floor, Lefty noticed The Magi Roost hosted few patrons, which was odd for this time of day. He sat down near the bar across from Gillem at a small table made for halflings, thanks to many pushy suggestions. Lefty hated that table, small chairs on long legs, surrounding a round table. Being small was bad enough, but sitting at a small table seemed ten times worse. But it had been just another distraction, not for him or Gillem, but for Kam and Joline. It was a devious game.

"Let's have something to drink, shall we?" Gillem said.

No thanks!

"That would be good," he said.

It was getting easier, the lying, cheating and stealing. His hands were steady, his mannerisms cool, and he swore he even had Gillem fooled. He rubbed his hands on his trousers and combed his fingers through his curly blond hair. Gillem's eyebrow lifted the ever slightest. *Good.* He'd been practicing for days, adding a subtle move here and there, figuring Gillem would think he was nervous. That would be normal with so much at stake, but he could control it, turn it on or off as easily as sheathing a sword in a scabbard.

"We'll get some cheese, too," Gillem said quietly. "It will help settle our stomachs."

Lefty nodded as Gillem motioned one of the girls over. The serving girl rolled her eyes before she made her way over, the sway in her hips gone. It was the one that had been quite fond of Georgio, and she was outwardly sad these days. As Gillem placed the order, Lefty cast a quick glance over his shoulder.

There was Thorn. Tall and leering, the man strolled throughout the tavern poking his crooked nose in everyone's business. Several patrons, including a dwarf, had already left, and more were certain to follow as the dangerous looking man in sheepskin vest and trousers continued to tap his ringed fingers on the metal pommels of his swords. It was all part of the plan.

"That'll be all, Dearie," Gillem said, slapping the girl's rear as she turned to walk away.

In the passing weeks Lefty had been involved with the kidnapping plan that was designed to wear Kam down to a nub. He and Gillem had become the friendliest nuisances in the world of Bish, and it came so naturally. Lefty had even reached a point where he felt no shame in it at all. Kam, as strong and alluring as she was, now showed signs of exhaustion. It was a cold reminder of what he was up to, even though he tried to deny it. Deep down, he'd thought someone would arrive in time to prevent all this, but no help had come. *Maybe Kam can save herself.*

The waitress returned, set a pair of small jugs and a tray of cheese on the table and departed. Gillem tore off a hunk of cheese, dipped it in mustard and ate. Lefty followed suit with a smaller portion, and after many long minutes the entire tray was gone. The cheese did little to settle the gnawing feeling that was growing inside him. The jug of hot tea was of little comfort, either. Something was wrong.

Lefty looked over at Gillem and said, "Shouldn't we send the girls up? Kam's very impatient these days."

"Give it a moment," the halfling man responded, leaning back in his chair, long fingers drumming on the table.

Lefty didn't like the way Gillem said it. There was something he didn't know. It was at that moment he noticed something else: his feet were sweating. *Oh no!* Gillem gave him a funny smile. *What in Bish?* The older halfling looked under the table where his dripping feet were making a puddle on the floor. As Gillem's eyes returned to his, a sliver of fear raced through him. What Gillem said next astounded him.

"You've done well, Lefty. A good student, one of the best, but now the real test begins."

What is he talking about?

"We will go upstairs, you and me, and pick the lock. Inside we shall find Kam, bound and gagged by magic. Baby Erin will be long gone."

Lefty could feel his thundering little heart collapsing inside his chest. *No!* How many days had there been to warn her? How many opportunities had he missed?

"She'll never suspect us, Lefty. She'll never suspect a thing thanks to yer damp feet. Thorn will take care of the rest."

Gillem hopped down from his stool, and on numb legs, Lefty followed.

"Too late to warn your friend now, Lad," Gillem said glumly. "Ye should've done that when you had the chance."

Chapter 37

Tunk-Tunk-Tunk-Tunk.

"What is that?"

Tunk-Tunk-Tunk.

Something was pecking on the exterior of Boon's standing metal cocoon. The old wizard had ignored the first several minutes of the strange sound, assuming it to be another delusion of his imagination. But, the persistent sound remained.

Tunk-Tunk-Tunk-Tunk …

"Am I some child's rattle? Another musing toy of a giant simpleton?"

He was talking to himself again. The giants kept a watchful eye on him these days, and he was happy that his lips remained free. His ramblings gave him company, but not freedom. No, the giants were privy to his tricks and his magic, which, for all purposes, was dormant. It had something to do with his cocoon, or sarcophagus; he didn't know what to call it: an upright metal husk with three bars in front of a face hole.

Tunk-Tunk-Tunk-Tunk.

"I'd curse right now if I remembered any curse words! And I know I used to know many!"

His prison didn't sustain him. The giants did. They let him out every few days for a few hours, which he spent strolling around an abandoned study of sorts: no books, just musty furniture for people ten times bigger than him, and a cold fireplace big enough to burn a village. It was there he sat, ate and drank. There was nothing to do, nowhere to go. He didn't even get out to toy with the latest captives, assuming there were any. He thought of Venir, on and off, wondering if the man ever escaped the Under Bish. Could he have made it back out of the Mist? It was of little curiosity to him now.

Tunk-Tunk-Tunk-Tunk …

"This is obscene. I've truly gone mad!"

That's when he heard the flapping and something bird-like landing near where he now rested, beside the fireplace's mantle. He squished his bearded face into the bars in front of him. He swore whatever it was had landed above him on the mantle. *What is it?* Boon shifted his weight on his aching feet, back and forth. His metal cocoon bumped against the stone hearth. It was torture, barely moving an inch inside, left to right, his energy within his frail body already spent. *I must see it!* He put what little weight his meager frame had into it. There was a scraping sound on stone as the cocoon teetered to the ground.

Thonk!

His feeble body paid for it, and his teeth cracked inside his mouth. Warm blood trickled over the wispy hairs on his mustache and into his mouth as his cocoon rolled and rolled before it came to a stop. *Painful and nauseating.* His eyes flitted open. There was a tiled floor, and the sofa's mahogany clawed foot could be seen from the corner of his eye. He was facing the wrong way.

He couldn't muster the energy to speak. He lay still, mentally venting the maddening frustration, trying to block out the pain of his broken nose and cracked tooth. He wanted to know what had been making that noise. He had to find out before the giants came.

Tunk-Tunk-Tunk-Tunk-Tunk ...

A sliver of the unexpected might just give him the advantage he needed. He might as well try to escape once more before he died. But for now, he wasn't going anywhere.

Chapter 38

"**T**HREE!"

Baltor closed the distance in two quick steps, head down, fists up. Venir shuffled on his feet, keeping his shoulders square to his opponent's, eyes down toward his head.

Whap! Whap!

Baltor slugged two right crosses into his mid-section.

The crowd of people roared.

Venir winced as the heavy blows banged into his arm. His thick blood was beginning to burn.

He jerked back from a haymaker that clipped his chin and slid aside from another body blow, catching it on his back.

"Punch the lout in the groin, Baltor!"

"Make the giant fall!"

"Kill the loud-mouth story-telling liar, and drag his carcass back to the Mist where he can hump giants, dragons and such!"

Pop!

Baltor's head rocked back on his thick neck, drawing an angry grunt. The man shook off the punch like a dog shedding water.

"Ha! That all you got?" Baltor spat blood. "I'll have Adanna back in my sack in no time."

There was something irritating about the man. Stupidity combined with arrogance. It reminded Venir of someone, but he couldn't remember who.

"Take him to the ground, Baltor!" Another yelled. "Break his neck! You got the juice! Do it!"

Rolling in the dirt with the powerful man was a bad idea. With only one arm, it would be difficult to subdue Baltor. The man looked like he'd wrestled in the Pit before. Maybe the man had even battled in the Warfield. One thing was for sure: Baltor was as tough as he was mean.

Venir shuffled away, his large hand slapping away Baltor's heavy blows before they got too close. The last thing he wanted was more busted ribs among those that were still not fully healed.

"Come on, Girlie," Baltor mocked, "take a swing! I won't bite after your little sting."

Venir jumped away as the brute ripped an uppercut through the air. A chorus of boos followed him, shuffling around the ring.

Venir paid them no mind. Baltor was a seasoned fighter, quick and powerful. One punch could land him on his back or in his grave. He had to be careful … or not.

"Fight, you cow sticker!" An orcen hag offered.

Venir's dander had risen. Fist clenched, he drew his arm back. Baltor's wild eyes widened as he rushed in and swung. Venir unloaded with all he had.

CRACK!

Baltor stopped dead in his tracks, his nose busted open like a tomato. Time seemed to stop as Venir's fist retraced its path and came forth like a rod of power.

CRACK!

Baltor's jaw broke.

The crowd gawped.

Faces were stupefied.

Baltor's arms flailed in a maddened frenzy, slamming into Venir's body with little effect. Baltor's punishment had just begun.

WHOP!

He lifted Baltor off his toes with a punch to the guts.

SMACK!

He felt the bones in the man's face shatter, followed by the next blow that felled the man like an ox.

POW!

He wasn't finished. His red rage began to consume him. He had a message to send. Baltor kicked and twitched as Venir kneeled down and squeezed the man's corded neck in one hand.

"This," he yelled, "is what happens to bad people! This is what happens to my enemies!"

Baltor's face had turned purple, and his eyes bulged from his sockets. Venir didn't care. The man was a menace. The man was evil. The man must die.

"Remember who you bet against, fools! I AM VENIR!"

Baltor's eyes rolled up inside his head, his last breath spent. Venir rose to his feet.

"Which one of you cut throats is next?" He said it wiping his sweaty locks from his eyes. "Anyone!"

None came forward, and most were gone. Venir took in a deep draw of breath as Baltor's body was dragged away. He looked around at the remaining faces, each face marred with guilt from countless crimes. It was clear his message had been sent, and he was certain someone wanted him gone, someone from his past, perhaps. Or, more underling treachery.

Hogan shook his head and tossed him a canteen.

"Did you have to kill him?" Hogan said.

"No." Venir took a drink and said, "but he was an evil bastard."

Hogan nodded and said, "By Bish Venir, what happened behind the Mist?"

"Giants, dragons and such, I tell you," he said, a fierce grin coming to his face.

Hogan shook his head and walked away.

The tall man who had run the challenge walked over and unfastened his arm. The skinny man, older, was looking down on him, his pale eyes sparkling with joy.

"Slim?"

"It's been a long time, Venir. Where in Bone have you been? Don't you know the underlings have taken over? Where are that axe and helmet of yours?"

Venir was still trying to take it all in. Slim, once youthful and strong, so many years ago, was worn and gray, double if not triple his age. The man's features were wrinkled, his skin spotted, but his voice was still strong and playful like children frolicking under a spring.

"Don't you worry about that," he replied.

Adanna had gathered by his side, arms wrapped around his waist, eyes filled with desire and admiration. Venir's blood was still running hot, but not for her. The mention of underlings, his helm and Brool, had ignited another fire. Something in Slim the Cleric's voice told him the fun was over. It was time to get back to work.

"Go get them," Slim said, his skinny arms pushing him forward.

Venir bristled.

"Easy, Venir." Slim looked him up and down. "How in Bish do you keep getting taller?" Slim asked, unable to hide his astonishment.

Hogan had returned and grunted, "Aye."

"I'm not as tall as you, now am I?" Venir said it looking up a little.

"Well, not yet anyway. Now tell me; I've got to know."

Venir shook his head and said, "I don't know. It just happens." He felt Adanna's warm hand playing with his hard belly.

"I bet I can make him grow some more," she said.

"Sheesh Daughter, is that all ye think about?" Hogan said.

"Only when I'm with him."

"STOP!"

Everyone jumped but Venir at the sound of the loud baritone voice.

A dozen feet away, an ominous figure blocked the pathway. Wrapped in a brown cloak, his face covered by a cowl, the man stood taller than Slim and broader than Venir.

Venir's instincts told him it was the figure he had noticed prowling in the background before the fight.

"What is it you want, you oversized scavenger?" Venir said.

The low and throaty voice that responded wasn't human, more monster than man.

"I have a message for the one called Venir," it said, pointing a finger covered in coarse black hair.

Venir stepped forward saying, "And what might that be?"

The creature unrolled a parchment of paper and spoke:

"You survived my first attempt. You and your comrades will not survive the next. Leave now or perish."

Venir noticed a look of concern growing on everyone's faces as they looked at one another.

"Who's the coward that sent this message?" Venir asked in agitation.

Venir watched as a large harry hand pulled the cowl from its face. There was a gasp behind him. *Can it be?*

"I'm no coward, Venir." The big humanoid's knuckles cracked as it crumpled up the parchment and tossed it at Venir's feet. "You will leave, or your friends will die. I'll break their backs like you broke my son's. I'll rip their arms off and bury them in the muck and mire. I am Farc!" The half ogre pounded his chest. "You have till nightfall." The ogre snapped his fingers. A small army of orcs, gnolls, and brigands appeared from behind the tents, brandishing steel of all shapes and sizes.

"And it looks like nightfall has come," Farc said, following within a rugged snicker.

CHAPTER 39

LEGS SHACKLED, HANDS BOUND AND stomach rumbling, Brak sat sulking on the dungeon floor. His stomach, as big as those of two men, let out a part roar, part rumble. It was misery. He couldn't remember ever being so hungry before.

The dungeon, vast in size, was superior in facility to his former home with the Slergs, below the city. The stone walls were gray, but dry. The metal bars that housed his cell were clear of rust and debris. Every day, small children, most much younger than he, scrubbed the blood, filth and slat from the floors. They were small and ragged, their faces gaunt, tired and worn. They looked as hungry as him, but fear seemed to propel their skinny little bones with purpose.

The guards, a handful of them, one just as cruel and intolerant as the next, kicked the children around like aging dogs. Brak would have killed them if he could, but he had no energy. He was dry, his tears gone, his fear replaced by apathy. There had been nothing but hardship for him in the City of Bone. His dreams had brought him to the City. His mother, Vorla, was dead now. Cut down. Thrown on a slab of metal. Dropped in a vat of fire. No more mother. A brand new life of survival and misery had begun.

Nearby, Leezir the Slerg, the one who had taken him in, snored. The man had no words of comfort. No words at all. The other one, Hagerdon, lay on rotting piles of hay, quivering beneath a pile of rags. Both men had been lashed a few days ago. Brak had watched from his cell as the men were strung up in chains and whipped until the blood ran down their ankles. The guards left only the little girl, Jubilee, who wailed like a frightened sheep as her grandfather was whipped again and again till the blood ran between his toes. She was flattened with the hilt of a blade crossing the back of her head, gagged, hauled off into a small metal cage and locked inside. It was the last he had heard from her. He nibbled at the skin on his fingertips. His nails were gone from his stubby hands that looked like they could crush rocks into dust. He tried to sleep, but his hunger pangs had gotten so bad they woke him up, and when he did sleep he didn't dream. The image of his father, Venir, had faded. It seemed that whatever had endangered his father had won. The chains scraped across the stone as he pulled his knees to his chest. His lids turned heavy, his small chin dipped and he fell asleep.

"Detective Melegal," Sefron said, "let us put our differences aside for the sake of the Almen family. After all, what choice do we have?"

Your death would be my choice.

Sefron had been both pushy and polite ever since he had been ordered to work with Melegal in setting up the Royal games. He suspected it was only a temporary lapse at best, but Sefron's efforts, for some strange reason, had come off as sincere.

"None, it would seem," he said as they walked down the hall, side by side.

Melegal was uncomfortable and very cognizant of the stares. *A shady stick and a pasty tub of goo. Something for the stupid sentries to gossip about between nose pickings.* The plans for the event were in order. Everything was set in stone, and nothing was left to be done, but still Sefron seemed determined to seek him out. The creepy man wanted something from him. What, he couldn't imagine, but it was important. Ever since Melegal came into service, Sefron's words and efforts towards him had been nothing less than poisonous. Why had that suddenly changed? Was it something Lord Almen had said or threatened? Was the castle Lord so pleased with his efforts in capturing and annihilating the Slergs?

Sefron stopped in the hall. Melegal watched the man's eyes shift back and forth as his snail-like tongue licked over his thin purple lips. It was barely a whisper when the cleric spoke.

"Detective, you and I have much more in common than I realized. We both serve against our desires."

This was new. Melegal never suspected the cleric to have been unhappy with his work. Still, he struggled to keep his hand from his dagger. *One blink. One slice. Ah … must I play this game with him!*

"Go on."

Sefron hunched over, drawing himself near, wringing his hands together. "There is something I *seek*. I cannot *retrieve* it. I cannot find it. A *key* of sorts. It can free us from the Royal powers. Help me find it."

What is this fool blathering about? He shoved in front of Sefron's desperate gaze.

"Say no more, Cleric. I'll not be dabbling with any thoughts of treason," Melegal said as he turned to walk away.

He felt Sefron's fingers on his hand and jerked his arm away. The cleric said, "Remember Detective, it is my word against yours. If you keep this between us I'll remember. If you don't, you'll have regret."

"I've had many regrets, but seeing your head removed from your flabby shape would not be one of them," Melegal said, walking on. "I'll not concern myself with your problems. I have my own. As far as I'm concerned, feel free to find your key and shove it where the suns don't shine. Just don't drag me into it or let Lord Almen find out about it."

Sefron watched the Detective disappear around the corner, and a toothy evil grin crossed his face. The seed had been planted. Now all he had to do was wait and watch it grow. Without even knowing it, Melegal would help him find the key. He was certain his spell had worked, as magic had seeped from his limbs and into the marble floor like mist. He rubbed his hands together and recounted his words. *There is something I seek. I cannot retrieve it. I cannot find it. A key of sorts. It can free us from the Royal powers. Help me find it.* He'd emphasized his words: Seek. Retrieve. Key. The spell was activated with a simple touch. He kissed his finger.

"Not long, Master. Not long." He murmured. "As for you, Detective, once it's delivered you'll be the first to go."

He rubbed his flabby belly, smacking his lips as he waddled towards the kitchen.

"All of this scheming makes me hungry."

CHAPTER 40

C HONGO, ONCE A VIBRANT, DANGEROUS and playful beast, was now a husk. Both of his massive heads were down, tongues hanging with a grayish tint above his saggy chins. Fogle Boon felt a wave of guilt. In the days since they had returned he had not even come to see the giant two-headed dog. Needless to say, when he entered its stable, things were awkward, as every eye seemed intent on him. Cass was down on her knees, brushing her gentle hand over Chongo's shedding belly. Fogle noticed the scolding look that she cast his way before whispering soothing words into the dwarven setter's floppy black ears.

He started to speak, but was cut off by Mood's meaty hand. Instead, he crammed himself alongside Mood within the confines of the stuffy stable. The thick-set dwarf, the size of a man, had a sad look behind his bushy red beard. Even within the dim torchlight, Fogle thought he could see watery green eyes behind the red.

There were others, too. He counted ten dwarven women, adorned in soft grey robes with lavender trim wrapped around their plump bodies. Their sweet round faces had intense looks as they held hands and hummed. Still, the body heat, stuffiness and straw-filled air made him uncomfortable. So did the feeling of death that lingered in the room.

He focused on Cass. She lay atop Chongo's back, hugging him with her arms and legs, muttering sounds that were not natural for a human to make. Chongo's diminished body shuddered; the muscle spasms rippling underneath his thinning hair. Fogle felt a swelling in his throat. It was both heads now, one as pitiful as the other. He had to admit: it wasn't easy being a witness to another creature's death.

He sneezed, loud and awful. Everything lurched except Chongo. Cass shot daggers from her eyes.

"Sorry." *Not good, Imbecile.*

Fogle, once again, felt horribly out of place as he rubbed his sweaty hands on his robes. He wasn't one to sweat, even when put to task, but it happened at funerals. *I hope this isn't a long ceremony.* He didn't mean it in a bad way, but rather a sad one. He had no desire to be around miserable people.

He didn't want to hear their sad stories or wipe any tears. *Well, I don't think dwarves cry, so that's good news.* He didn't want to be caught crying, either and wondered if it would be rude if he didn't. He hadn't cried when Ox the Mintaur died, or had he? It seemed like forever ago. He supposed it was only proper that he was present. After all, he had almost died trying to retrieve Cass in an effort to save the dog.

Cass rolled from Chongo's back. She had an exhausted look on her face. He hadn't even noticed this when she was up in his room, earlier. He was only thinking about himself these days, it seemed. He leaned back as she extended her hands towards him.

"What?" he said, more defensive than he intended.

Her voice was haunting when she said, "We need your magic, Wizard!" Fogle cocked his head and said, "For what?"

Cass's beautiful face turned into a pit of anger.

"To save the dog, you FOOL!"

He stood there unthinking for a moment. Why would she think that he could save the dog? If that were the case they wouldn't need her. It was preposterous. He was a wizard, not a healer. He looked at Chongo and chose his next words without thinking.

"He doesn't look like he can be saved. Have you not done everything that you can?"

He felt Mood stir at his side. Cass's eyes became daggers of ice.

"Besides—"

Smack!

Fogle's teeth clattered in his jaw. The slap stung. His face flushed red.

"Idiot Man!" Cass vented. "Do you want me to stick your entrails in your mouth? Did you drag me from my mountains so we could fail? You little wart on a frog's arse!"

Hands up, Fogle began backing away. Mood's big frame stepped between them.

"Druid, tell the wizard what you need. No time fer fussin'. Spit it out, Girl!"

Cass bit her lip as she pulled at locks of her hair. Fogle realized she indeed cared about the life of Chongo. His concerns were hardly important. The right thing to do was.

"I'll help," he said. "But you never disclosed the conditions which required my presence here."

Cass's hands were clenched at her sides. "I thought Fogle *Fool* wanted to save the dog, not play splish-splash with dwarven whores."

"Hey!" Mood said. "Ain't no such thing, Druid. Watch yer tongue about me women. Now get on wit it. This pooch is dying. He's my friend. Ye save him, ta' both of ya."

Fogle's narrow shoulders sagged as he sighed and said, "Cass, what would you have me do?"

She stood there, nostrils flaring, tapping her bare foot and biting her lip. She took a deep breath and said, "The dog has one heart, bigger than that of a horse. I hoped for two, but it only has one. It's poisoned. These underlings, or the albino urchlings, they are poison. The wounds were deep, the blood lost was heavy, but the dwarves did well with that. But the poison, a nasty thing, black and deadly, has made its way to his heart."

How do you know that? Fogle kept his mouth shut, however.

"I can extract the poison, but it will take magic, and mine is limited. I need more strength. I need you, Fogle Boon, to tether with me."

"Tether? I've not the slightest idea what you are talking about."

Cass stiffened. She looked like she was about to explode.

"Is there nothing but stupidity filled in that enormous head of yours? Lock minds with me. Mind Grumbles, you pompous imbecile!"

How would she know about Mind Grumbles? He rubbed his chin. Was Cass from the City of Three as well? Still, he was beginning to understand what she wanted, but it wasn't something he'd ever done with a woman before. He let out a puffy laugh.

"What are you laughing at?" Cass said.

"It's just … well … it's one of those other things I've never done with a woman before."

"Great Bish, will I have to show you how to do this, too?" She said it while taking him by his hand.

Cass sat down beside Chongo and laid her small hand on the big beast's belly. Fogle joined her on the ground. Her eyes fastened on his. *My, she's beautiful.*

"Wizard, there is no time for your fantasies." She squeezed the blood from his hand. "This must be done now. Lock with me!"

It was a simple spell, for a mage anyway: two willing minds becoming one. He remembered the last one, the battle with the golden-eyed underling. He'd been suffocated, dying, his awesome will being crushed like an egg. Somehow his battle with Venir had saved him. Maybe this was important after all.

The dwarven women surrounded them like a cauldron of warmth, locking arms and murmuring an ancient tune.

"Get on with it, Fogle. I don't like your sweaty hands."

He looked deep into Cass's eyes.

"*Impre ontu doskst,*" he whispered.

A wave of energy rushed through him like a spring. Cass was drawing from him, a warm hand reaching inside and taking hold. It was strong, but he was stronger. With control, he released his power. He saw her body, spinning, contorting and turning black. She plunged into an abyss and was gone.

Don't let me go, Fogle, he heard her mind say, *or the dog will die and I as well.*

Fogle's body broke out in a cold sweat. Cass's hand was burning like fire, and his mind was being stretched down to his toes. Something tugged at his mind, powerful and sinister. The fight for Chongo and Cass had just begun.

Chapter 41

I T WAS AN ENORMOUS THING, perhaps the largest living creature Verbard had ever seen, and he had to kill it, or rather, direct its killing. That didn't stop the massive stalactite from dropping into a barge filled with fifty underlings, capsizing the vessel. Of the fifty, it could only be assumed that most were dead, and the remaining passengers were swimming for the shore.

"BAAAAAAAAA-HAA-ROOOON!" the creature roared. It was a hulking bi-ped whose neckless fish head scraped debris the size of boulders from the stone ceiling as it attacked. Another volley of arrows and spears ricocheted off the creature's armor. It raised its leg and dropped its foot on the closet barge.

This is a disaster! Underling magi respond!

Robed figures floated over the waters, a dozen wielders of magic, their clawed finger tips burning with life. Verbard floated behind them, his mind and theirs one.

Burn his head! He ordered.

Lightning. Fire. Energy.

The entire cavern was aglow from the various explosions of power. The brilliant colors splashed across the fuzzy faced underlings, adding an additional gleam to their bejeweled eyes. The creature bellowed a deafening roar as it staggered backwards. It raised the fins of its thickset arms in front of its face as the mire and muck broiled on its grotesque body.

Don't let up!

Whatever it was, it was a force. A stupid unyielding one. Verbard took a quick glace into the fray below. The barges were filled with melee. The underling warriors, Badoon, Juegen and urchlings were at odds with a host of Trolls. Not a single underling screamed when it died, and not a single one yelled when it attacked. Instead, the chitters came in precise hissing commands.5 A single troll was drowning three underlings at once. Another underling, a metal-armored Juegen, was being swung like a club. The surprise was becoming an onslaught.

Verbard felt his own black blood begin to boil as another barge was capsized by the trolls. He wanted to scream. Instead, he did something else. *Enough of this!* He pulled a rod with a fist on the end from inside his robes. It was a two-foot long piece of inch-thick iron, cold and heavy in his hand.

He touched the metallic fist to his lips and muttered an incantation.

Jottenhiem, attention!

A Juegen, covered from head to toe in troll guts, stood at the bow of the barge below him. The underling raised its open hand as it ducked under the swing of a troll that had been rocking the barge.

Catch.

Verbard tossed the rod and watched it fall into Jottenhiem the Juegen commander's eager grasp. The rod burst from two to six feet, a fist at the point. As the troll climbed onto the bow, Jottenhiem rammed its skull with the rod. A flash of light erupted, followed by a notable thunder crack, pulverizing the troll's head, sinking the monster back into the current.

Much better.

Another troll had a pair of urchlings in his hands, beating them together like dolls. Jottenhiem hurled the fist in a streak of black light.

CRACK!

The troll fell back into the waves, dead as a stone, two smushed urchlings crushed in its clutches.

Verbard turned his attention back to the other magi. He could feel their energy ebbing. Ahead, in the dimness of the lake, the creature still stood, a smoking ruin of living scales and searing flesh. It stomped its finned legs and punched the jagged ceilings like an angry child. It should have been dead by now, but it wasn't.

That thing must have a heart a big as a barge.

Verbard's lip curled over his clenched teeth.

I can't invade an entire city with half an army.

Another rock formation fell, crushing one underling mage's skull, knocking it from the air and driving it into the waters.

Follow my lead, magi!

A bubble of yellow energy formed in his hand. A soft blow from his thin black lips sent the warbling globe towards the creature. Another series of the globes followed. *Well done, brethren.* The creature swung at them, catching them on its arms and legs, while other globes stuck like dew to its chest and face.

Now!

Bamf! Bamf! Bamf!

The creature roared out in sheer agony as chunks of flesh blew from its body.

Bamf! Bamf!

One arm fell into the murk.

Bamf! Bamf!

Its entrails spilled out into the water.

And for the finale …

BAMF!

Verbard added another hole in the back of its head. It wavered, mouth clutching open and closed, then splashed full force into the waters and sank.

Verbard sat on the beach holding his head. The trolls, what was left of them, had fled. The rod of smiting he had given Jottenhiem lay at his feet, a charred husk of steel. Sixty seven underlings were dead, two barges sunk, and his siege on the greatest city in the world of Bish had not yet begun. He watched in irritation as the magi levitated one barge from the Current, flipped it over and set it down with a splash. Three barges were ready now. The blockade in the tunnel was almost clear as more magi had begun using magic to remove the boulders.

How? Why?

The entire attack was unprecedented. It left him filled with uncertainty, and he couldn't help but wonder if Master Sinway was behind this. After all, it had been Sinway's suggestion to begin the siege from within.

He rubbed his temples.

"Jottenhiem," he said.

The Juegen commander stood at attention by his side, helmet off, long curved blades gleaming with blood at his hips. "Yes, Lord Verbard."

Verbard rose to his aching feet and faced his commander. Why they ached he didn't know, but everything seemed to ache these days.

"What is your assessment?"

Jottenhiem had ruby red eyes, typical of most Juegen warriors. The sides of his head were shaved, and his rat-furred face twitched with muscles. The Juegen, one of Verbard's longtime allies, was reliable. He spoke in a manner unlike most, deep and less chittering, almost slow.

"A troll trap for troll food."

"We are underlings, not troll food, Jottenhiem."

"It seems some of us are troll food."

"And what do you make of that other monster? Was it hungry as well?"

"I didn't get a chance to ask it."

Verbard turned away and watched as the underlings continued their preparations for the remaining journey.

"What do you make of our invasion of the human city?"

Jottenhiem formed a tiny grin of razor sharp teeth.

"It will be glorious and bloody."

"Assuming we get there in one piece," Verbard snapped. "Take the helm of the first barge and see to it we don't fall into more troll traps! Imbecile!"

Verbard floated away, filled with anger and frustration, but there was nowhere to go. He ducked into come caves. *I need help.* He couldn't shake the feeling he was being set up. Now, he should feel nothing more than elation for the opportunity to slaughter mankind with a single lethal strike. His brethren were almost glowing about it, but why was he not? He was an underling. He despised mankind, but this mission, this golden moment of underling kind, filled him with doubt. His fingernails dug into his palms. His teeth bit into his jaw. Something wasn't right.

Chapter 42

ELPLESS AND ALONE. KAM'S HANDS trembled as her stomach twisted inside out. Her baby girl, Erin, was gone. She wiped her eyes and nose as she sat at a table inside the Magi Roost. She did not recognize the man that sat across from her, but she'd caught his name, Thorn. His speech was slow, reserved, scary.

"This doesn't have to be difficult," he said in a rugged voice that was far from reassuring. "The ransom isn't what is important. The return of your child is."

The tavern was empty, other than herself, the crooked-nosed man, Gillem and Lefty, who sat fidgeting at the bar. It was Lefty that had come to her rescue, a bit conveniently. His story, sweating feet and all, was convincing. Gillem, in all his stock and grace, affirmed the history of halflings with sweaty feet in brief detail. Kam had no choice but to believe them, for now.

"As you know, the Prince of Thieves, Palos, my master, has been expecting a favor from you for quite some time …"

Palos. The name inflamed her anger like a hot iron. She knew him to be crafty, beguiling and deviant. No thief could be trusted, him least of all. His honor had less weight than a feather, and his greed was without rival. It appeared the rumors were true. But kidnapping a child, of a Royal, no less? That was as unexpected as it was frightening. Who was she really dealing with? She pushed her fingers through her hair, aware of Thorn's hungry eyes on her chest.

She couldn't stop her chin from trembling as she spoke:

"I owe that man no favors. Bring back my daughter, you dog!"

It was there, the magic, a festering blossom of rage ready to unleash itself. *Kill this ugly bastard!*

Thorn wagged his long finger in her face.

"Now, don't lose control. This is a negotiation, not a discussion, nor an argument. I'm just delivering the terms." The chair groaned as he leaned back. Thorn was tall, heavy boned and sinister in expression. He spoke better than his dull eyes let on. There was intelligent life behind his harsh and haggard expression, cunning and without mercy. "Your choices are limited as well as your time, Mistress of the Magi Roost," he finished, licking his tongue over his lips.

Pop.

Kam jumped as an ember cracked in the fireplace behind the man. She clutched her chest, which was fighting her ability to breathe. Thorn chuckled. It took a degree of self-control to not hurl the man aside. What would she do? Who could she turn to for help? Her family, Royals themselves, would be more than agitated by this attempt. But Palos would not have made such a move if he did not already have something on them. Her family, aloof with politics and position, had made it perfectly clear years ago that she was on her own when she made her choice. She had gladly accepted. If anything, she'd be too ashamed to ask for their help. She'd rather die than hear them say *I told you so,* even at the cost of her life or her daughter's.

"Palos knows I'll do anything to get my daughter back. I could not live without her," she said, her sobs becoming heavy again.

"My master is counting on that," Thorn said, leaning forward, entranced by her trembling curves. "What Prince Palos offers is more of a gift than a threat. It's just difficult to present it in any other way. He desires your company. He wants to bask in the glow of your beauty. I cannot fault the prince in his tastes, they are superb. Captivating." Thorn eased closer. "Even alluring on the darkest of days."

Inhaling deeply through her nose, Kam pulled her shoulders back and let out a slow shuddering sigh. She watched as Thorn's Adam's apple rolled up and down, his eyes filled with fantasy.

"So," she said wiping her nose on a rag, "how long have you and Gillem been planning this abduction?"

Thorn's eyes flicked over her shoulder where Gillem sat, then back to her.

I knew it!

"I've no business with the halfling other than this parlay."

Liar!

She let her energy swell behind her chest, a cauldron of boiling power.

"You know what, Thorn?" she said, unable to hide her simmering green eyes.

"Eh …?" he replied, edging back.

"You remind me of something that crawled out of an ogre's nose."

The vulture-like man stiffened in his chair, his hands falling to his sides.

Kam held out her palms.

"Wench! I'll carve—*oomph!*"

Thorn was thrown from his feet and heading towards the fire.

She felt him fighting against the bonds of her telekinesis spell, fighting to avoid the flames.

"Mercy, you wench!" he shouted.

Her anger swelled her energy. Thorn screamed as he was stuffed into the flames. Harder and harder she pushed. She felt small bones breaking as her power began to crush him like a vice of flame.

"YOU WILL PAY, RODENT!"

Bottles were rattled from the shelves, shattering on the floor. Thorn was wailing, burning and writhing with torment. Someone else was yelling as well. She caught a flicker of movement in the corner of her eye. Gillem was making haste towards the door. She released her hold on Thorn.

"STOP, GILLEM!"

A row of plates cut through the air, one by one, making a bead for the halfling's head. Gillem ducked, rolled, twisted and dodged as the air was filled with the sounds of breaking dishes. Master Longfingers leaped toward the window. Kam reached out her painted nails.

"*Kye-Noche-Liene!*"

Tendrils of white energy whipped out from her fingertips, coiled around Gillem's portly little body and snatched him from the air. He writhed within the coils, his aghast face aglow from the white hot light. She rolled her wrists, layer over layer, wrapping the halfling into a tight bundle. Gillem wasn't going anywhere. She let go. The harmless but steel-strong bonds held the halfling tighter that a bear trap.

Gillem rolled into sitting position, a look of bewilderment in his eyes.

"You fool hot tempered woman! What have you done? Ye'll never get back the baby Erin now!"

Chapter 43

"So be it, Farc," Venir replied, spitting on the ground. "Your stench is more threatening than your words."

The small throng of Farc's Outlaws erupted in a sinister chuckle. Venir, despite his blossoming hatred for his foe, didn't care for the odds. He glanced over at the worried looks on Hogan and Adanna's faces. Farc's threats had them convinced.

Farc snorted and looked up into the sky. The second dusk, a glow of radiant yellow light, was washing over the city. Dusk was almost gone. "Look at this human, men! A cheater. A coward. A liar. A murderer. This is the man who took my young son, barely twelve years old, and broke his neck."

Venir's neck warmed, his face flushed. He reached for the swords at his feet. The sound of steel scraping from sheaths and a bow drawing back caught his ears. He was as flatfooted as a horse was hoofed.

"Adanna, get our gear. Hogan, break down the rest. I'll wait."

Another series of chuckles came as Adanna and Hogan scurried into the tent. The sounds of rattling gear and unpleasant words were exchanged from within the canvas. Venir kept his eyes on Farc's one. The ogre, once as powerful a warrior as a warrior could be, was diminished. He stooped. His left shoulder dipped, and the fire behind his yellow eye no longer burned. Farc, at least a decade or two older than Venir, was in decay. He watched as the ogre wiped the drool from his jutting jaw. Farc's hand trembled as he swung it behind his back.

"Venir, I should kill you now."

"Then why don't you?"

"You know the rules in the Hide."

Outlaw's Hide was a sanctuary for the worst that Bish had to offer. There was a code among all, unless you were an underling: no killing without a challenge and don't rat out your neighbors. There was no judge and no law, but there was an unspoken civil order. Other than that, it was anything goes. Of course, if you were killed, which did happen quite often, there was little to defend you. And if you killed, you were asked to leave, or subsequently killed by a self- appointed militia. But, if you had control, which Farc seemed to have at the moment, you could do whatever you wanted.

"Why not challenge me then?"

Farc let out a gruff laugh.

"Time to go, Yellow Hair."

Venir looked over at Slim, who was biting his nails.

"You coming?"

Slim's wizened face looked around at all the outlaws and said with a shrug, "Well, it's either that or die."

Farc and his men followed as Venir, Slim, Adanna, Hogan and his wife trekked a mile north to the edge of the haphazard city, loaded down with all they could carry. The only things they were missing were the tents, water and rations. He heard Farc's final words:

"I sent the underlings my personal mattock to dig a grave for you. I only asked for your boots in return."

They traveled almost five miles north of Outlaw's Hide and made a fireless camp. The terrain, grasslands mixed with jungle, posed few problems. They all sat, wiping sweat and slapping away mosquitoes, or holding their hungry bellies. There was no food.

"What do you think, Venir?"

"They're gone. They followed the first few miles." He unrolled his blanket that contained the large leather sack. "I'm going to do some scouting." He tossed his borrowed broadswords on the ground.

Hogan cocked an eye and said, "With no weapons?"

"Too much noise." Venir stuffed his sack into a pack that Adanna had given him and slung it over his shoulders. "I'll need your cloak, Slim."

"But I like this cloak. Take Hogan's."

"Too small."

"First you get us kicked out of camp, and then you abandon us." Slim slung it from his knobby shoulders and said with a frown, "Fine."

It was past midnight. Outlaw's Hide was in full swing. Heavily armed and cloaked bodies swaggered through the dusty streets singing or crying out shouts of alarm. Venir swaggered as well, cloak hood draped over his face, a jug of wine swinging at his side, vengeance on his mind.

Where is that ogre!

There weren't too many half-ogres here. The sound and smell of them, a salty mix of manure and urine, would knock you down if you weren't ready for it. Venir sauntered in and out of the tents and shabby buildings, one muck and filth ridden alley at a time. Farc, like most ogres, would prefer his privacy. The big humanoid preferred caves, mountains and high places. If anything, Farc probably preferred the wide open spaces that Outlaw's Hide provided.

Venir took a deep draw through his nose.

"Ah!"

Venir followed his nose towards a ramshackle barn where many beasts for slaughter and burden were stabled. A canvas tent, large enough for a host of people, sat catty cornered to the edge of the barn. There was an inhuman squeal of delight coming from within, followed by a series of heavy smacks on bare flesh. Venir kneeled down inside the shadows between the barn and tent, his keen eyes scanning for sentries. An orc leaned against a pile of logs near the tent entrance, hairy hands draped across its bulging belly. It wiped its mouth and yawned, peering around before it tossed another log on the nearby campfire.

Venir pulled out the sack and withdrew Brool. Its razor sharp edges seemed to hum in the moonlight. On cat's feet he slipped around the back side of the tent and slit open a hole the size of a man. Pulling the edge of the canvas back, he saw the backside of Farc's hulking form, sitting on a stool. Bent over the half-ogre's knee was a squealing orcen trollop. Her dirty blonde hair cascaded onto the dirt floor as she squirmed underneath Farc's heavy wallops. *Please don't be Dolly.*

Venir took a breath and waited, avoiding the lantern light as he stepped inside. The shaft of his axe throbbed in his hand. His murderous thoughts began to consume him. His enemies, one and all, must go. Something beckoned him onward towards the removal of all evil. It was him or them. He took another step forward, axe hanging ready over his shoulder.

"Hrmm," Farc murmured, as his head, the size of three men's, swung back his way.

The tip of Brool met the ogre's temple, drawing blood.

"Sssssh," Venir warned the orcen woman, unfamiliar to his relief, jaw dropped open.

"Who dares?" Farc said in a huff, a nervous twinge in his voice.

Venir applied more pressure. Farc took a sharp draw through his nose.

"Ah … Venir," the half-ogre said, "come to assassinate me like a coward, I see."

"No, I came to get a better look at the orc's arse," he retorted. "Flat on your belly, Wench. Shut your eyes and think about bathing."

The trollop flopped onto the ground, thick forearms covering her head.

Venir flipped Brool's blade under Farc's trembling chin.

"What are you wanting, Venir? You beat me, cripple me, humiliate me, and that's not enough. Now come to kill me?"

"Aye, Farc."

Farc grunted. The half-ogre sat, hands on his knees, head tilted down.

Venir could smell the big humanoid's fear as he watched the blood drip from Farc's temple. *That's it. Sweat it out.*

"Tilt your big head back," Venir ordered, lifting Farc's chin with his axe. "I can't have you crying out before I get this over with."

Farc made an audible gulp. The orcen woman went into a fit of squealing shudders and sobs.

"Any last words, Farc? Care to give that hairy arse another good whack before your body's fed to the other pigs?"

The half-ogre let out a raspy sound.

Venir tilted his head down and said, "What's that?"

"S-Sp …"

Venir grabbed a handful of hair and growled, "Spit it out, Ogre."

Farc trembled as he managed to say, "Sp-Spare me."

"Say again?"

"Spare me, Venir. Spare my life," Farc pleaded.

Farc's monstrous shoulders sagged. His fingers were lifeless at his side. He was beaten.

Venir pulled his axe away.

"I'll need horses. Water. Rations. Your word, Farc. For your life, this grudge is over."

Farc nodded as he buried his face in his trembling hands.

What was it Mood said? he thought as he departed.

Never trust an ogre.

The first dawn's sun was rising as Venir galloped to his camp.

"Whoa," he said, pulling back the reins on a large chestnut steed. Sliding out of his saddle, he inspected impressions in the dirt and grass. The smell of blood was in the air, something rotting and foul as well. "Bone!"

On foot he dashed over the rugged terrain, pushing his way over the tall grasses and thick jungle of vines and trees. He donned his helm. Wind, blood and death whirled through his senses. A burning sensation raised the hair on his arms. He moved forward, heavy feet smashing down the thick grasses, his head on a swivel, his heightened senses alert for the unnatural. He heard the crickets, an owl, a slithering snake, buzzing flies, but none of the distant mocking chitter of underlings, far or near. He pulled the helm off and dropped it into the sack as he stood on the edge of the meager camp. His blood ran cold.

Dark stains were smeared over the patches of moss and grass. Hogan's head, eyes wide with terror, was lying on its ear in the dirt. The man's clothes and body had been severed in many places and made up into a mound of flesh.

Venir's knuckles whitened on Brool's shaft.

One ... Four ... Nine ... Eleven ...

The underlings were many. The footsteps of two women, Adanna and her Mother, were intermingled with the underlings. It was clear they had no concern of being followed. Venir cursed and spat, fighting his urge to howl.

He heard the frightened scream of a horse.

"Slat!"

Nothing could have prepared him for what he saw as he burst through the brush and into the clearing. A jolt of fear erupted in his spine as he scrambled to dig out the armament.

"Sweet Bish!"

Chapter 44

MELEGAL LAY FLAT ON HIS belly on a mattress of feathers inside McKnight's old apartment, exhausted.

A key. A key. What did Sefron mean?

Haze straddled his back, her fingers working masterfully over the knotted fibers of muscle on his back and shoulders.

"You sure are tight for a thief," she said, boring her thumb into the middle of his back.

It felt like the blade of a knife was being driven into his spine. *Outrageous.* He had never been anything less than supple before. Now, under Lord Almen's geyser of pressure, he was as taut as a bow string these days. He felt Haze's warm lips pecking on his knobby shoulders.

"Will you stop, Woman," he said, not a question but an order. "You know I hate that."

"Oh, but I like the little goose bumps it makes on your bony back. It's adorable."

"Rub, you wench! And don't ever use the word *adorable* in my presence again. I've removed tongues for less."

Haze giggled. "As you wish, Detective."

He felt her gyrating her hips in a rhythmic sway as dripped more oil onto his back. *Ah, that's nice.* The scent, something with cinnamon, elated his nostrils, and the warm oil opened his pores like a mild lava. It was one of the best moments he'd had in days. *Why haven't I let her do this all along?*

Melegal buried his face inside a small pillow, trying to envision what the key that Sefron mentioned looked like. How could a key free them from the Almen bondage? If there was such a key, one thing he was certain of, he would have it before Sefron. The half-naked pasty skinned cleric would have to fend for himself.

He let out a sigh.

"Feeling better?" she said.

"A little," he said, words muffled in the pillow.

If I were a key where would I be? Melegal noted every object from Lord Almen's study beneath the kitchens: A cupboard of maps and scrolls. Two desks, one used, the other abandoned, no chair and four deep drawers. A small armament of weapons in the corner. Nine lanterns. Eighteen Candles. A molding rug on the floor with a hollow spot below that he had noted because of the way Lord Almen always stepped over it. *Hmmm.* Two shelves full of small decorations and awards. Above, wooden rafters. A drop down ladder. The edges of tapestries concealing who knew what. A box, small as a hand. A chest of cast iron as big as a man.

"What are you thinking, Me?" Haze said, shoving her palms into the center of his back. A notable series a cracks followed, continuing up to his neck.

His eyes popped open. "Ahhh … nothing." *Key. Key. Key. Key. Key.*

Seek. Retrieve. Key.

Melegal held his hand on his aching head as he crept through Castle Almen. It was always quietest in the hours before the first dawn, long before the city roosters crowed. In the kitchen, a tiled expanse of wood-fed ovens and long maple tables, he'd wedged himself into the dark shadow between two cupboards and settled in. He could hear mice, a pair, their tiny nails scraping the tiles, small teeth nibbling into a silk sack of corn flour. Exterior shudders creaked from a nearby window pane where the two moons' glow added a gentle light in an otherwise dark room.

Listen, Fool.

Everything was quiet and natural, yet ominous and threatening. It was the time of day none should be trespassing within the walls of the castle, not even the heralded detective. Only the sentries and members of the Royal family roamed at night. It was foolish for him to do so. *Got to find that key.* He rubbed his fingers over his chin. *What am I doing?*

His compulsion was natural. The urge to find something of value, enhanced by magic, suggested by an enchanted mind, only charged the thief's natural tendencies. Whatever it was that Sefron wanted, he wanted it more, even at his own peril.

A sound of heavy footsteps made its way up the stone stairwell. Unmoving, eyes closed, Melegal remained one with the kitchen. The sounds of the sentry alone lent a picture as clear as daylight to his mind: a large man with a hitch in his step sauntered through the kitchen and began to rummage quietly through the cupboards. *Ah, good.* It made things easier. No sentry would dare abandon his post with Lord Almen within his chambers.

The sentry was chewing now, strong teeth chomping into a piece of hard fruit. Melegal could feel a shadow closing over the moonlight that was shed his way, the man's footsteps only a few feet away and passing.

"Hmmm," the man said as he stopped, his boots turning over the floor. "What's this?"

Melegal heard the man pick something up from the table. He cracked an eye open. The sentry held a long kitchen knife, its keen edge reflecting the moonlight. The sentry's head cocked back and forth on his bull neck. *Slat.* Like a beast in the fields, the man sensed something was amiss. Melegal could feel the tension rise in the man. Instincts beginning to fire. Oily sweat beginning to build.

Slowly the man turned, his sword scabbard thunking against a table leg. Melegal felt his heart begin to race as the sentry reached toward the cupboard he hunkered behind. He pulled his cloak tight and dipped his chin deeper into his chest. A heavy footstep landed inches from him.

Burp!

The smell of apples and tobacco wafted through the air, followed by a strange sounding fart.

"Mmmm … that's better," the sentry grumbled, tapping his fist on his chest as he continued to walk by, back towards the stone stair case.

Melegal slipped behind the man, matching him step for step, wading through the funk of odor. *One would think you'd get used to it.* The man was halfway to the bottom when he let out another burst, louder than the last, echoing within the corridor. *The fool could wake the dead with that.*

Melegal's hand slipped down to the pommel of his blade. He eased it from the sheath, making a scraping sound of metal on wood, like a whisper. Ten more steps he followed the man like a shadow, the small torches wavering light against the wall. The sentry stretched his arms high, turned at the waist and farted again. *Enough.* Melegal raised his dagger and poised the tip on the man's broad back as he slipped behind and cradled him like a child. *Sleep. Sleep. Sleep.*

His mind tingled. His thoughts raced. The man swayed. Melegal slid his dagger in the sheath as the sentry's knees buckled and he teetered forward. *Catch him.* He grabbed the man behind his girdle and scooped his arm underneath the man's chest. *Heavy bastard. Blasted chainmail.* Melegal sagged along with the man as they both crumpled to the landing. *Whew.* The man began to snore like an ogre. Melegal rolled the man onto his stomach. *That should do it.* Up the stairwell, the small torches, two in all, offered little light against the black stone walls. He withdrew a pair of steel gauged wires and dropped to a knee. Eyeing the keyhole, he stuck the two thin rods inside and began picking. Melegal was already aware of the mechanisms within as he had heard Lord Almen locking and unlocking the door before. It was a heavy brass key that worked the lock, and turned the tumblers. Still, it was not the average lock. Rather, it was one designed to give the utmost security ... *pop* ... except when dealing with the utmost thief. *Unimpressive.* Sliding the tools into the pouch with one hand, he depressed the thumb lever down with the other. He took a deep breath. *Why am I doing this?* And pushed the door open. *Have I gone mad?*

Chapter 45

Fogle's feet were anchored on the edge of the abyss. His arms and back were straining against a heavy mystical rope that he squeezed inside his grip. He wasn't the same man now, no longer a weakling of a wizard, but instead a titan of sorts. Inside his mind was another world within, one that he knew quite well.

A woman's high pitched scream echoed behind his thoughts.

Hang on, Cass!

Below him, a vat of vile looking green and black goo bubbled with anger. Little by little it sucked the rope he held, burning the fibers in his grasp. Fogle groaned, digging the heels of his boots into the dirt. He'd been here before. Another world. Locked in a mind grumble of the oddest kind. He liked it, but he was losing control. He cried out.

"Cass!"

No reply.

"Cass!"

He slipped the rope over his shoulder, feeling as if a giant, legs like trunks, filled with muscle, churned back at him from the abyss. Something was pulling back, stronger this time, the weight unimaginable. *NO!* Smoke rose as the rope slipped through his skin, rending his flesh. He screamed. *NO! Think, Wizard!*

He screamed for Cass one last time as he fought to hold onto the rope.

One second the druid woman Cass was there, wrapped up with the wizard Fogle Boon. In the next second she twisted, contorted and plunged inside of Chongo. It was possibly the strangest thing the King of the Blood Rangers, Mood, had ever seen in all of his centuries.

Mood huddled before Chongo's dreary heads, holding the beasts in the nooks of his arms. He could feel the dog's big body shaking, its body writhing with sickening sounds. The wizard, Fogle, sat with his face transfixed on a woman who was no longer there. Sweat was dripping from the man's forehead, his body straining against an unseen force.

"Hold on, Boy," Mood said into Chongo's ear. "Help's coming."

In truth, Mood had never seen a dog or anything so sick before. The beast was well past the point where any other beast would have been put out of its misery. Mercy had come to mind more than once. No animal or man should be made to suffer like that. He could only assume that Chongo held on for some reason. The dog was his friend, and he was his. "I got you!"

He looked over and saw the worried look on the lady dwarven faces. Each one was contorted, exerted, and intense. One had her arms around Fogle's waist, and the others followed suit in a chain from behind. Fogle pitched forward, tugging the entire group with him. Chongo trembled and shook, but Mood held on, feeling that the beast's bull necks were not quite as strong as before. That's when the smoke came. Fogle's hands were burning.

Agony. Never had Fogle experienced anything on this level. Chongo was the furthest concern from his mind. Cass was foremost. He couldn't let her go, not with the feelings he had. Not with so much unresolved between them. He wanted to know. He wanted to know how she felt about him. He wasn't sure how he felt about her. It seemed he was about to find out soon enough because his back was being dragged over the ground towards the acidic burbling of the pit. *Think or die. Isn't that what the oaf said?* All of this suffering over one man, one dog, one person. What was the meaning of that?

More rope raced through his loosening fingertips. *Just win, Fogle. Win!*

He dug down into his belly and began loosening the lid off a kettle of energy. *There it is!* A dormant power lay unused except when his life or another's was in peril. He'd found it when Ox the Mintaur died. He'd found it when he thought Mood was about to die. A bit by accident on both accounts. It had been there when the underling Catten was shutting his brain down. He didn't have the control then, but he was gaining control now. *The Bone with the lid! For Three!* He shoved the deposit of energy over.

Elation. Magic and mind intermingled, forming a coating over his mental body. A shiny coat of metal replaced this skin. His grip became hard as iron. He rolled the rope around his wrist and pulled. The sucking pit of goo let out an eerie wail of anger. Fogle rose to his feet, his face molded in steel, his muscles bulging of hammered iron.

"Cass!"

He tugged. Dug his heels into the turf and pulled backward. One step. Two steps. The pit hissed. Green and black acid erupted in splattering globs, splashing his hardened skin and sizzling into nothing. He took control of his magic, his anger, his will, pulling the rope back, hand over hand, faster and faster. The ground quaked beneath his feet. Something dark and deadly was furious with him.

He called for her again. The rope continued to coil, foot after foot, at his feet. Where was she? He dragged a man-sized gob of something, sticky, green and black, onto the ledge. He rushed over and picked the mass up into his arms, and the world exploded.

One second Fogle's hands were burning, the next they were not. Chongo's entire body writhed with violent seizures that tested the limits of Mood's mighty arms. In the next second the naked flesh of the druid spilled outside of Chongo, coated in a dark green and purplish goo. The smell had the foulness of an underling's marsh. Fogle wrapped his arms around the unmoving woman. The wizard was rocking her back and forth, saying, "Don't die. Don't die, my sweet."

Chapter 46

SMACK!

Lefty reeled as Kam's heavy hand knocked him to the floor. She wanted to kill the little betrayer, but she needed him.

"How could you do this to me, Lefty? After all I have done for you!" She screamed in his face.

The little blond haired boy said nothing, only holding his tiny hand on his reddening cheek. Kam's fists were clutched at her sides. She let her anger fight her panic. What else could she do? Her baby was gone, somewhere deep in the vile underbelly of the City of Three. Thorn, Palos's personal messenger, had been pretty clear on what the Prince of Thieves wanted. He wanted her, more so than gold and power. *Why? Why me?*

She could hear Joline sobbing inside the kitchen. The woman had returned violated and mortified somehow, unable to speak. Her thick gray hair was a mess, and her clothes were torn. The woman fell completely apart at the news of Erin's kidnapping.

"Fool woman. What do you suppose to do now?" Thorn said, grimacing. His face and body were burnt and broken, but there was still pleasure in his face. The rogue still had some control, bound by magic or not. "You've attacked me. Palos will kill you and your daughter for your transgression."

Thorn's mocking laughter was cut off with a wave of her palm. The magic cords that bonded him squeezed around his neck.

"Kam, you must stop this and listen," Gillem piped in, a nervous look in his eye. "We can't help you with your baby if you're dead. Just give Palos — *urk!*"

Similar bonds held the halfling, the sound of leather constricting around his neck. Kam let the halfling's eyes start to bulge from their sockets, his face turning into a turnip.

"Kam!"

Both Thorn and Gillem Longfingers were choking to death.

"KAM!" Joline shouted again, blocking her view of the men.

They both flopped and kicked on the floor, gagging and coughing for air.

Joline grabbed her face that was flushed and streaked with tears and said, "You are not a murderer."

The words affected her. The urge to tear something apart drained out of her. She released her hold. Gillem and Thorn gulped for air.

"What do I do?" Kam whispered.

"How much does Erin mean to you, Kam?" Joline said softly.

"Everything," she sobbed, "she's all I have left."

Joline gave her a look, and she knew what she would have to do. It was time to make a sacrifice.

She turned around and muttered something in magic. Her mind shimmered, searching for Erin, trying to bring her baby back. Nothing. Her powers, formidable as they were, had limitations in that regard. She had focused more on the aggressive arts, as opposed to the passive ones. She slunk down onto a chair. Her mind and powers were exhausted, and her grip on the two thieves on the floor was beginning to ebb. She needed time to regain her strength. Thorn had already made it clear her time was short.

She looked over at Lefty. He sat on a kitchen stool, his little head downcast, spitting out his nails. What had happened to the once innocent little boy? She cast a glance towards Gillem, the robust halfling, as deceiving as Palos himself. Georgio had been right after all. Gillem was at the root of Lefty's problems. How had the boy seen it and not she? Perhaps she hadn't wanted to.

She cursed.

Still, the responsibility was on Lefty. His deceit had led to all this. Lies and dishonesty would cost them all greatly. Maybe the boy didn't think he had a choice, but there was only one choice when it came to right and wrong. One had to discern the difference.

"Joline," Kam said, regaining her feet, "get me the City Watch. I'm sure Thorn's time would be better served with them."

She twirled her fingers in the air, and Gillem's bonds fell loose. The halfling man couldn't hide the surprise on his face as he quickly rose to his feet, soft eyes flitting back and forth. His long fingers rubbed at his wrists and neck as he said, "Kam, we must hurry. Palos is ruthless. He'll kill Erin and have you anyway."

"Aye, wench, she's probably dead—"

"*Chad-dah kin*," Kam spoke. Thorn's lips and ears sealed shut.

Thorn's newly deformed face had the most panicked expression.

"We can't have him blabbing my plans to the City Watch. For all I know they are bought and paid for. That should keep him quiet for now. "She looked at Thorn. "You're fortunate I left you your nose holes. As for you two," she motioned to the halflings, "I guess I don't have any choice. Take me to Palos."

A Gondola. It was something Kam had never ridden in nor known existed before. Small and wavering, the tiny craft cut through the blackness with only the green glow of the lantern providing light. She held her stomach as she shivered underneath a heavy cloak. Behind her, Gillem manned the rudder, his pie face almost hidden in the dark. In the front, Lefty paddled the craft, its small oars moving the craft over the black waters at what seemed to be an agonizing pace.

"How much farther," she asked, her voice echoing.

Gillem replied, "Not much longer, Lass. Not long at all," he said as his voice trailed off.

Erin. How would she save her baby? She was venturing far from her beaten path, below the city, into the unknown, where another world waited for her like an open maw. She had heard rumors of the Nest, but she had given little thought to its actual existence. There had never before been a need to concern herself.

"What is that?" she said.

Lefty gave her a glance. She could see the frown etched in his sad face. What had happened to the happy little blond haired and blue-eyed boy? He seemed so much older now, but filled with despair. She looked away. There was no time for forgiveness now. It was his fault.

"Archways, Lass. We are close," Gillem offered.

She fought against the creeping doom that was seeping into her bones. She had to be strong for Erin. Closing her eyes, she meditated, ignoring the sounds of the paddles dipping and pushing through the waters and the creaking of the boat. She had a few spells left. She always did. One by one she recalled the steps in her mind. Her vault of energy had strength, but it was no longer full.

It would take more than magic to escape from Palos. The man might be greedy, but he was no fool. He'd dealt with the likes of magi and wizards before. He wouldn't have gotten to be who he was if he hadn't been privy to their tricks. She thought of Venir. What would the man think if he knew he had a daughter who was abducted? Would he be as angry and vengeful as she?

She tucked her hands up under her aching breasts. *I'm getting closer. I must be.* She reached out with her mind for Erin. *Nothing.* For all she knew her baby was starving now. *Be strong.* Fresh tears began to stream from the corners of her eyes as the passed underneath the arches. *Concentrate.* Everything faded away as she stared at the tiny lantern, stroke after stroke. She closed her eyes.

"We're here," Gillem said.

Kam opened her eyes. A rotting city awaited them on a mound of dirt. A massive brick chimney was in the middle of it all, smoke seeping from a tiny vent hole on the side. It gave the otherwise hopeless and dreary slat hole the appearance of life. Docks jutted out and wrapped around the entire city where faceless men strolled, stood and talked. Light flickered from torch lit lampposts and the insides of haphazard storefronts and apartments. She couldn't believe her baby was here, in the dark and murk, among the city's most notorious ilk.

She glared at Lefty, then back at Gillem.

"Take me to Palos, rogues!"

She ignored the hard and gawping stares as she strode behind Gillem. They would all burn if she had her way: thieves, kidnappers and smugglers, all deserved to die. Many of them would if she did not get her way. She ignored the smell, the rodents and the screams of vile pleasure as they traversed the catacombs of the tiny city's alleys. All she knew was she was getting closer to her baby. *Hang on, Baby.*

Gillem pushed his way inside two swinging tavern doors. She followed, booted feet clomping on the planks, and came to a sudden stop. A dozen men wielding crossbows and knives greeted her: four on a balcony, the others on the main floor, spread out among the tables.

"Have a seat, Woman," one said from the balcony, sucking on a toothpick that dangled from his mouth. "Prince Palos will be with you momentarily."

"Tell that blood sucker I'll see him now!" she yelled.

Clatch – Zip!

Kam cried out. A small crossbow bolt protruded from her thigh, knocking her to the ground. An eruption of pain raced through her leg, and humiliation followed on the snickers of the men. She'd never been cut or stabbed by anything before, but she'd stitched a kitchen wound or two. *Blast, it hurts. I never imagined.* Kam fought to regain her feet. As Lefty reached for her hands she punched him in the chest, filling the room with uproarious laughter.

Two uncomely men dragged her up into a chair and bound her. Her leg was on fire. It was agony. *Help me.* There wasn't an honest face in the room to heed her call.

Then, as the man with the toothpick in his mouth reloaded, he said, "Any more blasphemy towards the prince and the next one will go in your neck. That will leave us to take care of your darling little baby."

Chapter 47

THE CITY OF BONE. A black monolith shimmering below the burning sky. Georgio wiped the sweat from his brow. *Home.* He sped up his pace, mouth watering at the thought of a stuffed biscuit and milk.

"Slow down," Mikkel said, peering through his spy glass. A look of frustration crossed his ebony face, his big smile many days gone. "Get a look at this, Billip."

"I want to see," Georgio turned back and headed for Mikkel.

"In a minute, Boy," Billip said, pushing him aside.

The journey from the City of Three had been nothing short of harrowing. Wind storms came and went; the nights were longer than the days and of all things, underlings. Georgio had killed three himself, and Billip and Mikkel had killed another twelve, but they weren't without casualties. One mintaur and two ponies were dead. Only they themselves and somehow Quickster still lived.

Billip, skin tanned by the suns, his sharp features hardened by battle, gawped as he peered at the ominous city.

"Let me see," Georgio pleaded. His stomach groaned. He was starving. They had started off with all they could carry, but after that last fight with the underling hunters most of their supplies were left to wither in the dust. He'd had little food in days. He couldn't ever remember being so hungry. It didn't seem possible.

Billip tossed Georgio the telescope, turned to Mikkel and said, "Those people are worse off than we are."

"What people?" Georgio said, "I don't see hardly anything."

Billip jerked the spy glass from his grip and hit him in the head.

"Ow! What did you do that for?"

"Wrong end, Stupid."

"Oh," he replied, rubbing his head as he raised the spy glass back to his eye. "What the in world of Bish!"

There were thousands of them. People. Huddled in a moving mass outside the City. He had never seen that many people in one place before. It was enough for an army. An army without a banner or siege equipment. An army that was starving to death. His belly let out another loud growl.

"You better get used to that," Mikkel said, "because we can't get in there. Bone!"

Billip kicked up the dirt. "Bish!"

Georgio could see the anguish in Billip's face as he clutched at the bandage on his side. Mikkel sat down behind Quickster's shadow and adjusted the sling on his busted shoulder. Georgio felt a little guilt as the two men baked in the sun, clearly in some type of agony—internal and external agony. He, however hungry he may be, was fine. Sure, getting feathered with a few crossbow bolts hurt like the dickens, but the look on that underling's face before he ran them through almost made it worth it.

I got to have a biscuit. So close.

He walked over to Quickster and stroked his think black mane. If the quick pony was thirsty or hungry, he didn't show it. The pony seemed as oblivious to the blistering environment as a stone. "We better not take you anywhere nears those people, Quickster. Those people will turn you into a roast."

"They aren't the only ones," Billip said, tossing a knife into the ground.

"Oh no you don't," he said. "I'm not eating my friend."

Mikkel added, "We may have to trade him, Georgio. It's the donkey or us."

"No!" He wrapped his arms around Quickster's neck. "He's not even mine … he's Melegal's"

Billip jumped up on his feet. "The beast is mine, Boy! Melegal stole him from me!"

"Did not!" Georgio screamed.

"Ah, but he did. What else would you expect from a thief?" Billip poked Georgio in his chest. "He stole my ass!"

Mikkel rumbled in laughter, adding, "You can say that again. Did he steal your tender heart, too?"

Georgio slapped Billip's hand away saying, "He's Melegal's, and under my care. You might as well try to kill me if you want to take him." He ripped his broad sword from his sheath. "And just to remind you … You can't kill me!"

Billip slugged him in the jaw. He dropped to his knees, sword falling from his hand. Then it hit him. He raised his finger. "I just remembered: I know a secret way in!" He fell face first into the dirt.

Chapter 48

I T WAS BIG. VENIR STOOD in helpless horror, his own marrow running cold, at the sight of one of the most ghastly things he ever saw.

"Bish."

One horse was being weaved into a cocoon while the other's life was being sucked from it. A spider, the size of four war horses, had its fangs plunged deep into the big horse's haunches. The grey mare kicked one last time as its strong and vibrant body was sucked down to a husk. The enormous insect rose up on four of its eight hairy legs and let out a frightening screech that would have run a giant's blood cold. *Run!* His instincts screamed, and he would have if not for something else.

Huddled down in the tall grasses, he strapped on his helm and withdrew his shield. There would be no running from that thing. Hide yes, but run … no. But, that's not why Venir stayed. It was something else: underlings. Six of them rode atop a basket impossibly embedded on the spider's back. The second dawn's light had risen to reveal the gleaming evil in their bright speckled eyes.

His helm began to burn and beckon. *Kill!* The black eyelets began their glow. *Them!* The bond between him and Brool became one. *ALL!*

Venir's muscles bulged; his veins writhed beneath his skin as his blood began to flow like lava. He took no notice of his heaving chest or prickling hairs as he fought to hold his position. The venomous spider glided over the grass, its long hairy legs touching the ground as soft as petals. It was the only barrier that came between Venir and the underlings. In order to kill them, Venir would have to kill it. It was time to fight. It was time for something to die.

As the spider tapped around the clearing on its fuzzy black legs, Venir crept forward. *Attack!* The black body and white-and-black-ringed orb of this spider wasn't very different than that of the sand spider had been. He was certain there was nothing but gooey green guts in there. From a hole on its tail end, spider silk shot forth, spraying and coating the dead horse. It turned again, the red glow of its eight eyes scanning over the grass and jungle. It felt like thunder behind his temple, exploding in his ear. *Attack!* The spider reared up on its hind legs almost fifteen feet in height and screeched once more.

The underlings were making short chittering commands as they tugged at many ropes on the saddle. The spider shuddered and shook, knocking one underling off its back and onto the ground. In the next instant, the spider's front spear-shaped leg pierced the underling in a series of lightning quick blows. Something in Venir quivered.

Avoid those.

The underlings chittered with anger as they jabbed long black rods into the insect, and they crackled with every strike. The spider's feet flailed as it reared and then it dropped and settled down. The underlings had regained control and turned the insect toward him. Venir remained still. His shield was pulled in front of him as he hunkered into the tall grasses and angled himself behind a small grove of jungle trees. Fear and rage intermingled in his mind. The spider was getting closer, each of its steps crushing down on the ground with power. He would have liked to be giant sized again so he could smash the insect under his toe. *Attack!*

Something bounded past him. The spider turned. A cotton tailed rabbit as big as a man stood up in the field.

A giant rabbit? What in Bish?

Spider silk shot out. The rabbit bounded away in a single leap that took it clear from his sight. The spider turned in pursuit, its rear flank exposed. Venir couldn't contain himself. The proximity of the underlings was killing him. *Attack!* Like a metal gazelle he bounded over the grass, closing the gap from him to the spider in two seconds. The spider flinched as he rolled under its belly, grazing its hairy coat. A spear-like tentacle jabbed at his head, glancing off of his shield.

"RAH!" Venir cried, ramming Brool to his knuckles into the spider's belly, then ripping it free with another bellow. An ear shattering screech followed. Spider guts coated him from head to toe, like spoiled milk or a toxic sewer. Something hit him hard, sprawling him to the ground, throwing spots before his eyes. He rolled onto his back as the spider crashed his way. *Move!* He screamed in pain as the spider fell down on his legs. He was pinned to the ground.

"Son of a Bish!" he yelled, drawing the bewildered gazes of the underlings. "Come on, you slat eaters! I've been waiting for this!" Venir raised his axe, chopping away at the spider's flesh with fury, black and green chunks of the beast flying everywhere.

As if they had a single mind, the underlings jumped from their saddle, drew their edged weapons and attacked. Venir sat up, catching the ringing blows on his shield. He chopped the legs out from underneath one underling, dismembering it from the knee. It chittered in agony, crawling away. Venir tried to pull his legs free. *Move quicker!*

The helm beckoned a warning. The underlings were circling behind his back.

Clang. Clang. Clang.

Venir fended off the nearest underling then shoved the edge of his shield in its mouth. *Move!* He flopped to the ground as a blade sliced over the top of his head. He cried out as something stabbed into his leg. He could hardly see from all the goo in his eyes, which also coated him from head to toe. He ripped his legs out from under the spider, rolled over one of the underlings and sprang to his feet.

The underling with a mouthful of busted teeth still fumbled for a weapon as the other three rushed him.

Chop!

One stopped to find its arm.

Stab! Rip!

One clutched at the gaping hole in its chest.

Slice!

The other fell to the ground, black-red blood burbling from its headless neck.

A sharp whistle caught his ears. The last underling, busted mouth and all, had managed a whistle. Brool shot from his arm like an arrow, cutting the underling's alarm short. Venir scanned the area as he wrenched his weapon free. He stepped away.

The spider's spear-like tendril poked at his side. The creature lived, its red eyes full of an evil intent. He sliced away the tendril. Webbing shot from the front and rear of the dying creature as he tried to force its bulk up from the ground. One at a time, Venir cut its legs off. He jammed Brool's spike in its skull.

"That's for killing one of my underlings!"

He whirled at the sound of something he hadn't expected to hear: clapping.

There, among the grasses and the gore, stood Slim. He had the ears of a rabbit sticking up from his head.

"You can't be serious," Venir said.

Slim held his finger to his lips and said, "Sssh … not so loud." The tall lanky man crinkled his bunny nose and added, "That smells horrible, and it's all over you. We've got to find you a river, a big one."

"Great idea," Venir said, slinging the goo from himself. "We need to find some horses and our women, too. At least you survived. What happened?"

"What happened," Slim said, his peaceful face showing a hint of anger, "is you left."

Venir shook his head. More people were dead or abducted because of him, and he'd only been back in Bish a few days. In trying to prevent one bad thing he'd opened the door to another. He shook his head.

"Slim, it's probably best you parted ways with me. Most people don't fare so well in my company these days."

"Bish happens, Venir. Get over it. Besides, I like you."

"Really? Why's that?"

Slim shrugged.

"Because you kill evil. You're good at it."

Venir took off his helm, surveyed the dead underlings and said with a smile, "I'd be lying if didn't say that felt really good. Hmmm, I say we go and find some more." He chopped his axe in the air.

Slim's ears perked up, and his nose began to twitch.

"I hate to say this, but I think more of those things," he motioned towards the spider, "are coming."

"Any chance you can turn into a horse so we can track these kidnapping fiends down?"

Slim's ears shrunk and returned to normal. An older man, with long earlobes and calming blue eyes, remained. "Not today, but if we live till tomorrow maybe I'll surprise you."

In the distance Venir could see three large black things creeping over the landscape. Killing one spider was one thing, but three? *Run or die.* He looked over at Slim, but the lanky cleric was already running.

Chapter 49

A KEY. A KEY. A KEY.

He held the continual light coin in his mouth. It made what otherwise would be a very dark room quite bright. The small, tightly wrapped coin gave off quite the powerful beam of illumination. Melegal had become very fond of it. *I wonder if McKnight knew about this key.* Lighting a lantern or candle wasn't an option. The smell of the burning oil or wick would linger and be a dead giveaway.

Melegal's hands ran up and down every nook and crevice of Lord Almen's office. He'd been inside more than a dozen times over the past several months and noted every detail. He could have done it blindfolded if he had to, but why show off when your life was on the line.

Noting the thin layer of dust on the floor, his keen eyes followed a trail unseen to normal sight. The office, virtually dust free and dry as a husk of corn, still left many signs to his naked eye that was as sharp as a bird of prey's. Holding his chin in the nook between his finger and thumb, he bent down on one knee, eyeing a row of books and baubles on the bottom shelf of a book case.

"Hmmm. ..."

Royal Lord Almen, when he was in his presence, rarely moved from his seat at the desk. Instead, the stoic man always remained in close proximity, never venturing far. In all likelihood, his most precious items were probably there. At the same time, it was likely the desk would be booby trapped. Setting a trap off was one thing, but resetting it was another. Melegal didn't have time to risk it, so he chose to run his search from the outside in.

This is interesting.

He removed the coin from his mouth and fanned his hand up and down the shelf. Tiny particles of dust glittered in his coin's bright beam. Some floated; others remained affixed to their objects. There were golden dragon bookends, precious metal candle sticks, several finely crafted letter openers and so on, but dust coated each and every discarded object of appreciation.

What would the key look like?

Melegal aimed the beam high and low. Its brilliance identified other details that his own eyes in the dim lantern light had missed. Tonio's sword, for example, was placed within a trove of weapons that appeared to have been discarded. The encrusted jewels on the pommel of the magnificent sword reflected with brilliance underneath the cloth Melegal had recovered it in. *The murdering brat.* The thought of the horrifying young man left his blood a little cold. What the monster had done to all of the sentries months back had been something he'd set up, the results more grisly than expected. But he lived.

The room itself, a five-hundred square-foot rectangle, seemed vaster than it first appeared as he shined the light around its edges. Another black case, somewhat ominous in its old mahogany finish, sat along the wall askew. The faintest of scratches could be seen at the corner of the case on the castle stone. A delicate breeze nibbled at his fingertips as he ran them along the back edges.

"Clever."

Indeed. It was one of the better concealed passageways he'd ever encountered.

"And where might you go?" He pulled the case outward, not scraping, but gliding over the stone. A small door, less than his chin in height, greeted him. He pulled on a silk glove, reached down and grabbed the brass knob that jutted out just above his knees. He felt cold metal through his glove. *Interesting.* The mechanism's springs pinged his ears as he twisted the knob and shoved it open. A whoosh of icy air nipped at his nose and ruffled his cloak. Chill bumps rose all over his body.

He ducked down and crept inside. A tunnel, tall and wide as a large man, greeted him like a large mouth. Steps carved from the ground descended in a steep decline before dropping out of sight. His beam of light, not withstanding, reached less than thirty feet ahead. The air was musty, chilly and damp. He rubbed his burning nose. Melegal was accustomed to the tunnels beneath the vast City, but this was different.

What am I doing? Why would the key be down here? Fool, I don't even know what the key looks like. Was this another one of Sefron's games? He took a closer look at things. On the landing where he stood were a staff, a cloak and a pair of curved swords on belts and in scabbards. *Cutlasses. Strange.* Two torches hung on the wall, and there was a peg on the wall as well, and hanging from it was … *A Key!*

It was slender, a hollow head, a row of teeth, as long as his hand and made of dark steel. He wrapped his silk covered fingers around it and removed it from the peg. He checked the brass door knob and the key hole below it. *Nope. Blast. This is either it, or it goes to something down there.* He craned his neck above the steps and closed his eyes. Something was scratching against the stone. There was an ebb, something like breathing, and dripping water. *I'm not going down there.* He stepped back inside Lord Almen's chamber and took a deep breath. His hand clutched at his heart.

No thank you.

He twirled the key in his fingers. It was different, certainly not like anything he'd ever come across before. A human locksmith could have made it, but the design wasn't human. The teeth were more round than square, and the rivets weren't smooth, but rough. How long would it be before Lord Almen missed it? Should he give it to Sefron? Draw a picture? *Yes.*

It was closing in on an hour, time to move. There was no telling how early Lord Almen actually came in. He made his way back through the small door and hung the key back on the peg. With relief he began to pull the door closed behind him.

A disturbance was coming from the other side of the main door in Lord Almen's chamber room. *No!* He could hear voices on the other side. One of them was Lord Almen's, and he was angry. He heard a thumb depressing the lever. *SLAT!* He began pulling the cabinet back into place. *Ow!* He pinched his fingers between the stone and wood from the effort.

"Remove that man's head at dawn! See to it all the sentries are in the courtyard to bear witness. Outrageous! Find his superior and remove his right hand as well. Move, Imbecile!"

Melegal heard another sentry racing back up the steps just as he closed the small door. He could barely hear a thing on the other side. The little door seemed as thick as the stones that surrounded it. That's when he closed his hand around the bright light of the coin. *Bone!* He felt for the key on the post and waited in the pitch black. What to do now.

He'll post two guards for this. Even after he leaves, I'll never get back out unnoticed. To make matters worse, he had a meeting with Lord Almen. He pressed his ear to the door. He thought he heard a muffled voice from within. It was hard to say. Lord Almen, more than likely, sat at his desk, plotted death and brooded.

I'm dead. He let his boots dangle over the first step. *If you can't go up, than you must go down. The only place I'm going is down.*

Chapter 50

Cass's slim, coated body was as stiff as driftwood.

"Somebody, do something!" Fogle cried.

The dwarven ladies removed Cass from his grasp and rolled her onto her stomach. Their strong little hands thumped all over the druid's back while another dwarven woman wiped the goo from her mouth. Fogle brushed his gooey fingers through his hair.

She can't die! She can't!

Death wasn't something he'd come to terms with. Ox the Mintaur had been the first friend he'd seen die, and that had been hard. Seeing this exotic woman—perfect in features and form—seeing her perish would be unfathomable.

"Do something, Mood!" he said, shooting the Blood Ranger a pleading look.

Mood stood, his solemn expression unchanged, unmoving.

Cough!

Cass's body shook and shimmered. The dwarves lifted the woman into a sitting position and continued their heavy taps on her back. Fogle watched her fingers writhe and her arms sling. Her body lurched upright as her head heaved forward to retch. Something vile, muddy, brown and black gushed forth like a geyser from the druid's petite mouth. She stopped, gasped, then heaved again with more violent fury that before. The putrid smelly substance seemed unnatural and endless.

Ew!

Fogle turned his nose away. He glanced over and away again. Something about the exotic nature of their relationship had been damaged. At least he thought maybe it had. *She lives. That's all that matters. Well, I'm certain she'll want to clean herself up. She's puking again!*

The retching and puking went on for another minute. The dwarven women had thin smiles growing on their chubby little faces. Cass had her legs wrapped beneath her, her body sagging into the arms of the women. She pulled her hair away and looked down at the massive pile of vomit she had created.

"That's foul," she said in a meek voice. "Burn it. Quickly."

The women dragged her back. Mood dropped a torch into the bile. It burst into a roaring flame. The fire burned green and orange, the smoke shades of deep purple and pink, the heat not hot but cold. It hissed and squealed in anger, like a living thing in its last hideous moments of life. Fogle shielded his face with his hand from the strange beacon of flame. It was evil, vile and deadly. Whatever poison Chongo'd had in him should have killed him. He looked over at Cass. It should have killed her as well. He felt fortunate to be alive.

The fire let out a final vengeful groan and then extinguished as fast as it started, leaving nothing but silence and an unforgettable smell. Suddenly, Fogle Boon felt as weary as he'd ever been. He fought to keep his eyes open. It was a degree of guilt that kept them open. How much had Cass suffered for the dog, and how much had Chongo suffered for … Venir?

That's when he heard Cass's purring voice speaking in a raspy, not-so-seductive manner. His eyes latched onto hers, and he tried to make out the words coming from her grotesquely coated face. Somehow she was both beautiful and disgusting at the same time as she said, "Come, give your *sweet* a kiss."

Something like a tiny mouse ran up and down his spine as he gaped. Then something huge shuffled at his side. Chongo rose to his feet. Fogle looked up and blinked, eyes growing as large as the moons at what happened before them. The dog's thinning grey coat thickened and darkened to a deeper brown. Its tongues turned pink, its big eyes grew alert. Fogle scooted back as Chongo turned, swayed over to Cass and began to lick the entirety of the muck from her body. She giggled.

Mood's big hand landed on his shoulder, and he could have sworn he saw the dwarf wipe something wet from his eyes. "Don't get too cozy, Wizard." The dwarf gave his shoulder a powerful squeeze. "The adventure has just begun."

"No time to celebrate? I've not even gotten a chance to take my bath."

"Better make it quick. Chongo's waited long enough," Mood said, pulling him up to his feet.

It can't be time to go already. It can't be.

Mood whispered something haunting in his ear.

"It won't be long before ta' underlings take Bish over. We must find Venir. The world's gonna need The Darkslayer."

As if the last few months hadn't been difficult enough.

CHAPTER 51

THE ORANGE FLAMES OF A fireplace danced in her green eyes as she struggled against her bonds. Kam, a proud woman, a little more than thirty, for the first time in her life was helpless. The only thing keeping her mind from collapsing was her baby, an innocent creature even more helpless than her. *What has he done with my baby?*

The rogues had taken her up the steps and set her down inside a lavish chamber. There, she sat alongside a massive table, bonds biting into her wrists, gagged with a dish cloth. High back chairs of precious wood and velvet surrounded the ancient table. Piles of gold, silver and other precious metals were stacked up from one end to the other. There were jewels, goblets, fine china, tapestries, art and statues—the equivalent of a Royal throne room. A great sword hung over the fireplace mantle, shadows flickering on its ominous blade. There was something significant about it, a story perhaps, but she did not concern herself with that now.

Her belly groaned. Her leg burned, but the wound had been bandaged. Still, she had been sitting for more than an hour since the last man left. Her tight bonds had numbed her wrists, and the rag inside her mouth was dry. Her breasts ached. She coughed and sniffed. *Where is she?*

She had tried to move her chair, but the ropes were too secure and the chair too heavy. Instead, she sat there, chin dipping downward before rising against her straining neck. She heard heavy footsteps outside the door, the murmuring of voices. *Come on!* Then they were gone, and only the sound of the dying embers of the fire accompanied her. Her gaze moved to another door in the room, closed and filled with nothing but silence behind. *What is he waiting for?*

The hot flames kept the sweat running down her clothes. Every inch of her body was soaked with sweat. Every inch of her body had also been groped as the cutthroats took their time and turns, bringing her up the stairs. It seemed that all had taken a squeeze, a grope, a poke added with a few lip licking lusty glares. She'd never been violated in any manner before. She had a bad feeling the worst was yet to come.

Be strong, Kam. Be strong. You can survive this. You have to, for Erin.

Everything had been a disaster since Venir left, most particularly her. She'd been falling apart for months. She could not figure out if it was because of him or her. She was a woman that always knew what she wanted, but lately all she had been doing was second guessing herself. *I'm a fool, and now my baby is going to die.* She couldn't help but think that was already a possibility. It was killing her inside. *No!* Her body shuddered and heaved against her painful bonds as fresh tears streamed down her rosy cheeks.

She flinched as something soft and delicate wiped the tears from her cheeks.

"Even in the most disagreeable situation, you are still the most captivating woman I've ever seen," a voice said from nowhere.

Palos!

She mumbled angrily behind her gag.

A sinister laughter followed as she felt a finger running across her lips. The hairs on her arms recoiled, and fear raced down her spine. Had he been there the whole time?

The voice of a gentleman charmer spoke again.

"It's a shame to bind your full and perfect lips. They are the color of my favorite wine, and I can only imagine that they taste all the sweeter."

She thought she had died when he said his next words.

"Welcome to your new home, Kam."

It's all my fault. It's all my fault. It's all my fault.

Lefty sulked within, his mind a place of misery. Gillem was quiet at his side. The tavern however, Palos's home, the prison of Kam, was full of rude comments and raunchy jokes. The things the men said about Kam and Palos were sickening. Vile. Evil. Incomprehensible to his young mind. All he could do was sit there like a mute, helpless and full of worry. There was absolutely nothing he could do.

Gillem, however, seemed content to smoke his pipe and drink ale after ale. His halfling mentor smiled and played along with all the congratulations of his brethren, like a wealthy brother returning home.

"Master Gillem, can you kidnap me one of those?"

"Who carried the left breast and who took the right? Take me next time; I'll carry them both."

"Her back must be strong from carrying all that milk. What meadow did you find her in?"

The master thief just slapped his knee, smiled and laughed. All Lefty could do was wallow within, a silly smile on his face. *Smile and everyone will think everything is all right,* Venir had once said. What would Venir do? What would Melegal do? Kill them? Stab them? Save them?

One of the cutthroats swayed into him, spilling ale on his clothes.

"Watch yourself, tiny one!" the man said before staggering away. "Yellow-headed rodent."

There's must be something I can do. If I could just find Erin.

He'd been concentrating as well. His mind was still at work beneath his thick locks of blond hair. The room was full of rugged voices, each expressing fantasies while the others commented in demented delight. There was no mention of the baby girl Erin, however. That worried him. *Please don't be dead.* Someone in the room had to know where the baby was. They all couldn't keep their mouths shut. What had Melegal told him long ago? *What they aren't saying, their bodies are showing. Watch close and see and hear as well.*

"Eat something, Boy," Gillem said in his ear, interrupting his thoughts. "Blend in. Yer suffering is showing. Palos has little need of you now, so ye act like yer a brother of the guild."

For the first time in his life, Lefty felt the urge to jam a dagger in another living person's body. *SCUM! They are scum. I am scum.* His eyes drifted past Gillem's bobbing head to the doorway about the stairs. It was hard to imagine what was going on up there. A tiny fire ignited behind his heart. It was his fault. He had to fix it. From the corner of his eye he noticed a man he'd not seen before, entering the tavern. A nasty scar went from his chin to his ear, and his left eye was milk white. He gave a quick nod to the crossbowman called Diller, on the balcony, then disappeared back outside. Lefty was certain that no one else even noticed, not even Gillem.

Diller headed down the stairs and had quick words with one rogue and then another. The two men finished their drinks before departing without another word.

"Gillem," Lefty said, another minute after the two men were gone, "may I take a moment?"

Master Longfingers' eyes were bloodshot and blurry from all the smoke as he said, "Er … well, don't go far or be gone too long. And come back with more tobacco."

He still had a heart, Gillem just couldn't let it show as he ignored the halfling boy's departure. There was little he could do to save the woman or the child, and he felt horrible for it. It was not natural for a halfling to do such atrocious things. They were simple people that had a knack for getting into trouble with the other races. Why they were drawn to them, he could not figure, but they offered them things the halfling world did not. And like a curious cat, Gillem found himself plunging deeper into the lowest of wells. He never figured it would have gone this far.

Patience, Gillem. Patience.

Even he'd been cut from Palos's loop. He'd been too close to this one, and the Prince of Thieves was privy to that. It didn't help matters that Thorn had not returned. That would only make matters worse for everyone: Kam, Erin, Lefty and him. It was a dangerous time, indeed. Still, Lefty Lightfoot just might have the stones to figure a way out. The boy could do things that he could not, and his heart was still good. Time, however, would be running out. He'd seen many women come to the Roost but never go, woman or child. So he laughed, swapped stories, smoked and drank. *Farewell, friends of fiends.*

One second there was nothing but a table of gold before her and in the next Palos had revealed himself. His face, still handsome, yet demented, glowered above hers. His image faded out, then solidified once more.

Invisibility potion? A waste of potent magic.

"What are you willing to do to see your baby, Kam?" He asked with hungry eyes.

She looked deep into his eyes that rested beneath two well primped brows and said, "Anything."

The Prince of Thieves flashed a handsome row of teeth.

"I find it hard to believe, but I like what I am hearing. Hmmm."

He kneeled down and tore the pants around her leg wound.

"We can't have this holding back your efforts." She groaned as he applied pressure with his thumb. "Still tender, I see." He grabbed a small jar from the table and pulled the lid off, revealing a light blue salve. He gently rubbed it into her leg.

A wonderful sensation, burning and soothing, filled her as she watched the wound close shut. He began messaging her thigh with his nimble fingers. It felt good, comforting, and her eyes began to roll up in her head. *No. Stop.*

"Relax, Kam. That salve will take away more than your pain." He kissed her knees. "It will subdue your vanity as well. Enjoy."

Her head began to roll along her shoulders as the euphoric sensation set in. She felt something being clasped around her neck. A collar.

"This will keep you from mumbling any nasty spells," he said, lips nibbling at her ear.

She had already made her mind up that she would do whatever it took to see her baby again. Her mind was still her own, but now she was so relaxed, as if she had slipped into a warm bed of fox fur minks. Palos slowly removed her gag and other bonds. She was free. Magic swelled within in her then flowed back again. The next thing she knew there was a goblet of wine in her hand. She gulped it down. It was good. She felt good. She felt guilty for feeling so good. *Focus. You've got to see your baby.*

"When can I see my baby?" she asked.

"Follow me," Palos said. He walked with grace that belied his girth, opened the door across the room and passed inside.

She rubbed her wrists and followed. The blood flowing through her body was almost painful from where the circulation had been cut off, but she felt loose. Palos closed the door behind her.

A large candle illuminated an otherwise dark bedroom. A large four posted bed covered in silk and cotton sheets seemed to await her. She fully expected her stomach to curdle, but it did not.

Palos spoke with the most calming and reassuring of voices. It suggested everything would be fine.

"What was it you were trying to say you would do to see your baby?" he said, dropping his robe and slipping beneath the sheets. *I can't be doing this.*

Part of her wanted someone, anyone, to come crashing through the door. The other part of her didn't.

She pushed her matted hair back from her eyes and took a deep breath. She let her clothes fall to the floor. Palos's eyes enlarged like saucers as she walked over, pulled the sheets from him and climbed onto the bed.

She could see his lips moving but heard nothing. She straddled the man, pushed his hands back over his head and dangled her breasts in his face. She gave them both something they'd never forget as a single tear dropped from the corner of her eye.

Chapter 52

IXTY-SEVEN.

Melegal slid his thumb back from the wrapped up coin of continual light and gazed in wonder. He was in a room: not a small dungeon only capable of hoarding a few prisoners, no, this was different. It was another world, capable of housing a tiny village. And that wasn't all. Mixed in with the man-made architecture were strange formations cut from the rock. It was alien compared to anything he'd ever seen in the city, or anywhere else for that matter.

Not at all what I expected.

He shivered. The place was foreign to his sharp senses. He wanted to completely unwrap the coin and let its full illumination blossom. For some reason, all he could think of was underlings. They'd forced droves of people to find shelter in the city. Maybe they were closer than he even expected. Why couldn't they be lying beneath the City of Bone itself? He flashed the beam of light over his surroundings and up the steps. The landing at the bottom of the steps had unlit torches at the ready on either side. *Somebody's doing something down here.*

He scanned his light across the room, noting the intricate patterns on the old tiled floor. There was something sinister in how the mosaic seemed to twist and writhe, the light reflecting as if the tiles were moving. He moved toward the exterior of the room, unable to shake the odd feeling drifting into his shoes. Ahead, an open chamber beckoned, and along the sides was a series of small wooden doors with heavy brass handles that were similar to the one he'd ventured through.

There had to be another way out. *Going back is not an option, Rogue.* But this far underground, where would any of these doors go? *What was this room used for? So strange. So odd.* He made his way along the perimeter of the oval room, every footstep light as the one before. The only sound was the occasional scuff of his boots and his soft breath through his nose. He stopped and inspected the key hole in one of the doors. The opening was large enough to insert the key from the top of the stairs. *Interesting.* He depressed the thumb lever only to meet with resistance.

Hmmm. It might even explain why the upstairs door was not secure as one would expect it to be. *The key!* Maybe that was indeed the key. He checked another door that was the same as the first. Pressing his ear to the door, he listened. *Nothing.* He tried another. Still nothing. He made his way to the open chamber and shined his light inside. *Keys!* Not one, but many, all lined on pegs along the curving wall, each the same as the first, but different. The teeth, similar to those on the key up the stairs, twinkled in the light. Each key head was different: round, oval, and rectangular shapes of some foreign sort, ancient and not of the common customs. Melegal sat down, crossing his legs, at the edge of the chamber. He'd need to think about this.

Trap. It must be. He rubbed his chin. *One. Two. Three. Four. Five. Six. Seven pegs.* He looked over his shoulder and scanned his light over the doors. *Six doors. Threes keys left and three right. Lonely peg in the middle.* Perhaps that was for the key at the top of the stairs, which still begged the question: why was the door at the top unlocked? Even worse, why had Lord Almen come to his study in the wee hours of the morning? Lord Almen would expect him early, but who did he expect before him? He wasn't one to track the man, but such a time of day was odd, even for him.

He ran his fingers over the mosaic tiles on the floor. The grey grout between the small tiles was thin, but solid. On his hands and knees he followed his light along the outer edge of the round room toward the first key on his left. At an agonizing pace his light and hands scoured over the wall and floor, feeling for loose plates or difficult to see holes. It seemed unlikely that such a place would not be protected by something. After several minutes he slid his way underneath the first key. *Good so far.*

He rolled onto his knee, shined the light on the wooden peg that jutted out above his nose and gave it intense study. His slender fingers glided over the tiles around the peg. *I hate traps. Hate them.* He took another long draw of stale air through his nose. *Just do it.* He lifted the key from the peg like a feather. A tingling sensation ran from his fingers to his toes. He rubbed the cold key in his grip. *Good. Now, let's try door number one, shall we.*

The squeak of a door came from nearby. *Slat!* It wasn't upstairs. Instead, it was one of the doors in the main room, a door slowly being shoved outward. Melegal dropped his coin of light into his black silk pouch and flattened himself along the floor. The glow of a lantern filled the room. The door, the closest one to the right, was fully open now. *I'm dead.* He pushed his body backward, slithering over the tiles like a snake, into the shadows of the opposing wall. Three pairs of heavy footsteps clomped loudly over the floor.

Clearly not here to steal anything. He reached his hand down his belly, to the pommel of a well concealed knife. The door clanked back shut. A rustle of footsteps echoed within the chamber. The smell of sweaty men began to linger. *Good. No underlings.*

"Follow me," a husky female voice said.

Melegal could see the lantern moving toward the stairs as he peeked from underneath his cloak. They were well armed, weapons jangling on hips, their strides confident without alarm.

He's expecting them. Excellent. But where did they come from? On silent feet he dashed across the room and caught sight of the two men and the woman heading up the steps before they disappeared around the corner. There was something familiar about the way the woman walked. The way she talked. The shadows in the darkness can remind the mind of many things. *Nah.* He crept from behind, up the winding stair case, from deep in the shadows, straining to hear any words that might help. A door opened. Three pairs of booted feet made their way through. The door closed, leaving him back in the utter black near the bottom of the steps.

Melegal leaned against the wall and fanned himself with his hat. He licked the salt from his lips. *I'm thirsty.* He ran the strange key through his hands. A feeling of satisfaction ran through him.

"Ah …," he clutched at his stomach.

A wave of nausea came, and he doubled over. A feverish sweat broke out on his brow. *What is happening to me?* He began panting for his breath.

The sound of a door opening burst in his ears. Whoever just went in to Lord Almen's was coming back. The sounds of booted feet were rushing down the steps, but Melegal was already on the bottom. Threatening voices began to shout. *What had happened? What am I doing here?*

He shut his eyes and recalled everything he'd already seen with the light. Through the pitch black he bottomed out at the stairwell, stumbled, and dashed through the dark to the last door he had the key for. Without looking over his shoulder he jammed the key in the door and turned. *Click.* A sense of dread filled him as the footsteps closed in. A cry and crash roared out from above. He propped the door open as he slipped off his boot, ran into the alcove, hung the key on the peg, ran back, pulled open the door, rushed inside and closed it. *I should have stayed home in bed.* He screamed, or so he thought he did. Something powerful lifted him from his feet, turned him inside out and hurled him through time and space.

"I saw nothing, Lord Almen," the woman said.

Lord Almen stood inside the alcove, touching each and every key. His instincts had never failed him. He had a sleeping guard in front of his office quarters followed by another coincidence.

He turned to the woman that stood a finger shorter than he and said, "But you did smell cinnamon, did you not?"

"As faint as the dew on a honeysuckle," she said, as the lantern light deepened the scars over her sensuous wine red lips.

Lord Almen walked around the room and said, "No man could have escaped so quickly, but we cannot be certain thanks to these two buffoons that stumbled in the stairwell."

"It will never happen again my Lord," she said, ramming her sword in the nearest man's chest. The other's eyes widened like saucers.

Slice!

Lord Almen hacked that one with his cutlass, biting deep into his shoulder and neck. The floor moaned with life, the tiles shifting and sucking. He watched in morbid fascination as the dead men's blood was sucked into the floor and disappeared. Their bodies withered and turned to dust. That chilling sight never grew old for the Royal. The chamber of death was as deadly as fascinating. He smirked.

"As for you," he said, wrapping his arm around the woman's waist and kissing her neck, "it's been too long, my little black queen."

"Don't you mean Brigand Queen?" She purred.

What happened?

The door handle Melegal had been holding was gone. Part of his mind should have been as well. He patted himself up and down. *Dagger. Boots. Belt. Coins. Knife. Hat.* He couldn't be where he was, though. The room was still black as night, but his ears were on high alert as his fingers found the edges of a wall. He fully expected to be inside of a corridor or tunnel of some sort, instead it was nothing more than a closet and another stone door. He ran his fingers over the keyhole, kneeled down and took a look. *Huh?*

He pushed the door open and walked through.

The woman in the room screamed and jumped so high her head almost hit the low ceiling. The startled look on her face was one for the ages.

"W-Where did you come from?" she stammered as she pointed at him.

Melegal shrugged, looking over his shoulder and said, "The bedroom."

He might as well have been a ghost in her eyes, and he liked it. *I don't know what happened, but that really was something.* "Perhaps you should sit down," he said.

Instead, Haze came over and wrapped her arms around him. He could feel her body tremble like a frightened animal in his arms. *Oh, this is good.*

"You're real. That's all I need to know," she sighed.

It was the kind of answer he needed for now, and if anyone should sit, it should be him. *Keys.* There were seven in his life now, one as significant as the first. Great power lay within one, but what power did one have with all seven? He pulled his hat off and tossed it on the peg with a little laugh. He'd managed to dodge certain death. *Not too shabby, Rat.*

Haze filled his hand with a glass of port.

He shrugged at her and propped his feet up, letting the crackling embers warm them and wondering. What kind of power did Lord Almen have? How desperate must Sefron have been to align himself with him? But, how could Sefron have ever known?

"Uh … I missed you," Haze said, rubbing his shoulders.

"Not now, I'm still trying to figure out how I got here."

"But, when did you … I was just in there."

"All in due time Haze, now shush, and relish in my presence."

He pinched the bridge of his nose and rubbed. His heart was still beating like a bunny rabbit's. His moment of doom had passed, but that wasn't all. His obsession with finding the key had moved on as well. Whatever possessed him to do something so foolish? As desperate as he was, he'd never considered breaking into Lord Almen's office, and he was certain Lord Almen would have his suspicions. Still, the keys had his undivided attention now. Where did those other doors lead? Could they take you anywhere you ever wanted to go? And what was with all of those strange markings on the wall, the floors?

The dawn's first light crept in through a small stained glass window over the tiny kitchen area. Its bright light ate at his brain. It was time to get up, but all he wanted to do was go to bed. There was something he had to do, though. *The Time!* Haze squeaked as he jumped out of the chair and grabbed his hat.

"Where—?"

He snatched the bottle of port from the table and headed out the door, bounding the steps two at a time. He had a meeting with Lord Almen at the castle, and he was already late.

CHAPTER 53

AFTER ALL HIS YEARS DREAMING of adventure, Morley Sickle'd had enough over the past few months. It was time to kill himself. He climbed willow branches. *Pickles. Pickles. Pickles.* Crawled out on a branch. *Cheese. Cheese. Cheese.* And dove headfirst into quicksand that awaited him below. *Jig. Jig. Jig.* The first moments weren't so bad. The murk was warm and comforting as he sank, ever so slowly, into its awaiting darkness. He could hear nothing save for his own heartbeat. In a few moments he'd be listening to his last. *Peace.*

Elsewhere, Scorch, the omnipotent man, was distracted. Swamp trolls, six in all, had taken them by surprise. Morley's man-sized captor, blond hair flowing over his shoulders, was swinging a glowing great sword he'd procured from thin air. The trolls piled around Scorch, twelve feet of evil and hate, teeth chomping at the man who'd invaded their swamp. The trolls didn't stand a chance, but Morley had seen his chance and fled.

Instinct seized his withering bones. His air supply came to an abrupt halt as he sucked his first taste of sandy bile down his throat. It was awful, choking and dying. Suddenly, life didn't seem so bad. *Help!* The quicksand continued to surge down his throat, burning his lungs, as he swam with utter futility in the puddle. *I'm going to die.* His body twitched and lurched. *Scorch!*

Morley hacked. A deep breath of air filled his sandy lungs. He coughed and hacked more. He was on his hands and knees, his body shaking in pain from his violent seizure. It was pure joy compared to where he was before. The grit of the land was a familiar companion as he wiped away the wet dirt that covered his eyes. The first thing he saw was gleaming steel sunk deep into the ground. A pair of booted feet straddled it.

"Morley, seriously, what did I tell you about killing yourself?" Scorch said, voice tranquil with a layer of agitation.

He tilted his head up. Scorch's gore splattered face was almost serene, eyes glittering like torches. He coughed and spit.

"Morley," Scorch said in his upbeat and authoritative tone, "what do you say?"

"Thank you."

"Ah, now that's better, and you're welcome," Scorch said, squatting down in front of him. "Can you not see now living is better than dying now?"

He spit another mouthful of grit away. Scorch was a manner of man like no other. Dressed in a common tunic of leather, the man made the miserable, fog-laden swamp seem like a palace. His voice was soothing, but pressing, borderline arrogant and annoying. Morley couldn't help but like the man and hate him just the same.

"I suppose."

"Morley, why despise me? I've brought you no harm. I've showered you with gifts and look," he stretched his arm over the surrounding landscape, "I've killed all these evil trolls."

He looked over his shoulder. A troll, grey and green as a toad, lay sprawled along the ground, decapitated. Another leaned against a tree, clutching a gaping hole in its chest, dead. Entrails hung from the branches, and the foul smell of a charred husk lingered in the air. He shook his head.

"What is it, Man? Why don't you like me?" Scorch asked, his voice more demanding.

"I don't understand you." He paused. Scorch gave him a pleading look. "Uh ... you read my thoughts. You're too powerful!" he yelled, then covered his face, cowering.

Scorch stood up and said, "Ah ... so you want my power."

Morley's dander began to rise.

No! I want to be left alone! I want you to leave me alone!

Scorch studied his nails and said, "I can't do that, Morley."

Why?

"I like you, Morley ... and, I don't want to."

Morley felt his mind going numb.

"But, I'll tell you what I can do. I'll make you the second most powerful man in the city."

It wasn't such a bad idea. After all, he had been a jig churning nobody all of his life. Now, other than his peace of mind, he could have anything he wanted: Women. Power. Gold. Women. Besides, Scorch didn't seem to mind what he thought. Of course, he'd gone that route before, only to see a lot of people needlessly die and suffer at Scorch's will and pleasure. It had gotten to him, but better them than him.

"Now you're thinking, Morley. Now you're thinking like those troublesome Royals. So, you ready to clean yourself up and head back to the city?"

Morley nodded. *There seems to be no other choice.*

"Excellent. I'm starting to miss my moldy cheese and pickles."

CHAPTER 54

T RINOS SAT ON THE WATER fountain's edge, her sensuous arm dangling in its cool waters, basking in the early sunlight. The fountain bubbled and trickled from the mouth of a large fish, endless and sparkling. Around her were many people, some carrying pots, others clay urns, all nodding or bowing in greeting. Corrin stood nearby, a gangly man of medium height and build, wrapped in a light grey cloak, his fingers tapping on his chest. The man had been a thief and cutthroat all his life, but that had changed now. His purpose had been redefined, but his doubts remained persistent.

"They're coming," he warned. "I told you they'd be coming. You can't just open up a fountain in the middle of nowhere and think the Royals won't find out. Son of a boar! There's a dozen of them!" He shuffled closer to Trinos.

She yawned as she gathered her elegant feet and stood. Stretched out in the light, she saw Corrin gawp at her magnificent framework. He had the look of a child seeing a rainbow for the first time. Of all the men she'd encountered, his mind, though savaged by the brutal world, remained respectful. "I'll handle this. You just see the others to safety."

"Er … safety?"

She gave him a look.

"Right away," he said. "Get your pots and go, rodents! The Royals come to fetch their water. They'll have your hides if they catch you with it. Skin you like hogs. Especially you," he said, pointing at a fat woman that waddled as fast as she could, carrying a full pot of water between her legs. "Yer gonna need more water than that to wash that thick hide of yours, Tula!"

Trinos smirked. Corrin was as effective a communicator as he was crude, and for some reason she liked the way he said things.

Two rows of horses trotted in a direct path toward the fountain. The men atop the mounts wore heavy armor, swords dangling from saddle scabbards. One lone man carried the banner whose gold and forest green colors she'd already come to know. They spread out, cutting off her path from going anywhere else, as well as Corrin's. She gazed up at a large man who was blocking her sunlight.

"Can I help you?" she asked.

Trinos could feel their needs: their hunger, anger and lust. The dark clad men weren't here for negotiations. Instead, they were here for humiliation and with orders to destroy, if need be, all the people she protected. In their sight, not one was worth saving. Six of the twelve men swung their legs from their saddles, dropping heavy boots onto the cobblestone road. Corrin became pale at her side as the formidable group of trained soldiers closed in.

The leader folded his arms over the neck of his mount and leaned forward. He had a thick head of yellow hair and a black mustache. He ran his eyes up and down her body, then flicked them towards the burbling fountain and back to her. He cleared his throat.

"This fountain is not for public use. It is property of the Royals." He took a closer look at his surroundings, his black brows arching. "District 27 is under the watch of the Kling household. You are trespassing. You must go."

The soldier's voice was cool and condescending at the same time, his thoughts wicked, but in control. He'd been with many fine women before, but nothing that compared to her. What did women think of such men? *Pigs.* She smiled and offered a suggestion.

"We are only serving the needs of the Royals. No harm is being done. Come, let your horse and men drink from this fountain of Bish's cooling waters. Perhaps you would like to help serve this purpose as well?"

The man blanched and swallowed hard. His face became knit with confusion. She could feel the others begin to thirst for something other than herself. Their eyes began to gaze over the water.

A feminine chuckle came from nowhere, followed by a clapping sound.

"Bravo, Radiant One. Bravo."

Trinos gasped. The horses stirred. Something humanoid shimmered in the air.

A short haired woman, clad in robes of deep purple with copper trim, appeared a few feet away. She was older, her face crinkled like a sun beaten hag, her eyes luminous and dangerous. Many earrings pierced her ears, and mystic power emanated from her persona. She was hunched over as she looked Trinos up and down.

"My, what a beautiful spell you have woven, Sorceress," she said in a voice as frozen as ice. "I myself may have struggled with such a powerful suggestion. You have all of these dogs' tongues hanging from mouths, and you have their tails wagging. Next, they'll be romping in the waters like children." The woman's bracelets jangled as she lifted her arm and snapped her finger.

Pop!

The soldiers blinked and rubbed their glazed eyes. Trinos cringed. How had this woman evaded her detection? It seemed Bish had surprises for even her.

"I only offered them a drink from my fountain, no spell required."

The woman let out a short laugh as she rubbed her knobby chin.

"A well versed liar too, I see. Hmmm … so tell me where you hail from," the woman said, fondling her platinum hair. "What is your name?"

"Trinos. And you are?"

"Manamis. Lorda Manamis Kling," she said, looking for a reaction.

"Pleased to meet you," Trinos said, extending her hand.

Manamis slapped it away. Her voice took on a more dangerous edge than before.

"Fool! You're about to be defiled and then shackled by these very same men. These pathetic people will be slain and fed to the furnace. You dare try to place your hand upon a Royal? I'll have your hands removed, your tongue cut out, your pretty eyes gouged—"

Trinos fell to her knees. Corrin followed suit, trembling at her side.

"I beg forgiveness, Lorda Manamis Kling!" she cried. "I only sought good—"

"Too late to grovel, you little necromancing whore! Soldiers! Seize her and slay these wretched people! Each and every one!"

Trinos kept her head down, hiding the smile on her face. She saw Manamis's feet shuffle back toward the men.

"What are you waiting for? I said seize … er?"

Trinos lifted her chin and watched the look on the stupefied woman. The men, each and every one, were gone.

Manamis looked like someone was pulling her tongue from her face. Her ringed fingers twitched and grasped in the air. Trinos could feel the woman's power growing, her fingers glowing. Manamis's power was dismaying. Trinos had yet to sense such a force before now. The woman's shout could be heard echoing over a quarter mile round.

"Impossible!"

She whirled on Trinos, hands on hips, as she looked down on her like a mother over a spoiled child.

Trinos's eyes radiated in the reflection in Manamis's sunken eyes.

"District 27 is under my good care, Manamis. Go in peace, and do not return ..."

Manamis hissed a reply, "Never! Your illusion does not fool me." The older woman flinched at the sound of horrifying screams coming from above.

Manamis looked up just in time to see the Kling soldiers falling from the sky. Metal and screaming flesh smashing into the cobblestone road was as sickening a sound as there ever was, and they splattered all around the street. Manamis gawped at the gore as the horses reared and galloped away.

"As I was saying," Trinos said, dusting off her hands, "go in peace and do not return, or die in a fashion far more horrible."

Manamis gave her one last look, eyes narrowing like needles before she screeched and disappeared.

Corrin stood up and said, "Think she'll be back?"

Trinos shrugged, "Certainly. She hungers for power. She won't be able to let that go."

"Why not kill her?" Corrin said, examining a nearby pile of flesh.

"She'll have an awful lot of explaining to do. For her, that's worse than death. After all, she might not survive her explanation."

Corrin yelled out, "Somebody get a cart and some shovels. Make it quick, else we'll have a swarm of flies all over." He put his hands on his hips. "What a mess, but I like it. The only good Royal is a dead Royal."

She resumed her seat by the fountain and let out a soft sigh. *Next time, I better be more careful.*

Chapter 55

Tonio didn't even notice the down pour of rain as he sloshed through the city streets. Tiny rivers were filling the sewers below, forcing him to abandon the sanctity of his rotting abode. The rain splattered on his scarred and split face as he looked up into the sky. The moons were not there. He'd grown fond of them, two beacons that he could trust. Their light gave him clarity.

His mother, Lorda Almen, used to walk with him through the castle gardens at night. She often commented on the moons. Her gentle arm always hung inside the nook of his elbow. He was walking in such a fashion now, down the flooding street, not paying any mind to the district in which he wandered. There was no cause for alarm. Few—barring all murderers and criminals— ventured out this time of night, and the rain made for an even more unlikely reception.

"Mutha," he said. "I come soon home."

He growled. His garbled voice was beyond comprehension. Yet he talked to his imaginary mother all the same. Reflecting on fragments of memory, he tried to explain to her what had happened: a two-headed beast had mauled him. He never contemplated how he now lived. He'd died once, or almost had. He'd been resurrected by an underling, only to be severed in twain by an axe as big as the moon. Spidery men had brought him back. Stitch by stitch, their threads laced with fine magic had meticulously taken his innards and put them back inside him. He told his imaginary mother how his throat had been severed and re-sewn, which was why his tongue was thick as leather. He told how somewhere in there, he'd fought a man with a spider's head to the death. His memories were a blur most days, but today they were good.

He looked up to see where his booted feet had taken him. A sign hanging on two chains swayed in the wind. A monstrous creature of color was painted on the wooden sign: a lion, serpent and goat all on one body.

"Kye-mar-ah."

A familiar feeling swept over him as he stepped inside the entry way. He pushed his way through the heavy double doors and found himself face to face with two men every bit as big as he. He paid the startled looks on their faces no mind as he stood dripping inside the foyer.

A bald-headed man unfolded his meaty arms from his chest, said, "Your fee is triple," and held out his hand. Tony reached inside the folds of his tattered cloak and handed the man a small purse. The two men smiled, parted and watched him pass. There was a familiar smell, sweet and musky. The interior décor was refined and uncommon. The smoky room quieted as he made his way to the bar and sat down.

The red-faced bartender recoiled. "Er … What will it be?"

Tonio looked over his shoulder at a table where a finely dressed and aghast couple sat. The table was filled with bottled wine and steaming food. He tipped his chin up.

"S-Sam get." He dropped a small gemstone on the table.

Sam's eyes popped open as the fire-burst gemstone disappeared under his rag. "Right away."

For several minutes Tonio sat, motionless, while the other patrons quietly made their way out.

One by one they rustled by, casting nervous glances his way, before disappearing through the front and rear doors. If he noticed, it didn't show. Sam the barkeep, in the meantime, filled a stone cut tumbler with a bottle of grog. Tonio sniffed it and drank. There was a burning sensation, and he coughed. He snatched the bottle from the counter and tipped it up. Down his throat it poured, one ounce after the other, burning like living fire and filling his belly. He slammed the bottle on the bar.

"More!"

More came, and food followed. He stuffed every tasteless bite inside his mouth and chewed. The steak, bread, cheese, and rice did little to fill him, but the grog and ale offered something good. That's when a strange feeling overcame him. He shifted his big hips on the stool as he turned.

Six Watchmen in brown hats with black bills stood soaked from head to toe, dripping on the floor. A net was stretched out by the two on opposite ends. He heard one of them say, "On my signal, men." Tonio's face offered a jagged smile, and he leapt behind the bar.

The net whipped through the air, its weights smashing into bottles and clearing the shelves as Tonio crawled down the barkeep's alley.

"You missed him, you idiots! Kill him! Kill him now!"

Tonio rose behind the bar and caught the tip of a sword being buried in his shoulder. He ripped his sword free with his other hand, sneered and stabbed his assailant's face. He rolled over the bar and squared up against his attackers. In a rush they came, their steel clashing into his.

Clang! Clang! Clang!

Their arms juttered like bowstrings as he swatted them away. He could feel something now. He was alive within, a swordsman.

Clang! Stab!

One man clutched at his bloody belly, his sword clattering on the floor.

He ducked under another man's blow and cut open the skin beneath a third man's chin. He punched a forth in the nose with the pommel of his sword. The men came on, one at a time, at a speed that seemed too slow to measure.

Cut! Stab! Thrust!

Down they went.

More men spilled through the back door as others screamed and scrambled to the front. His fingers closed around his other hilt, ripping the blade from his sheath, and the swarm of men began to fall even faster.

Chop! Chop! Chop!

Stab! Stab! Stab!

Thrust! Thrust! Thrust!

He was lightning in a bottle of blood. The screams of pain and cries of alarm were a symphony in his mangled ears as metal clashed and chopped through bone. The decorative room was getting a makeover, velvet curtains and polished floors now coated in red blood and grey guts.

One man, stout as a stone, came at him with a heavy war hammer, only to be sliced like a dinner roast. Tonio felt his sense of worth begin to return. He'd been there before, fighting and scrapping among his comrades, but now he was something else. He was powerful. Supernatural.

"TONIO!" he shouted as the men of the Watch ran.

Others tried to drag away their dying friends as Tonio noticed Sam the barkeep shaking with horror. The man's blood-speckled face said it all. The barkeep knew him, and more importantly he knew himself now. Smiling, he showed off his blood-stained teeth as he sat down at the bar, his work done.

"Grog."

Both of Sam's hands trembled as he handed over the bottle. To Tonio's surprise, the barkeep spoke, "Y-You killed about a dozen Watchmen, T-Tonio."

Tonio tilted the bottle to his lips and drank.

"Ah!" He wiped his armored sleeve on his mouth and said, "And I'll kill a hundred more … you included … if I don't find the man called Venir."

CHAPTER 56

"**S**INCE WHEN DO UNDERLINGS TAKE prisoners, Venir?" Slim was filling a small canteen from a drying stream bed.

They'd been running for what seemed to be hours, but Slim had reassured him they'd lost any pursuers by now. A simple spell, the cleric reassured him, would throw anything off their trail. The cleric, Venir knew, was very resourceful like that, but he still kept looking over his shoulder from time to time.

As for the man's question, Venir didn't have an answer. The women, Adanna and her mother whose name he did not know, most certainly were dead. If not, the torture would be unimaginable. He sat on a large stone, head down over his hulking shoulders, drawing with a stick in the dirt. He'd tracked the underlings as far as he cared to go. Any closer and there was no telling what he would do.

He huffed. "Since when does anything in this land do what it's supposed to do?"

"Good point," Slim said, standing up and stretching his long limbs. The man looked like a crane in his pale green robes and sandaled feet. "So, you aren't really going to try and rescue them, are you? It would be suicide."

Venir looked up with a grim smile, "For who?"

"Oh, listen to you. Ready to put on your shiny helmet and take on an entire regiment of underlings now, are we? Well count me out. I'll just flap my way north, like everyone else."

"I'd be lying if I said I didn't want to try and kill them all. As for the women, well Adanna stuck her neck out for me, else I'd be dead already. I have to do the right thing."

Slim laughed. "The right thing? Since when is dying the right thing? Venir, you can't do it all on your own. Your weapons can only take this fight so far. It's a thousand to one, not including all the other creepy crawlies. You'll be spider food by dawn."

Venir shrugged. "Anything's better than the Mist. Besides, I had time to realize that's what I do."

"Well, why don't you get serious about it, then?"

He cocked he head and said, "I am serious."

"No, you're being unrealistic. Raise an army and protect this land from the fiends."

The thought had crossed his mind, but that was long ago. Before Brool. Before he became his own one man army.

"I'd rather raise my one axe instead."

Slim shook his head.

"You said nothing lasts forever, what then?"

He looked up towards the suns. They were hot on his face, and it was good. He took a drink.

"I'll become a cleric like you."

Slim raised his arms over his head and said with exasperation, "You lunatic! Clerics don't chop the living up into little pieces. What am I going to do with you? I've walked these lands for decades, even before you were born, but I've naught seen one like you, Venir: half happy, half mad. All at the same time. I don't understand you." He kicked the dirt.

Venir didn't understand himself, nor did he care to. He didn't understand Slim's point of view, either.

"What difference does it make if I'm happy or mad? I'm still going to kill underlings."

Slim responded in a mocking voice, "I'm still going to kill underlings."

Venir slung his pack over his monstrous shoulders.

"Don't go all girlie on me now, Cleric. We've got some scouting to do."

They made their way over the slick greenery of the twisting jungle to a cliff face that dropped off behind the trees. Venir wiped the sweat that stung his blue eyes as he crawled to the rim of the edge. Slim slid up beside him as they peered down. Anger and fear began to churn inside his stomach as he scanned the scenery below. He looked over at Slim. The man looked like he'd just swallowed a crow.

"I'm not going down there," the cleric said, his voice barely audible. The cleric then handed over the small spyglass they'd salvaged from Hogan's belongings.

He lifted it to his eye and soaked in every detail. Down on the plains, less than half a mile away, were underlings. Hundreds of them milled between rows of small dark grey tents. Their shapes and sizes were indistinguishable, but that wasn't all. Venir recognized their different manners. The underling warrior hunters called Badoon were there. They had dark leather armor underneath heavy cloaks. The foulest of creatures, the albino urchlings, were there as well, hunkered beneath canvas shades. Four nostrils flared on their faces as their teeth gnashed, and clawed hands opened and closed as they stood chained to posts. They were the creatures that had most recently wounded Chongo.

A rock of guilt stuck in Venir's craw. He'd convinced himself that Chongo would be all right, that his dog and the rest of his friends were better off without him. He was dangerous. Reality hit him now: as far as he knew, he'd left his most trusted friend, Chongo, to die.

He caught an odd flash of movement in the glass. A half dozen of the giant tarantulas were heading away from the camp in pairs: south, east and west. A pair of floating magi were in tow, each to the side of the basket of underling soldiers mounted atop the spiders. It was a scouting party, and most likely they were looking for him.

"See any sign of the women, Vee?"

He fought the images of the women woven inside a cocoon of webs, every drop of water sucked from their bodies. Perhaps they'd been taken as food for the spiders. He couldn't imagine what else was needed of them. His head began to ache as the suns beat down on his bullish neck.

"No. I think we're going to need a closer look."

Slim's head snapped in his direction.

"We! No, you!"

"Slim, sometimes you just have to decide what's worth dying for."

The slender cleric's jaw fell open.

"What happened to you in the Mist?"

"I realized some things: Living for myself isn't as important as living for others. I've been at war with the underlings for a long time, and that will never end. I've come to accept that. I think I could have saved more lives, but I'd been trying to avoid the battle for years." He pointed his two good fingers over the plains. "I've a feeling they wouldn't be here if not for my being gone."

"Your friends stick with you. You should stick with them."

"It's dangerous being close to me," he said, closing the spy glass.

"Well, you are the Darkslayer … and this is Bish."

"I guess I am."

"So, what's the plan?" Slim said, rolling onto his back and closing his eyes. "Do you want me to fly over like a bird? Or … I could turn you into a snake. You could slither right through them? How about a beetle?" Slim's long fingers fidgeted in the air. "They won't mess with a beetle. I like beetles."

The cleric continued on with one ludicrous idea after the other. In the meantime, an enormous tarantula had broken off and was coming their way, along with a host of underlings and two magi. Whatever was going to be done would need to be done soon. It wouldn't be long before the spider began to scale the cliff they overlooked.

Venir punched Slim's bony shoulder.

"Ow!"

"Can you control the spider?"

Slim rolled back over on his belly. His peaceful face bunched up with fear.

"No. I only do that with animals and people. Uh … that thing's moving pretty fast, Venir. It'll be on top of us in no time. Shouldn't we be going? Or is there something else that you wanted me to do?"

Venir caught movement from the corner of his eye. Something was rushing over the plain from the north, a small cloud of dust behind it. Venir pulled open the spyglass. A pair of underlings were running for their lives on the backs of smaller sand spiders like the ones Venir battled near the Red Clay Forest months ago. His knees burned at the memory, and he still had the scars from the acid-like venom to show for it. Another quarter mile behind them came a host of riders on horses. A banner of deep red, light blue and white led the charge of a few score war horses.

"Slim, look there," he said, handing him the spy glass and pointing.

"I'll be! Royal Riders!"

Venir could feel the thunder from the distant hooves now. He wasn't the only one. The spider stopped, pivoted its eight legs and headed back north. The fleeing underlings on the sand spiders had made the edge of the camp and sounded the alarm. The underling army assembled in moments, rank and file facing the charge. Venir's heart began to pound in his temples. He rubbed his hand on the flat of Brool's blades then slipped it between his pack and shoulders.

"Now's your chance, Slim. Come on."

Venir slipped off the edge and began his descent over a hundred feet down where the open plain awaited him. It was more of a steep grade than a cliff, so he slid more than climbed, scraping up his legs and arms all the way down. He didn't feel a thing. He gazed north. The Royal Riders hand formed a single line formation. A Royal banner billowed in the hot winds at one end and the other. The Royal Riders were a mishmash of elite soldiers from all outposts that represented most all of the Royal Houses. It was good thing.

"Sweet Bish! I never thought I'd be happy to see Royals!"

He flinched as something skittered down the cliff along his side. A beetle as big as his hand hung on the jagged rocks. It was black, with splotches of olive green and white. Two pale green eyes flared at him as two protruding black antennas seemed to make an angry gesture. The black and gold wings hummed to life, and the beetle soared toward the underling camp and disappeared in the light.

"Humph …"

Another fifty feet down and Venir noticed something else. Something writhed beneath the clay patches of the sun baked plain. Tiny holes opened up in the ground. A funny feeling overcame his senses. Something lurked beneath the surface: spiders, snakes or more underlings. Maybe something worse. The mammoth sized spiders were returning to camp. The small army of horsemen would have a hard enough time with one of them, let alone six. The underlings, he knew, were full of surprises.

He hurried his descent and dropped the final ten feet to the ground. He pulled out the spyglass and watched the odd gait of the giant tarantula. He was still half covered in the guts of the last one he'd slain. Atop the creature was another basket of six underling riders, chittering and pointing back and forth. The underling magi floated six feet above the ground like shades, covered in robes from head to toe. His mouth became dry, and he wished he'd taken one last drink.

"Bones of the dead!" he exclaimed as more underlings began to pop up from the ground in the distance. Their jewel speckled eyes infuriated him. "Too many underlings, not enough Royals." He found himself longing for a saddle between his legs. *Chongo.* He had to find his beast. He swung the spy glass back towards the riders on the spider. Their faces were turned his way. The spider stopped and turned. His blood froze. *Slat!* The brass on the spy glass gleamed in the dipping suns. He slammed it closed. The spider reared up on its back legs and charged as the underling magi soared his way.

Venir yanked his shield and helm from the old leather sack, along with something else: Mood's scale mail shirt.

"Well Bish blast my eyes! "He pulled it over his head, arms bulging under its short sleeves. He stuffed the sack in his backpack and strapped it on his shoulders. The air went still as he strapped on the helm and felt his blood rise. He could see, smell and hear everything as he stood like a gleaming metal statue in the suns. His powerful legs churned forward like a charging bull, and Brool whistled at his side. One second the blue sky was clear in the horizon and in the next instant the underling magi raised their clawed fingers high in the air. The ground beneath him erupted in white hot light.

CHAPTER 57

MELEGAL HAD ARRIVED BACK AT Castle Almen in time enough to see the head removed from the shoulders of the sentry he'd put to sleep hours earlier. The gloomy feeling followed him to the meeting that involved himself, Sefron and a very irritated Lord Almen. As usual, he averted his stare, but his tardiness was not to be ignored nor his tawdry clothes and breath bathed in alcohol.

The Royal Lord shared with him a sincere concern, which was odd, about an incident that occurred within the city. He was a scowling hawk when he dismissed him, saying, "I shall deal with you later." Melegal silently promised himself to do his best to see to it that later never came. Without further courtesy, Lord Almen departed, leaving him all alone with Sefron.

Sefron had been a different matter entirely. There he stood, as the cleric sat, inside the confines of a dark but quaint living room. All of the preparations for the Royal Coming of Age games were in order according to Sefron, who rambled on with one detail after the other. The foul cleric with a mouthful of blackening teeth kept showing his tell, to Melegal's chagrin.

"The *key* to this event ..."

"... and another *key* moment ... "

"Where the guests are seated will be *key* ..."

Melegal kept his internal fervor in check. The deceit was confirmed. Without a word, he hit the streets and left Sefron babbling all over himself. *I've found the key to killing you, Sefron. Won't be long.*

The pressure behind his eyes began to ease the farther he traveled from the castle. *For a few more hours I live. How grand!* The merchant class was in full swing as he weaved his way in and out of carts, carriages and burly laborers. There had been a time, it seemed so long ago, when he'd been sleeping in with a belly full of wine and playing footsies with a run of the mill wench. Those days might as well have been ages ago. His simple life as a swindler had changed for the worse. Those memories erupted from within as he stepped inside The Chimera.

Retching wasn't the greeting he'd expected, but that's what he got. A Watchman, barely a man, was vomiting on the floor. Melegal's pale demeanor flushed at the sight of all the blood and gore. It looked like twenty men had been slaughtered on the battlefield, but he could only count half a dozen heads. This wasn't the homecoming he was expecting. Behind the bar was Sam, a stout man with greased black hair and a pock-marked face. Sam was puffing heavily on a fat cigar, nervous, his smoke reddened eyes trying to blink away the horror.

Another city Watchman was jotting down notes on a piece of parchment and nodding in dismay. Melegal walked over and snatched the parchment away, saying, "That will be all, Sergeant." *Buffoon.*

The bigger man whirled in anger, but then caught the brooch pinned on Melegal's cloak.

"You pardon, Detective."

"Take your hounds and get some air."

The man nodded, rounded up his green-faced men and departed.

Sam the barkeep gave Melegal a curious look. He was certain that Sam's memory was as keen as his business sense, so it wasn't likely he'd forgotten his face, no matter how long ago it had been. Sam's eyes lingered on his brooch and then on his eyes.

"Don't ask," he said, pointing to the top shelf. "How about some wine?" He looked around. "White. "The barkeep reached below the bar, saying, "The good stuff is down here." He plunked a crystal wine glass on the bar and filled up half the glass.

"Tell me what happened, Sam."

Sam rolled his sleeves up over his thick forearms and said:

"A man came in here, tall and blond, as out of place and ugly as an orc. He was like nothing I've ever seen: face split with a jagged scar ..." Melegal stopped drinking. "... but he had coin, plenty of it. His armor had the insignia of a Royal. He could barely sputter a word, so I gave him some grog." Sam made a sour face. "He smelled like death. We cleared everyone out just before the City Watch came."

It can't be. Tonio's out butchering grown men like children. Can the man be stopped? Are my own rumors true?

Sam kept wringing the rag in his meaty hands, and sweat dripped from his brow.

"Detective, he was that Royal, the one you and your brawny friend tussled with. I thought I'd never see another night like that night."

Slat. The barkeep's eyes flitted to the floor where new planks had yet to blend in with the old. Melegal could have sworn that thunderous crack had broken Tonio's back when Venir slammed him to the floor. Instead, it had only raised his ambitions to a new level. He never understood what possessed that man about Venir.

Sam poured himself a drink and continued.

"Not until tonight, anyway. It was a nightmare gone mad." The barkeep was a hardened man, a retired soldier, but he was choked up when he spoke. "He mutilated those men. Fast and powerful strokes. Even when they clipped him with a blade or stabbed him, he still moved without hesitation, unhindered by pain and showing no mercy."

The barkeep wiped his brow and refilled Melegal's glass.

"What did he do after that?"

"I'd never been so scared in my life, not even on the battlefield. After they were all dead, things got really weird."

Melegal leaned forward, careful not to catch his sleeve on any blood, and asked, "How so?"

"He screamed his name—Tonio. That's when I knew for sure the monster was actually him. Then he asked me where he could find Venir. He said he was going to kill every straw-headed man in Bone until he found him. I've got a brother with blond hair. He shaved his head weeks ago."

"Pah! He is the one killing all those people?"

"I suppose, but he's a Royal, right? Why would a Royal—"

Venir is not even here, and he still causes me trouble. Melegal whisked his blade under the man's double chin. In a very audible whisper he said, "Listen to me, Sam. If you want to live much longer, you will forget Tonio's name. Understand?" He said it while pushing the blade farther up into the folds of the man's chin.

The barkeep croaked in acknowledgment.

"Another thing ... who drugged Venir that night he came back, Tonio?"

"He paid me. I didn't want to do it, but he gave me little choice."

It was probably true; Melegal was confident about that. But it wasn't the first time Venir had been removed from a bar under another's power. Something else was bothering him about the barkeep, though.

"The night of the challenge, you were part of that. Was Tonio acting on his own will? It seemed very uncharacteristic for the Royal to take up matters with a commoner."

"Er ... well..."

Melegal drew a thin red line on the man's neck.

"Yes." Sam stammered. "There are lots of Royal houses here. Their brats come in and make sport of my women and other patrons. But the Slergs and Klings set Tonio up. I already told the other Detective—the one with the hat—the same."

Hah! McKnight held back from Almen. I can't believe it! The Klings have a hand in this. The plot thickens. Dead big hatted bastard had some stones after all.

"Not a word of this, Sam. Because if you think Tonio is scary, you don't want to meet his father." He could feel the barkeep's Adams apple roll over the blade just before he pulled it back and walked out the door. Melegal had things to do. The Coming of Age Games were later today.

The Slergs. All but extinct now. The Klings. The 2nd most powerful house in Bone. And they wanted the Almens dead. This card will be worth something.

He made his way down the street, thinking of Venir, the man behind it all. His son Brak was scheduled to die today, and Melegal had no way of saving him. *Seems the mute galoot won't have the fortune of his father.*

Tonio, a dead madman walking, was on the loose, still seeking vengeance on his missing friend. *Can the impudent bastard even die? Perhaps it's time to reunite him with his gorgeous, succulent and vile mother. I could arrange that today. By the way, Lorda Almen, your son is the murdering bastard. He's in that alley.*

And on top of all that, Melegal knew something else: there was indeed a key that would cut him for the grasp of the Almens. He just didn't know where it would take him. Not that it mattered. *I see no reason to let Sefron live a day longer. Perhaps he'll find his way into the deadly arena as well.*

He removed his hat, fanned himself and made his way into the shade of the alleys. *Blasted suns.* It was one of those days, just as hot inside as out. He noted a grey cat pinning down a large brown rat that was inches from a sewer drain. *Almost.* A small tickle ran unseen fingers up his back as a hooded man in a cloak cut off one end of the narrow alley.

Gaghk! What is this?

He slipped his hat back onto his head and slowed his pace as the big man came his way at a brisk pace, along with a gleaming piece of steel. *Perhaps another course would suit me better.*

He spun back the other direction on the heel of his boot and was greeted by more twinkling sharp steel coming his way. He thought of the assassin that had hemmed him in months ago. The day the halfling saved him. *Not again.* He was pinned in with nowhere to go but up, and that wasn't possible. Or, cry for help. *Blasted thieves!* He whipped out his short blades, the Sisters. *Perhaps I'll scare them away.* The appearance of his blades only prompted a lowly chuckle and a charge.

Chapter 58

"**T**HIS BEAST IS MAGNIFICENT!" Cass exclaimed for about the tenth consecutive time in a day. "I find it impossible to believe that it serves a man. A warrior, you say? Warriors are hardly known for good character. Nothing but sweat and seed spouting louts that swill too much ale and boast impossible tales."

Fogle rubbed his neck and smiled. "It seems you've already met with Chongo's master then? Hmm ... or maybe you're referring to the brutes that kept your tent in the mountains? Maybe your true feelings for big sweaty men are beginning to surface."

Cass shot him a dangerous look from atop Chongo's saddle as they traveled south from Dwarven Hole. Then she turned away. *Please ignore me. The trip couldn't be any more unbearable.* He'd become accustomed to the cool settings below the ground, so the burning sunlight was already wearing him down. He had been picking at Cass and she picking back for the past day. There was little thanks for his part in their efforts at renewing Chongo back to full health. He'd expected some gratitude but was granted only further disappointment. *Women!*

The woman and Chongo led the journey, to where, he did not know. All he could do was watch Cass's sensuous figure sway in rhythm with Chongo's gait. The big dog's thick pelt of brown hair had returned, and its tongues hung playfully from its mouths. Cass was right: Chongo was a magnificent creature, padding across the toasted landscape, stiff black tails whipping back and forth in the air. Without having any idea where he was going, he had a feeling Chongo did know.

"Mood," he said to the giant dwarf that was riding a horse along his side, "do you really think Venir is in the South? I'd think we'd be heading north, towards the Mist, where we saw him last, and let Chongo sniff out his trail."

"The pooch knows where he's going, I figure," Mood added along with a plume of pale blue cigar smoke.

"You figure?"

"Aye. Whether Chongo's tracking er huntin', it's all part of the 'venture."

"Well, what would he be hunting if he's not tracking?"

"Underlings."

Fogle stiffened as he pulled his horse to a stop.

"Whoa. Now, let's go over this, Mood. I want to find Venir. I don't want to hunt underlings." His bookish voice began to rise. "Which is it? I don't want to be prepared for one thing only to be dragged into another. I just want to find the man and go home."

"Ye've forgotten how to use the gray matter in that melon head of yers already, haven't ya? Ye can't be prepared fer everything. You survive with what you got. Now, the land's crawling with underlings. If Venir's in the land, he goes where the underlings go. If Chongo is in the land, it's the same. Chongo will sniff out the black little fiends. If we kill 'em first, it's a good thing. Besides, why you think I brought me kin along? To protect yer eccentric lady? If ye want ta' go home, then go. Ya can drink all yer mother's milk ya want when you get there." Mood snapped his reigns. "Yah!"

Fogle sat as glum-faced as ever while the rest of the party trotted past him on ponies that looked like Clydesdales: ten grim-faced dwarves with notable scars, beards hanging down to their bellies, dressed in chainmail, partial plate and leather armor. Bringing up the rear was the biggest one of them all, a Blood Ranger like Mood, except his skin was dark brown and his beard looked like a burning bush. The dwarf's deep blue eyes met his as he stopped his horse and stared. Fogle noted the two swords that crossed his broad back and the enormous crossbow that hung from the saddle.

I guess we'll be dining with underlings after all.

"Alright, Eethum, I'm going," he said, digging his heels into the horse and trotting forward. *Saddle sore already.*

As he made his way back toward the front, his gaze wandered to the small of Cass's supine back. The woman, pale as cotton linen, chose to wear little more than her abundant hair draped over a tight rose-colored travel tunic woven by the dwarven women. The garment enhanced her excellent features, adding a more rugged tone to an otherwise soft looking woman. As if in a trance, he made his way up beside her.

"Ahem."

She left her chin high, pink eyes forward, delicate hands rubbing two of the massive dog's four ears.

He cleared his throat again.

She glared at him and huffed, "Oh … what is it, Flippant Fogle? Have you come to insult me some more? Make light of my yearnings? Boast about your moments splashing in a Dwarven bath?" She turned away. "Please, *my sweet*, layer it on."

He blushed. *My Sweet.* Had he actually said that? It seemed like the entire world had heard. The strangest thing of all was that he was positive he'd never even used the word in conversation before. He didn't even have a sweet spell component. Once again he found his tongue thickening in his mouth. *Blast!*

He fell back.

"You fool!" she said, whipping her neck around like a striking snake. "Get up here!"

"But, you didn't seem like you wanted to speak with me," he stammered.

"I just spoke to you, did I not, Fogle Fool!"

"Well …"

"And we are talking now, are we not?"

He dipped his chin and shook his head saying, "Yes."

"Then say what you must say. The journey is long, and I don't think the dwarves will be providing much conversation."

Fogle wanted to say everything and nothing at the same time. The woman captivated him like a string makes a cat watch and angered him like a bee stinging a raging bull. *I have no idea where to start. I wonder what Venir would say. Ah … I can't do it. I can blast an earth elemental to smithereens, but I can't spit out a single word to speak to a woman I've slept with before. Speak or die.*

"Well, did I ever tell you that your eyes are as pretty as a bed of pink roses?"

Cass's body lurched as she let out an abrupt chuckle.

Chongo's massive right head loomed his way and growled. His steed nickered and stammered.

"Easy, Boy," Fogle said, rubbing the horse's chestnut neck. He could feel the horse's heart thundering the same as his. *I guess I should have expected the laughter, but I didn't think it would piss the dog off, too. Now what?* He stooped over in the saddle and trailed a little further back.

"I'm still listening," Cass said as she stretched her slender arms in the air.

He noticed a tiny grin forming on the corners of her mouth. *I think she liked that.*

"Er … your hair is more lustrous than the twilight moons. As brilliant in the day as in the night."

She flipped her hair over her shoulders.

"When I see you, I can think of nothing. When I can't see you, I can think only of you." *Oh, that's horrible. Here it comes. More giggles. What will she call me now, Fogle Failure with Pleasing Words?*

She gazed over at him with a twinkling curiosity in her eyes and said, "Is that true?"

He shrugged and said, "I suppose."

"Humph. I like it."

"Well, your bosoms are as—"

"Fogle!"

"What?"

"You've said enough. Speak no more, or else ruin it." She shook her head. "I think I shall savor that nectar that just crossed your lips for now."

She smiled at him, warm and welcoming, before turning away. A great bit of relief filled him. Maybe he was beginning to understand women better after all.

Chongo stopped and hunkered down with a growl. The beast's shoulders rippled with agitated muscle, his snouts bared dripping canines, ears alert. A shadow shot across the sky, blotting out the suns for a moment.

"What in the …," he muttered, turning his head to the sky.

A massive projectile of rock come crashing down to the ground, barreling into the small host of dwarven fighters. Dust and rock scattered everywhere, coating them from head to toe in dust and smoke.

"Mood!" Fogle yelled, "What in Bish was that?"

He could barely see a thing. Out of the dirty mist, Mood pulled his mount along his side, giant hand axes ready to go.

"You take care of yer lady! Me and me men shall deal with the giants!"

"Giants!"

"Aye! Huzzah!"

A battle cry rose up from the dwarves as the tiny army scrambled onto their mounts and forged ahead. Chongo and Cass were right behind them.

"Cass!" he cried out, just as another boulder crashed into the ground ahead. He couldn't hear anything but thundering hooves and bellowing dwarves intermingled with a woman's terrified scream. *Giants and dwarves and druids, oh my!*

Chapter 59

The call. It had come after what had seemed like another eternity. Every moment away from Bish was as dull as dull could be. There was nothing of interest where he was, only other creatures as discontented as he, bored, lonely and isolated. He avoided them all, watching the world of Bish, waiting for the call. And when it came, he was thankful, if such a thing was ever possible for the imp called Eep.

He hissed with joy as he said his first words on his return to the main world of Bish, "As you wish, Master."

Verbard, the entertaining one, had recalled him with a summoning spell. He'd grown quite fond of the Underling Lord, despite all the powerful mage had put him through. Lord Verbard didn't hold his reigns as tight as his presiding master, the underling cleric Oran. Verbard respected his needs to kill and destroy and never made him hold back. And now, he was on a mission to kill again and this time his prey was not as typical as he was accustomed to.

Kill! Kill! Kill!

Eep salivated as he zipped in and out of the black tunnels that surrounded the Current. His large mouth hung open with razor sharp teeth waiting to devour his prey, and his powerful taloned hands clutched in and out. He could see and hear everything within a quarter mile as his bat-like wings hummed through the black. The sound came fast before it was gone, echoing over the waters, and when his prey turned, it was too late.

A troll, twelve feet of monstrous mass, stood in the waters, a large stalactite club gripped in its hand. Eep's large orb of an eye opened larger before narrowing as he zipped underneath the Troll's clumsy blow and plunged into its stomach. Eep's tiny earholes were filled with its wails and screams as he blinked his little muscular body—almost four feet of muscle and taloned fury—into the troll's belly and tore it from the inside out. He twisted the troll's innards, gashed its lungs and ate its heart before he clawed his way back out and watched the dying troll sink into the current. *More!*

Troll's blood wasn't as delicious as a man's, and the smell, even to his hawkish nose, was quite awful as he sputtered the gore from his wings. It was the seventh troll he had killed today, and it never got old. He was hovering over the waters now, head looking back and forth, when he heard a voice in his head. It was Verbard.

Eep, return!

His long serpent tongue flicked out when he said, "Yes, Master."

The battle with the trolls and the fish golem had taken its toll on the underling army, but those that traveled on foot reported back they had been unscathed. Verbard stood at the helm of the middle barge, alongside him Jottenhiem, his most vicious commander.

Verbard's silver eyes flickered in the blue lantern light as his clawed index finger scratched at the pale fur on his cheek. He scanned the surface above him, the tunnel once again opening up into a massive cave. Humans. He could feel their nearness. Thousands of them, soft, self-indulgent, weak but irrepressible. Now, he was going to get to lead the first strike into their very heart: The City of Bone. *With no more than 500 underlings, at that.*

"Jottenhiem, you've had more dealings with Kierway than I over the centuries. What do you think his plan will be for me?"

The Juegen commander's ruby eyes flicked to his, a fierce smile turned up on the corner of his mouth.

"Lord Verbard, he'll try to take command by offering assistance. No fighter believes a mage can do what a soldier does. His plans, however, are always kept close to the vest, the true ones that is. After all, what kind of leader would he be if he told us everything?"

True. Regardless of outcome, one underling always held out on the other, and this grand event didn't pose any reason to be any different. But why would Sinway go to all this trouble to get rid of Verbard? Was it indeed possible that he actually wanted to take over the massive human city? He couldn't shake the feeling there was less to it than that.

Something fluttered and landed by his side. Jottenhiem stirred in his armor, but his feet remained unmoved. It was Eep. Verbard reached over and stroked the horned head. *My little equalizer.*

"Seems such a small army to take on tens of thousands," Verbard said.

"They're soft, untrained. They'll flee the city like rats in a flooding sewer. Even if we all were to die, the City of Bone would never be the same. I can already taste victory, and it tastes good."

"You seem ready to perish, Commander."

"All of us Juegen are, but we rarely ever do." Jottenhiem shrugged. "Soldiers are meant to die on the battlefield, necks and elbows deep in their enemies' blood. I can't think of a better way to go than into the belly of the vile men, seeing them wailing and crying, burning through the city as we cut them down." Jottenhiem filled his armored chest with air. "Once it starts we won't stop chopping until we're dead. It shall be so … glorifying."

"Hmmm … I, however, have no plans to see any underlings die in vain." Verbard lowered his voice. "Let me be clear, Commander: our siege shall be slow, precise and deliberate. I'll not be turning our kind loose on a suicide mission. You need to be certain of my orders."

Verbard's fingertips glowed red hot as he held them in front of Jottenhiem's face. The commander's tiny facial hairs began to curl and stink as his face beaded with sweat.

"My orders alone, else you won't be the one to lead the Juegen into any battle."

Stone-faced, Jottenhiem bared his teeth as the tiny hairs on his face burned and drifted away. He managed to say, "Lord Verbard, my allegiance to the one that vanquished the Darkslayer is without fail. I'll do as you tell me and no other. You have my word as the Juegen Commander."

Behind him, Verbard was oblivious to the strange look on Eep's face. His fingers winked out. "Very good. Eep, is the rest of the way clear?"

"Ack … Y-Yes, Master."

"Is something wrong, Imp? You look like you've had too much troll."

"No-No. Troll good." The imp patted his belly. "Yum. Yum."

Kierway rose to his feet as the first half of Lord Verbard's army floated into the gray sandy beach that ran alongside the Current. His knees crackled. He'd been sitting for days if not longer, his only company the Vicious who remained steadfast by his side. He dusted the sand from his hands and made his way down the shore.

"Impressive," he hissed under his breath. It had been quite some time since he had dealt with an army of any sort. Now, before him another two hundred men were at his disposal, and two hundred more should be arriving later in the day. He had been aware of that much, as well as many other things.

As Juegen fighters, underling magi, Badoon hunter warriors, albino urchlings and other Underland horrors made their way on shore, he spotted Lord Verbard and his Commander, Jottenhiem. A briar of envy began to jab at his insides as he watched two of his least favorite underlings approach. Verbard's silver eyes glinted with power in the cave's strange twilight, which cast a faint illumination below the city. Kierway rested his hands on the pommel of his sword and nodded a greeting.

"Welcome, Lord Verbard. I see your journey bode you good will, but I was expecting six ships, not three. What happened? Has it been reported to my father, Master Sinway?"

He could see Verbard's eyes flare as he hung in the air, looking down on him with a sneer.

"I see you miss your father too much, as always, Master Kierway. Perhaps you should take him the message yourself. After all, I know you are not accustomed to handling things without his direct supervision."

Kierway glared back and said, "My father expects—"

"Your father expects to hear about success! Not trivial matters. We've a mission above that needs our direct attention, Kierway. We've a city to take over, whether it be with five hundred or fifty. The siege on Bone begins now, unless of course, you'd rather wait on your father to lead the charge?"

Kierway couldn't have been more insulted if Verbard had pissed on his head. His claws wrapped around the pommel of his sword. No one should talk to him like that and live! He noted the mocking expression on Jottenhiem's face as well. The Juegen Commander and he liked little of one another. He'd better be more careful. *Never send a troll to do an underling's job.*

"I see," he said, opening up his hands, "so tell me then, Lord Verbard, how can I be of assistance?" *Before I have you killed.*

Verbard's robe-covered feet lowered to the ground.

"Other than this army, what is it you wait for?"

"A bigger army."

"Don't dally with me, Kierway. Your father's and my conversations have been deep. I'll have the knowledge that you prefer to hide. What do you have to offer me for this invasion?"

"The key. I've an associate bringing me a key that is a great source of power."

Verbard's features darkened. His silver eyes flared. "Shouldn't this key be here by now? What does it do?"

"It opens up a portal into the city." *The likes that none has ever seen in centuries. As I understand it, as explained by my father, the underlings can travel from the Underland to Bone in a single step. An army with the key would be invincible.* So he believed.

"And when can we expect this key?" Verbard interjected.

"Any day now."

Kierway's heart almost stopped at what Verbard snapped out next.

"Tell me everything you know, down to the last detail. I shall locate this key and make preparations with our soldiers. Kierway, my first wave of destruction into the City of Bone will start soon, with or without this *key*."

CHAPTER 60

SHAME AND WINE. THEY WENT well together. Kam sat beside Palos's roaring fire and rocked baby Erin. The troubles of the world had faded, all the hurt and humiliation gone now that her baby was safe in her arms. Never had she felt so strongly about any living thing than her beautiful daughter. The baby cooed as she tickled her nose. Now all she had to do was figure out how to escape.

"Your daughter will always be safe here, Kam, and you as well," Palos said. "It was never my intent to harm either one of you." His fingers continued stacking the coins, row after row, on the table. "And I must say, last night my desire for you at all costs was justified."

The rocking chair she sat in creaked as she hummed a dreary tune. His words, last night and after, meant nothing to her. The words she said to him meant nothing at all either, but it had an impact on him. Palos was in control, for now. She just had to make sure she didn't get used to it. She couldn't be too unyielding with him, either.

"I'm talking to you, Woman."

She continued, her humming only interrupted between sips of wine.

He flicked a coin that struck her on the top of her forehead, leaving a painful red mark. Her cheeks brightened. The collar on her neck restricted. Agony ensued as baby Erin almost slipped to the floor. Her magic, what little of it was left, extinguished, but her burning desire to kill the man did not.

"Must you be such a child!" She was shouting. Baby Erin began to wail. "Now look what you've done, my prince! Oh dear Prince Palos, master of the sewers!"

Palos struck the coins, scattering them across the room.

"Silence that baby, you red-haired witch, else I'll have it washed down the gutters. They make a fine cemetery."

"You wouldn't dare!"

"Hah! It wouldn't be the first time, nor the last." He stood up, pushed his chest out and rocked on his toes. "Kam, you can have a good thing here or a bad thing, but whatever the choice—it will be *here*!" He poked his pudgy finger into the table.

He was a snake. A handsome, charming, chubby snake, but not one to make idle threats, either. *Don't push him too hard. Be strong for Erin.* She hoisted Erin on her shoulder, patted her tiny back and said, "If I had a little magic at my disposal I could keep her more content."

Palos's chuckle was low, insidious.

"You have all the magic you need between those splendid thighs of yours." He wiped a dribble of wine on the sleeve of his robe.

Kam felt her face flush. *Repulsive pig.* "You could at least let me clean myself up. Bathe my child, too." She bit her lip and added more of a pleasing tone to her voice. "Feel free to watch if you like. I just need to bathe."

Palos's eyes became orbs of lust. "I'll see what I can arrange," he said, sandals flapping on his heels as he made his way to the front door. She wanted more than a bath, though. She needed scoured from the inside out. She began to recoil within herself. *I can't keep doing this. I need to get out!* Erin's cries began to subside as she pulled her down and hugged her to her chest. She hummed some more.

Palos yelled from the inside of the doorway. "Diller! Fetch the halflings and some water. Lots of water!"

Lefty sat inside Palos's tavern home alongside Gillem, fingers latched and thumbs rolling backward and forward. It had been more than a day since he fetched Gillem his last batch of tobacco, and his back ached from taking cat naps on the dirty wooden floor. His world was collapsing. *What can I do? I have to do something!* Indeed, he had. He'd scouted a little, but that wasn't enough. He had to do more.

"Gillem," he said. "Can I try some of that?"

The master thief's smoky eyes widened in a moment of alarm before shifting back to normal. "Eh … are you serious? You want some ale?"

"The pipe, too."

"Really?" Gillem said, sucking on the long stem of the pipe before letting it out.

Lefty studied the halfling man's face. Gillem, always energetic and cheerful, was exhausted. His cheeks sagged under his graying brows and greasy head of busy hair. Gillem looked old, which had seemed impossible less than a day ago.

"I've nothing better to do, and I just figured, you have to start some time. And I'm bored. This is killing me. Maybe you can teach me cards, too." Lefty straightened his back and leaned forward. "I've been paying attention to them," he pointed with his lips, "and I think I'd be good at the cards."

Gillem shifted his hips on his stool, head still turned away and surrounded by a yellow blossom of smoke. Lefty felt a tingling on his hands. Melegal had taught him how to draw suspicion from himself. *Don't sit and stare. Be a part of something. Stare from within.* Who would worry about a smoking and drinking halfling, anyway? Besides, he'd already figured out where they kept baby Erin. But she'd been upstairs ever since he found the location. It was pretty easy finding a crying baby, but the suffering sounds were horrible.

"Here," Gillem said, handing him the pipe. "Take a puff, but don't inhale just yet. The tobacco smoke will sink in through lips and gum."

He thought of Mood, Venir and Chongo and how much he wished they were here. Georgio, too. What he wouldn't do to have coffee with his best friend once more. He felt the warm smoke and burning tobacco leaves fill his mouth.

"Hold it."

His jaws were popping out as he nodded.

"Good. Good. Now let it out … slowly."

He blew a long stream from his mouth and said, "Like that?"

"Yes. Good. Now take a drink," Gillem said, replacing the pipe with his mug.

Just as Lefty lifted the mug to his lips he heard Diller shout from above.

"Gillem! You and the boy! Prince Palos wants you now!"

Gillem's eyes flickered with surprise before he turned back and said, "Right away!" He snatched the ale away, adding, "There'll be more time for this later. Come."

Kam's eyes glanced over and away as Lefty and Gillem quietly made their way inside Palos's little throne room. Lefty looked pitiful and Gillem mostly drunk as they both swayed and bowed. Palos, a man below average height, towered over them, hands on hips. She hated the halflings, but for some reason she hated the tiny boy more than the man. *Traitor.* When she got free she just might have to kill him as well.

"As you well know," Palos began, "the prince has found his queen, and she'll need watchful servants for her spoilings."

Gillem and Lefty nodded, wide eyed and eager. Kam sneered.

"The lady's pleasure is ours."

"Indeed," Lefty added.

She caught his eyes for a moment, but the stare seemed much longer. The little halfling had a smug look on his face, something devious. A puppet of thieves. Nothing more and nothing less. Just another male that couldn't be trusted. *What happened to that sweet boy? Where did I go wrong?* She pulled the blanket over Erin's face and snuggled her. *I won't ever let that happen to you. I'm just glad you're a girl. Boys are rotten to the core it seems.*

Palos had a bouncing step as he strolled around in his robes, pale eyes dangerous and full of wonder. He'd been doing more than drinking wine and counting gold over the past few hours. She'd watched him sniff the kind of stuff he smuggled in to ruin the Royals.

"Kam and, er … what is the little nuisance's name?"

"Erin," Gillem added, smiling and teetering up on his toes.

"Whatever. So, they'll need clothes, fine ones. I'll be needing fresh linens, too. One of those cribs or a bassinet, I believe it's called. They'll need bathed as well. Yonder is my tub."

He pointed to a large tub that appeared to be made from dark marble and inlaid with gold and silver. "She and the child can bathe there as soon as the water is fetched." He gave Kam a hungry look. "And there shall be plenty of room for the both of us to carry on."

Kam half-sneered and half smiled. It was bad enough she had to sleep with him, but now she would have to bathe with him, too. *Perhaps I'll drown you in that grand tub of yours.*

"Diller!"

Diller swung the door inward.

"Where is the nanny?"

"She's coming, Prince." He took the toothpick from his mouth. "Coming up the steps right now.

A husky woman shoved past Diller and made her way inside, her hard eyes dropping on the table of gold. Kam didn't like the looks of her. Her hair was stringy, her face worn and haggard. She wore trousers and shirts like a man and her bottom lip was jutted out over her fat greasy neck.

"Who is this woman?" Kam demanded, watching the woman fold her beefy forearms under her saggy breasts.

"Meet my nanny, Kam. She'll be your baby's, too," he said as if she was a member of his family.

"I don't need a nanny, Palos. I can take care of my baby just fine."

Palos made an open gesture with his hands saying, "Why, certainly that's the truth when the child is here, but she won't be all of the time, and that will be most of the time, especially when I want you all to myself!"

The rocker teetered to the floor as Kam jumped to her feet.

"I thought we had an understanding, Palos! I've given myself over to you for my child. We both stay!"

Palos had a cool look on his face as he brushed white flakes from his shoulder.

"A happy servant is a pleasing servant. But an unhappy servant is still a servant. Like it or not, the baby comes and goes as I say. And you'll do good to take care of my needs if you want me taking care of your needs."

"You filthy bastard!" she yelled.

Diller opened the door to bring in a bucket of water and set it on the table. She watched as Palos produced a corked vial with a pale pink fluid inside and emptied it inside the bucket. The wooden bucket rocked and reeled.

"Quick, Gillem," he said.

The halfling man snatched the bucket as he rushed over to the tub and poured the water inside. The water kept pouring, as endless as the waterfalls.

Foolish man! Wasting more magic. The reckless use of magic offered a degree of hope. She was trying to think up a plan when Palos interrupted her thoughts.

"Don't worry, Princess. You'll have plenty of time to clean this filthy bastard up shortly." Palos walked over and peeled back a portion of her robe. She recoiled as she felt his kiss below her ear. He stepped away and said, "Diller, if need be, subdue the woman. Nanny, take the baby!"

"No!" Kam wailed. Baby Erin began screaming as Diller strong armed Kam. The nanny snatched and wrestled Erin away, but the wretched woman screamed as Kam clawed a piece of her face off.

"Oomph!"

Kam folded over on her hands and knees as Diller whopped her in the stomach.

Lifting her chin, Kam watched her baby being carried away. She glared at Lefty and said, "This is all your fault, you little halfling bastard!"

The boy just smiled and shrugged. All her hope fled.

CHAPTER 61

T HE TASTE OF ROCK AND metal filled his mouth as he gasped for air. Venir clawed through the rock that had just erupted below him as his helm screamed at him to move. Disoriented and aggravated, Venir arose from his rocky grave, his entire body coated in debris and dust. His black eyelets smoldered as his body coursed with energy and rage. The Darkslayer was back, and it was good. He shook off the stinging pain from the lightning and yelled.

"Is that all you have, Fiends!"

He snapped up his shield as a small barrage of black missiles assailed him from the robed underling on the left.

Tink. Tink. Tink. Tink.

They reflected away and sizzled into the ground.

"Hah!"

Another urgent warning came to his mind. Power coursed from the other mage's hands, sending a streak of energy searing downward. Venir stepped into it, shield first, and laughed. The mage's power slammed into the shield with blue and white energy, rocking him back, his feet sliding back in the dirt before the power faded.

Venir flashed the two underlings a fierce grin and charged their retreating forms.

"Now it's my turn!"

He ran and leapt high in the air. The first creature howled as Venir's fingertips caught the bottom of its cloak and pulled it to the ground. A pair of clawed fingers left a burning gash under his chin as he pinned it to the ground and choked the life out of it in his mighty grasp. The other underling continued its hasty retreat towards the camp and out of sight.

Thwwhip! A cord of web caught his shield. He sliced it away. "Blasted insects!"

The giant spider with its basket full of underling warriors had arrived. Venir held onto his shield as the spider began to reel him in. The monstrous beast's fanged mouth dripped with acid that sizzled the ground, and its beady red eyes were filled with hunger. A javelin glanced off the side of his helm. Another stuck in the ground by his foot.

"I'm going to kill your pet! I'll kill you all! HUZZAH!"

He was an inferno. His mind, metal and magic one. Underling destruction was his game. Venir was his name. And no spider, no matter how big, was going to stop him from slaughtering them all.

Venir charged. Bolts and javelins assailed him, glancing off his armor and web covered shield. He didn't feel a thing. Covering the thirty feet between him and the spider in an instant, shoving Brool down to the handle into the spider's brain. Its enormous body lurched and bucked, tossing the underling riders to the ground before it collapsed. Something sizzled Venir's skin as he chopped more hefty strokes into the huge arachnid's brain. Then he whirled on the scrambling pack of underlings, each face aghast and angry. It fed him.

Two, armored in leathers and chain, rushed up from behind, swords clipping at his sides as he dove over the spider's twitching legs and rolled back to his feet.

"There's no insect bigger than me! *"Keep moving!* Venir still had his consciousness as he parried their darting strikes that clanged from his shield and clipped the dwarven scale mail. He fought on as all of the underlings closed in, waiting for a blinding rage to consume him. One hard chop followed another, faster and faster. His massive iron-willed thews struck in powerful cobra like stokes.

Slice!

Brool removed a yellow-eyed underling's head from its shoulders, black-red blood spurting into the sky.

Crunch!

He chopped the knees from beneath another, while catching a wild sword stroke swinging into his shield with a loud *clang*. Venir wrought death, anticipated every move, weaved in and out of harm's way, every strike a death blow. A taloned eagle fighting sparrows. He cracked an underling's head open with his shield, cutting its attack short. He kicked another in the groin. Spiked another in the neck and cut the last one in twain at the waist.

Venir labored for his breath. His oily sweat mixed with blood and gore, some his, some theirs. Underling bodies were scattered on and around the enormous spider, making up a revolting sight. The stench of baking death was heavy in the air. The fight lasted less than a minute, but it seemed to go quicker. Venir jabbed Brool's spike into the heart of an underling that was twitching nearby.

He ripped it out and said, "Seven's a good start!"

He swung his helmeted head around at the familiar sound of battle. Steel crashed on steel, cries of mayhem and triumph roared inside his helm. He'd never seen so many fighting underlings before. The dusty smoke from horse hooves rolled over the camp with a flair of mystic energy cracking in the air. The fight inside him propelled his legs forward over the wasteland, of his own will this time, not the helm's, yet Venir felt stronger than ever. Today was as good a day to die as any, especially if you were an underling.

Faster!

The tide was turning on the valiant Royal Riders as the monstrous spiders closed in on the camp and sprayed them down with webs and anger. Chittering underlings were still spewing from holes in the ground. Venir's powerful legs lengthened his stride, closing the gap at the pace of a galloping horse. He couldn't get there fast enough, and his black eyelets steamed behind his helm. Ahead, an underling mage reappeared, and he wasn't alone. Ten pale white creatures scurried beneath him, all heading his way on all fours, cutting him off from the battle, where he was certain he was needed. Albino urchlings, nostrils flaring and fangs gnashing, closed in on him with the speed of wild wolves. They were the same vicious beasts that had almost killed Chongo. Venir's head exploded in rage as he raised his axe high in the air and screamed …

CHAPTER 62

HEMMED IN LIKE A ROOSTER in a chicken coup, Melegal pointed his blades at the opposite ends of the alley, which was becoming smaller. The big one that blocked his original path raised a club over his towering head while the next man brandished a pair of knives. *Hunting knives. Completely inferior to my blades, but the man's forearms are strung like a fighter's. And there's another one behind him, to boot.*

"Drop those blades before you hurt yourself, you bloody rogue, or I'll have your hands for trophies," the short man in a forest green cloak said. "Hah, a man swinging steel thicker than his arm, now that's a laugh."

Melegal fought the smile of relief that was cracking open on his otherwise stern expression while the other man's baritone voice rumbled.

"Ho! This can't be the man we seek; surely it's an illusion. Melegal would never play with swords, unless he stole them."

Melegal couldn't believe his eyes when Mikkel revealed his cheery face and leaned his club along the wall. Billip pulled back his hood, his crafty features still hard, as he stuffed his knives under his belt and began popping his knuckles. *Oh, how annoying.* But who was the other man? *Soon enough.*

"It's good to see you both, "he said, sheathing his swords and bumping wrists with the men. "What are you doing in Bone? And who is that?"

"It's me, Me!"

He didn't recognize the deep voice, but he knew the tone. Georgio's curly brown hair was down past his shoulders when he revealed his hooded face. The extra meat he had carried was gone from his pie face, and his broader shoulders suggested solid muscle underneath. The boy, now a man, was at least a foot taller and fifty pounds heavier than last he saw him.

"Where's Quickster?" he snapped.

Georgio's happy face turned into a frown. "Ah, don't start, he's—"

"My pony's fine," Billip intervened.

"He's mine and always has been!" Melegal almost yelled. "Where is he?"

Georgio wasn't finished.

"You gave him to me."

"No, I gave him to Lefty. Where's Lefty?"

An odd silence ensued.

"What?" Melegal asked.

Mikkel slapped his big hand on Melegal's shoulder and said, "Listen Me, Lefty's back in Three. When we heard about all the trouble in the South, we decided to head back down to get my son, Nikkel. That's why we're here. Stocking up for the final leg."

The four men stood in the alley looking at one another for answers to many questions. Melegal had the most, as he'd not seen Billip or Mikkel since the hunt for the Brigand Queen more than five years ago. But they still hadn't answered the primary question.

"Where's Quickster?"

"Same place you'd expect him to be," Georgio answered.

"I can only hope you're not still eating his food. It appears you've still been eating plenty."

Billip had to hold Georgio back as the man-sized boy came after him.

"You better shut your rat hole, Me! I'll pummel your skinny arse. You can't hurt me, but I know how to hurt you!"

Melegal let out a shrill little laugh. *Slat! The boy's changed, indeed. His threat's far from idle.* "I don't think so, Boy," he replied, making a quick cutting motion across his throat. Georgio's eyes widened and his body softened.

"You're still an arse, Melegal," Georgio said, turning away.

"What is this on your cloak ... Detective?" Billip said, grabbing the brooch pinned on his cloak.

Melegal snatched it away saying, "Long story, men. I only have time for you to get me up to speed. How'd you wind up in the City of Three? Where's Venir? And how in Bish did you find me in this pit?" He sat down on a crate that was sitting against the wall. It felt good to sit among old friends for the moment, but time was pressing. "And give me the short version."

Mikkel opened his mouth to speak, but Billip put him off.

"He said the short version."

"Mine will be short."

"Yours are as bad as Venir's."

Mikkel bristled.

"And yours are as boring as Georgio's."

"Huh ... what?" Georgio came over, a bit confused. "I tell good stories."

Mikkel and Billip laughed, but Mikkel stepped aside with a graceful bow. "Fine, I just want to go eat."

"Me too," piped Georgio.

"We know!" the three other men said.

Billip began.

"First, fortune favored us finding you, as we weren't even looking for you. Georgio caught you ducking into that tavern. Our ears have been filled with stories about the Yellow Hair Butcher. We were snooping around, thinking Venir might have returned. You haven't seen him, have you?"

"No," Melegal said dryly. "Not since the last time I saw Quickster." *Slat!* A little bit of guilt swelled inside his belly. Georgio had been tormented, for all he knew by Tonio. It would shake the boy up if he knew the foul man still lived.

Billip caught him up on how they arrived in the City of Three to begin with, which was surprising as they were southerners. Melegal found it difficult to hide his amazement as he learned about their liaisons with Jarla on her hunt for Venir and the trip to Dwarven Hole, where they all last parted. The falling out between Lefty and Georgio left him hollow inside. He missed the time he'd spent with them both. Billip told him about Kam, a woman he'd consider the journey to see, and Venir's daughter, Erin. *Spreads his seed like a dandelion.* Then he remembered Brak and his upcoming engagement.

"It's all fascinating, but I've no part in this now. I've got my own troubles," he said, tapping his brooch, rising to his feet and unfolding his arms. "Mikkel, traveling south is impossible right now. A death trap they say. You'd be lucky to make it alive to the Red Clay Forest. The Royals are up to their elbows in figuring out how to deal with the underlings."

"Venir will take care of it," Georgio interjected.

"It wouldn't surprise me if the big lout was behind it," Melegal shot back.

"You better watch what you say about him. He saved your skinny neck plenty of times."

"And he's almost gotten me killed ten times more, Foolish Boy. You too!"

Georgio fell silent, but Melegal continued on.

"I'd say there's a good chance your son fled north. For all you know he's right outside these gates. You're bound to see a familiar face or two if you scour the crowd."

Mikkel landed another heavy slap on Melegal's shoulder, saying, "Good advice, thanks."

"Aye, if we find him maybe we can collect that bounty on this yellow haired butcher," Billip said, his greedy eyes dancing with thoughts of more gold.

"Stay out of that," Melegal warned.

"You'll not be collecting what I can collect for myself. Care to put a wager on the bounty, Melegal?"

I'm an idiot. Should have just sent them away. Billip was just as greedy as was he, but of a different make-up. The man had hunted for hefty bags of underling bounty, so a bounty on a man would give him little to fear.

Mikkel frowned at Billip and said, "I'm not getting into that, Billip. I told you that once already. We find Nikkel! If he's not here, we're heading south. That's what we agreed on."

"Fine. Melegal, for the time being Georgio has led us to the place called The Octopus. We'll be there if you need us."

Perfect.

Melegal's steely eyes were dancing behind his lids.

"That's a pretty dangerous hole during these times. I had to leave, no thanks to a man called Jeb. Beat me silly in an Iron Hands contest."

"What?" Mikkel, Billip and Georgio were all incredulous.

"Took my room and my table, so I've heard.

Mikkel's guffaws of laughter echoed up and down the alley.

"You expect me to believe you fist fought someone? And lived?"

Billip clutched at his stomach.

"I gotta see this guy."

"Pah! Both of you sots will fare worse than I did."

Mikkel was leaning against the wall, bowled over in laughter.

It's good to see some things never change. Georgio was frowning at him as he walked away. "I'll get down there to see Quickster, Georgio. Stay close to those two. Bone is more dangerous than ever now. And there's one more thing that I'd like to say."

"W-What?" Georgio stammered a little.

He wanted to warn him about Tonio, but that might do more harm than good. He changed his mind.

"Go back to Three and live. Stay in Bone and die."

"Aw!" Georgio turned and walked away.

Melegal's mind was already elsewhere.

Keys. Keys. Keys. The Coming of Age games. Death to the Slergs and Brak. Slat. He felt guiltier now that ever. After all, the boy had a half-sister and father he'd never know. *Stay focused. Live one day at a time. Kill Sefron!*

Chapter 63

A RIVER OF BLOOD STRETCHED ACROSS Bish's open landscape as far as he could see. One side of the bank was an endless sea of underlings; on the other side stood his father, Venir: razor sharp axe in hand, screaming with a maddening look in his blazing blue eyes.

Whack.

Brak jumped up, clutching at his side as the warden kicked him hard in the ribs.

Whack! The ugly man did it again.

"Get up, you big fat headed Slerg! It's time for the end."

His stomach rumbled as he rubbed his blurry eyes. Leezir and Hagerdon shuffled by, wrists locked, ankle chains dragging over the floor. Leezir's head sagged, and his shoulder stooped. Hagerdon, once proud and cocky, wheezed and coughed, his lips thin and pale, almost morbid.

"You won't have to worry about being hungry anymore after this, Boy," Hagerdon said, "because soon you'll be dead."

Leezir didn't even look his way as he watched them go.

The warden and two others shackled his wrists, ankles and neck, like the other men, and hooked him to the prisoner chain.

"Criminy, you're a big bastard!" One of the guards said, looking up at him. "Warden, you ever seen this one standing before? He's like a tree, just not as smart. Heh-heh."

"Shaddup, Morg," the warden said, smacking a lash into Brak's back. "He'll be an easy target for the Royal wretches. Chopped into firewood soon enough. Now get the girl and get 'em moving. I don't want to be late, and I'm hoping to get a look for a change."

There had been nothing but dread and misery in Brak's brief life since his mother Vorla was killed. Each day had been worse than the one before. The smells, the food or lack thereof, his itching skin, the gummy taste in his mouth. His fingertips were bloody.

"Come here, you little wretch!" The guard said from ahead, snatching Jubilee by the leg and dragging her from her cage, kicking and screaming. "Oh … them boys will have great sport of you. Sad for such a weensy little thing."

They were all shackled now, moving forward, Jubilee sobbing and sniffling every step of the way. He felt her tears under his bare feet as he walked over them. Her grandfather, Leezir, got smacked in the mouth for trying to comfort her. It seemed that everyone making their way down the tunnel was broken, metal shackles and chains scraping over the cold stone. Brak thought of his father one last time when they stopped in front of a large wooden door. His stomach groaned so loud it made an echo.

"Shame to see a man fight on an empty stomach. Maybe we should have fed him the girl. She'd make a delicious little morsel for somebody," the warden said, playing with her hair.

Brak could hear noises on the other side of the door. There were many people on the other side, and he had good reason to think they all were going to kill him.

He heard Hagerdon say, "I can only assume I had this coming, but I never imagined my end coming in this manner." He went into a fit of coughing. "Bish give me the strength to kill one

Almen before it's done." Hagerdon looked back over his shoulder and said to Leezir, "You got anything left?"

"Just a few rotting teeth to throw at them," the once vibrant, now glum-looking man said.

The guard made his way to the door and talked to another guard through a small sliding wood portal in the door.

Hagerdon turned and offered Brak some final words.

"Brak, I hate to admit it, but I wish your father was here. You'll have to do. You see Boy, on the other side of the door is a death so certain, so inevitable I can already feel the heat blistering my bones in the furnace." Hagerdon motioned to the big door.

"I've been there before; your father's been there before but not under these dire circumstances. Whatever you have left—let ... it ... out! I deserve what's coming, but you don't. Fight ... and die! Just take some of them with you."

Hagerdon fell to the ground as the guard jammed his spear butt in his belly.

"Save your breath if you want to beg for mercy, Slerg."

"And save your breath for your orc-faced wife. I'm sure she'll enjoy it as much as a roasted gnoll's gonads."

The guard lowered the point of his spear again, saying, "Why you—"

The door popped open.

A glow of light and the feeling of warm air wafted over Brak, giving him chills. There was the smell of food and what he believed was perfume. The guards prodded him forward. Bleachers greeted his eyes, three rows deep going up, plank after plank forming a circle. Most seats were filled with the rumps of people in elaborate clothes, chatting back and forth and muttering as a strange silence began to fall.

It seemed like every eye was on him. It made him uncomfortable. There was a wall inside the circle, higher than his head, guards posted every few feet at ground and bleacher level. Below them were small men, plus a few notably bigger, in polished armor, pointing in their direction with shining blades, laughing. They weren't men, more like boys, his age possibly, maybe a little older. There was something sinister in each and every one of them. Cruel, cunning and sneering, young hunters wanting that first kill. Brak could tell each of them was hungry for the glory of his death. One of them, bigger than the rest, spat on the ground, glared at him with steely eyes and said, "I'll be gutting that barrel headed galoot as soon as we finish beating him into a bloody rug. His head's going over the mantle, the big mantle!" The others' shrill laughs pierced his ears. Something about the young man frightened him. His body began to tremble as he hunched down behind Leezir. *Mah! I miss my Mah!*

"Welcome to the Royal arena," Leezir said under his breath. "Your final resting stop in Bone."

Chapter 64

THERE WERE THREE OF THEM, taller than trees, throwing boulders like skipping stones at the band of dwarven men. Fogle's horse reared up as they were showered with rock and dust, and another boulder tumbled by. There was no sign of Cass and Chongo.

"Cass!" he cried. "Cass, where are you?"

Ahead, Mood and the other Blood Ranger, Eethum, were closing the gap between them and the giants. A rumbling cloud of dust was behind them, and ahead the band chopped at the giants' knees. Fogle blinked hard. *They're real!* He pictured the statues in the former grand square of the City of Three in his mind. He knew the stories, how the magi tricked the monstrous men into building their city and trapped them. He assumed, like so many other things, they were tales to tell children, legends, like dragons and even underlings. It was time he grew up; he should have known better by now. What had Mood said? "Bish happens."

He pulled the reins on his mount, bringing the noble beast to a stop. A giant's club, a heavy piece of carved wood, came down on the head of a dwarf, crushing it and shaking the ground. Fogle was less than fifty yards away when he summoned the energy inside him and let it fly. Two streaks of coiled energy sprung like geysers from his hands. He spoke the words, harnessed the power and guided it straight into the giant's chest, knocking it from its feet and to the ground with a tremendous thud. A cry of cheers arose as the persistent dwarves piled on.

A wave of nausea filled him as his power winked out. Bright spots flashed in his eyes, and he held his aching head.

"Where'd that come from?" He muttered, fighting for his breath.

The giants, hairy chested men wearing little more than a fur cloth about their waists, stood fifteen feet tall, hammering at everything in sight. The one he felled rose to its feet, angry, and shed dwarves like water before stomping them into the ground. "It's not dead?"

A shadow fell over him.

"Move, Fool!"

A lithe figure knocked him from his horse a split second before a spiked club crushed the beast into the ground.

Cass was on top of him, then him on top of her as they rolled out from under the next devastating blow.

"Do something, Fogle!" she screamed inside his ear.

Energy filled him as he summoned his next spell. This time he opened the gate inside him further and let loose the words of power. A ball of swirling energy, a brilliant red light, formed in his grasp. He threw it at the giant's gaping mouth.

Clonk!

The giant batted it away like a stone, sending the ball of energy into the rocky hillside where it exploded in a brilliant flash of light.

"Oh no," he muttered as the big giant smiled and raised his club high.

"Run!" Cass cried, trying to pull him up. Fogle couldn't move. He watched the giant's head descend back down towards Cass. His razor sharp mind told him it was too late.

Boom!

Knocked from his feet, he tumbled to the ground. Everything was loud and dusty. The giant, bald-headed, bearded and ugly, raised its club once more. Fogle had just enough time to look over where Cass once was. All he could think of was Ox the Mintaur being squeezed to a bloody pulp.

"I'm so sorry," he said, reaching out, but there was no sign of her. The giant's club was coming back down.

He muttered another word of power that added a translucent shield before him. The club glanced off the shield, drawing an angry grunt from the giant. Fogle felt like his elbows were about to break apart when another blow came, then another. It was like when he dealt with the snow ogres, but two tons worse. He'd already spent most of his energy this time. Pinned down and with nowhere to go, he tried to yell for help, but his voice was muffled when the giant raised its booted foot and stomped on him like a snail.

"Go for the toes!" Mood ordered back to his men.

There was nothing that got his dander up more than the hill giants. They were a cruel race that was crafty and cunning. His hatred for Horace, his recently dispatched foe, would never settle, nor would his anger ever subside. Most of the giants were as bad as ogres and trolls most of the time. No exception for most hill giants, either. They treated the dwarves like snacks, and sometimes snatched them and enslaved them like pets.

He hunched down at the sound of a powerful energy that slammed into the giant nearest by, felling it like a tree. The dwarves poured over the giant, axes and hammers chopping into it like a piece of wood.

"Eethum!"

The black Blood Ranger and two dwarves swiped at the flesh on the other giant's ankles. Eethum ducked under the giant's clutching grasp, missed a swing at its wrist with his axe and watched in horror as the giant snatched one mailed dwarven warrior up and crushed it in his hands. The dwarf didn't even scream. Mood heard its bones crack and pop.

"Eethum! Over here!"

Eethum waved his battle axe back and forth over his head, catching the giants' eye. It swung its monstrous head around and roared.

Clatch-Zip!

Clatch-Zip!

Rocking back on its heels, the giant cried out in fury. Two large crossbow bolts, one in its right eye, the other embedded in the bridge of its nose, were buried deep.

"I'll be a halfling's uncle; I missed one!" Mood said, tossing his crossbow aside and charging into the fray.

The giant flailed its arms and legs, roaring like thunder, scooping up dirt and debris and showering everything close by with rocks. The third giant jumped into his path, jaw jutting, both hands coming together and smashing Mood like a fly. His ears popped. His bones clattered, and half a dozen ribs busted as he sagged to the ground. The last time he'd taken a direct hit like that he'd lain on his back for weeks.

"Get up and fight, King of the Dwarves!" he growled to himself.

All he could see was Eethum, hacking with fury into his monstrous assailant's knees. Hunks of skin, fingers and muscles scattered the sky as the giant teetered back and wailed. Mood raised himself up, pulled his shoulders back and charged the one he had shot. It was regaining its composure and closing in on Eethum. Feeling like daggers pierced his chest, he side stepped the giant's charge and chopped his axes into the back of the giant's knees. He cut a tendon and could feel it snap like a bowstring. The giant pitched forward, smacking into the ground and rock. The giant began to push itself up, but Mood scrambled up its back and brought both his blades down with all his might. The first blow cracked open its skull. The second pierced its brain. Despite his victory, his instincts suggested they were losing. Something wasn't right. Weary, dizzy and body wracked with pain, Mood wiped the blood from his face, tumbled from the giant's back and fell face first into the dirt.

Chapter 65

THERE IT WAS. A SCINTILLATING rainbow of colors encircled a strange view that hung in midair before them. Verbard heard Kierway let out a sharp gasp as the view cut through windows, people, walls and doorways like an apparition of lightning. Jottenhiem's rugged chin hung over his shoulder, his nostrils snorting over the back of his neck. The mighty fighters of the Underland gawped in amazement.

"I've never seen so many humans before," the Juegen commander said.

Kierway swallowed hard. "Nor I, either. But that's just more to kill for me."

"Pah, I'll take ten of those white devils to your five any night, Kierway."

Eep, slow it down!

Verbard ordered, shrugging off a wave of nausea.

"Kierway, what is the name of this human you are dealing with, again?"

It was strange, underlings dealing with men, but it had been done before. Even he himself had indulged in human encounters, though he lamented it. The humans were weak and greedy, as easy to bribe with shiny objects as a newborn taken to mother's milk. It worked on some, but not all, however.

"A shabby man, as pathetic as the rot between an urchling's toes," Kierway hissed. "A practitioner of dark healings, named Sefron."

"And how did you come to know this man? How long ago?" Verbard said in a demanding tone.

"We've always had our spies among them, searching for what my father seeks. That and other things. Didn't you and your brother discuss these things?"

Lies. Verbard held a spell on his tongue that would turn Kierway's eyes inside out. *Save it for the mission.* He fought down his bubbling anger. Everything was wrong. Every gesture of Master Sinway's son made him uncomfortable. His words had been accommodating, but not convincing. Now, he, Lord Verbard, one of the most powerful underlings, had just learned that he was not privy to a secret mission that had been going on for decades, if not centuries, beneath the City of Bone. *And within as well.* He wanted to kill someone. *Save it for the humans.*

"There were many things we didn't share with one another, Kierway, but one thing we did always share was our displeasure of your company. Now, tell me, where does this Sefron reside? Certainly you've been there in some shape or form." Verbard turned his silver eyes on Kierway's tightening face. "Oh, I forgot, you're but a fighter, incapable of hiding from anything but a fight."

"Watch your words, Verbard." Kierway warned. "I've had high ranking heads for less."

Verbard's eyes narrowed as he rose from the ground. "And I've destroyed Underland's most powerful enemy of all. Remember that the next time you shove your steel into sleeping men, crying women and one-armed children, you little gnat. Now answer my question!"

The hulking Vicious bristled behind Kierway's back as Kierway's sword flashed from its sheath.

Clang!

Inches from carving a chunk from Verbard's face, Jottenhiem caught the blow on his sword in a shower of sparks. *Excellent*, Verbard thought, floating backward but leaving up his shield. He twisted the enchanted metal ring. *One can never be too careful. Thanks, Brother.*

Clang! Clang! Clang! Blades licked in and out like serpent tongues as the blows got faster and faster. Single handed, they exchanged blows back and forth, one striking, the other counter striking, the next counter striking the counter strike. *If only they both were on my side. Ah, what splendid devastation they'll wreak on the humans.*

Verbard brought his clawed hands together with power.

CLAP!

The entire cavern shook.

Kierway and Jottenhiem stopped.

"Save your energies!" he said in an angry hiss. "We've more planning to do."

The Juegen leaders sheathed their blades and nodded, iron and ruby eyes still narrowed as they backed away. Verbard could see the tiniest glimmer of sweat on both their brows.

"Castle Almen," Kierway said, snapping his fingers. A pair of robed underlings scurried up with a heavy rolled up parchment that looked to be part paper, part quilt. "A map of the entire city," Kierway said, motioning to the underlings who quickly began unrolling it on the ground.

"That will do," he said, turning his gaze back on Eep's vision.

Almen? Almen! Hah! Was that not the name of the human Castle that had given Oran the whereabouts of the Darkslayer? Underling Oran the Cleric had dealt with these men before and had even kept records of it. Still, there was nothing mentioned of a key. He'd known Oran had previous dealings with Kierway, and as he recalled, it had been the Almens who'd been bribed in taking over Outpost Thirty-One. Perhaps Oran knew of the key, and maybe Eep knew something as well.

Eep!

Yes, Master.

Did Oran ever mention a key to you?

No, Master.

Are you certain?

Yes, Master.

I see.

Verbard felt the spell beginning to drain him. He looked down on the map and focused on the banner that Kierway showed of Castle Almen.

Eep, take us into Castle Almen, and find this cleric. We've little time.

One second the vision spiraled above the castle spires, the next second they were diving through the block, zipping in and out of corridors, lavish bedrooms and servant quarters.

"Slow your foul pet down, Verbard. I cannot make out an image, and my stomach churns with grubs," Kierway said, clutching his stomach.

Eep's eye glided into an arena where the faces of many men sat upright in their lavish clothes and women chatted soundlessly with painted lips and faces.

"There he is!" Kierway pointed.

"My, he is a slug, is he not?" Jottenhiem commented on Sefron's flabby, half-naked form that was eyeballing a man as skinny and rigid as a rail. "Send me in, Lord," Jottenhiem pleaded. "I'm ready to kill them all."

Verbard shifted his gaze to Kierway and sighed.

"This is your liaison to mankind? He's the one to acquire this key, and for decades he's been promising to deliver but has not? I cannot help but doubt your wisdom, Kierway."

The underling Master shot back.

"The key's in the castle. Of that, I am certain."

"How can you be … certain?" Verbard sneered.

"Because Master Sinway told me so."

I think your father has gone mad. Does he want the key, or the city? Or, is it the key to the city? Doubt subdued his thoughts as he let the scintillating image drift away. The underlings, thousands strong, were overtaking the land of Bish. All he had to do was wreak havoc and destruction from within. But it all still made little sense to him. The humans and the other races were bound to fight back at some point, were they not? Then again, perhaps Master Sinway was right. Perhaps now was the time to strike a blow from which the humans would never recover.

"Kierway, as I can see on the map, I believe the Current leads below this Castle which you are so fond of," he said, his feet now lifting from the ground.

"Indeed, and your point is?"

"The point is," Verbard clutched his fists, "you are going inside that castle to fetch the key. Take all the underlings you need."

Kierway raised his voice, saying, "And what will you do while I'm gone?"

"I'll do what I said I was going to do," his voice rising to the level of thunder.

"I'm leading this underling army into the City of Bone! Death to the humans! Death to them all!"

A thunderous chorus of chitters rose up, shaking the streets above.

Chapter 66

Tunk. Tunk. Tunk. Tunk. Tunk ...

It had been going on like this for hours. One peck after the other. Boon, once the mightiest wizard in the lands, so far as he knew, couldn't help but envision devious children outside his metal cocoon, pounding away with hammers.

"Dear me," he cried, but his words of desperation did him no good. The pecking would not stop, despite his angry urgings. He let out a long rattling sigh and resumed sucking the blood from his split lip.

The giants, of all the times for them to be tardy, had not come to his aid. When they did, he'd beg to be dropped in the labyrinth to let his suffering end once and for all. Of course, he wouldn't be here if he'd just let Venir die. The might of the warrior gave him hope for escape from the Under Bish that—for all intents and purposes—he had banished himself to. But the sack, the mystical power it contained, he hungered for once more. With it he could escape, even destroy the giants if that was what it was meant for. Its power, so divine, unrelenting and unending was worth dying for.

Tunk. Tunk. Tunk. Tunk. Tunk ...

"NOOOOOOO!" he moaned, but it kept on going. It seemed there was no escape. If he could will himself to die, he would. Boon was certain most of his sanity was already gone, and it seemed that losing the rest wasn't far behind.

Tunk. Tunk. Tunk. Tunk. Tunk ...

Barton was mad. He ripped an apple tree up, roots and all, and slammed it into the ground. For hours, days, he did not know how long, he'd been searching for the toys that Venir had hidden from him.

"Venir cheated! Venir bad! He make the game too hard!" The one-eyed boy moaned, ripping the branches from the trees. "Venir gonna pay for this! Venir will give me my toys!"

Boon's bloodshot eyes had been staring at the same grey tile—for how many hours he did not know.

Tunk. Tunk. Tunk. Tunk. Tunk ...

He'd drifted off to sleep several times, only to be awakened by the same chronic sound.

Tunk. Tunk. Tunk. Tunk. Tunk ...

No life was worth living like this. Nothing was worth this. He should have let the underlings take him long ago.

"OH, GO AWAY!" he yelled from an otherwise dry throat. He said it, but he wasn't sure he heard it. All he had to note it was a sore throat, busted teeth and, he was pretty certain, a foot full of broken bones, not to mention that his head still ached from the initial contact he made when he fell to the floor.

Something flustered and flapped, and the chronic tapping was gone. A shadow fell over the room, leaving everything dark. *Finally, they're here. Certainly my punishment won't be as bad as the tapping.* Something powerful snatched him from the floor and shook him like a rattle. Pain erupted in his eyes.

"OW!" he cried, his head smacking hard into the metal. Something was looking at him as his vision blurred and everything went black.

Fresh air, pain and annoyance.

Tunk. Tunk. Tunk. Tunk. Tunk …

"Aghk …," Boon said.

It was bright now, so bright he could not see. The air was warm, no longer dank and moldy as he was accustomed to. Still, the new scenery did little to improve his bleak situation. Something was still pounding on his casing, and his brittle bones ached at every joint. *Where am I now?*

The giants. It seemed likely that only they would relocate him to another place, something more secure. But outside? Now that was hardly likely. *Hmmm ….* He recalled a black shadow falling over the room and leaving a dozen knots on his head, each of which throbbed like a painful cyst. What had befallen him? But the smell of grass was good.

SPLASH!

Panic seized him. *They're drowning me! All the things I've done for them and they drown me.*

SPLASH! SPLASH! SPLASH!

That's strange. Does one usually hear splashing when they're sinking?

A wave of water cascaded over his sarcophagus, icy and drenching. A sound of beating wings flapped away. *Where in all of the Under Bish am I now?* Boon knew little about the Under Bish other than what he'd seen in the Ziggurat. Everything was enormous in scale, odd and strange, the river he knew was wider than the eye could see. There was Blackie the dragon and little more that he knew.

THOOM!

That was a giant's footstep. At least now he could get some answers.

THOOM!

Closer it came, shaking and shifting him.

"GO AWAY, TINY BIRD!"

The voice was unfamiliar, strange and garbled. A shadow came, a glimpse of skin, then the dark again.

"Hello!" he yelled.

He was suspended in the air, a feeling he'd gotten used to, but it still jostled his innards, leaving him queasy. He couldn't remember the last time he'd ridden on a raft in the river, but this felt something like that. Slowly, he heard the sound of skin peeling away from the metal, and for the first time he came face to face with his oppressor. And for the first time in years he let out a curse word.

"Slat."

A large droopy eye squinted and shook him around.

"You in there? I heard you. What did you say, *Smat*?

Boon realized that his situation, bad as it had been, just got worse. *Barton! Of all the giants, why Barton?* The one-eyed boy man, a giant miscast of sorts, was a trouble maker he'd sought to avoid in all of his time in the Under Bish. Boon knew Barton, but Barton, who was never around the Ziggurat for long, did not know Boon. The giants had seen to that. As far as he understood things, the giant boy man, for lack of a better word, was cursed, dangerous, and maligned. And based off the look of things, Boon didn't see any reason to take him at his word. *Perhaps they'll find me and rescue me.*

"Hello!" Barton yelled inside his cage, his breath as foul as waste water.

Boon sighed. *Perhaps I deserve this.* "There is nobody home. Now take me back to the Ziggurat!"

"Huh!"

"Take me now or the giants will be very angry!"

Plunk!

"Ow!" Boon screamed. Everything inside him shuddered painfully as Barton dropped him to the ground. "You blasted idiot! You're going to kill me! Then how angry will the giants be!"

THOOM! THOOM! THOOM! SPLASH! SPLASH! SPLASH!

Icy water drenched him inside his casing. Barton had run away, leaving Boon all alone.

Tunk. Tunk. Tunk. Tunk. Tunk …

Boon learned one thing: *It's a bird.* The hours kept passing, and the bird kept pecking. *I can't take this anymore. Where are you, Barton?*

SERIES 1 · THE · BOOK 5

DARKSLAYER

· FIGHT OR DIE ·

Outrage in the Outlands

CRAIG HALLORAN

CHAPTER 1

NERVES OF STEEL. *WHERE ARE they?* Melegal swore he used to have them; even in his own darkest hours, he'd had little fear. Ever since he was a boy he'd been beaten and abused to some degree, but it only reinforced his steely resolve. For some reason, as far back as he could recall, he'd always figured he could wriggle his way out of anything, until today.

The Royal Coming of Age games were about to begin, and every face that sat along the benches was eager for blood. Royals—pompous, arrogant, extravagant, impossible and powerful—loved nothing more than seeing their falling brethren hacked down like rabid dogs. Melegal stood leaning against the wall, inspecting his fingernails, five rows up from the bottom of the arena. *Say nothing. Talk to no one. Avoid all contact. It will be over soon.*

The arena, nothing extravagant but fairly large, was a small compound where the Royal sentries did much of their routine training. The Royals and sentries sat behind a wall that was about eight feet in height, along wooden benches where one was no more distinct than the other. Above them, a dome rested on a network of limestone pillars where sun and moonlight could gleam in through the litany of tiny windows, making for a majestic affect. Other than that, it was a place of seclusion. A safe place from prying eyes and a good place to muffle the cries of death. Melegal clutched his fingers in and out, pumping blood into his lengthy fingers. *What to do?* He felt obligated to be doing something. *When all else fails, listen.*

Lord Almen sat in the first row, broad shoulders pulled back proud as a peacock, looking stately as well as deadly in his exquisite black silk jerkin laced with threads of gold. Along his side and spreading out were another twenty people who Melegal hadn't seen before. More Royals, some gray-headed, others bald-headed, both young and old, each having a smile when Lord Almen had their attention and a sneer when he did not. Staff, young women, attractive and revealing, served wine, food and other pleasantries to the men who gathered around one another like a host of evil colleagues. Melegal wanted to spit. *Blathering men.*

The arena itself had other guests, ones that Melegal knew all too well. Sefron sat alone, near the front of the flock of garish Royals, neck craning back, and hanging on their every word, wearing more robes than Melegal had ever seen him in before. *There is still time to kill you today.* He brushed his fingers over his wrists, feeling the contraptions hidden beneath his sleeves and fighting the urge to launch the darts he'd acquired from the Slergs when he took them into custody. Elation had filled him when he came across them. They were prized weapons, indeed. When the right time and place presented itself, he'd be ready. *I'll feather that laggard's flabby back full of them.*

A pair of heavy double doors were pulled open from inside the arena. The contestants of the Coming of Age Games were pulled inside, heavy chains clanking, to a small chorus of cheers.

"Booooo!"

"You're going to die, you wretched Slergs! You killed my brother," one Royal shouted, rising to his toes and hurling a goblet of wine at Leezir.

Here we go.

Melegal wanted to crawl into a hole, such a dreadful feeling overcame him. He'd been in an arena similar to this before, but on the other side of things, when he was an urchin serving in the Slerg castle, watching his one and only friend, Venir, take ritual beating from the Slerg boys. He'd never forget that day, during another ceremony, when Venir stuck it to the twins, Hagerdon and Creighton. That was the day he knew if he was to ever be free of the Royals, or to live a long life, his road to freedom was through Venir. He fought to keep his eyes away from the men inside the arena. *Don't look. Don't look. Don't look.* He looked.

There they stood, two Slerg men and a Slerg girl, beaten, downcast and destitute, except one, Hagerdon. Fighting a hard cough but known to be quite a swordsman, the man kept his chin up, green eyes still ablaze. *Always hated him and his brother. Such scrappy arses. You'd think I'd be happy to see them go.* Instead, Melegal felt pity. *Venir's bloody seed. The man still makes my life impossible.*

He looked at the man who he should be trying to save, Brak. The man, or boy rather, was a monster by comparison to the rest. Tall, sullen-eyed, big-boned with a tuft of blond hair hanging down past his jaws. He stood still, shoulders stooped, eyes gazing at the ground like nothing more than a common mute. Melegal had at least seen to it that he wasn't whipped, but he swore he heard the man's stomach growl from where he sat.

Melegal rubbed his chin. He could see little of Brak's father in him, other than his blue eyes. *I'm not so sure he's Venir's seed.* But he knew that he was. Something eerie about the man's presence told him so.

He fanned himself with his cap and took a seat a few benches down, all alone from the rest of the crowd. Lord Almen's hawking eyes caught his for a moment. He swore the man was going to kill him any day now. He bowed his chin, turned, and refocused his attention on the inner arena, where six well-armed youths were conducting routine exercises with wooden weapons along the wall.

"Look at that one's head," a haughty voiced boy said, swinging a heavy club. The others all looked over and laughed. "Ten gold says I crack it open first."

"I'll take that, and raise you fifteen more. My, his face is three times bigger than mine," another said, strutting around swinging his wooden sword.

They were all laughing and practicing quick little moves.

"I'm in for twenty. They should have just given us cows and sheep to slaughter. It would last longer."

"But we aren't supposed to kill them," one said, his black hair as straight as an arrow.

There was a pause among the boys and then an outburst of laughter.

"Tell you what," one said, freckled and brown headed, "we can take the little Slerg girl back to our quarters and give her something to feel good about after we've killed what's left of her family. She's cute for a Slerg. Has all of her teeth anyway."

"Not for long," one said, whacking a wooden mallet into the wall.

They chattered back and forth like gossiping women, but Melegal could hear the nervous twinge in their voices. It was their first trial against men, unknown men at that. And even though the cards on the table were overwhelmingly in their favor, there was a wild card, Brak. The bastard son of the unstoppable Venir. And Melegal swore it had been Brak's hands that bent those bars in the sewers. *I hope he at least snaps a few necks before he perishes. Alas.*

The bench felt abnormally hard on his skinny butt as he shifted in his seat the ever slightest. Normally, the skinny thief had ice water in his veins, but now his dexterous poise had been violated. Keys. Sefron wanted them. He'd seen them and taken a trip from one side of the city to the other with them. He'd broken into Lord Almen's office to find them, against his will, something he was certain was Sefron's doing. *I'll never follow the reason behind that.* Now, he was certain that Lord

Almen suspected him. *He'll have me dead as a toad sure enough. Wicked Royals.* He clenched his fist. *I've had enough.*

He cocked his chin and watched another unsettling figure from the corner of his eye. Another unanticipated obstacle. A woman, tall, sinewy, with short raven hair and maroon lips sat several feet over from Lord Almen. A sheathed sword lay over her lap where she scowled. He noticed Lord Almen's eyes drifting to hers from time to time. *Interesting.*

Melegal was certain it was the same woman from the chamber room, the one he'd thought looked so familiar. Still, he found himself looking over at her, and she was looking back at him. Dark blue eyes as sharp as razors. Face scarred from injury or mishap. Scowling at him like he was the plaque of the earth. He knew who it was: *Jarla the Brigand Queen.* He scowled right back and turned towards the other notable woman in the room, who was scowling at Jarla. Lorda Almen.

She was picture perfect, legs crossed below her short white and rose colored tunic dress, revealing her sensual calves. The Lorda was a marvelous woman who stood out among the rest of the Royals, her lithe frame feline in grace, her every movement accenting her generous curves beneath her snug but appropriate garments. Melegal could see poisoned daggers behind Lorda Almen's glaring expression on the raven-headed interloper. *Fascinating, even when hating.*

She flipped her dark hair behind her shoulders and locked eyes with Melegal. His heart pounded with new energy. The Lorda had become quite fond of him over the passing months. He'd saved her from her own son, Tonio. He'd killed an innocent man that day, Gordin, a commander of the Almen Castle watch. Stabbed him in the back. Duped the Lorda into believing Tonio was at fault and had gone from being a goat to a hero. His plan had worked, and so far, he lived.

Still, Lord Almen and Sefron he was certain remained unconvinced. But, as time passed, Lorda stayed fond of Melegal and treated him less like a servant and more like a confidante. He'd even walked through her gardens with her once, and her exotic nearness had almost curled his toes. If not for her interventions, he was certain he'd be nothing but charred or rotting bones. He read her full and perfect lips as she spoke to one of her servants who got up and headed his way. *No, not now!*

The servant was a pretty little thing, light hair pulled back in a bun, her servant robes ruffling over the bench as she squatted along his side and whispered in his ear.

"The Lorda would like a moment with you, Detective," she said, bowing, then gracefully walking away.

All the men inside the arena were lathered up in conversation, pointing and goading one another as Melegal made his way over with sagging shoulders. Despite the pleasure of Lorda Almen's presence, she still had her own way of being as demanding as her husband. *Who must I spy on this time?* He glimpsed at the back of Jarla's muscular back. *I can only imagine.* He huddled beside the Lorda, catching the full effect of her arousing perfume. *Perhaps I can swipe a drop or two for Haze.*

"Detective, it is good to see you," she said with a pleasant smile. "I've heard that you and Sefron have worked hard together on this venture. Is that true?"

No.

"I do what must be done in hopes it pleases the Lords."

"I see," she said. "But, are you not the one who brought in all of these Slergs? Tracked them down one by one and saw to it that only these few remain? The cleric had no part in that, did he?" She eyed Sefron, frowned, and returned her gaze to Melegal. "We can never get the fiend from the castle, it seems. All he does is ogle the women and creep up on the girls." She reached over and grabbed his sleeve. "He's a disturbing one, and I can only imagine he's hard to work with."

Ha.

"It is true, Lorda, that I am responsible for capturing these men, and the cleric played no part. He did manage the risky task of inviting Lord Almen's guests and picking out the wine and appetizers for this event. I think he even has a blister on his lips to show for it."

Lorda pulled him in closer, laughing and pressing her soft bosom into his arm, sending a wave of passion through him. He wanted to pull away, but she was holding him fast. What if Lord Almen saw? *Cripes! Just toss me in the arena, why don't you?* But Lorda's servants obstructed the view. Lightning raced down his spine as Lorda Almen's lips nibbled at his earlobe and she whispered to him, "See that black clad whore over there?"

There's only one Jarla.

"Yes, Lorda, "he managed.

"Kill her."

There's too much blood rushing to my head. Did she just say—

"Kill her," she squeezed his arm, "… and I'll be so very grateful. Don't kill her, and I'll be disappointed." She let go. Returning to her stately posture, her voice was a cold as stone. "And you don't want to see me disappointed. Now go."

"As you wish," he said, turning his steely eyes way. Jaws clenched, he got up, and his mind started thinking. *Madness! Why me? Kill the infamous Brigand Queen. Watch a friend's son die. I need to at least try to save him. Possibly die in the process. If anyone is to go before I expire, it will be Sefron. I've had it with these Royals.* He took a place on the bench adjacent to the back of Jarla, allowing his hand to slip to one of his daggers. *Let the Lorda think I'm at least going to try. Women!*

Chapter 2

Brak cast a glance at the leering faces in the crowd. He looked back down. At his side, Hagerdon and Leezir stood in as bad a shape as they'd ever been in before. Leezir hacked and coughed, a trickle of blood coming from his lips, his breathing crackling and raspy. Hagerdon, battered and bruised from head to toe, eyes almost swollen shut, stood chin up and chest out, glaring at his enemies.

The Slerg fighter's eyes locked on his as he said, "Brak, get your chin up. Your father'd be ripping those chains and whipping their scrawny arses with them if he were here. They're going to take you down. Rip you apart. Take some of them down with you." Hagerdon fell to the ground when a spear butt cracked him in the head. A chorus of laughter followed.

"Shaddup, Slerg!"

Brak reached out to Hagerdon and caught the tip of a spear in his ribs.

"Don't move, Mute! Else I'll poke a hole in you before the fight begins."

He shuffled back, chains jangling at his feet, as Hagerdon struggled to rise. He looked around at the people in the seats in the arena now. One woman was stunning, another one scowled. His mouth watered. He could smell the food that robed servant girls carried to the men adorned in the most extravagant clothes. His stomach sounded like a bullfrog as it growled. He'd do anything to eat again, just one last meal and he'd be happy to die. He just didn't want to die hungry. It seemed like such a sorry way to go.

He glanced over at the young men, most of whom he swore were his age, and something else stirred in his hungry belly. Anger mixed with fear. They'd said the crudest things about the little girl, Jubilee. Things he couldn't even imagine. At the same time, he suspected much of what they said was true. Yet, he had no desire to fight them. He just wanted to leave this place. He just wanted to eat. He wanted to see his mother, Vorla, again.

"Hoy! Big Face!" one of the young men said. "We're going to chop you up and feed you to the pigs! Ha-hahahahah!"

Brak looked down at his toes. He'd gotten accustomed to Hagerdon's insults over the passing months, but these young men's tongues made the Slerg fighters sound like honey.

"His face looks like an orc's butthole!" another one added.

"His head is shaped like a cracked ogre's egg!"

He blocked it out and glanced into the stands once more. A flabby man, odd like a hairless bird, was trying to run his hand up a slender girl's robes. Then he noticed the skinny man with steely eyes, the one who knew of his father. *There's sympathy in the cold man's face.* This awareness brought him more fear than hope. It was as if the man who captured him, the one they called Detective, was looking at a corpse. He couldn't take it anymore.

He pumped his big fists in the air, and his voice filled the arena, "LET ME EAT! PLEASE, LET ME EAT!"

A stark silence filled the arena. Food dropped from the mouth of one man, and a young royal dropped his wooden club.

"I DON'T CARE!" Brak moaned. "JUST LET ME EAT ONCE MORE BEFORE I DIE!" He wiped the tears from his face and fell to his knees. "PLEASE!"

Creighton hissed a fierce whisper at him, "Pull yourself together, you imbecile! Die with dignity!"

Brak didn't know what that meant and did not care. He was miserable, alone and starving.

A murmuring began among the men and soldiers, but it was the one in the middle, the broad shouldered vulture of a man dressed in the most ornate clothes, who spoke first.

"I thought you said he was a mute, Detective Melegal?" Lord Almen said, looking back over his shoulder at the skinny man who knew his father.

The thin man shrugged and said, "I figured he'd eaten his tongue, and why wouldn't I, Lord Almen?"

A small chorus of laughter erupted.

"I see, Detective." Lord Almen let out a chuckle and turned his attention back on Brak. "Hmmmm … Brethren, I say we let this former mute eat. Perhaps a plateful of pig's innards would do."

"Nay, Lord Almen, a spoonful of slat would be better."

The suggestions continued, one after the other, and Brak could feel himself slipping into the ground beneath his chains.

"Get up, Brak! Die on your feet, not on your back like a coward!" Hagerdon said.

He heard one of the Royal youths speak up and say to the onlookers, "Don't worry, my Lords. I'll cut out his tongue and feed it to him. Then he'll not complain about being hungry anymore!" The young warrior ran over and cracked him across the skull with a wooden sword.

Brak's head exploded with white lights. Pain filled his eyes. Yet, his hunger was the worst feeling of all. He looked at the faces of the laughing men and women. Compassionless. Cold. The young man that swatted him pumped his fists in the air to a chorus of praise and jubilation. Brak didn't even wipe the blood that ran down into his eyes. How much more would he have to suffer before he died?

"Get up!" The sentries said, jerking him to his feet.

Lord Almen stood up, raised his arms, and said, "I think we've had enough enjoyment from the mute, er, former mute," he bowed, "but the time has come to let the Coming of Age games begin. We've all been there, when were young, oh so many decades ago that seem like yesterday."

"For you maybe, Lord Almen, you old Griffon!" one of his colleagues offered, hoisting his goblet in the air, then sucking it down.

"Ah … but my locks don't share the same gray as yours, Reginald, you son of a Slerg's milk maid."

Laughter

"But now the time has come for the next generation of our Brood to earn their stripes, and who the better to earn them against than some of our former allies turned enemies, the sacrificial Slergs."

Boos

"The Slergs, each and every one save these four, are no more. The House of Almen has seen to that. Now, the time has come to see them pay for all of their betrayals. First," he emphasized, "there will be death!"

The men with decorative weaponry rattled their scabbards.

"Second will come their much overdue deaths!"

Brak could see their faces bearing down on him and the Slergs like they were nothing more than sheep being slaughtered for a feast. He clutched at his groaning belly. He just wanted it all to be over with. He just wished he could see his mother, Vorla, one last time.

"You!" Lord Almen pointed at Hagerdon. "Step forward. You'll be the first to suffer and die, Hagerdon."

The guards shoved the Slerg fighter forward and pulled the rest of them back against the wall. Jubilee's sobbing started up again.

Hagerdon, busted up with drying blood on his filthy clothes, spoke up.

"Why don't you come down here and give me an honorable death yourself, Lord Almen. I'll even leave my back open for your slat eating—*urk!*"

The sentry yanked the collar on his neck. The Slerg fighter jerked away.

"Assassin!" Hagerdon slipped away. "Sending children to do what you don't have the guts to do yourself. I challenge, blade for blade, until the bitter end!"

Brak never realized that laughter could be so annoying. He'd often laughed at his mother's stories during his short fourteen years of life and at other recountings on the farms, and he was pretty sure that laughter wasn't meant to sound like this. It disturbed him.

Lord Almen, in the meantime, remained poised, hand folded across his lap, a smile forming on the corner of his lips.

"I'll tell you what, Hagerdon Slerg. I'll grant part of your wish. We'll begin this contest not with wood, but with steel." He looked over at the sentries and the young men and pointed. "Give those three blades." Then he tossed something into the arena that Hagerdon snatched out of the air.

A wooden sword. A short one at that, carved as a complete replica of a real one. The Slerg fighter's chin bobbed up and down as he studied his useless blade and shrugged, "Better than I expected. May you burn in the furnace soon, Lord Almen," he said, making an offensive gesture as the three young Royals surrounded him. Brak held his stomach and cringed.

The young Royals wore leather cuirasses, short over their well-defined stomach muscles, round bucklers strapped to their sinewy arms and light swords Brak believed were called rapiers. Each sword gleamed along its ornate hilt. These were all studded with gems and pearls. The young Royals cut the blades through the air with sharp *swish-swish-swish* sounds as Hagerdon shuffled in his chains, head whipping back and forth. The Slerg fighter, taller and broader than his opponents, looked over-matched by comparison in his tattered clothes and wooden sword, but he had the look of a seasoned fighter in his hard eyes, which watched them look back and forth at one another.

"Come on, Boys," he growled, "haven't you ever fought a living man before?"

"Do as you've been taught!" one of the Royal trainers ordered. "You've done this before, now make this man bleed!"

The tallest of the three thrust his rapier forward and darted back again. Then the next followed suit, then the other, each blade coming inches from Hagerdon's belly as he shuffled away. Brak watched their every move. He'd seen these moves before.

Step. Lunge. Retreat. Step. Lunge. Retreat. Step. Lunge. Retreat.

Hagerdon dodged the tip of one blade and smacked away another, just in time to twist, parry and dodge out of harm's way.

"Is that all you little slats have?" he said, wiping the sweat from his brow. "I've seen dogs handle blades better than that."

"Press! Faster!" the trainer ordered.

Step. Lunge. Retreat. Step. Lunge. Retreat. Step. Lunge. Retreat.

They were getting faster. Their blades were getting closer, cutting and poking at his unprotected body. For the first time, Brak was seeing what Hagerdon had taught him about how a sword can easily whittle down an unarmed man. *Sword versus no sword strategy. Run.* But the Slerg fighter had nowhere to run.

The small crowd began cheering in eager anticipation of the first drop of Slerg blood being spilt. Hagerdon was gasping for air, chains rattling and clanking, a most desperate sound. Brak knew the heavy chains were wearing him down. It was just a matter of time. Fighting the urge to watch the inevitable, he nonetheless watched on, feeling like the room was about to explode at any moment.

Step. Lunge. Retreat. Step. Lunge. Retreat. Slice!

The arena erupted in a chorus of cheers as one Royal tore a sliver from Hagerdon's shoulder.

"You got first blood, Boy!" one man cried.

"Finish him!" another said.

The trainer yelled over them all, saying, "Keep up the pace! Don't stop!"

Hagerdon was grimacing underneath his thick head of hair, ducking, dodging and parrying in a more desperate fashion now. His fluidity had become stiff, and his efforts in vain. Brak stood solemnly as he watched the man quickly being whittled down without a fight.

Slice! Lunge. Retreat. Step. Lunge. Retreat. Step. Lunge. Retreat.

There was a roar of applause when the Slerg fighter began to bleed from half a dozen wounds. Blood was dripping from his chin to his belly. Brak couldn't help but wonder if this was the kind of death that awaited him. Not only would he die with an empty stomach, it would have a bloody hole in it, too.

Step. Lunge. Retreat.

Whack! Whack! Whack!

Hagerdon burst in a tornado of blood and tattered clothes, cracking one Royal with his wooden sword so hard he broke his sword arm, drawing a howling cry. For a split second, everyone froze but Hagerdon. He tore the buckler away from one man and whacked the throat of another. Two other young Royals were down on their knees as the Slerg fighter twisted the rapier away from the third and stabbed him in the knee.

"Stop him!" everyone seemed to shout at the same time, but Hagerdon kept on going.

One of the young Royals reached after him and had his fingers sliced off. The trainer pulled his sword from his sheath just in time to try and parry Hagerdon from skewing his heart, but he was too late and fell to his knees wide eyed while the Slerg ripped his blade free. A little blood became a lot as he spilled into the dirt and Hagerdon charged towards his nearest opponent.

Churk!

Hagerdon's eyes widened like moons. A spear burst through his chest. One of the sentries from the stands had hurled the deadly weapon into Hagerdon's back. Brak was face to face with the man as it happened. The rapier clattered to the ground as he fell to his knees and said through blood soaked lips, "That's how you go out, Brak."

Brak shook within his shackles. He filled with horror as he watched the remaining young Royals came over and take their turns at hacking the dying many down. He closed his eyes and tried to ignore the warm blood splattering his face while he clutched his groaning belly.

Chapter 3

Albino urchlings. Venir had only seen them once before. That had been the last time he saw Chongo, and it seemed like ages ago. He'd moved on. He hunted the ones that would have him dead, as did his comrade and his best friend. Now there were ten of them. Teeth gnashing, claws barred, ready to rip him to shreds. The translucent white little brutes were nothing more than muscles, fangs and claws as sharp as razors charging at him full speed and leaving behind them a trail of dust.

Venir was red hot with rage. Muscle, steel and magic intertwined and forged the ultimate fighting machine. Brool was singing in his grip, pulsating with power. The eyelets on his helm oozed with a mystic radiance as he crossed the dusty parallel. Man, monster and mayhem met in the middle.

Venir's bulging arms chopped into the face of the first screaming urchling, dropping it like a bloody stone. The smaller creatures ducked and rolled away from the deadly arcs of Brool's sting. Venir could feel their rage and fear intermingle as he plunged his spike into another one's chest. *Two!*

Something else lurks nearby, the helm warned.

Slat! There's more! Another urchling jumped on his shield, its fangs biting into the rim. Two more clawed and nipped at his feet like starving hounds.

Chop! Chop!

They hungered no more, twitching in their own blood.

A heap of them piled on top of him, tearing into his back and biting into his legs. The scale mail saved him from being ripped to shreds as they tried to pull him to the ground and feast.

"NO!"

He pierced the skull of the one hanging on his shield and slung it to the dirt. *Five!* The little monsters were strong! They latched onto his knees and squeezed him while two more assailed him, howling with bloodlust. He couldn't let these underlings stop him from getting in the larger fight with the Royal Riders.

"Fiends!"

With one urchling hanging on his arm, he hacked into the chest of another. With his shield arm, he grabbed the one hanging from his arm by the neck, squeezed, and pulled it off him. It clawed and scratched like an oversized angry rat in Venir's arms. He reversed his grip on Brool and began stabbing the two that wrestled and gnawed at his knees.

Scrunch! Scrunch!

Eight!

The tongue of the one in his clutches was juttering from its mouth in an awful hiss as Venir crushed its throat and dropped it to the ground. One still hung on his back, trying to rip the scale mail from his body. The air shimmered around him. All the hairs on his body stood up. Venir whipped his head around. *Where is it?* He looked up in time to see the underling hovering ten feet above him, hands pointing downward on him, radiating with power. *Move!* It was too late.

Venir balled up on the ground, back up, head down.

CHA —KAOW!

It felt like lightning was shooting through his nose as everything around him exploded in white hot light.

Slim the beetle buzzed through the effort to coordinate the chaos of an underling army that was under attack. His charge: to find and lead to safety two women who had been taken prisoner by underling hunters. As his black and gold wings buzzed through the air, none of the multicolored eyes that gleamed with evil paid him any mind. He soared over their heads, searching for the prisoners.

The camp, a series of dark grey tents lined up row by row, proved to be a bigger search area than he expected, and it was even more challenging when you were the size of a beetle.

If I were an underling, where would I hide two humans?

As the sounds of battle clashed nearby and the giant sized spiders were making their way back, he noticed every underling was moving except for a handful of guards. Armed with serrated spears and adorned in black leather armor, three underling warriors with eyes like hard sapphires chittered back and forth with one another. Behind them was a large pit with a wooden grate dropped over the top of it. Slim flew over the underlings' heads, dropped to the ground on the other side of the pit, and crawled inside.

His insect senses were aroused at the scent of waste in the air, and his instincts told him he was hungry. *I'm craving excrement. I'm not a dung beetle. Just a beetle.* He crawled down the dirt wall, his black shell with olive and white color blending in as he went farther and farther down. The pit was deeper than he expected, and he noticed hand and footholds dug into the dirt on the other side. What purpose did the underlings have for keeping the women alive? For the most part, anytime underlings came into contract with humans, or any other race, they left them for dead.

Making his way to the bottom, he let his antennas start feeling around. He could see the light coming from the top of the cage, but the shadows below left everything pitch black. He sensed vibrations of movement in the area, and sounds vibrated through his butt and into his head. He couldn't tell if the women were in there or not, but something was. There was only one way to find out.

Here goes.

His shell started cracking. His body expanded, warbled and returned to normal. Slim arched his back and stretched his long limbs. "Ah … that's better." He peered through the darkness where two huddled figures shivered.

"Adanna?" he said. "Is that you? It's me, Slim," he said, squatting down and touching a woman's leg.

She flinched.

As his eyes adjusted, her form took on a more distinct shape. Both of the women's figures became more defined, but there was something unnatural in the air. Slim shuffled back, hands out as an overwhelming sense of evil lurked within the pit. As his heart began pounding in his chest, he mumbled a protection spell. The suffocating shadow of the unknown retreated as Slim stepped forward, summoning more magic, and a soft glow erupted in the palm of his hand.

The two women, Adanna and her mother, trembled as they held on to one another for their dear lives. They were bound together with silky cords, like webs that spiders shoot and something else. That's when he heard a sucking sound, and Adanna let out a heavy sob. The mother's body lurched. That's when Slim noticed red eyes glimmering along the walls and on the women's bodies. Dozens of them popped open all at once. Spiders, bigger than his hands like tarantulas, began to detach themselves from the women and scurry towards him. *Oh my!*

He glanced above. The day's light looked like it was a mile off. He looked down as a spider sped his way, and he stomped it under his sandal. The pit erupted with a sound like squealing rats as the tiny horde of spiders darted at him. Above, the underlings chittered, gemstone eyes peering downward, the soft glow of his hand giving him away.

"Not good," he said, stomping each and every spider he could into the ground. The blood sucking spiders bit into his ankles. "Ow! Dratted bugs!" There was no sense in holding back; the underlings knew he was in there. "Enough!" He summoned more energy into his hands, and both burst aglow in white hot fire. The spiders burst into char as he grabbed, crushed or swatted them away. "How many of these things are there!"

They burned. They fried. They died. One palmful at a time. He burned the webs away from Adanna and her mother and shook them both. The mother was dead. An empty feeling overcame Slim, and Adanna sobbed as he wiped her nose with his robes. "Come on. I have to get you out of here." The buxom woman didn't move, quivering. People on Bish, no matter how hard they were, were never prepared for what the underlings had to offer.

He looked her over. Wounds, dozens of spider bites, covered her in red welts from head to toe. They weren't poisonous, but they fed off her blood. Some spiders were like mosquitoes, and others ate flesh like rodents. A few dozen spiders could easily kill a man as big as Venir if you didn't kill them first. He cupped Adanna's face in his palms and muttered under his breath. He felt his skin tighten as he fed his life force into her, sealing her wounds and charging her blood. He sagged to the ground.

"Slim?" she said, reaching down and hugging his lanky bones. "Are you all right?" she said, pulling him up to his feet.

He leaned on her and said, "I'll be fine in a moment." He looked up through the pit at where the underlings had removed the grate. "But I'm not so sure we have that long to wait."

They came. Two sand spiders as big as large dogs, tan with white ringed tails, scurried into the pit and cast a blanket of webbing above them. There was no way out now.

Adanna squeezed her arms around Slim's waist, looked up, and screamed just as the new spiders made their descent.

CHAPTER 4

"*F*IDDERBAY! *FIDDERBAY! FIDDERBAY!*" FOGLE BOON chanted as the giant foot stomped him into the ground. His face smashed into the rock and dirt. His body shuddered under the weight as it squished and contracted but did not bust. His bones didn't crack, and his skull wasn't crushed. The magic spell had worked. Fidderbay was an odd spell, made more for trick and fun than anything else, something he'd mastered as a young boy when they played games at school. The Fidderbay spell made you and your attachments soft and porous like a sponge. Still, he could feel the giant's foot trying to grind him into dust. *Think and Live!*

He shifted onto his back, and the giant lifted his boot up. The giant cocked its head as it stared down on him, eyes full of confusion. Fogle tried to yell for Cass, but his mouth felt like it was filled with cotton. The spell rendered any other incantations impossible, but it didn't last very long. The giant raised its club over its head and swung down with all its power. *Please keep working.*

Wham!

The giant struck him full in the chest. All of his blood rushed to his head, fingers and toes, stretching his skin to the limits. It fell like a geyser was trying to burst through his skull, and his eyes bulged from the sockets. His brain screamed, but his body remained intact, retaking its natural shape. Fogle was panting as he started to pat down his chest. *I live.*

He shook his fist at the giant and screamed, "I live!"

The giant roared and rotated back for another swing.

"Bish Almighty," he said, realizing that his tongue, along with the rest of him, had lost its cushiony vitality. He backpedaled, stumbled over a rough stone, and fell. He tried to scramble to his feet only to fall again. *Time to die!*

"Mood!" he yelled, but he knew already the Blood Ranger wouldn't come. "Cass!" But it was too late. The giant leered down on him and swung.

There was noise: wails of battle, mountainous bellows and the sound of rock and bones being shattered. Mood struggled to rise to his feet with the bitter taste of a mouthful of blood and dirt, which wasn't so bad for a dwarf. Especially a Blood Ranger no less. Still, his vision was blurry, and everything was a haze, and he couldn't tell if he walked or ran as he reeled toward the sounds of battle. The giant who had smashed him like a fly was dead, but the damage had been done. Mood, born and bred to fight, had been in some bad scraps before, but this last one got him.

"Eethum!" he yelled, but it came out in more of a garbled sound.

Ahead was another giant, bigger than the rest of the hill giants, one he didn't remember seeing before. The black bearded dwarves hurled spear after spear into its legs, but the giant didn't slow down. They looked like grim faced puppies attacking a man. The giant was big, with muscular trapezoids up to his pierced ears. He swung a hammer like a well-trained soldier, each blow ripping the rocks from the ground and sending Mood's brethren flying.

"Retreat! Retreat!" he yelled, but not one dwarven fighter turned.

The giant snatched one fallen dwarf from the ground, clenched his leg in his mouth, and shook him like a dog.

"No! Blasted giant!" Mood said, fighting to regain his feet.

The giant dwarves unleashed another assault of missiles into the giant's face as their comrade kicked and punched within the monster's mouth.

The hammer came down, crushing the nearest dwarf to a bloody pulp and shaking the ground. As Mood ran, it felt like the inner fiber of his being was tearing apart. He didn't notice his clavicle sticking out from his skin or the ribs jutting out underneath his arms or that his face was blackening underneath his bushy blood-red beard. All he knew was if that giant didn't die soon, he and his brethren would.

He banged his axes together and yelled as loud as he could.

"Come on, Giant!"

The monstrous man stopped and spit the broken dwarf from his mouth.

"That's right! I'm talking to you!" he said as the wind picked up and billowed his beard.

Another sharp clang of battle axes came together as Eethum appeared from underneath a pile of rubble, caked from head to toe in dirt and blood.

The remaining black bearded fighters backed up, dragging their comrades out of the way. The giant stuck its chest out and laughed. It looked more like a man than the others, cunning like a hunter, whereas the typical hill giant was more brute than brains. Mood now realized this wasn't a common hill giant that mixed with the ogres. This giant was something else: the real thing he'd rarely seen before. The last time he battled a full bred, he'd barely survived. No doubt this battle wouldn't be any different.

"AH ... BLOOD RANGERS! HA! HA! HA! WHAT A PLEASURE IT WILL BE TO KILL YOU BOTH," the giant said in a voice that was commanding and full of power. "YOU LITTLE INSECTS WILL NEVER LEARN, WILL YOU?" The giant was twirling its massive battle hammer around like a stick. "I AM TUNDOOR ... HA-HA-HA ... AND I'LL BE CRUSHING YOUR HEADS!" It swung its hammer over his head and slammed it into the ground with incredible force. The ground exploded, knocking Mood and Eethum from their feet as a billow of dusty smoke rose, thick as soup.

"HA-HA-HA!" the giant's booming voice mocked. "I CAN SEE YOU! SMELL YOU! AND HEAR YOUR DYING BREATHS!"

A sliver of uncertainty raced through Mood's spine. The smoke was confusing. One moment the giant was there, the next moment it wasn't. He could usually track a giant blindfolded, but at the moment he couldn't sniff out a single thing at all. Either his senses had been damaged, or the giant was using some of its tricks.

Eh? he thought, a split second before he dove to the ground.

The giant's hammer whooshed over his head.

Mood rolled left and kept going. It felt like a bag of knives was rattling inside his chest. He spat his blood into the ground.

The giant's foot came down inches from his head.

He struck, axes cleaving through skin and deep into muscle.

"OW! THAT STINGS, LITTLE RANGER! HA-HA-HA! TUNDOOR HEALS FAST! YOU'LL NEED A BIGGER AXE THAN THAT!"

CHAPTER 5

H E WAS TOLD HIS OLD room, the one he, Lefty, Melegal and Venir had shared, was now occupied by a brood of sordid men. It left him empty. Georgio stood on the stairs looking down inside the Drunken Octopus and wiped his sleeve across his forehead. It wasn't the same. The roughshod tavern's atmosphere was as dead as the candles on the chandeliers. He was used to more activity mid-day. Instead, he, Mikkel and Billip were greeted with hard stares from faces he didn't recall. It was as if the tavern had received a makeover. Mikkel's broad face was smiling as he shoved Georgio towards the bar.

"Move it, Boy. I'm as thirsty as a fish on a hook."

"Aye," Billip said, brushing past him with a greedy look in his eye, "let's eat, drink, and get a room." He cracked his knuckles in front of him. "And let me do the talking. I'm not paying coin if I can find some fool to do it for me."

"Fine," Georgio said, frowning and taking a seat at the bar. His stomach rumbled. "They have good stew, but the bread is always stale."

"Perfect!" Mikkel said.

One table at a time, he scanned the room. Not a face was familiar. But something was. His heart almost stopped as he locked eyes with a man in a wide brimmed hat. *McKnight!* His regrown fingers tingled as he stared at the man whose hat was the only thing that resembled the Detective. This man had a shaggy head of hair spilling out from underneath the brim, and there wasn't a single tooth left inside the mouth of his sagging face.

"Here," Mikkel said, shoving a mug of ale into his hand. "What's wrong with you? You look like you've seen an underling."

Georgio shook his head and took a sip of the bitter ale. "Nah … just thought I saw that guy who chopped my finger off, is all."

"If Melegal chopped him up and fed him to the pigs, then I'm pretty sure you're not going to ever be seeing him again." Mikkel patted his shoulder, looking around. "So this is where Venir used to stay, huh? No surprise, but you'd think there'd at least be some pretty girls."

Georgio scrunched his face up as he looked around some more. He'd never spent much time on the main floor. Someone his age wasn't allowed, but he'd changed. He took another drink. He felt like more of a man now. A sad one that missed his friend, Venir. He was hoping he'd see him here.

"Say, Sam," Billip said to the pock-faced barkeep, "tell me what you've heard about this Blond Haired Butcher? What's the bounty up to now?"

Georgio remained facing the fireplace on the other side of the bar. It had always blazed with a big orange fire, but now it was filled with long dead ashes. Beside it was Melegal's table, now occupied by the men who had taken over the room upstairs. They slammed their fists on the table and guffawed over a bunch of senseless jokes. A few meaty women kept them company, and they had no shame when it came to keeping the men's attention. Georgio had brushed shoulders with the leader while passing down the stairs. Jeb. That's the name Melegal had said. Georgio laughed at the thought of Melegal boxing him. *I wish I could have seen that.*

"The City Watch is offering a thousand gold for this man's head," the barkeep said, smoking a cigar and twisting the water from a rag.

"A thousand gold!" Billip exclaimed. "For one measly man? Pah, that's a bunch of lies. Last I heard, it was a hundred." Billip twisted the hairs under his chin. "Still, a hundred or a thousand is a lot of money. I could live well off that. For a while, anyway."

Mikkel clonked his empty tankard on the table.

"Another," he said, twisting his large frame in the stool towards Billip. "One hundred or one thousand, Billip, it would all slip through your fingers as easily as sand in a grate. You've never kept a hoard longer than a month, I'd say."

Billip rattled a sack of coins in front of Mikkel's face and said, "I've still got more coin than you. Now tell us, Sam," he slid a few coins across the bar, "you know something else, don't you? I can tell by the look in your eye. I've owned a tavern myself, you know."

Georgio locked eyes for a moment with Jeb, the man across the room who was whispering something into the ear of one of his comrades. Jeb, a stout man with a brawny build underneath his jerkin, seemed like just the kind of person looking for a fight. Something about the man's coarse black hair, mustache and sideburns didn't sit well with Georgio as he watched a larger man, almost as big a Mikkel, make his way across the tavern and take a seat at the bar. He didn't like the look of that man, either. He turned around and folded his hands across the bar.

"I've heard the man can't be killed," the barkeep said, "and he's got a scar that runs straight down the middle of his face."

Georgio's blood ran cold. *Tonio!*

Chapter 6

"**I**'VE SEEN SUCH MAN IN here, months ago. A tall one, as tall as you," he said, nodding towards Mikkel, "came in here and stabbed a troubadour through the back. The blood's still on the table. Things haven't been quite right around here since then, if you ask me." He refilled Mikkel's tankard and pointed at Georgio. "Not since that boy's big friend left, that is. Venir. I sorta miss having that big lout around here. He kept things interesting, if not even friendly, so to speak."

Mikkel and Billip looked at each other, then at Georgio.

"What?" he said, trying to hide his trembling hands.

"I think that man, whatever sort of evil he may be, has a vendetta on your friend. Why else would he be going around and killing all the yellow-haired people? He's even killed members of the City Watch. People have seen him do it. The urchins say he lives in the sewers. I've not seen a yellow hair in this tavern in weeks, if not months."

Georgio swallowed hard and rubbed his throat. Maybe that's what Melegal's warning was about. *"Go to Three and Live. Stay in Bone and die."* But Tonio wouldn't be after him. He'd be after Venir, and no one had any idea where Venir was. Georgio slumped in his seat.

"Ewww!" Mikkel said, "I'm not going into any sewers, Billip. Let's drop this nonsense and go find Nikkel. We haven't even checked outside the wall yet."

"Quit nagging me, will you? We'll look for your boy then. It'd just be better if I had some additional booty, is all. Besides, I'm beginning to like it here. Reminds me of the Orc's Elbow."

"Stay if you want," Mikkel said, poking Billip in the chest, "but me and Georgio will go."

"What?" Billip cocked an eye and looked over his shoulder. The large man from Jeb's group was walking away with something cupped in his hand. He took a quick look at Mikkel and said, "That big bastard just lifted my purse."

"Serves you right."

Billip flung his tankard into the back of the man's head. The man crashed head first into a table, Billip's coins spilling everywhere.

Georgio jumped from his stool while men and women erupted from Jeb's table. He could hear blades whisking from leather as they knocked over the tables and charged. Georgio stood brandishing a tankard in his hand. Mikkel right behind him.

"Don't any of you dogs move, or I'll skewer this mutt of yours," Billip warned, holding a dagger at the man's throat. "And you better get your foot off my gold," he eyed one of the thugs, "or I'll add some holes into you."

"Back off!" Jeb ordered in a rugged voice. "Back off, I say." His gang of men pressed behind him, a half dozen in all, one looking just as tough and ugly as the next. Jeb held out two knives with wide blades and brass pommels, waggled his wrist, and stuffed them behind his belt. The rest of his men followed suit. "Now let my man up, Little Man," he added, folding his arms across his broad chest.

"I'll collect my coins first," Billip said, flexing the muscles in his wiry forearm, "or this little man's going to skin this big man like an antelope. Then comes you." Billip nodded at Georgio. "Gather my coins before I let this lout up."

Georgio shook his head, but obeyed.

Jeb snorted a laugh. "Is that so?" Jeb scratched at his side burns. "We'll see about that. Tell you what, Little Man."

Georgio looked up at Jeb and then noticed Billip's cheeks flaring. Billip wasn't small for a man by any means, but Georgio had noticed that he now stood as tall as him. Even Kam was taller than the wiry archer. He scooped up all the coins he could find and retook his place beside Mikkel.

"That's enough, Jeb." The barkeep interrupted. "I'm not having any more of my customers run off. You've run off enough of them already."

"Shut it, Sam, or I'll see to it you'll have no more customers at all. Now let my man up from the floor."

Billip clonked the man's head off the hardwood planks and rose to his feet. Georgio tossed his coin sack over, and Billip snatched it from the air. Jeb's hands slipped back to his knives, and Mikkel was breathing down his neck as the tension began to thicken. Billip cracked his knuckles and popped his neck as he walked over and stood face to face with Jeb.

The brute looked down on him, sneered, and said, "Well?"

"Georgio, Mikkel, look at this man. He's awful pretty for an orc, wouldn't you say?"

"What?" Jeb said through clenched teeth.

"Knock him out, Jeb!"

"Jeb? You're the man called Jeb? The Jeb. The best brawler in Bone?" Billip said, stepping back a half step and holding up his palms. "Oh, I've heard about you."

"Yeah, what about it, Little Man?" Jeb replied with a half-smile.

Billip shrugged, his face turning from fearful to whimsical.

"I heard you beat an old woman with the iron gloves, but judging by your face, I'd say she got the best of you!"

"That's it!" Jeb roared, ripping out his knife and lunging forward.

Billip caught him by the wrist and twisted the blade free in one fluid motion. Billip cracked his head on Jeb's hard chin.

Georgio pounced on the man's legs, sending the three of them sprawling to the floor.

"Stop!" The barkeep screamed.

Someone ripped Georgio free from Jeb's legs, a brute of a man with arms of corded iron, and slung him into the nearest table.

"Bone!" he exclaimed, rising to his feet and wiping the blood from his nose

Billip and Jeb were hammering away at each other, one hard punch after the other. Mikkel picked one man up over his head and tossed him into the other three. The women screamed the vilest of things as they slung whatever they could find at Mikkel.

The Drunken Octopus was in a frenzy now, with everyone fighting for themselves. Georgio jumped onto the back of the nearest man and dragged him to the ground.

"CHALLENGE! CHALLENGE! CHALLENGE!"

Mikkel clocked a man in the jaw whose eyes rolled up in his head as he fell like a stone.

"I SAID *CHALLENGE!*"

Every one stopped, even Billip and Jeb loosened their grips around each other's throats, but their eyes were still hot with rage.

"You'll be paying for all this damage, you fools!" Sam said, standing on the bar and holding a large club. "But there will be no more. No fighting in this place without a challenge. Now you, troublemakers," he pointed to the three of them. "Get back over to the bar, or get out."

Georgio slid off the man's back and headed over. Billip and Mikkel joined him.

"Jeb! You make your challenge. You three, that includes you, Boy, accept or go!"

"Fine by me," Mikkel said, flexing his arms.

All eyes fell on Jeb. The burly man had his hands on his knees, sucking for air, when he pointed at Georgio.

"I challenge the lad then, Sam!"

"Coward!" Billip blurted out.

"I'll say," Mikkel added, holding Billip back.

The barkeep added, "Sorry, but he's in this. Of course, you don't have to accept. You can just go if you want to."

Georgio felt every eye in the tavern upon him.

Mikkel laid his heavy hand on his shoulder. "You don't have to do this."

Georgio shoved his hand away.

"Yes, I do. I'm a man the same as the rest." He pointed at Jeb. "What's your challenge, Man with a Face Like a Goat's Behind?"

The women snickered, as well as a few of the men.

Jeb tucked his thumbs in his belt and laughed out loud as his disheveled men joined in. Georgio's cheeks flushed red. His hand slipped to his sword.

"None of the lad," Jeb said, teetering on his toes, "but I tell you what. I'll let you draw from the cards. But, first you need to make a wager." Jeb looked over at Billip and said, "That purse of yours will do."

"Ah! Stupid Boy!" Billip said, eyeing the sack in his grip. "Fine, I'll put it up, but you're going to owe me, Georgio. He tossed his purse to the barkeep. "I'll be shuffling those cards first, if you don't mind." He extended his hand."

Jeb shrugged.

The tavern's old vitality was rekindled. The fireplace was lit as a trove of new faces filled in from the streets. This was more like how Georgio remembered it. He took a long sip of ale. *I wish Venir was here.*

A woman with long black hair and a sultry voice pressed her body into Georgio's back and whispered in his ear, "Why don't you let me draw for you, Handsome?"

Georgio swallowed hard and said, "Certainly."

Billip just shook his head, shuffling the cards like a magician. "Let's get this over with and draw."

Sam the barkeep hopped down from the bar, dragging his club behind him, and headed towards the middle, where he stood puffing his cigar. "Get over here and draw, Velvet."

The woman kissed Georgio on the cheek as she wiggled her way up to Sam, who fanned out all the cards on the table. Georgio's feet twitched and jangled as she bent over to some *oooh*'s and *ahhh*'s while walking her fingers over the cards.

"I think I'll take ... this one," she said, sliding the card from the deck and nuzzling it between her breasts.

The crowd jeered with lust.

"Show um' to us, Velvet!" one man shouted.

"The cards, too!" another added.

She peeked at the card, and her bright eyes began to dim.

What? Something was wrong. Georgio could feel it in his bones.

"Show us the card, Wench!"

She was biting her lip as her sad eyes looked on Georgio and she rose the card up over her head. A gasp filled the air.

A black card faced them, showing a burning skull with a pair of fencing blades stuck through it.

"The Flaming Fence!" the barkeep cried.

Georgio felt a heavy shadow fall over him as every eye in the room turned toward him and the barkeep added, "Ye might wish to yield unless you want to die."

Chapter 7

K AM WAS NUMB. HUMILIATION WAS something she hoped she never got used to as she soaked in the cooling waters of Palos's golden tub. Since becoming a captive, she'd been shot with a crossbow and punched in the gut by a man named Diller, and she wasn't sure which was worse: taking the pain or succumbing to Palos's erotic needs. She scrubbed the soapy water deeper into her skin with a wash cloth.

"Lefty!" she exclaimed under her breath.

"What was that?" Palos said, knotting the belt over his long black bath robe.

It was only the two of them now and the sound of a roaring fire underneath the nearby mantle. Things would be much better if Venir was here, but there was no chance the man could come to her rescue now. Nor any man for the matter. Besides, for all she knew, the father of her daughter was dead, even though that didn't really seem possible.

"I said, 'When can I see Erin, Palos?'"

He huffed as he dried his hair with a towel and took a seat at the table.

"It's not even been a day," he said, rolling his pale eyes and pouring a jeweled goblet of wine. "Now, let's take a moment to talk about things, Kam. I think it would be better if we had a fresh start." He poured another goblet. "Come on over and join me for some wine, and let's talk about something different. The past, perhaps."

Deep in the water, her nails dug into the palms of her hands. *Just go along with it. What choice do you have? Just don't make it too easy.*

"Fine," she said, grabbing her robe and standing up in the tub while taking her time slipping it on over her soapy body.

Palos' eyes were every bit as hungry as moments earlier.

"We can talk about the past, but not forever." She walked over, grabbed her goblet, and stood by the fire. Its burning logs warmed her from head to toe. It felt good, revitalizing, almost cleansing.

Palos smiled at her. "Feels good, doesn't it, Kam? The fire, the wine and the touch of a man. I know, Kam. I can tell how lonely you are. You've always been that way. You never wanted to get too close or have the kind of fun the other girls had. You were such a serious person, a dreamer within your own little world. I've wanted you since the moment I first saw you, but unlike the rest of your feminine breed, you never dropped your britches for me." He gulped down his wine. "It just made me want you so much more."

"And, now you have me?" she flipped her hair. "Does that mean there are no more pastures of women to conquer? Is it just a matter of time before I'm tossed dead into a gutter when you don't fancy me anymore?"

He lifted his palms up and said, "Easy. Easy now, Kam. I've promised you that no harm will come to you or your daughter."

"So long as I play your little whore."

He shrugged his satin shoulders and smiled.

"Well, that's one way of putting it, but I want more than that with you, and over time you will see that."

I hope not. She ran her fingers under the choker on her neck. If she could just get it off, she'd turn him inside out with a single word. Her power dwelled inside her, and she'd memorized quite a few spells. But she couldn't hang on to them forever. Still, she'd always have some power. Her sorcery allowed for that.

"So, would you like me to rub your feet now, Prince Palos?" She batted her eyes.

"Oh, I like the sound of that! But don't patronize me."

She strolled over behind him and placed her hands on his shoulders.

"How about I rub your shoulders, then?" she whispered in his ear. She could see the hairs on his neck stand up on end.

"Eh … well, I suppose that would be all right."

She rubbed deep into the supple muscles under his meaty neck. The man, despite his additional girth, moved with the grace of a swan. As much as she wanted to choke him to death, she knew taking the opportunity would only meet with failure and with that would come more time away from Erin. She rubbed harder and deeper.

"Aaaahhhh …," Palos moaned, "it feels so good."

She pulled him back into her chest and said in a soft voice, "After this, can I see my baby? It's nursing time already."

"We'll see. But I'm going to need more of these muscles loosened first."

She brushed her hands through his flaky hair. She remembered when Palos never had a thing out of place. Compared to most men, he'd been divine. And he'd been right about her, too. She was a prude. She didn't do things like the other girls in school, but not because she thought she was better, but more because she was afraid.

"Perhaps I could trim this hair of yours? I think it could use a woman's touch." *You vile and fattened beast.*

"And have my own scissors rammed through my eyes, Kam? I don't think so. Besides, when the time comes, I'll have my nanny do it for me."

"So be it, then." She continued her rubbing, minute after minute as Palos slunk deeper into the chair. *Just relax, Pig.* Getting Palos out of her hair was one thing, but escaping the Nest would be another. There were hundreds of cutthroats out there: murderers, slavers, smugglers and thieves, and if Palos fell, no doubt someone would take his place. And she was certain she'd have Palos's father Palzor to deal with after that. There had to be another way.

Palos's eyes rolled up in his head as she rubbed his temples with her thumbs. *Cocky bastard.* The Prince of thieves was as loose as a goose in her hands, and it made her uneasy. The man had no fear of anything bad happening in his own house, it seemed. It left her feeling more helpless than ever. She scanned the room looking for anything that might assist her to escape. Empty bottles of wine, stacked piles of coins, candle stands, and furniture all of the finest quality. But nothing of a useful sort. The magic Palos had displayed had been tucked away somewhere her keen eyes had yet to find.

"What are you thinking, Kam?" he said, raising goose bumps on her arms. "I can feel you thinking, and frankly it's only making it harder for me to relax."

"I want to see my Erin, that's all. Of course I wouldn't expect you to understand."

He puffed a laugh and said, "Why, because my breasts are not yearning to be suckled?"

Something was uncoiling inside her. Her emerald eyes blazed on the great sword that hung on the mantle. Something about that magnificent sword was speaking to her.

"Don't stop now!" Palos warned, "Or you won't see your baby until the morrow', maybe later."

"Of course, Prince ..." *of swine*

He reached back and snatched her by the hair and jerked violently down.

Face to face, she saw a deranged look in his eyes that was not there a moment ago.

"And if you don't stop thinking of escape, Dearie, I'm sure my servant Diller and his men will be more than glad to suckle that swelling chest of yours!"

She cracked her head on the table when he shoved her to the floor.

"Now, rub my feet, you red-headed cow, and think of nothing more!"

Kam shivered and averted her eyes from his. *He's mad!* One second he was as smooth as a stone in a tranquil river and in the next he was an impulsive maniac with murder in his eyes. It scared her. It was one thing to deal with a wicked person that was sane, but it was quite another to deal with one that might just be crazy. Her body trembled as she rubbed and rubbed and rubbed and her doubt at ever again seeing her daughter grew. All she wanted to do was get her baby to safety now, but trying to do that might cost her life.

Got to save them. Got to save them! Lefty sat beside Gillem at a table full of cards and coins, his blond hair disheveled, trying to hide the weight of the world from showing on his face. He faced the steps that led up to Palos's room and cast a casual glance up now and again.

Diller was there, crossbow folded under his arms, toothpick dangling from his mouth, eyes surveying each and every person below.

But how do I get past that man?

"Drop a card, you little rodent," the man with a skinned up face sneered across from him.

"Oh my," he said, running his tiny fingers through his hair before plopping a few coppers on the table. "Tell you what, Scratch, why don't you drop a card instead?"

Scratch glowered at him with beady eyes and said, "You're a little fool, Boy. Master Gillem, why'd you bring this rodent to us? He's as stupid as he is short."

Gillem sat on his stool, his pie face a humble grin, puffing on his pipe.

"He's learnin,' Scratch. Nothing better to teach a youngling quick than to snatch his coins. And since when did you ever care about someone losing to you? Take all his money you want. It's mine you should be worried about." He slipped a silver coin onto the table.

Scratch grunted as the remaining figure at the table, a black-eyed dwarf with a braided brown beard, shoved a matching silver coin across the table.

Lefty showed his teeth to Scratch and said, "It seems fortune's on the side of the little people. Call or withdraw, Scratch."

The card game they played is called Three. Ninety-nine cards fill the deck. There are nine symbolic face cards, each a different animal or creature, numbered from one to eleven. Each player is dealt three cards face down. One can look at them, bet or withdraw. The highest card wins. In the event of a tie, the deck is shuffled and dealt again, and the pile of bets grows.

Lefty's eyes flicked over all the cards turned over on the table. Gillem showed a rooster and a dog, and had withdrawn. The dwarf who had not revealed his name, as he didn't speak, but grunted, had done the same, showing only a pair of weasels. All low cards. Scratch showed a bear and a ram, high cards. Lefty had a dog and a rat. He rubbed his chin. "Hmmmm ..."

There were three of each animal represented. A rat was the lowest, and the dragon was the highest. No dragons were played, and Gillem and the dwarf had withdrawn. He could feel all eyes on him. *Good.* He looked at his last card again. A lion. Only a dragon could beat it. Out of the twelve cards on the table, only the dragons were loose, and two lions would tie.

"Watcha going to do, Lefty?" Gillem asked, his blurry eyes watering as he stuffed more tobacco in his pipe.

"Ah … I'm thinking, Master Gillem," he said, scratching his head, "but this is pretty hard."
Wham!

Lefty jumped as Scratch rapped his fist on the table and said, "Think faster, you little turd. I'm getting tired of waiting on you. Gillem, teach him cards elsewhere!"

Gillem glared at the man and said, "That's Master Gillem, you son of a pick pocket! You best remember the order of things around here."

Scratch sulked back in his chair as the roughhewn dwarf stuck a wad of chaw in his mouth.

"Apologies, Master Gillem. I'm just getting tired of his halfling's good fortune, is all. He's fared well for someone that's never played before," he said, pouring more grog into his tumbler.

So I have him fooled, after all. Now all I have to do is figure out how to fool them all. His hand that he drummed his fingers with slid down to his tell. *Do one thing so they think you are going to do another,* Melegal had said. Lefty was beginning to understand all of these little lessons better. He'd been observing all of them, taking notice of what they did with a good hand or a bad hand.

Scratch's tell was that he drank a little more with a good hand, and bit his inside cheek with a bad one. The dwarven man was a stone, however, and Lefty had the hardest time figuring him out. He didn't talk; he grunted. He didn't blink at all. All he did was chew and swallow the nasty tobacco juice. But, come to think of it, on a good hand he could hear the dwarf sucking the juice through his teeth, and on a bad hand he switched his chaw from one cheek to the other. And that left Master Gillem, who, as it turned out, had the easiest tell of all. Or was that just what he wanted him to see? On a good hand, he let out a plume of smoke, and on a bad hand he sucked the smoke in from his mouth and in his nose.

He took another peek at his card. *Better let him win one. This is too easy.*

"What's the matter, did you forget what you got, Stupid?"

"No!" Lefty shot back. "Are you certain you don't want to withdraw Scratch? I've got a pretty fine card!"

Scratch pushed another silver coin across and said, "Let's see it, then."

Lefty added his silver to the pile and flipped over his card.

"Ha!"

Scratch slapped a dragon card on top of his lion.

"Beat you again, halflings!" he said in elation, scooping the small pile of coins his way.

Lefty frowned, chin down, and said, "I'm sorry, Master Gillem. I really thought I had him. I really did."

Gillem reached over, rubbed his head, and said, "That's all right, Lad. You're getting better. But sometimes you need to know when to withdraw and wait for the sure thing."

Lefty nodded, locked eyes with Gillem, and said, "I know. Can I take a moment, go outside, and stretch my legs? Besides," he said, fanning the smoke from his face, "I'm getting a bit of a headache."

Gillem was shuffling the cards. "Be quick about it. You never know when Prince Palos will call. We must be ready."

"Hah! I bet he's having some good fun with her up there! I'd give a mouthful of silver just to watch," Scratch said with a lusty look in his yellow eyes. "Give her a week, and she'll be just as common as the rest of his whores."

The man's cold words felt like daggers in Lefty's back. Kam's situation was his fault and his alone. *Do something or die,* Melegal had always said. He patted his belly. There was something in there he'd been careful to conceal from the rest of the guild, especially Gillem. Magic. He could use some, a little bit at least. And he knew that Palos had plenty of items at his disposal as well. If he could just get in there and get his hands on some, he could help. *If I could just make it back to the Magi Roost.* He fought an inner sob. *What have I done to my friend? If I can't do anything else, I'll at least save her baby.* Whether his eyes were watering from tears or from the smoke, he did not know as he stepped over the threshold and outside.

"Ulp!" A pair of strong hands picked him up by the hair of his head.

He clutched at the hands that held him as he looked into the burnt and angry face of the man called Thorn.

"You halflings are going to die," he said in a garbled voice.

Lefty kicked him in his crooked nose.

"Ow! Blasted Halfling!" Thorn swung him by the head of hair, sending him flying back inside. He crashed into a table and whopped his head on the floor so hard bright spots burst forth. The sound of a sword slipping through the leather filled his ears as Thorn cried, "Gillem! You and this little boy are going to die tonight!"

Chapter 8

THE CITY OF BONE. It wasn't a place Verbard ever would have imagined setting his foot in before. As he walked down a narrow alley followed by two dozen of his men, the feeling he had in his gut wasn't something he had ever dealt with. He reached forward and tapped Jottenhiem on the shoulder. The underling fighter turned, a fierce grin under his ruby red eyes.

"My Lord," he said.

Verbard raised a finger, his silver eyes flickering in the shadows of the midday sunlight. The city smelled far worse than he imagined it. *How do men live in this wretched place?* The underlings were notoriously clean by comparison. There were no slums in the underworld, just caves and caverns filled with creatures united in the working cause of destroying mankind.

"Let me send Eep ahead," Verbard said. "We are getting very close to the people; I can hear them now. Many, many people." He stuffed his fingers in his pockets and secured them on some magic objects. *I have a feeling I'll need all of this. Eep, what is ahead?*

Somewhere, Eep sat on the ledge of a building at the end of an alley, peering downward.

People, Master. Many people, working, eating and waiting for me to kill them. Can I kill them all, Master?

Any soldiers?

No. Just sacks of soon to be rotting flesh. So many, Master. I cannot contain myself. Release me!

Be still, Eep. I have other plans for you.

Does it involve killing more people?

Certainly.

Verbard turned to his commander, Jottenhiem. "Our time to strike has come." He looked back over his shoulder at the small group of underlings.

The swords of the twelve Juegen armored in black plate mail from head to toes gleamed in the dim light. Six badoon underlings in black leather hauberks stood with small crossbows and knives at the ready, and behind them were six magi, fingers glimmering with radiant power, eyes flickering under their hoods. No human could possibly be ready for this. Not even The Darkslayer, himself. A slender smile broke over Verbard's lips. He was ready.

"Let's take as many as we can. There will be no time for burials. On my command, we'll retreat. You know what to do."

"This will be glorious," Jottenhiem said, lowering a full iron helmet over his skull and cutting his swords through the air. "On your command, my lord, and we shall remove the skin from their bones."

Verbard felt a charge of energy surge through him at having his natural enemy so close, as if he were running with a pack of timber wolves who were taking down a tired elk.

I can't believe I'm actually doing this. Yet, it feels so right somehow.

Eep, lead us to the largest group of people.

The City of Bone was moments away from never being the same again.

Kierway, the Vicious, three Juegen and three underling magi departed from the barge and the current.

"Stay here," the underling ranger said with iron eyes that seemed to glow.

Another twenty underlings, well-armed and ready, remained on the barge as Kierway drew his sword and led the way through the dark caverns beneath Castle Almen. Oran had described his dealings with Royal Lord Almen before, and he knew the way inside, but still, the very thought of entering the castle of his enemies was a bit unsettling. It was one thing to strike in the dark of the Outlands that he'd been so accustomed to over the decades, but striking within their walls was another matter entirely. *This should be Verbard, not me.*

He led the way up a set of stone stairs to a man-sized wooden door trimmed in discolored iron. He chittered a command and stepped aside as an underling mage floated up to the threshold. The mage's clawed hands flared with energy as it pressed them on the door.

Kierway noticed all the hungry looks on the faces of his troops. Each was a mask of concentration, starving to be the first to strike a lethal blow on behalf of underling kind. Maybe his father, Master Sinway, wasn't being so frivolous after all. Things seemed natural, as if he was returning to regain his home. *Impossible. But maybe the key will explain what is going on.*

There was a flash of energy followed by a sizzling sound when he found himself staring through the other side of a gaping hole. Warmth and the scent of human sweat filled the air around him. The instincts of his black blood pulsated with new life as a craving for battle consumed him.

"Kill anything that moves," he said, pointing the Vicious forward. Everything tingled from head to toe as he stepped through the door into an uncharted battle ground.

CHAPTER 9

VENIR FELT LIKE HE'D BEEN struck by a hundred hammers as he struggled to lift his hulking frame from the ground only to collapse again into the turf. He spit dirt and blood as he pushed his chest from the ground and rolled into the light of the blaring suns. He could smell the charred flesh of the underling that was on his back, a rancid smell like that of a burning skunk as he pinched his nose, fighting nausea and rising to his feet.

He mumbled as he took a step forward, staggering and dazed. Above him, the underling mage let out an angry hiss. Venir's helm beckoned action, but he could hardly move as he fought through the numbness and pain. He glanced up as a coat of webbing fell from the sky. *Move or die.* He slung his shield into the net of webbing and dove to the side.

The underling hissed as the shield carried the webbing to the ground, negating the spell. Venir let out a triumphant growl as he felt life begin to flow back into his fingertips and tried to spit the taste of nails from his mouth.

"What else do you have, Fiend?" Venir said, twirling Brool in the air.

The underling floated backward now, slowly retreating towards the battle at the camp, its yellow eyes burning with hatred. Yet, Venir could feel its confusion and sense its doubt.

"That's right! Your moments left on Bish aren't many. I've returned!"

The webs dissipated as he drew Brool's keen edge over his web-coated shield. Strapping it on over his back, he began chasing the underling down. In the dusty distance, the clashing sounds of battle rung inside his helm, and the wind whistled through his ears. He was gaining on the underling. Somehow, Venir could feel its magic fading as its dark robes dipped and brushed over the barren landscape's stones.

"Ha!" Venir cried, churning ahead, long stride after stride, gaining speed.

Twenty Feet. Ten Feet. Five feet. He dove forward, crashing into the back of the much smaller creature and driving it to the ground. Venir wrapped his fingers around its neck and squeezed. The blue veins in his arms rolled up like snakes as the underling kicked and flailed beneath his waist. Its black tongue jutted from inside its mouth as its citrine eyes bulged. Venir felt the taut wiry muscles in its neck heave then slacken as its wind pipe was crushed in his grasp.

"Eleven!" he said, wiping the sweat from his eyes and rushing for the battle. His long strides couldn't get him there fast enough as the Royal Riders were swarmed and ripped down from their saddles.

"BONE!"

The tide had turned. The element of surprise was gone. The riders were outnumbered three to one, and that didn't include the giant spiders that shot webbing from one side of the camp to the other. Horses nickered and neighed as the hairy black creatures from the Underland cut and stabbed at their thundering legs.

From the distance, Venir saw one Knight catch a spear in the neck and tumble into the fray. Another's head was blasted open by a barrage of mystic red missiles. Venir's inner core burned. A knot of fury needed release as he witnessed the battle unfold, blow by blow.

Seek! The helm urged him. *Destroy!*

Thirty yards. Twenty yards. Ten yards. Brool pulsated with life as he hefted it back behind his shoulders and exploded.

A throng of underlings were pulling another rider from his horse. Venir slammed into them, carving into them like canoes. A giant spider as big as a horse had a rider pinned down, its two protruding tentacles poking holes through the man's plate mail. Venir disemboweled the creature, leaving it twitching on the dusty floor. He was in the thick of the fight, powerful arms chopping left and right, splitting dark faces and cleaving through bone. Brool was humming now, a living thing weaving a path of destruction like black lightening. *Seventeen!*

Venir was bigger, faster and stronger than them all. His mind and the armament merged as one, punching holes into the army of underlings one by one.

Glitch!

Hack!

Slack!

Chop!

Chop!

Stab!

The underling bodies piled up at his feet, yet they kept coming on, in pairs and triples, crossbow bolts careening off his helmet, darts bouncing from his shield. Venir snarled down on them and growled like a savage beast, swinging his war-axe in an arc of death that ripped two underlings' heads from their shoulders.

More! The helm pleaded as black blood fertilized the Outland ground.

Still, unlike before, Venir's vision was clear, his mind concise, his body and armor taking all of the punishment he could handle. He could sense their worry; he fed on their fear, his hulking frame moving as fast as thought, a half second faster than everything the underlings threw at him. He kept swinging; they kept coming. His mind forgot about all of the others engaged in the battle.

The helm's black eyelets smoldered like blazing fires; Brool's black blade was a tornado of steel. *No mercy!*

Venir felt in control, his body as strong as a gale, the helm telling him when to duck, twist and turn, but he stayed on the offensive. *Move and die, Underlings! Run and die! I'll have you all!*

They screamed. With rage. With defiance. With fear. Their evil faces were twisted with hatred as they realized their old foe had returned, his vengeance like they'd never seen before. Still, with gnashing teeth they piled on, blades arcing high and low.

He jabbed Brool's spike through one and ripped its heart out. "RRRRRAHHH!"

In the back of his mind, he remembered the Warfield, the Vicious, and Georgio. The armament had propelled him there and pushed him past his limits to where he had collapsed and died, or almost died. Now, he felt invincible. He should be exhausted by now. What was different this time?

He snapped his head around as a massive shadow fell over him. The biggest spider of them all's eight eyes looked down on him like a treat as a burst of green fluid shot from its mouth. Venir bounded away, the splash of the acid sizzling into his legs. He roared as he scrambled into another wave of underlings. *Slice! Chop! Glitch! Twenty-Eight!*

The smoldering helm screamed a warning.

"What!" Venir yelled, casting an upward glance.

Four magi hovered above, a net large enough for twenty men in their grasp. One second Venir was a blur of destruction. The next, he was a helpless heap, trapped like a fish in a net full of piranhas.

There was no time left. Slim sagged alongside Adanna as the spiders crept down the walls and out of the light. Adanna had screamed herself hoarse as she trembled at his side, her body drained of all the rush of fright.

"Wrap this around your face," Slim said, tearing the sleeve from his robe.

She didn't respond. He covered her head with his sleeve and whispered something in her ear. He could feel the tension in her chest ease as she slipped to the floor. Slim covered his head with his robe as well and huddled over Adanna, muttering another spell, and then he had nothing left. His magic was spent. He let his body slacken in the dim light of the pit. He could hear the clicking and sucking sounds of the spiders as they made their way down the walls. He clutched Adanna tight as her body recoiled.

"Don't flinch. I've got you protected," he whispered in her ear. But he didn't. Not from their acidic or blood-sucking bits. But with something else. A gamble. *I hope they've been well fed today, or else I'm going to be spider crap real soon.* He lay still, huddled over the warmth of Adanna's body as the spiders began to coat them with their silk. The strong creatures pulled him and Adanna apart from one another and covered them from head to toe, one by one.

CHAPTER 10

ONCE, HE'D BEEN NOTHING MORE than a common rogue who pilfered in the streets and enjoyed cheap wine. Now, Melegal sat in utter misery inside his calm exterior as the loud and distraught pleas of Brak ran loops in his thoughts. *Pitiful. Sick and pitiful.* Down in the arena, the young Royals were hoisting their swords in jubilation and chanting praises to one another as the sentries dragged the bloody corpse of Hagerdon the Slerg across the floor and out of sight.

Disgusting little wretches!

He shifted on the hardened bench beneath him as they paraded around, wiping the blood from their swords before tasting it. Lord Almen and his cohorts were standing and applauding, offering congratulations to the young men. Melegal couldn't help but be disappointed. This seemed beneath someone like Lord Almen. He shifted his attention back to Lorda Almen.

She bit into some sliced fruit, a catty smile on her face as if nothing in the arena was going on. Her servants fanned her face and wiped the sweat glistening on her brow. She'd made him an offer he couldn't refuse, simply because he had no choice. *Just as wicked, twice as beautiful.* But he still couldn't help but be tempted by what her offer meant. *Kill the Brigand Queen. What an honor! For a fool.*

"Who shall we kill next, Lord Almen?" one of the young Royals shouted up into the stands. "The taste of Slerg blood is divine!"

Melegal's fingers caressed the triggers on the dart launching bracers concealed inside his clothes. How many times had he been tolerated and chastised by their kind as a child? The whippings and humiliation were nothing to be forgotten. He'd seen all the things these young men got into: defiling, lying, cheating and stealing from one another like it was their rightful cause. If part of that lingering sentiment made it easy to watch the Slergs go, then they could all die for all he cared. He'd been a part of their castle up until he and Venir escaped, but he'd never desired vengeance upon them. He'd gotten away and left them alone. Now he sat watching them die, one by one, with nothing but an empty feeling inside. *I hate Royals!*

"Leezir the Slerg," Lord Almen spoke, disrupting his thoughts, "my old foe, come … step forward."

Leezir, now a haggard man, once short and shifty, shuffled forward in his chains, head down and fighting the shivers and a cough. He stood in the middle of the arena and lifted his chin up, his pale eyes no longer intent and filled with power like the man Melegal once knew as the fearless and callous leader of his house.

"Ah, Leezir, it seems your final game is over," Lord Almen said with smug satisfaction in his voice. "You attempted to overtake my castle, yet you failed. And now, I, Royal Lord Almen, noble and wise …"

"Hear! Hear!"

"… now stand willing to entertain your pleas. And …" he held his jeweled fingers out, "perhaps I'll show mercy."

Leezir opened his mouth to speak but was overtaken by a fit of coughing.

Lord Almen chuckled, the others as well.

"Come now, Leezir, certainly you can do better than that?"

A hearty burst of laughter filled the room.

Leezir raised his head once more, his eyes drifting into the stands, taking in every face one by one. Of all the Slergs, Leezir was the most reasonable, and he'd be the last one Melegal wanted to see go. After all, Leezir'd had a small hand in freeing them, which was something Melegal had never make sense of.

Stopping on Melegal, he locked his gaze for a moment, sending a jolt to his senses, before moving on. Lord Almen gave him a casual glance as well.

Thanks for that, Slerg! As if I wasn't a greasy blemish already. Blast, I'm getting a headache. What is wrong with me?

"Lord Almen," Leezir managed with a voice that belied his calm appearance, "you are as vile as a pit of vipers. A snake within the roses. Your black heart is filled with nothing but treachery and darkness. You betrayed me," he pointed into the stands, "and he'll betray the rest of you as well. Mercy, you say!" Leezir spat on the ground. "Pah! You don't know the meaning, you murderer of old women and children in their sleep!"

Hear! Hear! Melegal thought, fighting the urge to applaud. *Remember, never sleep near an Almen.*

Lord Almen's body noticeably stiffened at the resounding truth in those words. His glance drifted over to his Lorda, who now sat up glaring. Sefron gaped, and his lips looked to be mumbling a spell, while Jarla the Brigand Queen sat with her legs crossed, hands clasped on her knee, smiling.

Almen cleared his throat and smiled.

"You've an interesting way of pleading for mercy, Leezir. Perhaps your tactics are why all of your negotiations failed. It's almost a shame to see such a slow-witted family go. I'm sure you'd have made excellent grape pressers," Lord Almen needled his chin in pose, "or grave diggers."

"Let us kill him, Lord Almen!" the same youth as before said.

"Arm the young Royals with their bows," Almen ordered. "I think I've found an excellent practice target."

Leezir shouted back, shaking his fist. "I'll not run like some rabbit, Almen! I've seen this game before. You might as well take me as I am!"

"Perhaps you won't, but I'm sure your … granddaughter will," Almen added.

"Let the child go!" Leezir's face reddened as he fell into a fit of coughing. "She's not guilty of anything. She's only a child."

"Oh, but she is guilty of being a Slerg though, isn't she? And I can't have any legacy Slergs hanging around my castle. As you know, I think we all do, revenge can be such a powerful motivator, and I can't have that kind of weapon scurrying around my city. It's best to end this once and for all. It's for the better."

The young Royals, excluding the one who had lost his fingers earlier, had formed a line. One by one, they nocked their bows. Melegal leaned forward on the edge of his seat. He remembered seeing this game before, played with blunt arrows. He and many urchins had suffered welts and bruises from it, even an eye out or two. He stiffened and frowned. In this case however, the arrows were steel tipped.

"You'll burn for this, Almen! I'm not your last enemy standing, you know. *Cough-cough* There will be more, and your blood will run red into the sewers down below, I swear it!" Leezir didn't struggle as the guards dragged him and the wailing girl into the middle of the arena.

Her high pitched screams were unnerving. Melegal fought the urge to cover his ears. He looked to Lorda, but she had her head turned away in chatter. *No mercy there, either. I see.*

"What about the big one?" one of Almen's' guests asked.

Brak!

Time was running out to save Venir's son. He had no plan, nothing at all. It would almost be better if he dove in the arena himself and caught a few shafts in his chest to get it over with. *Way to go, Rat. If I can't save myself, then how can I save anyone else?* He felt a pair of eyes on him and looked down. Jarla's dark blues probed his, like a cat cornering a mouse. Her nostrils flared, and her lips twitched, standing Melegal's hair on end. She narrowed her eyes and turned away.

Witch! What does she know? I think the Lorda has it right, after all.

"We'll save the big one for last. The main event," Lord Almen said. "Carry on!"

The guards knocked the chained figures of Leezir and Jubilee to the ground and backed away. One of the sentries in the arena began counting down.

"Five!"

They could at least take off the chains.

"Four!"

Melegal could read Leezir's lips as he clutched the girl in his arms. He was saying, *Don't run, Jubilee. Stay close to me. I'll keep you safe.* That wasn't possible, Melegal knew. Every blood thirsty Royal knew that, too, but it was still the right thing to say.

"Three!"

Melegal took a quick glance around. For some reason, he thought Venir would come bursting through the door at any moment, axe high, screaming for the heads of every last Royal.

"Two!"

All of Melegal's hopes fled as Leezir hugged his granddaughter with all his might.

"One!"

Twang. Twang. Twang. Twang. Twang. Twang.

Leezir's body lurched forward, six arrows piercing his back. Cheers erupted from the small crowd as Leezir's hand fluttered and he moved no more.

Jubilee crawled out from beneath him, eyes wide with horror, tears streaming down her face, clutching at her grandfather's face.

"Reload, Lads!"

I can't watch this! Melegal's head dipped down at the sound of the wooden shafts scraping along the arrows in the rest of the bows. The sound of the stretching bow strings clenched the muscles in his jaws.

"One at a time," the soldier said, "Let's feather the little Slerg like a goose, shall we?"

The first young Royal, the one with the boasting mouth, let his arrow fly. Melegal's grey eyes watched with deep remorse as the arrow seemed to sail across the arena in slow motion and hit the wall above Jubilee's fragile shoulder, sending her running and tripping over Leezir's corpse. Somehow, she still staggered back to her feet.

Stay down!

Twang.

An arrow narrowly missed her leg as she screamed.

Amid the rousing cheers and cries, a triumphant and most unnatural sound occurred.

Melegal's back straightened as a snake of ice slivered through his spine. The sounds of groaning metal and snapping chains cut through the arena like a lightning strike. Brak, once huddled and forgotten, was in full motion now. His hulking frame was tearing his metal bonds away like cob webbing, and his big face was a raging inferno the likes of which no man had seen before.

Brak stormed across the arena, slamming into the row stunned young Royals. His blue eyes blazed like a man possessed, and his thickset arms were knotted in fury, hammering at the young men who were awestruck by the raging bull.

Melegal had seen a similar look on Venir before, but this was different, a frenzied beast out of control. *Go, Brak!*

A young Royal's neck was snapped like a branch. Brak bent another one's head back over his shoulder.

Melegal remained frozen in his seat, aware that the woman, Jarla, remained poised as well, her hands falling to her sword as she scooted forward. Melegal held his fingers tight on his triggers as madness overcame the crowd.

"NOOOO!" a guest from the stands screamed, his arm stretching out.

In the arena, two soldiers lay dead, and Brak had his hands filled with their swords, chopping down everything, living, moving or breathing. Big and frightening, he came at them with speed that defied the natural boundaries of man.

CHOP!

He cut one soldier in twain.

SLICE!

A young Royal's head was severed from his shoulders.

A durable soldier in chain armor launched an arrow into Brak's shoulder. He ripped it out, charged, and jabbed it into the soldier's neck.

Lord Almen was on his feet now, barking orders as his precious Coming of Age game quickly became a Royal blood bath. The servant girls were scrambling up the stands, dragging the distraught Lorda behind them. By the time they reached the top, he'd seen two more Royals felled under Brak's devastating blows.

Think, Detective! He scanned the arena for Sefron. The vile cleric was scurrying through a door above, his sagging face agape in terror. *Slat!* Melegal contemplated his move, if he had one at all. The Royal guests, the softer sort, adorned in fanciful robes and far from prepared for battle, scurried around the arena stubbing their sandaled toes. Lord Almen was the only calm one among them as Brak skewered the last young Royal and hoisted the dead young man high in the air on his sword.

"Somebody stop him!" Lord Almen cried. He looked back over his shoulder.

"Detective! Get in there!"

Almen sneered at Jarla and pointed inside the ring.

"You get in there as well!"

Jarla looked at Melegal, and he looked at her. He stood up and made his first step. An impossible thought occurred to him. An urge that felt right, good.

I've had it with these Royals.

Jarla unsheathed her sword and took another look at him.

Melegal's mind glimmered with life, filling his body from head to toe.

Sleep! Sleep! Sleep! Sleep!

Jarla's eyes rolled up in her head as she swooned, her sword clattering on the seats.

"What is this!" Lord Almen said, reaching for the collapsing woman.

Everything was in slow motion. Lord Almen's back turned to him. Melegal grinned from cheek to cheek. *Might as well start at the top.*

Stab!

Lord Almen's expression was one he'd never forget as he plunged his dagger deep in between the Royal's ribs.

"Welcome to my arena," he said, twisting his blade.

Lord Almen's handsome expression paled as he tried to twist free, arms pushing away Melegal's face. He held Almen tight by his robes and pushed the blade deeper.

"Urk!"

Almen's eyes widened in alarm as fear filled his eyes.

"You'll pay for this, Detect ..."

Lord Almen's eyes rolled up in his head as Melegal lowered him to the floor.

"But you won't be around to see that, will you?" he said, head whipping around.

Whop!

Brak was in the stands now, arrows jutting from his back and shoulders as he smashed two of Lord Almen's guests into each other and hurled them over the wall.

He slipped his dagger from between Almen's ribs. The man was dead. He couldn't believe it. *I killed him. I actually killed him. Have I gone mad?* The memory of Leezir's eyes flashed in his mind. His cap tingled with alarm.

Slice!

He sprung backward as a sword stroke almost cleaved him in half.

"Murdering coward!" Jarla yelled.

It seemed his suggestion hadn't worked so well. What a willful woman she must be.

As Brak continued to hack the Royals down one by one in a maddened frenzy, Melegal dashed up the stairs and down again as more guards and soldiers spilled into the arena from high and low.

"Bone!"

Jarla's steel nipped at his toes as he bounded past her and down into the arena. Ten more able soldiers made their way into the arena and blocked every door. There was no way out for Melegal unless he took out the angry swordswoman coming his way.

Think!

Chapter 11

FOGLE'S LIMBS WERE FROZEN AS he watched the giant's club descend.

Poof!

The giant roared as its club burst into sawdust, and it fought to wipe the plume of grit from its eyes.

Fogle Boon clutched his chest and frantically began to speak. Something fierce had clamped down on the collar of his robes and was dragging him backward over the sand. He tried to think of a spell, all the while kicking and flailing his arms and legs. Something snorted a gooey mist over his robes. He strained to look behind him. It was Chongo.

"Quit flapping like a fish, Fogle!" Cass yelled. "I've come to aid you. You called for me, didn't you?"

"Er … Yes!" he said, gathering his feet.

"Well, here I am. Now get out of the way, will you!" she said, raising her hands above her head, soft pink lips muttering a quick incantation.

Fogle jumped out of the way and fell alongside Chongo as the giant clenched its monstrous fists and charged. Cass's body shimmered and convulsed in a captivating matter as a shadow of life erupted beneath the giant.

It moaned as it sank waist deep into the quick sand that had been solid ground moments before.

Impressive!

The giant's free hand clawed at the ground, ripping it up like sand as it sunk chest deep into the dirt. It seemed the last moments of the giant's life were coming to an end as it sank farther and farther and then stopped when the quick sand began to solidify around its neck.

"Looks like you got him, Cass! Amazing!"

The giant's hand burst from beneath the ground.

"It won't hold him forever, Fogle Fool! Do something, before he pulls himself out!"

Fogle's hands rummaged through all the belongings inside his robes. He wished Ox the Mintaur was there. He'd always kept things handy.

"Hurry!" Cass yelled as the giant began pushing itself out of the hole.

"I don't have anything!"

Two stocky black bearded figures charged into the giant's path and began jabbing at its neck with spears.

"Thank Bish for the Dwarves," Cass said, sliding from Chongo's back.

The giant two-headed dog sped towards the giant, attacking with both heads and four lion-like claws. The giant swatted one dwarf away and sent him spinning over the ground. It snatched the other in its palm.

Cass was rummaging through Fogle's robes.

"What are you doing?" he asked.

"Something!" she shot back, producing a vial of luminescent liquid from his robes.

Chongo yelped as the giant sent the big dog sprawling.

Cass winded her arm back with the vial.

"Don't throw that!"

It was too late. The vial sailed into the giant's mouth and disappeared down its maw.

Cass looked over at Fogle and said, "What was that?"

The giant jerked upright, eyes bulging as it clutched at its throat.

"What's happening?" Cass yelled, stepping backward to Fogle's side.

The giant went into a fit of spasms, its big mouth gulping for air as it released the dwarf from its grasp. The dwarves and Chongo backed away from the giant as it swung away at everything in its path. Fogle watched with avid fascination. The giant was choking to death.

It snorted and gurgled as water began spilling from its mouth. Finally, the giant's head pitched forward into the hard ground with a thud. It moved no more.

Fogle and Cass eased their way over and gazed at the pool of water spilling from its mouth.

She grabbed him by his arm and asked again, "What was that?"

"Oh, just about a year's worth of water rations."

She pinched his face in the palm of her hand and said with a glowing smile.

"I knew that, Fogle."

"I don't think—"

"TUNDOOR's GOING TO KILL YOU PESKY DWARVES!"

Fogle whipped his head around. A giant with bulging muscles from his shins to his neck was inside a dust cloud, swinging a hammer as big as a man.

"Where in Bish did he come from?" he said, unable to hide the fear quivering in his voice.

Cass wrapped her arms around his waist and exclaimed, "We're going to need a lot more water to stop that giant!"

Mood had seen many things in his long lifetime on Bish, and the giants were among those, just not giants this big.

The ground erupted where the giant's hammer came down less than a foot from his feet, knocking him to the ground.

"I CAN SMELL YOUR FEAR! YOU CAN'T HIDE FROM TUNDOOR! HA! HA! HA!"

Mood's boots moved toward the sound of the giant's bellowing voice. There were only two good ways to fight a giant: from a long distance or right up close. As he made his way through the dust, the ground erupted once again. Mood's hand axe lashed out, chopping deep in the giant's hand. He swung again, missing as the giant jerked its injured hand away.

"ARGH! A nice sting, you fuzzy red mouse, but it will take more than that to stop Tundoor. HA! HA!" the giant said, raising its leg and stomping the ground. "OUCH!"

Eethum had struck a nasty blow from somewhere nearby. If Eethum was working one side, Mood needed to be working the other. *Got to get him to the ground!*

WHOOM!

WHOOM!

WHOOM!

WHOOM!

Tundoor hammered all over like an angry child. Mood jumped left, right, backward and forward, each leap as painful as the next inside his rattling chest. The hammering moved away from him as he caught a glimpse of the giant's hairy shin in the dust. He chopped into the giant with all of his might.

Whack!

Tundoor jerked his knee up and let out a deafening roar. Mood thought he was listening to the world coming to an end ...

Whang! In the next moment, he was skipping over the hardened ground. He stopped with a mouthful of grit, two dislocated shoulders, and maybe worse. Everything hurt. The world was rumbling beneath him, and for the first time in three hundred years he felt the urge to retch as his blood trickled down his broken face. He tried to speak, but no words came out.

Got to get up! Must kill that giant!

But all he could do was watch the blurry spots in the dusty sky and feel the land-shaking steps getting closer.

Chapter 12

"**B**RING ME THE DUSSACKS!" SAM the barkeep yelled.

A hunchbacked woman with wispy white hair teetered into the middle of the room with two knife-like swords hanging in her fragile arms. They clattered on the floor as she turned to walk away.

"Get the oil, too," the barkeep ordered, "you old hen, and don't drop it, either."

She teetered away, waving her hand over her head.

"And a flame as well!"

Georgio stood within a circle of pressing people, Billip and Mikkel both at his back. Across from him stood Jeb, a stout brute with a neck of iron, his cutthroats behind, eyes and lips full of mockery. He didn't like them. They weren't the kind of men who had standards. They were takers: cold, merciless and cowardly. He could feel that in his bones.

"You can walk away, Georgio. There's nothing to be gained by this," Billip said, cracking his knuckles.

"No, I'm going to fight."

"You are not ready! This man, he's a seasoned beast. He'll cut you to ribbons. You pick up that Dussack," Billip squeezed his shoulder, "you're on your own."

Georgio looked down at the blade lying on the floor. It was a wide blade of steel, about thirty inches long with a gentle bend towards the tip. It had a loop for a hilt wrapped in leather that reminded him of half a pair of scissors. It was different, but he'd been training with Mikkel and Billip for a while. How different could one sword be from another?

Mikkel stepped out into the center, his broad shoulders and muscular back heaving. He pounded his chest with his fist.

"Take on a man, Jeb! Fight me instead! He's untrained."

Jeb squatted down, plucked his Dussack from the floor, and said, "All knew the risk the moment you stepped in here. The boy can walk away," he thumbed the edge of the blade, "just leave your purses and go."

"Coward!"

Jeb laughed.

"Your words are talking any thoughts of mercy from my mind. I suggest you talk some sense into your young friend … or give him a hug before he dies."

Mikkel turned and said, "Georgio, this man is a killer. You don't have to do this."

Georgio pushed past Mikkel and picked up the sword.

A cry of cheers went up.

"Thatta boy!"

"Kill him, Jeb, and cut me a lock of that curly hair!" A surly woman cried.

"Don't kill him, just punish him," a harlot said, "I want to pinch those cheeks one time at least."

Coarse laughter erupted as the bar maids bustled, refilling the tankards of ale. It wasn't often action like this happened so early in the day.

That's when Georgio noticed the sullen look on the face of the woman who had drawn the card, Velvet. It as if she was looking at a dead man. Shoulders slumped, he looked away. He didn't know why he was doing this, but he felt compelled to, as if something inside him was driving him forward. But the words Melegal said had haunted him, *Go back to Three and live. Stay in Bone and die.*

Mikkel put his heavy hands on his shoulders and said, "Stay on the defensive, and wait for an opening. You cut him good, he'll yield. Be patient, Georgio." Billip gave him a final squeeze. "You can do it, Georgio!"

"Aye," Billip said," you've learned from the best. This man's a thug. One good cut and he'll run."

"Thanks," Georgio said, unable to hide the dullness in his voice. He searched for Jeb's eyes and found them staring back at him. His men were all offering encouragement, pointing and mocking at him. Something about the looks on their faces and the sound of their voices began to charge his blood.

"Ah!" the barkeep's voice cut through the noise of the crowd, "our favorite retriever returns."

The old woman's arms quavered as she handed him over a jar and a candle.

"Come here, young warrior," the barkeep said, dousing a rag in the oil. "Let me see your blade."

Georgio stuck it out. The barkeep coated the blade halfway down with thick oily residue. It had a pungent smell, like the glue used to seal stones.

"Step back," he said, holding out the candle.

"Fire them up, Sam!"

Sam the barkeep stuck the candle under the blade's tip, igniting the blade.

Georgio's eyes widened as he watched the wispy black smoke rise from the orange flames.

The crowd started chanting as the barkeep did the same to Jeb's blade.

"Jeb! Jeb! Jeb! Jeb!"

"Take your places, men!" the barkeep said, guiding them both to the middle of the circle.

Georgio looked up into the face of the man leering down on him with a flaming sword in his hand. *Fight or die! That's what Venir would say.* He pulled back his shoulders and clenched his teeth.

"Let's go over the rules of the Flaming Sword. The Dussack is a cutting weapon, but stabbing is allowed. But you only get one poke."

"Aah! Give 'em three pokes, Sam!"

The barkeep waved the comments off as he allowed his words to arouse the crowd.

"I've seen men slashed to ribbons! I saw a woman whittled down to the bone! No Mercy! A merry old man sliced off his best friend's fingers! Be alert! A woman cut her husband's neck open! Be wary!"

Georgio blanched as his hand rubbed his chest below his neck and his forehead burst into beads of sweat. *Fight or die!*

"And there will be no dancing and delays, Men! The flame gets hotter as time goes on. It will seep down the steel until that handle's as hot as a poker. It will cauterize your skin to the metal. The first challenger to drop his weapon loses. Or the first one to yield."

Georgio could feel the warmth growing in his hands.

The barkeep took a long draw on his cigar and exhaled a plume of smoke in the air. There was a glimmer in his sagging bloodshot eyes as he spoke.

"Ready yourselves, then!"

The room stiffened with tension.

"One!"

"Two!"

Georgio raised his flaming sword.

Mikkel's muscles were as taut at bowstrings as he watched his young friend Georgio lift his Dussack from the floor. Over the past few months, a bond had grown between him and Georgio, who served as a reminder of his own son, Nikkel. He couldn't help but think. *What would it be like if Nikkel were out there, about to get cut to ribbons by a man?* So far as he could tell, Jeb was a cold-blooded killer. His hands clenched at his sides. One poke was all it took.

"Come on, Georgio!" he said with encouragement.

Billip's eyes narrowed at his side, flitting back and forth as he twisted the hairs under his chin. Billip wasn't much of a sword fighter, but he'd fair better than Georgio, who was still swinging steels like hatchets. Whatever possessed the boy to take this fight was beyond him. Maybe it was his fault. After all, he'd been saying for weeks, *You have be a man sometime.* People grew up quick on Bish, and it had been no different for him than any other.

"Put these on the young man," Billip said, filling a bet taker's hands with coins.

Mikkel pulled Billip up by the cloth of his shoulder and said through his teeth, "What are you doing?"

"Gambling."

"On the life of our friend?"

Billip shrugged and said, "I can't help it. I just like long shots. You know that."

"That's sick, even for you."

"It's quite normal; you know that. Besides, I've bet for and against you, too."

"I was a man. That was different."

"It seems our Georgio is a man now, too." Billip brushed his arm away. "Now pay attention."

Georgio was squared up with Jeb as the barkeep backed away. Jeb's round face with the squared jaw leered down at Georgio, who stood chest out only half a head shorter. Georgio's thickset frame was almost as broad, but his muscles weren't developed like those on the hardened criminal across from him. Jeb's body was covered in thick hair. Corded muscles bulged under his heavy jerkin, and Georgio looked soft as a lamb by comparison. Mikkel could feel the fight was going to go bad really fast as all the betting was shifting against Georgio.

"Two!"

Oil from the burning swords dripped to the floor, sizzling on the planks. Georgio's back foot slid back, and his stiff legs began to bend. *Good stance. Be ready!*

"Three!"

Georgio leapt back as the flaming tip of Jeb's Dussack ripped at his neck.

"Move, Georgio!" Mikkel cried as Billip grabbed hold of him and pulled him back.

"Ha! You're pretty fast for a chubby one," Jeb said, clashing his sword into Georgio's and almost ripping it from his grasp. Oily flames scattered and fell, leaving sizzling little fires on the floor. "You got sticky hands, too!"

Georgio wrapped both hands around the hilt, feet shuffling back and forth, shoulders rocking left and right.

Clang! Clang! Clang!

The crowd roared in jubilation as Jeb hammered his heavy blade down, juttering Georgio's arms at the elbows. Mikkel could feel the steel ringing his teeth. *He's a sitting duck.*

Jeb sprang away, cutting his sword in arcing flames back and forth like a sickle.

"Is that blade getting hot on those soft hands of yours, Boy? I've got callouses as thick as an ogre's hide."

Georgio's chest was heaving as he wiped the sweat from his face and said, "It seems you've got the ogre's breath, too."

"Har!" One man laughed so loud he dropped his tankard.

"You're funny for a dead man," Jeb said, lunging forward.

Slice!

The flaming blade ripped a gash in Georgio's thigh.

Mikkel wanted to stop the fight, but it was too late. *Live a man, die a man.*

"He'll be fine," Billip said. "He's got skin as thick as his skull."

Mikkel shook his head. Healing took time, even for Georgio, and no matter who you are, getting cut and stabbed always hurts like fire.

Georgio cried out as Jeb cut his arm. The smell of burning flesh filled the smoke-filled air as the red hot sword tip instantly cauterized the wound.

"Feel that, Boy! Wait till I drive this blade into that soft belly and scorch your innards like coals. Won't that be a fine way to die?"

Jeb swung downward in powerful orange flamed strikes, one after the other, driving Georgio to his knees. Tiny flames singed holes in his clothes and burned dark patches on his skin. His arms began to sag, and Jeb knocked his sword back into his head.

"Let go, Georgio!" Mikkel warned. "Blast your pride."

Jeb was toying with the boy, but now his voice took on a deadly tone as he lifted his arm up for the final strike.

Georgio fought for his breath as sweat trickled in his eyes. His arms and legs burned like they were on fire. Jeb was killing him. But he wouldn't let go of the sword. *Fight!* He hadn't even taken a swing. Was this what fighting was really like? He'd never felt so exhausted before. He could feel the sword heating up in his hand. It seemed every inch of him hurt. He felt like he'd fallen in a bucket of knives. *Take the pain! Fight! Get one piece of him before you go!*

He gathered himself to his knees as Jeb's sword came arcing downward, and then he lunged. Something bit deep into his shoulder, cutting it to the bone.

The crowd reeled with delight as Georgio screamed on the floor, his shoulder inflamed with pain, his body going into total recoil. He looked for his opponent. Jeb was shuffling back, flaming sword in hand, patting out a flaming streak across his belly. *Yes!*

He heard Mikkel's voice booming over the rest.

"You got him, Georgio! Go after him!"

Georgio rose to his feet. As a blinding pain erupted in his shoulder, he moved his sword from one hand to the other. It was hot now. Like the handle of a metal coffee kettle. *Don't let go!*

He staggered forward, his shoulder feeling like an anchor was tied to it, his other arm barely able to lift his flaming sword. The steel was glowing red hot to the end.

Jeb switched his sword from one hand to the other, shaking his former sword hand. He snarled, spit coming from his lips, and charged.

Clang!

Georgio parried, but the jabbing pain erupted in his shoulder. Jeb was slower now, and Georgio felt his wind returning. He parried the next series of blows as Jeb's face became wracked with anger and pain. He locked him up, flaming swords inches from their faces.

"I'm going to gut you, Boy! Yield, before I fill your belly with steel."

"Not if I fill yours first!"

Crack!

He head-butted Jeb in the nose.

Blood flowed over Jeb's teeth and lips as he staggered away.

The crowd cried foul.

"It's a fair move!" the barkeep shouted.

Jeb spat the blood from his face, grimacing as he switched his sword from one hand to the other, then back again. A desperate look was filling his eyes.

"Kill him, Jeb!" one of his men said.

Georgio held his sword up and out and said, "I can do this all day."

It felt like his entire hand was on fire, and the steel was beginning to stick to his skin. He fought the urge to switch hands after one person said:

"He's not even switched hands yet. Jeb's done so three times!"

Jeb charged.

Georgio backpedaled away from Jeb's lunging swings and misses.

"Getting hot, isn't it, Jeb!" Georgio said.

Jeb's sword clattered to the ground as he fell to his knees and cried, "Sweet Mother of Bish! Water! I yield! Water!" The thug was blowing his smoldering hands.

"Somebody piss on the baby's hands!"

Billip strolled over to Jeb with a bucket of water and said, "Ah- Ah –Ah ... pay first, then take this bucket and get your arses out of here!"

"Georgio! Drop the sword; you won!" Mikkel exclaimed.

Georgio was stunned. His hand kept burning until it was almost done. He looked over at the barkeep, who nodded, shook his head, and walked away.

He flung the blade from his palm, felt his legs buckle, and then the strong hands of Mikkel dragged him away. He thought he heard someone cry out something about underlings as he started puking in the floor.

CHAPTER 13

THORN SUNK ONE BLADE INTO the plank floor were Lefty was a blink ago. The halfling boy leaped from table top to table top as the big rogue ran roughshod through the tavern.

"Somebody grab that little bastard," Thorn yelled.

The big thief's face was pink and white, the raw skin exposed. It was pretty clear Thorn blamed them for his demise. But it had been Kam who shoved him into the fireplace, not them. Of course, they'd had a little something to do with the fact that he was jailed. Gillem had walloped him over the head, and Kam's spell had silenced him for a while. But it seemed Thorn's corrupt connections had won out. He was free to avenge himself.

"Settle down, Thorn. We've got nothing to do with you!" Gillem said from atop a table. "I'm still the Master here, not you. Sheath those swords or be trialed!"

Thorn lowered his short swords by his side and sneered under his burnt and crooked nose as he walked towards the table.

"The Bone I will, Gillem, you little halfling toad!"

Gillem ducked under the first cut and leaped over the other.

Lefty threw a wine bottle that careened off the side of Thorn's head.

"Blast you two rodents! Somebody grab them! That's an order! They're traitors! They left me behind!"

Gillem leapt to another table and surveyed the room. Lefty watched from behind a chair. There was a shift in the room as everyone got a closer look at Thorn's face.

"They watched the woman burn me and did not come to my aid," Thorn whined. "Had me jailed, my lips sealed by magic, and dragged away by the Watch." He spat. "Gillem, you're not the thief you used to be. Nothing more than an aging mushroom."

Gillem stood his ground, stuck his pipe in between his lips and laughed.

"Is that so, coming from the man who guards a door? One trip up top, and you come back roasted like a log, blaming me."

The older halfling had the room's full attention now. His voice the father of all fathers. A thief among thieves. "How embarrassing that must be for you. And naturally, being the bully that you are, you take the fight to the tiniest man in the room, Lefty." Gillem puffed a smoke ring. "And when you can't manage to lay a finger on him, you come after me, and asking for the aid of your brethren as well. I'm ashamed. Ashamed for you and ashamed for the thieves' guild."

Thorn's swords were quavering in his hands, his knuckles white, his face full of shame and anger.

"Why you little liar! Fraud! You're cohorts with that wench up there! When I speak to Palos, I'll prove it."

The rogues in the house looked back and forth between the two men and each other. Lefty remained still. He knew Palos wasn't going to take Gillem's word for anything anymore. He could tell. The way the man spoke to Master Gillem was often harsh and uncalled for. It was clear to him the Prince of Thieves didn't like that halfling anymore.

"Talk all you want, Thorn. Please do. I'm sure Prince Palos has nothing better to do than hear your petty excuses. It was my plan that snatched the child, and my plan that got the woman here. You come back with nothing but a sack full of blame ..."

Lefty looked down at his watery feet on the floor.

Oh no! What's wrong? Why are my feet sweating?

He scanned the room. No other daggers were drawn. *Where's Diller?* He looked up at the top of the stairs. The man was there, toothpick and all, a devious look on his face, but he wasn't alone. Lefty's tongue clove to the roof of his mouth as he tried to yell out.

"... Ha!" Gillem continued, chest out, hitching his thumbs in his pants. "I'm sure he'll enjoy that more than gold."

Clatch-Zip!

Thorn jumped five feet backward. Gillem stood with eyes as big as the moon as he looked down at the bolt protruding from his chest.

Clatch-Zip!

The next one caught him clean in the throat. Gillem swayed left and right as the pipe fell from his mouth and clunked on the table. Lefty caught him as he fell, and searched his eyes, only to find an empty blank stare. Now the only friend he had left in the world was dead. *No! Just like that! How? No!* He looked up and saw the leering face of Palos. Cold and crazy.

"The trial has begun and ended, in the favor of my newest Master, Thorn!" Palos said, handing Diller back over his crossbow. "Now, bring me the halfling boy, and dispose of the other one in the cemetery beneath the water."

No hope. Drained of all vitality, Lefty was limp as several rough hands dragged him up the stairs.

Kam sat, chin dipped, huddled in a rocking chair by the fire, arms folded across her chest, rubbing her shoulders. She was an empty vessel as Palos got up to check the commotion outside.

"Don't move an inch," he ordered, slipping a thin dagger through the belt on his robes and strutting to the door.

Think, Kam!

Fear ruined her hopes as Palos crossed the threshold of the door, his back to her, but Diller, long and sly, stood just outside the doorway, leering at her from time to time. She ran her fingers between her neck and the choker Palos had imprisoned her magic with. It was a wispy thing that tightened like a garrote if she tugged on it.

"Ugh!" she growled.

Time was running out for her; she could feel it. Not only her, but Erin as well. It was only a matter of time before Palos tired of her, unless of course, she played his little strumpet. *No! I'll die first!* She scanned the room. Certainly Palos had hidden things that she could use. He'd just produced a dagger from nowhere. That meant there had to be something else. Paintings, a great sword, etchings in the marble mantle, fanciful rugs over a polished hardwood floor, statues, candelabras and more.

"Hmmm ...," she muttered, eyes flicking towards Diller, who at the moment seemed to be enthralled with the commotion on the lower floor. There were marble ashtrays as big as her hand. A poker for stoking the wood and coals in the fireplace. An onyx figurine of a part woman, part fox stood over a foot tall on a pedestal. It seemed there were some things, unconventional things, she could use to bash his head in, after all. She picked at her lip. Then what? She'd still need help to remove the choker, and how would she escape after that? *It can't be hopeless.*

Clatch-Zip!

She jerked in her chair, biting her lip. Immediately, her thigh began to throb, and her heart pounded like a fearful rabbit's.

Clatch-Zip!

She jerked again, more so than the last time. She pulled her legs up and curled into the chair. She heard Palos's words to the men below before he strolled back in, sneering and angry.

"Good!" he said, walking in and taking a seat at the table. "You didn't move. I'd hate to have to cut a toe off, but I've had it done before. Now, make yourself presentable. We're having company."

A lurking figure filled the doorway. It was Thorn. He leered at her like a hungry dog as he stepped inside and took a seat at the table. *I should have killed him.*

Diller followed, chewing his toothpick, dragging Lefty by his collar like a heavy sack.

Kam felt her heart sink. *Is he dead? No, it can't be!* Her nose started to run as the door was closed from the outside. She sniffled.

"Don't start blathering, Kam." Palos took a quaff of wine. "Your little friend is alive, for now. But, I'm sorry to say, it seems Master Gillem has had a most unfortunate accident." Thorn and Diller snickered. "He impaled himself on a pair of crossbow bolts. One of the most bizarre things I ever saw."

Kam's eyes drifted to Palos's. There was nothing but the cold-blooded look of a butcher in his eyes. He enjoyed seeing her suffer. He thrived on his power over people. She could feel it. She looked over at Lefty as Diller lifted him to his feet by the scruff of his neck. The little liar's feet were dripping wet, and his swollen eyes were glued on the floor. She almost felt bad for him. He sobbed. Her heart opened as the boy stood there ... broken. She turned away, head towards the burning coals under the mantle. She realized it couldn't have all been his fault.

"Kam, Dear, please come and sit at the table with the rest of the family. We've much to discuss," Palos said, stretching his arms over his head and yawning. "Whew ... the hot bath you gave me took a lot out of me."

Slime! She rocked forward, shuffled over, and slid into a chair, head down. She'd never been in the presence of people she actually hated, and now there were three of them. The most hated men in the world.

"When can I see Erin?" she said, trying to hide the quivering in her voice. "You were about to send for her before all the commotion."

She jumped as Palos rapped his fist on the table.

"That can wait! We've business to discuss. It seems Master Thorn has brought a different story forward as opposed to the one spun by the former Master Gillem and his apprentice ... er ... Lefty."

"What would you know?" she said, the fire rising in her voice. "Both men are liars. What difference does the truth make at this point? You have me. Does it really matter how I got here?"

"Well ..."

She sat up and pulled her shoulders back and twirled her hair.

"What does this roasted oaf have to offer you that I cannot, Prince Palos? It seems quite peculiar."

"Why, you!" Thorn said, drawing his swords.

"Stop!" Palos ordered. "Thorn, my woman speaks. You do not. Continue, my dearest. Please."

Diller covered his mouth, eyes glimmering from beyond.

"This ugly fool tried to seduce me. Pawed at me like a hungry lion."

Palos's eyes narrowed.

"I defended myself. Launched him into the fire. It was Gillem who stopped me from turning this lout … that you call Master … into a charred log. I should have killed him." She clenched her fists and shook them at him. "But Gillem had him spared. I melted his lips and ears, a minor incantation, and had him dragged off by the City Watch."

He shifted back toward Palos, who sat slunk forward, eyes glaring at Thorn with suspicion.

"Prince, I never laid a finger on her," Thorn said, his eyes shifting back and forth between her and him. Behind him, Diller lowered a crossbow on his back. "I swear, my lord. She—"

Palos sprang on top of the table. "She was to be defiled by no one, Thorn!" Thorn stood at rigid attention as Palos poked the tip of his dagger at his nose. "Which hand did he touch you with, dearest Kam?"

"Both, my Prince."

"Hold them out, Thorn."

"B-But …"

"Hold them out! Diller!"

She could hear Diller's finger squeezing the trigger.

Thorn lifted his hands, palms up, parallel to the ground.

"Yes, Milord."

Stab! Stab!

Stab! Stab!

Like a striking snake, Palos dotted two holes in each palm.

Thorn's bloody hands quavered in the air, fear and agony growing on his face.

"Easy, Thorn," Palos looked down on him and patted his shoulder. "If the daggers had been tip triggered, you'd be dead from the venom already," Palos said, needling the bronze snake-scaled hilt beneath the fang-like blade as he tucked it away from sight.

"Uh … thank you, Prince."

Palos whirled towards Kam and said, "Is there anything you wish to add, Dearest?"

Kam shook her head. There had been enough blood shed for the day. Another death, even the likes of Thorn's, was not something she cared to partake in.

"Go …, Master Thorn, and patch your wounds. I want both Diller and you to return back to your posts."

"And the halfling, Pal—'"

Palos shot Diller an angry stare.

"Er … Prince Palos?" Diller corrected, shifting his toothpick from one side to the other.

"Oh …" Palos said looking down at the tiny sad-eyed boy as he resumed his seat at the table. "Bind him up. Leave him here, and let him mourn the loss of his kindred friend." He drummed his pudgy fingers on the table. "Thorn, I've had a change of heart, given the evidence presented. See to it Master Gillem is given a proper burial. After all, he was my own mentor, and it's possible I'll regret my actions tomorrow, or next week maybe. But remember this, you over-sized rogue. My doubt can be quite deadly."

He's mad! Kam struggled with the fear that coiled within her belly. She ached from head to toe. Somewhere, her baby girl hungered. She could feel it. Within her, she had the power to stop it, but couldn't use it without killing herself. She knew full well what the collar around her neck did: it used her power against her.

"Have a drink, Dearest. You look quite thirsty," Palos said, taking another guzzle of wine, the gentility returning to his voice. "You see, running a kingdom, albeit a dark and secret one, has many consequences, and a ruler like me can never be too careful." He reached over and patted her hand and licked his lips. "But being in charge gives you all the power you want and so many, many rewards.

Kam swallowed hard and gave a slight nod while Diller shackled Lefty with a network of rope like chains made from absidium, a thin metal that was stronger than hammered iron. Lefty stood in silence, narrow shoulders sagging, his mop of yellow hair cast down ... defeated. The boy had come to the City of Three like a shining beacon of life, but nervous. Adept in magic, quick-witted and sure-footed, a promising little sparrow—now with both wings broken.

"Where do you want him?" Diller said, pulling Lefty up on his tip toes by his hair.

"Hmmm ..." Palos said, looking up from the coins he was stacking. "Well, hitch him by the foot of my tub over there, and don't leave any slack in it, either."

Kam didn't turn as she heard Diller dragging Lefty away. A wave of guilt washed over her. The boy had lost his real family once already, to the underlings. He'd lost his friends from the Magi Roost as well. Now, his third family had betrayed him. *Maybe he didn't know better, but he should have. Blast Venir for leaving those boys with me!*

As Diller started to leave, she asked, "Can I please see my baby now, Prince Palos?"

"Can I please see my baby now, Prince Palos?" he said, imitating her voice.

"I've done everything you've asked of me."

"I've done everything you've asked —"

"Palos!" She rose from her chair. "You gave me your word! Now bring me my baby!"

"NO!" he slammed his fists into the table. "NO! NO! NO! NO! NO!"

She saw a feverish look in his eye, and his steady hands began to tremble.

"Diller!" he shouted. "Bind her as well. I need rest."

He got up, calmly walked into his bedroom, and closed the door.

He's crazy!

Diller was coming her way, chains wrapped around his hands, toothpick rolling in and out of his mouth.

"Alone at last ..."

CHAPTER 14

T HE MARKETPLACE WAS HUMMING WITH activity as the merchants hoisted their voices high in the air, competing to sell their wares. The people of Bone, hundreds, a rugged lot, were well prepared for anything. They stumbled, rumbled, bristled and hissed at one another, fighting over fruits and metal pots. The pickpockets and urchins were out in full force, squeezing their fingers into tiny crevices and snatching purses one at a time. It was all expected in the course of doing daily business in the harshest city in the world. After all, the citizens of Bone were prepared for anything, so they said, until today.

A woman shrieked. The crowd slowed, heads looking around for the source of the outburst that was suddenly cut short.

KA-CHOW!

Something exploded. A cart of fruit was thrown high in the air. A unified gasp followed as all eyes turned to the sky. There, Verbard hovered, feeding on their sudden fear. Each face was a puzzled knot of confusion. He let them have it.

A frizzy brown-haired woman holding a large melon gawped at his appearance a split second before she exploded. Verbard and his fellow magi floated above chaos, spraying their deadly magic from one street corner to the other. Juegen soldiers, led by Jottenhiem, black armor glistening in the sunlight, spilled from the alley's shadows like a pack of hungry wolves. The census in Bone would be lower this year. Men, women and urchins fell beneath the precise cuts of underling blades. Necks were opened, hands and arms lopped off.

Eep snatched a boy from the ground, black wings buzzing as he lifted him high in the air and dropped him into the fray below. Behind Verbard, another mage summoned his power. The sewers, cracks and crevices began to fill with large ants and cockroaches, insects of all kinds. They scurried over all things living and dead, a terrifying army of another kind.

The badoon underlings, naked from the waist to the shoulders, fired missile upon missile into even the fleetest of feet, sending their bearers reeling to the ground. A heavy man with hunched over shoulders, bolts piercing his back, waded through the desperate crowd, grabbed a heavy rope at the corner, and started ringing a brass metal bell.

Let them come, Verbard thought, silver eyes charged with energy.

As he floated over the chaos where the streets began to slicken with blood, he felt nothing but satisfaction. As Jottenhiem led a wedge of blood coated Juegen soldiers, the humans kept piling up. But fear outweighed their forces, and within moments of the beginning of the onslaught, the entire marketplace was cleared. Like rats, the humans had disappeared into their dark little holes. Only the dead and the twitching remained.

Verbard and his men surveyed their surroundings. The small buildings had every door secured and every window shut.

Jottenhiem put an ailing man out of his misery as he shouted up in underling, "What are your orders, Lord Verbard? We're ready for more!"

Eep, come!

The one-eyed imp hummed to his side with an arm hanging out of his razor sharp mouth.

Scout. Let me know what comes. If anything.

The imp nodded and buzzed away.

Brethren magi! Set fire to everything you see!

The black robed underlings fanned out over the market square, toes hovering over the ground as high as the buildings. All hands, twelve in all, ignited with fire. Verbard could feel the radiant heat of pouring flame erupting from the magi surrounding him. Below him, the Juegen and Badoon decapitated the dead and tossed the heads through the windows.

Excellent!

Verbard rose higher in the air overlooking the vast city and the castle tops that surrounded the walls. He felt small in the presence of it all. Below him, the smoke and fires were growing, but it was little more than a campfire compared to the rest of it all. His strike seemed futile compared to what was needed to take this city. *Suicide mission.* Master Sinway couldn't be serious. There were so many people.

Eep hummed along his side, crunching an arm between his teeth before swallowing.

"A large host of armored riders on horseback come riding under Royal banners."

"How many?"

"Two score or more," Eep hissed, wringing his clawed hands.

An arc of light struck Eep full force in the chest and sent him spiraling downward, his small body disappearing into the smoke. Verbard felt the power of many minds converging on him at once. *Suicide Mission.*

Inside Castle Almen, another battle raged. The human soldiers fought hard but were incredibly slow. Kierway's sword flashed twice for every one of their heavy strokes. He sank his blade deep into the heart of one man and sliced out the neck of another. It seemed he and the Vicious, as well as the Juegen and Magi, had come upon the barracks confined within Castle Almen. Their surprise was short-lived. The humans were well fortified and prepared, barricading the tunnels and sealing the doors. Still, in such an enormous place it would take quite some time to find what they were looking for. That's the other reason the magi came.

"Find me that cleric," Kierway ordered, withdrawing his blade from the armored belly of his last victim.

At his side, the Vicious, the black hulking brute with skin as hard as armor, was crushing the neck of another soldier whose feet twitched above the ground.

It felt good, killing all these men. His natural enemies. His most hated foes. But he was in unfamiliar territory. The walls were closing in as time elapsed. He had to find that cleric and get those keys before the Royals, and their total garrison, cut them off completely. Based off all that he had seen, there must be more than seventy fighting men, if not a hundred, who guarded the castle, and they wouldn't all be push overs.

A mage with bright blue eyes drifted in from the door of another room and beckoned towards him.

Kierway smiled, looked over to his soldiers, and said, "Follow me."

Clatch-Zip!

Kierway ducked as a bolt ripped past his head.

Clatch-Zip!

Clatch-Zip!

The blue-eyed mage was shot down, spilling to the floor in a heap, two bolts embedded in his head. Three soldiers armored in plate mail emerged on the other side of the room, tossing down their heavy crossbows as they drew their bastard swords.

"Bish blast my eyes!" one of them yelled, "Underlings in Bone. I'd never have believed it if I weren't seeing it for myself."

"They bleed the same as men!" said another.

"Attack," Kierway ordered in underling.

The Juegen soldiers rushed in, swords flashing out as they cut into their foes. The men, tall and heavy, leaned into the smaller people. Broad arcing swings came from heavy handed blows as the Juegen shifted and ducked away.

The armored Royal soldiers chopped down, their blades clanging from the stone floor. The underlings shifted their stances, swords licking out like snakes, glancing off the heavy mail of the bigger fighters.

"Put your weight on them. They're small and fast, but we can wear them down," a Royal said, taking a swing into the chest and knocking down a Juegen fighter. The underling rolled back to his feet.

"They don't bleed," one soldier yelled.

"If you can't cut them, stab them!"

Kierway rolled his eyes. The underling armor was as hard as it was light, but it didn't make them invulnerable. He was running out of time. If more heavy soldiers rushed in, they'd be cornered. He needed to keep his small group together. He chittered an order. The Juegen pressed the man left of center, blades licking out like a pit of striking snakes.

Kierway attacked. In one fluid motion, he sidestepped one soldier's swing and jammed his blade backwards into the lower abdomen of the other. One soldier remained, backing towards the door as the Juegen peeled away the armor and skin of the other with their swords. One second three men stood valiantly, in the next only one remained. The soldier glanced at Kierway, a determined look under his helmet.

"You're fast, even for a little one, I'll grant you that—"

The Vicious leapt over Kierway's back and landed on top of the soldier.

Wham! Wham! Wham!

The Vicious punched the soldier's head into the wall, denting the metal and crushing the man's skull.

"Well done," Kierway commented, sheathing his sword.

Another underling, eyes bright like sapphires, glided to Kierway's side.

"I think we've located the man you're looking for," it said, extending its hand.

Kierway gazed at a vision on the underling mage's palm. A vision of Sefron the cleric was there. Brow sweating, belly bulging over his tiny belt, glossy eyes filled with fear.

"That's him. Lead the way!"

Five more heavily armored soldiers spilled into the barracks' front doorway.

"Take them out!" he said to the three Juegen soldiers.

They burst into action, hurling their bodies and swinging their swords into the big men with heavy arms. Their chitters were filled with rage as they tried to whittle the force of men down one by one while Kierway, the Vicious and the two remaining magi made their escape through the castle passages with the sound of heavy boots coming from all directions.

CHAPTER 15

WRIGGLING IN THE HEAVY ROPES of the net, Venir managed to get his hands around the neck of one underling soldier and squeeze. The underling's orange eyes bulged out of its sockets while it stabbed into Venir's arm with a dagger. Venir held tight as he and the other trapped underlings were dragged over the rugged terrain.

The underlings thrashed, hissed and howled, their sharp claws stretching through the heavy netting trying to carve off a piece of his hide.

Venir upped the pressure, fingers crushing his victim's windpipe.

"Tell your fiend brother good-bye, you black jackals!"

He felt the underling's throat collapse. The remaining brood surged within their bonds.

"Have at me, then!" he yelled.

Venir wrenched the dagger from his arm and sawed at the cords. His muscles tightened in his neck at a sucking and shrieking sound that froze the marrow in his bones. The underlings were dragging him toward another enormous spider ahead that feasted on a horse and rider. He sawed faster.

All around him, the sounds of battle still surged. The underlings chittered in anger and pain, and the Royal Riders thundered past, shouting battle cries at the top of their lungs.

KA-CHOW!

A wave of energy knocked several from their horses.

"Bone!"

Venir could feel the tide of battle turning. The shock and surprise had worn off, and the underlings, they were a well-oiled machine: quick, efficient and deadly. From all directions, they swarmed the men three to one.

"Cut faster, Idiot!"

Venir cut through one piece of the net, but it would take at least ten more to free him.

Nearby, an underling squirmed closer, clawed fingers grabbing his shield. It began pulling him back, its rancid breath on his ear. In his other hand, Brool was useless, bound up in the netting. Another cord broke.

A Royal Rider cried out, "Retreat! Retreat!" waving a banner from atop a white horse.

"Slat! You cowards!" Venir yelled, sawing faster as the underling tugged harder on his shield, stretching him back.

He caught the rider in the corner of his eye, spinning around his horse, and chopping down into an underling with his sword.

"Over here, Rider!" Venir yelled again.

The man peered through the dust as Venir was dragged right past him. The man pointed at him, saluted and galloped away.

"Bone!"

It seemed it was down to Venir; the remains of the decimated army of Royal Riders was now in full retreat.

"Cowardly Royals!"

He cut through the third cord, then the fourth. Something blocked out the suns. Above, a hairy belly was straddled over him with a man in its mouth. A wrenching sound tore at his ears as the creature sucked a rider down to a husk. He cut the 5th cord and then the 6th. *Got to escape!*

The helm began to burn like fire on his head.

Visions of being buried head first in the dirt leapt forward in his mind. Not that again. Not ever. He cut through the 7th and 8th cords. Being sucked down to the marrow didn't sit well with him, either. *Cut faster!* The feisty underling grabbed hold of the eyelets of his helmet, nails cutting the skin around his eyes. A series of angry chitters surrounded him from everywhere. He looked up. Underlings surrounded him. Weapons raised, gemstone eyes glowing as they began pressing closer. *Saw or die!*

Please don't be hungry. Slim struggled in his bonds, but he wasn't going anywhere. *I've got to escape!* He could hear his heart pounding in his chest. He took a deep breath. The cloth on his face kept his lips from being sealed, and the spell he'd cast allowed him and Adanna to breathe much longer. *Just need enough time to get my energy back, and I'll remove these insects from Bish forever.*

"Mrmph!" he exclaimed beneath the cocoon.

A spider bit deep into his ankle, setting his leg on fire as the sucking began. Slim felt the blood being drained away from his body.

NOOOOOOO!

Excruciating. Slim's eyes fluttered in his skull, each second pure agony. He shuddered inside his cocoon, convulsed, then his body stopped. The pain was gone now. The spider was sucking on his limbs. As ghastly as that sounded, it was a merciful predator after all. Their poison subdued whatever man or beast they got hold of, but Slim's body slackened as a mild euphoria settled inside him.

Don't fall asleep. Don't fall asleep. Don't fall asleep.

Slim had never taken into consideration that he'd be eaten by a spider. He always figured he'd die of old age one day. After all, he was never really one to get in trouble. He just liked to help out now and again. He jerked in his web-made cocoon. A shot of fire raced from his toe to his brain as the spider's fang bit farther down.

That will keep you awake!

Now, the battle of wills began. The mind of a man versus the instinctive needs of an insect. Slim felt all sensation leave below his knees. He meditated on his elements. As a healer, a man born attached to the mystic powers of the world, Slim could draw upon the power of the living. The grass, the trees, the birds, even men. At the moment, the pit he lived in was barren of any living forces other than him, Adanna and the spiders, which made it all the tougher to renew his inner power.

Don't fall asleep, or you're dead, Slim the Cleric!

The spell he had cast to keep air in the cowls over his and Adanna's heads wouldn't last much longer. He'd already felt the air beginning to thin. It was dark and warm where he was, his only company now was the sharp sucking sounds from the sand spider gnawing on his calf.

Sssckt! Sssckt! Sssckt!

The numbness rolled over his waist and into his belly.

Maybe this isn't such a bad way to go. Mmmm …

Sssckt! Sssckt! Sssckt!

He thought of Venir. Adanna. All the lives the underlings had taken. The tiny fire inside his mind began to twinkle.

Got to fight it. Fight or die! Fight or die! Or, become a beetle. Mmmm ... Flying was enjoyable.

Slim felt himself sinking deeper into a bath of warm goo. *Maybe the spider won't suck all the blood from me. See you tomorrow, Bish. Or never again. What does it matter?*

The fire in his mind began to dim as his lips twitched with the last word of power he remembered. *I better use this before it's too late. Ah ... but just another minute. It feels so nice.*

Sssckt! Sssckt! Sssckt!

Zip! Zip! Zip!

The dagger fell from Venir's hand as a small crossbow bolt punctured through it. He cursed. He'd just cut the ninth cord. Another bolt ricocheted from his helmet, and one stuck in his calf.

"Bone!" he roared.

A spider abdomen loomed over his head, and dozens of underlings had him surrounded. He thrashed like a fish in the net that held him. Brool, still hot in his grip, was useless. His eyelets still smoldered like black fire. He'd never been at the mercy of this many underlings before. They had him.

The spider's face lowered before him.

"I'll make your belly sour, you eight-legged underling!" he said, kicking in the net.

The underlings approached, spears lowered, wicked faces chittering back and forth, a look of astonishment in their eyes. Two of them, heavy laden in black armor, approached with spears. Venir fought harder against his bonds. They cocked their elbows back.

"I see you got big plans for those toothpicks! Turn around and I'll show you how to use them," he said, tugging at the bolt protruding from his hand. "Slat! I suppose this is it."

Venir's mortality began to soak in. He was trapped like an animal. A hundred hunters had boxed him in. He was certain he wasn't going to live a moment longer. He just wanted to take a few more with him, however.

"Fight and die." He looked into the horizon. "So it is."

Venir felt the ground rumble. The underlings' heads snapped up. A chorus of surprised chitters was smothered by the sound of galloping horses. Two columns stormed through the camp. The first Royal Rider plunged a lance into the face of the giant spider. The spider reared up and caught two spears in its belly just as the horses trampled over it.

The underlings dove, rolled and died under the thundering hooves of the horses. The riders raced by, spears ripping through the air. One underling caught a spear clean in the throat. Another caught two spears in the chest.

Venir yelled out, "Get me out of this net you Royal Bas—*urk!*"

As the last two riders rode past, they reached down and grabbed the net, dragging Venir and the surviving underlings behind them. Being dragged by horses was a painful way to go. It seemed the Riders had a harsh death in mind for the underlings as their small bodies scraped and bumped over the rough stones, faces screeching in terror. Venir balled up, trying to keep his legs up as he was dragged roughshod over the dirt.

"Blast you, Royals!" he said through gritted teeth.

Behind him, the underling camp was falling farther away. After a mind numbing mile, the

Riders came to a stop. Beasts were nickering and stamping their hooves. Horses, all noble, all good, were never comfortable around underlings. As Venir wiped the dust and dirt that caked his eyes, he saw half a dozen well-armed men standing around him.

"Kill them. Kill them all," a rider ordered, his voice full of authority. A gold crescent stained with blood gleamed from atop his helmet.

"Even the warrior?" another rider said, hoisting his spear.

"No, you idiot! Kill the underlings. Why in Bish would we kill a man?" the commander said.

The remaining underlings fell quickly as the spears jabbed into them more times than were needed. Weighted down under the net, Venir struggled to rise.

"Someone cut this big bastard free! Do I have to do everything around here?" the Commander said, unsheathing a broad hunting knife on his belt. In three quick slices, the net fell away.

Venir rose to his full height and said, "Nice knife."

The Commander snorted under his red-brown mustache that hung past his chin and said, "Nice axe," eyeing Brool and stepping back.

Venir groaned. Everything hurt. He could barely stand. His arms and legs were raw. He looked back over his shoulder.

"Why aren't the underlings pursuing us?" he said, looking around at the remaining Royal Riders. There looked to be about thirty or so of them left, all blood splattered and wounded, some broken.

"They won't be coming. They've got more to worry about than us. Look over yonder horizon," the Commander said, pointing towards the northwest. The sound of Royal Battle horns now carried through the air as the banners of more Royal Riders appeared on the crest of the dusty hills.

"My gratitude, Commander," Venir said, nodding "I didn't figure on any Royals coming back for me."

"Ha!" the Commander said, reaching up and slapping him back. "I don't know where you came from, Man, but we'd all be dead if not for your timely arrival. Those underlings took to you like stink on a pig, but it didn't do them much good. I swear I saw you chop down ten of them. I've never seen a man as big as you move so fast. And the axe." He couldn't hide the incredulity in his voice. "It cuts though bone like butter."

"Underling bone that is," Venir said, grimacing as he plucked the bolt from his calf.

"Let us suture that wound, er ... what is your name, warrior?"

"Venir," he said, pushing the other bolt through one side of his hand an out the other. "And I don't need stitches. I need a horse!"

"But you need to stop the bleeding," the Commander said, waving a pair of soldiers over. "Those Riders over there will have the underlings routed. This isn't our first assault."

"I don't care about that. I've got friends taken prisoner in there. Now, give me a horse, Commander!"

"Underlings take no prisoners. No chance they're alive."

Venir glared down on the man.

"So be it!" The Commander handed him over the reins of a big brown mare. Venir grabbed the saddle with his bloody hand and swung up with a moan. The Royal Riders bore down on the underlings from the northwest and ran clean through the underlings' first defensive formation.

"Yah!" Venir said, digging his heels into the horse's sides and galloping away.

"Get back on your horses, Soldiers!" the commander ordered. "It's time to finish what we started! Yah!"

Venir didn't hear a thing but the wind whistling through his helmet as the horse galloped in full charge. The underlings were already scurrying into their black holes, possibly dragging Adanna and her mother down with them. And where was Slim? He didn't remember seeing any beetles on the battlefield. He had a feeling something was horribly wrong. *Got to find them!*

CHAPTER 16

"**S**EIZE HER! SHE KILLED LORD ALMEN!" Melegal shouted, pointing at Jarla the Brigand Queen.

"What!" she exclaimed, freezing in her tracks as the sentries surrounded her.

His mind was still glowing beneath his cap.

"Take her down, Men! Kill her if you have to!" he ordered.

A half dozen sentries armed with spears and swords formed a line between him and her. Jarla's face was a mask of rage as her twisted lips fought to find the right words to say. Hah! Melegal was in charge now. After all, he was the head Detective of the Royal Almen house. And what had Lorda Almen ordered him to do? Kill Jarla.

"A hundred gold to whoever can bring me her head! She's a murderer. An Assassin from the guilds. A defiler from another Royal house."

His words carried. Melegal could feel the power he had over the simple minds of the 'take orders first, ask questions later' sentries. He had her right where he wanted. Jarla the Brigand Queen was fighting for her life. Her blade flashed and parried as the small force of men closed in on her. Left and right she went, cut off from every direction she wanted to go. Melegal folded his arms across his chest and watched as the men began picking the woman apart. But where was Brak? Something blocked the suns' light from the windows above.

Move!

Melegal sprung right.

"Ooooof!" He was too late. A mound of man and muscle pounced on top of him, driving him to the ground, knocking the wind from his lungs. Melegal squirmed onto his back only to face the berserk face of Brak. The slumped over figure who had been begging for food minutes earlier was now pure monster.

Do something before he breaks your head apart!

Mindless and savage, the boy-turned-man raised both his fists over his head.

Melegal pointed the dart launchers into Brak's chest and belly.

Have to do this!

Brak brought his fists down with all his might.

Whoof!

Two soldiers almost as big as Brak barreled into him, knocking him to the ground. Melegal gasped for air, crawling on his knees. There was a sharp crack in the air. He whipped around. Brak bent another man's head over his neck. *Slat!* Melegal wasn't going to stick around to see what happened next. The berserker was already wrapping his fingers around the hilt of a sword and charging into the nearest warrior. *Move far, move fast!*

Melegal scanned the room. Two sentries had fallen under the deadly strokes of Jarla's sword. *No!* She moved with the feline grace of a panther and struck with the power of a cobra. A man screamed out as his sword hand was sliced off at the wrist, gaping at the sight of all the blood. Up in the bleachers, another commotion was stirring.

Sefron!

The slimy cleric waddled down the stairs, two men in full armor guarding his back shoulders as he made his way down the steps to where Lord Almen had fallen. Melegal slid out of sight along the wall.

Slat!

For all he knew, the cleric could save the man, and he couldn't let that happen. He couldn't let Jarla survive, either, but time was running out. His nose twitched as Sefron hunched down over Lord Almen's body and began to mutter something. Lord Almen's fingers clutched in the air. Melegal's heart lurched in his chest. *Blasted cleric!*

He stuck his hand out, pulled his sleeve back from his wrist, and squeezed the trigger on the dart launchers.

Zing! Zing! Zing! Zing! Zing! Zing!

Sefron jumped up, squealing like a pig, clutching at the darts embedded in his neck and face. The two soldiers reached out for the ailing cleric, who staggered down the steps, smacked into the arena's rail, and fell over the wall.

Yes!

He turned his attention back over to Brak. The over-sized young man stood in the center of the arena, coated in blood and gore, staring around in wide-eyed wonder. The monster was gone. Only the young man remained. A tiny little figure raced out to meet him. It was the Slerg girl named Jubilee.

"Come on, Brak! Come on!" she said, grasping his fingers and pulling him towards the doors at the bottom.

The two soldiers were over the wall, one helping Sefron to his feet, the other, long sword ready, was heading towards Brak and the girl.

On the other side of the arena, a badly limping Jarla had whittled six men down to two. Blood was running down her leg from a nasty gash on her thigh while she grimaced and parried each and every blow. *She can't survive this. She can't!*

Melegal yelled at the fully armored soldier and pointed at her, saying, "Finish that assassin! I'll take care of the mute!"

The soldier stopped for a moment, then took another step towards Brak and Jubilee.

Melegal stuck his finger out again and said, "Now!"

Sefron screeched out, "Get me back over that wall!" He whirled back towards Melegal, plucking a dart from his face, and added, "Curse you, Thief! I curse you and the womb you crawled out of."

Melegal drew the sleeve back over his other hand and raised it towards Sefron's throat.

"Not if I curse you first, Dead Man!"

The soldier stepped between them as Sefron scrambled over the wall.

A door at the top of the stairs exploded open, and a dark energy filled the room.

Melegal crouched back along the wall. A black creature as big as a man, cat-faced and knotted in muscle, stepped through the threshold.

An underling! It cannot be possible!

An underling with short black hair and eyes like burning iron glided in behind the Vicious, two razor sharp swords unlike anything he'd ever seen hanging in his hands. Melegal was already moving for the door when two cloaked underlings floated inside, fingertips glowing with power.

Run, Melegal! Run!

Jubilee was pushing Brak through the nearest doorway, but it was Melegal who shoved them through. He closed the door and barred it shut.

"Follow me!" he snapped.

Down the corridor they went. Brak stumbled along, arrows still embedded in his back, moaning with hunger. Melegal led them down into the dungeons and snatched some shackles from the wall. They all fought for breath. *Think, Thief!* He had to come up with something fast. He also had to figure out what was going on. What were underlings doing inside the castle?

"Listen to me; we have to act quickly. I need you to put these on Brak."

"No," Jubilee shot back.

"It's the safest way for me to lead you through. We'll be stopped. There'll be questions."

Brak's eyes narrowed, but he couldn't hide the exhaustion on his face. The man had just killed a dozen men as easy as a devious child could drown a dozen kittens.

"Brak," Melegal said, trying to sound calm and not in a hurry. "I lied. I know your father, Venir. I know him well. If he were here, he'd tell you to listen and do as you're told."

"Don't listen to him, Brak. He's an Almen. Almens are liars," Jubilee said, tugging at his hand.

"So are Slergs, Little Dear. And I'm not a Royal." He poked her in the chest. "I'm an overgrown urchin that was once a slave that swabbed the blood from the dungeons in your dubious castle." He slapped the first cuff on Brak. "If we live through this, I'd be happy to describe each and every last detail, but for now, we better go … or die."

Brak looked down on Melegal as he slapped on the second wrist cuff and said, "My back hurts."

Melegal looked around at the two arrows in his back and said, "Just a couple of scratches. We'll patch you up later."

A chorus of screams was followed by a series of explosions coming from the corridor they'd just cleared.

"Let's move!"

They were all running in step, through one corridor and down another. In one doorway and out the other. A pair of dead Royals lay dead on the floor, gashed and bloody. The sounds of booted feet seemed to be echoing from every corner, and shouts were haranguing out from down the halls.

"Get in here," Melegal said, shoving the both of them into a closet.

Four sentries in chainmail hauberks drew their broad swords and came at him. Not every person knew who he was, as most of his dealings with the Almens had been discreet. Melegal held up his hand and pulled out his brooch.

The men stopped and eyed him warily.

"Detective," one managed, eyes shifting in every direction at once, "what business do you have in the Castle?"

"That's no concern of yours. At the present, mine is self-preservation. Yours is to stop the underlings that are running through this place like jackals in a hen house."

KA-BOOM!

Paintings fell from the walls and vases full of flowers tipped from their pedestals and crashed on the floor. All the soldiers were looking around at one another, their faces turning as white as their teeth.

Melegal continued, "I believe that's from the Arena." He clapped his hands together. "Are all the exits sealed?"

Drat! There'd be no way to smuggle Brak and Jubilee out.

"We'll catch those black fiends yet! Now go!" he ordered. *So willing to listen, those sentries. If only more people did as they were told.*

"Yes, Detective," they said, trotting down the corridor and out of sight.

Melegal opened the closet.

"Come on!"

"Where are we going?" Jubilee asked, her little toes on his heels. "They said all the exits are closed."

"And so they are, as far as they know, but if you have any better ideas, I'd like to hear them."

"Well—"

Melegal grabbed her by the wrist, saying, "Shut up!" as he whisked her away.

"Hungry," Brak said, holding his stomach.

They dashed down the corridor that led them to the kitchen.

Two sentries stood alone at the top of the steps.

"Halt!" one said, lowering a spear at Melegal's chest.

"You men need to secure the arena, Lord Almen's under attack," he said, holding out his brooch.

"We're not going anywhere, Detective."

Leave. Leave. Leave.

Melegal pinched the bridge of his nose. He suddenly had a massive headache.

"Are you all right, Detective?"

Lord's no! "I'd be better if you did as I said. I caught these prisoners trying to escape, but the dungeons are filled with underlings. We need every last man to get them under control, and you two fish faces are standing here letting your entire future fall into ruin. Lord Almen will have a fit when he hears about this."

The sentry poked Melegal in the chest with the tip of his spear.

"Sounds like a bunch of horse slat if you ask me. The last man who failed this post was guillotined, and that man was my brother."

Not good. These sentries weren't going anywhere, even if the Castle was on fire. He had to think of something else, or kill them.

Melegal had opened his mouth to speak when one of the worst sounds he'd ever heard came from down the hall. The sentries' faces drew up in horror. He peeked around the corner and down the hall. A man covered in flesh-eating worms was running his way, his own fingernails digging into his face. Behind him were the hulking form of the Vicious and two cloaked figures dragging the disabled form of … Sefron.

Melegal grabbed the shaft of the man's spear and pulled him forward, slipping behind him in one motion.

"Every man for himself!" he said, shoving them down the hall.

"What the," one man said, falling over the other.

Brak, stuffing a loaf of bread in his face, and a terror stricken Jubilee bounded down the staircase.

They learn fast when death is so close.

At the bottom, Brak and Jubilee were pounding on the door.

"It's locked!"

"Get out of my way," Melegal said, shoving through them and dropping to his knees.

Another painful wail billowed from the top of the stair.

Click. Clack. Click. Melegal's slender fingers worked his tools in the keyhole. *CLICK.*

He shoved the door open, spilling Brak and Jubilee inside. He slammed it shut and locked it. Lord Almen's study was empty and undisturbed. Jubilee ran over to the desk and snatched up Leezir's ash white cudgel. She hugged it and looked at Melegal.

"It's yours!" he said. "Brak, pull open that bookshelf."

"Hmrph?" he said, trying to swallow a mouthful of bread.

"Slerg Child, help him!"

WHAM! WHAM! WHAM! …

The hinges on the heavy door were shaking loose.

Melegal rummaged through the objects tucked away in the corner and wrapped his hands around Tonio's sword and something else he'd noticed before that he tucked into his belt. *What have we here?*

He jumped over the desk and slid behind the open bookshelf. The hammering at the door stopped, but the hinges and fixtures were glowing red hot.

He stepped through the threshold of the tiny doorway and closed it behind him. It was pitch black.

"I can't see anything," Jubilee complained.

Melegal stuck his coin of light in his hand, handed Brak the sword, and snatched the key from the peg.

"Follow to the bottom," he said as fast as he could, running down the steps into the darkness.

Keys. Keys. Keys.

Leaping down the next stairs and landing on the bottom, he dashed across the threshold in the dark. What if the keys aren't there? What if Lord Almen removed them? Were these keys what the underlings were after? Why else would they be here? *Sefron!* Melegal's quick mind was putting things together. It couldn't be a coincidence. Light spilled out into the room. Jubilee and Brak were coming, but they weren't alone. The sound of wood splintering came from above.

Melegal ran his hands over the alcove wall. A cold piece of metal brushed against his fingertip. He plucked them from the wall one at a time. *One. Two. Three. Four. Five. Six. I have them!* He bolted for the last door, unlocked it, and entered. Brak and Jubilee made it to the landing, running toward the opposite side.

"This way, you two idiots!" Melegal screamed.

Jubilee whirled, shining the bright beam of light in his eyes.

"Point that down, and hurry!"

He could hear a fierce snarling coming down the steps. Ahead of him, Brak and Jubilee were moving horribly slowly. *They're going to die and get me killed.*

As they ran past the landing, speeding his way, an underling mage appeared, teeth gnashing, fingertips glowing, the air beginning to shimmer with power.

"Faster!" *They're not going to make it!*

He felt the air begin to split as the mage's bright magic coiled around its arms.

Zing! Zing! Zing! Zing! Zing! Zing!

It shrieked in rage as Melegal filled its face full of darts.

Brak and Jubilee raced into the closet, and Melegal closed the door.

"What!"

The door wouldn't shut. Eight claws had hold of it and ripped it open. There the Vicious stood, tall and nasty. Melegal felt his heart stop. They were dead.

Wham!

Pain exploded the creature's face as Jubilee blasted it in the knee with the glowing white cudgel. Melegal jerked her back and slammed the door shut. Melegal couldn't tell their screams from his as his mind twisted inside out.

CHAPTER 17

HOW DO YOU KILL A tree with arms, legs and muscle? Fogle Boon couldn't help but marvel at the man who towered at twenty feet tall.

"Do something, Fogle!" Cass urged him as they both stepped back from the smoke.

WHANG!

He flinched as Cass dug her fingers into his arm and an object came careening towards them, stopped, and settled in the dust.

"It's Mood," Fogle exclaimed, his feet moving faster than his lips. Chongo galloped past him and bared down, growling at Mood's side. The over-sized dwarf's body was trembling as he tried to rise from the ground.

"HOW DID THAT FEEL, RANGER? HA! HA! HA! ARE YOU DEAD?" The giant said as its footsteps thundered closer.

Chongo was barking and growling, the hairs rising on his massive necks, two sets of canine teeth bared. But Fogle had a feeling it was going to take more than dog bites to stop that giant. *Where in Bish did that man come from?* Fogle lurched at the giant's thunderous step. Mood was struggling to rise and mumbling something under his bloodied face and beard. That's when Fogle noticed the bone sticking out of the dwarf's shoulder. His stomach became queasy.

"Cass, shut Chongo up and drag Mood out of here!" he said, fanning the dust from his face.

"What are you going to do?" she said, rushing over to Chongo and swinging her legs onto his back.

"Something! Now go!"

"But—"

"Hurry!"

Chongo bit down on Mood's foot and started dragging him away as Fogle fell to his knees and filled his hands with dirt and sand. He closed his eyes and summoned the little power he had within. Swinging his hands around in big circles, he chanted the words and let the sand fly free.

The dust and dirt lifted from the ground, thickening and swirling. A small sand storm encompassed the giant, and it covered its eyes in the nook of its elbow. Fogle fell back away from the storm. The entire area was nothing more than a swirling white brown smoke. Fogle brushed the dust from his hands. *That should buy us some time.*

"HA! HA! HA! TUNDOOR SMELLS A WIZARD! MMMM ... I SHALL EAT YOU AND HAVE YOUR MAGIC! HA! HA! HA!"

Fogle ran, catching up with Cass, Chongo and Mood. *I'm not getting eaten by anything.* What he wouldn't do to have the underling power of floating.

"Now what?" Cass yelled at him.

"We've got to lift up Mood. Send him away with Chongo! Are there any horses or dwarves left?"

"I don't see any."

"Just help me get him up," Fogle said.

"He's too heavy in all this gear!" Cass complained. "I'm not an orc!"

The hairs on the back of Fogle's neck stood on end as everything around them went perfectly still. It was as if time stopped. He turned to look back where the giant was. The storm, the sand, and the smoky air were all gone. Not even the giant remained.

"Where in the world of Bish did—"

"HA! HA! HA!" the giant bellowed as it materialized behind them, war hammer raised over its head, trapezoid bulging on its neck.

"CASS!" Fogle screamed as the giant swung the hammer down with all of its power.

WHAM!

Fogle felt his world coming to an end as Cass exploded into thousands of tiny white, black and yellow butterflies that sputtered and fluttered in every direction.

"Cass!" he yelled as the giant raised its hammer once more. There was no sign of the woman, only a large indentation the soil. She was gone.

"TUNDOOR CRUSH YOU, TOO NOW, WIZARD!"

"NO!" Fogle yelled back, raising his arms forward. "Wizard blast Tundoor now!"

A white hot missile left one hand, striking the giant in the knee.

Tundoor roared.

Fogle let out another and another.

Ssszram! Ssszram! Ssszram!

One missile followed the other, the next bigger and more powerful than last. The magic shards created holes in the giant's leg and tore the flesh from his bones. Tundoor toppled backward, falling hard like a massive catapult stone.

Sweat dripping in his eyes, Fogle fell to his knees and fought for his breath. Smoke was rolling from his fingers, and the magi fires had singed the edges of his robes. A series of heavy booted footsteps rushed past. It was Eethum the Blood Ranger and a pair of black bearded dwarves, axes hoisted over their shoulders. Chongo charged forward, digging and clawing into the face of the reeling giant.

Fogle couldn't make heads or tails of all of the thrashing that was going on. All he wanted to do was figure out what happened to Cass. The butterflies, or at least what he thought were butterflies, were gone, his energy along with them. He spit the dust from his mouth and tried to speak. He doubled over. Retching came instead. *What is wrong with me? Where's Cass?*

"TUNDOOR KILL YOU ALL!" the giant said, face full of anguish as it rose to one knee, hammer swinging into a dwarf soldier that was too slow to dodge. The small man's teeth shattered as his skull was driven into his neck like a nail.

Fogle winced and looked away. *Cass!* He looked around and caught sight of Mood rising to his feet, hand axe dragging in his bloody hand as he staggered into the fray. There was nothing Fogle could do to stop him. He could barely hold his throbbing head up for the discomfort behind his eyes.

"ALMOST DEAD! ALL OF YOU WILL FEEL TUDOOR'S POWER!"

He smashed the hammer into the ground where Eethum was just standing.

"FEEL MY WRATH!"

The hammer cracked a pile of boulders into rubble.

"MY FURY!"

Fogle lifted his chin up and stared. The enormous giant—with jewelry the size of barrels hanging from its ears, teeth as big as Fogle's head, and the maddened look of a bull on its snorting face—didn't seem real. It was something that appeared in nightmares. It couldn't possibly be real.

He wondered if his grandfather Boon had ever taken on such monsters before. Boon had at least survived long enough to become old, gray and crazy. Fogle was pretty certain his life wasn't going to last that long. Maybe a few more seconds at best.

Eethum, black-faced and red bearded, went spinning to the ground as the hammer clipped him on the shoulder.

Chongo's claws tore into the giant's chest, but the giant grabbed him by the nape of one neck and flung him away.

This is it, Fogle thought with a sinking feeling.

"TIME FOR TUNDOOR TO EAT YOU, WIZARD. MAN WITH MAGIC TASTE GOOD!" He said, reaching towards him with a hand as big as a cart. "HA! HA! URK!"

Tundoor's eyes widened like big white moons. Atop his massive back, Mood was hanging onto a handful of the giant's hair and chopping into the giant's skull with unfettered fury.

"LET GO! STOP!" The giant cried out, arms flailing back towards the pest that was carving a canoe in his skull. "PLEASE! TUND—"

Mood sunk his axe wrist deep inside Tundoor's head and wrenched it free.

The giant's body convulsed then pitched forward like a toppled tower. His big face crashed inches from Fogle, his eyes gawping in wonder. Mood lay still on top of the giant's back.

Fogle rubbed his aching head. Only he, Chongo, Mood, Eethum and a single black-bearded dwarf remained.

"Does he live?" he asked.

Eethum stumbled over and slid Mood from atop the giant's blood smeared back and lowered him to the ground. He wasn't breathing.

"Well?" Fogle managed to say, despite his dry mouth.

Eethum shook his head.

"Pardon me for saying, but he should be dead." Fogle said, rubbing the numbness in his hands. "We all should be. How did he manage that?"

"He summoned the *Odenson.* Part of the Blood Ranger craft where our mystic blood allows us do things beyond our natural power. Some use it for great feats in contests, others to turn the tide of a battle. But there is a price." Eethum tried to pull the axe from Mood's grasp, but it would not budge.

"What is the price?" Fogle said, managing to rise to his feet.

Eethum eyed him with fierce green eyes and shook his head.

"The Everslumber overtakes him."

"How long is that?"

Eethum snorted.

"The last time it happened, a Blood Ranger slumbered for years."

Fogle gulped. He'd finally gotten used to the ancient dwarf, and now he was gone.

"Now what?" he asked.

"I'll take him home."

"But what about our journey?"

Eethum reached under Mood's battered figure, hoisted him up in his arms, and said, "It's your journey now, Wizard. I have to take care of my king." The Blood Ranger started limping away.

"But, where are you going? What if there are more giants? I can't take them alone."

"Make a fire, rest, gather your resources, Wizard. Be better prepared next time."

Fogle felt like he was the only man left in the world as he surveyed the carnage. Four dead giants lay baking under the suns. The black bearded dwarves, all but one, so far as he guessed, were dead. *Cass!*

He hurried over to the spot where Cass had stood before she was pulverized. He sat down at the edge of the big indentation in the ground and ran his fingers though the dirt. There was no sign of her, but there was blood. He looked over at the hammer the giant wielded. There was a lot of blood on that hammer. *I hope it's only dwarven.* Yet a sad feeling overwhelmed him. He sunk his head in his hand and clutched his fingers in his hair.

"No." he panted. "No. She can't be gone."

Chongo lumbered behind him and was panting down his neck.

"This is your fault," he said, pushing away his nose.

"It certainly is not!" Cass snapped.

Fogle jumped to his feet.

The beautiful druid woman sat perched on top of Chongo's saddle. Tiny black, white and yellow butterflies adorned her long white hair.

Fogle shuffled to her side, grabbed the warm ankle of her sensual leg, and gaped up at her.

"I'm real," she said, smiling down on him. "You're handsome when you smile, Fogle. You should try it more," she said, sliding down into his arms.

All of his passions flooded him when he felt her sensual body slide along his. He kissed her deeply, arms tightening around her waist as she melted in his arms. After a few long moments, she broke way.

"Hmmm ... Fogle, you are learning," she said in his ear. "But right now we have more important things to worry about."

"How did you... "

"Burst into butterflies? Oh, that's something for only druids to know. We're about as easy to kill as we are to understand," she said with a bewitching smile.

"It's just us now," he said, stepping away and stroking the big dog's necks. "Sorry, Chongo."

Chongo licked him in the face.

Ugh!

Cass giggled. "He's forgiven you, but it looks like he's ready for the next leg of the journey. You look worried."

Fogle looked around, lost in a world that he didn't understand. Rock, dirt, clay and the suns that always sizzled. His robes, a fine gift, were almost in tatters, but all things considered, they'd held up well. Still ...

"I am. I'm used to Mood being around, but he's going to be out for a while. Eethum left me with good advice, the likes of 'Be better prepared next time.'" He began pacing. "No one said anything about giants in the Outlands. Underlings I was ready for, but not giants. Where on Bish did they come from? Why'd they attack us?"

Cass shrugged her slender shoulders. "They hate dwarves."

"Have you ever seen giants before?"

"No. But just because I hadn't seen them didn't mean they didn't exist."

Fogle couldn't even begin to imagine all the things he'd never seen that might exist. Back in the City of Three, there were images of monsters and beasts everywhere: giants, griffons, chimeras, minotaurs, trolls of many sorts and so on. He traveled with a giant two-headed dog after all, so why'd he rule out the possibility of other things?

He looked at Tundoor. The giant's earrings alone were worth a fortune. Who'd forged items such as those?

"I believe those jewels would be too big for my ears, "Cass said, "but I like the way you're thinking."

"Huh … oh, well, I think you deserve something a hundred times the worth of those."

Cass brightened at the remark, took a deep draw into her chest and said, "It's just us, you know, and it's going to be dark soon. Perhaps you can tell me more about what I deserve beside a nice fire and under the moons."

He smiled again. "I'll fetch the wood." He scurried away, then came to a stop. He turned back and said, "I'm assuming we're not going to pitch a fire around here?"

She shook her head.

"I'll find a place for the fire. You just fetch the wood. Hmmm …," she needled her chin, "we have to take care of the fallen dwarves."

"No, leave them where they lay. Eethum will send for them soon. The dwarves are very picky about the dead. The family will want to see the place of battle. I have a feeling all of these frowns will be upside down when they see it."

"Then I'll see to it they remain undisturbed. Make haste, Fogle."

Make haste, indeed. My, surrounded by the dead and thinking only of my lustful yearnings for a woman. How can that be? Maybe that's why they say the 'The castles rise and fall between the legs of one maiden or another." I never understood those perverts until now. Slat. What is becoming of me?

Fogle's weariness returned. He felt his skin sagging over his bones. His head hurt, and his stomach was still queasy as he picked his way over the battle ground. The journey had just begun, and almost everyone was dead. Mood had looked more dead than alive. He looked to the south. Nothing but the barren Outlands, a place where only the cacti, bone trees and red toads thrived. Wouldn't it be better to just let the dog go to find his master on his own? Did the dog need them, or did they need the dog? *Maybe it's time to head back to the City of Three.*

He picked up a few more pieces of wood and headed back over to where he'd last seen Chongo and Cass. They were nowhere to be found. An unsettling feeling overcame him.

Somewhere, Chongo was barking like a dozen hounds.

He heard a harrowed scream. It was Cass.

NO! Not again!

He dropped everything and ran.

CHAPTER 18

VERBARD COULD SEE THEM NOW: men, robed and wizened, converging on his location. *Impressive.* The Royals, the guardians of the city, were better prepared for the unexpected than he'd anticipated. Across the skyline the wizards came, one rising up behind the other. Verbard could sense their power and their fear as well. It wasn't likely any of them had even seen an underling before, and they couldn't possibly have imagined one like him. His silver eyes shined as he ran his black tongue across his top row of teeth. *Underling Magi, to me!*

One by one, the underlings rose up from the smoke, heavy cloth robes billowing over their toes. Verbard felt a collective attack coming from the human wizards. They were here, but they were far from ready. The first barrage of energy came. Balls of blue light scorched across the sky, blasting full force into the mystic shield of the underlings and ricocheting harmlessly away.

Follow my lead!

Coils of red energy laced around Verbard as he summoned is power. The air crackled above the streets as he unleashed the first bolt of power, which streaked across the expanse and blasted into the wizards' pale blue mystic shield, splitting shards of magic from its edge, rocking a wizard back. The next bolt hit the wizard again, shattering his shield and sending him spinning through the air. Verbard's next bolt disintegrated the wizard completely. One down.

The human wizards huddled behind their shields together, hesitating. Verbard sensed their weakness and something else. He knew the humans couldn't float as the underlings could. Someone or something else was using power to keep them afloat. Another mind, stronger than the rest, was pulling the strings from somewhere else.

Finish them!

Eep, where are you?

Verbard drifted downward towards the burning building tops. Below his dangling feet, Jottenhiem, the Juegen and the Badoon were clashing with a heavy force of well-armored soldiers that had charged into the market place. The war was on. Men were toppled from their horses, and underlings were trampled under hooves. The keen edge of Jottenhiem's sword split through the skull inside a fallen rider's helmet, and another soldier's head was ripped from his shoulders. Still, Verbard could see that as quickly as the men fell, two more replaced them.

Eep buzzed to his side, rough skin singed and stained with blood.

"You calls me, Master," Eep hissed.

"I need you to find someone, a mage, somewhere nearby. And be quick about it."

Eep was wringing his clawed hands as he said, "You want me to kill him, Master?"

"Just sniff out the strongest source of magic and lead me to him," he ordered.

Buzz! Zip!

Eep blinked out of sight.

A barrage of arrows ripped through the air around Verbard, most bouncing harmlessly away. A row of archers had lined up along the wall, nocking and firing at his chest. He called the lightning within him. A white silver light streaked from his finger tips and passed through one soldier and into the others, cooking their bodies inside their metal armor. Verbard surveyed the battle below with wisps of lightning still dancing along his fingers. Jottenhiem and his men had the soldiers hemmed up in corridors, but couldn't hold them back forever. In the distance, Verbard could sense more forces were coming, and coming fast.

Eep reappeared and hissed excitedly.

"Found him, Master! A fat one. Like a giant grape. Let me eat his belly."

"Is he guarded?"

"By many. Sits on a pillow like a toad. Face is fat and sweaty. Red face ready to explode." Eep pointed his clawed finger down the road over the heads of the soldiers. "I can kill him."

"Perhaps." Verbard took a moment. "Nay. I'll handle this man myself. You, however, are needed above. Go."

Eep blinked away.

Verbard kept his energy ready. It was time he got a better feel for how much power the humans wielded. He sailed through the smoke, a shadow that was hidden from sight, whereupon he spied the man that Eep had described. On a wagon bed sat a man as tall as an underling but ten times as round. Three rows of chins hung beneath his bald-headed face, which was beet red with concentration. Surrounding him were ten soldiers: swords and spears ready, chainmail suits from head to toe, eyes wide and jittering at the sounds of the battle and the colorful explosions that came from above.

Verbard let loose the chained lightning. The searing bolt cracked into one man, passed through the next, then fizzled out. The blood-shot eyes of the fat human wizard in orange silk robes snapped open and locked on Verbard's through the smoke. Verbard felt a force surround him, drawing him closer, downward into the throng of soldiers that waited to chop him down.

He hissed. It appeared the fat wizard was as powerful as he was heavy, like a massive anvil wrapped around his neck, weighting him down. Verbard's straining eyes drifted to an orb which sat in the wizard's lap. It gleamed and swirled with intensity. His silver eyes widened. *An Orb of Imbibing!* He was trapped.

Not only did the orb consume magic, in this case it seemed to be feeding the wizard as well. Verbard was getting weaker, and the man, a useless sot by all appearances, was getting stronger. Much stronger. Verbard wrestled against the forces that were wrenching his power from him. His descent to the ground became quicker.

EEP! EEP! KILL THIS HUMAN SLUDGE PILE!

An arrow whizzed past his nose.

All of Verbard's strength was fading as he descended into the awaiting swords and spears.

EEP! HURRY!

Blink!

The imp was standing on the man's bulbous belly, hanging onto the man's ears, poking his clawed fingers into the man's neck and throat. The man wailed and squealed like a hog on fire.

Another arrow crashed through Verbard's shield and into his leg. He hissed. Yet, the blanket that absorbed his power had faded. His strength renewed. More arrows came, but ricocheted away. He realized it was time to go. He sped through the air, back towards the alley from where they had come.

Retreat! Retreat!

At the end of the alley, Verbard summoned a black dimensional doorway. One by one, the Badoon, Juegen and Magi survivors passed through. Verbard made one final command.

Eep, fetch that orb!

Jottenhiem was the last in line, breathing heavily, slick with blood and ailing.

"We have failed, my Lord."

Verbard gently pushed him through, saying, "Only if we were supposed to succeed."

Behind him, Eep was running his way, his wing broken, the orb wrapped in his hands, a wave of soldiers on his tail. "Wait, Master, wait!"

Over Eep's head, Verbard sent a bolt that slammed into Eep pursuers as the imp jumped through the door. Verbard dove in behind him, collapsing the door as a dozen arrows clattered off the alley walls.

Kierway stood inside the ancient chamber below Lord Almen's study, swords sheathed and clenched fists shaking. At his side floated two underling magi, both of whom he wanted to kill, but he needed them if he was going to get out of this castle alive.

Trembling near his feet was the flabby form of the human cleric, Sefron. Groveling.

"My Lord. Apologies. I've never been to this chamber. I never knew there was a secret door. I was never privy to the study. Please, my Lord, don't kill me," he whined, his high voice echoing all over the chamber.

Kierway slapped him across his face.

"Quiet, you failure!"

Kierway made his way over to the pegs in the alcove and touched them with his clawed finger, one by one. Seven keys, not one. His father, Master Sinway, had only required one, but which one would that have been? It hardly mattered now; they had failed.

The Vicious threw his weight into the door where the three humans had escaped. The creature's powerful talons clawed and swiped, its heavy shoulders shaking the door on the hinges, but it held. The magi, both of them, tried spells and incantations, but the door remained sealed. So did their fate as well. There was no escape from where they stood.

"Enough!" he said. The Vicious and Magi fell at attention. He kicked Sefron in the head.

"Who was this man that took the keys? It seems he knew more about them than you knew? I'm curious: why was that?"

Sefron wiped the blood from his mouth and gasped a sickly wheeze. It bothered Kierway's iron eyes to even look at him. Certainly, he could have found someone better to serve him, but the cleric had been the most willing.

"Melegal is his name. He serves Lord Almen as his detective. He's of little importance. Nothing more than a little rat, is all. *Hack. Hack.* A fool with fortune on his side this day."

Kierway reached over and plucked a dart out of Sefron's face.

"A fool. A fool that has seven keys to our none. A fool who it seems is much smarter than you." He grabbed Sefron by the back of his head and held the dart tip to his bulbous eye. "You will find this man, and quickly." He jammed the dart in Sefron's eye. The cleric let out a howl like a wounded wolf. "Or you'll lose the other eye, as well." Voices could be heard over the top of Sefron's pain-filled wails as he kicked and wallowed on the floor.

Kierway drew his blades as the Vicious bounded toward the landing on the stairwell. One of the magi muttered a powerful incantation, and they were gone.

CHAPTER 19

THE GLOWING FIRE WAS HOT on his face, but Georgio, though exhausted, was all smiles. Sucking down a tankard of ale while chewing a mouthful of food, he felt like he'd reached another plateau in his life. He felt all grown up. He'd survived a one-on-one battle with a brutal rogue, and he'd won.

"That was something," Billip said, shoving a small pile of coins across the table. The older man, grim-faced and wiry, looked as uncertain as he was pleased. Running his fingers through his coarse black hair, he leaned back in his chair and added, "Stupid, but something. I'm not sure what possessed you, Boy … er … Georgio, but I'm certain you've sprouted more chest hairs today." He hoisted his goblet up and drank.

Georgio hardly noticed a word that he'd said. His attention was elsewhere.

"Something?" The dark sultry woman by his side had her leg draped over his lap. "Amazing. That's what I'd say."

Her name was Velvet, the one who'd drawn the cards. Raven-haired, sensuous and captivating. She stirred his blood by running her gentle fingers through his hair and down over his chin.

"And to see such a handsome young man thrash such an ugly brute. I must say, I'm grateful. Jeb and his goons have been nothing but a menace to us girls and all the other patrons around here."

Georgio was smiling all over himself when he said, "Aw … it was nothing."

Billip humphed from across the table, folding his arms across his chest.

Velvet reached down, grabbed his hands and began inspecting them.

"How can you not be burned? Your meaty hands are soft like butter, yet there's not a single scorch mark." She started massaging them. "Are you a mage of some sort?"

"Well, I can't exactly—"

He felt a boot smack into his shin. Billip was eyeing him.

"Ow! Er … I'm from a family of blacksmiths, is all. I've been around the furnaces all my life. Tough hands. It runs in the family." He shrugged.

"Impressive," Velvet purred. "And my hands are from a long line of … well … personal services, and they're all yours. I'm sure you have plenty of bumps and bruises that I could," she squeezed his thigh, "remedy."

Georgio scratched the back of his neck.

"Uh …"

"Alright," Billip interjected with a smile, "can you give me and the young warrior a moment, Velvet is it?" He slid her a coin and winked. "And we could use another round if you'd please oblige, Pretty Thing."

Velvet kissed Georgio on his forehead, shot Billip an aggravated look, huffed, and walked away.

"What'd you do that for?" Georgio said, gawking at the sway of Velvet's hips.

Billip reached over and punched him in the arm.

"Ow! What'd you do that for!" he exclaimed, wiping his face.

"No time for fooling around, Georgio! Underlings! In Bone!"

Georgio surveyed the room. The people, what was left of them anyway, were drawn up as tight as bows. Stories and chatter of the vicious creatures were spreading from one chair to the other. There was talk of a mass exodus that had begun, but Georgio had a hard time believing any of it. And the only thing that mattered to him was getting closer to Velvet. He shrugged.

"I don't see any underlings in here."

Billip punched him again, harder this time.

"No, but you're about to see stars."

"Ha! I'd like to see you try."

Billip's eyes narrowed, his voice as deadly as a pit of vipers.

"You think beating that curly haired slug has you prepared for the likes of me ... Boy?"

Georgio gulped. He'd seen Billip angry before. On the trek down to Bone, they came across a nomad band of half-orcs that tried pushing them around. Billip skewered one in the neck with one throw and another in the belly with the other. It all happened in the blink of an eye. "Er ... only teasing, Billip."

"Fill your belly. Cop your feel, but we're getting out of here ... soon. Mikkel's checking the stories out, and when he returns, we're going after Nikkel." The wary archer looked over his shoulder. "Something about this city just isn't right. The whole world isn't right and hasn't been for a while. Underlings in the City of Three and now underlings in Bone. You're young, Georgio. But I'm telling you, this is crazy."

Georgio was weary again. The fire was soothing, but his spirits began to dull. He could tell by the grim looks on the people's faces that something wasn't right. Normally, the people of Bone, though hardened and somewhat criminal, had a more positive tone about them. Now, they spoke in whispers, under their breath, jumping a bit at every unusual sound. It only made sense. The citizens had never seen an underling before, and according to rumors, no one lived to tell about seeing one, either.

"What's going on inside that big melon of yours?" Billip said.

"Ah ... I'm just starting to get the feeling that maybe you're right, Billip. What if the underlings are overrunning the city? What if they've overrun Bish? What will happen to us?"

An uncertain smile broadened over Billip's thick black goatee when he said, "Well, I guess we'll all eventually be buried arses up and heads stuck in the ground. Cheers!" He reached over and clonked his tankard against Georgio's.

Reaching for his mug, Georgio saw a group of distraught men burst inside the door.

"Underlings! Hundreds!" a man dressed as a laborer shouted.

"Thousands!" the other man, thick in muscle and skull, added at his partner's side.

The Drunken Octopus fell silent.

"The entire 21st District is overrun. Burning and mutilated. Thousands of Royal Soldiers are dead."

The short stocky one waved his hands over his shoulders.

"All of their heads are gone. Half eaten most of them. You must flee! They're coming!"

A small quiet group of people turned into a frenzied hoard when the entire room made for the stairs and the doors. Georgio was rising to his feet when Billip pushed him back down.

"What?" he asked.

"We'll go when Mikkel returns."

"What if they got him already?"

Billip's lips twitched as he popped his knuckles.

"We wait. Those fools over there are just creating a panic. I'd say there's only ten at most out there, if that."

Velvet glided back into her seat, trembling, and draped her arms around Georgio.

"Will you protect me?"

He could feel her shivering. Her painted eyes were full of fear. His heart began to swell.

"Sure. I've killed underlings before. Just stay close to me," he said, running his arm across her back.

Billip shook his head as the room behind him began to clear out. Velvet's arms tightened around Georgio's neck as the screaming in the streets began to rise. Something was going on out there. Something bad. Something evil.

That's when Sam the Barkeep spoke up.

"Everyone out!"

His usual expressionless countenance now unfurled as he took rapid puffs on his cigar.

The few who remained didn't waste any time heading out the door. Sam stormed over to the table, smacking his club in his hand.

"It's time to get your arses out of here, too. My tavern's closed."

Billip said, "But we've already paid for our room."

Sam cracked his club on the table.

"Tough!"

Chapter 20

"**Y**OU TRY ANYTHING AND I'LL scream," Kam said as Diller shoved her towards the tub. "I don't think Palos would be too happy with you accosting me. You saw what happened to Thorn."

Diller shoved her hard to the floor. She kicked at his knee. He slipped past and swatted her hard in the back of the head. His calloused hands were strong. He grabbed her by the wrist and dragged her kicking across the floor. One again, she was powerless in the quick and deadly hands of one of Palo's top men. Still, she managed to bite his hand and wriggle free.

"Ahhhh!" He said, wincing. "You keep struggling, and I'll see the little baby starved, you spoiled wench."

Kam froze, chest heavy beneath her robes as she drew her legs up to her chin.

"You leave my daughter alone."

She smacked her in the face, drawing more blood in her mouth.

"That's the plan, Princess."

Kam fell silent. Numb inside. Her courage dissipated as quickly as it had started. There was nothing she could do. Diller reached down, fetid breath on her neck, groping her body while tying her to the legs of the tub with the absidium chains.

"You sick, wretched pervert. Wait until—"

"Until what? You go ahead and tell Palos." He kneeled down in front of her, elbow relaxed on his knee, toothpick rolling back and forth in his mouth. "Princess, you'll be begging to have me once Palos is through with you."

Her green eyes lit up at the matter-of-factness of his statement.

"Ah … that's right. I hope you don't think you're the one and only pretty thing he's ever drug down here. You certainly aren't the first Royal, and you won't be the last."

She swallowed hard and slunk back.

"Yes," he brushed the back of his palm against her cheek. "It's only a matter of time. No woman can ever satisfy a man like that for long." He laughed, a mocking one. "Then you'll certainly be mine … or Thorn's. Ah … there will be suitors aplenty to bid on you, my dear. But you better hope it ends up being me."

He grabbed her chin. She jerked it away.

"Never," she said with trembling breath.

His knees cracked as he rose to his full height and leered down on her.

"I'm a patient man," he said, walking away, dusting off his hands. "You'll be mine, and fortunate for you, I'm much easier to satisfy than him." He gave her a lusty look over his shoulder. "And I'm sure I'll satisfy you as well, not that it will matter."

Kam fell into a fit of tears as soon as he closed the door.

This is my fault. My fault. My fault.

Lefty gently banged his head over into the clawed foot of the tub.

My fault!

He hit it once more, harder this time. It hurt, but it didn't ache near as much as his heart, which was slipping inside his chest as Kam's sobs became deafening. He wanted to reach out. Touch her. Comfort her. Say how sorry he was, but he couldn't. The truth was, he was too scared. If anyone deserved to die, it was him. And if anyone reserved the right to kill him, it was her.

My fault!

He struck his head once more. *Perhaps I can spare her the effort.*

"Stop doing that," Kam managed from beneath her sobs.

Huddled under the tub, he tilted his head back.

"Don't!" she said, her voice stronger, regaining its fiery luster. "I might have use for that little head, after all."

Lefty sucked up the courage to look up into her eyes.

Tears filled his eyes. Kam, still as beautiful as the first day he saw her, was misaligned. Her glorious auburn hair was a tangled mess, and her high cheek bones were now bruised. A split lip accompanied the dark circles under her eyes, and her polished nails were chipped and chewed. She was a lovely white dove now covered in soot and grime. Her robe barely covered her skinned up features and none of her shame. She'd been through something. Something bad. All because of him.

"Stop crying, you little bastard. I've cried enough for all of your years and mine put together."

"K-Kam … I'm sorry," he sobbed, wiping his runny nose. "I didn't …" Tears streaming into his face, he curled up into a ball.

She rankled her chains.

"I said no more crying, Lefty! Now get up."

He didn't move. He just lay there trembling like a frightened bunny.

Kam leaned back against the tub, pulled her legs under her hips, and tried to make herself more comfortable. She blew the locks of hair from her eyes. *I must look horrible. I am horrible.* And now she'd terrified a boy, or at least someone who looked like a boy, but was certainly much older. She wasn't even sure how long halflings lived, and she had no idea how old Lefty actually was. But he was helpless. Far more helpless than her, or so it seemed at the moment.

All men, no matter how big or how small, are trouble.

Lefty. His haggard little face told it all. He was exhausted, weary, over-run by the dangerous life that one can easily encounter in Bish, especially when you're not careful. That must have been what happened to him. Or, maybe he was just trying to deceive her once more. That grin. The one he'd shown earlier, when Gillem was around. The face stuck with her, leaving an unfavorable impression. But at this point, what did they have to gain from her? Was Lefty spying on her? Why not let Diller do that? It seemed odd that they'd just leave him here with her. What else would they want from her?

She scooted over, stretched out her leg, and pushed him with her toe.

"Stop crying, you little sot."

He kept on. She shoved him again.

"I'm miserable enough already, so don't make it worse. Now tell me something. You owe me at least that much. Have you seen Erin?"

His trembling stopped as he pulled himself to his knees. Tears dripping from his tiny face to the floor, he nodded.

"I'm s-s-s-soooo sorry! I know it's all … all my fault."

The next question was the hardest for her, but she had to ask it.

"Is she alive?"

Her heart stopped as she watched him gulp and take a breath.

"I'm certain of it."

Kam gasped. She would have hugged him if she could.

"Do you know where she is?"

"I do, Kam. It was the first thing I did, finding that out. Kam, I swear I was trying to think of a way out of this. I really was," he pleaded. "But they killed Gillem." His eyes watered again. "And I was scared they'd kill me and you and Erin. They all lied to me, Kam. They tricked me. The kidnapping. Everything. I never, ever would do anything to hurt you or anyone. I really wouldn't. But, I – I just didn't have a choice. Palos … he's so mean and cruel and scary." He dragged his sleeve across his wet face. "He killed Gillem for no reason at all. I've seen him kill other men, too. And he keeps the dead bodies in the lake. Gillem showed it to me. Told me that was where I'd live, at the bottom of the lake. I've seen them all dead. Skin hanging off of them. It's horrifying. Terrible. I didn't want to be drowned and staring forever up at the living. I'm sorry. I'm so sorry! I just—"

Kam nudged him with her foot and tried to sound reassuring.

"That's enough, Lefty. I'm starting to understand."

Lefty was always a jittery little man, a victim of seeing things that were awfully horrible. She actually was beginning to understand. If she were a little girl in the same situation, what would she have done? *No. I would have made the right choice. He made the wrong one. You're better off dying for the right reasons than living for the wrong ones.* That's what her mother taught her anyway, and she remembered passing that along to him and Georgio a time or two. The question now was, could she trust him again?

"Do you think Erin is well?"

He shrugged his small shoulders and said, "I think so. That old woman, she's not so bad, at least not compared to the rest of them. Just ugly is all."

It gave Kam little relief, but it was better than nothing.

"Well, you're a thief now, right? Can't you undo these bonds?"

"I've tried. This absidium is really tough, like living wire. Master Gillem could have undone it, but I haven't figured out how yet."

Kam winced as she fought the chains that bound up her wrists. The more you wriggled, the more they bit. It was strange that the metal wasn't magic, but it sure did act like it, and Lefty was bound up worse than her. Still, she noticed he could wiggle his fingers and toes. It gave her an idea.

"Do you think you can cast a spell?" she asked.

"I think, but can't you?"

"No, this choker prevents that. If I try, it will kill me."

His blue eyes lit up.

"Maybe I can help. If you lie down, maybe I can get it off."

"No, only magic can unseal it."

"But I don't know any spells. And I haven't practiced in a long time."

"True, but I can give you the words, and maybe you can harness the power."

He nodded. "Let's try."

She looked over at the doors. If Palos or Diller stepped in, it would be all over.

Better try something small.

"Lefty, repeat after me."

She started speaking in a slow and rhythmic series of syllables, very quiet, very easy. Lefty's lips followed her, uttering everything as if she spoke it herself. She chanted faster now, repeating the same phrases over and over.

"Urk!"

The choker around her neck seized up like a python, turning her face red as she kicked and reeled on the floor.

"Kam! Kam!" Lefty shrieked, stretching his fingers out to save her.

The choker was like a living snake around her neck, insidious and in control. All she could do was think of Erin and never seeing her baby's face again. *No! No!* The choker released her. Whatever little bit of magic she'd summoned fled her just in time. Now, she lay on the floor gasping, sucking for air.

"I'm so sorry! I'm so sorry!"

It took more than a minute before she recovered herself. She looked over at Lefty and said, "Lefty, don't worry about me. If you can do anything, save Erin. Escape and free her."

"I have to help you, too. If I take her, they might kill you," he said with such a sad look in his eyes she felt like she was dead already.

"That's my choice, not yours. If I can't save her, then you are the only one who can. It's the only way you can make things right with me."

"But Kam—"

"Promise me, Lefty!"

He nodded his head.

"I promise."

She sat there and let her fate sink in. Palos had her. Without her magic, she was nothing. Just an ordinary woman turned into a madman's whore.

Lefty started retching.

She ignored it. Whatever could possibly be wrong now didn't even matter. *Bish.*

CHAPTER 21

GALLOPING ON HORSEBACK, VENIR SWEPT Brool into the nearest underling's chest and shattered another's teeth on his shield. All around him was chaos. The underlings were fleeing. A screeching black army scurrying as fast as they could into their dark little holes. Venir hewed them down, one by one, preventing the escape of all he could. Left and right, they fell under his swath of destruction. He was a black knight filling a moat with their blood.

Kill them! Kill them all! The helm urged him on.

His hatred pushed him further.

Horses, dozens of them, spears and lance tips lowered to the ground, ran over and through one underling after the other. The Royal Riders, the stoutest cavalry in the world of Bish, had the underlings undone. The underling army fragmented. Spiders, underlings, Juegen and magi fled, bled and died. Their bones, guts and entire camp were trampled into the dust.

A desperate underling, fleeing for its life, sent a spear into the rump of Venir's horse. He cried out as the horse bucked and sent him careening to the ground. The underlings, the closest ones that still lived, piled on him, tearing at him, their bright eyes wild for his destruction.

Venir's arms and shoulders ached, and his wounded hand felt like it was on fire. Exhausted, he struck onward, upward, downward, until his arms gave out. His wounds many, he pressed on.

Fight! Fight! Fight! The helm urged.

He couldn't go on much longer.

CHOP!

The last underling fell beneath the weight of his axe, its arm dangling from its shoulder. Laboring for breath, he fell to his knees. He checked his surroundings Every last one was dead or fled.

"Finally," he huffed. Brool was sticky and bloody in his grip as he slipped his blood-soaked hand from the shaft and reached for his canteen. It was no longer there. *Bone.*

It was a macabre scene the likes of which he'd never seen before. Dead underlings in their dark mail armor lay baking in the suns. Stout men had fallen to weapons, and others' skin had been sizzled or melted off by powerful magic. Over-sized spider legs were twitching, and webs were scattered everywhere.

Someone stepped into his sunlight and tossed something on the ground before him. A canteen.

"You owe me a horse," a strong and familiar voice said.

Venir looked up. It was the Commander of the Royal Riders, coated in dirt and blood, leaning over the neck of his horse, a meek but broad smile showing.

Venir grabbed the canteen and gulped down every last drop.

"And some water too, it seems," he said, rising on shaking feet. Then a thought jarred his aching head. "Adanna!"

"Who?" the commander asked.

"Can you begin a search? Two women were taken and possibly a man as well."

The Commander shook his head and said, "I'm telling you, underlings don't take prisoners, but I'll see what I can do." He turned in his saddle. "Men, begin a search. Two women and one male survivor!"

Venir walked a few steps away. He need to search as well.

"You can at least give me my canteen back. I'm sure you can pluck a good one from the dead. Huh, I hope that broad back of yours can use a shovel as well as it swings that axe, Stranger. We've got many good men to bury."

Walking away, Venir tossed the man up the canteen. "And many enemies to burn as well."

The underling camp was a small city filled with rows of dark grey tents that no longer stood. Venir limped to the nearest collapsed tent and lifted it up. A bunch of small black spiders scurried out, and he stomped them into the ground. He had an uncanny feeling. Underlings setting up camps like men. It wasn't normal, not above ground that is, at least in his lifetime anyway.

Searching one disheveled tent after the other, he cursed his luck. And, as far as he could tell, the Royal Riders weren't doing their best to look, either. Instead, they sat tending the wounded and catching their breath. Another hour passed, and Venir had covered little ground. His temper and vitality were wearing thin as he limped from one tent to the other. *Blast, there's so many.*

It was beginning to feel like a lost cause. The underlings didn't often take prisoners, but when they did, they usually weren't heard from again. As the first sun sunk down over the horizon, the likelihood that his friends survived darkened as well. He hoisted up the heavy canvas of the tents, one after the other, his wounds festering and burning. His leg was so stiff he could hardly walk, and the insides of his cheeks stung from where he'd bitten them in battle. He pulled off his helm. The throbbing in his head subsided, but he groaned as the other aches and pains intensified. He eased himself to the ground as exhaustion quickly settled into his bones. He just wanted to sleep. He closed his eyes.

"Warrior!"

The voice sounded like an explosion in his ear and made his entire body flinch on the ground. Everything hurt. It even hurt when he blinked. He rose into a sitting position and looked up at the sky. It was dusk, with little more than a few minutes of daylight remaining.

He found the commander's face. "What?"

"Better come with me. I think we've found who you're looking for," he said in a somber tone.

With the help of a strong armed soldier, Venir made it to his feet and followed the man, who was still riding his horse. The commander led him alongside a deep pit that was too dark to see inside. The smell of death and decay filtered up through it. Another bottomless pit opened up, this one in Venir's stomach, and that old guilty feeling rose its ugly head. All his friends were better off without him.

The commander slid from his saddle at his side, stroked his mustache, and said, "There's more of them. Not as deep, but the bodies were many. No women, though. This is the last one we found." He motioned toward a dog-sized sand spider that lay dead on its back, a pair of spears shoved through it. "That thing was crawling out when we got here. Its belly's full." The man spat. "I've seen plenty of them spiders in my day, but not so many nor so big all at once."

He made his way to the edge of the pit and prepared to lower himself inside.

"Give me a torch," Venir asked, strapping on his helm.

A soldier nearby handed one over, and Venir tossed it down inside. It stuck on a bed of webs and then slowly dissipated as it fell all the way through. The pit wasn't as deep as it looked. He uncoiled a rope, tossed it over the side, and started climbing down. That's when he noted the steps cut into the walls, underling size. Reaching the bottom, he noticed the pit was quiet and rank.

When he bent to pick the torch up, the marrow in his bones chilled and the hairs on his neck stood on end.

Sssckt. Sssckt. Sssckt … A sand spider was sucking on the cocooned figure of a man.

Venir's instincts fired. He limped over and rammed Brool's spike dead center into the spider's bulbous body. It detached with a screech and died. Venir shuffled around the bottom of the pit, waving the torch back and forth, but no other spiders were in sight. Three figures were wrapped up in spidery cocoons, one of them stretched out at least seven feet. *Slim!*

Venir lowered the torch along the webs and watched the spider silk shrivel and dissipate.

"I'm going to need a hand down here," he shouted upward. "I've got three bodies!"

He found the cloth around Slim's face and pulled it away. His face was gaunt, and no breath came. "Come on, Slim." He slapped the skinny man's face. Nothing happened. Then there was a twitch behind his eyelids.

He lowered the torch to the next cocoon and pulled the sticky webbing away from another face wrapped in cloth. It was Adanna. Her once lustrous hair was dry as bone, and the skin around her once full figure was tight as sun dried leather and sunken in all places. Venir's chin dipped down. She was dead. Besides Adanna, her mother was gone as well.

"Blast my pride-filled hide," he grumbled.

If he'd only stayed with them, they'd probably all be still alive. Instead, he'd doubled back to deal with Farc. Now Hogan, his wife and his daughter were dead. That guilty feeling renewed the fires within him.

"Nay," he said to himself.

It wasn't him that was responsible. It was the underlings. And he was going to make them pay. Every last one.

Venir sat by the campfire, guarding Slim. His friend looked dead as a tombstone. Above him, the moons had risen, both full and glowing in pale shades of blood. He'd just spent the last several hours shoveling shallow graves for Adanna, her mother and many of the hundreds of Royal Riders. It had been a long time since he'd been part of such a big battle, and the feeling inside his gut told him there were many more battles to come.

He took a deep breath and let out the ragged sigh of a tired lion. The throbbing in his hand made it feel like it was about to explode.

"You're going to need to take care of that wound before long."

Venir looked over his shoulder. It was the commander. The man took a spot along his side and stoked the crackling embers of the fire while he stroked the long ends of his mustache

"Quite a battle," he added, reaching out his hand. "By the way, my name is Jans. Commander Jans."

Venir took the man's grip in his and said, "Venir. Underling Killer."

"Ha! You can say that again. You've got most of my men talking about you already. I've even found myself making a comment or two, and I'm not a man of many words."

Jans ran a cloth over the bald crown of his head and took a deep draw from a sack of wine. Venir could see the hardened face of a battle tested soldier who wasn't like many Royals. Some were good, most bad by his account, but Jans seemed alright. An old soldier who put his trust in steel, more so than men.

Slim moaned. It was faint, but at least he was moving. Venir checked the wound on the man's leg. The spider bite, four holes each as big as the tip of his finger, had swollen the man's ankle to the size of Venir's arm. Slim's head was dripping with sweat. Venir let out a grunt.

"He's made it this long, I'd say in a few days he'll be moving, maybe just not walking," Jans said, "but we'll have to clear out first light tomorrow. You sure you don't want someone to look at your wound?"

"No. I've had worse." Venir shrugged.

"So, what were you doing with these people?"

"Heading north. There are some people I'm looking for."

"They must be important if you plan on traversing these jungles that are thicker with underlings than they are mosquitoes."

Venir shrugged. "It looks like you and your men have survived. Certainly there are more Royals to come."

Jans laughed. "Our days are numbered, and our supplies run low. Almost half of our outposts in Southern Bish are either under siege or over taken." Jans tossed him the wine sack and cleared his throat. "The underlings cut through here like a black storm one night. They burned, killed and destroyed everything living and moving for miles. This batch we just ran over," Jans looked over his shoulder where a pyre of burning underling bodies smoked and smoldered, leaving a foul stench lingering in the air, "is only a small roving force. There are underling armies numbering in the thousands out there. The only things getting us through are that we know our lands better and horses travel much faster than underlings and spiders."

Venir knew it to be true. The jungle-like forests of the south were difficult to march an entire army through. Filled with high hill tops that jutted outward in many places and formed steep cliff faces in other places, the southern lands were a place of sanctuary to those who knew them. As well, the deep ravines and vines thick as trees made it tough for travel.

Venir's face turned grim as he asked, "So, what are the Royals doing to deal with this mess? Still sitting on their thrones and spinning lies to the masses, or are they gearing up for battle?"

"They're fortifying the north."

"And leaving the south to die."

"Well, it's mostly gnolls and orcs these days. But, Venir, without Outpost Thirty-One, any attempts to hold the south are in vain."

Venir let out an angry snort. He still didn't understand why the Royals never attempted to retake their most strategic stronghold in the south. If it had been up to him, he would have rooted the underlings out before the underlings were dug in too deep. Now, it seemed like it was too late for that. Besides, it was the Royals who had abandoned their own kind. Jarla the Brigand Queen, in unison with the underlings, led the fort to its fall. As far as he was concerned, the Royals deserved what they got. But now, more than five years later, the issue had a new significance. Something needed to be done.

"Where were you when that Outpost fell?" Venir asked, taking a sip.

"Twenty-Four. And you?"

"I was there. I was part of that small group that gave the early warning."

Jans's brows lifted as the fire reflected on his oily face. "Ah … I know you, Man. At least, I knew of you. Are you one of the rogues who took down the Brigand Army? Hah! That horde, now that was something the likes I hope I never see again. Orcs, gnolls, kobolds and men fighting as one."

"Under the direction of the underlings."

Jans grunted. "Aye, of course. I think that us and the other races are in the same predicament now."

"Have you seen any evidence of that?"

"Yes, but very little. As much as I hate the underlings, I have no sympathy when they carve down the other scum, either. Bish would be better off without all of them."

Venir felt a little irritated at the remark. As despicable as the other races could be, he still had difficulty dealing with the Royals and their attitude of superiority. As much as he hated to admit it, it was the underlings and the other pesky races that kept the Royal egos in check, at least if that was possible. Now, as these soldiers struggled for a foothold for their own survival, he could only imagine that the Royals were too busy pointing the blame at one another instead of acting. As the underlings gained ground and dug in deeper, he imagined the Royals wouldn't do a thing until the last moment possible.

He put the wine sack to Slim's mouth, squeezed out a few drops that soaked right between Slim's lips, and tossed it back over to Jans. Something about what Slim had said to him a day earlier was sticking in his craw. He'd been fighting underlings on his own for the most part. Now, maybe it was time he added some more people to help shoulder the load.

"So, what are you going to do when you run out of supplies?"

Now it was Jans's time to sigh.

"I can feel it, Venir, deep in my belly." He tapped his stomach. "Time. Our time is running out. We've kept on the move knowing full well if we take a fort and hold out the underlings will starve us out."

Jans took out a wetting stone and began running it across the edge of his sword.

"My men are becoming weary with worry now, as I've run out of answers. All I've been able to tell them is that help is on the way, but no aid has come. We send riders north, but none have returned." He stretched his booted feet towards the fire. "The truth is, I figured this battle would be my last. None of my men had planned to survive, either. It was our choice, our sacrifice to distract the underlings so the rest of the force could clean up." He became solemn for a moment, rugged face looking up into the sky. "The fewer mouths to feed, the better. We die so others can live a day or two longer and have one last belly full before battle."

His words sank in. Jans and his men were unlike most men he'd known.

Jans slapped his leg and spit out a laugh.

"And then you show up, and here I sit, ready to live another day and die on another. I just didn't want to die from starvation, holed up in a fort. And the thought of my own men eating one another didn't sit right with me, either. I've seen that happen before, long ago." Jans's head sagged down to his chest as his eyes got all misty.

"What happened?"

"Oh … I was a boy, my brothers and sisters starving, trapped in Bonehole by brigand orcs that had seized a small outpost leagues northwest of here. My father and mother said they were leaving to gather food, but only one returned. The meat got us through the next few days until the Royal Riders showed up, and I've been one of them ever since."

Venir thought he saw a tear on the man's cheek.

Staring into the fire, Jans finished his thought. "I'd rather burn than ever do that again."

CHAPTER 22

BRAK'S STOMACH FELT LIKE IT was being turned upside down in his belly, and he swore his head was spinning on his shoulders, but it all ended abruptly. Darkness. The rustling of bodies and the scent of something wonderful. Baked food. Brak noticed light creeping from beneath a doorway and shoved it open.

"Wait!" the skinny man interjected as he pulled on the back of his pants.

A dozen men couldn't have stopped him from stepping out into the smokehouse, wrapping his blood-stained fingers around a hot blackberry pie, and shoving it into his mouth. The café owner didn't contain his dismay or fury, shouting, pointing and crying out for the City Watch. He didn't care. He ate and ate and ate.

"What have you done? Where have you taken us?" Melegal asked, holding his aching head.

Melegal stood behind Brak, watching the big young man stuff his face like a hungry pig. The baker, a man in a flour coated apron and with coarse black hair down his arms and over his knuckles, drew back a butcher's knife, aiming to ram it into Brak's back. *Drat!* In a fluid motion, Melegal wrenched the weapon from the baker's hand and drove his elbow across the man's chin. He didn't bother to slow the man's fall, just let him collapse on the tiles.

Melegal stepped outside the kitchen into the small store front, took a seat on one of the stools at the bar, and let out a sigh. He was still in Bone, and not only that, but he knew exactly where he was as well. He watched as the citizens of Bone scurried along with unusual activity. It was the time of day they would normally be working, but many of them were packed up. Fleeing from an unseen force. *Underlings.* He leaned against the bar to hear what they were saying.

The streets run red with blood.

The Royals have failed.

Thousands have taken over.

They shoot fire from their eyes and insects from their breath.

Thousands of women and children have been killed.

They are bigger than men and ride on the backs of Chimera.

They cut off my uncle's head and devoured his brains.

Something tugged at Melegal's vest. It was Jubilee: pitiful, with big brown eyes and Leezir's flat nose.

"What do you want?"

"Can I have something to eat, too?"

He looked over his shoulder at Brak, whose face was stained in blackberries and crust as he sucked down a jug of goat's milk. The over-sized young man with the face of a hardened soldier seemed awfully content, almost serene for someone who'd just butchered more than a dozen people. Melegal had seen Venir have his own fits of rage, but he'd never seen anything like what Brak was capable of. *Ew! What he did to those people?* He couldn't erase the thought of the man being bent backwards until the back of his head touched his arse. Or that Brak had almost killed him, Melegal, a moment earlier. He'd never been pinned down by such raw power before. He'd heard the term *berserker*, but before now it had seemed like a silly notion: a man so battle crazed that he'd fight, even without limbs, like a ravenous dog until dead. It seemed the stories were true.

He patted Jubilee on the brown-haired head and said, "Yes. But you better hurry before it's gone."

"Thank you," she said, smiling up at him, "for saving us." She wrapped her ginger little arms around his waist and hugged him.

Melegal cocked a brow over his steely eyes. After all the death, all the horror, the little girl still found a reason to smile and be grateful. He peeled her arms away, saying, "Fond of me all of a sudden, are we? Well, little Slerg, you are on your own now, so get a belly full, and don't ever hug me again."

He set Tonio's sword on the bar, felt the pommels on his swords, *the Sisters*, on his hips, took a deep breath, and rubbed his temples. Underlings. They were actually inside the City of Bone and attacking people. The improbable had occurred. Outside of the city walls were thousands of people who had fled the south to find sanctuary in the north. Inside the city, the citizens were scrambling to find a way back outside. No doubt, the Royals would permit them to leave, only never to return. He reached inside his vest, produced new darts, and reloaded his launchers. *If I'd only used poison, Sefron would be dead by now.*

Though thankful for his escape, he still had immediate problems. Lord Almen. Was he alive or dead? Sefron had come to the man's aid, and Melegal had witnessed his moving hand. *Slat. I should have cut his throat.* It wasn't his style, however, and killing wasn't something he was accustomed to, but sometimes that was the only choice if you wanted to live. Jarla the Brigand queen had witnessed the entire ordeal, and he'd tried to dispatch of her, but she had still been fighting when he'd fled. *Should have just done what the Lorda said and killed her. I'm not sure what possessed me to gut Almen.* He looked over at Jubilee, who was chomping on a biscuit. She had Leezir's eyes as well. Melegal grabbed a loaf of bread and had started picking at it when two surly men walked up, eyeing the food.

Melegal's eyes narrowed as he slid Tonio's sword from the sheath, saying, "Keep walking. This store's closed."

"We'll pay," one man said, licking his lips as the other fidgeted at his side.

"I only take blood," he replied, twirling the sword over his wrist.

The men grumbled and shuffled along.

He stuck the sword in the ground and resumed his thoughts. The underlings had been his unlikely ally in all this. They must have slaughtered all of the living in the arena, which should include Lord Almen and Jarla. They'd taken Sefron prisoner and pursued him. They wanted the keys.

"Ha!"

All this time, Sefron, of all people, had an alliance with the underlings. Sefron wanted the keys for the underlings. Melegal ran his hands over the hidden inner pockets of his clothing. *One. Two. Three. Four. Five. Six. Seven. All present and accounted for.* He pulled a key out, fingering the topaz gem encrusted in the square head. It was the one he'd used on the last door. Then he remembered something. The Brigand Queen. She had arrived through another door with her men. *How did she manage to do that? Were there more keys? Or did she get there by some other means?*

"What is that key for?" Jubilee asked, crawling up on the bar, her legs dangling over the edge, mouth full of a biscuit and appearing happy as a lark.

"Trouble," he said, sliding it back into his clothes. "Now don't bother me. I'm thinking."

"All right," she said, beginning to hum a tune.

Now where was I? Keys. The underlings want the keys. Which means, the underlings will be coming after me. Slat! He couldn't shake the image of the Vicious, the beastly creature that could rend through stone with its nails. Was that creature coming after him as well? He remembered that the last time he saw one, at the Warfield, the nasty thing had slit Georgio's throat. *Oh my.* That made for two things even he'd hope the boy'd never see again: the Vicious and Tonio. He counted his enemies again. *Kill Sefron. Fail. Lord Almen. Fail. The Brigand Queen. Fail. It's only safe to assume that all live. After all, evil has an uncanny ability to survive. And now the Underlings. Aren't they supposed to be the problem for that brutish friend of mine?* He turned towards his friend's son, whose eating pace was now a slow chew. Brak's Venir-like eyes drifted into Melegal's, leaving a haunting feeling in his gut. Was he sane or a madman?

"Er … Jubilee, uh, how well do you know this man?"

She perched her eyebrows, smiling, wiping the crumbs from her lips.

"Brak? He's good. Nothing like my uncles or my grandfather, who weren't too bad, but still did many things I thought were questionable."

"Is that so?" *How interesting for a little Slerg.*

"Hagerdon said Grandfather Leezir had gotten soft in his age, but I never thought of him as old, not for a man, anyway."

"Hmmm … an interesting observation for such a young person. I'll tell you something else about your grandfather, Leezir. You are right. He wasn't one of the worst, not when it comes to Royals. Not that he had a soft side, he didn't, but, uh … how should I put it? He was reasonable and resourceful, just flawed."

Jubilee dusted the crumbs from her hands and hopped down on the ground.

"Everyone is flawed. If they weren't, then the world would be perfect. But if that were so, we'd be quite bored."

"You are smart for one so young."

"I know. Say, where's everybody going?"

"Why don't you go ask them?"

Jubilee didn't say another word. She just stood and stared at the crowd.

"My back hurts," Brak said.

Melegal turned and looked at the man's grimacing face.

Two feathered arrows still protruded from Brak's' back. Moving like a sloth, he made his way over and rested his arms on the bar.

Melegal looked up into his big face with the thick tuft of hair that was marred with blood. "Are you sure the hurt is not your stomach? You just inhaled enough to fill two cows."

"No …"

Brak's speech was a little garbled, low, and his pronunciations were long. It irritated Melegal.

"… it's in my back. It hurts. Did someone stab me? I can't remember."

"What do you remember?"

"Seeing Hagerdon killed. Leezir getting shot and Jubilee screaming. The next thing I remember, my back was on fire, and I was following you through a castle." He lifted his chin in repose. "Those paintings were wonderful. I'd never seen anything like them before."

A brute with an eye for art. Utterly ridiculous. But what isn't these days?

Jubilee wandered back over and gasped. "Brak! Your back! We have to do something!"

Brak's eyes narrowed on Melegal.

"You said it was just a scratch."

"Well it is, in a manner of speaking."

"Take them out," Jubilee demanded.

"You're the smart one; you take them out."

"Give me a knife, and I will."

"Pah … just get out of the way." He removed Brak's' shackles and inspected his back, needling his fingers around the wounds. Though they were not well defined, he could feel the brutish muscles of an ox beneath the meaty skin.

"If your arms were long enough, you could pull them out yourself," he muttered under his breath.

"What?" Brak said, cocking his meaty neck.

"Nothing." He wrapped his fingers around the shafts. "Now be still. This shouldn't hurt a bit."

Yank!

Brak roared like a savage beast, sending everyone nearby scattering in all directions. Melegal was twirling the arrows through his fingers as Brak whirled on him, snorting with rage, fingers clutching in the air.

Melegal took a step back and said, "You'll be fine. Target arrows. See?" He banged the bloody tips together, showing that they were only pointed, not serrated. "It's what they use to kill baby deer with."

"Or my grandfather!" Jubilee sniped, arms folded over her chest, frowning.

Brak snatched the arrows from his hands and snapped them in front of his face.

"Don't ever do that again, or else I'll break you in two."

"Sure. In the meantime, try not to get shot again. And with that, I think it's time we went our separate ways."

"What?" said Brak.

"What? No!" said Jubilee.

Melegal tossed the girl a small purse of coins.

"Get cleaned up and find a private place to live in this big city. I've got problems of my own. They'll be coming for me."

"The Royals will find us and find you no matter where you go. It's best we stick together. They'll be after all of us now. You know that. You tracked us down."

Indeed, she was smart. Street smart to say the least. There would be no hiding Brak, however. He'd only get bigger and bigger. But it wasn't his problem. And what about the Almens? Maybe none of them had survived. Was it possible the underlings had wiped them out? If Lorda Almen lived, she'd expect him, unless she assumed him dead. But without a body, what proof was there of that? He looked up. Dusk had begun. Where had the time gone? It was as if the last few hours had been lost. Where had the past few hours gone? If they did indeed come looking for him, they'd know where to look first. Then he took off in a run. *Haze!*

CHAPTER 23

EXHAUSTED, FOGLE BOON FORGED AHEAD, Cass's screams giving him the energy he'd lacked a moment earlier. So far as he was concerned, she was his woman, as he'd never been with another, and as things would have it, he probably wouldn't live long enough to meet another. Instead, the impulse to rescue her overcame all reason. He ambled over a dusty hilltop on weary legs.

Not again! It can't be!

But it was. Another giant. Cass kicked and screamed like a wild woman in the monster's clutches. But where was Chongo? He could hear the dog barking, the sound as powerful and carrying as a dwarven gong, but the two-headed beast was nowhere in sight.

All around he looked. Nothing, but all he was truly concerned about was Cass.

"Let go!" She yelled, kicking the side of the giant's nose.

It sneezed, getting a spray of snot all over Fogle, as well as on Cass's magnificent face.

She shrieked in fury!

"AAAAAAAAAAAAAAH!" she yelled, her lungs recharged to their full power.

Fogle stumbled down the hill, his mind racing, trying to figure out what the best course of action would be.

"FOGLE!" Cass cried, "get me away from this behemoth! Now!"

He closed in about thirty feet away, summoned all the energy he had left, and flung a small barrage of glowing missiles from his hand.

The giant grunted and sneered when the missiles struck its leg, fizzled, and extinguished like drops of water being poured on a campfire.

He caught the worried look in Cass's eyes. *I've failed.* His shoulders sagged, and he could barely lift his chin up to face the inevitable death of his lover. *Chongo. Mood. Where are you? We need help!*

Chongo's barks were in full agitation, yet the beast was nowhere in sight. Perhaps he was trapped by more giants, but there was nothing nearby where the creatures could hide. He looked up at Cass, whose struggles were as futile as an infant's in the arms of a man. *She's going to be crushed.* He tried to summon that well of energy he'd tapped before, but unable to find it, he stumbled forward on weak knees and pitched face first into the ground.

Cass let out another blood curdling cry as he rose back to his feet into the blinding light of the setting suns.

"FOGLE! SAVE ME!"

He tried not to look. He didn't want his last memory of Cass to be a picture of her head exploding. He fought the urge to plug his ears. The sickening sound of Ox the Mintaur's bones being snapped and pulverized still rung there.

Chongo was still barking, a little closer now than before.

"Where are you, blasted beast?"

He shielded his eyes from the suns with his hands.

"What?"

There was Chongo: a giant two-headed dog suspended forty feet in the sky, running in mid-air, but going nowhere.

Who in Bish did that? Underlings!

"Look out behind you, Fogle!"

As he tried to twist around on his feeble limbs, something hard and painful cracked him in the back of his head. The lights of Bish went out.

"Ow!"

Fogle stirred. A throbbing headache greeted him. He had no idea how long he'd been out, but night had come, and it was dark, very dark. Unnaturally so. *Where am I?* He blinked and tried to wipe the grit from his eyes, quickly learning he could do no such thing. *Slat!* He was bound. *Cass!* There was nothing. Only his muffled efforts to speak could be heard. He struggled against his bonds once more, only to feel his strength fade from the effort as he slumped over and sucked for air.

Think, Fogle. Use the over-sized clump of brain matter in that over-sized skull of yours. One of the main things Mood had taught him in their many months together was not to panic. *When goininta the unknown, don't ferget ta use yer udder senses, he could hear him say.* Without having anything better to do and no other options that mattered, he rolled onto his back with a sigh.

Blinking his eyes and staring upward, or at least what he thought was upward, he allowed his eyes to adjust. *Black. Still black. Even blacker.* He closed his eyes and slowly drew a long whiff of air in his nose. *Dirt. Mud. Hmmm … a foul odor mixed with salt. Oh … it's bad. Not the scent of an animal.* A chill air drifted through his robes. *Underlings!* An unseen force coiled around him like a python and squeezed out all of his courage. The story came to mind of what underlings did to men way down below, under the ground. Why else would he be here in what must be a cave of some sort? He'd been dragged underground by the most deviant race of all. Mood had said that Bish was now crawling with them—and how easy it would have been to find him after all the commotion they'd caused, battling the giants. And now that they had not a single dwarf in tow, the underlings had struck the weakened party.

He could feel his heart pounding in his ears now. A tide of panic was rising. It only made perfect sense that the underlings worked with the giants, sending monstrous men then springing the trap as the giants wore their prey down. *Chongo was floating, and Cass was being crushed by the last giant. No! She's gone!* He wanted to scream out. He wanted to say he was sorry that he had failed. *Why me?*

A little fire ignited inside him suddenly as a vision of Cass's light vibrant features, sharp and picturesque, drifted into his thoughts. Her slender hips, sensuous legs, pale lips and perky breasts had left a life-long impression in his mind. He swore he could almost smell her. The faint smell of flowers and a twinge of an exotic perfume mingled inside his nostrils. *I'll kill anyone that hurt her! I just need out of here.* He fought against his unseen bonds until, exhausted, he fought no more, slumping to the ground

In the distance, something he hadn't noticed before echoed. A muffled crunching sound like a dog chomping on a ham bone. All he could think of was the giant. He recalled seeing one stuff a dwarf in its mouth and bite down. He winced. *Cass!* He had to get out of there. He had to find her.

He summoned his mystic power into his thoughts and reached out for the minds that held him prisoner. He jerked up off the ground. *What?* Something strong, very powerful, unlike anything he'd encountered before, now mingled with his thoughts. His invading powers surprised it and it was coming, coming for him right now. Merciless, unrelenting and formidable. He clutched at the dirt. *A sharp stone or anything.* Nothing. Nothing there to help him at all but the dark.

"Who are you?" He sat up. "Where are my friends?"

The presence remained. Strong and silent.

"What do you want?" he asked.

Nothing.

He struggled within his bonds. The ropes that bound him did not seem natural.

"Huh?"

He could feel the presence growing impatient, and his wrists began to burn as he renewed his struggles.

The mind intertwined with his let out a frustrated groan.

In the distance, the chomping sounds became louder, like tree branches snapping in a storm. He shivered.

Fogle muttered a quick series of words. Part of an old binding spell. His wrists and legs became undone.

"About time," a familiar scratchy voice commented.

Fogle sat up. *Can it really be?*

"Grandfather?" he said, pushing away a thin veil of cloth that was wrapped around his head. It dissipated like twinkling dust. He rubbed his eyes and allowed them to adjust to the dim light that filtered in through the mouth of the cave.

Before him stood an older man with a long wispy white beard: tall and broad shouldered with forearms as stout and wiry as a pit fighter.

"It is you!" he gasped.

"Aye, Grandson." Boon's eyes twinkled as he reached down and helped Fogle back to his feet.

He gawped at his grandfather, whom he hadn't seen in over a decade. The man seemed a little older, yet his grip was as strong as iron.

"Where have you been?" Fogle asked. "Wait! The giant! Cass!" He began to shuffle around.

"Ah … your woman. Yes, she is fine," Boon reassured him. "Very fine, indeed. Fine like a crystal vase pouring chilled wine. Fine as the hairs on a baby's head. Fine like the scintillating, titillating colors of a rainbow." Boon smacked his lips. "Fine like a —"

"Enough already, I know how *fine* she is," Fogle said, irritated.

Boon looked down and patted him on his head.

"I'm sorry, Grandson. It's just that I haven't seen a woman in an awfully long time, and I'm certain the last one I saw didn't look anything like her. She's absolutely gorgeous."

Fogle shoved his grandfather's hand away and said, "It's Fogle. And she's a druid."

"Interesting," Boon said as he turned and teetered deeper into the cave. "Come on."

"But what about the giant?" he objected, looking around.

"Come on," Boon said, beckoning for him, moving more like a man of his wizened years as he shuffled over the loose footing, holding his deep blue robes up over his toes.

Unreal. Unlikely. Weary from head to toe. Fogle tried his best to assess his situation, wondering if it was real. Then he threw his hands up and swung them down through the air. *Just take what the adventure gives you. Trying to make sense of it is of little help,* Mood had said. "Never mind."

"What was that? Did you say something?"

"No."

Boon motioned for him. "Come along then."

The farther they traveled downward through the tunnels, the more Fogle noticed something. There was no source of light. No torch. No suns or moons. No candles or lanterns. Yet the walls were dimly lit with a soft blue hue. In three long strides, he caught up with his grandfather and grabbed him by the elbow.

"Did you do this?"

"Do what?" Boon said, this time a little irritation in is tone.

"The light. What is making this light?"

"Ah. That's the underlight. Incredible, isn't it?"

"Do you mean *under* as in *under*ling?"

Boon looked at him as if he was stupid and said, "Of course. What else would the underlight be?" Boon jerked his elbow away. "Now come on. Your friends are down there."

Fogle didn't move. He was in a cave, an underling cave, being led downward by his grandfather, who he hadn't seen in well over a decade. Nothing tingled or raced down his spine like a trickle of lightening. His senses had heightened over the past few months, yet nothing told him anything was wrong, but something had to be, certainly. If anything, the moment seemed quite ordinary, and that's what worried him most of all. And now the strange munching sound returned, echoing up the massive cavern which he was being led down. Boon was already moving on. Fogle looked back toward the mouth of the cave. It was gone.

"You'll be lost if you don't follow," Boon said. "Don't be such a baby. You always did worry about everything that could possibly go wrong. You can't control everything, just like that whack I gave you on the back of your head. You should know that by now."

Fogle rubbed the small knot on his skull. That was real. By why had his grandfather hit him and brought them all into this cave?

"Your questions will be answered soon enough. Now come. You're beginning to annoy me."

Fogle followed, one slow step at a time, through an enormous cave illuminated by the strange blue light. As the munching sound became louder, the scent of vegetation and water wafted through the air. One second Boon was wandering up ahead, then the next second he dropped out of sight. Fogle rushed over and found himself standing on a ledge overlooking a strange garden. There were trees whose leaves glowed and bushes filled with bright red berries. A stream passed over glittering stones and disappeared from sight. Boon was traversing a narrow pathway that led into the garden more than twenty feet below. And that's when he saw her. *Cass!*

She was lounging alongside Chongo, a curious and happy expression on her face, watching a giant stuffing something that looked like bamboo reeds into his mouth.

"Cass!" he yelled.

She jerked her head up and waved, saying, "Come down, Fogle! This is the most amazing place."

"But," he started to object, looking at the giant as he made his way down the path.

"Come on! His name's Barton. He won't hurt you. He's a friend."

He made it into the garden, dashed by Boon who'd taken a seat on an oversized mushroom, and embraced Cass. She was the real thing. Smelling like honey and roses as her pale eyes and lips seemed to glow in the underlight.

"I-I thought," he looked away, "I'd failed you."

She grabbed his chin and smiled, saying, "I thought so, too, but it seems fortune found us anyway." She eyed Boon. "Hmmm ... now I see where you get your striking looks. Your grandfather is quite ... interesting, to say the least."

"I guess you could say that. So, are you well? Did that giant hurt you? I thought you were going to die."

Pulling Cass into an embrace, Fogle got his first hard look at the giant, Barton, who was ripping more of the bamboo reeds from the stream bank and stuffing them in his mouth. One of the giant's eyes was disfigured, an impression of scarred flesh, while the other stared right at him, unblinking, a little deranged.

"You burned Barton with magic. No-No. Barton not like that. Do that once more, Barton smash you good. Understand?" Barton said, balling up is meaty fist and snapping the bamboo within.

"Er … yes," Fogle said.

"Grandfa—Boon," he said, turned his attention aside, "where have—"

"I been?" Boon responded less than a foot from his face.

Fogle flinched, then folded his arms behind his back and started pacing around.

"Don't do that again … and yes, where have you been? What are you doing here? Where did this giant come from? How did you find me?"

"Easy Fogle," Boon said, "you always were as uptight as a dwarf. Just give me a few seconds, and I'll explain. I'm tired, you know. Running from giants isn't the easiest thing to do. It takes a lot out of an old man like me, but I tell you what … It sure feels good to be back."

Fogle folded his arms across his chest and faced his grandfather, saying, "What do you mean, 'running from giants'? Why would they be chasing you?"

"I've been their prisoner, and I've befriended one of their own, Barton. I guess you could say that I'm an escapee and he is a fugitive, and a bushel of men twenty feet tall want to kill us. Well, me at least. Sorry to have to drag you into this."

"Wait a second," Fogle motioned to himself and Cass, "we didn't want any part of this."

"Well, you probably didn't want to be my grandson, either, but you are."

Cass giggled.

Boon slapped his knees and sat back down.

"Now, let's get some rest. We're going to need it for the journey ahead. Say, where's my spellbook? I need to bone up on a thing or two."

"It's *my* spellbook," Fogle said, looking around, "and where is it?" As he looked back at Boon, it was laying in his lap, where the old wizard's eyes glimmered with admiration. "Give me that back." He snatched it.

"Pah," Boon shooed him away, "I still remember it all, anyway."

As Fogle opened his mouth to speak, Boon was already snoring. He looked at Cass, who shrugged and lay down on a grassy bed.

What is happening? Is there anything I can control?

Chapter 24

VERBARD SAT ON A ROUGHHEWN throne of stone beneath the City of Bone, enjoying the celebration. The underlings had struck a nasty blow to the world above and lived to tell about it. Commander Jottenhiem stood at his side, holding a bottle of underling port up in celebration. Verbard was moved. He'd never seen his kind, reserved yet tenacious, so charged up before. Now they bragged, one underling to the other, of the exploit, and the news spread like fire. Perhaps leading underlings into battle wasn't so bad, yet he still couldn't shake the feeling that something was wrong.

"Some port, Lord Verbard?"

"Certainly," he replied. "I see no reason to exclude myself from this celebration. After all, a handful of us just slaughtered hundreds. Just think what we can do with the entire army."

"I've been wondering the same thing," Jottenhiem said, handing him the goblet. "I think with a thousand more underlings we could take the entire city." Jottenhiem ran his black nailed fingers though his short coarse hair and showed him a fierce grin. "My sword arm is at your will and command, my Lord. I'll take all the soldiers you can give me back above right now. The more dead humans, the better."

"I agree, Commander." He picked up the object resting between his legs. The orb of imbibing. "But they will be ready next time."

"They won't be able to anticipate our strikes. They'll assume it's only a handful, but next time it will be hundreds. Whoever responds first will be wiped out."

But Verbard wasn't listening. Instead, he stared into the orb. The human mage wasn't nearly as powerful as he was resourceful, but the fat man's resources almost cost him his life. The magic in Bish was formidable. More so than he'd suspected. If a few more seconds had passed, he'd have been undone if not for Eep. Plus, the imp had followed his command, retrieving the orb to him. A costly move for Eep. The orb prevented him from teleporting, and Eep had a severed wing to show for it. Now the little horror sat behind the throne, mumbling in anger. Eep couldn't return to his world to heal. Verbard chuckled within, stroking the dark mirror-like surface of the orb. He'd had something to do with that. *It was worth the death of all those underlings combined.*

"We have company, Lord Verbard."

It was Kierway, escorted by the Vicious and two magi.

"Where are my Juegen?" Jottenhiem demanded, hands drifting to his swords.

"Dead, Jottenhiem," Kierway fired back, iron eyes smoldering. "Perhaps with better training from the likes of a true swordsman they'd have fared better."

Verbard rose from his throne, silver eyes flashing like lightening.

"Those are my men! And I'd also know the whereabouts of my other magi. Did they perish as well?"

"They died in battle, taking ten humans at least to their one," Kierway said, eyes flitting back and forth between the two. "And I see plenty of other soldiers missing on your watch as well. I'd judge not if I were you, Verbard."

"And yet I don't see a single scratch on you, Kierway. With so many fallen, I can't imagine how you'd come out unscathed. Yet here you stand, like a babe drawn from the refreshing waters of a cave bath. Pah!" Verbard let out a long seething hiss as he struggled to keep down his rage. "Well," he added, "can I at least see the key that my soldiers have died for?"

Kierway took a half step back, fingering his bandolier of knives.

"YOU DON'T HAVE IT!"

Every underling stopped as the dust and bat dung from the cave ceiling drifted downward.

Kierway pulled his shoulders back as he braced his fists on his hips.

"There were no keys! Only an empty chamber!"

Verbard fought the urge to shove the Orb of Imbibing down Kierway's throat. The underling was nothing but lies and disappointment all wrapped up together.

"Ah, so am I to understand that Master Sinway sent us on a fools run? Is that the case? And what do you mean by *keys*? I thought there was only one."

"No, many. Seven pegs, no keys."

Liar. Verbard resumed his place on the throne. For all he knew, Kierway had the keys. Or, there never had been any keys, and Master Sinway had sent them both to meet their final fates in Bone. After all, Kierway was clearly the biggest disappointment in Master Sinway's family. Kierway was a skilled swordsman, the stoutest of fighters, yet his career in leadership was marred in failure. His bloodlust led to the demise of more underling troops than most army commanders combined. Now, here he sat, paired with the most unpredictable underling of all. *Might as well play this ruse through.*

"And what of this cleric you mentioned? Is he dead … alive? I see no prisoners."

Kierway showed a grin of sharp teeth and lied, "He paid the ultimate price."

"I can only assume you mean he's dead?"

Master Kierway nodded.

"So, let me understand this. There were seven pegs and no keys. The only lead you had was this human, which you now claim is dead. Hmmm … I'm having a hard time believing you, Kierway."

Verbard pulled out a brass amulet with a clear crystal in the center. Kierway took a sharp draw in his nose.

"Of course," he added," I'm not going to take exception with your thin explanation. I'll let Master Sinway handle that."

Kierway's eyes filled with hatred as Verbard draped the amulet over his neck, clasped his hands around it and chittered mystic words. The amulet felt like black fire in his hands as he let go. The humanoid image shimmered to life between the stone throne and Master Kierway. Verbard abandoned his throne and bowed. Master Sinway's apparition was as real as if he was standing there. Verbard's silver eyes drifted onto the amulet that was warm in his hand, radiating with black power, before turning them back to the all too realistic shade.

"What an unexpected surprise," Sinway said in his powerful voice as he gazed upon his son, "and all this time I thought you were undone. I can only imagine that the delay was because you have taken over the entire City of Bone." Sinway's head glanced around. "But, this hardly looks like the interior of a castle." The Master of all underlings turned his attention towards Verbard.

The iron eyes of Master Sinway were a swirl of copper and black, his expression cold and snake-like. Verbard found his tongue cloven to the roof of his mouth as he began to speak.

"I've led one small force inside, and we decimated hundreds. Among them, Royals and many magi. All ours that went in returned alive, and are now rejuvenated and craving the destruction of the Humans and their vile city more than ever. At this very moment, plans are being laid out for the next strike," He bowed again, "Master Sinway."

"Excellent, Verbard, and now, my plans of conquest shall be even easier with the acquisition of the key. Let me see it!" Master Sinway clawed and clutched at the air before him.

"Master Kierway led a small force into Castle Almen to recover the key," Verbard said as he looked over at Kierway, whose eyes bore into him like lances of fire, "but his mission failed. He—"

"WHAT!" Sinway yelled, his vocal power frightening the bats from their roosts and bringing the buzzing underling army to a standstill. He turned on his son. "Kierway! Is this true?"

Kierway opened his mouth to speak, but Sinway cut him off.

"You are a failure! An imbecile! If you were not my son, I'd have you chopped up and fed to the urchlings. But, your mother insists I keep you around. That you will redeem yourself. Instead, you find another failure, this one grander than all the others!"

In a flash, lightning coiled around Master Sinway's arms and blasted into his dumbstruck son. Kierway was bewildered as the bolts passed through him without so much as a singe. Sinway let out an angry hiss and turned his attention back to Verbard.

Verbard wanted to look away but didn't. *Don't say it! Don't say it!*

"I want that key. You," Sinway pointed at him, "will get it for me."

He glared at Kierway. The underling had smirk on his face.

I knew it. The fool fails, and I now have to bear the full responsibility. Is this what success breeds? Escapades of conquest outside the realm of even dreams. He wondered if he should mention there were seven keys. It seemed strange Master Sinway wanted only one, yet Kierway seemed truthful there were seven. *It will be easier to find one that seven. The best laid plans are kept to yourself.*

Master Sinway turned his focus back to his son.

"As for you, Kierway. You are now at the will and pleasure of Lord Verbard, as is my Vicious."

"No, Father!" Kierway objected as the Vicious took his place along Verbard's side.

Verbard looked up at the Vicious. *Things are looking up all of a sudden.*

"Your life is in his hands, Kierway. Failing me is one thing, I'm your father. Failing him is another. He's not." Master Sinway's image began to fade away.

Yes! Perhaps I'm not being set up, after all.

"Father, a moment!" Kierway said. "I've seen a grand chamber that hosted key pegs. There were seven in all, not one. I assumed Lord Verbard would have mentioned that. I thought you should know."

Bastard manipulator!

As Sinway faded away, his gaze locked on Verbard's as he said, "I only need one, but now I want them all. Get the keys. Continue the assault on humans! And await my next orderssssss …"

Verbard squeezed the amulet with all his might, sneering at Kierway, who snarled right back.

CHAPTER 25

L EFTY BARFED OUT TWO GLOBS the size of eyeballs into his tiny hand.

Kam turned her head away, only to turn it back to him.

"Ew … what is that? Have you got a sickness, too?"

Lefty just stared at the objects in his hand, unable to hide his fascination. The look in his eye worried her. It was as if the halfling was possessed. Perhaps he was. He'd been awfully strange, after all.

"It's disgusting, Lefty. Are you ill or not?"

He shook his head and began polishing the murky color from the stones. A flare of red light lit up the entire room, then winked out.

"What was that?" Kam said, exasperated. *Magic!*

Lefty concealed the gems under his clothes as the front door creaked open and Diller entered. Lefty curled back into a ball, and Kam glared at the man.

"What was that?" Diller said, looking around.

"What?" Kam replied, sneering.

"There was a light. A red one, spilling out from under the door."

Kam didn't say a word. Diller walked over, grabbed the chains that bound her, and pulled her up. He ran his rough hands over her bound wrists, brushed his paw all over her, squeezed open her mouth, and looked inside. She decided right then and there that if she got the chance she would kill him first. He shoved her back to the ground.

"You better not try anything foolish, Pretty Lady. I'd hate to bury your fine corpse," he said, walking away and closing the door behind him.

"Lefty, where did you get those gems?"

The halfling rolled up into sitting position with a playful look in his sagging eyes. He looked more like himself that she'd seen him in days. The youthful energy in his voice returned when he spoke.

"The first time I met Venir, there was this underling. A powerful one …," he looked up, "uh …, yes, I wrote it down in my tome."

"I don't care about your tome."

"Oh … well, sorry, but I found these gems in the dead underling's robes. You should have seen that underling, Kam. Venir cut his head in half with Brool. Really gross. So, I've had these gems ever since, and I know they have power; I can feel it. And I meant to tell you about them, but I was always worried someone might steal them, so I stored them in my stomach."

"In your stomach? You can do that?"

Lefty made a cheerful shrug.

"Melegal said it was a gift. Just like my light feet."

Kam cocked an eye at him and said, "Well, did you ever think to store a key to those chains in there?"

"Huh … no," he said, looking sad.

"What else do you have?"

"Nothing, just these gems. Do you think they can help us?" he asked, holding them out in the palm of his hand.

Kam motioned with her hands to put them on the floor.

"We don't need that glow again. Something you did triggered them before." She shook her head. "I can't believe you've had them in your belly all this time. And you never got sick?"

"No."

"Or pooped them out?"

He made a disgusted face, shaking his head.

Kam's fingertips drifted closer to the gems. She wanted to grab them so bad. Find out what kind of power was within. Underling magi weren't anything she'd ever toyed with before, but she'd been taught that all the mystic powers in Bish came from one source. There must be something within them that she could use.

"What do you think they do?" Lefty asked, nosing closer.

Kam hunched a little closer, too. The gems were a deep red like rubies, and their cut wasn't the quality of gemstones, but more rounded on the edges, similar to river stones. Inside each one was a black swirl, like a tornado that she swore either pulsated or throbbed, like a living thing. Dark and mysterious, it beckoned her closer. Her fingers fanned out over the tops of the stones.

"Don't Kam," Lefty warned.

She bit into the soft flesh of her lip as her fingers curled up into a fist. There was power there. Dangerous. Seductive. Liberating. She could feel her heart pounding faster in her chest as beads of sweat burst on her brow. *Take them. They can help. They will help.*

"Kam?" Lefty said, pushing her hand away.

"What?" she snapped.

"We need a plan. For Erin's sake."

She held her aching head in her hand as she eased away while Lefty tucked the gems back under his clothes. *Erin.* Now wasn't the time to be reckless, but what other chances would she get? What would happen if she and Lefty were separated and she didn't get a chance to get her hands on the gems again? She couldn't let that happen. She had to do something. *Die doing something or die for nothing.* Isn't that what Venir once said? Maybe that was Billip or Mikkel, even Georgio, maybe.

"Lefty, do you think you can get those chains off, or not?"

"I think I can, but it might take a while. Why? Do you have a plan?"

She nodded as she shifted her hips to face him, saying, "I want you to free yourself. If you can do that, you can free me as well."

"But then what?"

"Then I'm going to find out what those little gems can do, and when I do that," Lefty's blue eyes were looking right into hers, "I'm going to use it, if I can, to help you fulfill your promise to me. Whatever power I can give you, or me, you are going to use it to get Erin to safety."

"No Kam! Using magic will kill you," he objected. "I can't let that happen. Maybe you can teach me to use the stones."

She ran her finger underneath the choker on her neck and sighed.

"No, if you could use them, you'd have known already. Lefty, you're going to have to be strong," she pointed at him with her shackled wrists, "for you, for me, and especially for Erin."

"But I mess up, Kam."

"No, you messed up." She poked him in the chest. "Now you fix it. Now you use all of your know how to make things right. Whatever happens, get Erin to safety. Find Joline; she'll know what to do."

The distraught look on Lefty's face left a sad feeling inside her, sadder than the one she already had. How hard it must be to do the right thing when evil had you in its grasp. Now, surrounded by thieves, liars and murderers, she'd asked a tiny boy to somehow save her daughter. She shivered under her robes as she pulled them tight and leaned back against the tub. Guilt washed over her as her chin sagged above her breasts. She could have gone to her family for help. She just hadn't wanted to. Over the years, she'd convinced herself they didn't care for her anymore. But now she was in over her head. *Blasted pride!* Now her daughter had to suffer for it. And she had to trust in a halfling boy who didn't look much older than ten, if that.

She sat there, eyes closed, unmoving, gathering all of her thoughts and plans. What would it take for her and Erin to escape? It seemed every plan and scenario met with a dead end.

The sound of Palos's door creaking open brought her chin up. The Prince of Thieves emerged, arms outstretched over his head, yawning in all his glory.

Disgusting.

"Well, it seems I can't sleep with all the excitement going on," he said, tying the belt around his robe, taking a seat, and pouring more wine. "I just love cat naps, so refreshing, brrrrrr. But Kam, my dearest, I couldn't stop thinking about you. Diller!"

Swift as a ghost, the man entered, crossbow ready, concerned eyes drifting towards Kam, before returning to Palos. "Yes, Palos?"

"Prince Palos, mind you. Now, remove her chains and take this little person to the Quarter. I, well, we, will be needing some privacy. I'm in the mood for another extravagant bath already." He rubbed his skin and leered at Kam as he guzzled his wine. "It leaves the skin so smooth." Lefty and Kam glanced at one another as Diller made his way over.

Kam rose to her feet as Diller unbound her, his hands much lighter to the touch this time.

Palos tipped his chin at her, and he swaggered over and said, "Fetch those warming salts. I want my water to make you sweat. It glistens so well on your body."

I need those stones.

As Diller bent over to unshackle Lefty, Palos said, "Better leave him in the chains. I don't want him wandering around here stirring up trouble. See to it the Quartermaster keeps a close eye on him."

Kam almost dropped the bowl of warming salts when she caught Lefty giving her a wink.

"Enjoy your bath, *Princess,*" Lefty said, tongue hanging from his mouth.

She reached down and grabbed a handful of his thick yellow hair and said in his face, "I should kill you, little halfling Bastard!"

"Alright you two, cut that out!" Diller sat, pulling Lefty away, leaving Kam with a fistful of his blond hair.

"Ow!" Lefty said in an angry cry.

"Get him out of here, Diller! And as for you, Kam, you need to calm yourself and focus on me. Get those salts in the tub. Now!"

Kam dabbed her hand in the bowl of bath salts as Diller slung Lefty over his shoulder. A sinking feeling settled in: that she might not ever see the boy again, or the gems either, for that matter. She tossed a ball of bath salt in the tub, bringing the water to a sizzle. The next one she grabbed was as hard as a stone. She looked at it and almost gasped. It was one of the gemstones. The other was resting in the bowl.

When the door closed behind Diller, she realized she was alone with Palos, but with a glimmer of hope this time.

"What are you gawking at?" he said, disrobing as he slipped into the tub. "Throw in more salt; it's not hot enough, you lactating witch."

I'm not going to live another moment like this. I'm sorry, Erin!

She tossed the rest of salts in the water and let the bowl clatter to the floor.

"Ah, that's better," Palos said, closing his eyes.

Inside her hand, the red stones throbbed. The choker around her neck began to tighten. *Summon it! Do something!* The gem stones' magic made contact with the magic within her and rose her to another level. Kam felt more power than she'd ever felt before. Dark and wondrous. Magnifying the magic within her. Her face purpled, and her knees began to buckle. *Hang on, Kam! Think!* But no words came to mind.

Palos wasn't paying her a lick of attention as she hung back to the side of the tub. The water was all bubbles, fizzles and steams. But any second he was certain to notice that she was about to choke to death. *Think!*

Gems in hand, she touched them to her neck and focused her thoughts on the choker. *Remove this harness from me!* She envisioned it unraveling in her mind. The choker squeezed her neck so hard she swore her brains were oozing from her ears as she fought for her life. One magic force in a fierce battle against the other. Her body a punching bag. She summoned all her anger, all her hate, every bit of desperation, and turned it on the white hot line on her neck. Something inside her mind screamed.

Snik-ting. The choker slackened on her neck, yet remained there, its magic spent. She'd won.

She gasped for air, saying, "Oh my."

Palos turned his head," Did you say something?

Kam disrobed, swung her legs into the tub, slid into the bubbling waters, and began rubbing his head with one hand as she pressed her breasts into his back.

"Just a little choked up is all," she said. "It's been a long day."

"Ah … that's better," he said, leaning back into her. "Nothing like being a Prince."

The steam from the sizzling hot water did little to relieve the tension in her taut muscles. Filled with power she'd longed for, only one question came to mind. *What now?* She had her magic. She had more power. But she still didn't have any idea where her daughter was, and she couldn't go blasting her magic through the tavern like a bull gone wild, even though that's exactly what she wanted to do.

"It would feel much better if you used both hands, Kam!"

She tossed the red gems on her robes and twitched her fingers at them. The robes moved, concealing the gems.

I should kill you now. She grasped Palos behind the muscles on his neck. *But I just don't think it would be that easy.*

She dug her thumbs deeper into Palos's supple muscles. The man might have gotten hefty over the years, but his svelte feline muscles were still at work under there. She had to be careful, very careful. The man could overpower her in a second.

She brushed her lips against his neck and said, "Feel better?"

"Without question. My, it's a sudden twist in your attitude. Why so sudden?"

"I just want to see—"

"Pah! Of course. You just want to *see your daughter*," he said, mocking her. "Pathetic. It would be best if you lied about liking it. It would make things better for the both of us."

"I see," she said, kissing his neck. *Bastard!* "Does this feel better?" She kissed it again. *Like kissing swine.*

"You're learning."

As much as Kam longed to see her baby and get her to safety, she'd have to play along a bit longer. And hope her shameful acts wouldn't lead her to kill herself in the meantime.

Chapter 26

"OUTPOST THIRTY-ONE!" Jans shouted, slamming his helmet to the ground. "That's Absurd!"

Venir wasn't surprised at the reaction. He'd grown accustomed to it over the years, seeing how he'd suggested it a few times before.

"It's the only foothold the underlings have, Jans," he argued. "And by the looks of things, I think it's the best choice. You are low on supplies and getting lower on men. No word has come from the Royals."

"You are a madman!" He pointed at Venir, gesturing to his men. Each and every one of the commander's top leaders was stark-faced and glum. "I know you swing a mighty axe, but that's hardly enough to take on an entire underling army. They're thicker than thieves in those forests. Thousands if not tens of thousands."

Venir shook his head. "You don't know that, and I don't believe it. The Royals have done nothing but turn tail and run since the day it was overtaken. One swift assault from the beginning would have gotten it back. Instead, they went back home, hid in the castles, and left all the rest for dead." He looked down at Jans. "You know I'm right."

"That's treason, you renegade," Jans warned. "I'd be more careful what you say."

Venir balled up his fist and started to draw back, but stopped. Now wasn't the time to fight with fists. Maybe, for a change, he could try using words.

"Now is not the time to worry about upsetting a bunch of pouty Royals. Now's the time to figure out how to survive. You can't keep running through these hills and jungles until your horses drop dead. You can't wait for orders from the north. They aren't coming. What you need to do is take care of these men. If we can get into the Outpost, spread the word, then a greater force might come."

"You can't possibly believe we can penetrate an impenetrable Outpost? Hah! It's not possible. Not even if I had another thousand riders. We'd need siege equipment, too. You can't really think we can pull this off, can you? Be reasonable. I say we make a bee line for Bone and don't look back."

Venir wanted to stick his fist in Jans's mouth. Certainly the man realized the Outpost had already been overtaken once before.

"They'll expect that. What they won't expect is battle at the front gate. We only have to take one gate, and I wouldn't be surprised if it isn't as heavily defended as you think. The hilltop's been as quiet as the dead since the Royals departed." Venir lifted his brow. "Besides, I think we can take it back the same way they got in."

"I'm not getting all my men killed."

Venir looked around. The Royal Riders were a proud group of hard riding adventurers who had battled more than a few times in their lives, judging by the looks of them. Battered and weary, armor dented, chinked and gashed, they looked like they were up for another fight or two.

"You men," he said, standing tall, "you didn't become Royal Riders because you wanted to live forever, did you?"

No one said a thing, but the crowed began to stir.

"Do you want to sink your spears into more underling bellies?"

"Aye!" a few responded.

"Have you burned enough of their stinking hides to last you a lifetime?"

"Nay!"

"Are you ready to trample their bones into dust? Stomp their guts in the mud? Or do I have to light a fire under your arses!?"

"Nay!" all of the surrounding men chanted, raising their spears and swords.

"Do we need more forces to show us how to kill the underlings, or do we just need the sound of thundering hooves under our feet?"

"Aye!"

"Are you ready to fight?"

Aye!"

Are you ready to die?"

"Aye!"

"But most of all, are you ready to make the underlings pay?"

"Aye!"

"Aye, Venir, I'm with you!"

"I want to stick my spear so far up their arses I poke their eyes out!"

The Royal Riders shouted and cheered. The entire camp bristled with energy.

Venir hoisted his axe high in the air.

"Release the Hounds of Chaos!"

Chapter 27

THE DAYS OF CARING ABOUT himself had evaporated over the past few months, now replaced with a strange sense of nobility. *Slat! I'm going to save my woman. Well, a woman. And she's not even that pretty, at that!* Melegal traversed the city streets like a grey ghost, the shadows of the dipping suns quickly leaving the street mysterious and deadly compared to the day time.

Looking over his shoulder and ducking into alleys, the city's craftiest of thieves felt pressed for time. The city had never been like this. The people's faces and voices were full of panic, and a chronic series of alarms was being raised. The underlings were here. He'd seen them. The rumors and stories were so rampant he'd have sworn the entire city was on fire. *This can't be happening,* he thought, running up one narrow set of steps and down another. *Underlings in Bone. Insanity!*

He climbed up the window sills to the top of an apartment building, then jumped across from one rooftop to the other. Huffing for breath, he hunkered down in the shadows of a chimney stack and peered at his building across the way. *Haze shouldn't be in there.* Below him, people were pushing and shoving, gathering their gear and heading towards the gates. He could hear windows being nailed shut and deadbolts sliding into place. Not all of Bone's residents were going to flee. He assumed most would fight to the death before they moved. Still. *I've never seen it this bad before. But I don't see any underlings, either. Oh my!*

For the first time, his steely eyes noticed the smoke in the distance and the flames licking from the rooftops. He'd seen plenty of fires in Bone in his lifetime. Civilian riots were the main cause, but they were small and easily quashed under the boots of the City Watch. This, however, was big: an inferno by comparison. He shook his head. *What in Bish is going on?*

Haze. She'd been nothing but kind, in an odd sort of way, since the first time they met, and he'd almost chopped her fingers off for it. Now, he felt compelled to save her, and for all he knew, she wasn't in any real danger. He wouldn't figure they even knew where he lived. It was McKnight's apartment, after all, the former detective's secret place of privacy. But, the Royals' reach was as long as it was deep. After all, they'd found him once before.

It wasn't likely that with all the commotion the Almens would be focused on him. And if anything, they were all dead. Lord Almen, Sefron and the Brigand Queen should really already be eliminated from his life, after what happened in the arena. He should be a free man. He could, perhaps, return to the Castle and console Lorda Almen. *Who knows, maybe the Brigand Queen is dead.* He grinned. *Now that would be special.* He glanced at his apartment building. Nothing was out of the ordinary. Taking a seat, he leaned back, closed his eyes, listened to the chaos in the streets, and tried to relax. *Give it some time. Just a few minutes of peace and quiet.*

In his lap, he laid a long rectangular case that he'd removed from Lord Almen's study. He gently ran his fingers over the edges. *I wonder if this is what I think it is.*

"What's in that case?"

Melegal's eyes snapped open. It was Jubilee.

"How did you get up here?"

"I climbed."

"You couldn't have kept up with me," he said, hiding his incredulity.

"But I did. Why, were you trying to abandon us? I thought we were sticking together," she said, frowning.

"Little Slerg, just to be frank: yes, I was trying to leave you." He looked behind her. "Where's Brak?" *Maybe he's dead and I won't have the blame for that.*

"Hidden in the sewers. We can go back after him later. Unless he gets hungry again. Then he'll leave," she said, taking a seat beside him.

"We aren't going back after anyone. You are."

"I'm not leaving you, and you can't get away from me. I'm a shadow. That's what my grandfather said."

"Do shadows have wings?" Melegal asked, narrowing his eyes.

Jubilee made a strange face and said, "Uh … no. Why?"

Melegal snatched her by the cuff of her shirt and dragged her across the rooftop towards the ledge, saying, "Because you're going to need them after I toss you over this edge."

"No! No! I'll scream!" she cried.

Jubilee's toes were scraping the ledge.

"I'm not worried; no one will listen. Now, are you going to leave me be, or am I going to have to drop you like rotting cabbage?"

She eyed him, saying, "You wouldn't drop me. I'm a girl."

"No, you're a Slerg," he said, shoving her farther out. "Are you going to … eh?"

He pulled her back. The sounds of heavy boots were coming down his apartment stairs. Three Watchmen emerged from the entryway and onto the street. One wiped his bloody dagger on his pants leg. Melegal felt his heart in his throat. *Haze!* The man shoved his dagger back in his sheath, adjusted the black-billed brown cap on his head, laughed, and motioned for his men to follow. Down the street they went. Melegal gawped at his bricked up apartment window.

"Who lives in there? Your wife?"

"No."

"Your whore then?" Jubilee asked.

"No. Be silent, will you?"

"Well, you look very sad. It must have been someone that meant something to you. So it's either your wife, a whore, or your mother, and it couldn't be your mother because you already told me you were a bastard. So which is it? A whore or a wife?"

Melegal heard, but he wasn't listening. He made his way back down onto the street. Jubilee followed him down, still talking.

"Grandfather says there are only four women in a man's life: his mother, his wife, his whore … Ah." She snapped her fingers. "Your sister. But, it couldn't be your sister, seeing that you were an urchin. So," she proudly said. "It's a whore. Grandfather says there are wives and whores and whores that become wives — *eek!*"

Melegal wrapped his fingers around her neck and said, "What do you call a woman that is not married. A whore? No. Are you married? No. Are you a whore? No."

"But I'm a sister," Jubilee squeaked out.

"No, you are an urchin now. And not being married doesn't make you a whore. Being a whore makes you a whore. And your grandfather, well, it sounds like he knew a lot more about whores than he did about women. Now shut your mouth and come on."

Melegal was accustomed to seeing the dead, but the thought of Haze covered in blood with frozen eyes affixed to the ceiling caused a feeling of fluttering moths in his stomach. Crossing the road and taking the steps up three at a time, he found himself at the top staring at a busted door. *Please, no!*

Stepping through the doorway, the fireplace was the first thing he saw, its embers cold. A table was overturned, two flower vases were shattered, and his easy chair was turned over. Anything that wasn't affixed to something was broken, except the door to the tiny bedroom. In two long steps, Melegal made it from one side of the room to the other and stepped inside.

Haze lay face down on the bed, unmoving, the sheets red with blood.

He touched her bare leg, noting the bruises on her ankles. Gently, he rolled her onto her back and studied her battered face. She looked like she'd fallen face first down a stone staircase, but she was breathing, barely. Her skinny legs had been sliced and poked. But she was alive.

"Is she dead?" Jubilee said, peaking in the door.

Melegal said nothing.

Jubilee stepped up to the foot of the bed and watched the feeble rising of Haze's chest. The little girl's eyes traveled from Haze's toes to her head. "You do have a sister. I'm sorry. I had it all wrong."

Haze's good eye fluttered open as she tried to say something.

"It's Me. Don't talk. I'll get you some aid, Haze."

Haze's voice was garbled, and she winced as she spoke, but he could still understand what she said.

"No. I'm fine. I've taken heavier beatings from Sis and Frigdah before. Just get me up and find me some wine, water or something. Oooh," she moaned, "face feels like it got hit with a sack of gravel."

"It looks like it, too," Jubilee added.

"What?" Haze looked at the little girl, then up at Melegal. "Who in Bone is she?"

Melegal helped Haze back to her feet. "I'll explain when it matters. I suppose those men were looking for me?"

"Yup," she said, pulling out a loose tooth and flicking it away. "Why?"

Slat! That meant either Lord Almen, Sefron or possibly the Brigand Queen were looking for him. But how had they managed to find his apartment so fast? Very little time had passed since he'd left Almen Castle. But that door, something about that door, the magic portal they sailed through. He was certain it had been later in the day when he arrived than when he'd left. At least a couple of hours had been lost. He led Haze to the living room. "What did they say?"

"They wanted to know where they could find you."

"And what did you tell them?"

Haze managed a smile. "I told them you had a woman in District Seven and you stayed there sometimes. I told them you were a dirty bastard that had a thing for bloated whores. I told them your—"

"I get it," he said, patting her on the backside. "Why District Seven?"

"Just a place where someone I don't like lives, is all."

"Good girl," he said, stopping to take one last look at his apartment.

Haze hugged his side and said, "We had good times here, didn't we?"

Sadly, he said, "Some of the best."

"You're an awfully strange brother and sister," Jubilee added, "but don't worry: I have a nice place you can stay with me down in the sewers."

And the rat returns from whence he came.

CHAPTER 28

"H OW MUCH LONGER ARE WE going to wait out here, Billip?"

Since being tossed from the Drunken Octopus, Georgio felt tired and agitated. The entire city, a place he'd become quite accustomed to at one time, screamed insanity. The City of Three was so much better. Now, he sat on a melon crate, twiddling his thumbs.

"Stop fidgeting," Billip said, cracking his knuckles for the 1000th time. "We'll go shortly if we have to. Whatever he's doing, he's taking his sweet time about it. Wouldn't surprise me if he was lost."

That wouldn't surprise Georgio one bit. He'd gotten lost in Bone a few times before, himself.

He looked up at Billip and said, "Do you ever get a funny feeling that things aren't right? I mean, I just don't feel like myself right now."

Billip slid an arrow from his quiver and started scratching the tip in the dirt. "Ah … that's just your young loins talking. That girl, Velvet, got you all stirred up down there. Don't worry, you'll get used to it. It'll show till the day you die. A woman does that to a—"

"No Billip. Not that!" Georgio pressed his hands to his ears, shook his head, and then let them back down. "That's all you and Mikkel talked about coming down here. It's disgusting."

"One day, you won't think so." Billip smiled, then snapped his fingers. "I bet he's with a woman!" His green eyes widened. "Oh no!"

"What?"

"I just remembered. I think his wife lives in this town."

"Mikkel's married?" Georgio asked.

"Used to be. Hmmm … but where in Bone would she be? You should see her. Something else." Georgio leaned forward.

"Really pretty, huh?"

Billip made a sour face. "Bish, no! She's squat legged like a kobold and as barrel chested as an ogre. Feisty as a hungry badger. I'd rather cut off my arm than spend a night with her."

"She couldn't be that bad," Georgio said, laughing.

"Well, every woman has her graces. Mikkel's woman just hides hers much better than the rest. Like a squirrel hides a nut, that is."

Georgio chuckled so hard he fell off his crate. Billip had the funniest way of putting things. He tipped the crate back up and resumed his seat.

"Billip, really, do you have a feeling that things are not normal? Lefty's feet used to sweat when things weren't right. Right now," he patted his tummy," I'm not even hungry. I'm always hungry!"

Twirling the arrow in his fingers, Billip said, "Whatever it is, I'm sure it will go away. Now let's go."

"What? Already?"

"I'm not waiting on the brute a minute longer. It wouldn't surprise me one bit if he was frolicking with that heifer," Billip said, slinging his bow over his shoulder and walking away.

Georgio jumped to his feet and followed.

"He said he was going to look into things. Maybe he ran into underlings."

"I don't see or smell any. Now come on. He's smart enough to know where we'll be."

"The stable?"

"Yes, but first, I want to check out the main gates."

"Why?"

"Look around. All the people are gone."

"What about Velvet?" Georgio said, stopping to turn around and look. She'd made quite the impression on him, and he hated to leave her.

"She isn't going anywhere. You can look for her when we come back."

Billip led; Georgio followed. Ahead of him, the man strutted through the alleys and down the abandoned streets, elbows swinging and head on a swivel. Billip looked like he was trying to keep an eye on everything at once. Not nervous by doing so, but casual. Georgio found himself looking around, too, but he didn't notice anything. *Just ugly buildings that should be torn down.* He missed his bed in the City of Three. It was soft and warm. He wondered how Kam was doing. *I bet she's glad I'm no longer around.*

"Quit gawking, Boy. We're almost there."

When they rounded the next corner, Georgio was bewildered by the sight. Thousands of men, women and children now crowded the inner gate. They had pack mules, carts and wagons loaded, fighting and pressing as hard to get out as what he'd seen on the other side to get in.

"I've never seen so many crammed together before. Not even for a hanging," he said.

"Look up there," Billip said, pointing at the top of the wall.

Georgio had never seen so many soldiers before. Where there were normally ten spaced out along the perimeter, there were at least a hundred, if not more.

"There really must be underlings in this city," he said, looking at Billip and all around. "What do we do now?"

"If I had a business set up, I'd be making a mighty profit now!" Billip said, clenching his fists and teeth. "Now I'm missing out. Nothing like a crisis to fill a smart man's pockets. Nothing, indeed. Wouldn't surprise me one bit if the Royals were the cause of all this." Billip eyed the spire of the nearest castle. "No. Wouldn't surprise me one bit at all. Bloody thieves. Come on. Let's lay low in the stable. We aren't going anywhere this way."

"What about Mikkel?"

"He'll figure it out."

Georgio followed on heavy feet, trying to make sense of what was going on around him. Underlings had invaded his last two homes, and that unsettling feeling was only growing in his gut. *Where are you, Venir?*

It wasn't long before the scent of hay and fresh manure wafted into his nostrils, and some of that odd feeling drifted away. The old barn was quiet and dark. Billip slowed his pace, eyeballing his surroundings. Nothing seemed out of place to Georgio, but as he started to speak, Billip cut him off with his hand. The archer slipped an arrow from his quiver and notched it on the string. One thought raced through Georgio's mind. *Underlings!*

Georgio had just slid his sword from the sheath when a stark realization hit him like a pan in the face. Every stall and gate was the perfect hiding place for an … *ambush.* Had he not seen it used for the same purpose? The time had come for him to start thinking fast for a change. *Should we retreat? What about Quickster?* He had to make sure the shaggy pony was well. The hilt of his sword was slippery in his palm as they crept farther into the barn.

Billip stopped and pulled his bowstring back as a stall gate creaked nearby. Something darted across the dirt: black, brown and grey. *A cat*! One moment there, the next it was gone.

Billip looked back at him and gave him a wry smile.

"I almost shot that thing. The poor light can be tricky if you're not careful. I'd hate to waste an arrow."

Georgio swallowed hard and wiped the sweat from his brow. After a few dozen more steps, they stood at Quickster's stall. Billip guarded the corridor, and Georgio swung open the stable gate. In the dimness, he could see the shaggy pony lying on its back, legs upward, knees bent downward, without a care in the world.

Georgio entered, bent down, rubbed the pony's shaggy black belly, and said, "Can I light a lantern?"

"Go ahead; just don't burn down the place. Wait a minute."

Georgio froze.

"Someone's coming."

He stepped out of the stall and looked down towards the end of the barn. A man carrying a bottle was swaggering their way.

"Where'd he come from?" Georgio whispered.

"I don't know. He just slipped out of those shadows."

Georgio remembered the old stable hand who'd always been there over the years. The old man, a toothless dullard with flakes and lice in his hair, hadn't been present when they arrived. It was odd. He usually saw the man most of the time. But this man was different. His gait was somewhat staggered, and his tall frame slightly hunched.

"Looks like a drunkard or vagrant," Billip said from the corner of his mouth. "I'll handle it."

But Georgio couldn't stop watching the silhouette that approached. The closer he came, the bigger he was, bigger than most men, almost as big as Mikkel. *Venir?* He took two steps forward, and that's when he heard it. The sound of a ragged breath, like someone exhaling broken glass. His fingers started to ache, and the muscles in his body froze. It wasn't Venir. It was Tonio.

"You! Tonio pointed Georgio's way, his voice garbled and broken when he spoke. "I know you. I knew someone would be back. I wait. I find. I kill."

"Sh-Sh-Sh …," Georgio tried to say *Shoot* but couldn't.

Twang!

Billip's arrow plunged into Tonio's armored shoulder. The split-faced man locked his hand down on the arrow, took a swig from his bottle, and yanked it out.

The sound of the shaft pulling from the muscle and bone made Georgio's innards flex.

"Who is this man?" Billip said, pulling back the next arrow.

"T-Tonio …," Georgio said, sputtering.

"Ah, I see. One more step, and I'll add a third to your head," Billip warned, pulling the string back along his cheek.

Tonio dropped the arrow to the ground. Georgio's eyes froze on the half-dead man. Tonio was tall, plated from the waist up in mismatched armor. Two swords hung on his hips; another was sheathed on his back. His jaw hung to the right side of his mouth. In the twilight darkness, his black eyes sparkled, demented.

"Shoot him again," Georgio managed.

Tonio held up his hand. "Tell me where the Vee-Man is, and I might spare you."

Billip said, "Oh, so you are the Yellow Hair Butcher, are you not? There is quite a nice bounty on your head."

Tonio's chin dipped down as he eyed Billip.

"You'll never collect it. Tell me where the Vee-Man is … NOW!"

Tonio's voice scattered the pigeons from the rafters.

Billip let another shaft fly.

Tonio snapped his forearms in front of his face.

Chink.

The arrow juttered on the metal bracer.

"Impossible!" Billip nocked another arrow and fired.

Chink.

Tonio took another step forward. Georgio took a step backward, trying to blink the living nightmare away.

"Tell me where the Vee-Man is!" Tonio growled, ripping a sword from the sheath on his back. "I remember those fingers, Boy. They might grow back, but your head won't. Not after I eat it."

Twang! Twang!

Billip pinned one foot to the ground, then the other.

"Pah! You'll be out of arrows soon, Little Man."

Tonio guzzled down what was left of his whine and tossed the bottle aside.

"Shoot him again, Billip!" Georgio said, shuffling behind the man.

Billip unloaded another feathered shaft at Tonio's face. Tonio knocked it aside in one fluid motion with his sword, reached down, and pulled the other shafts from his feet. He drew his other sword. "When Vee-Man comes, I'll be eating your bones." He pointed one sword at Georgio. "But I'll be saving yours for last."

"Run, Georgio!" Billip said, backing away as he reloaded.

Twang!

This arrow caught Tonio full in the chest, but he was already running. Tonio's bigger body slammed into Billip, driving him hard to the ground. Billip had his fingers wrapped around one of Tonio's wrists as the other sword hand came down. There was a sickening sound of metal meeting bone as Billip cried out and went limp. As Tonio rose his arm to deliver the next deadly blow, Georgio charged.

"NOOOOO!"

He whacked Tonio full in the chest with the edge of his blade, knocking the man backward. With one mighty swing after another, Georgio drove the monster man backwards. Tonio parried again, again and again, then let out a frightening laugh.

"Tired are you, Young Man? Do not fear, you'll not feel fatigue much longer."

Tonio swung.

Georgio parried. The powerful blow stung his hands. Gasping for breath, Georgio took another swing.

Clang!

Tonio swatted it away like a child's rattle.

"Come, Boy, just lead me to the Vee-Man. His head is all I want. Vengeance I must have for what he did to me. See?" He ran his finger down the face of his nasty scar. "Vengeance so I can rest. Tell, and I shall go away."

Georgio's arms quavered as he rose his sword up. He'd never been so tired before, not even during the challenge. There was quite a big difference between swinging a heavy sword and swinging a Dussack knife. Huffing and puffing, he said, "You won't find him. You'll never kill him. He's gone."

Clang!

Tonio knocked his sword from his hand, grabbed him by the throat, and lifted him from the ground. Georgio couldn't get over the putrid smell of rot and alcohol as he gawped for air, his face turning red as a beet.

"He must come back. I must kill the Vee-Man."

Tonio looked as cunning as he was deranged, horrifying Georgio, who kicked and struggled, but Tonio was too powerful. Unyielding. Unnatural. It was like that final moment with the Vicious before it cut his throat was happening all over again. *I can't let him eat my head. Fight or Die!* He kicked at Tonio's belly harder and harder, but the man was like a statue.

"I wait for Vee-Man. But you die."

He could hear the leather in Tonio's gauntlet squeak as the pressure began to build behind his eyes. *I don't want to die again.*

Clatch-Zip!

Something rocketed past his ear, and he found himself on his hands and knees, coughing. He rolled to his back and looked up to see Tonio reeling, a large crossbow bolt lodged in his neck.

Clatch-Zip!

Another bolt ripped through the air, hitting Tonio in the leg, sending him spinning to the ground. A large man with a heavy studded club started pounding the man into submission. The club rose and fell. *Wham! Wham! Wham!* It was Mikkel.

Georgio reached for his sword and rose back to his feet.

"Who is this man, Georgio?" Mikkel cried out, bringing down his club with all he had.

"It's the Yellow Hair Butcher," Billip said, blood dripping from his mouth. "And the bounty's mine."

Mikkel hit Tonio again, harder than the last. Georgio could see the sweat glistening on the back of the man's neck. Tonio was regaining his feet, a golem that would not be put down, swords still dangling in his hands.

Whack!

Billip hit him in the arm.

Whack!

In the knee.

Whack!

Upside the head, but Tonio kept on coming.

"What in Bish is this man made of?" Mikkel said, laboring for breath.

"Hit him again, Father," an unknown voice cut through the darkness, or maybe that was the torch being carried by a young man, about Georgio's size, who was also holding a heavy crossbow.

Whack!

"Good thinking, Nikkel."

Whack!

"Enough!" Tonio groaned, swords flashing in the light.

Slice! Slice! Slice!

"Argh!" Mikkel roared, dropping his club. Tonio cut deep into his arm, leg and across his belly.

Clatch-Zip!

Tonio stopped. A bolt was planted square between his eyes. He teetered backward and fell to the ground.

Mikkel was gasping for air, blood dripping from his wounds. "Great shot, Boy."

"That's my bounty," Billip managed. The archer was grimacing in the torch light. His arm dangled from his shoulder. "I'll need money to stitch my arm back together. Pah!" He spat a mouthful of blood. "Well … what are you looking at? I'm about to die over here. Do something!" His eyes rolled up in his head as he slumped back to the ground.

Georgio dashed into the stable and led Quickster out. Mikkel was carrying Billip in his arms. "What do we do?" Georgio asked, worried.

"I've never seen him this bad before. We can head for the nearest castle," Mikkel shook his head. "We'll just have to ask the Royals for a favor."

"What about Tonio?" Georgio asked.

When he looked back. Tonio was gone.

Chapter 29

"Delicious, simply delicious," Morley Sickle said, nibbling on another morsel of food. It was the finest dining he'd ever had. He'd never imagined there was so much that the tongue could experience. "The bread, the roasted meat and those vegetables that you … er … what did you do to it?"

"Sautéed'," a prosperous man replied, sitting by his side at an unusually long dining table.

"Yes, yes! Sautéed. Excellent. I'd never known food could be prepared as such before. Marvelous."

"More wine, My Lord?" a blossoming servant girl asked, with hands and face as delicate as the fine cloth draped over his lap.

Morley licked his teeth and said, "Absolutely," while reaching over and patting her on the rear. *My. A man could really get used to this.*

"Are you enjoying yourself, Morley, my friend?" the most dashing man asked from the far side of the table.

It was Scorch. The man who could do anything it seemed, which included making him a Royal.

Morley could feel his face stretching into a smile as wide as a canoe. *It must be this wine!* He couldn't contain it, marveling at the excellent dining hall. The chandeliers, each candle lit, hung twelve feet high in the air. The walls were cut limestone, where the most extravagant painted scenes of landscapes and battles were displayed. His wine goblet was pure silver, and his plates a fine porcelain. He never imaged so much wealth in the world. The Royals did well to keep that hidden from the citizens.

"I am, Scorch, but … I don't think the rest of us are," he said, sucking down more wine as he eyed the others seated at the table.

"No! Er … excuse me, no, ahem, Lord Sickle. It's just been a busy day, is all," said one Lord dressed in a tunic and pants as expensive as a suit of armor. On each side of the man, two others were face down in their food, dead. "And, ahem, quite frankly, I'm not accustomed to eating in the presence of the dead." The Lord's head lurked back on his neck. "Not with my brothers, anyway."

"Well," Scorch said, rising from his chair and tossing his long blond hair over his shoulder, "perhaps they should have known better than to interrupt my friend, Lord Sickle. And," Scorch twitched his finger on his nose, "I'm not so sure what to make of your tone, Lord Ashlorn. I sense agitation in your tone."

The satin clad women at the table, five in all, one just as pretty as the next, let out gasps. All except one, quite weathered, almost ancient. She was scraping her spoon on the soup bowl.

Slurp. Scrape. Slurp.

Lord Ashlorn dabbed his forehead on his cloth napkin, shaking his head.

"Forgiveness, Lord Scorch—"

"Lord Sickle is over there," Scorch nodded. "I'm not a Lord. I'm well above this drivel."

"Er … yes, forgive me, Lord Sickle. But, I must confess, I am somewhat … uh," he eyed his dead brothers, "frightened."

Morley hiccupped as he waved his wobbling hand at the man. "Oh, phish-posh, Lord Ashlorn. How could I ever be upset with my father-in law? Especially after he's blessed me with such beau—beautiful brides." He reached over and patted the trembling arm of the woman on his right. She was young, barely a woman, hair long and black like a sparrow. Her chin was quivering as she closed her eyes. "Hah. Now that's pretty."

In the other chair on his right, another woman sat, older, full figured, with a frown as big as a hat. She was Lorda Ashlorn, Lord Ashlorn's wife. Morley leaned over, puckered his lips and kissed her half on the lips.

"Heh-heh, I kissed her. I haven't kissed a girl since I was a young man," he said, licking his lips. "And she was as ugly as a mountain goat." He tried to kiss her again and slipped from his chair onto the floor. "She kicked like one, too. Heh-heh."

"SOMEBODY HELP HIM UP!" Scorch ordered, the polish in his voice turned hard as a wetting stone.

Everyone at the table moved, aside from the old woman, whom Scorch resumed helping with her spoon. Morley felt several pairs of hands helping him back up into his seat and dusting off his clothes.

"Thank you," he said.

Every face was stark, leaving him with an uneasy feeling. Before in life, most people hardly noticed him, now they were all terrified of him. Friendly or not.

"Oh, this is ridiculous. I don't belong here," he said, dropping his face into his hands.

"Certainly you do," Scorch said. "You've as a much reason to be here as the rest."

"Certainly," Lord Ashlorn agreed.

"Absolutely, here, let me rub your shoulders. They must ache after that fall," his eldest bride said, showing a slight smile.

But Morley, dispatched as he might be, could still feel their uncertainty. Their fear was mixed with loathing and self-preservation. They only did what they did because they had no other choice. It was either that or die. He snorted. He'd not spent much time around many people, but he'd been an avid listener over the years. The Royals in Hohm City, though not as intrusive as the others, still did not hesitate to exert their will. *Serves them well.*

"What was that, Morley?" Scorch said.

Pickles. Pickles. Hic. Pickles.

"Nothing, I just … I just want to lie down. I think I'm getting sick."

"Have they poisoned you?" Scorch said. As he did so, all of the knives and forks on the grand table rose up on end.

A collective shiver filled the room. Even Morley, as dull as his senses were, blanched at the sudden height of danger.

"Scorch! Blast you! I've no quarrel with them," he said, watching the forks and knives slowly rise from the table. "Please, put the silverware down. I've seen too many die today. I don't want to see any more."

Scorch looked at him, blue eyes shining as bright as the sky. "But these people don't like you, Morley."

"No, we do like you," Lorda Ashlorn fell to her knees, "You are excellent, Lord Sickle. Worthy of the most high on highs." She clutched the silk of his pants and whispered. "Please don't let him kill us. Please."

The desperation in the pretty woman's voice and face sunk Morley's heart down between his knees. In a matter of hours, Scorch had over taken a castle, wiped out an entire garrison of guards, and delivered unto him everything he could ever hope for: the finest wine, women and clothing a man could find, but in all its splendor he was still not content. All he wanted was peace. *Pickles. Pickles. Pickles.*

The women trembled and sobbed, huddling close to one another while the knives and forks flashed and spun in the air. Every Royal was wide-eyed with terror when their heads weren't hunkered down. All accept the leathery old woman, whose satin sleeve now rested in the bowl of soup she scraped, determined to get every last drop in her mouth.

"She's lying, Morley," Scorch said, his silvery voice as hard as stone. "She wants you to leave. You repulse her. She thinks you are unworthy of the dirt beneath a chair."

"No," the Lorda said, rubbing his thighs, "It's not true, Lord Sickle. I've no such inclination. Your will and pleasure are mine. I assure you. I'll show you."

"Hah! She's a convincing one. Aren't they all?" Scorch said as the knives and forks continued to spin over their heads. "Come now, Morley. You have everything you want now. A beautiful woman grovels on her knees. Your belly is filled, and you've drunk wine pressed from mystic vineyards you didn't even know existed. Yet still, you are unhappy. Why is that? Is it these people?"

"NO!" Morley shouted. "NO! NO! NO!" he slammed his fists on the table. "It's YOU, SCORCH! Why won't you leave me alone!" Morley rose to his feet and began tearing off his clothes. He ripped his shirt off. Scorch replaced it with another. He pulled of his shoes and tossed them across the room, only to see them reappear over his toes. "STOP IT! STOP IT!"

"MORLEY!"

The entire castle shook as Scorch rose from the floor, his eyes flashing with anger. All the Royals who lived were scrambling for the doors.

WHAM! WHAM! WHAM!

The Royals fell to their knees, begging for mercy, waning at the threshold of the secured doors.

For the first time in his life, Morley felt something overcoming his fear: anger. He didn't care what Scorch said, what Scorch did. He could not take it anymore.

"Leave me be, Scorch or whoever you are! Be the curse of someone else. Follow these people! Read their thoughts! Leave mine alone! *Ulp!*"

Morley stood as still as a tree as the whirling knives and forks lowered around his head. The look on Scorch's face was one he had not seen before. Impatient. Dangerous.

"I suppose you would rather die than spend another moment with me; is that it?"

Morley swallowed hard. His sweat dripped into his mouth. Scorch had given him everything he ever wanted, except the power to make his own choice. He couldn't take it anymore. No life like this was worth living. Not like this. He just wanted his old life back. To be left alone to make his jig. He nodded.

The silverware hummed to life, spinning faster and faster, the circle narrowing around his neck. Morley heard a woman scream. He shut his eyes. *Pickles. Pickles. Pickles. Blasted Pickles!*

One eye snapped open at the sound of silverware clattering to the ground. The first thing he noticed as he scanned the room was that Scorch was gone. He let out a strange little laugh, like a man whose sanity had returned after a long absence. He opened his mouth to speak. *No! Don't say his name. Don't even utter it. Don't even think it again.*

Lord Ashlorn was the first to rise back to his feet. Hawking, long-limbed and heavy set the man ambled over, casting quick glances all over the room.

"Is he gone?" the Royal said, placing a heavy hand on his shoulder.

Morley showed a bewildered smile and said, "Yes, I believe so. Ur ... Lord Ashlorn, I am sorry for all of the — *urk!*"

Morley felt a dagger being rammed through his stomach and out his back. His knees weakened as his body slid from the blade, and he crumbled to the ground. He could see his brides, young and old, sneering down on him as if he was an old rabid dog. His lips stammered under his nose as he tried to summon his last gasping word. *Scorch.* There was no reply, and he died with the taste of blood and pickles in his mouth.

Hohm City was such dreary place. Devoid of the suns' brilliant light and the moons' soothing glow thanks to the chronic company of mist and fog. No. It wasn't something that was going to be missed by Scorch. But Morley Sickle was. Why the man wouldn't accept all that had been given him, he didn't understand. It was clear though: the people of Bish were a stubborn lot. They would rather die than change.

Scorch made his way on foot through the marsh until he passed through the great pillars that marked the entrance to the road to the city. Before him, a hot dry land of cracked mud and hard ground awaited for miles in all directions. He'd learned enough about it before, when he traveled to Hohm City. The kind folk he'd traveled with had taught him a lot about the lands in the world of Bish that they knew. Certainly, there had to be a better place than Hohm.

"Where would you like to go?" he asked.

A woman, maybe thirty, with light brown hair down to her wide hips, strutted like a warrior by his side. *She's a gutsy woman, big boned, rough-handed and durable. Perhaps she'll better handle what Morley Sickle could not.* Plus, she had a funny way of talking, and Scorch liked that.

"Well, I've been south, as far as the settlements beyond dwarven hole. Met my first husband there, but buried him here." She thumbed the marsh. "Well, not really buried. Just killed him for cheating and dropped his bones in the swamp. He's a troll's booger now. Naw, I says we go to the City of Three. I hear it's really pretty there. That's where most all the nice things come from anyway." She tied her hair up in a knot and swung it back over her shoulder. "Of course, you already knew that, didn't you?"

Scorch smiled.

"Indeed, I did. So, Darlene, do you prefer to walk or ride?"

She set her hands to the hunting knifes at her hips and looked around.

"Well, I don't see any horses. Do you? Besides, I don't mind walking. My mother says my father was a dwarf, but I just think she says that 'cause I'm not very pretty. Besides, with these new boots you got me, I feel like I could walk forever." She scratched her head. "Can you make horses, too?"

Scorch chuckled.

"I can make anything. I just can't make you happy."

"Aw, don't worry about that." She spat on the ground. "I'm always happy so long as there's game to be tracked, shot, fetched and skinned. I'm going to feed you like a mountain king. You'll see. I can shoot a swamp rat cutting through the marsh at fifty yards. I once killed a bobcat with my bare hands. I smashed a boar with a log ..."

CHAPTER 30

T HE CITY OF BONE. PANIC. Chaos. Confusion. The Royals were walled up in their castles while the soldiers and Watchmen marched through the streets in heavy armor and heavy hands. The underling strike had shocked the very core of the hardiest citizens in Bone with its effects spreading and long lasting. District 27 wasn't any different, but the people there, long forgotten, were not in a panic. Instead, they went about their business, rebuilding one block at a time.

Trinos was perched on a bench facing the soothing waters of the fountain. Her platinum hair was brilliant in the light, along with the rest of her as well. The people who served her had worked hard all day long, and now they sat along the busted roads and dipped bread into soup bowls. A little girl, no more than six, was filling a pitcher with water. Her little smile was as warm as the suns as she curtsied towards Trinos and scurried away. It felt good, seeing people get things done, despite themselves. If only more of them would act the same.

"Ahem … Trinos?" said Corrin, taking a seat beside her.

She continued her gaze into the fountain and replied, "Yes."

"The people, well, they are getting nervous, despite their graces. Frightened, unlike anything I've ever seen." Corrin pulled the cloth coif from his head and held it to his chest. "The Royals are one thing to deal with. But Underlings, well that is quite another. They say they are the most atrocious creatures in all of Bish. Vicious. They eat people as they live!"

The underlings. Yes, they indeed were vicious. After all, she was the one who'd created them for such intents and purposes. Well, they were a loose creation copied from another world. Just a spice to give the boiling pot more flavor. Now it felt odd being among the people witnessing and hearing the testimonies of personal terror. She ran her delicate fingers through her hair then patted Corrin on the knee. The man's grim face brightened a little as he pulled his narrow shoulders back and offered a toothy smile.

"Corrin, tell the people they'll always be safe with me. As for the underlings …." She stopped and cocked her head. Someone close by and coming their way was near death. "Corrin. A man needs aid down Warrow's street. Lead him and his companions to me."

Corrin's heavy lids blinked as he said, "But, we've helped enough—"

"Corrin," she warned, narrowing her eyes.

He nodded.

"As you wish."

Stubborn man. They all were. But Corrin was faithful. Being a man of notorious ilk left his compassionate side as barren as a burned bee hive. But he kept the people working, much harder than they cared for, but as he reminded them, he was merciful compared to the Royals. Even though he really wasn't. They were just better fed and not whipped, at least not that she saw.

She rose to her feet and watched down the street. Four men approached her sanctuary: two young, two older including the one who was near death from his wounds. As Corrin led them from the street buildings' shadows and into the courtyard, she got a better look at them. They were a durable group, not attached to anything like the other people, with an amount of unusual pain and suffering carrying on their faces, unlike the rest of the people.

The biggest one, built like a black marble statue, was the first to glance her way. She saw the whites of his eyes as he gawped and stared. She felt him fight the urge to fall to his knees and beg for her hand in marriage. Yet, his concern for his friend prevented him from doing so.

"This one's wounded," Corrin said, "very bad. His arm's almost chopped in two. I'd say he's pretty much dead already by the look of him. Shall I get a shovel?"

Trinos stepped around the bench and made her way over to the man on the shaggy pony. The wounded man's clothes were soaked in blood, and the young man behind him strained to hold him up.

"Hold him still," she said in a soothing voice.

The wiry man moved his head around the back of his comrades to gaze upon her. "I'll be still," he sputtered, "so long as you stay right there. But I go where you go." He gawped and grimaced, continuing his stare as if he'd seen a woman for the first time.

She laid her hand on the wounded man's bloody shoulder and let her power run its course. The sound of muscles and bones stitching together was sickening. The man lurched up in the saddle. His chin cracked back into the face of the man behind him, but that man held on.

"YEE-OUCH!" the man cried as he gulped for air and blinked a dozen times.

No one said anything. All the men just stood in the courtyard watching her, eyes filled with wonder, lust and amazement. Corrin stepped in front of her.

"Your man is healed. You can all leave now." He held his hand out. "But, I'll be needing a contribution ... a big one. It's not every day a man gets brought back from the dead."

"I-I wasn't dead," Billip said, craning his neck to get a better look at Trinos. "I was dreaming, and even in my dreams I've seen nothing like you. Will you—"

"Marry me!" Mikkel interjected.

Trinos let out a polite laugh.

"You are a passionate pair, I'll say that much. But I have other things in mind for the both of you."

Billip slid from Quickster's back and started rolling his shoulder.

"My hitch: it's gone." He opened and closed his fingers in front of his face. "And I feel stronger, more like when I was young." He looked at her and said, "Whatever you have in mind, I'm up for it."

"So am I," Mikkel said, stepping in front of his smaller friend.

"But we have to find Venir!" Georgio objected.

"Venir doesn't have legs like that," Mikkel said, smiling from ear to ear.

"Father!" Nikkel said, giving Mikkel an odd look.

Billip's head snapped at the tall black young man with pale blue eyes and broad shoulders and said, "Nikkel! Where'd you come from? Why, you're practically a man!"

"I've been with my mother for the past few weeks. Made the trek with the merchants." He slapped the steel on his hip. "I worked as a guard."

Trinos took her place back on her bench as the men got reacquainted. They were unlike the rest of the men in the City of Bone: fearless, dangerous and even jovial, they spoke with coarse words and high spirits. They were men who had seen it all. They were just what she needed.

"Come, men. Sit and drink from the fountain," she said. "Corrin, please find them food and goblets."

"But ... Eh, as you wish," Corrin said, frowning.

"And fetch some bandages for this man's wounds." She nodded at Mikkel. "Are you well, man of many thews?"

Mikkel almost blushed as he said, "Ah, the bleeding stopped, but I could still use a stitch or two."

With a snap of her fingers, two women appeared almost in an instant, sitting Mikkel down and getting to work.

The other men seated themselves on the fountain's edge, the youngest sampling the waters.

"Billip. Georgio. Mikkel and son, Nikkel. It's a pleasure to meet you all. My name is Trinos, and I'm the caregiver of this District. I could use a few men such as you."

They all stared at her as if they'd never heard language spoken before, except one. The younger man called Georgio. He had other things on his mind, though he still found her fascinating, just not to the point where it bridled his tongue.

"We are trying to find *my* friend, Venir." He glared at the others. "And we were, well, about to leave, when Billip was wounded. But now that you've healed him, I think we can continue on."

"Will you hush your mouth, Boy?" Billip said. "This lady saved me, and I'll not be leaving her side to find Venir. Nor would he expect me to. Whatever he's into, I'm sure he'll be just fine."

"Yeah, be quiet, Georgio, and show some respect to this fine woman," Mikkel said, gesturing toward her with his hand, "whom I'm certain I'd eat my hand for. Pardon me, Trinos, but not in all of Bish has a woman such as you touched her toes on this dirt. I'd fight an army of underlings for you."

It was Billip's turn to step in front of Mikkel. "I'd fight ten armies!"

Trinos smiled. The men's passion rose like waters from a dam, almost blocking out all reason. They'd kill for her, and she knew it. It seemed foolish to think a man would go to such great lengths over a woman, even though it was her. Maybe it was time she put a damper on things. She shifted her face and figure into something less bewitching.

Corrin arrived with two women who set food and goblets at their feet.

"Men, eat and drink," she said, flipping her brown hair over her shoulder.

"Ah," Corrin said, gaping at her, "see what you two did? I hate it when she does that."

Billip and Mikkel blinked and stared, eyeing her less pronounced features. She could feel their thoughts returning back to normal.

Billip clutched at his shoulder. "Mercy. I hope your healing is not an illusion as well."

"Oh, I assure you your arm is healed, yet your vile thoughts, well, they need some work." She eyed Mikkel. "Yours, too. After all, you've a son to set a good example for."

"Uh …," Mikkel said, staring blankly back at her, "yes."

"So, you men have fought many underlings, have you not?"

"Er … well, of course. We've slain a great many," Billip said, pushing his chest out.

"I've slain more than him, Trinos. At least two to his one," Mikkel interjected, flexing his muscles. "He's never fought any face to face."

"What! I've saved you from more underlings than you killed."

Mikkel stood up and pointed in Billip's face.

"One time! One time you saved me. I've peeled those black leeches from your back a dozen times. In the mud. In the water. You're a dead goose as soon as they get within ten feet of you, Billip. You know that!"

Billip jumped to his feet and started poking Mikkel in the chest.

"You're as stupid as a troll with the memory of a slug and the accuracy of a toad. I've seen kobolds that shoot, slat and fight better than you!"

"That's it!" Mikkel pulled off his shirt and snatched his crossbow from Nikkel's hands. "We're gonna see who's the better shot, right here and right now!"

Trinos liked the bravado. The men were fearless and full of fire. It wasn't something she'd experienced much of in the City of Bone. The young men, Georgio and Nikkel, were all smiles as well. But Corrin, his hands fell to the pommels of his blades, eyes and feet shifting around as if the fountain was about to explode.

Billip snatched up his bow and snagged three arrows from the quiver.

"Georgio, take the pitcher and hold it up over your head, yonder."

"I'm not doing that! Go hold it up yourself, you knuckle cracking fool!"

By this time, a crowd of Trinos's people had gathered. She sensed their emotion rising at the thought of the competition. It was the most energy she'd felt from them ever. It shouldn't have been a surprise to her. After all, it was a big part of their makeup. She stepped between them.

"Men, I have no doubt about your prowess—"

"My prowess is bigger than his prowess," Mikkel said, snarling.

"Is not!"

"Stop it, please!"

Everyone fell to their knees, except the newcomers. Even Corrin kneeled.

"Listen everyone! These men, Billip and Mikkel, have slain multitudes of underlings, and they are here to protect us."

Mikkel and Billip's bodies slackened as they looked around and lowered their weapons.

Trinos raised her arms and continued.

"So, treat them as one of us. Fear the underlings no more. Fear the Royals no more. You have food, water, and now, protection." She lowered her arms back down. "Now, rest. We've much work to begin tomorrow."

"What about the competition?" a thickset woman with a head full of curls asked.

"Aye! I want to see them in action!" a man added.

"I've got ten coppers on the bald headed one."

"I'll match that!"

"I'm taking the bowman!"

The wave of emotion began to sway even her as she raised her arms and said, "So be it then! Let the competition begin!"

With that, a red ball of energy appeared in one of her hands and a blue ball in the other, each scintillating in its own brilliant color.

"I call red," Billip said, nocking his bow.

Trinos flicked her fingers up, sending the balls soaring into the night, getting small as lit fireflies as they went.

Twang!

The red ball burst into a thousand sparkles of light, much to the delight of the crowd.

Clatch-Zip!

Mikkel's bolt ripped through the air and disappeared into the night.

"Blast!" he roared

Twang!

The blue ball burst in the dark sky; its shards of magic raining down on the people in tiny light blue speckles.

Billip bowed as the crowd applauded.

Mikkel looked at her with a frown.

"Alright, Mikkel, one more time," she said as two more orbs flared up in her palms.

Mikkel loaded his crossbow as Billip nocked another arrow.

"From the hip," Mikkel said. "You aren't getting a jump on me this time."

"Hah."

Up the balls of energy went.

Clatch-Zip!

The red one burst into sparkles of light not even twenty feet above.

"You shot the wrong one, Mikkel!"

"I didn't shoot it," Mikkel said. *Clatch-Zip!* His bolt sailed into the night, disappearing with the blue sphere as well.

"Well then who shot it?" Billip said.

"I did."

It was Nikkel, standing on the fountain's rim, holding a crossbow.

"That's my boy!" Mikkel exclaimed, thumbing his chest.

"Well at least *he* can shoot. You couldn't hit a frog's arse on a Lilly pad from ten steps."

"I've seen cats swing steel better than you," Mikkel retorted.

Trinos resumed her seat on the bench. All the people were in good spirits, except the young curly haired one. He was glum. *Strange.* Still, she had the kind of men she wanted, including Corrin. She would need them to keep things in order. *I can't always be here.* But that wasn't all she needed them for. Royals and Underlings were a problem. There were other things as well. *They've much to offer, but will it be enough?*

CHAPTER 31

CHONGO LED THE WAY OVER the Outlands, tongue wagging, his big faces panting. Cass, as radiant as a beam of light, sat atop his back, her lithe body swaying along with the beast's rhythm. She was still the most fantastic thing he'd ever seen, but now Fogle was bitter. On one surviving Clydesdale pony, he, and on the other, his grandfather, followed her and the dog. Behind them, the giant Barton ambled along, silent, yet disturbing like an avalanche ready to fall. His grandfather Boon had said little, other than restating that they must go. Fogle complied, and that was what disturbed him the most. *Let it be. Just let it be.*

"You look troubled, Grandson. You haven't spoken all day. Care to tell me what's going on?"

Fogle gave his grandfather a disgruntled look and said, "No."

"I tell you, if I were you, I'd be talking with the pretty woman, instead of sulking back here alongside me."

Fogle glared at his grandfather. Every time he rode along Cass's side and started speaking, his grandfather joined the conversation. And her ears were all Boon's, not his.

"Oh … well, you have to realize, I've not been around people very much. As a matter of fact, I'd hardly even said a word in years until your friend, Vuh …," Boon glanced over his shoulder at Barton, who was busy staring at the clouds, "you know who, showed up. He's a funny one. Grim, but funny."

Fogle had heard enough about Venir as well. His grandfather had been rambling on about him and Cass ever since he'd arrived. And when he wasn't doing that, he wanted to stick his nose in the spellbook, which had been his at one time, but he'd given it to Fogle. He could have shown more thanks, more respect, but he didn't want to. *Just be silent, Old Man. Your ramblings give me a headache.*

"The sack. Have you seen that sack, Fogle? The things that it can do. The power that it contains!"

"What?" *This is different.* He saw a lustful look in his grandfather's eyes, like a vagrant thirsty for more grog.

"That staff," Boon motioned with his finger. The broken staff slid from Fogle's pack and sailed into Boon's fingers.

"Quit taking without asking. First my spellbook, now this."

Boon wasn't paying him any mind. His eyes were locked on the staff, living in the past, searching for a future. "It's from the sack."

"Excuse me?"

"Yes, from the sack, something I know quite well. Your friend told me about it, but I wasn't so sure that I believed it. But Barton confirmed what I was told. Your friend wields a power so great," he ran his fingers over the weathered wooden shaft, "I think it could destroy anything in this world."

Except your chatty mouth, I'm certain. He huffed. Fogle recalled his dreams of his grandfather, battling before an abyss and blasting through a coven of underlings. It was that staff he had wielded, with braces and an amulet as well, glowing with gemstones like fire. Boon had wiped them out with a single stroke and hurled their corpses into the abyss like a blood mad warrior. Fogle could see the muscles rippling in Boon's forearm as he clutched the staff like a hoard of gold. There was still much fire in there. Uncontrolled fury lurked deep within.

"I had the power, for years. I hunted underlings, and they hunted me. Back and forth we went until my last battle. The day this staff shattered and the sack disappeared. Gone, like a wisp of smoke." Boon's eyes were smoky and lost for a moment, his wispy white beard blowing in his face. "So many underlings were dead and fled that day. I'd won, so it seemed. Those fiends hunkered back down in their caves and me, hee hee, well, I wandered the world, lost, purposeless, unable to reconnect myself."

Boon's worlds weighed heavy on Fogle. He could feel his grandfather's anguish, so it saddened him a little. Only a little.

"So, what is it you want?" Fogle's voice began to rise. "To re-acquire the sack and resume your fight with the underlings? Is that what this journey is all about? Just to be clear, I'm here to find Venir and reacquaint him with his dog. And then, I'm heading home." He looked back at Barton. The giant, now the oddest thing he'd ever seen, trudged along, scratching the nose on his disfigured face. "You and the giant can fend for yourselves."

"There's strength in numbers, Grandson."

"They are looking for you, not us!"

"You are foolish, Fogle. Much like your father. How many more giants do you think you can handle without the dwarves to aid you? You'd be dead without them."

"Well, as you said yourself, it wasn't likely more giants were near. That they were an initial assault. You said there are not so many."

"The giants will want to avenge the deaths of their kind. Most likely, they will take it out on the dwarves."

"What? Well then we should warn them!" Fogle said.

"Hah! You fool, the dwarves are fully aware of the giants. They've fought them all their lives. Besides, they like it."

Fogle couldn't imagine anyone liking to fight giants. Of course, he couldn't imagine many things that he'd already experienced. How can one prepare for the unexpected? He sighed, wishing Mood or Eethum were still there. "Will you do something for me, Boon?" he asked, looking up at Cass.

"Ah … I see. Go on. I'll stay back. Of course, I'd never have left her side in the first place if I were you."

Fogle trotted up alongside Cass and Chongo, smiled, and said, "How are you doing, uh, Cass?"

"Never better," she said, chin up, eyes forward.

He looked up into the sky that was streaked with white clouds. In the distance was nothing but more dry land, covered in rock, sand and caves. He'd never been this far south before, either, and by the looks of things it was dreadful, judging by the mountains that were east of them.

"So, is Chongo leading, or are you?"

He scratched the big dog's necks and smiled, saying, "He is. His friend is out there; he knows it. I don't see how he could smell it, unless the man is close. But he senses it. Such an amazing beast. Strong and faithful. You can learn much from a dog, you know."

"He looks tired," Fogle said.

"He's not tired; he could walk for days," she said, looking at him like he was foolish.

"True, but perhaps his back could use a rest. I think my pony could handle the two of us," he said, swallowing as he looked at her, "for a little while, anyway."

Cass kept riding and said nothing. For the past few days, they'd had very little contact with one another, which was bad. With all the dwarves around he talked even less. Now, Boon kept talking and talking until Cass was fast asleep, barely taking a breath so Fogle could get a word in with her. As difficult as it was to communicate with a woman, it was even worse doing so with his least favorite elder appearing from out of nowhere. Him not getting close to Cass was like a thirsty man unable to reach the waters of a waterfall. He couldn't take it anymore.

He rode close, his leg brushing against hers.

"What are you—"

He wrapped his arm around her waist and with great effort pulled her into his saddle and held her tight.

"Are you a brigand who snatches women now?" she exclaimed.

"No, I'm a wizard who only snatches the most beautiful one in the world," he said, looking down into her pink eyes.

"I should kill you," she said, sliding in behind him and wrapping her arms around his waist and squeezing him hard.

"Ulp!"

"But I think I'll let you live," she said, brushing his ear with her lips.

Fogle felt the tightness in his back and neck fading away. It was the best he'd felt in days. He found it astonishing how a single woman could turn this upside down adventure upright so easily. *No wonder houses rise and fall so quickly.*

Chongo led, his stiff tails snapping back and forth, large tongues dangling from his mouths. It was strange, following a dog into the unknown and what for. He was pretty sure the dog didn't need them anymore. *Maybe I should let the dog do all the thinking for a change.*

"What are you thinking, Fogle?"

"About you."

"No, I'm pretty sure I know what you think about with me!" She giggled. "What else is going on in that over-sized skull of yours?"

"Life is so different in the wild. I don't know how you do it."

"I was born in the wild. It is my way," she said.

"Do you want to return to your icy home in the mountains?"

"You just got me, and now you wish to be separated from me?"

"Never," he smiled. "I just wondered what your plans are when this journey's over. Assuming we all survive." He tried to turn back and look at her, but she evaded his attempt. "I don't want to be the cause of any harm coming to you, Cass."

She squeezed her fists into his gut, draped her chin over his shoulder, and said in his ear.

"It's my choice, Fogle Fool. My home is where I choose it to be: the mountains, the forest or the Outlands. It's all fine by me. Now my home is here, with you and the dog. Besides, did you ever think that maybe it is me protecting you and not the other way around?"

"No," he admitted.

"And to think, you have far less experience in the wild than me. I've lived outside the cities most all of my years, yet, in less than one, you suppose to know more about survival than me."

"Ah … I didn't suppose anything. I just thought protecting you was the right thing to do."

"Because you are a man?" she said, digging her nails into his side.

He fought against his laugh as her fingers half hurt, half tickled. He squirmed in his saddle and replied, "No, because you're my woman." Her fingers went still.

As they trotted along, she didn't say a word. Fogle was trying to be strong, to say the right thing, without pissing her off. But, so far as he could tell, his chances were usually half wrong and half right. *Oh, Bish. She's gonna hop off any moment now.*

"I don't recall giving you any claim to me," she said. "Did I mutter such a musing to you in my sleep?"

"No, but for crying out loud, I like you is all. And you like me."

"I do? Since when, Fogle?"

"Ah … never mind it then. I'm sure my grandfather or Barton could find better words to say than I. Perhaps I should mumble uncontrollably more," he said, stiffening in the saddle.

Cass wrapped her slender arms around his stomach and held tight. "Oh, don't be so impossible. I'm just teasing you. And it's not as if my wiles are so hard to come by. After all, I did deflower you the first day we met. Do you think I'd have done that if I didn't like you already?"

"Well, those Mountain Men, —"

"Don't mention them again if you know what's good for you. They were protectors, nothing more, nothing less."

But what about the snow ogres? They were an evil brood according to Mood. It didn't seem likely that someone as unique as Cass would take up with such a race. Yet she had, and that was a disturbing thing that stuck in Mood's craw. Something about Cass was odd, dangerous, but he couldn't help but be captivated by her. He knew he needed to be more careful, but it was hard. After all, she was the only woman he truly knew, and he should be wary of that. His memories flitted to Kam. *I bet she's not so complicated.*

"Are you still with me, Fogle? Has a nymph got your tongue?" Cass said.

"No, I just—"

Chongo's ears perked up as the two-headed dog snorted the air and let out a rumbling growl. A split second later, the dog dashed ahead, plunging into a rocky gorge and out of sight. Cass jumped from the back of his saddle.

"What are you doing?" he said.

Cass rubbed her hands together, muttering an incantation. She transformed into a large slender dog with a grey and white pelt that sped after Chongo's trail.

"Wait!" he shouted. But Cass and Chongo were gone. "What did she do that for?"

Boon led his pony along his side and said, "That's a woman for you: unpredictable."

"We'll never catch them on these ponies if we don't get going!"

"Looks like a good place to have an ambush up there. I'd proceed with caution."

"Then you do that," Fogle said, digging his heals into his mount. "YAH!"

He could hear Boon say as he thundered ahead, "Barton, make sure you keep up."

CHAPTER 32

"**H**OW ARE YOU FEELING?" VENIR asked.

"Like my veins are filled with sewer," Slim said.

"Ah ... you're getting stronger then. Yesterday you smelled like a sewer, but now, look at you, a full seven feet of Bones and manure, living and breathing like a new born calf."

Slim let out a raspy grumble, reached out his hand, and said, "Help me to my feet, will you?"

Slim was light as a feather as he pulled him up onto his sandaled feet. The man was pale as a wight and skinnier than a post, but he was alive. Venir was relieved for that. Adanna and her mother hadn't made it, and he hadn't told Slim that yet.

Slim was leaning against his side when he said, "They didn't make it, did they?"

Chin down, Venir shook his head.

"How'd you know?"

"I didn't think any of us would make it, but I could see it in your eyes. Your voice. Don't blame yourself, Venir. The underlings did this, not you." Slim patted him on the shoulder, his bird-like face peering around. "Say, where are we, anyway? And who are all these people?"

"Royal Riders, remember?"

Slim shook his head.

"This forest seems oddly familiar. Are we?"

Venir nodded. "Just south of Outpost 31."

Slim went into a fit of coughing and spit black bile. He wiped his mouth on his sleeve and said, "Ech ... tastes like a spider's butt. Nasty things. I hate spiders. Never hated them before, but I hate them now." Slim teetered up on his toes, stretching beyond his full height, stretching his fingers into the sunlight that peeked through the branches. "Ah ... that feels good. The suns are like warm rainbows. Venir, I was so cold. Colder than I'd ever been before. I never would have imagined one could be so cold. Ah ... those beams are a blessing. I'll never complain about the heat again."

An older man, stout in frame but shorter than Venir, walked up and nodded.

"You're a survivor I see?" He extended his hand towards Slim. "Commander Jans. Uh ... my, you are tall as a crane. How are you feeling?"

"Better," Slim said, then turned back into the light.

Jans stroked his mustache and said, "Say, I understand you're a healer."

Slim nodded.

"I've got some men that are ailing. Do you think you could help out?"

"Certainly, Jans, but I'm unable at the moment. That spider pretty much sucked out all the power I had left in me. I should be dead, you know."

Jans's grunted.

"So should we all. But today, we live."

"And tomorrow, if you stick around Venir much longer, we die," Slim said, laughing.

"And who gives a slat about tomorrow," Venir added, taking a seat on a log. "I'm not going to give it consideration anymore."

Jans pulled up a log and sat beside him. "Certainly you don't care, else you wouldn't be running to your death at Outpost Thirty One."

Venir shot Jans a glance, but the older warrior shrugged.

Slim frowned at him and said, "What? We're going to the outpost?"

"No, *I'm* going to the Outpost … alone."

"Of course you are. After all, that's what you do: leave everyone behind."

"They need you here, Slim. And you are far from fit to travel. I'm not saying I wouldn't let you come, either."

"Let me come!" Slim threw his lanky arms in the air, smacking them into a tree branch. "I've been here many lifetimes, and no one has ever let me do anything. I'll come if I want, Brute. You need me."

The last thing Venir wanted to do was rile the man. He'd just sent him to his death once, and he didn't care to see it happen again. Three had died: Hogan, his wife and Adanna, since he'd returned. It wasn't his fault, according to Slim, Mood and many, but he couldn't help but feel that way. Still, it was their life, they could choose to do as they wished. And if they wanted to tag along, so be it.

"Fine. Come along, then. I'd be glad to have you."

Slim eyed him.

"Really?"

Venir smiled. "Sure, if you want to do something as foolish as following me to a certain death, then who am I to stop you?"

"Well," Slim sputtered as he pulled his robes tighter, "I'd at least like to know the plan first."

Jans was laughing now.

"Not so eager, are you now. Heh-Heh. You'd be wise to stay back here with us and await the signal … though I doubt it will ever come." Jans tossed a wooden canister he had in his hand at Venir's feet. "We'll be able to see that for miles all around. But," he pointed at Venir's face, "don't you dare use it if you don't open that gate. We aren't a rescue party. We're a stronghold storming army, no thanks to you."

"Hold on," Slim said, stretching his long arms in the faces of the two of them, "am I to understand that Venir is going to infiltrate the Outpost and open the gate from the inside?"

"Yes," Venir said as Jans's nodded.

"Venir, you've lost your mind."

"You're the one who suggested I lead the fight against the underlings. Getting back that Outpost is the best place to start the battle."

"Venir, there may be thousands of them in there."

Venir stood back up and grabbed the canister.

"And there might not be that many. Besides, they won't be able to see me. If it's not possible, I can always come back."

Jans stood up and said to Venir, "You better not waste any time with that, either. My men are exposed down here. We'll need all the time we can get to gallop out of here if you fail and the entire underling army spills out. You've got a day. If not, we're gone."

Venir slung his pack over his shoulders.

"I know." He bumped arms with Jans, picked up his axe, and strapped the helm on.

"What? You're going right now?" Slim exclaimed.

"Why let underlings live a second longer than they deserve to?"

Slim's jaw dropped to the forest floor as Venir jogged into the woods and out of sight.

The hunt. It had seemed like a lifetime ago since Venir had been on his own, hunting the underlings. As he passed through the brush, it didn't matter if it was one or a thousand of his enemy. The only thing that mattered was that many more would soon be dead. He'd had enough of the underlings to last him a hundred lifetimes. He wanted them gone.

He kneeled down, took a swig from his canteen, and checked his bearings. He was near the base of the hill, less than two miles from the actual fort, with no signs of underling activity or tracks for that matter, which was odd. The road that led to the southern gate was overgrown when he crossed over. It was strange. He was certain the terrain would be buzzing with underling activity, yet it was not. The metal on his helm didn't even throb.

He rubbed his bearded chin then renewed his journey up the hill, his mind focused on one thing: vengeance on the underlings. All his life they'd been a jagged thorn in his side. Now, he'd just as soon be rid of them once and for all. And now he was free. Unshackled. Unfettered. Simmering with inner fury. And it was good. Alone, in the woods, war-axe singing in his grip with only the remote sounds of nature filling his ears.

He pressed his large form beside a tree. He heard a rustling sound. Brool was warm in his aching grip as he held it tight to his chest. There were other creatures in the forest that were as dangerous as underlings: razorback bears with claws as sharp as steel, forty foot snakes and ten foot lizards with poisoned bites and tails. Any one of them could kill him if he didn't strike first and fast. A drop of sweat fell from his nose into his beard as a ringed python as thick as his arm wound around the tree and over his toes. Venir shifted Brool's shaft in his hand, point down, as the creature's crushing weight slithered over his boots.

Hurry up! Ringed pythons, all black with bright yellow rings, unlike most of their kind, were not only fast, but fanged and poisonous. Venir knew the slightest tremor in his body could set the thing off. As the serpent slithered on, he noticed a bulk under its scales. The serpent's bloated belly dragged over the leaves, not slowed by the hump. *I hope it was an underling.* Venir exhaled through his lips as he watched the tail of the serpent disappear down the slope.

He tugged at the buckle under his chin and resumed his trek. He noted he wasn't so far from where he'd left the last time as he made his way into a ravine. The water that once trickled in the creek was gone, its surrounding greenery withering and dead. Over the past five years, the lush landscape had been forever changed, now darker and quieter. He tightened his grip on Brool. Underlings had to be near. They just had to be. *Where are they?*

In the dim forest, Venir's keen eyes could pick up what the average eye could not: deer droppings, animal impressions, and critters' burrows hidden within the ferns. He patted his palm on the helm. *This has to be working.* Yet not the slightest murmur came within his iron skull. Certainly the underlings would not have abandoned the Outpost? The Royals would have known about that.

He huddled down in the brush at the sound of rustling in the trees. *Spiders!* He'd seen enough of them to last him a lifetime already. Peering up, he noticed two black squirrels, jumping from tree limb to tree limb. He grunted. *Getting rusty.* He crept up the ravine another half mile before he stopped again. The humidity had the sweat dripping from him like a waterfall. He took another drink. Eyeing. Listening. Smelling everything around him. *Nothing.* It was as if the hilltop was dead.

Pressing through a row of man-sized ferns, he found himself alongside a patch of bright green, black and brown mushrooms as tall as his knees. They were unlike anything he'd ever seen before.

Not even the Red Clay forest that was filled with wondrous plant life, or even what he'd seen in the Under-Bish. *This is different.* He'd scouted these forests all his life and wouldn't have forgotten something like this. Backwards he retraced his steps and froze.

The mushrooms began to warble with tiny tremors. Their tops sprouted with strange trunk-like mouths.

Venir's ears felt like they were about to split open as the mushrooms ripped out a howling whine. He pressed his palms over the metal of his ears. *Slat! Madness this is!* His knees buckled, and his stomach churned as he stumbled up the bank and crashed into a pit of mud. Trying to regain his wits, he crawled from the mud hole. The underlings would be here at any moment. On his hands and knees, he crawled up the hill at an agonizing pace. The shrieking sound was agonizing and distorting. His stomach churned as he spit up bile. That's when he noticed movement above him. His enemies were coming, and he couldn't hardly move.

Chapter 33

PALOS'S APARTMENT DOOR CLOSED SHUT, and for a change Palos was on the other side. *Finally!*

Kam let out a sigh of relief and slumped her head down on the table. *I thought he'd never leave.* Quietly, she observed Thorn and Diller bringing in purses of coin and other treasure. Palos always moaned that it was never enough, each and every time. It was sickening. The man had more gold than most Royals and then some. To make matters worse, she'd had little time with Erin, despite every defiling attempt she'd allowed from him. Palos would not let the baby girl stay.

"You aren't broken yet, Princess," he'd said.

Now what? The room, despite its gaudy décor, was comfortable. The fire, warm and soothing with the slow burning Everlogs, was her only source of comfort most of the time. She stared at it for hours while Palos napped, conducted business and so forth. It was there that she planned, conspired and contemplated her next move. She flicked her fingers towards the fire. It roared with new life, hungry for air, the same as the mystic power in her belly. She released her magic, and the fire returned to normal.

Diddling with her choker, she said, "It would be a deserving home for Palos in there." Rising from her chair, she paced around the room. She wiggled the handle on the bedroom door, but it was locked. She couldn't help but think that Palos would have a secret exit from there. After all, sometimes he appeared to be in there for hours, and she swore she never heard him make a sound. He couldn't just be in there doing nothing.

"Think, Woman! You must be smarter than these stupid men!" she whispered to herself. She shifted the gems in her fingers. Their power should help. It had to. She tucked them in a small pocket in her robe. Now that her anger had subsided, she found herself missing Lefty. And now was one of those times he would be quite resourceful. If there was a secret door in here, Lefty would find it. Another thought crept into her mind as well. What if Lefty was dead? She had not seen him in days, and she was worried. No one ever said a word about him, either.

Another hour passed as she wandered around, contemplating her ideas. Her first imaginings were always of Palos dying: drowning him in the tub, choking him to death, casting him into the fire, running a snake of mystic energy through his groin and out his nose and ear holes. There were more passive options as well, such as an illusion that she was there when she wasn't. Would that fool him? She shook her head and beat her hands on the table. She knew very little of what was behind the wall. She had to secure Erin first. *I've got to save my baby!*

Once again, she found herself by the fireplace mantle, this time staring up at the great sword that hung above. It fascinated her. Its blade shone of the brightest steel, its pommel and hilt guard were worked with the most intricate metals. She knew little about weapons and combat, but she knew a fine piece of work when she saw it. Whoever forged the sword must have been as much an artist as a weapon smith. She reached up, touching the blade.

A flood of emotion washed over her.

Free me!

Gasping, she jerked her hand away. *That's not possible*, Kam thought to herself as she watched her fingerprint disappear from the blade.

"I must have imagined that," she mumbled. "A trick of the thieves, maybe."

Her reflection in the sword's blade shimmered, contorted to an image of another person, then faded away. She blinked. Rubbed her eyes. Her reflection was now gone, as well as the other. *That's not possible. Not possible at all.* Her teeth dug into her lip. She reached out to touch the blade one more time, trembling.

Free me! the sword moaned, its eerie voice not discernible as a woman's or a man's.

Kam jerked away. Her finger tips were ice cold, which didn't seem possible from touching a metal object that hung over a mantle filled with burning wood.

She combed her fingers through her hair, trying to decide if the voice was real or some kind of delusion. *Why would a sword need to be freed? Perhaps it's one of Palos's tricks.*

Her gut told her not to touch it again, but she leaned closer. *Here we go.* She took a quick glance over her shoulder, saw the door was secure, and grabbed the great sword by the hilt. A thousand thoughts and images assailed her, standing her hairs on end. The room spun around her. She thought she was screaming as she tried to tug her hand free, but the sword would not release her.

The Quarter was the working quadrant of the Nest. It was there that the worst of rogues, urchins and smugglers hammered crates filled with stolen goods under the stern supervision of the Quarter Master.

Crack!

"Hammer those nails faster, else I'll hammer them into you, Halfling!" said a full blooded orc, snapping his whip in the air for the hundredth time in a day.

Lefty had never worked so hard before. All day and night he worked. His gentle hands were calloused, and his back was sore. So tired he was, he could barely lift a hammer, but he did anyway, somehow … someway. *How did this happen?* He paused to wipe the sweat from his eye.

Crack!

He didn't even flinch.

"Halfling! No break! You nail! Or I break you!"

Tap. Tap. Tap.

He hammered. Both hands wielding the heavy hammer, shoulders aching. All the others, working near the end of the docks, hammered away with tools no bigger than his. Men, dwarves and mintaurs were there: all had failed Palos at some point, and this was part of the punishment. But all of them, excluding the enslaved urchins, left for the night when each day's labors were done. He sighed. He'd never sighed before in his life he didn't think, until now. Now it was a habit.

Don't quit, Lefty! You've got to free Erin. You owe that to Kam! If he could only get some rest. Clear his head so he could think straight. He was given a few hours a day to sleep, but it always ended as soon as it started. And it was uncomfortable sleeping in these absidium chains he was bound with at all times. The more you moved, the more they constricted. He thought of Gillem. He missed his halfling mentor, who, though bad, had still been good to him, as best as could be expected, anyway. He sighed. He swore it was his fault that Gillem had died, too. He shook his little head. *No! Palos is a madman. I'm going to get out of here.*

Tap. Tap. Tap.

Crack!

"Work faster, you ugly toads!"

Lefty snorted a laugh. The quartermaster was the ugliest person he'd ever seen. A warted toad was handsome by comparison. The orcen quarter master's face was pock-marked and lumpy. His skin was covered not only in warts but also in moles, and his teeth were half missing. Worst of all, he always scowled like he'd just eaten a basket full of lemons. The only thing the orc had going for him was a lash and the frame of two stout men in one. He'd seen the quartermaster snap a chain anchor off the deck. *Every bit as strong as he is ugly. I won't ask what his parents looked like.*

Crack!

"What are you looking at, Halfling?"

"Nothing, Quarter Master. Nothing at all."

Tap. Tap. Tap.

His tummy rumbled. He never remembered ever being so hungry before, either. Had Georgio always felt this way? All he'd eaten the past few days was gruel, and unlike the rest, he wasn't given any honey. He blinked the tears from his eyes. *How can I help anyone if I can't help myself? Ugh, somebody help me.*

Chapter 34

BRAK NIBBLED THE LAST BIT of meat from a ham bone and tossed it into the corner. His stomach still rumbled, but it wasn't nearly as bad as it had been a few days ago, in the arena. It was just him and Jubilee, basking in the feeble glow of a lantern tucked away beneath the streets of the city.

"Brak," Jubilee said, "You weren't supposed to eat all that. Melegal will be mad. Again!"

"He's always mad," he said, rubbing the hairs on his arms. It was always cool down in the sewers. He preferred the heat. He missed the suns. "And he looks like he has an aversion to food."

Jubilee giggled.

"You're funny, Brak. And 'aversion' is a good word. You're learning," she said, teetering around the dank little room, draped in a dirty blanket that barely covered her arms. "Here's a new one to learn. Abhorrence: detestation, indisposition."

A long look formed on Brak's big face.

"Don't worry, Brak, they all mean the same thing as aversion. Lots of different words mean that same thing. The more you know, the smarter you'll be. That's what Grandfather told me."

Jubilee had led them back to the exact same room he'd been brought to when they met. It was here he'd trained with Hagerdon, Leezir and the other men. It was little more than a moldy storage room with a few chairs and a table, but it was far better than the dungeon. It was the only home he'd known since his mother, Vorla, had departed. Every time he thought of her, the sadness within returned.

"Abhorrence." He paused. "Detestation."

Jubilee nodded, lips beginning to mouth the next word.

"Indisposition."

"And," a cold voice interrupted, "don't forget disinclination, disfavor, *loathing* and horror." It was Melegal, scowling as he tossed a bundle on the floor. "For example, my disinclination festers as I return to a man who always hungers and a girl who cannot seal her tongue."

Jubilee crossed her arms and stuck out her tongue.

"Bish, Brak!" Melegal gaped. "You've eaten the entire ham." Melegal grabbed Jubilee by her shirt collar. "Teach the man what rationing means, you little Slerg. Allowance: apportionment, consignment, provender." Melegal slung his cap against the wall. "Next time we need supplies, I'll send you two dally wiggles to get them."

"A dally wiggle's a ne'er-do-well, Brak," Jubilee explained. "Or a wastrel or a loafer. I had many uncles with that quality."

"Oh, shut up!" Melegal said, taking a seat at the table, frowning as his steely eyes drifted away.

Brak wasn't fond of the man, but he didn't dislike him, either. Despite the man's dour demeanor, he was always relieved when Melegal showed up. Especially since the rogue always promised he was leaving them. Plus, he brought the food.

He reached down and unraveled the bundled sack. It was filled with bread loaves, hard biscuits and dried meat.

Jubilee's quick little hand snagged a baked apple tart that she quickly stuffed in her mouth.

"Save a crumb for me, you brats," Melegal sneered. "Food's not so easy to come by now, with or without money. Especially when this entire city is spooked."

Brak picked up the sack and stood. Bending his bullish neck down beneath the ceiling, he walked over towards Melegal and set all the food on the table.

"Thank you," he said, returning to his seat.

Melegal waved his hand at him in a downward motion, lightly shaking his head.

It was odd. Brak couldn't tell if Melegal liked him or not, but he treated him better than the Slergs had.

"Morning, youngins," Haze said, entering the room and tossing a small sack at Brak's feet. The woman was in much better shape than she had been a few days ago. Her black eye was no longer swollen, but the red in her eye remained. "That's some good stuff there. I had to slip it away from Frigdah while she slept. You'd like her, Brak. She likes to eat as much as you do, but she evens it out with ale and all." She placed her hands on her narrow hips. "Enjoy."

Melegal huffed.

"What?" Haze said.

"Melegal's been lecturing us about rationing. Saying that Brak eats too much."

"Oh, well, I see his point." She took a seat by Melegal and rubbed his arm. "Sorry."

Brak felt guilty. If anything, he ate even more than he used to. He just didn't want to be so hungry, ever again. He rummaged through the bag. A cake of fruit and nuts was in there. He tore off a piece and stuffed it in his mouth. It was good. Not like the pies in the bakery he devoured, but better than dried meat and hard cheese, for now.

"So, Me, have you come up with any bright ideas yet?" Haze asked.

Melegal pulled his arm away.

"No. But we can't stay here much longer. If they're coming after us, which they are, it's only a matter of time before they find us."

"I don't know about that. It was you and me that found the Slergs the last time."

Jubilee glared at Haze.

"And I don't think they have the man power to pursue right now. If anything, they're more worried about underlings than you. Those castles are under full guard. Everywhere."

Melegal pulled out a knife and began cleaning his nails.

"I know that. We can't stay in Bone, however. They'll catch us. The Royals always get their man."

"They never got your friend Venir, the fighting man."

Melegal shot Haze a look. He'd told her not to say anything.

Brak jumped to his feet and banged his head on the ceiling.

"Venir! You said you didn't know my father!"

"Brilliant, Haze!" Melegal said, scooting back in his seat.

The time for silence was gone. Melegal was a liar! And Brak was going to squeeze the truth from his throat.

The last thing Melegal had wanted to do was trigger the rage within the young giant. Brak had almost killed him once already, and he wasn't about to risk it again. But now, as with all things, the truth he'd been trying to hide, for Brak's safety, had surfaced. Melegal found himself within the big man's cross hairs. Big meaty hands and short powerful arms clutched at his throat.

"Easy now, Brak!" Haze squeezed her narrow body in between them. "If Melegal isn't telling you something, I'm sure there's a good reason."

Brak pointed at him.

"He told me my father was dead!"

Slat, where's my hat? It was out of reach. *Soothing words. Be honest. Distract the beast.* "I only said I thought he was dead."

"Well he isn't," Brak said, clenching his fist.

"I've no way of knowing that."

Brak thumbed his chest, saying, "I do! I see him in my dreams. He's fighting, fighting for his life, out there. Somewhere. He must be."

A silence fell in the small room that's only illuminating source was the glow of a small lantern. Brak was convinced that Venir lived. Melegal could feel the truth of it in his bones. If anything, news that Venir lived gave him one thing nothing else could. Hope.

Melegal showed a wry smile.

"Is he fighting underlings?"

Brak shrugged his shoulders.

"I don't know. But I must find him. I want to meet my father. My mother is gone," Brak said, choking out the last word.

Jubilee reached over, grabbed his meaty hand with her tiny ones, and said, "I'll help you find him, Brak.

Haze grabbed the other.

"I'll help you, too."

Brak's head dipped into his chest as he started to sniffle.

Both of the women were eyeing Melegal now.

Melegal, tossing his hands out, said, "I don't know where he is! And I'm not going to look for him. If he's still out there, I'm certain he'll show up here eventually. He always did before."

Haze added, "You always said he'd be wherever the underlings were, didn't you?"

"Yes, Haze. I did. And right now, there's thousands of underlings out there. And they're probably trying to kill him. What are you suggesting, we walk up to them and ask them if they've seen The Darkslayer?"

"What's The Darkslayer?" Jubilee asked.

Brak's face was a mask of curiosity.

"Oh ..." Melegal rubbed his head. "...I thought these days were over. That's what the pig farmers call him. He's their hero. He's rousted as many underlings into beds of death as an entire army. The truth is: when's he's got that get-up on, that massive axe and helm, he becomes, oh, disturbing. Dangerous, but dismaying, foreboding, ominous—"

"Vexing?" Jubilee piped in.

"Well, that's not the best word to describe him, but partly. It's rather hard to explain. All I know is you'd better be on his side." Melegal cleared his throat. "Brak, your father, despite his brutish and impulsive intellect ... is a hero to many."

The small wooden chair groaned as Brak sat down.

"The Slergs ... they told me Venir was a fighter. My mother said he was good. A hero?" He looked up at Melegal.

"Barring all of the ideal characteristics of a hero ... yes." Melegal leaned over, grabbed his hat, and put it back on his head. "It's not something you hear very often in Bish, but your father tends to save as many lives as he takes. Which isn't really a good thing, especially if you get it wrong. In his case, so far as I know, his bloodshed's been on the right side of things. Though some sources might disagree."

"So, what happened the last time you saw him?"

I was hoping you wouldn't ask that. To lie or not to lie. Still, everyone was looking at him.

"His last trek was to the City of Three."

"Ooh ... I've always wanted to go there," Jubilee said. "They say it's named after waterfalls as big as the mountains. And they have otter cats there. My grandfather said so."

Haze grabbed him by the vest.

"I want to go there! Please, Melegal, take me!"

Melegal huffed.

"And separate you from your stupefying siblings? Your detachment would be overwhelming." He pulled away and stood up. "I'm not entertaining any thoughts of traveling. The Outlands is far from ideal for traveling for a man like me. I need shelter." He looked around. "And even this is better comfort than the Outlands."

"It's not so bad," Brak said, "It's how I got here."

Of course. The young are always so hopeful.

"With your mother's aid, I presume?"

Brak started to rise from his seat.

"Don't be a child, Brak. At least you knew your mother. That's far better than many of us." As Brak sat back down, he added, "Besides, the last I heard, your father wasn't there anymore. He'd gone on to Dwarven Hole. Never to be heard from again."

"Who told you that?" Jubilee piped in.

Such a dreaded little girl. I'll not be getting anything over on him with her around. At least Haze knows how to keep her mouth shut. He glanced over at Haze who nodded without even moving her head. *At least she realizes I'm trying to protect them.*

"Men. Acquaintances. Associates. Colleagues. Comrades. Cohorts."

"I know what that means. When did you see them last? Perhaps they will be willing to help us," Brak said.

That's actually a really good idea.

"They wouldn't want to fool with a little rodent like you. They've their own quests and charges."

Brak stood up and banged his head again.

"Ow!" he rubbed it. "I want to meet these ... *cohorts* ... too."

"I've no idea where they are." *At this very moment. But I can find them. The Octopus.*

Haze opened up her mouth to ask a question when her tongue froze.

"Haze?" he said, "Are you well?"

That's when he heard it. A faint hiss. A hiss he knew all too well. *It cannot be!*

He turned his head the direction of his eyes. Two underlings, bright yellow-eyed, sharp weapons in their grasp, cut off the exit from the room. Melegal's blood ran cold then froze as Jubilee let out a stone shattering scream.

CHAPTER 35

S EVEN KEYS. DOES IT EVEN *really matter?*

Verbard twitched his fingers together, igniting them in blue fire.

"Nooo …," a human mumbled, head down inside his robes.

Verbard touched his finger tip to the man's head, searing the skin as the man cried out, his moans echoing through the caves.

How many humans would he have to torment to find the man he sought? A man with skinny bones. Pale complexion. Salt and pepper hair. Moved like a ghost. So Kierway had said. *So, maybe Kierway had lied.* For all he knew, there was no man, or keys, for that matter. But, he had to find out.

"Human, is there such a man as I speak of?"

The man, a Royal dragged against his will from the Almens' very castle, shook his head. He was a tough soldier, but human. He'd sent in some of his kindred to snatch the man out from the night. It was all part of the wave of terror he'd begun from beneath the city. Underlings, in pairs of two and groups of three and four, spread out in the sewers, striking quick and returning with reports. Above, the humans were in full panic, torn by whether to stay or go.

"No …"

Verbard jabbed his burning blue finger into the man's cheek.

Again the man cried out in pain.

"You lie, Human. I can see it in your eyes, which you are about to lose."

The man's eyes opened wide as Verbard waggled his burning finger close to them. He knew the man was lying; he could tell. But the man's aversion for underlings was strong. Natural. He was loyal to the humans and a natural predator of the spawn of the underworld. Not all men were like that, but this one was.

"Bring him," he said, floating back through the cave until he found himself in a room with a pit.

Two underling soldiers dragged the Royal soldier by the nooks of his armpits. Inside the deep pit, illuminated by the underlight, were two albino urchlings, fighting over a bone. A human one, still covered in sinew and flesh.

"That," he emphasized, "is the last human who did not cooperate. So, answer truthfully, or be eaten alive. And, just so you know, while one holds you down, the other starts devouring your toes."

The man sobbed, shaking his head, quivering from head to toe.

"He is a Detective. Melegal is his name," the man stammered. "That's all I know."

Excellent. There is such a man. Kierway's words are true. But how will I find the man? It's a very large city. Eep … to me!

A buzz filled the air, and in a blink the imp appeared, hovering. "Human, tell this creature what you know of this man. Every last detail, starting from the top of his head, down to his toe, and I'll set you free. Maimed. But free."

The soldier looked down in the pit, up at Verbard, and nodded.

"Uh ... uh ... he wears a floppy cap ... d-d-d-dark gray ... that hangs down over the side of his face. Hair more white than black. A dimple in his narrow chin. Eyes like cold steel. Fingers long and slender, almost like a g—"

"Master!" Eep hissed, "I know this man of which he speaks. I've seen this man before. He's the man who travels with The Darkslayer."

Verbard felt his stomach tighten in a knot.

"How can you be certain?"

"It's him, Master. He's the one," Eep wrung his taloned fingers in his hands. "McKnight, the detective, was to dispatch of him that day."

Verbard felt his silver eyes begin to twitch inside his head. The mere mention of The Darkslayer was unsettling. After all, the man never perished. He'd only been banished into the Mist.

"What else can you tell me of this man? How dangerous is he?"

Eep's serpent tongue licked out and around his mouth.

"He's a pest. Nothing more. Just a man. A stick with flesh and bones. I can hunt him and kill him if you like." Eep hovered towards the disheveled Royal soldier and chomped his razor sharp teeth down. "I'd like a meal first."

Of all the things in Verbard's life, the only one that gave him an ounce of security was Eep. The heartless horror of Bish brought him as much security as delight. He thought of his brother Catten, 'the wiser of the two,' most had said. He regretted all the times he'd wanted his brother dead. It was one of those things he'd never imagined possible. Now, without him, he found himself lost. Catten'd had focus and purpose. He missed those glaring evil eyes and all of the conspiracies they'd plotted together.

"Eep, find this Melegal, and you shall have a treat upon your return."

"But, you said you'd let me live!" the soldier said, struggling to rise. The two underling soldiers shoved him down.

"Toss him in the pit," Verbard ordered, floating away from the edge.

The man screamed as he was pushed over the edge. Not a moment later, his cries were cut short.

"Master! I wished to have that one!" Eep screeched.

"Be silent and fill your charge, Imp," Verbard said, floating out of the smaller caves. "Contact me when you find him. Not a hair is to come off his head. I want him alive. I want those keys."

"Yes, Master, but there is something I must tell you, first," Eep said.

"Be gone!"

The imp's black wings buzzed with new life. It zipped away and blinked out of sight.

Verbard looked at his soldiers.

"Dismissed." As he watched them go, he muttered like a curse, "The Darkslayer." Somehow, someway, that impossible man had managed to creep back into his life.

Making his way back to the shoreline, he watched his commander, Jottenhiem, organizing the small army. The Royals would be better prepared for the next strike, but not for one of this size. Not for one that could overtake and fortify an entire castle. Jottenhiem's ruby eyes caught his. He waved the commander over.

"We are ready, Lord Verbard. Master Kierway, I believe, delays our tactics," Jottenhiem said, sneering.

"He'll be back as I've ordered, else, as he well knows, he'll have my Vicious to contend with." Verbard almost smiled as he said it. With the imp and the Vicious under his full control, even he felt invincible. "Despite his shortcomings, he's an excellent tactician. He'll find out which castles will give us the superior advantage."

"It shall be a hard fought battle, my Lord. The castles have many soldiers, hundreds in some cases according to Kierway. And how can we be certain he won't set you up for failure?"

"As it is with all of us, Kierway hates humans vastly more than he hates even me. No, he'll plan this one right."

The thought of overtaking an entire human Castle was both frightening and exhilarating. He couldn't imagine the humans ever having the audacity to occupy the Underland. That was unthinkable. But, with the Current, the underlings could run endless supplies, and within a solid fortress they could hold out forever. Perhaps this was what Master Sinway had in mind to begin with.

Verbard continued. "How are our agents performing beneath the streets, Jottenhiem?"

"Every day we quietly fill their sewers with their own dead. We cornered a small force of men in their own streets and slaughtered the frightened dogs."

"Excellent," Verbard said, stretching out his arms, resuming his feet from his stone throne. "Your efforts are appreciated, Jottenhiem. Enjoy the sanctuary of the caves for now." He looked to the cave ceiling above. "You might not be seeing them again for a while."

As Jottenhiem saluted and sauntered off, Verbard's clawed fingers fiddled with the Orb of Imbibing. "Such a precious possession."

Master, a voice sounded in his head. It was Eep.

Have you found the human already?

No Master. Soon, but I fear there is something I must tell you.

What could it possibly be? If you are so ravenous, have one of those urchins.

Master, I've news I failed to mention earlier.

And?

The Darkslayer, Master. He lives.

Verbard didn't feel the orb bounce off his toes as it rolled down the stone steps of the throne. "*NO!*"

CHAPTER 36

THE CHAMBER WAS ILLUMINATED BY a single crystal chandelier that glowed with the light of a lone candle. It was Lord Almen's bedroom. Inside, the Lord of Castle Almen lay still, gray skinned, the gentle rise and fall of his chest the only signs of life. Sefron rubbed his throbbing eye. Now blinded in it, he seethed within. *Melegal's fault.*

"He is strong, Lorda. I'm certain he'll survive his predicament." Sefron replaced the warm damp wash cloth on Lord Almen's head with a cool one. "He needs his rest."

Lorda Almen was in charge now. Graceful. Demanding. Demeaning. She did not hold back her revulsion from him. But for now, she needed him, and he needed her.

"If he dies, you die, Sefron. Are we clear?"

Sefron couldn't fight the lump that formed in his throat as he swallowed and replied, "Certainly, Lorda Almen. I'd rather die than live with my failure." As Lorda turned away, he couldn't tear his gaze from her legs underneath her garish tunic dress.

I'd die just to run my fingers along those thighs of yours.

The Lorda was perfect. Everything a man could desire and then some. For many long years, Sefron had longed for her, spied on her and fantasized of her. *The Lorda of all Lordas.* There was none like her. She, among the women, was revered and reviled. Most Lordas held true power: Magic. Skill. Poison. Words. Lorda Almen was different. She used nothing to control the wills of men and women but her comeliness ... and cunning.

She snapped her fingers in his face.

"Sefron! You ghastly cleric! Pay attention!"

Sefron shook his head. Her magnificent perfume had unhitched his fantasies again.

"Yes, ahem, my Lorda."

"I need Detective Melegal found and brought to me," she ordered.

Biting his lip, he nodded. She had a fancy for the man who he loathed with all his might. Melegal had foiled him. The rat from the streets had managed to snare the Lorda's attention. Had saved the woman from her own son, so witnesses had said. Sefron never believed any of it, but he'd yet to prove otherwise.

"As you wish, Lorda," he said, adjusting the patch over his eye. It ached to do so. "The City Watch is scouring the streets as we speak, and I cannot rule out the possibility that the man, stricken by fear, fled the castle. He should have defended it. Instead, he's gone."

Lorda remained expressionless, stroking her husband's arm, beautiful eyes in contemplation.

"No, he would do no such thing. He's fulfilled all of his charges with the utmost proficiency." Lorda stared into his eyes. A dangerous intent was there. "If you know something, you'd be wise to tell me now, Sefron." She glanced back at the other men in the room. Shadow sentries, presence dulled by their ghost armor, stood eyes forward and at rest. "If I'm given the slightest doubt you're lying to me, on my word, I'll have you chopped into bits."

"No worries, Lorda. If he lives, I'll find him. The Watchmen—"

"The Watchmen are not capable! Laggards! Over trained thugs is all they are! Hire the Bloodhounds if you must. Just see it done!"

"*The* Bloodhounds?"

Lorda pointed to the nearest Shadow Sentry, then at him.

"Oh ... mercy Lorda—"

Two quick strides, and the tall warrior walloped him in his saggy gut. Sefron couldn't breathe as he fell to the floor, but he could still hear.

"I want that black-haired witch, Jarla, accounted for, too. Dead."

Sefron petted the rug that broke his fall as he watched her sensuous legs walk away. *So pretty. One good eye is all I need.* The two shadow sentries remained as she departed with two others who bowed to her in the hall. After a few more minutes, he clutched at the spread on Lord Almen's bed and rose back to his feet, wheezing.

"Shew," he said, wiping the sweat from his pasty forehead. It hurt to even do that. *Thank goodness I can still heal things.* He scratched at one of the places were one of Melegal's many darts had found a new home. *Find the rat. Trap the rat. Kill the rat.* No lying needed to be done in the 'pursuit of Melegal' department. Lorda Almen wanted him. Kierway wanted him. And Sefron wanted him, too. It wasn't likely any man could avoid all those clutches for long. But the Bloodhounds? That was a reckless call.

He dipped a small cup into a bowl of water and whetted Lord Almen's lips.

"That's better. Can't have you drying out on me."

He did it a few more times before setting the cup back down.

"Bloodhounds," he whispered. "Of all the stupid ideas. Those cretins will foil everything."

The Bloodhounds were a guild of henchmen bounty hunters that every Castle used, from one side of the City of Bone to the other. They were the best at what they did, but the price always ended up higher than the gold you paid them. Lord Almen never dawdled with them. He considered their ilk, "Gormandizing Bastards." Sefron couldn't agree more.

He peeled the bandage back from the wound beneath Lord Almen's arm. He could have let the man die, and wasn't fully certain why he hadn't. He'd managed to stop the bleeding, but Lord Almen had lost an awful lot of blood. Still, he hadn't figured out who had stabbed the man. Melegal had accused Jarla, and it was likely the woman was an assassin. But what about Melegal? Could he have the stones to have done such a thing?

"Fiddle me," Melegal muttered, replacing the warm wash cloth on Almen's head with another cold one. "This will help you rest well as you recover, Lord Almen." He glanced back at the two stone-faced Shadow Sentries. They looked like they could break him in half just by staring at him. "It helps if you talk to them. Sing him a delightful song, if you like," he said, waddling out the door holding his finger to his lips, "I won't tell." *Slat sucking soldiers!*

Down the hall he went, limping and wheezing, carrying one lie on top of the other. It was hard lying to the Lorda, given all of her powerful wiles. But, lacking any witnesses from the torrid massacre that had befallen the victims in the arena, he'd convinced Lorda that Lord Almen had fallen battling the underlings. As for Lord Almen when he awakened? Sefron chuckled. *I'll let the man awaken when I'm ready. But it's my castle for now.*

Chapter 37

"**W**INE!" JARLA SLAMMED HER FIST on the table.

The young man jumped out of his stool, wiped his hands off on his apron, and blinked at her.

"Why do you stand and look at me so stupidly, Fish-face?" she asked, carving the tip of her dagger into the table.

"We've no more wine," he stammered, wringing his hands. "Perhaps—"

"I've never been in a tavern that ran out of wine. Where is it, Stooge?"

The young man crouched behind his hands.

"You drank it all … er … what we had left, that is."

Jarla slung the nearest wine jug at him, followed by another. The man scurried behind the bar. "Get me something! Else I'm going to carve another hole in your nose!" She slung the last remaining jug, and it slammed into the shelves behind the bar with a crash. "Idiot!"

Jarla was rattled. She'd faced death before but nothing quite like what had happened the other day in Castle Almen's arena. Madness. One second, she'd been watching the decimation of the Slergs and in the next, a bullish man exploded in a fit of frenzied rage. Her head ached still from the moment she'd momentarily blacked out. Fighting the sudden urge to sleep, she'd come to, only to see one of the skinniest men she'd ever seen sliding a dagger out from between Lord Almen's ribs.

She picked up her goblet and tilted it over her lips, catching the last remaining drops on her tongue. "Where's my drink, Boy?" She slung the goblet across the room.

Lord Almen was probably dead. He was one of the few allies she still had. They'd served together long ago as soldiers in the Royal forces. He'd taken her under his wing and then some. They'd learned to use each other for their wants and needs over the years. An alliance of great mutual benefit. He'd been the one who financed her Brigand Army from the outset. She dispatched of many of his enemies, and hers as well. But it had been her deal with the underlings that took it to another level. The demise at Outpost Thirty-One. When she'd come to Almen later, she'd been pleasantly surprised that he hadn't even seemed to mind. She hadn't figured that one out. But for some reason, he'd always been there when she needed him, until now.

"Slat!"

That detective had foiled her and escaped. Out of nowhere, the underlings came. One moment she was fighting for her life, spilling blood of the Royal soldiers, then came the underlings and she was overwhelmed. Something had struck from the air. A glimmering black javelin had sailed into her chest, searing through one end and out the other. She'd blacked out, only to awaken in excruciating pain. Alone but alive. She'd crawled over the dead, the slaughtered, the mutilated, managed to make it to her feet, and stumbled through the corridors.

The tavern boy interrupted her thoughts.

"I-I found this," he said, holding a bottle out with shaking arms.

"Grog will do."

He set it down, pushed his sweaty locks back, and backed away.

She scanned the room. The fireplace was dead, and the tavern was absent of all people. She liked that. It was only her and the boy, as far as she knew. She pulled the cork out of the bottle with her teeth and drank. It burned all the way down her throat and into her wounded belly. "Ah."

She wiped her sleeve across her busted lip and recalled her thoughts. Bleeding from a half dozen wounds and wracked in pain, she'd dragged her sword over marble floors in the halls. The sounds of battle had been ringing out from all directions. Distancing herself from the sounds, she'd made it to the garrison, into the lower courtyard, and slipped past the abandoned post out into the streets. She took another swig from the bottle.

"Now what?" she said to herself, tossing her head back.

She was alone again. Lord Almen had given her comfort, sanctuary and pleasure after she'd sought him out, but now that was gone. She reached inside her cloak, pulled out a key as long as her hand, and set it down on the table. The key was crafted with brass and iron with a rectangular amethyst setting. Lord Almen had given it to her, not a gift, but a charge.

She twisted a matching ring that was on her finger.

When the gem twinkled, it meant Lord Almen summoned her. The Key, once entered into any key hole, would take her back to the ancient chamber. At some point, Lord Almen might summon her back into his chambers. But she wasn't going to wait around.

Chapter 38

"Why so glum, Young Man? Are you not enjoying the food?" Trinos said, running her fingers through his curly hair.

A rousing sensation raced from his head to his toes. He panted out his words.

"No. The food's great." Georgio took a breath. "I just want to find my friend, is all."

Trinos set him down on the bench alongside her and patted his knee as she looked him up and down.

The woman was the most beautiful thing he ever saw. Prettier than Kam even, and he felt wholly inadequate in her audience. Small. Miniscule. Her long platinum hair seemed to cascade over her shoulders like a living waterfall. Her light blue eyes changed from green to gold in the light.

"Tell me about this friend. What is his name?"

Georgio swallowed hard as he tried to avert his gaze from the plunging neckline on her perfect chest, but had difficulty doing so.

Trinos flipped her hair forward, smiling as she repeated,

"What is his name?"

"Uh … Venir."

"I like that name. It's a strong one."

Georgio's thoughts shifted back to normal. Excited, as he'd felt for days, he said, "He's the strongest. The strongest man that ever lived!"

"Is that so?" Trinos said, crossing her legs and placing her hands on her knees. "Stronger than your comrade Mikkel?"

"Hah! Venir whipped him once already. He's beat an ogre with his bare hands, too."

She reached over and squeezed his bicep.

"You look like you're going to be a strong one, too."

"Well, I guess so." He couldn't help but smile. "I'm still growing, and I'm already big for my age."

"Uh-huh," she nodded, "So then what do you need your friend Venir for? By the looks of things, you can take care of yourself. And by the sounds of things, he can take care of himself. So why do you think you need him? You seem to be doing just fine without him. I'm certain he'd even be proud of the young man you're coming to be. I know if I were your friend that I would be."

Georgio shook his head a little, scooting back from her. Why did he need Venir? He'd never thought about it that way before. When he looked back up at Trinos, her face was a warm ray of sunshine.

"I don't need him." He felt his heart stiffen in his chest. "I miss him. You see, he's my best friend. He's my hero."

Trinos felt her heart tug inside her chest. Since she'd inhabited her world, she'd found little of the qualities she'd find to be noble: love, loyalty, friendship. It was a hard world, filled with as much good as evil, but the good ones, the defenders of right, had trouble showing it. This young person, not yet fully a man, still blossomed with all the things right in the world.

"Georgio, this Venir, I hope he knows how fortunate he is to have a friend like you. You are a true friend, and I'm grateful to know you."

"Me?" Georgio said, looking at her funny.

She laughed and said, "Yes, you. Your loyalty blinds you from all the other circumstances, and that is a good thing. It can be a dangerous one, as well."

"Why?" he said, grabbing a baked biscuit and stuffing it into his mouth.

"You don't want to be loyal to a fault. If Venir were to do bad things, would you still follow after him?"

"*Phmpf* ... Venir would never do anything bad. But Melegal would. Now, he's bad news. All he does is pick on me, but I'm almost as big as him now," he smacked his fist into his hand, "and I'm going to get him good."

Georgio was a breath of fresh air compared to the rest of her crew. He was naïve, yet weathered. His round face was beginning to chisel, and the handsome ruggedness of a man was beginning to show. He combed his fingers back through the long locks of curly brown hair and dusted the crumbs from his chest. Noting his grubby but otherwise perfect complexion, something puzzled her. He was different. Vastly so from the others.

Reaching over, she dug her nails into his wrist, drawing blood.

"Ow!" he cried. "What did you do that for?"

Holding his arm tight she watched the minor wound instantly heal up.

"I apologize, Georgio, but my curiosity got the best of me. Forgive me."

"Ah ... sure thing. It wasn't nothing anyway. I've had my fingers cut off and even had my throat sliced open, too."

Trinos slapped her hand over her chest and said, "That's awful. When was this?"

He shrugged.

"No so long ago. I was shorter and chubbier back then, but Venir took care of all that. Melegal too, though I hate to admit it."

"What did they do?" she asked.

"Venir has a mystic sack, and inside it he keeps his battle axe that he calls Brool. He went after that underling thing ... some black monster ... and chopped it to bits and pieces. Chongo ate what was left of it."

"Who's Chongo?"

"That's Venir's giant two-headed dog. Anyway, Melegal chopped up Detective McKnight into chunks and fed him to the hogs."

Trinos formed a bitter face. What a horrible thing for a child to go through. Was this her intention when she created Bish? All of this suffering for her entertainment? It all seemed quite dreadful when standing on the ground, where it occurred.

"You don't look well, Trinos. Here, have a drink," he said, holding a jug forth.

"No, I'll be just fine, Georgio."

But she wasn't. Guilt. She felt it stronger than any other emotion she'd felt before. Something knotted in her stomach. Compassion and mercy were one thing. You could act and feel good about yourself. But guilt was an entirely different monster to wrangle. *Perhaps it's a good thing, knowing how they feel.*

Georgio tapped her on the shoulder and said, "Trinos, I'm well. I heal. I've been through some bad things, real bad, but I'm better for it now. This is Bish, Lady. The land of fight or die. And like my friend Venir says, "Every day you live is another day to make the underlings die." He shook his fist at the ground. "And I'm going to kill underlings, like my friend, because they're the source of all the problems in this world."

His strong words not only brought her comfort but relief as well. *Perhaps that is why I've made it so tough.* Something else he'd mentioned seemed familiar. "You mentioned a sack, Georgio. Tell me more about it."

CHAPTER 39

THE FAST RIDE INTO THE pass was cut abruptly short by treacherous terrain that was difficult to navigate. Fogle cursed. At this pace, there was no way he'd be able to catch up to Cass and Chongo. All he could do now was hope they'd come back, and come back soon. The fragile muscles behind his narrow shoulders knotted up again when he saw Boon opening his mouth to speak.

"Haste is the mother of destruction in a situation like this. We need to be careful," the old man said, swatting a fly from his nose. "There are narrow passes like this all throughout the valley. Havens for underlings and other recreant life."

Fogle didn't turn, focusing on what was ahead instead. Cass was gone, and Chongo was the one that was supposed to be leading them to Venir. *If Mood were here, this would not have happened.*

"On a better note," Boon continued, "Barton will provide much protection. The smaller creatures, even underlings, are fearful of the giants. Their odor scares them. Not because it smells …

It does smell.

"… but rather because they are unfamiliar with it. That's why dwarves are such good giant hunters. They can smell them."

Fogle brought his pony to a halt and twisted his back around, glaring at his grandfather.

"Then why didn't the dwarves sniff them out before the attack?"

"They were down wind, as were Barton and I. But they were close, so very close to our path. It's a good thing you came along, or I'd have been back to the Under-Bish."

"The dwarves are dead!" Fogle snapped.

"And the giants are, too. The dwarven people couldn't be happier. There's nothing they enjoy celebrating better than giant soup," Boon smiled, patting his belly. "Makes me hungry to think about it!"

"WHAT?" Barton said, shoving his way through the trees. "WHO EATS GIANT SOUP?"

"Just a joke, Barton. Nothing to get excited about," Boon said a bit nervously, then turned back towards Fogle with a wink, saying, "Oops."

Barton the giant was strange. Harmless like a child, yet threatening as an angry bull at the same time. Fogle had seen what giants could do to a fully grown dwarf. He'd eyed this smaller giant's powerful hands. They could crush him like a squirrel. Still, he pitied the creature. Its large head was stooped over, and the skin was mangled over its eye, keeping it closed, and the jaw was askew. Barton was discarded. Alone.

"BARTON want to find Venir. Barton wants to find his toys, Hee. Hee." the giant said, pulling bushes from the ground and tearing out trees.

"Will you tell him to stop doing that? We don't need the entire valley to know we're here. And what is he talking about now? Toys?"

"Eh," Boon twisted at his beard, "seems that your friend tricked Barton in order to escape from The Mist."

"And?"

"Well, Barton's upset. It seems that Venir was supposed to leave him the contents of the sack, but failed to do so."

"And?"

Boon looked over his shoulder. Barton's back was to them as he chewed on a blue-berry Dackle Bush. "So Barton wants to kill him."

"What?" Fogle was aghast. "Why in Bish are you helping him?"

Boon put is fingers to his lips.

"Ssh. Ssh. Ssh. Don't fret it. I'm sure he won't follow through. Just don't mention Venir's name around him. It upsets him."

"What do we do when we find him?"

"If we find him." Boon corrected.

Clenching his teeth, Fogle dropped his head in his hand. He wanted to take out his spellbook and slap Boon in the face. *Idiot!*

"Don't worry, Grandson. If we find him ..."

Fogle shot him a look.

"When we find him, I'm sure I'll have figured out something."

"Just come on," Fogle said, digging his heels into the ribs of the pony.

He'd tried to look for signs of where Chongo and Cass had passed. After all, he should have picked up a thing or two from Mood. There was nothing, though. The dirt, rock, trees and bushes that went up one side of the pass and down the other all looked the same to Fogle. The problem was, he couldn't find his way back, despite all the wreckage Barton had created. *Come back, Woman!*

Because the pass seemed to narrow the deeper they traveled, he muttered an incantation under his breath. A feeling of security enveloped him, easing his mind, but it did little to shield him from the hot suns as he sweltered in his own sweat. He jerked.

Something twirled by his head, a radiant swirl of orange energy that buzzed through the treetops, up one side of the pass and down the other before it disappeared around the next bend. He stopped, looking back at Boon.

"What was that?" Fogle asked, frowning.

"A scout."

"Is that so?"

"Sort of. It's good for finding underlings, that is."

Barton was standing behind Boon and his pony, scratching his bald head.

"Where did the pretty light go?"

Boon bent his head backward, looking up into Barton's face. "Keep your eye up in the sky, Barton, and you'll see another pretty light ... possibly."

Fogle lifted his chin upward. There was nothing but blue skies for miles all around. But his mind began racing through the pages of his spellbook. The Scout. What was that incantation from?

Turning his attention back to Boon, he asked, "What does the Scout do?"

Boon's left eyebrow was cocked as he gazed into the sky, his wizened face unable to hide his concentration.

Fogle felt the air around him begin to prickle, and his mouth was suddenly dry.

"I don't see anything," Barton said, in his slow way of speaking.

"Ah ... Yes!" Boon exclaimed.

"What are you doing?" Fogle said.

But Boon was no longer there. Instead, the feeble old man sat tall in the saddle, tanned and sinewy arms raised high in the air. Eyes shut, brows buckled, he pulled his elbows down, then shot his fists back up and shouted in a voice of thunder:

"STRIKE!"

Fogle had both hands gripping the saddle when Boon's voice carried down the pass. Above, it sounded as if the sky had split open. The air thinned around him, and the ponies stomped and nickered.

What has he done!

A black slit opened up in the blue sky, and a roaring tower of flame emerged, striking the distant ground of the pass. Beautiful and terrifying, the orange-yellow-red torrent of flame came down upon the land like a powerful waterfall.

Fogle shielded his eyes with his hands. He could feel the heat on his knuckles and through his robes. As quickly as it had started, it stopped. He took a breath.

Beside him, Boon's eyes were glowing with energy, burning with new life and an old hatred. Pure intensity.

"Let's go, Fogle," Boon demanded, snapping the reins on his pony, "there will be survivors. There're always survivors, but not for long. Prepare for battle, Grandson. Yah!"

Chapter 40

H E KNEW SOMEONE WAS COMING, but that hardly mattered now. Venir, for all his efforts, was immobilized. He fought it, though. *Move or die* racing through his mind. The cocoon of caterpillars writhing in his stomach did not fade, nor did the shrieking sound of the mushrooms subside, either. Venir dug the mud from his eyelets in the helm as he crawled on his hands and knees up the hillside. It was miserable, the sound, the sweat, everything. Bish proved once again to be full of surprises.

What am I doing?

Straining with tremendous effort, he rose to his knees, leaned forward, and stepped slowly up the hillside. The mushrooms screamed louder and louder with every hard fought step as his mind began to dizzy from the maddening sound.

He screamed, but not even his own voice could be heard. He might have jammed Brool's spike in his ear if it were possible. His tortured mind had a better idea. He tore his helmet off and threw it to the ground.

REEEEEEEEEEEEEEEEEEEEEEEEEEEEEEEEEEEEEEEEEE!!!!

The sound amplified. He'd expected the opposite. *BAD IDEA!* He fell to his knees, fingers in his ears, Brool slipping from his grasp as he kicked and writhed on the ground.

REEEEEEEEEEEEEEEEEEEEEEEEEEEEEEEEEEEEEEEEEE!!!!

The blue veins rose in his forearms as he clutched for the helm. Fighting the madness, his fingers clawed at the dirt, getting him closer, inch by inch, when he swore he heard a chitter. *They were here.* The deep instincts of his mind spoke to him a warning.

Underlings!

A pair of underlings appeared, eyes glinting like blue sapphires. Hunters. Armed with small curved swords, metal bucklers, and wearing odd helmets, they scanned the forest. Venir got his fingers around the chinstrap of his helm and dragged it towards himself. That's when the first underling's eyes locked on his. The underling hit his comrade in the arm, who in turn hissed, raised his sword and charged.

Venir's fingers were numb when he realized he didn't have Brool in hand. The deafening sound sapped the strength from his arms and legs. The first underling was on him, sword high and chopping downward. Venir ran the helm's spike into its chest, bowling the smaller humanoid over. The other's blade hit him hard but glanced off his scale mail. Fighting through the dizzying blackness that was trying to overcome him, Venir grabbed the creature by the leg and jerked it down to the ground. The underling bit his hand, kicked him in the face, and twisted and writhed in his grasp. Venir's grip slipped.

REEEEEEEEEEEEEEEEEEEEEEEEEEEEEEEEEEEEEEEEEE!!!!

Everything was fuzzy when both the underlings pounced on him, claws digging into his arms and face. Venir grabbed whatever he could, holding on for his life. His strength was fading. He reached back and caught the lip of something in his fingers. The underling's helmet. He ripped it off.

The underling jolted to its feet, fanged mouth wide open, clawed fingers inside its ears. It was screaming, but there was no sound other than the high pitched …

REEEEEEEEEEEEEEEEEEEEEEEEEEEEEEEEEEEEEEEEEEEEEEEEEEEEE!!!!

Black blood trickled from the underling's nose as it fell to the ground and pitched forward, face first.

Somehow, Venir jammed his bloodied helm back down on his head and secured the strap under his chin. The high pitched wail was dulled, but far from no longer being annoying. *Brool!* Where was his axe? Certainly more would be coming.

REEEEEEEEEEEEEEEEEEE—

It stopped. The screeching stopped. Venir felt the weight of the world vacating his broad shoulders, aside from the ringing in his ears. He retched. Then retched again.

"SonuvaBish … that was nasty!"

Venir picked Brool back up and skewered the unconscious underling. Ripping the spike free, he put as much distance between him and those mushrooms as he could. Finding a cleft along a pile of moss-laden boulders, he tucked himself inside, gasped for breath, and took a long swig from his canteen. *Better lay low awhile.* He smashed a large mosquito that landed on his cheek and flicked it to the ground.

The underlings. Certainly, the hillside would be crawling with them by now. At any second, he expected to hear the angry mutterings of at least a score of underlings searching for him. *Where are they?* A drop of underling blood dripped from the helm onto his toe. One minute passed. Another drop fell. Two minutes passed. *Something's wrong.*

He closed his eyes. The forest smelled like a rotting log, and even the bugs in the air were thinned. He heard something. The sounds of dogs. And voices. *It can't be!* Human voices? But it was.

"Come on, men," he heard a gruff voice say from the bottom of the ravine. Dogs were sniffing and snorting, paws rustling the dry ground.

"What about the shriekers?" one man asked.

"No need to worry. These are old ones. My, pretty big, too. No wonder that shrieking was so bloody loud. Huh … dead now. Look at this …"

Venir slid out from the rocks, craning his neck forward.

"… see, they're dead now. Once they blow, they blow until they're dead. Haha. And so you'll be as well."

Another voice from the small party said, "A comrade got too close to one of those once. A littler one that is. He said that blasted thing turned his guts into worms and his ears ring to this day. Well, he's dead now, so I don't assume he can hear anything, I suppose."

Venir heard the jangling of weapons and boot steps stomping over the dirt. Whoever they were, they weren't trying to hide from anything or anyone. There must have been five of them at most. What on in Bish were men doing outside of Outpost Thirty-One? And where were the underlings?

"Hah," one said, his voice higher than the others, "we got two dead over here."

"Underlings?"

"Come take a look for yourself."

Venir eased his way back down the hill and bunched himself over a rocky outcropping.

"I'll be!"

"Aye!"

"I'm taking their eyes!"

"Fools!" the one that sounded like a leader said, "They'll have our heads. Slat! This is trouble.

Nothing but trouble. It's been bad enough up here, but at least it's quiet and the food's hot. Now this." Venir saw a man's arm chop down a sapling with his sword. "Slat on it! They'll have our heads!"

Venir crept farther down the rock edge as the man below smashed the sapling down under his boot. He got a view of the men, who were less than thirty yards below. *Royal soldiers? It can't be!* They were in full view now. He could even see the royal insignia on some of their shoulders. *Bone if it isn't.*

The leader wore a crested metal helmet, a full shirt of chainmail, bracers on his arms, and steel worked shin and thigh guards strapped to his legs. A bastard sword hung in his grip. He was a sizable man, Venir noted, when another one stepped along his side. *Sweet mother of Bish!*

The second man was bigger, taller than Venir and heavier, thick thewed and iron-jawed. A thought of Farc entered his mind at the sight of the man's bald crown rimmed with thick black hair, wearing a leather cuirass that bulged some at the gut. Venir noted the pair of long swords strapped at his sides and the thick coarse black hairs on his arms. *A part orc with Royals? What madness is this?*

The other three men were in similar uniform to the leader, one holding the leash to two large hunting dogs. All bigger than the average man, typical of Royal soldiers, each holding a small buckler and longsword. Venir bit into his lip as he tried to make sense of what was going on. Did these men occupy the outpost with underlings? How many more men would be up there? How many more underlings?

One of the men poked an underling with his sword.

"Don't do that," the leader kneeling among the dead said, "it's dead. Look at the hole in it. Bish! What kind of weapon hit the vermin?"

"Spear."

"Lance."

"Who'd be carrying a lance in these woods, Fool?" the leader said to the smallest of the soldiers.

They all looked at the half-orcen man who stood like a statue with oversized biceps crossed over his chest, chin up, nostrils flared, not paying them any mind.

"Have the hounds got a scent yet?"

The big dogs, both with medium coats of black, brown and white, snorted at the ground. He'd worked with such dogs before. They were excellent trackers and hunters, fast as gazelles. It wouldn't take them but a few seconds to track him down. Unless the armament protected him from dogs, which it wasn't known to do.

"Everyone spread out, and look for some signs. We need to get an idea of how many men we're dealing with before this hunt begins."

Venir remained frozen on the rocks and watched. Less than a minute later, the part-orc spoke. He voice was dry and deep.

"One man. Big." The soldier had his hand in the impression where he'd fallen in a mud hole. "Must be pretty strong to survive the shriekers."

"A mage, maybe?" the leader asked, eyeing the area.

"No mage has ever been that big. Not a fat man, either. Big boned. Wearing armor."

"Seeing how there's only one of him … er … it *is* a him, isn't it?"

The big part-orcen man shrugged.

"Could be a part ogre woman. Har. If that were the case we'd've all smelled her rotten crack by now. The flies would be thicker, too."

The soldiers showed a disturbed look.

"What?" the part orc said, chuckling "you men haven't lived till you've made woo-wu with an ogre."

Venir hunched back behind the rocks. All he'd wanted to do was make it to the Outpost wall by nightfall and try to slip in. Now, he was trapped. If he ran, there would certainly be more patrols out there. *There's got to be another way.*

"Let loose the dogs then," said the leader, tipping a flask to his lips, eyeing the hill.

"No, I'm not sending them into the unknown," a feisty voice retorted. "Whoever it is has killed two underlings. It can certainly kill my dogs."

"Fine, keep the dogs leashed, but you'll still be taking the point."

Great! Time's running out!

Turning to flee, Venir sent a small boulder tumbling down the hillside.

All the eyes in the ravine locked on him, and the dogs howled. Swords scraped from their scabbards as the leader yelled, "Cut him down!"

Chapter 41

"**D**on't despair, huh."

Lefty kept his head down, ears open, hammering away.

Tap. Tap. Tap. Tap. Tap. Tap. Tap. Tap.

"Huh. You listenin'? Huh."

Lefty peeked over the crate. The quarter master was farther down the dock, lash cracking with rhythm and fear. Still hammering, he glanced to his right. An old dwarf with a short white beard tied off in black and white tails hiding his chin was staring at him with beady black eyes. He looked like he was a thousand years old as he chewed the bottom of his mustache that hung inside his mouth.

"Huh. You seein'. Huh. You hearin' now, too? Huh."

Lefty remembered every face he'd come across, but this one he didn't know. The dwarves he'd been acquainted with, they were always gruff or short, unless of course they were telling a nasty joke. He held his tongue and hammered away. *I don't need any more trouble.*

"Listen to me, Boy. Huh. I knows many secrets. I've been here very long. Huh. You listen, Halfling. Huh," the dwarf said, his voice drawing a few curious stares from the other workers.

"Keep it down, Codger. I have no reason to converse with you. I'm in enough trouble already," Lefty replied, shifting his aching body away. The last thing he wanted was a lash on his back to add pain to his misery.

"You do listen. Huh. Good. Jubbler talk. You listen. Listen good. Huh. Jubbler. Me Jubbler. Else I'll talk louder. Huh."

"Yes. Huh!" Lefty said as his hammer slipped free of his sweaty hands and clattered on the planks. "See what you did?" he whispered, glaring at the old dwarf man as he snatched up his hammer.

The orcen quartermaster was coming back, a whip in one hand a leather lash in the other.

Tap. Tap. Tap. Tap. Tap. Tap. Tap. Tap.

"What was that racket, Halfling? You trying to skim off some work?"

Crack!

Lefty felt the whip's tip licking a foot from his back.

"No. No, Quartermaster. A little slip is all. It won't happen again.

Tap. Tap. Tap. Tap. Tap. Tap.

The Quartermaster was eyeing him when he noticed the dwarf.

"Ho. I see you've found some help, Halfling." The orcen man showed him a toothy grin. "Jubbler will have you wanting to drive those nails in your head within a few hours." The Quartermaster leaned down. "Tell you what, though. Once you feel you can't take it any longer, let me know. I'll be glad to drive the nails in your skull for you."

Jubbler jumped up on the crate, faced the quartermaster and started beating his chest like an ape.

"Huh! Huh! Huh! Huh! Huh! …"

The Quartermaster cocked his arm back and laid into Jubbler with the lash.

Jubbler curled up into a ball as he continued his insane mutterings.

After about ten lashes, the orc kicked the old dwarf off the crate, sending him crashing onto the planks with a thud.

"Remember, Halfling. I'll drive those nails for you," the Quartermaster said, holding his big paw of hand in front of his face, "but I'll be needing a bigger hammer." He turned and farted as he walked away.

Melegal had told him, "People often say, 'Misery loves company, unless you're me.'" Lefty looked at Mumbling Jubbler the Dwarf and couldn't agree more. More people and more problems to follow.

Jubbler rocked back and forth with his arms wrapped around his knees and head tucked in between, muttering, "Huh. Huh. Huh. Huh…"

I am Zorth the Everblade. Mind … Magic … Metal … now one.

Kam's arms trembled as she held the great sword before her.

Once I was a dying man, ages ago, a Royal on a throne of blood and gold.

Kam felt her will intertwined with another. A mind grumble of sorts. She fought against the foreign entity with everything she had. Nothing would control her. No man. No woman. No sword.

I asked for longer life, and a mage did this to me. It was not what I had in mind.

A great sadness filled her as tears streaked down her face. She could feel a cold metal tomb surrounding her, forcing the icy breath from her lungs. Long, cold and lonely Zorth's life in the sword had been.

I am thankful for you, Kam. I've not spoken for so long. I know your dilemma. I can help you if you can help me.

Help. It was the word she'd almost given up on. It wasn't someone who could help her it seemed, but rather something.

"How?" she asked.

Lend me your magic. I need strength.

She could feel the sword's hunger nibbling for her power. An invasion, but unobtrusive. The will of the sword was weak, like a fire lacking fuel.

Free me! Kam, please! the sword moaned inside her head.

She was stubborn. She fought back. She wasn't going to freely give what Palos had temporarily taken. She wouldn't be anyone's slave ever again. If only the sword had a woman's voice and not a man's, it would have been much easier; she was certain. It would be hard to trust men anymore.

"You release me first," she ordered.

I cannot. I will not. I cannot risk this torment any longer. I implore of you, Kam, a woman who is good, intelligent and mystic. I know you can feel my suffering." The sword whined inside her head, miserable. *"You must HELP ME!"*

Kam winced as the word bit deep into the recesses of her mind.

"I will not, Zorth Everblade!"

Alas, Kam. I mean you no harm. I can help. Give me power, and I shall release you. Such is the word of Zorth. Think about it, quickly, if you will.

Zorth. The name seemed as if it should have been familiar. Perhaps that was only what the sword wanted her to think. The thought of a mind infusion by magic with metal was another thing. As far as she was concerned, that wasn't possible. It wasn't even heard of before. As she struggled, her numb fingers remained frozen to the blade. She didn't like being controlled. She was sick of it entirely. She remembered what Joline had said time and time again. "Sometimes, you have to give in a little before you get what you want." She never liked that saying. She'd been giving way too much of herself lately, and it hadn't helped at all. The thought of Palos pawing at her made her mind recoil.

He is less than the crust between an orc's toes. I'd never let a man such as that within a league of a noble woman such as you. I'll make him pay ... if you let me.

"No, I will make him pay!"

Her anger was boiling over. Strengthening her. Filling her with new power. She wasn't going to have a man to do things for or against her ever again. Her fingertips lost their icy touch as new warmth flowed through her hand.

No Kam! Please! Help me! Free me! I need—

The giant sword clattered to the ground.

"Blast!" she said, flapping her hands as a headache came on. "I can get out of here all by myself!"

In her heart, she knew that wasn't true. She needed something or someone. The sword, however, was nothing but another problem. A big one. How was she going to explain why it wasn't on the mantle? She certainly didn't want to pick it up again.

"What am I going to do now?"

The long blade gleamed back at her, tantalizing like a diamond. The fire's light on the metal reflected and wavered on it like a living thing. She brushed her hair back over her ears, wondering how she could even consider carrying the massive thing out of there. It was the biggest sword she'd ever seen. Shaking her head, all she could think was how badly she needed to get out of here, somehow, someway.

Erin! She wanted to see her baby girl. When Palos found the sword on the floor, he'd be furious. He might not let her see her baby again. *Think of something, Kam.* She'd have to have an answer and have it soon. Her heart jumped as the door knob turned, the door opened, and Palos and Thorn appeared.

Chapter 42

S TAGGERING THROUGH THE STREETS, TONIO paid no mind to the gawping stares, nor the bolt jutting from his forehead. Something had rattled his mind, making it fuzzy again. A big black man with a knotted club had beaten him like a drum, jarring his skull and his bones. He needed something, but what was it that would help him focus?

"Whoa, Man. Watch where you're going!" a drunken bystander he jostled said.

Tonio leered at him, tall, ugly and scary.

The man rammed his knife into Tonio's shoulder, not once but twice, eyes in full alarm.

"What are you?"

Tonio backhanded the man in the face, spinning him to the ground, and then picked up a jug of wine from the ground and staggered on.

He muttered to himself but couldn't talk. A woman with one good eye and a head full of yellow hair passed out as he yanked the bolt from his head. He groaned an awful sound as tiny webs of flesh filled in the hole.

"What am I?"

Ducking into an alley, he found a narrow set of stairs and went down.

"Who am I?"

He sat down in his suit of battered armor, watching the big rats scurry beneath his feet. He tipped the jug of wine to his lips and drank. It was not long before clarity came. Memories of his mother flashed in his mind. The haughty face of the Vee-Man angered him most. He bashed his fist into the wall over and over, screaming, "What has happened to me?"

There was no answer, and not a single rat scurried. He used to be somebody important, but then the Vee-Man ruined it all. He had to kill him to make things right. He remembered the men back at the stables. The place where it all began. Where the beast had mauled him. And then the underling had healed him, bringing him back less than a man. And what had those spiders done to him? The arachnamen, McKnight had called them. What part did they play in all this? *Mother.* Should he not seek her out? And there was another woman in his life. Significant. Meaningful. *Rayal.* Raven-haired and beautiful.

He hungered, grabbed a rat, and bit into it as it squealed. *Plecht!* He spit it out, wiping his mouth and staggering farther down the stairwell where a sewer grate awaited him. He ripped it from the ground and crawled back in. The sewers, as foul as they were, he could not smell. He washed the taste of rat from his mouth with a swish of wine. Traversing through the corridors, he managed to find his spot. A small cell with many jugs, some empty, some full. He took a seat by his stash, closed his eyes, and drank.

He remembered the boy saying that the Vee-Man was gone. If that was true, then what would he do? Where would he find him? If the Vee-Man wasn't in the city, then where? He was confused. Angry. Without purpose now.

A thought drifted into his mind. *Home.*

"I am a Royal. Am I not?" he said in his raspy tone.

He swallowed down another jug of wine and smashed it into the wall. From now on, he was going to walk like a Royal, talk like a Royal, and take whatever he wanted like a Royal. Rising to his feet, he strapped on the sharpest sword he could find in the hoard he had gathered. He filled two flasks of wine and slung them over his shoulder. He didn't need any more confusion. Why the wine helped, he could not explain, but it did, or so he thought. Without it, his mind was rubble.

"I'm going home," he said. "Whether they want me or not."

And back onto the streets he went, picking his way through the alleys, ignoring the desperate faces, and ready to fight anything that stood in his way. A mile into his journey, he forgot where he was going. *Vee-Man!*

Chapter 43

Everyone was frozen or screaming, aside from Melegal. *Move!* His swords, the Sisters, slipped from their sheaths in time enough to deflect a blow that would have split his skull. The underlings were quick and taunting, playing with him, the living shield between the underlings and the others.

"Defend yourselves, fools! They're killers!" he exclaimed, chopping his swords in the air as fast as he could, keeping the underlings at bay.

The dark creatures jangled his nerves. Lithe and fluid, rippling in muscle, with sharp teeth chomping the air, they fearlessly came at him. If they got him on the ground with their sharp claws, they'd rend him to pieces, if they didn't chop him to death with their small curved swords. *Clang!*

He parried one blow.

Clang!

Then another.

He was quicker and taller, but they were smaller and stronger, a better fit for close quarters.

Jubilee was still screaming.

"Shut up, Jubilee!" he yelled.

She didn't.

Clang! Clang! Clang! Slit!

A sword tip slashed through his shirt, cutting him under the arm. *Sheesh! Fast little monsters!* Already, Melegal's arms were tiring. The underlings were cunning and content in their efforts to wear him down. He needed help.

"Brak, have you a sword or not?" he shouted.

Brak remained huddled back in the corner with the women. *Sonvuvabish!* Even Melegal couldn't choke down his fear, but it wasn't his first *Fight or Die* moment, either. If he was going to do something, he was going to have to do it fast. *Think!*

The underlings chittered back and forth with each other and one of them broke off and dashed for the lantern, grabbed it, and tossed it to the ground. Everything went pitch black.

Melegal lunged, driving the tip of his sword into the last spot he saw the underling's chest a split second earlier. A ghastly hiss filled the air as he felt the sword tip plunge through muscle and bone. Clawed fingers ripped into the skin above his eyes. He cried out in pain when a metal blade whisked across his side, but he felt the wicked creature give and die under his blade.

Haze moaned out his name.

"Melegal … help!"

He heard a chop into flesh, chittering and screaming all bound together in commotion. In the dark, they were helpless while the underlings tore into them like weasels in a chicken house.

Panting for breath, blood dripping into his eyes, fighting the burning gash in his ribs, Melegal rummaged through his clothes.

There was a sick chopping sound coming from the corner, and the screams of the women were no more. *Haze!* Jittery fingers found the hidden pocket in his vest, the silk pouch within.

Glitch!

No, don't be dead!

He dropped the magic coin into his hand, letting the light spill out.

Melegal was dismayed. The blood. The wounds. The twitching. He was at a loss for words, his thin lips twitching.

Brak had the underling pinned up to the ceiling with its own sword. The dark blood was dripping on Brak's face. Haze and Jubilee were huddled together, but breathing. Brak was squinting, head turned away from the brilliant light.

"I think you got him, Brak," Melegal said, hustling over.

"Haze!" He grabbed her, shaking her quivering shoulders. "Are you hurt?"

She shook her head. Jubilee opened her mouth to speak but was cut off by Melegal's hand. He looked over his shoulder at the entrance. No underlings. "No more screaming, please."

He helped the women up.

"We need to go. Gather all the gear and supplies."

No one wasted any time.

"I'll get the food," Brak said, while Melegal was gathering the rectangular case he'd taken from the corner of Lord Almen's study.

"Uh, you do that, Brak," he said, turning around to look.

The mangled underling remained pinned to the ceiling.

Melegal sniffed a chuckle. "Seems you have some of your father in you after all, Brak. Well done."

Jubilee hugged Brak's legs. "You saved us."

"All right, enough of that. Let's go," Melegal ordered. "As Venir used to say, Brak, 'Where there's two underlings, there's a dozen more waiting.'"

"Slat," Haze said.

Melegal pulled his blade from the underling he'd killed. Its citrine eyes seemed more alive than dead. People always said it was best to burn them or cut their eyes out, but Venir said that wasn't the case. 'Just chop them up till they move no more, and you'll be fine,' Venir'd said. A bad feeling still hung with him, though. Bone was under attack, and for the first time in months he missed Venir.

"Hurry, we need to leave," he said, leading the way out the door.

It was dark, but Melegal allowed a little light from the coin when needed. He cupped his ears, expecting sounds of underlings. Nothing but the scurry of rats and dripping water. *Better make this fast.*

Jubilee's hiding spot beneath the city streets was adequate but not as far removed from the heart of the city as he'd like. Popping up into the streets now would leave them exposed to any soldiers or Watchmen who were looking for them. To be safe, they'd have to travel farther down below the city.

"It stinks down here," Haze commented, holding her shirt up over her nose.

"Life stinks," Melegal replied with a wry smile, reaching back and grabbing her hand, "you'd think you'd be used to it by now."

She squeezed his hand back. "I'm worried about my sisters, Me." She was still shaking. "I've never seen anything as scary as an underling before. I'm scared, and my sisters are probably guarding that Everwell. They'll die before they abandon that post."

"We can't fret that at the moment. Let's make it topside first. I've got another spot to roost. They'll be fine until then, I'm certain," he said, trying to reassure her.

Bish! All I need is another big mouth to feed. Melegal and his family of big bellied urchins. What you won't eat, they will.

Twisting and turning, Melegal quietly led them through a half mile of tunnels and stood at the threshold of an abandoned door. There were stairways all over the city like this, all part of a long failed infrastructure filled with catacombs. Melegal had learned much about it as he chased down the Slergs. It was another world: dark, dank and lonely. Most tunnels were caved in by dirt or heavy rubble, making it impossible to move farther down. Whole families resided there, the most desperate citizens Bone had to offer. Still, despite the sanctuary, not as many people haunted the tunnels as one might expect. He wasn't sure if that was because of the underlings or something else. He remembered the presence he'd sensed months earlier: powerful and evil, unlike anything he'd ever known. Perhaps that's what kept it purged of more life.

"Put on your cowls," he said, making his way through the door and up the stairs.

One by one, they went by him, up the stairs on heavy legs. Using the coin's light, Melegal took one last look down the tunnels. The bright beam cut through the muck and slime covered walls, giving it an odd radiant shine. He exhaled through his pursed lips. *Ah …*

"Where are we going?" Jubilee asked, eyes bright and curious beneath her cowl.

"Be quiet, and you'll soon find out."

The southern part of the city was humming with activity. Crowds of people were pressed down the main street towards the gate. There was talk of nothing but underlings, unexplainable deaths and misery.

Perfect.

Melegal led them to the barn, taking the side entrance, avoiding all the traffic at the other barns where Royal soldiers were preparing horses. There was shouting, ordering and hollering from the barns next door, but this barn was still quiet and abandoned near the south entrance of the wall. He looked up into the rafters and saw the rope he'd used to kill McKnight. It was eerie.

"You sure didn't do a very good job avoiding the stink," Haze said. "Why would you bring us here, anyway?"

He opened the small door that was Quickster and Chongo's stable and ducked inside. No Quickster. That wasn't a good sign. The little bit of hope he had fled. Maybe they'd taken off.

"Now what?" Jubilee said, plopping down in a bed of hay.

"We wait," he said, closing the small door.

Jubilee and Haze both pulled the cowls from their faces, saying, "How long?"

At least Brak was quiet. The big man moaned like a wounded cow and sank to his knees, holding his belly. His fingers were covered in blood. How had Melegal missed that wound?

"Brak! Brak!" Jubilee jumped and pulled the cowl from his face. His face was grey and pasty, and his eyes fluttered up in his head.

Melegal braced himself behind the man to keep him from falling.

Brak was panting. "It's all right, Jubilee. You … you'll be better off without me. M-More food that way. S-so ssssad, dying and st-still being hungry."

"Don't wail, Slerg," Melegal hissed in warning, "or we'll all be dead as well."

He lowered Brak into the hay and ripped off the man's dirty shirt. The wound was deep and fatal. How had the man made it this far? It didn't seem possible. Brak might be a thick skinned slow bleeder, but time was running out. He looked at Haze, who only had a haunting look in her eyes as she shook her head. The son of Venir was a goner.

CHAPTER 44

"VENIR CALLS HIS HAND-AND-A-HALF AXE Brool. It's the deadliest weapon of all. I saw him chop an underling in two with it... more than once. One time, he chopped off a forest mage's head and batted it down the path. It was the funniest thing I ever saw, in a weird sort of way. I'll never forget that." Georgio slapped his knee. "And those Forest Magi won't, either; I'm certain."

The young man kept rambling, and she let him go. I was good to be in the presence of someone more cheerful than dour for a change. But Trinos's mind was racing, recalling what she knew about the sack, the tool she'd created to keep Bish balanced between good and evil. She rubbed her arms and shoulders. An unnatural chill was in the air, raising goose bumps on her arms as a stiff breeze tangled her hair.

"And the helm. It can heal him. Brought him back from the dead—at least I think he was dead—at least once. I saw it for myself."

Trinos wouldn't have thought she'd let such an important detail slip her mind. But it had. In her own crude way, she'd put it upon one man, one person at a time, to use a mystic power that would sway the balance back and forth forever and ever. What a charge that would put a person through, handling such awesome power. Yet, it seemed to do its job. And here sat a young man who'd witnessed it in action.

"Melegal was there. I swore he was crying over my almost dying, but he'd have sworn it was sweat. He's still mean, though. Lefty was there, too, along with Mood and Chongo," Georgio's voice trailed off. He had a saddened look on his face.

"What is it, Georgio? What's wrong?" she asked.

"Ah ... nothing."

"No, please tell me."

"My friend Lefty, the halfling I told you about, the one with sweaty feet."

She giggled and nodded. It was another one of the touches from her creation she'd forgotten about.

"He caught up with another one named Master Gillem." Georgio's face bunched up. "Turned him rotten, that halfling did. Always lying and stealing. And no one said a thing about it but me. They were all stupid to it or something. Ah, he acts happy, but I know he's not. Just a miserable little halfling."

"You really care about your friends, don't you?"

"Sure, I guess."

"Georgio, I care about people, too. Perhaps we can bring them all here, and I can help you keep them out of trouble."

Georgio looked around, frowning.

"I don't think Venir would like it here. He likes the Octopus and drinking the nasty tasting Grog. Lefty might like to come back, though, but I don't see how that's possible."

"Ahem," a voice interrupted. It was Corrin, holding his hat to his chest.

"Yes, Corrin?" she said.

"Trinos, ah … well, the people are worried about the underlings. They think we need some … er … fortifications. Some are even talking about leaving, but I don't let them. I tell them if they go, they can't ever come back," he finished with a firm nod.

"Corrin, must you always be so harsh? They are just frightened."

"Yes, I fear I must be," he said with a bow, "unless you say otherwise. And, those men, Mikkel and Billip, well, they're getting frisky with the women."

"And how do you know this?" she said, closing her eyes and raising her face to the sun.

"I can't find any of them, aside from the new boy, Nikkel. He's working with the others, as well should be this one." He tipped his chin at Georgio.

Trinos huffed as she rose. There were many things to consider now that she'd become involved. The people needed protection. They also needed self-control. Georgio, who she liked very much, wanted to leave rather than stay within her sanctuary, and Corrin was nothing but a worry wart. It was a wonder that her world managed to keep it all together, yet it did, and somewhere on Bish, a man named Venir unknowingly had that responsibility now. It didn't seem fair.

"I must leave you momentarily. Get along and behave, Corrin. And Georgio, I hope you're still here when I return."

Georgio was wiping his clammy hands on his trousers, admiring Trinos's beautiful face and tranquil speech, and then she was gone as if she wasn't ever there.

"Huh?"

He looked at Corrin, and Corrin looked at him, both looking around. He'd never seen anyone disappear like that.

"I'll be. Not again!" Corrin said, wringing his hat. "Why did she just do that for?"

"She said she'd be back," Georgio added.

"Sure, and the last time she did that she was gone more than a week. And that's no picnic when these people have to survive without her. They get antsy. And with the talk of all the underlings, it'll be much worse than the last time."

Georgio didn't know what to say. It seemed Corrin had his hands full as he stomped his feet, hands on hips and twirled around. It couldn't be that bad, though.

"We can help, Corrin."

"Who, you and those leg chasing louts? I'd rather you didn't bother. It'll only make things worse. If anyone asks, you don't know anything about Trinos. She often comes and goes. Pah!" Corrin spat on the ground and started walking away, "Just stay out of my way and keep your mouth closed. Blasted responsibility. It used to be so much easier: killing them rather than taking care of them."

All Georgio wanted to do was go and find Venir. He needed to find Billip and Mikkel and convince them it was time to go. As he walked around the District, the only person he could find was Nikkel, who was pushing a load of stones with a wheelbarrow.

"Do you know where your father is?" Georgio asked.

Nikkel shrugged his broad shoulders. It was clear he was growing into a sizable frame like his father. "No, why?"

"I want to get out of here."

"So, go already," Nikkel suggested. "You're a man, aren't you? You can do whatever you want to. Me, I have to do what my father says when he's around, but not when he's not."

Father! With all the commotion, Georgio had forgotten about his own family that resided south of the Red Clay Forest. He wanted to check on them as well.

"Tell Mikkel and Billip I'm heading home, to the Red Clay Village."

"Don't be stupid!" Nikkel said, tossing a large stone from the cart. "Underlings are as thick as a hive of bees out there. Besides, last I heard, the Red Clay Village was gone. Even if your family survived, they wouldn't still be there now."

Georgio fell down on his butt. Nikkel's words stunned him. In all these months, he'd given little thought to his family at all. And now, for all he knew they were dead. He'd given little consideration to them before. All this time, he'd been more worried about Venir than his own family. What kind of son did that?

"You aren't going to cry, are you?" Nikkel said, sitting down by his side. "Father says crying's for women and scrawny little men. He also says 'You're safer dead than alive in this world.'"

"What in Bish is that supposed to mean?" Georgio said, wiping his eyes.

"I don't know. It just seemed like the right thing to say about now," Nikkel stretched back up and resumed unloading the wheel barrow. "Want to help?"

Georgio missed his family. He wanted to see them so bad right now. He wanted to find Venir as well. Mikkel and Billip, as well meaning as they were, weren't the most reliable. And Trinos, as captivating as she might be, could certainly handle herself. Venir had said, 'If you want to be a man, act like a man. If you can't take care of yourself, how do you expect to take care of others?'

Georgio got up and said, "No. I'm getting out of Bone."

Chapter 45

"WILL YOU GET DOWN?" DARLENE said as she settled her wide hips behind the rocks. "Please?"

Scorch didn't feel the need to do any such thing. Why would he bother to hide from anything? Still, he didn't want to ruin all the woman's excitement by not participating. As Darlene had told him on the trail, 'It's not sportsmanlike.' He huddled by her side, watching her beady eyes shift back and forth under her uni-brow.

"Good," she breathed through her puffy lips, "just be still and quiet while I sort this out."

Scorch locked his fingers behind his head, lay down and closed his eyes. He'd gotten used to this. Darlene was a devoted hunter. She'd killed a boar, a hawk, and a pair of rather large horned rabbits. She'd convinced him she was quite the fisherman, too. Her pale brown eyes were always filled with energy as she tirelessly skinned the bloody meat from the bones. She was truly content with her role in the world, even though the meat she cooked wasn't particularly good.

"Scorch," she said in a harsh whisper as she nudged him.

He popped open his eye and looked at her. It was hot, just like any other day, but Darlene's head was always bone dry. Now, beads of sweat adorned it like rain, and her tanned cheeks were flushed. He rolled over to his belly and peeked over the rocks.

"Hmmm …" he said.

Over a hundred yards below their rocky perch, a squad of small, well-armed grey skinned people were digging holes in the outback ground. They weren't human, but the frightened screams of their prisoners were. Scorch rolled onto his back and closed his eyes. He could feel Darlene's uncertain rustlings at his side.

"Er .. well … um … Scorch … uh, I think those are underlings. What do we do?"

He could sense her heart pounding inside her chest and the fear of the unknown in her sweat. But that wasn't all.

He spoke in a calm and reassuring voice, saying, "We are safe here, Darlene. No worries at all. Just keep an eye on them, and when the moment is right, we will go."

"I guess you're right," she replied, her voice more steady than before. "You're safe with me... Yet," she said, sitting down beside him.

He could feel the intensity of her eyes on him. He re-opened his eye.

"Yet?"

"Um … you see, I can't just sit and watch those people die. It wouldn't be right."

"Why not?"

"Why not!" She grabbed his clothes. "Underlings are evil. All they do is kill people. They torture and mutilate them. I can't just sit here and not do anything. It wouldn't be right."

He propped himself up on his elbows. "But what makes you think those people need saving, and why would you put yourself in peril? You've known bad people, like your husband and such sorts. What if they're just as bad as them?"

"It doesn't matter if they're good or bad." She pulled an arrow from her quiver and loaded her bow. "They're men, not underlings." She stepped over Scorch and took a step down the hill, looking back at Scorch with a smile. "Besides, I've always wanted to kill an underling before I die. If I don't make it back, I'd appreciate it if you buried me instead of them."

Scorch found himself perplexed as he watched her go. The woman, durable and crafty as she might be, didn't stand the remotest of chances. And the men and women prisoners, though not as bad as some people could be, he sensed were hardly worth saving at all. Still, the hearts of the underlings were unlike anything he'd ever encountered. The things they did and were capable of.

Below, as silent as a deer, Darlene had closed within fifty yards of the underlings when she let the first arrow fly. It sailed true, catching a shoveling underling in the throat and knocking it into the grave. The next arrow caught an underling in the chest, piercing through its mailed armor. The black creatures scurried up the hill now, zeroing in on the doomed woman.

Scorch rose to his feet, shaking his head. Darlene was terrified, but she kept on shooting when most people would have fled. Her next arrow buried itself in a tree, and the following in an underling skull. He had to admit she was pretty good with that bow, but her wisdom lacked the same accuracy.

Now, the human prisoners were on the run. *Good for them. She's spared them momentarily from their agony.* At least she'd given them a few more moments of freedom and the hope for escape. But Darlene's daring was only seconds from coming to a chilling end. Once the underlings got a hold of her, they'd rip her to pieces.

Scorch sighed. Was she brave or foolish? If she'd stayed with him, no harm would have come to her. He could have given her anything she needed, just about. So he stood in contemplation, wondering if he'd grant her request to bury her or not.

CHAPTER 46

SHARDS OF LIGHTNING BLASTED A pair of underlings that were crawling from the fiery scene. Their bodies sizzled and popped as muscle was charred to a crisp on their bones. The smell was as malodorous as Fogle had ever experienced, so he held his nose under his cloak. The underlings, more than twelve of them, were nothing but remains.

Boon's eyes were filled with energy; his arms were draped over his head, fingertips crackling with power. He was a man possessed, standing in the middle of a smoldering hole on a mission to destroy every black thing that tried to crawl out.

Fogle held a spell on the tip of his tongue, eyeing the ridges and the sky. If there were more underlings about, they would come, unless they were scared. He led his horse by the burning trees and smoking bodies on a direct path for Boon. A moment later, the old man's eyes returned to normal.

Boon took a deep draw in through his nose and said, "Ah, there's nothing quite like the smell of roasting underling in the morning, is there?"

Fogle didn't know if it was a question or not. He didn't know whether to be upset or glad. But he didn't hold back the words on his tongue.

"At least if the giants and underlings are trying to find us, they know where to look."

"I hope so. I'm just getting warmed up," Boon said, trying to shake the radiant wisps of energy from his hand. "Oooh, that felt so good."

"Do it again!" Barton said, stomping the remains of an underling to ash. "Smelly. But bad things always smelly." Barton held his nose, stomping another and another.

Fogle grabbed Boon by his robes and said, "Did you even take a second to think that you could have hurt Cass or Chongo? You could have scorched them as well!"

Boon scratched the thinning white hairs on his head and replied, "Well, no, but I wasn't trying to destroy them. I sent my Scout to destroy the underlings ... not them."

"How could you know if they were engaged with them or not?" he said.

Boon grabbed his wrist. The old man had a grip of iron that Fogle struggled to twist away from, hurting his arm in the process.

Boon then said, "Instinct, Grandson. You worry too much. If they wish to run off, let them. We'll catch up ... eventually. Barton!"

Barton had pulled a pine tree from the ground and begun sweeping the underlings up. "What, Boon?"

"Do you smell anything?"

Barton scratched is head. "Huh?"

"Do you smell anything?"

The giant took a long snort through his nose.

"Just underlings. Dead ones," he said, brushing more of the bodies aside.

"No other giants, then?" Boon asked.

Barton didn't say anything as he swept more piles into the flame, stirring up the dust.

Fogle caught a mouthful of the tiny debris.

"Barton! Quit that, will you?" He shot a look a Boon. "Stop him, will you? He's your child, not mine!"

"Oh, you'll be fine." Boon hopped off his horse, stuck his hand into the skull of an underling, and pulled out its eyes. He rubbed the soot covered eyes on his sleeve. A dark blue color was underneath. Boon's face crinkled up when he twitched the marble like objects in his fingers. "Eh, just hunters, it seems. Hardly any magic in them at all." He tossed them into Barton's fire.

Fogle spat the grit from his mouth and asked, "Do they really have magic in them?"

"Finally, a question worthy of my attention," Boon said, taking a seat on the ground. "Just wait a second. We can't just be sitting around. We may be downwind from the north, but I'm certain the south can smell us coming by now."

"Oh, even if they do, they'll proceed with caution. We have a giant, after all. Even underlings are unsettled by giants, being so small and all. Plus, I'm tired. That took a bit more out of me than expected."

"We need to keep moving. It's risky to stay in this spot too long."

"I need rest!" Boon huffed. "Oh, if it makes you feel any better, I'll procure some additional security. Barton!" The giant swept with a mind of his own.

"BARTON!" Boon tried again.

Barton stopped and turned. His face was scrunched, and his head cocked as he slung a tree onto his shoulder.

"Yes, Boon Wizard."

"Will you be so kind as to keep watch on the south side of the fire? It's possible more underlings will come, and I'd like to be prepared."

Barton started tearing the branches from the tree he carried with his bare hands. Fogle felt miniscule in the presence of the giant's raw strength and power. *How did we ever overcome giants even bigger than he?* He felt a small amount of pride realizing he'd pulled off the incredible.

"Yes, Grandson, they are big and powerful on the outside, but it's better to be big and powerful on the inside."

Fogle combed his fingers through his hair. He realized it had never been so long before. Not even when he was a boy. "What's he doing to that tree?"

"Barton!" Boon yelled up at the towering figure, "What are you doing with that tree?"

With his good eye, Barton looked at them both like they were stupid, and said, "I'm making a club so I can smash the underlings." He slapped the club into the meaty palm of his hand and disappeared through the smoke.

"Feel safer now?"

Fogle sat down and replied, "Actually, I do."

"Good then. Now, what was your question?" Boon looked up into the sky. "Yes, yes the underlings' eyes. I'll tell you all about them. Of course, if you'd read all of my spellbook, most of it you'd know."

Fogle pitched a stick over into the fire. He'd always been reluctant to delve into the works of his grandfather, seeing how he believed, as did the rest of the City of Three, that Boon had gone mad. How could a madman be a great wizard? But even in his own young age, he knew that the dynamic power of magic could erode the mind. It seemed improbable that it could happen to him, so he'd considered such accounts weakness. Yet, here was his grandfather, quirky but in control. He sensed he was in the presence of the most powerful wizard he'd ever known. And for the first time in his life, he decided he would listen. The way things were going, he could stand to learn a thing or two.

"Not all underlings use magic, but they have it. Some can use it, some can't. Those we just killed were hunters. I'd need a dozen pairs of their eyes at least to cast the simplest of spells."

"They hold power?" Fogle asked.

"They can give you a charge if you know how to use it. But you don't want to carry too many of those eyes around." Boon said.

"How come?"

"They're heavy. Like rocks or gemstones. No, it's best to burn them like the rest. The underlings hate that. Seeing their kin burned. It makes them extra mad, and they're mad enough at men already."

Fogle wasn't even going to ask why that was. Even if Boon somehow knew the answer, he was pretty sure he wasn't ready to know. He had enough on his plate already.

"But, if you kill an underling mage, well, then you have some power. For the strangest reason, underlings leave power in their eyes. I collected them like a dwarf hoarding gold." Boon's fingers tickled the air. "Oh how I enjoyed turning their own power against them. Delicious," he said, licking his mustache.

Fogle felt a prickling sensation on his neck.

"What color eyes did you collect?"

"Now, there were all sorts. Of course, underlings, whether it be fighters or magic users, still have a variety of color. But the magic users tend to be the lighter shades than the others. I've seen many colors, some like rubies, others like sapphires, peridots, or an odd violet quartz in color. The oddest I ever came across was rose-colored pink. You ever seen a pink gemstone before?"

"No."

"A fascinating thing—"

"Boon, have you ever seen golden-eyed underling eyes before?"

His grandfather looked like he'd swallowed a bug.

"Aye …" he said with a loathing sound under his breath, "and silver, too."

Fogle felt a chill race up and down his spine. He and his grandfather had more in common than they'd realized.

Boon's eyes were intent, and his voice had a dangerous tone. "Tell me what you know, Grandson."

Fogle grabbed his grandfather by the arm and said, "Why don't I show you instead?"

Boon grunted, a wry smile coming to his lips.

"I like this way of thinking. So be it then, Fogle. Take my mind away."

It was a mind grumble of a different sort. Two willing minds coming together with no concern or conflict, only the sharing of knowledge. The trick was keeping your most closely guarded secrets from coming loose, as it was difficult for invading minds to fight their natural tendency to pry. Muttering, Fogle opened the doorway, and Boon quickly stepped through.

Boon tugged at his mind, strong but not forceful. Fogle shoved back, bringing forth a hollow chuckle. *Show me.* There they stood, two apparitions sharing one mind, one memory of a cataclysmic sort. Fogle showed him the battle he'd shared with Venir and the silver and golden eyed underlings.

Ha! Boon exclaimed. *It cannot be. Catten and Verbard!*

Fogle could feel his grandfather's respect for him building.

A grumble! With the most powerful of underling Lords, and you live?

Barely, Grandfather.

Fogle showed him the rest. The grave of boulders. The underling's corpse. The battle with the earth elemental and the exchange of the eyes for the spellbook.

Fogle felt a tremor of anger rippling through his mind. There was a brilliant flash of light, and his mind was again his own.

Boon punched him hard in the arm.

"Grandson, I cannot tell whether I want to hug you or *kill* you!"

The word kill stung, and the dark look in Boon's eye didn't leave him feeling very comfortable.

"Kill me? Why?" he asked, rising to his feet, readying a defensive spell on his tongue.

Boon swallowed hard before he opened his mouth to speak.

"OOOOOOOW!" Barton cried out from beyond the smoking crater.

Bang! Bang! Womp!

"What now?" All he wanted to do was track down Cass, and now something else had to happen. Fogle dashed towards the sound of the commotion with Boon on his heels. Emerging from the trees, he spied Barton with one hand full of an underling and the other swatting the club.

Wham!

Barton pulverized the underling into a greasy black smear. The bones of the other one cracked in his mighty grip before Barton bit its head off and spit it into the oncoming horde.

Fogle lost his breath. He'd never seen so many underlings before. They were coming from up one side of the ravine and down the other. If those underlings were alive, were Cass and Chongo dead? He felt the strong hand of Boon squeezing his arm.

"Whatever you used to save yourself from the gold and silver eyed underlings, you better unleash it now, Grandson!"

With so many underlings, Fogle didn't even know where to begin. *Cass!*

CHAPTER 47

"COME ON THEN, RABBITS!" VENIR said, rising to his full height, staring down on the men. "The first one up will be the first one down!" He whirled his axe around his body. "Any takers?"

The scouts stopped their advance, but the dogs howled on.

"Let your mangy curs loose, you raggedy man! I've not eaten in days!"

The soldier yanked back on his dogs' chains. They fell silent.

Venir had their attention. Their eyes passed back and forth between one another. Even the large part-orc slid a half-step back.

"What! I'd expect better from Royal soldiers. Is there not a valiant one among you?"

He hopped off the rocks. The small band shifted back.

"What about you, Orc? A big one, I see. Looks like your mother was diddled by trolls, I'd say!"

The orcen man's eyes darkened, his canine teeth flashed, but not a muscle moved.

Venir chopped Brool back and forth, low strokes beneath his knees that trimmed the foliage like wheat.

"Awfully quiet for an orc. I'm used to more talk and bravado."

The leader, tall and rangy, made a quick nod with his head. His men, aside from the half-orc before him, began to spread out. Venir's veins were charged with energy as they pulsated under his skin. These men, shady in movement and décor, disturbed him.

"Who are you, Man?" the leader spoke up, lowering his sword.

"Man? Aye, indeed, I am a man! I'm not some slug that crawled from the sewage to cavort with underlings. I'm a killer of such things, along with their cohorts, such as you."

The leader stuck his bastard sword in the ground and said, "You have us wrong. We are not cavorters but slaves. We'd just as well see these vermin skinned the same as you. But we've over a hundred men—"

"And orcs," the orc said.

The leader nodded up the hill and continued, "shackled, starving and half-dead. Mostly depraved. It's better to serve moving on two legs than serve with none at all. There are many of our brethren living with less than that already."

Venir sensed some truth in the man's words. But he was going to need more than that before he lowered his blade.

"Tell me then, Soldier, how many underlings hold that Outpost?" Venir asked.

"Oh, well, now I can't readily answer that, nor my colleagues. Such talk would be treasonous and put all of our heads at the mercy of our masters. No, you over-sized metal shade. I'd rather die that let you be privy to that." The leader pulled his sword from the ground and flicked the edge of the blade. "And at this point, a meaningful death in combat is vastly more preferable than facing the consequences of failure."

Treason! How could any man stand to be accused of treason by an underling? Venir had been deceived before by Jarla. The woman consorted with them. She'd been ready to turn him over to them and collect a bounty they had on his head. It was beyond him how any man could serve an underling, willingly or even unwillingly. Certainly death would be preferred. His knuckles whitened on Brool's shaft, his blood bristled, and the air became hot and stale. The shadow of death hung in the air. The men spread farther apart, blades ready, creeping in.

"Why don't you drop the axe and come quietly, Fool? You cannot defeat as all," the orc said, stepping up the hill.

"Maybe, but I'm certainly going to kill you," Venir said, pointing Brool's spike at the part orc's chest. .

Venir was never comfortable killing men, no matter how rotten they were. It was something he sought to avoid over the years. But sometimes, it couldn't be avoided. He hadn't hesitated to kill the brute Baltor; he'd sensed the evil. But with this group, he was uncertain. He couldn't just kill every man he didn't trust, or like, for that matter.

"Turn the dogs loose," the leader ordered.

Bish! And killing dogs was another issue. He was used to Chongo settling such matters. He shifted his feet down into the dirt.

The orc raised his arm and said in his rough voice, "Perhaps a challenge then, Stranger?"

"No, I like the odds I have at the moment, and I don't gamble with swine."

The orc was buying time. Not only for himself but for all of them. The men, as rugged as they appeared, now lacked the overbearing fortitude of being Royal soldiers.

The orc laughed, his brown teeth breaking into a grin.

"Heh-heh. You've got a sharp tongue for a man. Brassy as a lantern. But a fight is not what I had in mind."

"True," the leader interjected. "Stranger, we've no quarrel with the murderer of our tormentors, but our predicament is dire." He held a hand up. A sign of peace and welcome for some. "I don't want to die any more than my men, or you, for that matter. Perhaps we can sort this out." The soldier pointed up the hill towards the outpost. "And, time is short. The shriekers alerted more than us and them." He chopped a sapling down. "We're only the first patrol. There will be more, and they'll be in no mood to parlay."

Venir didn't sense any such thing, however. The soldiers were still making their way up the hill. The dogs' necks were straining on the leash, claws digging up the loose soil. The threat wasn't there. But something about the man's body language wasn't right. The leader was nervous, more desperate than a moment before.

"I'm beginning to think there are not so many up there as you say. Over a hundred Royals, you say, prisoners? I'll tell you what. How about you name me some names?"

The leader rubbed his leather gauntlet under his chin and said, "How about I start with mine first, then?"

"No, I don't know you, but I've known men inside."

"I see, so you were a soldier like us once?"

"No, nothing like you."

"A mercenary then?"

"A hunter. Now, let me hear some names." He waved his axe in the air. "I'm getting antsy."

The leader said nothing at first, then he began, "Well, it seems unlikely your sort of character would have known any of those honorable men. Perhaps if you removed your garish helmet, one of us would know you?"

"If you knew me, you'd have recognized me already," Venir said, stepping back up the hill.

His mind was beginning to catch up with his brawn. For all he knew, these men only wore the uniforms of the Royals. Only the leader, aside from the orc, offered much talk. At first, he'd thought they might be holdovers from the Brigand Army, but he would've recognized them. They didn't carry themselves with the gaits of soldiers, either. Their movement was not refined or disciplined. Even the dogs seemed more savage than trained. Who in Bish were these men?

"A challenge, Stranger?" the orc said again, sheathing his blades. "You and I."

Venir looked at the leader and said, "I thought you said more would be coming. It seems you have more time than you bargained for." He hefted his axe back over his shoulder. "What exactly did you have in mind, Orc?"

At the moment, Venir didn't have many options. Whoever was running the Outpost would be alerted to his presence soon enough. He seethed inside. His plan had been to slip past the underlings like a ghost. He'd assumed only underlings would be there, but there were humans and orcs, too, the occupants of the Outpost, men and underlings, and only Bish knew what else. The smart thing to do would be to abandon his plan, but then what would Jans's Royal Riders do? It was times like this he could have used a mind like Melegal's. He could hear the rogue's voice in his mind, saying, *Think first, Brute! Fight as the last resort. Fighting only increases your chances of getting killed. The gray matter is what counts, not the red meat that hides your bones.*

"First the terms. I win, you come quietly. You win, you go quietly," the orc said.

Venir countered, saying, "I win, I go in peace and you tell me all that I want to know about what lies within the fort. After that, I'll be on my way."

"Huh," the leader said. "Why you'd care to know is beyond me. Only death and misery are in there. Hmmmm … I think I see. You're looking for someone, aren't you?"

Venir didn't reply.

The leader added, "I'll have my men keep an eye on things up the ravine. Far enough away to only use the whistle call. That way, you don't need to be concerned with any interference. My word on that and my men's as well. Men?"

The other soldiers nodded.

"It seems like a risk. Odd, foolish, even for an orc," Venir said. "Makes me wonder if your situation is as precarious as you say."

"Heh … well, Stranger, the truth is I'm bored. We all are. Might as well make things as interesting as I can in the meantime. You win, it's on us, or me rather. I win, I'm taking you up this hill to suffer with the rest of us." The orc dropped his sword belt to the ground and pitched away a few knives. He unbuckled the straps of his leather hauberk and slipped it from his shoulders. The part-orc was knotted with muscle, but his ruddy skin was bare. He cracked his neck in his hands and smiled, a large canine popping up from the bottom of his mouth.

"Don't get his hopes up," the leader said, leading the other soldiers away. "He'll suffer far more greatly than us. He killed two underlings, remember. There will be a price for that. A leg for each perhaps, but maybe just his ears or eyes. One never knows with them. Fiends."

It was a surreal situation. A subtle churning in his gut made him think of his time in the mist, the unnatural atmosphere that had cloaked him like a blanket. At some point in the mist, he'd become used to what was expected, but now he wasn't certain what to expect at all. *I should just run.* But where? There was nowhere to go, and a host of men depended on him, including Slim. He had to play things out, wait and see where they went. Isn't that what Melegal would do? Perhaps when he won, he could get more information from them.

He shuffled up the hill alongside the rocks, where he'd spied on the soldiers before.

"Where are you going, Stranger?" the half-orc said, eyeing him with intent.

Venir held his axe out and said, "Just disposing of my gear. You don't want it too close. I might get tempted to jam it down your throat."

"Hah! Take that scale dress off, as well. What is that, Dwarven?"

Venir nodded.

"Hmmm," the orc rubbed his chin, "looks like it'd fit me just fine. Can I have claim to it if you don't survive... the hill?"

Venir unbuckled the side straps, slid it off, and tossed it to the ground in front of the orc.

"If I die this day, it's yours."

The orc's eyes filled with glee as he eyed the scale like a mound of treasure. As he did, behind the rock and out of sight, Venir slipped his helm, axe and shield into the sack and stuffed it into his pack.

When the orc turned his attention back to him, he grunted.

"Not often do I see another as big as me, Stranger. Or one so ugly, either. That yellow hair of yours is considered a weakness among my race."

"And every aspect of your race, from your hair to your toes, is considered a weakness by ours," Venir said, combing his fingers through his beard before he put his hands on his hips. "So, Orc, what will the challenge be, then?"

The orcen soldier glanced up the ravine. The other soldiers were out of sight, but their rustlings could be heard. The orc held his long arms up and extended his fingers. They were a good bit longer than Venir's.

"I must say, I never thought I'd get another chance at this game. As soon as I saw you, I didn't want to fight, I want to beat you in a game of Mercy."

Venir would have laughed normally, but this orc wasn't going to be a push over. Besides, Mercy wasn't a challenge he'd ever done before, and it seemed that this orc had, judging by the grin on his ugly face. He looked at the insides of his hands, then rubbed his palms together.

"What are the rules?" he asked, stepping down the hill and coming face to face with the orc. "

"Very simple. First one to cry Mercy loses."

Venir eyed the wrists on the orc, which seemed twice as thick as his. *Not good.* None of it was. He was fully exposed. His plan had washed down the gutter, and there weren't any options available other than to fight or die. Of course, he hadn't had to volunteer to be there in the first place. What had he been thinking, "Do the right thing"? *Preposterous!* Yet, here he was.

He asked one final question before they locked fingers.

"Have you ever cried *Mercy* before, Orc?"

"Heh-heh-heh ... not even to an ogre."

CHAPTER 48

TAP. TAP. TAP. TAP. TAP. *Tap* …

Head down, shoulders aching, Lefty resigned himself to his duties. Jubbler had quieted, opting to pick the flecks of sawdust from his hair and eating it momentarily. The Quartermaster made his rounds back and forth, but at the moment he'd moved to the far end and was talking, having struck up a conversation with smugglers departing with goods from the dock.

Any plans he had of helping Kam and Erin were abandoned. He had to find a way out of this jam first, and that wasn't likely any time soon. Tapping with one hand, he toyed with the absidium chains that kept him shackled. He was the only one shackled on the dock. All the others were free. He wasn't sure why they worried about him so much. He was hardly a threat.

Rolling his wrist, he felt the metal bonds slip down past his wrist and onto his hand. He swore there was just enough room to slip his hand free. He jerked his elbow back. The chain constricted faster than thought, pinching deep into his hand, almost turning his fingers blue. His eyes started to water. It hurt.

"Whatcha doin'? Huh. Huh. I saw. I saw that. Bad chains. Huh. Absurduim. Huh. Seen 'em squeeze a head off … huh … before." Jubbler gawped at Lefty's hands and patted his own hands together.

"Go away, Jubbler," Lefty said with all the venom he had in his voice.

"Huh."

Whack! He crushed a nail head with his hammer. "I said … ah, never mind." *Whack! Whack! Whack!*

Perhaps that's what they wanted. To make him crazy. Erode his mind like they'd clearly done to Jubbler.

"Don't despair. Huh. Listen to your elders. Huh. I've been here longer … Huh … than you've lived. Huh. Many lifetimes. I know where the smoke is. Fire makes smoke. Huh. Smoke, smokey smoke." Jubbler diddled with his beard as his eyes drifted away. "Smoke. Smoke. Huh. Smoke. I like smoke. Huh. And chicken."

Lefty grabbed two nails and stuck them in his ear holes. It caught the eye of Jubbler, who cocked his head like a curious bird.

"Huh. Why you do that? Huh. Nails don't go there. Huh. Huh. Huh."

"Can you use a hammer, Jubbler?"

"Huh. Yes. Huh."

Lefty handed the dwarf his hammer and said, bowing down, "Would you be kind enough to drive these nails into my ears, so I don't have to listen to you anymore?"

There was no reply. Not a mumble, a grumble, a huh or a sigh. Just silence among the resounding sounds of hammers hammering. Lefty closed his eyes. He envisioned the jabbering Jubbler taking him up on it and whacking him upside the head. *I bet Melegal never would have thought of this.*

"Well," Lefty started, "what are you waiting for, Jubbler? Tack them in."

He felt two gentle hands remove the nails from his ears and heard a soft soprano voice say, "Master Gillem was proud of you, Lefty. It would be a shame to waste your brain. You're going to need it to save Erin and Kam."

"What is the meaning of this, Kam!" Palos's paunchy face was filled with fury. "Have you found a new hobby, polishing swords?" In three quick steps, he came across the room and backhanded her in the mouth. She spiraled to the floor.

"Apologies," she said through her split and bloody lip. "Palos, I was only curious—"

Smack!

He hit her again.

"Silence, you red-headed heifer! Do you take me for a fool?" He grabbed her under the chin and leered into her eyes. "I know you've been trying to escape. I know you plot in your mind. You aren't the first whore to reject my musings."

"I'm sure I won't be the last either—*ulp!*"

Palos shoved her to the floor, both hands wrapped around her neck, squeezing her. She could have bit her tongue, but she couldn't take it anymore. The abuse and humiliation had finally snapped her cord. She forced the words out. "Kill me then, Coward!"

Palos's face became darker.

"Oh no, my pretty. You'll not escape life so easily. Suffer you shall. Suffer you and your baby like you never suffered before! Thorn!"

"Yes Prince Palos," the tall man said, stepping into view.

"I'm here as well, Prince," Diller said, arriving on the other side. "The door is secured."

Kam couldn't muster a spell. The pressure on her neck was too much. What had she gotten herself into? The sword. The sword of Zorth had caused this. *Cursed thing!* She strained against her captor.

"She struggles. Always struggles. I tire of that." Palos kept her pinned with one hand and brushed his hair from his eyes. "It seems she was not broken entirely, as I suspected. Too much fight in the lass." His eyes drifted back towards the sword for a moment then back on her. A blank look came on his face. "What did you possibly think you could accomplish with that sword? Put her in the chair, men, and hold her still."

Diller grabbed her by the hair and jerked her up from the ground. Thorn stuffed the chair beneath her legs, bringing a sharp pain to the backs of her knees. Both men leered at her like hungry dogs as they held her down. Diller winked. *Pig.* But at least she could move her mouth now and wriggle her fingers, too. *Concentrate.*

Palos kicked the sword along the floor with his toe, a milder tone in his voice.

"It's magic. The Sword of Zorth." He looked back at her and smiled, hands clasped behind his back. "One of my most prized possessions, actually. Would you like to hear how I acquired it?"

"No." *I want to kill you!*

Diller grabbed her hair and pulled her face up towards Palos.

"It's quite interesting, really." Palos leaned back on the table. "And you might not believe this, but I came across it honestly."

"Pfft," Kam stated. She wasn't going to believe a word he said. Not that it mattered. She wanted to summon something, but his eyes were all over her. *Stop looking at me.* She only needed a few seconds was all. Why hadn't she prepared a spell earlier?

"It was given to me by my father, a gift. As the story goes, Zorth was the founder of the City of Three. Yes, it was he who led the battle against the giants. It was he who subdued them with this, his magic blade. They yielded to him and his army, and in exchange for their lives, they built this city, which would explain why the towers are so tall and unique." Palos smacked his lips. "All of this talking has made me thirsty." He nodded at Thorn.

The man found a bottle and a half empty goblet, refilled it, and handed it over to Palos.

"Mmmm ... now, I must say, this wine is something. I could drink it all day."

Kam snarled, "You do drink it all day, Louse."

Palos wagged his finger at her.

"Oh Kam, you'd be wise to show more interest, because once this story ends, the genuine suffering of you and your child begins."

Kam couldn't fight the lump in her throat as her lips tightened. *I can't let this happen! He's a madman!*

Palos looked at Thorn and Diller, saying, "You see? You just have to know the right words to keep a woman quiet, men. Now, oh yes, where was I?"

Diller tugged at her hair.

"The sword, the giants and the towers. So, the wizards and the Royals wanted the giants to look up to them, not down. But the ruins outside the city show a different thing. Many towers were felled there, busted, broken and overgrown. You didn't know about that, did you?"

Diller and Thorn looked at one another, but Kam didn't say a thing.

"I've been there. Many secrets of the old ways lie hidden there as well as untold treasure, too. I've been there before and even spied a gem as big as the moons." Palos' eyes glossed over, and his hands were reaching out to grab something that wasn't there.

"What happened to the gem, Prince?" Diller asked.

"What kind was it?" Thorn added.

"A ruby as fiery as a dragon's breath. As bright as the daylight suns. Like an apparition, it appeared," his fingers tickled the air, "and like the wind, it was gone."

A strange silence fell on the room. Even Kam found herself captivated by his words. She shook it off.

"The Star of the Rising Suns," Kam murmured. "A bedtime story told to children, the same as giants, dragons and magic swords. Do you dogs wag your tails at everything he says?"

Diller cracked her in the mouth with his knuckles.

She glared up at him and spat a bloody tooth out, saying, "You'll pay for that!"

Diller drew his hand back again.

"Stop!" Palos held out his hand. "I've not finished my tale."

She'd had enough. There wasn't much she could take of this anymore. She had to do something and do it now. *Stay focused. You have to be smarter than these fools, Woman!*

"Oh, please do, Mighty Prince. I've nothing better to do, and your hounds are all ears. Perhaps you can add in the tale of the Dragon Clawed Throne or the Hive of Everwonder. Please spoil us with your tongue."

Diller pulled back on her hair, harder this time.

"Is that all you have, Diller? My daughter's stronger than that."

Diller turned red-faced.

"Palos, my Prince, must I stand for this?"

Kam stretched her fingers toward the small pocket in her robes.

"Be patient, Diller. You as well, Thorn. She'll be all yours after my story is done."

"What?" Kam exclaimed.

"You mean it, Prince?" Diller added.

Palos drained and tossed the goblet on the table.

"I've no need for a battered and toothless strumpet. I've a reputation to uphold. What would my men think if I was caught with her? But for you men, well, she's quite a prize, being a Royal."

"Palos, you Bastard! You mangy dog! YOU'LL PAY FOR THIS!"

He was laughing.

"And just think of when her daughter is fully grown, if I let her live that long. Ha-Ha-Ha. Now, where was I?"

Kam couldn't take it. She wasn't going to live with this a moment longer.

Diller leaned down in her face saying, "I told you that you'd be mine." He stroked her hair and tugged it, too.

She cringed. Biting her tongue wasn't an option anymore. She was going to get her fingers on those gems and let them have it. *Just do it!* Her fingertip touched the first stone.

" ... so, you say the tales are not true, Kam, but I'll have you know that I saw the very Star of the Rising Suns as well, and I'll make my trek back one day, much better prepared than last time. But that's not where I was going, however. No, the sword," he opened a drawer in the table, removed white cotton gloves, and put them on. "My father says it's not to be touched by human hands, well, skin rather. It could burn you to the touch."

Her fingers wrapped around one of the gems.

"Which I see is not the case," he said, looking at her, "at least for a woman. But magic has its own mind, all the same. The important part I wanted to mention was that this gift, the Sword of Zorth Morgwaggyn, was a gift to me from my father Palzor, who received it for services rendered to ..."

Kam had both stones between her knuckles, the magic surge tickled her nose.

"... your father, Lord Kamdroz."

"What?" she said as a glimmer of light twinkled inside her hands.

"She's got something!" Diller wrenched her wrist. Kam felt all her hope flee as the red stones clattered to the floor.

Chapter 49

"Is he dead?" Melegal asked.

Jubilee had tears streaming down her face. The child had seen enough death in the past few days. It was amazing she kept it together at all.

Haze wiped her bloody forearm across her head.

"He breathes, but the bleeding is only staunched, not stopped. Just stitched, and poorly at that. If he's bleeding inside as bad as he was on the outside, I don't think he can make it much longer."

All eyes were on Melegal. *What am I to do? I'm no healer … I'm a stealer.* Melegal couldn't ignore the feeling in his gut, however. He had to do something. He didn't want to, but felt compelled to. "Stop staring at me. I'm thinking." He stepped over into the corner and sat down. He'd stitched his fair share of wounds in his time, but nothing quite like this. It was just one of those things where you gave a man some water and let him bleed out and die. *Why me? I just want to leave this place.*

"You can make it, Brak," Jubilee was saying, over and over again.

The man's head seemed monstrous in her tiny lap.

Like a woman tending an ogre.

"We need water," Haze said. "I can fetch us some." She started to get up.

"No," Melegal said, rising to his feet. "I'll go. He needs the likes of you, not me."

As he made his way through the door, Jubilee said, "You will come back, won't you?"

"Of course he will," Haze said.

But Melegal didn't say a thing as he left. *Smart child. Even for a Slerg.*

Dreams. Nightmares. Most experience both. Brak only experienced the latter. He hung on the edge of an abyss, a great fire licking at his toes as he struggled to pull himself up. On his feet, a man hung, long and broad, a bearded face full of fire. It was Venir, his father, hanging on for his very life as he held on for his own. Brak had never felt such weight before, like a cart of heavy stones.

His father was screaming up at him, but he didn't understand the words. All he could do was try to hang on, his strength fading, the pain in his arms and neck excruciating. If only his father would let go, stop screaming, he could save himself. But he knew if he did, he would forever lose his face. He hung on. His father began to slip and fall. Still screaming at the top of his lungs.

The next barn was a stark contrast to the one he just left. It was a hive of activity. Horses were being led up and down the concourse. Royal soldiers were adorned in armor from head to toe. Commands and shouts rang out from one end to the other. *No City Watch, at least.*

Melegal threw a coarse blanket over his head, pinched it below his neck, stooped down, hunched his shoulders, and shuffled forward. *Eyes down, ears up!* From one stall to the other he went, doddering along with a discarded rake he found. All he needed to do was snatch a bucket, refill it in a water trough, and disappear as easily as he came. *Why am I suddenly responsible? He's not my bastard child.*

An urchin stumbled into his path, carrying a metal pail.

That will do. He grabbed it by the handle and said, "Child, is that your stall?"

"Let go of my pail, Hag. I'll be whipped if I stall," the boy said, trying to rip it away. He was quite strong.

"Nay, Child. I shall fetch it for you," Melegal suggested.

"Nay, Hag!"

"I'm no hag," he warned, ripping the pail free from the boy's grasp.

The boy opened his mouth wide. Melegal shoved a large silver talent in it.

"Taste that silver? Hush your mouth. Fetch another pail, and run along."

The boy had the strangest expression on his face as his eyes shifted back and forth. "Ulp." He swallowed the coin.

Melegal snorted. He'd have done the same back in those days. Royal urchins could not have coins, but it would serve him well.

"Go along now. My master's horse is thirsty," he said.

Ahead was a row of troughs where a few lathered-up horses drank. It would have been better to get water from an Everwell, but that was too far away. *What good is a bucket of water going to do, anyway? 'Keep the fever down,' they say. Pah, he'll be dead before I return.*

He waited a moment, along the outside of an abandoned stall. Two Royal soldiers chatted from horseback by the troughs. Four stable hands, men and boys, checked the fasteners on their saddles and harnesses. *Hurry up!*

"On good report, the underlings number in the thousands leagues south, outside the city walls. They say hundreds lie below," one soldier was saying.

"Thousands, you say? By my sources, there are tens of thousands and even more below," the other responded, slapping his comrade on the shoulder. "Ha Ha Ha! My, the tales grow taller all the time. I say we ride south into their belly and they'll never come this far north again. Black fiends. They fight like girls with steel and armor. High time we stopped toying with the brood. The pests are getting annoying. I've lost two of my finest house boys."

"Yes, I lost the same. I thought I was going to have to polish my own boots," the other soldier let out a laugh, "I've not done that since my training days."

The banter. It was that tireless banter that he'd grown accustomed to in his childhood, and he'd never grown sick of it. All the boots he'd shined until his arms were numb. And now, it seemed the soldiers weren't going to move. Their chatter continued.

I've got to move.

Melegal rambled over, a little hitch in his step, and dipped his pail in the water. The soldiers paused their conversation. He could feel their eyes on him as he withdrew the pail filled with water.

"Ahem," one of the soldiers said.

Melegal shuffled back.

"I don't think she heard you."

Why do they insist I'm a woman!

"A fragile thing."

"A husk with skin."

"Deaf. Mute. Rankled."

They were getting under his skin now. *Just go!*

He teetered away, turning his back to them.

"Perhaps it's an underling," one soldier said, leading his horse around and blocking his path. "Show me your face, Old One."

"My pail! My pail!" a little girl screeched. "That hag has stolen my urchin's pail!"

It would have been easier to fetch water in the Outland. *Of all the fool things!*

"Elizabeth," one of the soldiers said, chuckling, "Has your pail been stolen?"

Melegal kept his head down, shuffling his feet, trying to go around. *Seem confused. Sell it, Man, sell it!*

"Dullard!" Elizabeth snapped up at the soldier, "Of course I've been robbed. This hag has stolen my property, and my stable hand is now with a broken arm. Now, I'm shorthanded."

"I'll summon the Watch and have this one arrested," the soldier said, dismounting.

"I'll have the hag whipped now!" Elizabeth screamed.

Of all the ridiculous things. Whipped over this? A child no older than Jubilee, nonetheless.

"I think this matter is better served in the hands of the Watch," the soldier added, "and I'm surprised you are out with all the trouble of late. It's not safe—"

"Be silent, Cretin! I'll have you whipped as well. How dare you address me like your child? I am a Kling! And you are a soldier! A pawn to my whims. It is you who has to worry about the underlings, not I."

The air was ripe with tension. Melegal noticed the man's hand falling to his sword. *Split her skull. I would! Impudent Royals.*

"Elizabeth!" a familiar voice cried out. "Mind your tongue! You are creating a scene, as usual!"

"Stay out of this, Rayal! This old bitch stole my pail, and I'll have her head for that! And this soldier sneered at me! No man does that to a Kling and lives. Now give me my pail!" Elizabeth stormed over and wrapped her fingers on the handle.

Melegal held it tight in his grip as the girl, about as big as Jubilee, tugged away with all her strength.

"Give it to me!"

He let go.

Elizabeth lurched backward and tumbled onto her rear, the pail of water spilling all over her. Everyone fell silent as her face erupted in red rage, except Rayal, who was holding her belly and laughing.

Elizabeth pulled out a knife, raised it over her head, and charged.

"I'll kill you, Hag!"

Rayal caught the girl by the wrist and twisted the knife out of her hand.

"Enough of this, Elizabeth! You've gone too far. Men, apologies for my sister's trepidations. She gets carried away with her evil self!"

Elizabeth took the metal pail and swung it into Rayal's knees.

Bang!

"OW! Blast you, Little Fiend!"

Elizabeth ran away, screaming and pointing. "You still owe me a two-headed dog!"

So that's the one. Now what? He'd encountered Rayal before, briefly, and was certain that she would remember him. Rayal, another beauty, was unlike the typical Royals. Not only did she display strength, but grace and kindness as well. But what if she knew about the treachery at the castle? Melegal stepped around in his own private circle, showing he was uncertain where to go.

"Milady," one of the soldiers said. "Shall I send for the Watch? After all, she did, it seems, take a pail?"

"No, but I am curious why this one hides her face," she said, walking over, "and why she took the pail in the first place."

"Er … Milady, she could have a sickness, or a horrible face."

"A spy perhaps," the other soldier suggested.

Melegal swayed in place, looking down at her booted toes. Her perfume was incredible, just like the Lorda's. *I can't risk it.* He concentrated, sending a tingle through his mind.

"No," she said. "But I've run into the strangest people that shuffle around here in cowls and cloaks. You'd be surprised. Please, men, go about your business, I think I'll be fine. Thank you."

"As you wish," the men said, trotting away, their stable hands in tow.

Melegal let his mind ease.

She huffed. "Now, tell me, Old Woman, are you thirsty?"

Melegal didn't reply. *I can't tell her to sleep, run or look away. The first two would look odd, and the latter wouldn't be enough. Think!*

Rayal turned, picked up the pail, and handed it to him.

He grabbed it, shuffled over to the trough, and refilled it, then started to shuffle back the way he came. Eyes down, feet moving forward, not looking over his shoulder, he continued on. Rayal was right behind him. Melegal could hear not one set of footsteps, but three, trailing close behind him. *Drat! An Escort.*

"I'll be curious why this person is so desperate for water that they'd cross a Royal," she said under her breath. "And there's always something strange going on in that barn over there."

Just as he made his way over to the doorway that traversed between the barns, Rayal said, "Halt!"

Melegal kept going.

"Detective Melegal," she said again, "I suggest you stop."

His heart jumped a beat. *Not possible.* He kept going.

"Don't think to fool me; I'd recognize those delicate hands anywhere, especially those scars on your knuckles."

He didn't slow.

Her voice turned cold. "You are a wanted man, Detective. And with a word, I can have every soldier in these barns coming after you."

Mercy, is there no limit on my pursuers!

Chapter 50

THE UNDER-BISH. *PREPOSTEROUS.* VERBARD SAT on his throne deep in thought. Eep had filled him in on The Darkslayer. It seemed the man lived after all, but in another world below his. One that he never would have believed for himself. Eep had given him few details, other than the fact that he'd bitten the man's fingers off, or a portion of them rather.

He's no longer a threat. Could he escape the world beyond the Mist? Perhaps, but I cannot worry about that now, without proof. I'll forge ahead and press on. Stay on course.

Eep was still after the keys. Kierway still made preparations to overtake a castle. Jottenhiem kept his men in good order, biding their time. With or without keys, a living Darkslayer or not, he was going to press on. Bring the wretched humans to their knees, one citizen at a time.

Eep, have you found that man yet?

No, Master, but it won't be long. Do you require anything else? I hunger. A quick bite, perhaps?

Stay on course!

At his side stood the Vicious: tall and silent with the musculature of a hairless feline. How many of these powerful creatures did Master Sinway have at his disposal? *How many, indeed?*

"If I had a thousand of you, this would be much easier," he said, rising to his feet and drifting away. He cast his silver eyes above. How many thousands of humans could they take out with one lethal strike? With enough force, could they take the entire city? Eradicate the humans once and for all. If anything, he just wanted to get his charge over with.

Now wasn't the time to second guess himself. No. His plan was sound: take a Castle by force, and have a stronghold. It would work, but Kierway was an important part of that plan. He didn't trust him. No, once the castle was located, he'd send a portion to invade. He would lead a full scale assault on the world of men above first, in one giant wave. The castle would not expect an attack from within.

He rolled his fingers. The orb of imbibing floated from the ground and into his grasp. Then he noticed someone was coming. It was Kierway. *That was quick.*

"You have good report?" Verbard said.

"Castle Almen," Kierway stated, running his clawed fingers over his shaven head.

"Again? Have we not drawn enough attention to ourselves at that point?"

Kierway sauntered up, poured himself a glass of wine, and slumped down on the makeshift throne of rock and stone. "Fitting for you, vastly inferior to the one I'll inherit from my father. But for a lesser family, it will do."

Verbard sneered. "I believe your father was very clear with your role and mine. You are beholden to me, and you'd be served well to remember that."

The Vicious stepped forward and bared its fangs. Kierway remained in place.

"You need me as much as I need you, Verbard. Now, let's set our differences aside. I want to fulfill this quest as much as you."

"Go on."

"Castle Almen. Yes, its access to the Current is now overfilled with guards, but they number

less than a hundred. Still, it would be difficult to penetrate that small but heavily defended port."
Kierway took his first sip and spit it out. "Pah! Did an urchling make this? I wouldn't let a cave
dog drink it."

Verbard's silver eyes flashed. It was his favorite port. "Get on with it, Kierway."

"The strange thing is," he tipped his finger up, "the passages to the other castles are quite
narrow, and most castles don't have any access at all to the Current. Most are sealed off, as if no
passage was ever there to begin with. It wasn't always so. That leaves us with taking one from the
upside in, or from the downside up. Castle Almen, it seems, is the only choice."

Kierway kicked his legs up on the armrest and leaned back with his arms behind his head.

"I say we attack from the up and the down. We have more than enough w—"

Kierway's eyes were full of alarm as he sailed from the throne to the ground. Copper eyes filled
with rage, he jumped back to his feet, swords ripped from his scabbards.

Verbard rose from the ground, spikes of energy fueling his claws. He'd had enough of the
impudent Kierway, and he didn't have to take any more if he didn't want to. The time to let it loose
was now.

"Take him out!" he ordered the Vicious.

The Vicious sprang like a cat, claws ripping at Kierway's feet. Kierway twisted away, sword
chopping backward, clipping off a pair of the Vicious's fingers. It did not howl or slow. It pressed
on. The edges of Kierway's blades danced through the air, licking across the hardened skin of the
Vicious, sending black slivers of flesh into the air. The creature's ears matted down on its head. It
wasn't accustomed to fighting a faster opponent.

Curse those magic blades. Verbard watched in amazement and alarm. Kierway was a split second
faster than the Vicious at every strike or blow. It was as if he'd fought against one before. *I should
have known. What an excellent sparring partner one would be.*

"It's only a matter of time before I whittle him down," Kierway said, shifting, juking and
parrying. "I can do this all day, but he won't last that long; trust me."

No. Verbard could see that now. But once the Vicious pinned the man down, it would be all
over. *Perhaps it's time to intervene. Good-bye Kierway!*

The fluid motion of the Vicious's body had begun to slow.

Slice! Slice! Slice! Slice!

Kierway rolled his wrists with the rapid rhythm of a drummer, whittling two fingers off. The
Vicious was hobbled, chopped and gashed like a wounded dog.

Verbard summoned his power. *Let's even the odds, shall we?* The rock beneath the combatant's
feet turned to mud.

"No! What are you doing, Verbard? There is no honor in this!" Kierway cried out, sinking to
his ankles as the Vicious closed in.

Verbard waved good-bye.

Kierway's blades chopped and parried, keeping the pressing Vicious at bay. A look of concern
formed in Kierway's eyes, his legs now sunk knee deep in the sludge. The Vicious was not slowed.
Its mighty limbs still lunged. Kierway clipped its ear off as the Vicious wrapped one good arm
around Kierway's neck and drove him into the mud.

Excellent!

Kierway thrashed like a fish on a line, small daggers from his bandolier rising up and down
in his hands, blades breaking on the hardened back of the creature. Kierway shouted a plea with a
mouthful of mud.

"I yield!"

Verbard dusted his hands off. He wanted to laugh out loud as the Vicious pushed Kierway face down below the mud. In but a moment, it would all be over. One of his least favorite underlings would be gone forever. Bubbles of mud popped on the surface. Verbard glided back to his throne. *So be it.* Taking a seat, he brought a cup of port to his lips. *Might as well enjoy this.*

"STOP!"

Verbard went numb.

Chapter 51

BAMF!

One underling burst into dust.

Bamf!

Another did the same.

Bamf!

Followed by another. The rest of the underlings fled back down the hill, leaving Darlene's shattered body bleeding over the pine needles. Scorch took long strides down the slope, over the slippery terrain, watching the underlings go. Several black heads were running at full charge, one exploding into black dust after the other until they were nothing but fertilizer for the terrain.

Darlene lived, blood trickling over her puffy lips that sucked like a catfish out of water. How disturbing it was to see such a lively person dying like this. She tried to speak, lips struggling to form words. The gashes in her belly and chest prevented the effort.

A shame.

Scorch looked over the bright horizon towards the east. It was still a long walk to the City of Three. He kneeled down, grabbed her bloody hand and smiled.

"I still require company on my journey, Darlene. But I can't have you doing whatever it is you want. Stay close to me and live, drift away and die."

Darlene's rugged frame twitched with spasms. Despite the evident pain within her dying body, she nodded. Relief overtook the anguish in her face as Scorch pulled her up into her sitting position. Her eyes were wild with fire as she licked her lips and wiped the blood from her mouth. Then she began fingering the places where the puncture wounds had just been. She gaped at him. Blinking a hundred times before she spoke.

"You don't have to tell me twice, Scorch!" She lunged over and hugged him.

It was the strangest feeling. He couldn't remember ever being hugged before, but the affectionate gesture was touching. He struggled to peel her arms from his waist.

"That's enough of that," he said in a firm tone, "but my, you are strong as a dwarf, I'd say. There may be something to that." He patted her on the head.

She smiled back.

"I'm strong for a girl." She looked around. "I got five of them, I think," she said, shuffling down the hill and inspecting the bodies of the fallen underlings. "WOOOOO HOOOOOOO!" She hoisted a bloody arrow in the air. "I killed me some underlings! There ain't nothing I can't kill!" She rushed over to all the bodies and retrieved all her arrows, then went for the eyes.

"Stop that," Scorch ordered.

Darlene looked up at him and froze.

"But there's magic in their eyes. We have to cut them out and burn the bodies."

"No you don't. It's time to go."

"But ..."

Scorch felt irritated, and his power ebbed the ever slightest, but he didn't like it. It made him feel vulnerable.

"It is time to leave, and there will be no more of this savage talk. Come Darlene, or not. I'll entertain no more chatter."

Darlene slammed her knife into her sheath, fetched her bow, and returned to his side as he walked about the hill and onto the path they had abandoned. They traveled over a mile before Darlene broke her silence.

"I'm with you, Scorch. You saved me. I'm grateful. I saw what you did, too. Turned those underlings into smoke and dust. Incredible," she said, strutting along his side.

That's more like it.

"But …" Darlene hunkered down a little as she said it.

He felt that mild irritation return.

"What are you going to do about them?"

Scorch looked down on her. She was eyeing him and the path behind her. She pointed.

A small huddled group fell to their knees as he turned. It was the people that Darlene attempted to save earlier.

"Want me to shoot them?"

"What? You almost got yourself killed trying to save them!" he said.

"Well," she licked her lips, "I was mostly looking for a fight, is all. And I really wanted to kill an underling. Plus, I owe you." She readied her bow and arrow.

"Ask them what they want," he said, combing his fingers through his long locks of hair.

"What do you idiots want?" she screamed, pulling back her bowstring.

"Service!" One man shouted back. "We owe you our lives! We seek only to repay the debt."

Darlene looked up at Scorch from the corner of her eye and said, "Just say the word, and I'll put a red dot in his head."

Scorch could feel their willingness and sincerity. He liked it.

"Tell them they may follow, but they must do as they are told."

Darlene eased the string on her bow.

"Does that mean I can tell them what to do?"

"Certainly, but that doesn't mean they will listen," he said, turning forward and continuing his journey to the City of Three.

Darlene started barking orders.

"Don't get closer than thirty paces!"

"Keep up because we ain't slowing!"

"You get your own food and water! And no singing! Unless I say so!"

CHAPTER 52

"**W**HAT DO YOU MEAN HE left?" Mikkel said.

Nikkel rammed the wheel barrow of stone into the wall and dropped the arms down. He wiped his hands on his knees and shrugged.

"He's going to find Venir. He seemed pretty determined. But I just think he didn't want to help out with any of the work."

"Why did you let him go?" Billip said, slipping away from the woman who held his waist. "He's not supposed to go anywhere without us. You should have stopped him! Bone!"

"I'll handle this, Billip," Mikkel said, holding out his arm. "Nikkel, what did he say?"

"He just said he was going to 'get out of Bone'."

"And then what?"

"He left."

"Which way?"

Nikkel shrugged. Mikkel swatted him in the back of the head.

"Ow!" Nikkel pushed his father in the chest. "Don't do that again!"

Billip stepped between them as the fires ignited behind the eyes of both father and son.

"Let's not come to blows—"

Mikkel shoved him aside, hooked his arm under Nikkel and slammed him into the ground. Nikkel fought back, but it was over before it started, and Mikkel shoved his face into a pile of dirt.

"Son, you already had my attention, but it seems I didn't have yours. Do I have it now?"

Nikkel nodded, spitting out a mouthful of dirt. Mikkel lifted his son back to his feet.

"Georgio is my friend, Nikkel. Venir is, too, and he wants us to look after him. I'll need your help, too. Do you understand?"

"Sure, Father. And I'm—"

Mikkel cut him off as he helped his son up.

"You don't have to say it, Nikkel. I want you to stick up for yourself, but don't pick a fight with your father. Your mother, maybe?" He slapped his son on the back. "But me? No, no, that's a bad idea." He squeezed Nikkel's arm. "Don't worry, in due time, you'll be more than I can handle."

Nikkel nodded, pointed down the road, and said, "He was trying to find the both of you, but," he looked over his father's shoulder at the giggling women, "you were indisposed. I'm not so sure that man, Corrin, is too pleased with that, either."

"Ah, it's none of that rogue's business." Billip pushed his woman back. "Give me a moment, Jess." She backed away with a giggle. "As I was saying, we need to retrieve Georgio. The streets are dangerous out there. Blast!"

"What?" Mikkel said.

"He's taken Quickster with him," Billip said. "How long's he been gone, Nikkel?"

"An hour, I'd say."

"I bet he's back to the stables by now," Mikkel said. "We can catch up if we hurry."

"No, don't leave me," a brown-haired woman said, tugging on Billip's arm.

Two other women draped their arms on Mikkel. "We can't let you go! You must protect us."

Billip popped his knuckles. The thought of the stables unsettled him. What if that man, Tonio, had returned? He was inches from his death the last time they clashed. It was possible the deranged man could still be waiting at the stables. At the same time, he felt very compelled to stay back and help Trinos.

"I'm sure he'll come back," he offered.

"What? You can't be serious, Billip. You know that boy's as hard-headed as a bull. We have to go and get him, and my pony Quickster."

"I'll go," Nikkel said. "I can run. I might even beat them back to the stables. Assuming that's where they went."

"Has anyone seen Trinos?" Corrin yelled, storming their way. The man looked beside himself.

"No," Billip said, "we were about to ask you the same."

"Why would you be asking me?" Corrin said, looking at the hungry-eyed women, "... fornicators. Perhaps if you weren't diddling the help, you'd know. But know this," he pointed at the three of them, "with Trinos gone, I'm in charge."

Billip and Mikkel laughed.

"I am!" Corrin stomped his foot. "This isn't a brothel, mind you. Chip in, or get out!"

"You better watch yourself," Mikkel said, pointing his finger down in Corrin's face. "I could break you in half, Little Man."

"Hah! Then you better be able to sleep with one eye open," Corrin said. A pair of blades blinked out of his clothes and back in. "The both of you." He twisted around and walked away.

"Huh," Mikkel said, swallowing.

Billip perked up his eyebrows. It seemed there was more to Corrin than originally appeared.

"If we're going after Georgio, we might as well all go, and make it fast. Daylight is burning."

"Yeah, we'll all go," Mikkel said, putting his hand on Nikkel's shoulder. "I could use the run myself."

Billip saluted the women as they went, saying, "I was sure looking forward to keeping one eye open on them. Eh ..."

The women in all directions started screaming. A sea of rats was scurrying over the cobblestones by the hundreds, if not thousands. Mikkel and Nikkel stopped in their tracks, eyes wide, watching the vermin run over their booted toes. He and Mikkel looked at one another as the ground began to shake.

"What in the world of Bish?"

Ahead, cutting off the road that lead south towards the stables, the streets erupted. The stone and dirt bulged from underneath with a popping and grinding sound. The men joined the women with shouts, screams and yells as a monstrous hairy bulk unlike anything Billip had ever seen before emerged.

"Sonuvabish!" he cried.

CHAPTER 53

FEAR. IT WAS AN ADVENTURER'S enemy and friend. Fear could drive a man to crawl within himself in despair, which was precisely what Fogle Boon wanted to do right now. Or, Fear could spur action and powers deep within you that you'd never known. That furnace was depleted, replaced with a reservoir of icy stone. *Help me. Help us all!*

"Oh my!" Boon said, his hands charging up like fire. "If you have a helmet tucked somewhere in those robes of yours, you better strap it on. You're going to need it!"

The underlings, they weren't all in one spot, but they were many, black forms scurrying all over, spread out from one side of the ravine to the other. A dozen here, a small squad there, all peeking out from behind the rocks and trees, their gemstone eyes twinkling. Shiny steel weapons glinting in the suns' light. There were at least a hundred, if not more, and almost twenty had surrounded Barton. *Think, Fogle! Think!* He crouched down and huddled in his robes.

Boon let the first blast go.

Ka-BOOM!

Fogle cringed and held his hands over his ears as shards of rock and wood scattered all over.

A shower of debris cut his hand, and a chunk of rock clipped his shoulder, sending him to the ground. He hurt all over.

"I cannot do this without you!" Boon was screaming as a litany of small bolts filled the sky. "HOSLOMAN-DEEK!"

A transparent barricade shimmered with flecks of blue and green, deflecting and vaporizing the underling volley. On the other side of that barrier, Barton swatted at a small horde of underlings with his club and had moderate success. Quick and fast they were, driving javelins into his legs and lassoing ropes around his arms and neck.

"YOU CANNOT STOP ME WITH THREAD," Barton roared, grabbing hold of the rope and slinging two underlings across the ground. "YOU CANNOT HURT BARTON! I'M A GIANT, AND YOU ARE COCKROACHES! HA!" Barton stomped on another.

The underlings retreated, reformed, and slung javelins and shot bolts into his face. Barton shielded his face with his arm and stomped the ground, shaking the trees, and screamed at them all.

"Have you finished gawking yet, Grandson? More come! Come to your senses, Man!"

Death. The thought of if dulled his senses. Thrusting oneself into peril with no future knowledge of the outcome could sap the will of a man. Slowly, he rose to his feet, trying to grasp the chaos around him. How could he protect himself with so many things going on at once?

"Courage, Fogle! Have courage!" An array of bright green missiles burst from Boon's finger tips.

A knot of underling soldiers stormed up the ravine, small bucklers raised. They caught the full force of Boon's missiles and chittered with rage. Some were dead, others twitched, but they were still on the move. Fogle managed to make his way alongside his grandfather, where the air was thin. He couldn't breathe, think or do anything.

Boon grabbed hold of his arm.

"Now is not the time to be idle, Wizard. Now is the time to fight! What is wrong with you? You've fought underlings! You've fought giants! What are you waiting for?"

Fogle flinched. Another barrage of bolts slammed into the magic barricade a foot from his face. The underlings were less than a few dozen yards away. They were the most evil things he ever saw. What if he had to fight them with his fists? They'd cut him into little pieces.

He gave his grandfather Boon a blank look. The strong features on the elder's face were beginning to weaken. The wrinkles deepened, the pressure built. Boon couldn't hold up the barricade much longer. *Just cast something. Anything!*

He closed his eyes, muttering the words to the first spell that came to mind. Magic swelled inside his chest and throat, and something eerie oozed in one side of him and out the other. He opened his eyes and found the oddest expression on his grandfather's face.

"It's a start," Boon said, panting "Now do something with what you have done."

Fogle was beside himself, literally. To his left he was, to his right he was, and behind him as well. Three identical Fogles awaited his beck and call. It was an illusion he'd hoped would throw off the giants when he encountered them again.

Fogle pointed down the ravine with both fingers.

"Spread out and attack."

The three Fogles sprang into action.

I can't even move that fast. Concentrate. What shall I have them do?

Illusions were tricky things. Sometimes they worked, and sometimes they did not, depending on the mind of the other. Much of the time, it had more to do with the minds of others than your own. Fogle concentrated on his vision, gave his idea life, and let it go.

The underlings surged toward the direction of Fogle's apparitions, blades slashing, overwhelming the figures. The first one rose into the air, dousing the underlings with rays of arching light. The second fled, evading underling pursuit. The third multiplied from one to three, then fifteen more, all fighting for their lives against the masses.

"Impressive," Boon shouted. "You've bought us some time at least. But how much?"

Fogle half-smiled, "It's the least—"

Boon's barricade fizzled out. The old wizard shrugged. "Well, it was going to happen, but I thought we'd have at least a dozen more seconds or two."

Fogle took a deep breath. He had regained control for the moment, but Boon was right: the illusion wouldn't work forever, a minute more at the most. "What's the plan, Boon?"

"I was hoping you were thinking of one as I doddered around. My plan however, is simple: kill them all." Boon's hands were on his hips as he took a deep draw of air. "But, I'm afraid I'm lacking the firepower at the moment." Boon gritted his teeth. "Seems I don't have as much juice as I used to."

Fogle started to reply, "I'm not so—"

"RAAAAARGH!"

Barton cried out as he crashed into the ground and underlings piled all over him.

"GET OFF ME, PESTS!"

The giant's arms were pinned to his sides by ropes.

Fogle had to do something. Scanning his surroundings, he noticed his apparitions beginning to disappear. The underlings cried out in triumph and confusion. Some broke off after the apparitions that continued to multiply. There were more than twenty scattered throughout the ravine. He retrieved his pack, withdrew his spellbook, and tossed it to his grandfather.

"Find something in there," he said, making way to help Barton. "And get our arses out of here!"

"Giants are friends of fire, Grandson!" Boon shouted.

Fogle shook his head. He didn't see how that would help. Knowing a better weakness for underlings would have been better.

"HELP BARTON! HELP BARTON, WIZARD!" The underlings were on him like a hive of angry bees.

Fogle's heart went out. The giant was big, deformed, but more child than man. It was torment to watch him suffer such savagery as the underlings struck with all the venom they had. Barton cried out again, sending shivers down Fogle's spine. Barton began to bleed.

Move, Fogle! Act! He's about to die!

Four underlings hoisted a rope behind Barton's neck and yanked his chin back. Three others chittered with wicked glee as they hoisted their javelins back and took aim at Barton's last good eye.

CHAPTER 54

U ENIR COULD HEAR THE LEATHER squeak as the bald orc twisted his bracers on his wrists. Venir had a similar pair once that he discarded, never feeling the need. Maybe now would have been a good time to make use of such things.

"I am called Tuuth," the orc said, cracking his bullish neck in his hands. "It's best you know the name of your opponent." The orc bared one magnificent fang.

A fitting name. Venir stretched his limbs one last time. He couldn't have beaten an ogre, not a full one anyway. Yet there was truth behind Tuuth's words. Of course, orcs were notorious liars. Venir couldn't afford to worry about that now. He'd beaten ogres before, Farc and Son of Farc, in mortal combat and won. And if anything, he felt much stronger now than he did then.

Tuuth eyed him.

"No name, huh?"

"My name has many enemies," Venir responded, coming eye to eye with the orc.

Tuuth was rangy and powerfully built, as fine a specimen of his race as Venir had ever seen. Still, the thought of calling out mercy to anyone, even if a ploy, wasn't an easy one.

Toy with him. See what he's got.

Venir looked back up the ravine.

"They won't be near. Heh-heh. It don't matter."

Venir took one last look over his shoulder. Hidden behind the rocks, in the sack inside his pack, the armament was safe. No one could get to it but him. But being without it was disconcerting. *I don't need it. Not for this. I never met an orc I couldn't handle before.* He raised his arms up and spread his fingers out.

"Ready?"

Venir nodded.

He and Tuuth gripped hands. He felt the raw power behind the orc's squeeze. *Bish!*

"You make the count to three, Stranger."

Both man and orc braced their legs in the dirt, arms pressing, but holding back.

"You strong for a man," Tuuth muttered, showing an evil grin.

"One," Venir started.

"Tuuth strong for an orc."

"Two."

"Very strong. Not too late to back out, Stranger."

Jaws clenched, eyes filled with fire, he said, "It's not too late for you either, Orc. THREE!"

Tuuth's hands felt like dried leather and were as strong as vices. He pulled Venir's hands up and drove him back. The pressure built quickly. Tuuth squeezed his fingers at the same time, pinching the bone. Sweat beads burst on Venir's brow. *Blast! What kind of orc is this!*

"Say the word, and I'll make this easy," Tuuth mocked, pushing him backward, crushing his hands.

Venir wanted to tear his hands away, but held on. *Fight, Venir!* Tuuth dug his fingernails into the backs of his hands, drawing blood. Venir fought the urge to scream. He was losing. *NO!*

Blocking out the pain, he shoved back. Tuuth grunted, muscles knotting up in cords. Venir squeezed back, fighting with everything he had. Tuuth's feet slid back over the dirt. No, Mercy was not his game. Not in this case it wasn't. Either Tuuth never sweated, or he hadn't broken one.

"Give up you, Stranger? Ha. Just ask for Mercy."

Venir couldn't find the breath to respond. He put everything he had into forcing the orc's wrist back.

"Maybe if you had all your fingers it would help," Tuuth huffed in his face.

Venir couldn't remember the last time he'd been mocked. It stoked the fires in his belly. Spit frothing from his lips doubled his efforts, legs surging and driving the orc backward. Tuuth's eyes widened as Venir began to bend his wrists backward.

"Harrumph!" Tuuth exclaimed. He jerked Venir's arms left then right. Bullish shoulder against bullish shoulder. The orc gave no more, his thick wrists again forcing Venir's backwards.

"Come on, Tuuth!" The leader said, appearing from the brush. "No man can beat you!"

"What game is this?" Venir managed to spit out. "I'll not be bushwhacked!"

"Peace!" The leader said. "Battle on. My men can't pass on a show like this. We'll keep our distance. Our word, Stranger!"

"Aye," the soldier with the dogs said. "I've never seen Tuuth have a struggle before."

Venir blocked them out. The jeers and cheers had no meaning as he and Tuuth struggled back and forth. Keeping his breath and strength up was enough to worry about. *Bone! What strength!* His hands were killing him. It felt like they would break at any moment. A stone gargoyle didn't have a mightier grip.

"You tire, Stranger! Your chest heaves like an excited woman!"

Venir's wrists were back more than before.

"Ye've got him, Tuuth! Now break him."

Fight, Venir, Fight!

He fell to one knee.

A chorus of triumph burst out.

Tuuth towered over him, leering downward, powerful arms pulsating with life and vitality.

"Say it, Stranger!"

Melegal would kill me if he saw this. All the gold he would lose. Hang on! He must tire! He cannot be so strong!

The soldiers said, "Cry mercy! He'll cripple you! He will!"

"Pride's the doom of a man!"

"Tuuth will show no mercy to the foolish."

Venir's sweat-coated face was red and purple. His wrists were bent fully backward. The pain was becoming unbearable.

"Slat!" he yelled.

Tuuth's hot breath was in his face.

"Give in, Stranger! My patience runs out!"

"NO!"

Venir had suffered so many things. The Mist. The underlings. The Marsh. The Pit. A shallow grave. How could he not survive this? How could he be beaten? His heart was ready to explode in his chest. Big purple veins rose inside his temples. His nose bled, and his eyes rolled up in his head. Was it the armament? *Fool!* Was he weaker without it?

"Do it, Tuuth! Break him!" the Leader cried.

"Say the word!" Tuuth snorted.

Venir knew that he had to hold on. Just a little longer. The orc was soon to tire, he was certain. *Save your strength, Venir. He can't keep this up.* Certainly he'd have a second wind. He always had. But the orc shouldn't.

Tuuth shouted in his ear.

"Last chance, Stranger!"

"For you maybe," Venir spit through his lips.

Tuuth roared, wrenched downward and twisted.

Snap!

Venir's wrist broke. His fingers bent back to the edge.

"NOOOOOO!"

The soldiers jumped and hollered.

"Say it!"

Venir's right wrist was folded up to his arm. He might as well have been stabbed in the gut. That much he could understand. This wasn't possible. He screamed as the pain of a thousand fires shot up and down his arm. His stomach repulsed as he choked down the urge to vomit.

Snap!

Agony! His other wrist now shattered. *How!* He couldn't take it anymore. Dazed and defeated, he looked up into Tuuth's face. The orc's chest was heaving as he wiped the sweat from his brow. Venir didn't even realize his hands were freed. He couldn't feel them. They hung limp as his sides. He couldn't bear to look at them. Broken. Foolish. Ashamed.

"I didn't say mercy," was all Venir could manage to say.

Tuuth shook his fist, saying, "No, Stranger. I've no words for it. But you'll wish that you did." Tuuth then let out a cry of triumph to the cheers of his fellow soldiers.

Venir closed his eyes. *I can't believe it. What happened?*

The dogs howled.

The leader said, "Button it up, men."

Venir opened his eyes in time to see the small party scrambling around. Tuuth shoved him face first to the ground, held a knife to his throat, and said, "Keep silent, Stranger, if you want to live."

In all his life, Venir had never felt more helpless than when the underlings arrived.

CHAPTER 55

DID JUBBLER JUST SAY THAT?

No one else was around. Lefty removed the other nail from his ear. Jubbler picked at his beard and twitched his large nose.

"Did you say something?" Lefty asked.

"Huh."

Lefty huffed. He muttered. He cursed.

"I see you've picked up a few words in the Nest, now haven't you?" Jubbler said. The rugged dwarf's maniacal tone had turned around into something serene and wise.

He looked over at the Quartermaster, who was still down the dock.

"You did say that!" Lefty exclaimed, picking up his hammer. "Do you really know Gillem, or are you just acting crazy?"

Jubbler reached over, took Lefty's hand in his, and said, "I'm crazy because I want them to believe me to be. But I'm quite sane all the time. Now Lefty, pay attention. You don't have much time." It was Jubbler's turn to peer around. "Keep tapping. I'll start talking."

Tap. Tap. Tap. Tap. Tap ….

Lefty didn't know what to make of it, but the sound of a friendly voice energized him. Connecting with another living person elated him. All of his aches, pains and hunger subsided under a tide of hope.

Jubbler cleared his throat and spoke in a low and rich tone, his comments quick and direct.

"Master Gillem. Murdered. Let me say he was my friend and yours as well. But, he and I were doomed scoundrels from the start. Nothing but bad blood running through the both of us, most all the good parts long gone …" Jubbler drifted off and wiped his eyes.

Lefty scooted away. Was this dwarf someone he should be listening to?

"… but even the worst of us have some honor and loyalty. A code, you might say. A redeeming quality we can take to our deaths one day. Master Gillem served us all well, but he had enemies: Palos, Thorn and that dreadful Diller among them." Jubbler punched his gnarled fist on the deck. "It wasn't always this way in the guild. Palzor followed the code, but his deranged son does not. At least not anymore. It's one thing for a thief to be greedy, but Palos has taken it to another level. Our tributes and contributions are outrageous, almost triple what they'd been. And the clientele above, the additional costs for their commodities, well, they aren't so happy. Heh. Heh. Not happy at all. They ask for less for the smuggled goods, and Palos charges more."

Tap. Tap. Tap. Tap. Tap. Tap …

Lefty was enthralled. His small body filled with new energy. *I cannot believe the same person speaks.* From roughshod and rambling, Jubbler was now a polished stone, poised and in control.

"Us pick pockets are getting antsy, and with your arrival, the Royal woman and her baby, well, our bones were unsettled. Something must be done. The thin ice he's put us on is about to break." Jubbler clenched his hand and teeth. "Master Gillem was a friend, and many want him avenged." He stuck his knotty finger at Lefty's nose. "Most thieves come and go, their lives given as little consideration as their deaths. We've seen Palos snuff members out before. The man rules with an iron gauntlet. Cruel and unpredictable. But killing Gillem," Jubbler wiped his eyes and cleared the lump from his throat, "that was wrong. Wrong as a dwarf mating with an orc."

Crack!

The Quartermaster was coming back their way, eyes baring down on the both of them. Lefty picked up the pace.

Tap. Tap. Tap. Tap. Tap. Tap. Tap. Tap. Tap …

"Do some work, Jubbler, you babbling runt!"

Crack!

Jubbler squealed as the lash licked across his back and shoulder.

Lefty kept his head down and hammered away.

Crack!

"Ow!" Lefty cried out, the hammer slipping from his lashed wrist.

The orcen man growled, "Pick it up, Halfling!"

Tears streamed down Lefty's face as he reached for the hammer.

Crack!

Fingers an inch from the hammer, the lash caught him across the fingertips.

Blasted orc!

"I said, 'Pick it up!'"

Lefty snatched it like a snake strikes its prey.

Crack!

The Quartermaster missed.

"You'll pay for that, you blond-haired rodent."

Lefty balled up. Anchored down by the absidium chains, what else could he do?

Splash!

"What the!" the Quartermaster said, head and big shoulders whipping around. "You hooved fools. Clumsy as blind kobolds!"

Toward the other end of the dock, a wooden crate of goods found its way into the lake. A small craft capsized. The Quartermaster stomped down the dock, saying, "Someone's going to die for this!"

"Are you well?" Jubbler said, rubbing his shoulder.

Lefty shook his hand. Red and swollen, it hurt worse than it looked. He opened his fist in and out a few times. "I'm fine, but that hurt! What about you?"

"Heh, nothing but a sting, is all. A dwarf's hide thickens as he gets older, but it's not as flexible." Jubbler winked. "Just can't stay out in the sun too long. It can dry you up like a seed. Now, we have the get you out of here. Plans are now in motion."

"What do you mean?" Lefty said. "What plans?"

Jubbler snorted.

"You don't really think a bunch of cutthroats and smugglers accidentally dropped crates of goods into the lake, do you?"

Lefty perched his eyebrows and said, "I suppose not.

Jubbler grabbed him by the shoulder and gave it a tug.

"The Quartermaster, well, he's another Palos recruit. Not one to belong here. He'll have his hands full for now. But we have to get you going and out of here. Once it starts rolling… we can't stop it now."

Lefty had no idea what Jubbler was talking about, but he was willing to try anything to help

Kam and Erin. Anything at all, he was ready. He held up the absidium chains that dangled in his fingers.

"Ah, yes." Jubbler rubbed his chin. "I never figured those out, not like Master Gillem. I was certain you would figure it out, however. Can you not do it, Boy? You have to be free if this plan's to roll."

Lefty looked at his bleeding, swollen and throbbing hand.

"How much time do I have?"

"Little! Make haste. You can figure it out. Gillem said so."

Lefty began to fidget his fingers and tug at the bonds. The chains constricted like a living thing. "Why would you and Gillem talk about these chains? Seems odd. Did he foresee my incarceration?"

"Ho-Ho. No, not at all. We had a bet, was all. He said you could, and I said you couldn't. I've never seen another trick the chains before, but Gillem was like a magician. Juggled ten coins at once, he did."

"Really?" Lefty continued wrestling the chains, twisting and turning his tiny wrists all sorts of ways. The more he twisted, the deeper they dug. It was killing him.

"I saw it for myself," Jubbler said, a smile turning to a frown, "but I never seen my coins again, either.

Lefty huffed out. "Blast! I can't do this, Jubbler."

"Hurry, Boy," Jubbler urged, motioning his finger in the air. "You have to trick it. That's what Master Gillem said, but I could never figure it out."

Sweat glistened on Lefty's face. Maybe Gillem broke them, but they'd said they were unbreakable. *Oh no, I cannot do this. I cannot!*

"Hurry, Lefty, time is short! You must save the baby before they take her."

"Take her where? Ow!"

Lefty's hands were purple and red, both wrists bleeding now.

"Palos has another deal. He's ransoming the baby girl. It seems there are people above that want her. Much money they shall pay."

"Who? Don't they want Kam?"

"No, just the baby. Hurry now, there's little time before they move her."

He had promised Kam he'd take care of Erin, first and foremost. But he couldn't leave Kam behind. How was he supposed to get out of here? What if Jubbler lied? He didn't know what to think or believe anymore. *Think! Move! Act!*

"Did you see Gillem use anything?" Lefty asked. "Maybe he had a key hidden."

"Maybe a pick? But I didn't see." Jubbler reached inside his vest and produced a small key, similar to the one Diller used to lock the chains. "Perhaps this will work."

Lefty snatched it.

"It's too big! What's that for, anyway? Drat! I'm undone. I … Am … Undone."

Jubbler tossed the key in the lake and sighed.

"I don't remember. An unfortunate thing this is, very unfortunate. Still, the plan moves forward. You must go, chains or not."

Lefty eyed the shackles on his wrists and feet. It wasn't possible. He'd be seen. But what choice did he have at this point? He at least had to try and save Erin.

"Jubbler, what do I do? How can I even get her out of here? It will be impossible to cross the lake unnoticed." He held up his chains.

"There is another way." Jubbler eyed the giant smoke stack. "It's dangerous, but if you can get the baby, you can take her up there."

Lefty looked up at the massive smoke stack, red brick marred by soot, smoke puffing from gaping holes in the brick. "You can't mean that?"

"I do. And you have to move. Your feet are forming a pool."

"Bone!" Lefty's heart was pounding in his chest. Something was wrong. He could feel it. Kam and Erin both were in grave danger.

Chapter 56

"**W**HAT HAVE WE HERE?" DILLER said, shoving Kam to the ground.

She cried out as Thorn twisted her arm and shoved his knee into her back.

"Let go of me! Palos! Have you not treated me badly enough?"

Palos's soft eyes revealed something darker inside as Diller handed over the gems.

"She's turning into a thief, it seems," Diller said, chuckling. "Perhaps we're wearing off on the Royal wench."

Kam scraped her chin on the floor as she got a better view of Palos. The Prince of Thieves studied the gems in every detail, eyes dancing in the firelight. He kneeled down before her and spoke with a venomous tone.

"Where did you get these? I've never seen the likes before."

She held her tongue.

Thorn grabbed a handful of her hair and snapped her head back.

"Stop doing that!" Kam said.

"Answer the Prince."

"Certainly," she said, spitting blood. "I took them from your own coffers, you sot. Not that you could ever keep track of every bauble in your hoard." She laughed. "I thought you'd craft me a pair of earrings. I think I've earned them," she batted her eyes, "dear Prince."

"Diller," Palos ordered, "bring me that halfling. I'll be having words with him." Palos grabbed Kam's face with his pudgy fingers. "I've a feeling you and the boy are conspirators, Kam. And when I discover the truth, I've a feeling another halfling will be dead." He smacked her hard across the face. "Earrings, my arse. Though, they certainly have a unique twinkle to them. Perhaps they'll make a fine gift for my next Royal conquest." He snorted as he rose up. "One of your sisters, perhaps?"

Kam remained silent as Thorn picked her up and slammed her into the chair. At least Palos hadn't mentioned Erin again. But now Lefty was in danger. *What a clumsy fool I am. I should have attacked when I had the chance. Now, things are worse than ever!*

Palos sat down at the table, placed an eye piece in his head, and held up the gems.

"Fascinating. Hmmm …. The inner core sparkles like a piece of broken coal." He let out a haggard moan. "The cut is unlike most stones. Polished. Oval." He muttered and groaned, switching stones and studying every last detail.

I need those! I must get them back. She glanced at the sword. Had her father, Kamdroz, really given Palzor that? She didn't have the best relationship with her father. He was a withdrawn and mysterious man who dabbled in politics and other powers she didn't care for. And there were many things she never understood or cared about in the Castles and Towers where her family resided. People of all questionable backgrounds and character came and went in the night. Palos had revealed many things. The thieves were the main vein of supply for wizards' spell components. She had always wondered where the weird and rare items came from, and now she knew.

"Tell me more about my father, Palos, and the sword. I don't think you were finished with your story."

"Quiet!" Thorn said, pressing knife to her throat.

Don't push it. The last thing you need is a gag in your mouth. Think up a spell. Have it ready.

"It's quite alright, Thorn," Palos said, still looking at the underling eyes, a softer tone in his voice. "This is quite a find. I'm possibly grateful. Huh, yes, your father and the sword." Palos set the gems down on the table, locked his fingers on his chest, and teetered his chair on its back legs. "One doesn't reach the top without playing dirty, you naïve woman. He's had help, much help from the likes of me and my father. You might even say, to some degree, we're Royals as well."

"You can fill your mind up with all the lies you want, but it still doesn't change the lowly person you are and ever will be," Kam remarked.

"Said like a true Royal. Always justifying their position." Palos laughed. "Perhaps you'd be more tolerable if you understood your own family's history. As I recall, all in this city were beggars and thieves at one time. You'd do well to remember that." Palos coughed. "My throat is dry, and it seems my last bottle is empty. Thorn, grab two more from the rack."

Thorn twirled his knife into his belt and lumbered away. Palos picked the gems back up, juggling them in one hand, eyeing them with glee. *This is it, Kam. Do it now!*

Thorn returned, back towards her, blocking Palos's view. She whispered and muttered as Thorn refilled the goblet. A spring of mystic energy came forth. Remembering Palos's words about the sword burning skin and also the sword's promise to help, she let her suggestion out. *Thorn.*

The tall man stiffened, turning his chin her way.

She had his attention. Eyeing the great sword, creating a perfect picture in her mind, she made a powerful suggestion.

GRAB.

Thorn turned, looking at her, his burned face a mask of confusion. Kam felt another level of exhaustion seep into her bones. She was almost spent. Her consciousness drifting. She needed those gems. The underling's eyes. Thorn bent over, hand reaching for the great blade.

Palos stopped juggling, set the stones on the table, and said, "Thorn, what are you doing?" He glared at Kam. "What have you done, Witch? Thorn, don't touch that blade, I COMMAND YOU!"

Thorn wrapped his big hand around the hilt and lifted up the sword. A rush of energy filled the room, blowing the hair back from all their faces. Thorn turned, a dark look in his eyes, his mind no longer his own.

"Drop that blade, Thorn! Drop it now!" Palos jumped on the table and drew his dagger. "What have you done to him, Kam? Make him stop now!"

Swish!

The heavy blade cut where Palo's legs a moment earlier had been standing.

"I am Zorth, an Avenger, a King, a Giant Slayer." The voice was unnatural, strong, powerful. "You," Thorn's body pointed at Palos, "are a flea."

Kam had never seen fear in Palos's eyes before, but it was there, real, his forehead crinkled.

Palos lunged in, stabbed Thorn in the thigh, and jumped back.

Slice!

The blade licked out over Palos's head, clipping his ear.

"Bone!" Palos said, holding his bleeding ear. "Thorn, stop this madness!"

Kam fought to rise on her weakened knees. The spell had taken a toll on her. She needed strength. *Get the gems!*

The possessed Thorn jumped over the table and chopped.

"The time has come, Rodent Prince. Your evils shall be undone."

Kam slipped behind Thorn and grabbed the stones. *Yes!*

"No! Help! No, you witch! You cannot use magic! How did you do this?"

Thorn, great sword of Zorth in hand, chopped and sliced, but Palos was quicker than a rabbit to his oppressor's charging bull. The prince of thieves evaded all of Thorn's lethal blows, but they were getting closer.

What does he have in his hand?

Palos had a vial. He dove away from the next decapitating blow.

Kkk-rang!

The sword of Zorth chopped into the metal tub, hewing half way through the metal until it stuck. Thorn fought to free the blade.

Kam rushed over to the front door. *Where's Palos?* Scanning the room, the man had disappeared. *No!*

"You cannot escape your evils!" the possessed Thorn yelled. "There is no escape for your kind. I shall purge this city once again."

She summoned the power in the gems. *Clatch.* Palo's bedroom door locked shut. The front door was still sealed. *Where is he?* Her body turned clammy. She realized what had happened. The vial must have turned him invisible.

Wham! Wham! Wham! Someone pounded on the front door.

"Are you in there, Prince? We heard you shout!"

"Death awaits you, fools! Come and greet him!" Thorn cried.

A silence came from the other side of the door.

Kam backed towards the corner, stones clenching in her fists, glowing like fire. *Where are you, Bastard!*

"Er, Thorn, was that you? Let us in. We'll sort it out," a man said from the other side.

The great blade slipped free of the tub, and the possessed man said, "A moment in life … a moment in death … comes the cold kiss of vengeance." Thorn strode across the room to the door and shoved the sword through one side and out the other. Men wailed behind the doorway.

Kam shivered. *Oh my!* Something grabbed her from behind by the neck and squeezed. *No!* It was Palos. She knew his grip, his scent, every vital detail.

"Drop those gems, Witch! Drop them now!" he warned. One arm held her tight by the neck, the other held the dagger at her belly. "I'll not waste another moment on you. I'll gut you and let you watch your innards spill out!"

She could feel his tongue on her ear. *No!* This was her last chance. There would not be another. It had to end here, one way or the other. *I'm sorry, Erin!*

"Kill me then, you bastard!" Her hands became brilliant balls of energy as she summoned the power forth.

"So be it, you crazy whore!"

Palos choked her with all his strength and slid the dagger in her stomach. Her eyes popped open. The gem stones dangled in her grip. She clenched them one last time. *Come, Snake! Come!*

A glimmering snake of green and yellow burst from the fireplace, eyes a brilliant white fire. It came fast, slithering over the planks like living fire and coiled itself around Palos and Kam.

Palos screamed. His grip slackened, the dagger clattering on the floor. Kam fell to her knees, holding her belly, eyes watering. "No," she murmured. "I can't die."

Behind her, the snake struck and squeezed Palos, who she could now see, wailing and thrashing like an animal gone mad. *Good!*

Thorn pulled his sword free of the door, the blade streaked red in blood.

"Come! It's time we free ourselves!"

Kam was numb. Washed over with nausea. She was dying, she was certain this time. "You must take my..." she gasped, blood spitting from her mouth, "find my baby. Save her, Zorth. Save her ..."

"You'll pay for that!" a man screamed from the other side of the door. "That was my brother!" *Wham! Wham! Wham!*

Something heavy hit the door.

"Just pick the lock," another cried.

Straight and true, Zorth rammed the sword through the door again.

Zorth's voice was hollow, loud, direct.

"No evil shall escape. No power can stop my edge. I am Zorth."

The unseen force of Palos screamed for mercy. None came.

Kam collapsed on the floor. *Erin. I tried. I'm sorry.*

Chapter 57

"A WANTED MAN, YOU SAY?" MELEGAL said, righting his slouch and facing Rayal.

Rayal smiled, her teeth white, her face as pretty as a rainbow.

"Certainly wanted. However, I've heard nothing but the highest of comments from Lorda Almen. She's very keen on you." Rayal stepped over and pulled the blanket from his shoulders and straightened his cap. "And she is far from easy to please, Life Saver."

Why must they smell so good? Gives me the weak knees of a swooning woman, it does. How do they do that?

"I only do what is expected of my service, Rayal," he said with a slight nod. *She does not know. A lift in fortune for one miniscule moment for the day. Still, persistent and nosy. Aren't they all? Scars on my knuckles. Should've stuck them in a hog waller first.*

"Odd, Detective, seeing you in the barns, and going to great lengths to steal a pail of water … my bratty sister's at that." She took a deep breath into her chest, straining the leather cords on her riding corset, and yawned. "I'd hoped Elizabeth's enemies had the best of her. So, is this an investigation of some sort? And don't be coy. The Lorda and I share many things."

Rayal's escorts, one tall and lean, the other stocky and gruff, fingered the hilts of their long swords, eyes on Melegal. Between them, Rayal stood out like a sunflower planted between two beds of jagged rocks: hair and features dark, warm and mysterious. Was she not the one betrothed to Tonio? Such an odd situation that all their lives were intertwined. Clearly, *beauty cannot compensate for good senses.* He didn't sense the same level of cunning Lorda Almen had, either. But it was clear Rayal was sharp. *In another decade or so, she'll have it down. For now, take advantage of what she lacks.*

"I'd rather not trouble you," he said, switching the pail from one hand to the other, "but perhaps I can fill you in later."

"No. Now would be a good time. After all, trouble abounds from all corners with underlings about. They press from within and without. Many fear the great walls of Bone will come down. And I find it peculiar you are not within the walls of Castle Almen, affording protection." Her escorts bristled as she tossed her hair and folded her arms over her chest.

I don't have time for this. Brak is dying. I must act. Do something!

Melegal gave another slight bow. Added a nervous stammer and some desperation to his voice. "I-I apologize. As a commoner, I've my own troubles I'm trying to, oh how can I say it?" He grabbed his hat and wrung it, then placed it back on his head, "Rectify. I'm certain it would be frowned on by the Lorda, as it's outside of my tasks. I've much to do and little time."

Rayal's eyebrows perched.

"Perhaps I can help? I insist."

Melegal let out a slight sigh.

"A friend is injured. He lies in the stable bleeding and hot with fever."

Rayal's hand fell over her heart as she gasped. "Take me to him. I can help."

"But, Rayal, I could not impose."

With a hot look in her eye, she grabbed him by the arm and said, "Ooh, those blasted Almens only care about themselves. Just take me to this friend of yours. I'll help in spite of them."

"Eh," Melegal said as she pulled him away.

"I bet this is the barn, isn't it?" She gasped. "That's a lot of blood."

Large drops were just outside the door, but they weren't noticeable to an untrained eye.

"In here?"

Melegal nodded. *Play it through, and be ready to run.*

"Rayal," one of the soldiers said, shoving past Melegal, "let me enter first."

The other soldier stood holding his arm out between Melegal and the door.

"It's clear," the soldier yelled.

Rayal stepped inside, followed by Melegal and the last soldier.

Brak still lay in Jubilee's lap, pale as a sheet, unmoving. Haze was holding a bloody rag on his belly. The smell of death was in the air.

"Melegal," Haze said, her voice cracking, "I don't think." She sobbed.

Rayal looked at him and said, "Is this your family?"

NO!

He gestured.

"So to speak."

Rayal kneeled down alongside Brak and pulled off the chain that was around her neck. Haze glared at Melegal. He shrugged. At the end of the chain was a locket of some sort. Rayal popped it open.

"Let me see the wound," Rayal ordered in a firm but pleasant tone.

Haze revealed a gaping hole with blood seeping out.

"Mother of Bish! And yet he still breathes," Rayal dumped the contents of the locket, ground herbs of a strange pink and blue hue, on the wound. She rubbed it in and snapped the locket shut.

"What was that?" Jubilee said, wiping her eyes. "Will it help him?"

Rayal shook her head and sighed, "Not if I'm too late, Little One. I hope that I am not."

Brak's body remained still. The sweat that once beaded his face was now gone. Silence crept into the stable. Everyone took a moment to look around at one another.

Strange group. A stallion among the hounds.

Rayal broke the silence.

"Are you the Detective's sister?" she said to Haze.

Haze looked at Melegal, then back to Rayal and said, "No."

"Look," Jubilee gasped, pointing at Brak's stomach.

The bleeding stopped.

"So much blood lost, yet he mends," Rayal said, incredulous.

Brak's chest began to rise and fall again. His eyes snapped open as he rose up.

Melegal felt the sadness in his heart melt away with exhilaration. One life was saved today. *Now what am I going to do with them?*

Rayal rose to her feet and said, "It seems you owe me now, Detective." She smiled at him and looked down at Brak, who had Jubilee all over him. "What an odd looking fellow. I've never seen the likes of him. And he's got blood all over him. Some of it black. Who did you battle?"

"Underlings." *And Royals.*

Rayal made her way past him and said, "A moment outside, Detective. Ladies," she looked at Haze and Jubilee, "I'll just have him a moment."

Haze frowned while the soldiers followed him outside.

Good thing Haze is not a lycan. She'd tear Rayal's head off. Nothing like a jealous woman to tear the skin from your bones.

"I'm grateful, Rayal. My friend's loss would have been quite difficult to bear, I'm afraid. And I'm not one to mourn." He hated to say the next line, but he felt compelled to. "How can I repay you?"

Rayal leaned against the stable door and twirled her fingers in her hair. She licked her tongue over her perfect apple-red lips, thinking. Melegal quickly glanced from her toes to her head. Riding clothes couldn't be any snugger, from her long leather brown boots to the stitches in her leather breeches. He would have ridden with her anytime, anyplace, anywhere. *No need to be smart if you don't have to.*

"Tell me more about these *friends* of yours," she said, looking him dead in the eye. "The girl, in particular. She has the mannerisms of a Royal, among other things."

Oh my, she's one of those. Melegal knew the type. Rare, but honest. Rayal was proficient at discerning the truth from a lie. *Slat.* She'd caught every last detail up to this point. It wasn't likely she would miss one now. Of course, Melegal was as good a liar as any, but why risk it now? It was time to gamble. He didn't owe Jubilee anything, anyway.

"Can we have more privacy?"

"Give us some space." Rayal ordered.

The soldiers walked out of earshot.

Melegal continued in a quieter tone.

"Rayal, it may disturb you to know that my service with the Royal Almens is questionable."

He watched her eyes, but her expression remained unchanged.

"There was an incident. A battle in the Royal Arena that went wrong."

Rayal clenched her fists, "Ooh, I hate those bloody games. Cruel it is. Savage! Am I to take it that man in there is a survivor?"

"And the girl, but the woman, she is my friend."

Her brow perched over one eye.

"I see. And then who are those ..."

Melegal held his finger up.

"A moment, I've hardly finished. Underlings. They infiltrated the castle and attacked. Lord Almen fell, but his condition remains unknown. It seems no one has been accused of this infiltration but the Castle Cleric, Sefron."

Rayal's eyes drifted away from his as she looked at her guards.

Get ready to run, Melegal!

She returned her gaze back to him.

"Oh, he's a sickly one. Bulbous and perverted. I could wear ogre skin, and his bulging eyes would still strip me naked." She slapped her hand on his shoulder. "Detective, the Almens are my allies, but they are not my favorite people. The Lorda, I enjoy: how could one not? She's the most charming creature I've ever known."

The both of you, I'd say.

"But, I only owe them one thing."

"And that is?"

"My hand in marriage to her beloved Tonio. My beloved as well."

Melegal could feel the palpitations under his skin, but he kept his eyes on her. *Can my shallow grave go any deeper? This woman betrothed to a murdering abomination. This world will not be rid of him soon enough. Slat if that impudent man isn't what got us into this mess in the first place.* Melegal cleared his dry throat and said, "I've a feeling I know what you'll require of me, Rayal."

"So you can read minds, then?" She came closer. "Tell me what I ask for."

"You want to know what happened to Tonio."

Rayal combed his hair behind his ear, bringing an erotic shiver through his spine.

It's not fair. Not fair at all.

She said, "I've had many conversations with Lorda Almen. She said if anyone could find him, you could."

I wonder if she told Rayal the brute almost killed her. That I saved her? So to speak. How can this woman notice every last detail, yet be fooled by Tonio?

"Eh, did she say anything else?"

She came closer, lips so close he could feel her breath on his ear.

"She adores him as much as I do, but, I know of all the things rotten in his core, and if I am pledged to marry him, I'll be a dutiful Almen. It will strengthen my family as well as theirs." She reached over and ran a hand down his shoulder. "But if Tonio does not appear, our alliance will erode like a rotting log."

What is going on in that head of hers? She makes no sense at all.

"I need you to find him, and both you and I will be served well," she said, stepping away.

Bah, I don't need to play such games. She's more likely to marry a kobold than that butcher. I'll not find the man! Not for Lorda. Not for her. Not for a thousand gold. Well, maybe.

"So, Rayal, I'm not certain where we stand," he said, frowning.

"Check with me in a few days. You know where to find me," she said, waving to her guards, walking away.

Zip!

Melegal ducked. Something very fast flew through the barn, stirring up hay and dust. An eerie fluttering of bat-like wings came from the rafters above.

"What is that thing?" one of the soldiers said, drawing his sword and shielding Rayal.

Melegal got his first look at the creature. The muscles in the small of his back knotted as his hands fell to his swords. *Slat!* He'd taken them off to complete his disguise. The eye, a single eye bigger than his fist, was fixated on him, blinking. A hulking little creature about three feet tall hissed, clutching its black-clawed fingers in and out. Whatever it was, it was evil, menacing, dreadful, and from all appearances more than capable of ripping him into shreds.

"I've never seen such a thing!" one soldier exclaimed.

"Is that an underling?" the other added.

Something about the creature seemed both horrifying and familiar, as if Melegal had seen it somewhere before. Venir had mentioned such a thing during his battle at the great Forest of Bish. Melegal felt his bones turn cold as it licked its eye with its serpent tongue, pointed its clawed finger at him and hissed, "Time to eat!" Its red snake-like tongue whipped about as it patted its belly.

Chapter 58

"Who dares?" Verbard said, unable to shake the nervousness in his belly. *What is Master Sinway up to now?*

Kierway crawled out from under the Vicious, gasping and wiping the blood and mud from his face. No one else moved, not one soldier, Juegen, albino urchling, or the other creatures that creeped and crawled.

Stone-faced, Verbard dusted the debris that had fallen from his robes. A robed apparition floated his way, eyes gleaming in the darkness. The Vicious, hobbled, rose along his side. *Strange, I've not ordered the Vicious to stop. Only one underling is superior in my command.* Verbard squeezed the Orb of Imbibing, which pulsated in his hand. It wouldn't surprise him one bit if Master Sinway had shown up to execute him. Maybe killing his son wasn't such a good idea after all.

The closer the apparition came, the more solidified it was, robes black as night with intricate patterns of silver woven in, similar to his own. It floated past Kierway, who was stuffing his knives back into their sheaths.

You only have one superior, Verbard, but you also have an equal ...

The underling pushed back his hood, revealing his golden eyes.

Brother.

Verbard let out an audible gasp. He'd experienced many things in his life. Shock. Amazement. Pain. Joy. Elation. Dismay. But what he felt now could not be explained. His brother, Catten, once cinder and ashes, now lived. There were no words for that. None at all.

Kierway slogged his way from the mud, arms dangling at his sides, shaking his head. At Verbard's side, the Vicious stood like a mute, studying its missing fingers.

Catten's smile stretched from one side of his head to the other as he softly landed on Verbard's throne.

"Verbard, I can see you weren't expecting my arrival, but here I am. And it would not have been so without you." Catten motioned him over.

Verbard remained where he was. Catten, yes, it was his voice, his eyes, but the body was not what it had been. The body was taller, thinner, the chin more knobby at the end. But there was no mistaking that the mind of Catten was within. It was eerie. It was his brother, yet it wasn't.

"Have you checked in with your family?" Verbard asked of his brother, smiling. "I'd be curious to know their reaction. I'd think they'd be even more overwhelmed than I."

Catten bounced his fingertips together and said, "Oh, that can wait, Verbard. I've a more important mission right now. And I don't think Master Sinway restored me for the sake of reuniting me with my family, aside from you."

"Why are you here, then?" Kierway said, stuffing a knife back inside his bandolier.

Catten spoke with a sinister look at Kierway.

"To save your life for one thing, you fool! If your brain acted as fast as your swords, you'd be more useful, Kierway. Not only are you under my brother's command, but now mine as well."

Verbard came forward.

"This is my command, Brother. Not yours. Your timely appearance garners you nothing without Master Sinway's express authority."

"It will all be clarified soon enough, Verbard. Please, Brother, I'm here to offer my thanks and assistance."

"Yet you sit on my throne," Verbard fired back. He didn't like his brother's tone. There was a lack of sincerity about it, more so than even before. "That's what almost got Kierway killed in the first place, until you interrupted."

They locked eyes. Gold glaring at silver. Silver at gold. Verbard felt Catten's gentle knocking in his mind. He opened the door.

Verbard, I cannot openly show my gratitude to you, my dearest brother. It would be construed as weakness. I am grateful. You saved me. Vanquished the Darkslayer without me. You did alone what we could not do together. I'm humbled, but still resourceful. This is your command, your charge, but I sense you need me, as I've needed you. You stand at the threshold of greatness, set to conquer the great City of Bone. You lead, I'll follow. I know to trust your instincts now.

Verbard was overwhelmed by the sincerity, but Catten was holding back. He knew it.

And as time permits, I'll explain more of what I know of Sinway. He revealed things to me I believe I was not meant to know. It might be just what we need. I need you. You need me.

Verbard liked the cunning thoughts behind that.

Now, let's join armies and release the Underland's greatest terrors on the world above!

Verbard returned his own thoughts.

I welcome you, Catten, but we still have much to talk about.

There was nothing like family to give one new strength. For months, Verbard had felt alone and wayward. Now, his brother, best friend and confidante had returned. For most of their lives, each had been the right hand to the other. Cocky. Calculating. Condescending. Cruel. They did whatever they wanted, whenever they wanted. Now, at the threshold of the most impossible mission of his life, he needed a friend he could count on. And if he could pick anyone in the world to see this through, it would be his brother, Catten.

"My Lord," Jottenhiem arrived at his side, "more barges of soldiers have arrived …" he noted Catten and grunted.

"How many soldiers did you bring, Brother?"

"Oh, enough to destroy a few castles or more." He rose to his feet. "And what lies on the outside of those walls is enough to destroy the rest."

"Even without the keys?" Verbard asked.

"Master Sinway said, 'What would be easier *with* them will still be done *without* them.'"

Catten rose in the air and put his hands on Verbard's shoulders.

"And, I've already sent a few terrors into the streets above. Consider it a gift. There's nothing like a few rain drops before the storm."

Master!

Verbard blinked his eyes. It was Eep.

I've found the human! Kill?

I need the keys, Eep! If he does not have them. Bring him to me. Alive!

Then I eats?

Verbard shook his head.

Only then! Do not fail, Eep!

"I see our little friend is still with you," Catten said, "and he bears good news, eh? I can see it in your eyes. Well done, Brother."

Verbard nodded, but having Catten around was going to take some getting used to. He needed to re-establish himself now.

"Master Kierway, prepare your soldiers for the underground assault on Castle Almen. Commander Jottenhiem, prepare yours and my brother's reinforcements for the surface attack above."

Kierway dug his sword from the mud and said in a smug tone, "So, one moment you're having me killed, and in the next, I'm taking back my command."

"Have you not learned your lesson, then?" Verbard said. The Vicious turned towards Kierway, teeth barred. "You can always pick up where you left off, but the mud will be deeper next time."

"Pah ... Verbard, it bodes you well to know that I'd rather see human blood than yours." He sneered at Catten, walking away. "The same goes for you."

"I like how you handled him, Brother," Catten said. "I couldn't have done better myself."

No doubt you really think you could have; I'm certain.

CHAPTER 59

"WHAT IS THAT THING?" MIKKEL yelled.

It was big, almost a story tall on its spider-like legs, a round horse-sized hairy circle with four fanged mouths above four hairy insect legs. A host of well-armed underlings now crawled out of the hole with it. It was the weirdest thing Mikkel had ever seen. There was nothing like the unknown to get your blood flowing. All his instincts told him to run. But the screams of the scattering people galvanized him to stay.

Twang!

Twang!

Two arrows sunk into the black bulk, but it charged on, unfettered, its barbed tongues, as coarse as wire, licking out over the streets. It snatched one man by the leg and sucked him screaming into its fanged maw.

"Find cover!" Billip ordered, stepping back. He sent two more shafts into an underling's chest. Mikkel was on one side, Nikkel on the other, crossbows ready.

Clatch-Zip!

Clatch-Zip!

Both bolts hit center of the monster's mass, but it didn't slow. Its tendrils whipped out, killing one person after the other.

"This is bad, Billip! Really bad! How can we stop that thing?" Mikkel said, taking cover behind the pile of stones Nikkel had been working on before.

The monster was having its way with the people. The underlings dashed over the cobble stone road, a swath of well-organized devastation. Trinos's sanctuary was coming undone.

"Father, I'm scared!" Nikkel said, his eyes wide with horror as he struggled to reload his crossbow.

Mikkel lowered himself beside his son, grabbed him by the neck, and bumped his head. "Listen to me. Find somewhere safe."

Nikkel, trembling, was shaking his head.

"No! I'm staying with you. Like you said. I'll live a fighter; I'll die a fighter. I'm not leaving you!" Nikkel locked the string in place and loaded his bolt. "I'll do the best I can."

Mikkel never had a prouder moment when he said, "Son, it's better to fight scared than not fight at all, but if you see me running, you better run, too."

"Slat!"

Twang!

"That monster's snatching up people faster than I can load my bow," Billip cried.

The monster dashed left, right, backward, forward in short bursts of speed. Mikkel had never seen anything so big move so fast. He kneeled down along Billip's side. The tide of chaos and blood was rising. He was used to the sounds of battle, but not the sounds of slaughter. The people of District 27 didn't stand a chance. One fell right after the other, some of them being devoured.

"Run, you idiots!" Mikkel roared. "Where in Bish are they going?"

Billip punched him in the shoulder.

"Fool! Better them than us! Now listen. Go for the underlings first. There's not so many. We'll just have to figure out how to deal with the monster later." He pulled the bow string along his cheek. *Twang!* An underling attacking a woman pitched forward, an arrow in the back of its head.

Clatch-Zip!

Another underling spun and fell.

"Good shot, Nikkel!"

Clatch-Zip!

Bolt Thrower's missile cut though the neck of one underling and into the chest of another.

Nikkel looked at his father and said, "Can I use that?"

Mikkel grinned. "One day, Son. One day soon!"

Twang!

"That's the last of them," Billip said. "Now let's get after that monster."

There it was, feeding on dead bodies. Its barbed tendrils swiped back and forth as its legs dashed left, right, back and forward, destroying everything in sight. Mikkel wasn't sure what to do, so he reloaded. He'd rather fight a dozen underlings than fight it. He understood them, but this thing was bizarre.

"What are we going to do?" Nikkel said, peeking over the wall. More than a dozen people were dead already, and at the rate that thing was going they'd all be dead soon enough. He looked at Billip.

"Keep firing and hope it stops?"

"Should we shoot the legs? The mouths? That's all that thing's got!"

Billip grunted a laugh and cracked his knuckles.

"I'll take the legs. The mouths are much bigger targets."

"Ten gold to the man who drops it, then," Mikkel added.

Twang!

Twang!

The creature wobbled, two arrows sticking in one leg.

"Easy," Billip said, "I shoot five to your one. I'll have this beast down in no time."

"Don't be so sure," Mikkel said, taking aim.

Clatch-Zip!

The bolt was true, sailing through the creature's teeth and into the back of its mouth. It lurched up, all mouths squealing in a high pitched frenzy.

Clatch-Zip!

Nikkel let it have another.

It shuddered and charged their way.

Twang!

Twang!

"Get of here, Mikkel! The both of you! We can't stop this thing!" Billip yelled, reloading.

Two tendrils whipped out, one wrapped around Billip's waist, the other catching Nikkel by the leg.

Nikkel screamed, sending a jolt of lighting through Mikkel's spine as the monster began dragging the men towards its snapping maw. "Father, help!" Nikkel cried, fingers clawing at the ground.

Mikkel snatched his club from the ground and charged, all concern for safety abandoned. He had to save his son. The first blow smacked the monster dead center over its mouth, jolting his arms. "Bish!"

He swung again.

WHAM!

And again.

WHAM!

The creature slung Billip aside, skidding him hard over the road.

"Look out, Father!" Nikkel warned.

He could see his son still being dragged towards the mouth, the rows of sharp teeth snapping up and down.

Skull Basher rose and fell, driving the body of the creature down. It hissed and recoiled.

"Hang in there, Son!" he gasped out. "It's almost—*ulp*!"

A tendril coiled around his neck and squeezed. Mikkel could feel his eyes bulging from their sockets. He tried to yell for Nikkel, but could not. But he caught his eye. He could see his son being dragged to his death. *NO!* He had to stop that.

He forced a smile and winked at his boy. *I'll live a fighting man! I'll die a fighting man! But I will save my son!* He raised Skull Basher high over his head and brought it down with all his might.

WHOP!

The tendril released from Nikkel's leg.

WHOP!

Billip was pulling Nikkel kicking and screaming away, fingers grasping wildly in the air. Mikkel's club rose and fell two more times and fell no more.

Chapter 60

FRIENDS OF FIRE. *What is that supposed to mean?*

Barton's deep voice was still crying out with childlike fear. "Get them off me! Get them off!"

More than a dozen underlings had the giant pinned down, piercing weapons poised to strike. Fogle's boots slid down the bank, where he stopped and drew back his arms. There was no time to second guess himself, or Barton would be permanently blind.

You better be right, Boon!

He drew his arms out and summoned the power within. The air in the ravine rushed over him, swirling his robes. A spark ignited in front of his face, turning from a small flame into a fire, the air and his energy feeding it. Before his eyes, a ball as big as his fist grew to twice his own size. Fogle poured whatever he had left into it and let it loose. The fireball roared over the ground and slammed into the unsuspecting underlings and giant.

KRA-BOOOM!

The entire area was engulfed in flame. The small bodies were afire, scrambling and screaming. Fogle shielded his face in his robes. The fire was real now, no longer the magic power he could control. It hit. It touched. It burned.

The underlings were decimated, dying, burning in a pyre of flesh. Somewhere beneath the flames lay Barton. Either alive or dead, he did not know which. The roar of the flames grew louder, and black smoke began to roll. The stench of burning underlings had returned to greet his nostrils.

He held his nose. His eyes watered.

"Ew!"

He fanned his hands in front of his face and coughed. The wind hadn't done him any favors, and he was well aware that underlings still abounded in all directions. He couldn't decide whether to shout or be still. *Find Barton.*

Fogle had taken ten steps when he found himself face to face with a pair of underlings patting the splashes of flame from one another. Their emerald eyes sparked to life as they bared their claws and charged. Fogle ran, caught his foot on his robes, and tumbled to the ground. He screamed as a claw ripped open the back of his leg. He rolled and swatted. He needed another spell. He caught one in the nose with his heel. The other drove its fist into his face.

Smack!

It was a sickening sound. Fogle swore his jaw was broken as pain filled the space behind his eyes. His scream gave him little reassurance as the underling pinned him down and dug its claws deep into his shoulders. It was his turn to make a plea.

"Boon! Hel—"

Crack!

It felt like a rock hit him upside his head. Maybe it was, but he was too dizzy to know. As his blood dripped into his eyes and onto his robes, he fought to cry out once more, but his efforts faded, and only the sound of evil chitters remained. He thought of Cass. *I'm certain she's safer without me. I make a lousy adventurer.*

The underling was ripping up his robes when a powerful force tore the underling from atop him. Through the corner of his eye, Fogle could see a giant naked form of a man with steam rising from his body. Through the smoky haze, he hoped it was Barton because the giant slammed the two screeching underlings into each other like dolls before pitching them away. Fogle found relief from his pain, but his limbs were spent, making him unable to rise.

"Come on, you fools! They close fast!" Boon said from atop one pony and leading the other.

"I can't move!" Fogle screamed.

Two big arms reached down, picked him up, and leaned him over a shoulder like a baby.

"Wizard help Barton! Now, Barton help wizard."

Odd and humiliating, but I live.

Boon led the mounts back over the hill where they'd started, and Barton's steps shook the ground as he followed. Fogle had a better view of the vast ravine now. Underlings, dozens, were in pursuit, and even one of his apparitions remained in chase. *Slat!* It wasn't possible to outrun them on horseback. In minutes, they'd catch up and overwhelm the party.

"Boon," he shouted, turning his eyes to the front, "where are were going?"

Boon did not slow. He charged ahead, white hair whipping in the wind. That's when Fogle saw it. Another swarm of underlings had cut them off from the north and were closing in.

"Boon, are you mad?"

Less than fifty yards away, the underlings closed in like a black sea of fury, hundreds if not a thousand. In moments, it would all be over. He was certain of it. Fogle tried to form another spell on the tip of his tongue, but the jarring steps of Barton only clattered his teeth. Two dozen yards separated them all now from life and death.

"Boon! What are you doing?" he yelled.

A black shimmering hole opened up, as tall and wide as Barton. Boon and the horse rode through and disappeared. Two giant steps later, Barton charged through. Fogle's entire world and life flashed before his eyes coated in black. A brilliant glare emerged a split second later, drawing colorful spots in his eyes.

Barton grunted and lowered him down onto the ground. Fogle rubbed his eyes and blinked. It was the Outland. Same time of day, different place, no underlings. But where, exactly? And where was Cass?

"Boon?" he said, holding his head and looking around.

A raspy voice replied, "Easy now, Grandson. We're safe at the moment. And you look like death rolled over you. Save your strength while I sort things out, huh?"

Fogle looked up Boon, who had a curious look on his face, his eyes elsewhere. Barton stood, blocking the suns, scratching his naked buttocks, and looking around.

"I better see if I can find a spell to remedy that, but that one I just used..." he shook his head and grimaced, "It's gone from the book forever."

Fogle pressed his robes onto his bleeding head and said, "Well, you always told me, 'You lose it, you lose it, so you better make it count.' My breath reassures me its magic was not wasted, and I'm grateful for that." He noticed Boon's face was unchanged. The old man looked like a master who'd lost his dog.

"You almost didn't use it, did you? You contemplated full peril after all!" Fogle grabbed his head. He swore it was about to split open. *He's crazy!*

"Well, don't misunderstand me, Grandson. I'm not used to fleeing from underlings, is all. I'd rather die taking as many as I can with me. I just can't stand the thought of them living in my daylight."

If Fogle had the strength, he'd have stood up and punched Boon in the jaw. The man was obsessed with the evil brood. His actions were dangerous and irresponsible. It was time to corral his grandfather's impulsive behavior, else they might not live to see another sundown.

Through the hole in his robes, he checked the gash in his thigh. It burned and needed stitches. *That will leave a scar. I wonder if Cass will like that?* His narrow shoulders were sore and bleeding as well. He grunted.

"Yes, Fogle, you fought hand to hand with an underling and lived. That feeling will stay in your blood now. The burn will always be there."

Fogle nodded towards Barton.

"I had some help, and *no*, I'm not on some mission to wipe out the entire race of underlings." He managed to make it back to his feet. "I'm going to find Cass, that man, and that dog—and after that, I'm going back to the City of Three, with or without any of you." He dusted the dirt from his robes and grimaced. "Except Cass … maybe."

The truth was, she was all he cared about now. It seemed the dog was all she cared about. And he wasn't so sure anyone cared about him other than himself. And what his grandfather cared about, other than killing underlings, he was the least sure about.

"Barton help you."

The giant spoke with his broad back to him, his voice somber.

"Wizard saved Barton from the tiny people who tried to poke out my eye. I help you little man with big head. Find dog, pretty woman," Barton scooped dirt into his hands and rubbed it into his wounds "and find the tricky man that hid Barton's toys."

Fogle couldn't help but feel touched.

"Well, thank you, Barton. It's good to know that someone is looking out for me, but I believe you saved me as well. I was as good as dead before you came."

"Ha. Saving people is easy. Saving a giant is hard," Barton said, resting his chin on his knees, and gazing into the dipping horizon. "I help."

"We need to find safe ground to rest," Boon said, "and, as for the dog and woman, I'm not sure as of yet how to track them down. A little more study in the spell book might be needed."

"I thought you had it memorized," Fogle said, shuffling towards one of the horses and reaching into his pack.

"Mostly," Boon said, smirking. "I'm still foggy on a few pages."

"The dog goes where the man is. And if we can find the man, we can find the dog and the druid," Fogle said, loosening the cords tied around an object in burlap. "And just because it didn't work last time, doesn't mean it won't work better this go around." He tossed Venir's long hunting knife onto the ground, reached under his robes, and dumped the totem of his bird familiar Inky beside it.

"Good thinking," Boon said, fingering the knife in the pile. "Interesting blade this is. Very interesting, indeed." He ran his finger over its keen edge. "A shame we don't have a lock of the dog's hair, or the woman's, for that matter. A shame, indeed."

Fogle snatched it away and tossed it down.

"Whether it works or not, at least we can have a scout. And who knows? Maybe they'll find us." He set some component bottles along the ground. "Otherwise, we travel south."

Fogle took a seat. He was battered and exhausted, but he was getting used to it. Underlings were everywhere, and it seemed unlikely Cass and Chongo could avoid them. *They're better prepared than me.* It wouldn't have been so bad if Mood was here, or Eethum. A few dwarf trackers would be good. Instead, it was he and his grandfather, relying on magic to do things for them their natural instincts could not. Weary and worried, he began to cast his spell, after he made a silent promise to himself. *I will see this through.*

Chapter 61

Empty. Empty as a dry gulch. Barren as the Outlands plains. Broken like a glass window pane. Tuuth grabbed him by the hair, pulled him to his feet, and bound his broken wrists behind him. Venir didn't respond. He was listless, eyes averted from his captors. Underlings. Two had become four, and four had become eight. Everything inside him recoiled, yet he had no fight left inside him. It was disgraceful.

"Two dead," one said, gesturing to the black bodies Venir had broken earlier.

He could feel the underling's eyes looking up at him, glowering. His typical urge to slaughter and destroy was gone. Now, only a growing concern for his safety remained. He closed his eyes and tried to remain confident. *Let it play out.*

The underlings chittered back and forth, checking the wounds on the dead bodies.

"Where are his weapons?" the underling said, its common accent clear as a man's. "What did he kill with, orcen one?"

Venir felt Tuuth shift in discomfort. He knew what that was about. Tuuth wanted his weapon for himself, but that wouldn't make for much of an explanation.

"Here, I have it," the leader of the men said, stepping forward, holding a long sword. "It's a fine blade, and I'd considered keeping it for myself."

The underling snatched it from his hand and ran his clawed fingers over the blade. He made a sharp chit, and the other underling soldiers spread out and began a search of the area. The underling lifted Venir's chin up with the tip of the sword. So many underlings he'd fought and killed, but he'd never gotten as close a look at a living one as he had now. Usually, they were dead before he extended any formal pleasantries. For the first time in his life, he gave an underling a study.

Its features were a smooth granite under its thin rat-like pelt. The nose, eyes, and chin were similar to a man's, more lithe and refined, but the features tight and calculating. Something primordial and evil lurked in the depths of its eyes. Natural. Deep. Compassionless. Cold. Maniacal. They were like humans, and the other races for that matter, but lacked the empathy of men, even of orcs. No, even as Venir had killed multitudes of underlings without mercy, he'd had a reason. The only way to stop their killings was to kill them. *The underlings hunt me, not the other way around.* They enjoyed killing and torture, it seemed. Venir, he only killed because he had to, or did he?

"Human," the underlings hissed, "and such a large one at that. You are even bigger than this orc, such a strong one at that. What brings you here? Here on this hill? A spy, perhaps?"

Think. Venir had to set his emotions aside. Having a conversation with an underling was foreign to him. It began to stir his blood. He leaned forward over the underling and said, "I was hunting wild boar, but I found this orc instead."

The underling jabbed the sword tip an inch into his thigh.

Venir clenched his teeth in silence.

"I don't enjoy your chatter, Human, but I do enjoy drawing your blood," the underling said, "Now, tell me: why are you here?"

Another underling appeared with Venir's backpack in his hand, along with the signal cylinder Jans had given him earlier.

"What's in that? Dump it out."

The contents were spilled on the ground, including the sack, which the underling opened and revealed nothing. Tuuth grunted in his ear. *At least that is safe.*

The underling leader picked up the cylinder and waved it in his face.

"Tell me what this is, Human, or else I'll make your life more miserable."

Venir was certain he was going to do that anyway. *Stupid. I should have put that in the sack, too.* He clenched his teeth. *String them along. Let them think they need you.*

Venir looked away.

The underling twisted the blade in his thigh. He screamed at the top of his lungs until his throat was dry. He sank down on one knee when the underling pulled the blade from his thigh.

"Bring him along," the underling said, flipping the canister up underneath his arm. "We'll let the underling master decide his fate." The underling turned and led the way up the hill.

"Grab him," Tuuth said to the other humans. Two men came over and helped Venir limp up the hill as Tuuth drifted back.

"Borsh!" Tuuth said. He was seething. He couldn't find the axe or the armor anywhere. All that was left was the leather sack, backpack, a pair of canteens and a few other supplies. There was something about that axe and helm, something powerful he craved. He looked at his trembling fingers. The Stranger had almost broken them, should have broken them with all the pressure he felt. That man was more than a man. It had taken much of his magic to bring the man down.

"Who is that stranger?"

It bothered Tuuth.

He rubbed the leather bracers on his wrists. The rich hide texture was beginning to fade, and the leather cords that laced them were beginning to wither. How many charges were left until the magic was gone completely? It was the only thing he had to protect himself and his family. He grabbed the shirt of armor and tossed it into the backpack along with everything else, slung it over his shoulder, and hoofed it up the hill.

The southern gate of Outpost Thirty-One was big, but nothing like the City of Bone. Venir couldn't remember being so close before. He half limped and was half carried under the metal portcullis, where another set of massive doors waited to be opened.

"Blind him," the underling ordered. "The Master always likes to be the first to see their reaction and expressions. Heh, Human, consider this compassion. It will take time for your mind to adjust to what lies within."

Venir would like to think that he could handle seeing anything, for he'd seen many horrors before, but the odd smell suggested otherwise. He offered the underling one last scowl as a burlap sack was tied over his head. The big doors creaked open. Limping, blinded, wrists broken, he was led inside Outpost Thirty-One. He must have taken a hundred agonizing steps in stark silence before they stopped.

"Lock him up and leave him," the underling's voice said.

A heavy device was locked around his neck and wrists, both feet bound and chained. *A stockade?* The sound of footsteps became distant and faded. Only the throbbing in his neck, legs, wrists and knees remained to keep him company. *Bone.*

Chapter 62

"Take this and go," Jubbler tucked a dagger inside his belt. "And this," the old dwarf said, stuffing a vial inside his pocket. "Now go!"

"What does it do?" Lefty said.

"Just take it when you need it."

"How do I know when that is?"

"There's no time," Jubbler shoved him away, "just go!"

Lefty ran. Small feet splashing over the docks and away he went, darting from one alley to the next, blending in, and avoiding prying eyes, just as he'd been taught. The odd thing was, not so many people were to be seen. The Nest was vacant.

Erin. I have to get Erin.

It took several minutes before he came to his first stop and caught his breath. It was the apartment of Palos's nanny. He'd sniffed out her and Erin's whereabouts early, while Gillem was still alive. He crept down the alley and hid beneath the stairs that led up to the nanny's door. Two guards had been posted there before, one at the top and the other at the bottom. No one appeared to be there now.

Lefty sprang up the steps in three hops. At the top, the door was cracked open. His heart fluttered in his chest. He was too late to save Erin. He pushed the door inward and paused. Inside, he heard the nanny humming a lullaby and a rocker creaking. *Yes! She's here!* He glanced down the stairs, over his shoulders and back and forth. No one was in sight, but his keen ears picked up a commotion in the distance.

He slipped inside the room that was dimly lit by candles and had no windows. A bassinet and cupboard stood alongside the wall, and a clay bottle rested on the table. The nanny was huddled up with the baby, facing the corner. *That's odd.*

Lefty felt a pinching on his wrists. The absidium chains would make things difficult. Strange that they were so light and quiet. He wondered what their true intention was.

As the old nanny hummed and rocked, Lefty crept behind the woman. He drew the dagger from his belt. A slight blue sheen illuminated his face. It was his dagger. The one he'd been given from Melegal. How did Jubbler get it?

"Eh? Who is there," a haggard voice said. "I'm feeding the baby. Do not disturb. Do not disturb the baby."

She's insane. How do I snatch a baby from a crazy woman? He looked at his blade. *What would Melegal do?* He made up his mind: he'd stab her in the leg if he had to. He stepped around her backside, rose on his dripping tip toes, and sought Erin's face.

"No," he said, unable to hide his voice. It wasn't Erin. The nanny was nursing a baby mintaur. The vulgarity of the moment dropped his stomach into his toes. It was another moment in the nest he hoped he'd never comprehend.

Wham!

Lefty jumped as the door slammed shut.

Diller stood before it, toothpick rolling from one side of his mouth to the other.

"I've been looking for you," Diller said. "Heh-heh. I see you're looking for the baby girl, aren't you?" He stepped forward, leveling his crossbow to his chin. "Well, she's been gone for a good while now. Not likely me, you, or even Palos will ever see her again. Now, come quietly, Little Rodent. Palos wants to see you, and I won't hesitate to skewer you and haul you in like a little beast."

Lefty fidgeted. Diller had him dead to rights and cornered. His heart sunk, realizing Erin was gone and even worse, that it was all his fault. Maybe it was time to give up, already.

"Diller, you hush, Old Fool! I'm feeding the baby."

Lefty positioned himself between the old nanny and Diller.

"Cut that out, Boy. I'm not in the mood."

"There now, he's a cute little fella. I'll nurse him, too." She started to pull the rest of her blouse down.

Gads! This can't get any worse. A thought struck him. It was Jubbler saying, 'Take it when you need it.' He uncorked the vial in his pocket and sipped it down. An airy feeling washed over him. He held his fingers up to his face. They were gone.

"Ack! Where did the little fella go?" the nanny cried, jumping from her rocker. "It's a ghost, a ghost I say!" She swatted blindly in the air.

"It's not a ghost, addle headed woman. Just a boy and a magic potion." Diller pressed himself along the door. "I don't know where you got that, but if it's one of ours, it won't last but a few minutes. I can hold the door that long. Heh-heh. I bet you've never used the stuff before. Makes you sick, it does. You'll pay for it. Soon pay for it, you will."

Lefty kept his mouth shut, charged across the room, and stabbed Diller in the leg.

The man let out an awful howl as Lefty snatched the keys from his belt, backed off, and unlocked his absidium chains. He slung them, hitting Diller in the face.

"Fool!" Diller slammed the chains on the ground. "You won't get away. The magic quickly fades! In a moment, I'll have you!"

Lefty checked his fingers. He was beginning to reappear.

Diller lunged, a slice of his dagger grazing Lefty's chest.

"The ghost is back! The ghost is back!" the nanny yelled and charged to the door. "I must protect the baby." She ran into Diller, and they toppled into the door.

"Blast you, Woman! Get off of me!"

Lefty grabbed the absidium chains, swung them around Diller's neck, and yanked back.

"Urk!"

Diller stumbled from wall to wall, trying to knock Lefty free. His back was slammed into one wall after the other as Diller fought against the chains. He was choking the man, giving it everything he had, but Diller was strong. Every blow his small arms absorbed weakened them further. *Hang on for Kam! Hang on for Erin!*

The nanny opened the door and stumbled through.

Diller produced a knife and stabbed blindly back behind his head, poking at Lefty's eyes and shoulders. He ducked and dodged, crying out as the dagger poked a hole in his arm and face.

Lefty heaved back with all his might. Diller let out a rasping sound, tongue juttering from his mouth. The door started to close shut. *Move or die!* He leap-frogged over Diller's head and dashed out the door.

Whew!

There was no way Diller could catch him now. His feet were moving as if they were on air. *I have to try and save Kam.* He had no idea where Erin was, but that was another matter. On magic feet, he sped into Palos's tavern, ducking underneath the swinging doors.

Chaos.

Lefty hadn't heeded the sounds before he headed in. He only assumed it was carousing run amok. It had happened before. This time was different. The tavern was a battlefield packed with cutthroats, cut purses, and thugs. Every man and woman fended for themself. Brigand fought brigand. Hidden knives whipped out and fell. Lefty crouched behind the bar as the shouts of pain and anger reached a crescendo. It seemed Jubbler was telling the truth after all. The rebellion was on.

Get up the stairs and inside. Now was his best chance to save Kam.

One voice, odd and eerie, could be heard above the rest.

"I am Zorth! I tolerate no evil! None shall remain that cross my path!"

Thorn! What is going on?

Lefty jumped away as a body was hurled over the bar. Thorn stood atop the steps, a man possessed. He swung a massive sword that flashed like lightning over a pile of dead bodies at his feet.

"Zorth, the Slayer of all evil things!"

The great sword arced down, hewing one man in half. Down the steps Thorn came swinging: The sword judge. Jury. Executioner. Lefty was certain all in the tavern were condemned, including him.

I'm small. Maybe he won't see me. His hand trembled. He had to summon his courage. He owed it to Kam. As Zorth made it to the bottom landing on the steps, he sprang over the bar, ducked a rogue's knife chopping at another's head, climbed beams on the back of the steps, and dove inside Palo's door.

"Whew!" he wiped his forehead.

"I am Zorth, the greatest blade of all!" The sound wasn't coming towards him, but away. *"Nothing can withstand the wrath of Zorth. No giant, no dragon, and no misguided pieces of flesh!"* Thorn's odd force blended into the chaos. *"I'll be free, but for vengeance I thirst."*

Lefty shook his head. So much had been going on. He had to get his bearings. *Kam!*

There she lay on the floor, unmoving, where a pool of blood formed.

"No! Kam!" In an instant, Lefty had her hand in his, holding it in his lap. "Kam! You can't die! Don't be dead! Please!" Tears were streaming down his cheeks. The wound in her belly was deep. He tried to stop the bleeding with her robes.

"Lefty," she said in a hoarse whisper. "Where's Erin? Did you save her?"

He shook his head, tears dripping down his cheeks onto her face. He wasn't going to lie to her again. He couldn't do that to her. Not again. Not ever.

"I went to get her, Kam," he sobbed, "but they have sold her." He shook uncontrollably. "For ransom, I'm told."

Kam's green eyes had a glossy look in them, her face expressionless as she grabbed his shirt collar and pulled him down.

"Promise me you will save her, Lefty. Promise me you will find her."

"I-I will! Oh dear, I promise that I will save Erin!"

Kam's eyes closed. Her fingers twitched, the gems twinkling inside her hand. Lefty blinked more tears from his eyes. Her chest rose and fell no more …

"Heh, heh, heh, heh …" laughed a wicked voice. It was Palos. He lay on the floor a broken man, clothes smoldering, all the hair singed from his body. He huffed a puff of smoke. He looked like a log that had been patted out.

"You'll never find the girl, Halfling. She's gone a hundred leagues by now already." Palos coughed. His body contorted in pain. "Much coin she fetched. Much, indeed! Hah-hah! Better for the girl. A favor I did. *Hack. Hack.* Seems she has no mother anymore. Tis a shame to see such a vibrant body like that go. *Hack.* But my blade was much sharper than her tongue."

Lefty's tears stopped. Rage swelled inside his chest as he pulled out his blue-bladed dagger and dove at Palos's chest.

Kam stood in a cold river, its waters black, the chill as deep as bone. Her thoughts were of Erin, her daughter's innocent face. It was all she could hold onto. Her last spring of life.

Live and serve? A voice from beyond said.

"What?" her voice echoed. She felt her strength fading. Her memories going. Only a faint red light remained.

Live and serve?

Erin. She had to find Erin.

"Yes." She felt her mind touching another's.

We are bound.

Kam lurched up, gasping for air. The gems in her hand washed the room in red light. The agonizing pain in her belly was gone. Her strength returned.

"I'll kill you! I'll kill you, Palos! You killed my friend!" Lefty was on top of Palos, the Prince of Thieves' arms holding him at bay.

Kam wrenched Lefty from Palos with a single thought, and gently set him down.

The bewildered halfling couldn't hide his shock and the elation that enhanced all the features on his face.

"How!" Palos exclaimed. "You should be dead, you red-haired witch."

But she wasn't. She lived and felt more power than she ever felt before. The potential to pull Palo's bones outside of his skin was hers. But for now she needed him alive. Her eyes turned to burning green flames.

"Where's my daughter, Palos!"

EPILOGUE

Time stood still. Melegal was certain of it. It was as if everything in the barn no longer moved except the dreaded creature that eyed him. It sat in the rafters gnashing its teeth and slowly flapping its bat-leather wings. It said it was going to eat him. Melegal had no doubt it thought it would. If Melegal could step outside of his body, into another, anybody at all, he would. He'd reached the limit on all the running, all the fighting, all the lying he could take. He couldn't do this forever. He was ready to die.

Beside him, Rayal huddled behind her guards, who stood firm, but fearful.

Within the barn's expanse, underneath the rotting rafters and accompanied by the smell of ripening manure, Melegal realized it was as good a place to die as any. Where McKnight had, his mentor. Melegal folded his arms across his chest.

"Come and eat me then, Imp."

The horrible creature's wings buzzed to life. It dropped from the rafters and hovered before Melegal like a giant evil hummingbird.

"Keys," it said in a raspy voice. Its knotted arms reached out with four taloned fingers that looked as if they could cut through stone.

One of Rayal's guards struck the imp over the head with a two-handed chop of his sword. The blade glanced off the creature's steel hard skin. The bewildered guard looked back up just in time to catch the imp's claw in his throat. The other guard, the taller of the two, lunged at the imp.

Blink!

It disappeared.

"Sweet mother of Bish!" the man cried out, eyes blinking wildly, scanning all directions. One second the man stood in astonishment, in the next he was fighting for his life. The imp appeared on the man's back, pulling the skin from his bones. In two seconds, it was all over. Only the blood splattered imp, Melegal and Rayal remained. He wasn't about to move, and Rayal wasn't about to, either. A clever girl Rayal was. As smart as she was beautiful.

The imp hovered in front of Melegal once more, reaching out, blood dripping from its claws.

"Keys!" It demanded this time.

Perhaps all of Melegal's problems before hadn't been as bad as he'd thought. Maybe doing dirty deeds for the Almens wasn't so bad after all. Now, the feeling in his gut told him he'd become a part of something much bigger. The keys he had, the underlings wanted. They needed. They'd invaded the city for them. Oh, how valuable they must be! Oh, the power that maybe he could wield. If he had something so truly valuable in his hand, something that had helped the Almens rise to such power, then that was something maybe he should keep for himself. His shock and despair were replaced by a greater feeling. A stronger feeling. One that a thief could clearly understand: Greed. If the keys had the power the underlings wanted, that the Royals protected, then there was no way on all of Bish he was about to let them go.

"What keys?" Melegal asked, allowing a gentle bend in his knees.

"Do not play, Human. My master awaits. Give me the keys, or I shall rip them from your flesh."

Melegal could feel Rayal's eyes boring into him and the imp. Her fear and worry was heavy in the air. His own palms began to glisten with sweat.

The small door in the stable opened. It was Haze.

Not taking is eyes from the imp, Melegal said, "Get. Back. Inside."

Haze screamed as the imp eyed her.

"I just kill the women then, Skinny Man." It hissed at Haze and Rayal. "I eat them. I eat you. Alive I do."

Melegal had no doubt the creature could do it. Its mouth was as bigger than a man's. Its teeth were like dagger tips. Despite its lack of size, it reeked of raw power. He had to be careful what he did next. *But you won't get these keys.*

Melegal held up his hands.

"Easy. Easy now. I'll give you what you want." He started to reach into his vest. The imp's head jerked left and right like a little bird.

"Hurry! Eep hungers!"

Eep. The little fiend has a name.

Melegal could feel his heart in his chest now. The imp was going to kill him. Keys or no keys. He was certain of it. But the imp didn't know he had them. It was time to play a game. *How smart can an imp be, anyway?*

"I'll have to take you to the keys."

The imp hissed. *Blink.* Disappeared. Reappearing with both its claws wrapped around Haze's scrawny neck. The pressure was building in her face. Her eyes filled with terror. Melegal expected her neck to snap at any moment.

Let go! Let go! Let go!

The inside of his mind was glowing. Commanding. Splitting. Haze was about to die. He could feel it in his bones. Blood dripped from his nose.

"Eep don't like when human lies. Keys or no keys, you all die now!

Crack!

Melegal fell to his knees as Haze's body sagged to the ground. He heard Rayal panting behind him and nothing else.

"No," he murmured, unable to hold his head up. "No ..."

Call it instinct. Brak wasn't old enough to understand such things yet, but he'd heard plenty of talk about it. It was another sense, they said. Something that made your hair stand on end.

While he and Jubilee huddled behind, Haze went to check on all the commotion. Once she made it out the small door, he only saw part of her body. Her entire body stiffened, petrified with fear. Jubilee gasped at his side. His hair stood on end. Grabbing whatever he could, he was moving. That's when he saw it. A bat as big as a dog, with horns on its head, arms wrapped around Haze's neck. He hadn't even crossed the threshold when he swung.

Crack!

He hit the foul creature square in the head with the white ash cudgel that glowed with inner life. Haze crumpled to the ground like a sack of rags. The bat-like thing looked up at him now, a large red eye with a black pupil, a ragged tongue lurching from its mouth. Someone was screaming at him.

"Hit it again!"

Womp!

It was the raven-haired woman who saved him.

Womp!

Why was Melegal on his knees, head downcast, holding his heart?

Womp!

Whatever the creature was, it didn't break. It just hissed underneath the weight of every powerful blow. It was like beating a sack of cow-hide filled with sand. He went to swing one last time.

Blink.

It was gone.

"It's gone, Melegal. It's gone."

He knew the voice. It was Rayal. But that gave him little comfort or reassurance. But she smelled good. Haze was there, too. Alive and well. She didn't smell so good, but he was fond of her anyway. Inside him was an urge. An urge to hug them both and whoever else. It seemed they lived to face the next tragic moment in their lives. But he wasn't sure that it would top this one.

"Me! Me!"

Someone was screaming inside his ear. A soft familiar nicker of a pony could be heard.

Huh! Quickster and Georgio. Where did you come from?

"Me! It's me! Wake up, you sack of bones!" Georgio said. He could feel the boy shaking him, but it didn't do him any good.

"If he's dead, I get his hat," Jubilee said. "Uh … sorry Haze. But if you don't want it."

No! Not my hat! And the keys! What happens if they find my keys!

He couldn't move, though. Not one muscle. He couldn't tell if his eyes were opened or closed, but he couldn't see anything. He could barely feel his fingers or his toes. He didn't understand what had happened, either. One moment, Haze was about to die. In the next moment, his mind exploded. All he had left was his ears. All the rest of his body was damaged parts. He was certain his hat had something to do with that.

"I'll take him to the castle. I can care for him there," Rayal suggested.

"And what about us?" Haze responded, her voice heated.

"I'll see what I can do, but we need to get him to safety."

"I'm not going in any Castle," Jubilee said. "And who are you, exactly?"

"I'm Georgio. Who are you?"

Melegal was fading. His head swirling. The conversation around him becoming incomprehensible. *Maybe I'm dying.* It was his second to last thought. *Georgio better be feeding Quickster well, or I'll bust that fat arse of his.* His consciousness sunk into the darkness.

SERIES 1 · THE · BOOK 6

DARKSLAYER

· FIGHT OR DIE ·

Chaos at the Castle

CRAIG HALLORAN

Chapter 1

BLINK.

Eep looked like he'd been chewed up by a dragon and spit out. He lay quivering on the cave floor. His eye was red. Swollen. The wings on his back were mangled, and many of his teeth were broken. He let out a ragged hiss.

"Masstersss …"

"I hope you have the Keys, Imp," Verbard said, his eyes glowering with silver fire.

Eep opened his palms. They were empty.

"Vicious!" Verbard snapped.

The hulking figure emerged from the shadows, snatched Eep by the neck and squeezed.

Verbard kept his rage in check as Catten chuckled at his side.

"Brother," Catten began, "we will get the Keys in due time, if need be, but let's find out what happened first before you pull the imp apart, like old times."

Verbard wanted nothing more than to destroy something or someone, but Eep was his most trustworthy servant. Master Kierway wanted his head, but Master Sinway had saved it. Jottenhiem was a loyal soldier and comrade, but even he couldn't be trusted. Now, his brother, Catten, had returned, and that only made him all the more uncomfortable. He should be relieved, but he was far from it.

"What happened, Eep?" he said, looking right into the imp's great eye.

Eep's eye bulged in the socket. He could not speak.

"Ease up!"

Eep gasped.

"Thank you, Mastersss—"

Verbard snatched his snake-like tongue and said, "It's Master."

Eep glanced at Catten, then back at Verbard and nodded.

Verbard released his tongue.

"Pardons, Master Verbard. Ah … the skinny man I found under heavy guard. I had him, but a man, a large man, smote me with white magic. Cracked bones. Eep had no choice. Return or be banished."

"Next time," Verbard said, "I'll have to keep watch on things. Can you find this man again, if you have to?"

"Certainly, Masterss … er … Master."

"You were supposed to bring the Keys or the man, Eep. You have failed," Verbard said, letting a wave of energy course through him. Eep wasn't of any use to him now. The creature was broken and would need time to heal. He couldn't tolerate failure. Not from the imp or any other. He'd make an example of the imp, and he'd do it now.

Save your energy, Brother. Catten had entered his mind. *Banish the imp. Bring him back later. The Keys can wait for now.*

Verbard wanted to smite his brother. Everybody. But, he let his magic ease.

It's time we talked about the Keys.

"Be gone, Imp!" Verbard ordered.

"But Master, I hungers," Eep hissed.

"Be gone!"

Blink.

Catten still sat on his throne, sipping port.

"Up, Brother."

Catten rose, poured another goblet and handed it to Verbard.

Verbard took his seat. Eyeing his brother, he sipped.

"Alright, Brother. Now that we are alone, tell me everything. And don't mince words. I want it all. Your resurrections. Master Sinway's plans. This ludicrous notion that the underlings once lived in this city, and what is so important about these Keys."

Catten's gold eyes brightened. His voice was almost cheerful. He said, "Certainly, Brother. Where would you have me start?"

Verbard patted the Orb of Imbibing that now rested within the folds of his robes. Its presence gave him comfort. An edge he didn't have before with his brother.

"And don't be humble, Catten. It's unlike you. It's difficult to think that you are actually you, seeing how you have changed bodies. It will take some getting used to. Now tell me about your resurrection?"

Catten held his fist to his mouth and coughed.

"Unpleasant. It was bad enough when the Darkslayer ran me through, but merging into another body was far worse than that. The pain was excruciating—"

"I don't care how much it hurt! What happened?"

Catten stiffened, a darkness falling over him as he came closer and said, "I was getting to that, Brother."

That's more like it.

"Good. Continue."

"Master Sinway was alone as he moved me from one body to another. It seemed not all underlings were fit for my powers. Some died and others remained blind in the process."

"I don't care," Verbard said, taking another sip. "What happened?"

"There is a tomb in his Castle filled with many well-preserved underlings. He merged me with one of them."

It was one thing to raise a dead underling, but quite another to raise one without a body. The eyes of the underlings held many powers, and on occasion those eyes, if powerful enough, would be collected and turned over to the master underling. Verbard always suspected he hoarded the magic in them. That they gave him power.

"He merged you with the dead?"

"Yes. The corpse with the best likeness to me. My eyes and essence filled his body." He fanned out his hands. "And now here I am." He coughed. "I lay catatonic at first while Master Sinway let me recover. He told me about your mission and that you would need help. I, like you, Brother, felt him to be insane, but the part about the underlings living above in Bone might be true. He showed me glimpses of his past. He took me across the world. I saw where we underlings finally have men on the run. They are collapsing. Darkslayer or not."

Verbard rubbed his finger under his chin. "There are many humans, Brother. The city above alone holds many more than all of us."

"But, they are not united. They squabble with one another. They fight over power and gold. 'We have corrupted them before, and we can corrupt them again,' Sinway says."

Men could be bought, that much was certain, but Verbard would rather kill them then work with them. After all, the greed of men had led to the fall of Outpost Thirty One and many others. But taking the entire city of Bone still seemed ridiculous.

"Am I to assume that we are to live among them? Make them our slaves?"

"We will use fear against them. Taking one Castle, this Castle Almen, will lead to the capture of others."

"Does this have something to do with the Keys?"

Catten smiled. "'The Keys are only one means to an end,' Master Sinway said. Having them could aid us in the battle, but they are no guarantee of victory. But, he insists that we acquire them, for they are powerful weapons in our enemy's hands."

"Or they are worthless baubles? Hah! Kierway has spent years trying to find them, and now we are being told we don't need them. Tell me more, Catten. Something is not well with Sinway. You know that. I know that. What did you find out?"

"We should not speak of such things, Brother," Catten said. He eyed the Vicious.

"What? Do you think the Vicious can send a message? It can neither write nor talk. They follow orders. They kill. Now out with it, Catten. What did Sinway reveal to you?"

I feel your suspicions are correct, Brother. He's going crazy.

Verbard sank back into his chair. Catten was lying. Or was he? Verbard hoped that he wasn't. If Master Sinway was falling to madness, that thought was comforting. It would lend a greater understanding to it all. Besides, destroying the humans and taking their city wasn't a bad idea. Just a grand one. A grander one than he'd ever imagined before, hence opening the doorway to his doubts.

"Why do you say that, Brother? Is it because of this conquest, or was it something else?"

"Brother, I'm elated with the idea of overtaking the city, if not the entire world. I'm tired of sitting beneath the world of men, and clearly Master Sinway is as well. There is something ancient that he knows, that he remembers, that has come to life and begun to burn. A vengeance hotter than the hottest of fires. An impatience that spreads like a forest fire on a gusty day. He's bringing them out, Brother."

A deep crease formed on Verbard's brow as he sat up and leaned forward.

"The legions."

Verbard nodded.

"How many?"

"All of them."

The Legions consisted of every armed force in the Underland: soldiers, mages, clerics armed with metal and magic from head to toe. They had defended the Underland in centuries long gone, and now they were coming above ground. They would be a black plague on the land. They would destroy everything in their path. If they won, they won everything. If they lost, they lost everything. The Underland would not be defended. It was an insane idea.

Catten shrugged.

Verbard smiled. He loved the idea.

"Well, Brother, let the havoc begin. Jottenhiem!"

Chapter 2

"**N**AY, RAYAL! THEY CANNOT ENTER. Your father left the strictest of orders," the sentry said. The tall figure stood, spear at his side, in the entrance of Castle Kling.

It was a spectacular thing. Spires jutting into the moonlit sky, copper tiles twinkling like gold. It was the tallest building in all the City of Bone.

Georgio gawped at its highest point.

"Let me in, Cletus!" Rayal shouted back. "I demand it."

"You can come, and your guards, certainly Rayal, but not the others. Klings and Royal Klings only," the man returned.

The sentry stood firm in his coat of mail and helmet that bore the Royal insignia. A longsword was strapped at his waist. Georgio could see callouses on the insides of his palms as he held them out. This soldier had seen many battles, maybe even been to the Warfield. There was just something about him, but still, he was mindful of the raven-haired woman who seethed with outrage before him.

Her fists were balled up at her sides. She said, "Cletus! My father has his affairs, and I have mine. I owe these two my life." She gestured to Melegal and Haze.

Melegal was draped over Quickster's back. Georgio held him tight. The skinny woman he thought he recognized as Haze. She was one of the women who had rescued him from Tonio and McKnight. She was draped over the shoulder of a large man, called Brak. A girl, Jubilee, hung on to Brak's arm.

Cletus shook his head. "I don't care if they saved your father, you mother, and the grand ones of your family. They are not coming in, Rayal. I'm not losing my head over them, and you might just lose yours as well if you don't get inside these walls now."

"Don't you dare talk to me like that, you oaf. I'll have you quartered."

Cletus tugged at his beard. His face flushed.

"Er, Rayal, you know I am fond of you, but I cannot abandon my duty, no matter how much I'd want to." He bowed. "Forgive my directness, Rayal, but underlings!" He peered over the streets behind them. "They crawl through the city now, leading monsters and horrors that I've not even heard of. I've seen underlings, Rayal. I've seen what they do to people. I cannot bear the thought of them getting hold of you. Please, come in so we can talk about this. We'll find another remedy for those people." He looked Georgio and the rest of them over as if they were little more than urchins. "Perhaps a supply of food and water will help."

"Pig," Rayal said.

Georgio heard the girl, Jubilee, giggle. He turned. Brak's eyes locked on his. There was something there. Something familiar. Something sad in the man's eyes. Blinking, he turned towards Rayal. Everything from her hips to her lips was perfect. The young woman was angry, but poised. She was one of the most gorgeous women he'd ever seen. How the sentry, Cletus, resisted her, he did not know, but he'd dive into a barrel of fire for her if she asked. Wiping his sweaty palms on his clothes, he realized something. *I like brunettes.* He cleared his throat.

"We'll go," Georgio said.

Rayal spun on her heel. "Excuse me?"

"Uh … I said, 'We'll go.'"

She reached over and twirled Georgio's curly locks in her fingers. "What was your name again?"

He blushed. "Ah … Georgio. Uh—"

"How well do you know these people, Georgio? Are you their leader?"

"No. I'm no one's leader, but Melegal is my friend." He patted Melegal on the back. "Well, not really a friend so much. More of an acquaintance. But we've been together a long time. I used to live with him and Venir."

Georgio saw that Brak's gaze fell on him and that his eyes narrowed.

"What?" He shrugged. "It's true." He looked back at Rayal, smiling a little. "I don't know those two so well, but the woman over his shoulder saved me once. She saved me from that monster, Tonio."

"What!" Rayal stood up to her full height. Her nostrils flared.

Cletus stepped forward, reaching for her arm.

She jerked away.

"Rayal, Please! You must come inside now. We've word underlings are all over. The menace grows, Rayal!"

"Silence, Cletus." She cusped her hands under Georgio's face and calmly said, "Georgio, tell me more about this Tonio. When did this happen? What does he look like?"

She smells so good. So beautiful.

Rayal pinched his cheeks.

"Tell me!"

Georgio swallowed hard and started blurting words out. "He's a monster! A murderer! Insane. He keeps trying to kill Venir. He's dead, but lives. He tried to kill us days ago in the stables. His face is split. Venir killed him once, but he lives again. No, he killed him twice, actually."

Rayal's eyes were wide as saucers. Her delicate fingers slid from Georgio's face.

"The boy rambles, Rayal. Come in," Cletus said.

She staggered back. Lost and uncertain.

"Did you know him?"

Rayal nodded. "Does Detective Melegal know all this?"

Georgio felt chilly. It seemed he'd already said more than he should have. And this woman was a Royal. No matter how wonderful she seemed, Melegal and Venir both had warned him Royals could not be trusted. *What do I do?* He wasn't a fast talker either. Not like Melegal or Lefty. He wondered how his former halfling friend was doing. He could use his quick wits right now.

"I can't say," Georgio said. "All I think he knows leads me up to the last time I left Bone. And I was getting ready to leave Bone again when I ran across him again."

That part was most of the truth. He'd seen Melegal only once before, this time in Bone, but they hadn't said much, and there'd been no mention of Tonio. Just the Blond-Haired Butcher.

"Sentries!" Cletus said. The soldier grabbed Rayal by the wrist and held her fast.

"Let me go, Cletus!"

"Stop that!" Georgio said. He jumped off Quickster and grabbed at Cletus.

Whop!

Cletus slugged him right across the jaw.

Georgio's knees wobbled. It might have been the hardest he'd ever been hit.

Rayal fought against her bonds.

"Cletus! Unhand me, you pig-headed soldier!"

Half a dozen men in coats of chainmail and brandishing spears stormed out the door. They shoved Georgio, Brak, Haze, and Jubilee back with the tips of their spears.

"That man comes with me, Cletus!" Rayal said. She kicked, thrashed and screamed. "Bring them in the castle with me, or all of your soldiers will suffer the penalty!"

The soldiers paused.

"Get her in there!" Cletus said. "Lord Kling will show no mercy to any who don't follow his direct orders. I won't either! The guillotine is wet enough with blood already."

"Unhand me!"

Catching her eyes, Georgio started to wave. The butt of a spear caught him in the back of his head. When he looked up again, it was pouring rain. The angry wails of the beautiful woman were gone. He rubbed the knot on his head. *I hope I see her again.*

The soldier named Cletus stood at the door with his hands on his hips.

"Get out of here, you over-sized urchins! Hide before the underlings get you. If you stick around any longer, we'll be more than happy to put you out of your misery ourselves."

Wiping the rain from his eyes, Georgio took Quickster by the reins and backed away until he could see the gate of the castle no more.

Brak and Jubilee followed.

"What are we going to do now?" Jubilee asked. Her eyes were bright. Inquisitive.

Georgio didn't know who the big lout Brak and the droopy girl Jubilee were, but he could only assume they were Melegal's friends. If Melegal woke up, maybe he'd know what to do with them.

Something exploded in the air. Everyone flinched. Despite the rain, smoke and fires could be seen lighting up the city in all directions. The City of Bone always had an element of danger, but now it was taken over by something dark and eerie. He wondered if Billip and Mikkel were all right. Perhaps they needed him.

He put his hand on Melegal's back. The thief was so scrawny he could feel his bones. *He's breathing, I think?* He shook him a little, but nothing happened. He knew what a light sleeper Melegal was. A dropped feather would wake him. *I just need to get out of here! That's what Me would do.*

Scratching his head, Georgio looked at Brak. "Don't you have any ideas? You're the oldest who's awake. I just want to get out of here."

Brak leered over at him. Big faced. Unreadable. "I just want to find Venir."

"What? Why would you want to find Venir?"

Jubilee started to chime in. "Because that's his—"

Georgio felt the muscles tighten behind his neck. Something creeped and crawled over the cobblestone road nearby. He ripped out his sword.

"Underlings!"

Chapter 3

"**W**HERE'S MY DAUGHTER, PALOS!"

It was Kam. Half naked. Bleeding. Green eyes blazing with mystic fury unlike anything Lefty had ever seen before. Earlier, she'd been dead; he was certain of it, but now she was alive. Alive as ever. Radiant. Powerful. But, one thing was different: the dark red gemstones glowing through her fist.

Palos chuckled. A bubble of snot formed in his nose and busted. The man's arms were tied behind his back where he sat on a high-backed chair alongside the roaring fire place. His ankles were bound to the chair legs. Sweat dripped down his paunchy face, and his hair was wet and matted on his head. Lefty had never seen the polished man so out of sorts before.

"You won't kill me, Kam." He coughed. "You wouldn't let the halfling kill me, nor would you. You are a good woman, unwilling to cross the line of evil." He eyed her cleavage and licked his lips. "But, you certainly have some very wicked ways. Mmmm. Very wicked indeed."

Kam shoved her fist under his chin. "I'll show you wicked, Palos."

"By all means—"

She slung her arm back and punched him in the nose.

Palos howled. "You broke my nose! You broke my nose, you—"

Smack!

Palos's head rocked back into the chair. He fell silent.

Kam shook her glowing fist in his face. "I'll bust every bone in your face if I have to."

Lefty flinched. Kam was already mad enough at him for getting her into this mess. He'd tried to make it up by saving her daughter, and he'd failed at that. He eased back towards the door.

Without even turning, Kam said, "Don't you move, Lefty. I'm not finished with you either."

A chair slid across the floor and scooped his feet out from under him. "Sit!"

His chin dipped down into his chest. "Y-Yesss, Kam."

Lefty had been nothing short of miserable for days, if not weeks. Palos had ruined his life. Even worse, he'd ruined Kam's.

But at that moment, Lefty felt a little sympathy for the Prince of Thieves. The man was rattled. His bloody nose dripped onto his chest, and his eyes watered in anguish. As much of a demented oddball as Palos had become, it seemed the man's glory days were at end.

Kam was going to find out what she wanted. Lefty was convinced. Even if she had to pull it out of the man one piece at a time. Something bad was going to happen. He sat still, his tiny feet dripping on the floor.

"Kam, you cannot do this to me," Palos said. "My father and your father are allies. Release me, and I'll see no harm comes to you." He shrugged. "Why, I'll even see if we can't somehow locate your daughter, or at least find one that bears a close resemblance to her." He flashed a bloody smile. "Eh?"

Palos was as disgusting a man as there ever was, but he was no fool. No, Kam knew he wouldn't give any information up that might lead to his death. Still, she could feel the fear in the man, actually feel it. And that wasn't all she could feel.

Lefty's heart pounded like a frightened rabbit's where he sat frozen in his chair. And beyond the door she had sealed, a revolution was taking place. Palos's loyalists were at odds with his usurpers. The Prince of Thieves was undone, unless reinforcement of some sort arrived.

She grabbed a log poker and stuck it in the fireplace

"What are you doing, Kam?" Palos said. He eyed her and the poker. "The fire is plenty hot from where I am sitting."

Kill him. I can find your daughter. Kill him. It's time to serve. The gems were speaking to her. The force within had saved her. And now, whatever it was, she owed it service. But at what cost?

Kam's hand drifted to her stomach where the hole that almost took her life had been. It recoiled. Her stomach was in knots. Something bad was happening to her. But the power was so strong! So fulfilling. The gems gave her strength and a confidence that she'd never felt before.

Not looking at him, she twisted the poker in the flames.

"Where is my daughter, Palos? And before you offer a foolish response, I'll remind you that I stuffed Thorn in a fireplace once and I'd have no reservations against doing the same to you."

Palos swallowed.

"Kam, I'm not privy to that information after it reaches a certain point. I merely give the order. Collect the gold. Many other hands work under my directions. Eh, it's a thief's way of avoiding attachment." He blinked the sweat from his eyes. "Ahem. For example, if I were to sell something or someone as precious as you, I wouldn't want to be privy to where you went. I might be tempted to steal you back. And that would not be good for my business."

She jammed the poker deeper into the fire, scattering the coals.

Her voice took a darker tone behind her clenched teeth. "Palos, where is my daughter?"

"Uh … er … Kam, surely even you can sense that my father will not stand for this. I am—"

"A wretch." She jammed the poker into the coals.

"A bastard." Again she did it.

"A swine," she said, pulling it out and eyeing the glow of the red-hot tip.

Kill him! I will find your daughter. Delay me further, and I will not aid. You serve.

The urgings were strong, compelling, even forceful. She tried to open her fist, to release the gems. She didn't need them now. Her fingers were locked around them like a vice. *Blast. What have I done?*

Kill him! I have waited long. It is time to go.

"Agreed, Kam," Palos said. He groaned and shifted in his chair, "I am all those things and worse. But please consider: you can make plenty more children with those lovely loins of yours. As a matter of fact, I would be a bit surprised if a new seed was not sprouting inside you now."

Kam took the red hot poker and laid it on Palos's seat between his knees and crotch. His eyes widened. His lips trembled.

"And I assure you, Palos: if you don't tell me where my daughter is, you'll have no more seeds to spill."

"I admire your obsession with my nether region, Kam. It's simply thrilling, even in my condition."

Slap!

"Where's my daughter, Palos?"

"Do you ever get tired of repeating yourself, you milk-laden whore? I'll tell you nothing!"

Kam grabbed him by the hair on top of his head.

"We'll see about that."

Twirling her fingers in the air, the leather cords that bound him groaned. His wrists and ankles turned blood red.

"Stop this, you maddened wench! I'll have your head for this!"

"Lefty, find Diller! Bring him here!" she ordered.

Lefty slid from his seat and looked around uncertainly. "But, how can I?"

"How can you not, halfling fool that lost my daughter!"

Quickly, Lefty made his way to the door, but it would not open.

"Uh, K—"

With a wave of her hand, the door flew open. "Hurry up, Halfling!"

Lefty dashed out onto the balcony, peeking inside one last time. The door slammed shut.

"As for you, Palos! Your misery has just begun if you don't tell me what I want to know." She stepped behind him and drove her fingers into his temples. She muttered. Incanted. Locked her mind with his. "Where is my daughter, Palos?"

Palos was a silver fox. Quick. Shifty. Darting through a dark forest laughing.

She tracked him down with hounds.

He evaded.

Her hunters shot at him with arrows.

He disappeared. One moment, Palos stood alone on a rocky hilltop, looking down on her, a fox with his eyes in his mouth. In the next moment he was standing behind her with a dagger at her throat.

"Clever, Kam, but like the lactating fool you are, you've done just what I wanted," he said, licking her ear.

Once a woman of power and fury, she found herself under his will. Bound by his vile thoughts. Penetrating her inner weakness. Bringing her to her knees. Once again, she was helpless. His prisoner.

"No, you shall not take me. You shall not take my baby!" she said, trying to yell back, but her voice was weak.

Palos smote her to the ground. "I take whoever and whatever I please." He grabbed her by the head and pulled her down into his suffocating darkness.

CHAPTER 4

"**F**INALLY!" CASS WAS PANTING.

How long and how far the druid woman had been running after Chongo, she didn't know, but she couldn't have been more grateful that he stopped. Transforming from a large, slender white wolf, she returned back to her lithe form. She rolled from her hands and knees onto her back, still fighting for breath.

Chongo, both tongues hanging out of his big mouths, panted over her.

"I didn't think such a big dog could run so far and so fast before." She reached up and patted on of his cold wet snouts. "You really are a thing of beauty. Like a gallant stallion and mighty lion in one."

He sneezed all over her.

"Uck! Yet lacking in their grace." She giggled. Grabbed him by thick fur under his neck and pulled herself back to her feet. "Now, Chongo, what is it you finally stopped for? I was certain you wouldn't stop unless I died. Maybe not even then."

Chongo moaned a little, noses sniffing in the air, tails stiffly wagging back and forth.

The land had been barren for most of the length of the run, not that it mattered. Cass didn't have the time to stop and smell the flowers, or rather the Thorn Brush Lilies and Bone Trees. At last, the landscape was becoming more accommodating. Tall fields of wheat grass were in the distance, and small trees and shrub groves were scattered over the valley. The brisk wind stirred her long white hair as she followed Chongo up the hill, toward the horizon of the setting suns.

"Where are you taking me?" She looked back over her shoulder. "Lords of Life, how far have I chased you, anyway?"

Nature gave Cass comfort everywhere she went, but there was still much on Bish that she'd yet to see. Behind her was nothing but the hot rugged landscape that was common in the Outlands, harsh and unyielding. Though she loved the warmth, there was little comfort to be found in it. She preferred the forest or the high mountains.

"Not exactly the kind of terrain I'd care to settle in, Chongo. I need more streams, flowers and creatures to feel more comfortable." She grabbed him by one of his tails and followed the big dog up the hill. "You'll just keep on going, won't you? I can barely move my legs. Oosh! I need some rest, Chongo."

One of the giant heads swung back. Drooping eyes gazing at her, tongues hanging from his mouths. Cass swore there was a smile in his big jaws. Chongo was more than a common animal. He had a deeper intelligence in his eyes. He was part of a race of his own.

She gazed up at the hill's peak. "Whew, I see we are almost there, wherever up there is. I must admit it seems strange, you leading me up here like this. Shouldn't we be staying in the valleys?"

Chongo turned away, lion-like feet padding up the steep slope, until they stopped at the crest. He snorted, yawned, and lay down on the ground.

Cass lay on his back and draped her arms around his necks. "This better be spectacular." She gazed over the edge. A stiff wind whipped her white locks of hair into her eyes. Pushing them aside, she held her fingers under her nose. "Such a foul and unnatural odor is about, Chongo. Ugh." She spat. "What is—?"

Her pink eyes widened into circles.

Down in the plains, small black figures moved with purpose through the landscape.

Cass dug her nails into Chongo's furry mane. Underlings. She'd never seen so many before. They were a swarm of black ants moving through their fields. Tending to their macabre garden.

"Are those …" she muttered.

She cupped her hand behind her ear. What she heard made her stomach cringe.

"Shovels?"

Shovels. Spikes. Screams.

Squinting her eyes, she couldn't hide her disbelief.

The underlings were chopping into bodies. Men, women, and children of all races. The blood watered their twisted version of a garden. They threw the dead bodies head first into their holes. Buried them head first. Legs jutting from the ground. Their tombstones were bloody heads on spikes. Row after row, the field went on and on.

Cass's hands turned clammy. She clutched at her head and squeezed her eyes shut. Nothing rattled her … ever, but this did. This churned inside her core. All of her sympathies and compassion for all things living had changed. It was one thing to fight for your survival, but it was another when you were cruel. A vicious child that pulls the wings from a beautiful butterfly. She'd never dealt with the underlings. She'd always figured they had their reasons to do things, just like any other race. Until now. Maybe men weren't so bad after all.

"Chongo, we must go." She tugged the fur on the back of his neck. She'd been weary before looking down there, but now she was exhausted. "This is too dangerous. We need to go back. We need to be with Fogle."

Fogle Boon. She hadn't given him a single thought since she chased after Chongo. Suddenly, he was all she could think about. She liked him, but now she felt like she needed him. Not that she ever felt she needed anyone for anything, especially a man, but she wouldn't mind having him around now. She felt like a fool. He must be days away now.

"I hope he's looking for me."

Chongo's ears perked up. His necks growled.

The hairs on Cass's neck turned to icicles.

Down the steep slope, a hoard of underlings armed with swords and shovels scurried up the hill. Their chitters meant death.

Chapter 5

THE SUNS SET OVER THE southern horizon like two bloodshot eyes before collapsing into the mist. Fogle Boon lay flat on his back, his pillow a pile of dirt and stone.

Barton picked at his skin and complained.

"Barton wants to go find his toys now, Wizard. Why's this take so long? Hmmm. I'm ready. Ready now." He punched his fist into the dirt. "NOW! NOW!"

Fogle coughed. He fanned the dust away from his face.

"Will you stop that, Barton! *You* wouldn't have to wait if *you* hadn't *crushed* my familiar in the first place. And putting him back together is taking longer, no thanks to *you*." He dusted off his hands as he stuffed many of his bottles into his traveling sack and groaned under his breath, "Dolt."

"What did you say?" Barton poked his finger at Fogle's chest. "Dolt? What is *dolt*?"

Fogle took a hard swallow, but he didn't back away. Barton, a deformed monster-child, was one of the scariest things he'd ever seen. Barton had once held Cass in his grasp like a children's doll. Fogle had seen the man smash and eat underlings like bugs. He swallowed again. Barton used to be that scary until they fought Tundoor. That giant was from another world. How they survived that, he'd never know.

Fogle raked his finger over his sleepy eyes and replied in a complimenting manner. "A giant with a man's brain."

Barton rubbed his chin, peering up in the sky. "Hmmm ... Dolt. Like a smart man, right? Like the man who took my toys, right?"

Fogle shrugged. "You could say that."

"But I'm a bigger dolt, right? Stronger dolt than him, right?"

"Oh, absolutely. There's no doubt about that. He is a pretty big dolt, but not nearly as big as you, Barton."

Barton stuck out his chin and grinned.

"Good. Barton is the biggest and strongest dolt of all."

Barton turned, thumped his chest with his fist, and walked away.

Fogle let out a sigh and took a seat by the fire. His grandfather snored on his earthen cot without a care in the world while he stewed with doubt and worry. Cass was long gone. Underlings were cropping up everywhere. He'd almost died a dozen times since he left the City of Three and wasn't so sure he'd live to tell anyone about it. *I must see this through.* He tightened his robes around his shoulders and rubbed his hands over the fire.

"Bish," he muttered, "I feel a hundred years old."

Alongside the fire, a small black figurine sizzled with mystic fire. It was his familiar, Inky, the ebony hawk he had made. Barton had crushed the bird days earlier, losing many of the key components.

"This better work." Fogle reached over and touched the object. The black bird was cold to the touch. "Ah, what am I missing?" He eyed the bird with his green eyes, scanning the ground. "Oh yes." Reaching over, he picked up Venir's hunting knife, and with a small scalpel-like dagger, he shaved off part of the carved horn from the hilt.

"Son of a Bish!" he exclaimed as the knife slipped and he gashed his thumb. The blood dripped freely to the ground. "Just a scratch, Fogle. A tiny wound of the flesh." He pulled the shaving from the hilt and pushed it into the figurine.

He checked his thumb.

"Still bleeding. Ugh. Stop bleeding."

Cass would be laughing at him if she saw the look on his face. He didn't care for the sight of his own blood running down his arm. *She'd probably laugh at me. That two-headed dog would, too. Toughen up, Fogle Boon.* He scooped a pile of dirt up in his good hand.

"I wouldn't do that if I were you," Boon said. The man blinked. Rubbed his eyes and sat up. "You aren't giant flesh, you know."

"Do what?" Fogle said. He dropped the dirt and stuffed his bloody thumb in the folds of his robes. His green robes, once garish in their own way, now looked little better than what a starving nomad would wear.

Boon stood up. His bearded silhouette was formidable against the night sky.

"You know what. You aren't made out of mud, you know." Boon reached over. "Let me take a look at it."

Fogle shifted away.

"I'll be fine, Boon."

"Well, at least wrap it up, will you? We can't have you dripping all over Bish. Underlings can smell the blood of men for miles, don't you know?"

Fogle sighed. It was pretty hard to believe that underlings could smell his blood from miles away. "It's more likely that they'd smell the odor of Barton long before my fragile wound. Besides, I wouldn't be surprised one bit if you were excited that they were right on our trail. Looks like you are plenty rested up for another battle, aren't you?"

Scratching his chest, Boon groaned. "Well… I admit that I wouldn't be against it, but I'd rather have a trap set first. There's nothing quite like seeing a look of surprise on an underling the moment before their face melts away. It tickles my teeth every time."

He's insane. I'm the spawn of a madman.

"Tell you what then, Grandfather. You stay here." Fogle pointed at the ground. "Set a nice magic booby trap while me and Barton go and search for our friends. Does that fit into your plan? Because I'm not sticking around so you can get us all killed. Sure, I realize the underlings are evil, but there is a time and place where you pick your battles."

"NO! You are wrong, Grandson. The time is anytime. The place is anywhere. Every chance you get to kill them, you take it. You don't let evil linger around. You can't let it take root. You must destroy it because if you don't!" Boon seemed as tall as a giant, but his voice was deep and cold. "It will destroy you."

Fogle tucked his chin into his chest and swallowed. He knew the truth when he heard it. Everyone did. The difference in most people was they ignored what they believed, rather than acting on it. He'd been locked inside the mind of one underling already. Even if it had only been a glimpse, an underling's mind was the darkest, most sadistic thing he'd ever seen. The underlings took pleasure in all the vile things they did.

"I understand that. We should kill them. We should kill them all. But right now," Fogle stepped nose to nose with Boon, "I need you to help me find Cass, that dog, and that man. I need your word, Boon. Will you help me find them first?"

Boon rubbed his bearded chin and made some clicking sounds with his mouth.

"Boon?"   Fogle   said.

"I … well … hmmm … well, you really are fond of that gorgeous woman, aren't you? I'd fight a thousand underlings for a woman like that."

"You'd fight a thousand underlings for pleasure."

Boon huffed a laugh.

"You take as much joy in killing them as they take in killing us, don't you?"

"Well, it's not worth doing if you don't enjoy doing it, Grandson. You wouldn't be pursuing the druid if not for her libidinous thighs. Certainly you enjoy them?" He perched his eyebrows up and down. "Hmmm? Hmmm?"

"I pursue her because it's the right thing to do, not because of anything else. Her thighs, her hair—"

"Her bosoms?"

"No—not her bosoms!" Fogle turned away. "And stop changing the subject!"

"I remember the first time I saw your grandmother. She had the most amazing bosoms, like those of three well-formed women in one. She was bathing at the Three Falls. I'd been trying to catch a peek for weeks…"

Fogle stuck his fingers inside his ears. In the process, he ripped his bloody thumb from his robes. "Ow!" *Blood maddened Wizard. He'll get us all killed. I wish Mood were here.* He kicked the dirt. "Bish! Bone! Slat!"

He looked north, where the moons were rising. How long would it take to get back home and sip some wine? *Will I ever see the City of Three again?* And how far was it, anyway? The truth was, he didn't have much of an idea where he was or where Boon had taken him. He paced towards the forest where Barton had trotted off. There was no sign of the giant, but he noticed a track. Mood would be proud. *I can track a giant.* He sniffed. *Humph. I think I can even smell him as well. Pah, why am I looking for the giant, anyway?* He headed back towards camp. For all he knew, he was on the other side of the world.

"Boon, where in Bish are we anyway?"

The old wizard pointed one finger toward the dipping suns and the other at the rising moons and spun around slowly three times. "Let me get my sense of direction. You know, in the Under-Bish, the suns and moons were quite different." He stopped and shrugged. "Well, I don't know where we are, exactly."

"So, maybe we are farther away than we started then? That would be convenient, now wouldn't it? Next time, why don't you send us straight to the Underland? You'd like that, wouldn't you?"

"Why don't you just rest, Grandson? Things will be better when you rise up tomorrow." Boon patted his stomach. "I could use some food about now. Say, where's Barton? I bet he could scare something up."

"Boon!" Fogle grabbed him by the arm and squeezed it. "Get your own food. As soon as my familiar is ready, we are moving in whatever direction it leads us toward Cass. And there's rations in the saddle. I don't think we need to be making too much noise about it. Have you forgotten that giants are still after us too? Not to mention the underlings and Bish knows what else that lies out there. Now, give me your word you will help me find her, or else!"

Boon peeled Fogle's hand off his arm. "Grandson, you have my word, but don't tussle with your elder unless you want to lose that hand."

"And don't tussle with your grandson if you want to keep yours!"

They stood eyeing each other. Unmoving. Unblinking.

Boon's eyes were as hard as diamonds: passionate, powerful and fearless.

Fogle admired them. He wished he had them.

Irritated, Boon said, "Tell me about those golden and silver-eyed underlings, Catten and Verbard. Why did you give those eyes back to them? Did you not realize what you had? Burning them would have dealt a blow to the entire Underland."

"How do you know their names?"

"Never mind that." Boon motioned him over toward the fire and patted the ground. "Just have a seat."

Fogle did so with a sigh. He'd forgotten the conversation they were having earlier when the hoard of underlings attacked. Now it was time for both of them to satisfy each other's questions. As for the golden eyes of the underling he'd given away, he was certain he'd done the right thing, but there was always doubt inside him. He remembered what Mood had said. *You cannot bargain with evil. Evil wins every time.*

With a wave of Fogle's hand, a small book floated out of his sack.

"It was the only way to get the spellbook back. A trade. The eyes for the book." He swallowed. "And the robes too."

"Pah!" Boon spat. "You cannot bargain—"

"I know! With evil! Yes, I know, but you can't sit there and honestly tell me that you wouldn't have done the same." Fogle waggled their spellbook under Boon's nose. "Huh? Wouldn't you?"

Boon took the book from his hand. "Well, I could always make another spellbook." He ran his hands over the leather binding. "And I know it wouldn't be the same, but there is only one golden-eyed underling. And he's one of the most powerful ones. He's the one known as Catten. The other is Verbard, and how did I learn their names? I discovered them when I fought some of their allies. Gold eyes. Silver eyes. The only two of their kind. They were close. So close. I felt them. They felt me. I was young, like you, decades ago." His voice trailed off. "I'd say Catten is fully restored by now."

"What do you mean?"

"Underlings can bring back their dead so long as they have the eyes. That's why people burn them. Why else would his brother, Verbard, have wanted them?"

Fogle shivered. He sprinkled mystic energy from his fingertips on his ebony hawk. It was almost ready. "He was killed once already, you know." He grabbed the knife. "He had this punched through him. Venir did that. And I say if he can be killed once, he can be killed again."

"Give me that." Boon snatched the knife away. "I knew there was something unique about that blade. I could smell it. I might even be able to track that underling down with it."

"No! You gave your world we'd find Cass! You won't be getting any help from me on that quest!" He grabbed the book and closed it. "And you won't be taking this book."

"Grandson, if we can catch them, surprise them, kill them, and burn their eyes up, then it will be the end of them. The underlings would sink back into their holes and not come out for decades."

"That's never happened, Boon. You're delusional." Fogle scoffed. "You have to quit obsessing over them."

"No." Boon's eyes glazed. Drifted. He ran his fingers over the blade. "They must be destroyed."

"You're mad."

Boon shook his head.

"You're a fool. You don't realize the peril this world is in. I've never felt so many underlings on the surface before. They have invaded. This is not some skirmish. It is full-blown war!"

"Well, if you want to kill them, then I think your best chance is to find Venir. Find The Darkslayer. And if you help me find Cass first, I think I can have a quicker way to find those underlings."

"Oh?" Boon grunted. "Tell me now."

"First, I'm going to prepare some spells for our quest, and when I'm done, you can prepare some as well," Fogle said.

Boon's forehead wrinkled. "Grandson, tell me what you know now."

Fogle tapped his head with the tip of his finger. "I'll keep it safe from you until the time comes." *I'm in control now, you crazy bastard.*

Chapter 6

TWO DAYS. LONG, HOT AND miserable. Slim had bitten his nails down to the skin since Venir left. He sat alone, despite being surrounded by a few hundred of the finest horsemen that had ever been. He didn't feel safe. Not because he feared them, but because he'd have felt safer with Venir. Since the warrior left, a feeling of dread had crept into his belly, and it wouldn't go away. *Come on, Venir. Send that flare up.*

The horses nickered. The Royal Riders muttered. The foreboding sense of doom continued to grow. Early in the day a scout had returned, reporting another small army of underlings was leagues away. Bigger than the last one they'd fought. The Royal Riders were bold, brave, fearless as any, but they wouldn't be trapped and slaughtered. They'd fight until they bled their last drop, but it would be on their terms. Given the choice.

"Cleric," said a large man with a long mustache and plate armor, "we can't wait much longer. It's time we go." It was Commander Jans. A good man. A better soldier. His eyes were hard iron. He stared up into the gloom of the forest. "He was a good man, your friend, Venir. A good one."

"Still is a good man, Jans. He's not dead, you know." Slim rose up to his full height and looked down on the weathered soldier. He felt woozy. His blood still felt as thick as mud. Those spiders had taken a toll on him. "You don't know him like I do. He probably hasn't made it inside yet."

Jans stuffed a wad of tobacco into his mouth, sucked on it, then spat.

"Mmmm… now that's worth dying for right there. I should have sent some with your friend." He held his tobacco pouch out, shaking it. "Care for some? It's the best. Dwarven."

Slim held up his hand. "No, I don't think my stomach can handle it. Besides, there are other things I can do to unwind, but now is not the time."

Jans sucked and spit. "Well, so long as I have some chaw in my mouth, I think I'll die a happy man. Of course, I want my horse between my legs and my lance down an underling's throat, too." He made eyes up the hill. "Used to be you could see the flags at the top from here. Seems two lifetimes ago."

Slim nodded. "I remember. The last five years have been long."

And they had been, even for Slim, who had been around longer than most men. Over the decades, he'd seen men, dwarves, orcs and underlings go at it time and time again, but he'd never seen anything like this. It was as if the world was coming to an end. The underlings were creeping up from every corner. In the past, they'd struck terror in the night, keeping the world on edge then moving on. Now, they were getting as thick as a plague of locusts, overtaking and devouring everything in sight.

"Jans, do you think you can hold off another day? There is nowhere for you to run. Our best chance is to see if Venir comes through."

"Another day? Hah! Man, don't you realize that this might just be our last day? All of us." He pointed his mailed hand at Slim. "Now you listen to me, Slim. When the scouts come in with the next reports, if it's not good, we're leaving. And when I say we're leaving, I say we aren't just leaving this spot, but we're leaving our bones to Bish. And we're going to take as many of those dark fiends with us as we can." He patted Slim on the shoulder before he walked off. "I suggest you do the same."

Slim squatted like a vulture by the campfire and scratched his fingers through his hair. He fully expected Venir to come through in his mind, but his gut told him something else. Ever since the rangy warrior dashed up into the forest, Slim couldn't shake the feeling that he'd seen his friend for the last time. Perhaps, it wasn't Venir who wouldn't survive. Maybe it was him. Maybe his time had come to perish battling the underlings.

What was I thinking? I shouldn't have let him go alone! I should have died with him!

He nibbled at his fingernails and took another long look up the hill where Outpost Thirty One sat.

"A thousand underlings against one man," he said. Sadness fell over him. "No one could survive that."

Chapter 7

"Rumph."

Venir's eyes fluttered open, but there was nothing to see. The bag on his head was still in place. His tongue was swollen with thirst, and the stinging sweat that once dripped in his eyes was gone. He groaned.

Every time he dozed off inside the stockade, a biting pain inside his wrists awoke him. The small bones in both wrists ached in a way that such small things had no business aching. His fingers were black and blue, but he could move them. Several hours had been tolerable, but now he'd lost all track of time. He couldn't tell which was worse: being in the Mist, or being shackled and wounded in a fort full of underlings.

Must escape.

Venir had been hopeful at first.

Just wait it out until my enemies reveal themselves.

But the nagging pain in his wrists kept reminding him that he couldn't do anything. He was crippled. Invalid. Diminished. And the Royal Riders who were waiting on him would be slaughtered. He had failed them. He had failed Slim. He'd failed everyone.

His stomach groaned. His tongue was as thick as wool in his mouth.

"Waterrr …" he moaned.

Venir had never begged for anything before, not even when he was a starving young boy, but his conditions were beyond miserable. He was shackled inside the darkness. Hungering. Thirsting. No chance for escape. He flexed his limbs and fought against the restraints. They didn't groan. Days ago, they would have.

Bish.

Hours ago, it had been *Son of a Bish*, but now his deteriorating thoughts couldn't even muster that. Memories of the Mist sprung forth, worsening his fears. In the Mist, at least he could move; he could walk and talk, and there was water in abundance. In the Mist, there were sounds of life. Here, there was nothing.

Here, it was black. Painful. Agitating. Eroding and sweltering. The minutes felt like hours. His great strength faded. His will was breaking. This wasn't like the dungeons in the City of Bone. This was much worse. A hundred times worse, it seemed.

Fool.

Images were coming and going inside his mind. Friends and foes, distinct and drifting. What had he done in life that had led him here? Into the belly of his very enemy? Georgio and Melegal, what had become of them? And the tiny boy, Lefty? He'd forsaken them so he could pursue his enemy. Perhaps Billip and Mikkel were still looking after them. It seemed like decades since he'd seen them.

His knees trembled. He sagged to the ground. His feet were numb from countless hours of standing. The middle of his back felt like an anvil was stuck inside it. He wanted to sit, rest, but his pinned and swollen wrists wouldn't allow it. He hung. Locked in the stockade. His suffering increasing by the minute.

No. Must fight it. Focus.

It was hard to even think, but the beautiful face of Kam found its way inside his mind. Why would any man leave such a magnificent woman? Only a bull-headed fool would do that. And he had no lust for her now. Only the desire to see her face and to know that she was alright without him.

Many other memories came to mind. The Battle in the Pit with Son of Farc. As devastating as that had been, he'd rather risk another beating than die like this. And the blonde-haired half-orc woman, Dolly, with the snaggled teeth. Why did he wonder about her?

Jarla.

Was that when all the madness started? The day of her betrayal? The day he took the armament from the sack and hewed down the gnolls, Throk and Keel? His swollen fingers twitched in the darkness. His life had been nothing but underlings after that. He'd hated them even before. They'd killed his family when he was a boy. They'd buried him alive. Yet he'd survived somehow.

Mood.

Chongo.

They had saved him before. He lurched inside the stockade. Rocked his bullish shoulders back and forth, on his toes.

"Grrrrr ... *umph!*"

Nothing moved but him.

He tried again with the same result.

"Bish!" His voice was more of a croak than a sound.

He'd failed his friends and his dog. He'd failed them all, and they would all die at the hands of the underlings in the end. Now, all he could do was sit in misery and wait for his slow death to come. His thoughts drifted back and forth, between reality and some other world, hour after hour, day after day for all he knew.

His inner fire was dim, but not out. Not as long as the scent of underling skin that he knew so well was about. Hatred kept his heart beating when most men's would fail. Vengeance stoked the coals in his belly. Somehow, if he could get ahold of one more underling, he could die satisfied. If he could even just sink his teeth around one of their throats.

Dead silence. His ragged breathing. His only company until the familiar sound of a key being turned in a lock clicked in his ears. It might as well have been a trumpet blast that jostled Venir from his sleepless slumber. Stiff as a board, every joint in his body ached. He tried to move. The gash in his thigh where the underling stabbed him throbbed with its own life.

"Water," he said. It wasn't audible. The deep recesses of his mind blurted out another warning.

Be quiet, Fool! Shut up! Listen!

A steel door swung open and banged against the wall. A rush of cool air followed. Chill bumps rose along his arms, igniting each and every hair.

I'm still alive after all.

Booted feet entered. Rubbing plates of armor and weapons jangling followed. It was music to Venir's ears—until someone poked him in the ribs.

He jerked in his shackles and moaned.

Bloody bastards!

"Check the cuffs on those leg irons, and unfetter the stockade," a man said. His voice was familiar.

Venir turned his head. It was the leader of the Brigands. The ones posing as Royal soldiers he'd encountered in the gorge. Venir tried to recall how many men the leader had said they had. Less than a hundred, was it? His blood thickened in his veins.

"Tuuth," the leader said, "keep that spear on his back in case he makes any sudden moves."

The orc snorted. "He's not going to move anywhere. He won't be able to walk. Look."

Venir could feel the light from a lantern on his face. The others came closer.

"Gad! That is disgusting!" the leader said. He covered his mouth. "Give me that torch."

"No," the orc said. "The underlings like this. It's not ours to mess with."

Venir felt a lump form in his throat. What was going on? What was wrong with his legs?

"Give me the torch, Tuuth," the leader said. "The Bone with the underlings. This man's a warrior, and he doesn't deserve to die with his legs eaten off."

"It'll be your legs sticking out of the ground, not mine, Fraggon," the orc said. "You humans are so soft. Like buttered bread."

"And you orcs are rotten like basilisk eggs. Look at this!" Fraggon held the light closer. "So vile."

Venir heard another man squat down beneath him and gag.

"Blecht!" Another one spit a mouthful of bile from his mouth. "All these years, and I still can't stomach it."

Tuuth shoved one man onto his back and hunched his big frame down in the light. "Bone. That is nasty. Heh. Heh."

Venir raised his neck from the stockade and groaned. His head felt like it weighed a ton. He mumbled something incomprehensible. He was trying to say, "What's wrong with my legs?" He couldn't even feel them.

"Keep him steady while I burn these things," said the leader, Flaggon. "Hold him, men."

Tuuth clamped his arms around Venir's chest. Pinning his arms at his sides.

The others grabbed his legs.

"It's for the better, Stranger. An act of mercy I don't normally give, but you've earned that much respect from me," Tuuth said into the bag over his head.

"Mercy?" one brigand soldier started. "He'll need more than that. These grubs have eaten holes so deep in his flesh I can see the bone." Venir heard the man swallow. "Ah slat, I'm getting sick again."

"He's lucky for the leaches; that much is certain," Fraggon said. "They suck the blood and numb the pain. Gad, you don't usually see both like this." He took a dagger out and sliced one off that was bloated with blood and as big as his hand.

"How this man lives, I'll never know," the other brigand said. He spit more bile from his mouth. "He should be dead."

"Well, the grubs eat the skin, but they cauterized the holes somehow. I've seen men with tunnels of holes all over them that still live. But you're right; he should be dead, and I don't think the underlings want that yet."

Venir felt heat on his legs. His heart pounded inside his chest like a war drum. He'd seen grubs and leeches and what they did to the flesh. It horrified him.

What have they done to me!

Fraggon continued. "You've been blessed and cursed it seems, Stranger. The grubs and leeches are enjoying their meal, and a big beefy man like you can feed them for days. Well, what's left of you, anyway. But I don't think the underlings want you dead just yet; else they wouldn't have sent for you. But, I can't guarantee you'll live through this next step either. I mean, you might live, but I don't see you ever walking again. A shame too. You have him secured, Tuuth? I'd say there be some fight in him."

"Should I take the bag off and let him breathe? Let him bite down on something?"

"Are you volunteering your finger, Tuuth? My, so compassionate you've become for the stranger. No, just leave it on. It'll muffle the screams well enough. Not that the underlings would mind that one bit anyway. Stranger, may Bish be with you."

I don't have the strength to— "YEEEEEEEEAAAAAAAWWW!"

It felt like the tendons of his muscles were being pulled from his skin. Inch by inch. It was unimaginable. Excruciating. Mind numbing. His body shuddered from toe nail to chin. The top of his skull was on fire.

Flaggon pulled cord after cord from within and seared his skin with the torch.

Venir screamed. Stopped. Screamed some more.

"My, he's a gusty one," Tuuth said.

"That grub's as long my innards!"

"Keep pulling it out!" Flaggon said. "It's almost out! Get the knife ready so we can cut the head off!"

It felt like a cord of thick rope was being pulled through his body. He yelled at the top of his lungs, "GET THAT BLASTED THING OUT OF ME!"

"There's the head! Oh slat! What's in the mouth of that thing! Keep it still!"

"Kill it!"

The sound of steel cut through the air.

Slice!

"You got it! Bish! Barely! It almost got us!" Flaggon said. "How's the man, Tuuth?"

Tuuth shrugged his broad shoulders. Venir wasn't moving. "He's breathing, not that it matters. He's crippled now. A peaceful death being eaten alive would have been better."

What have the underlings done to me!

Thoughts were racing through Venir's mind despite the agony. How much suffering would they put him through?

Someone pulled the bag off his head

When he managed to look up, it was into the big pale face of the orcen man, Tuuth.

"His eyes still have some fight in them, Flaggon. Look at this?"

Flaggon stepped into view, eyed him and said with avid curiosity, "Can you stand, Stranger?"

"Can underlings die?" Venir said. He pushed against the stockade. Wobbling on his feet.

Tuuth and Flaggon looked at each other, astonished.

"Can you walk?"

Venir took his first step and collapsed face first to the stone floor.

"Help him up," Flaggon said.

"No!" Venir said.

He was free. Despite all the pain, he was going to enjoy it. Unable to use his hands because of the pain in his wrists, he rolled onto his elbows. He pushed himself over and sat himself up. He felt like he would pass out.

Bone!

He saw his legs. They were raw. Scarred. Pale as the orc. There was a hole in his thigh that led to the bone. That was the first one he saw. To the side, the grub lay dead on the floor, six feet in length. It looked like a hairy earthworm as thick as his thumb. Its head as big as his knuckles and filled with tiny teeth. His stomach churned bile up to his throat, but nothing came out.

"Well, Stranger," Flaggon said "you can't walk, but we'll let you crawl if you like. Else we can carry you."

"No," Venir said.

He was numb. Looking at his arms, the bracers on his aching wrists were loose. The bulges in his arms were gone. What had been done to him? The only thing left whole on him it seemed was his beard.

"Then get moving, Stranger. The underlings are expecting you." The brighter tone that Flaggon carried changed. "And seeing how you survived this much, I can only warn you that the worst is yet to come."

Venir swallowed hard. On elbows and knees, trembling, he crawled forward.

Tuuth rubbed the bracers on his wrists. The haggard form of Venir crawling stirred him. In the little amount of time the man had been imprisoned, he'd become a husk of the man Tuuth had battled earlier. Tuuth would never forget the shock in the man's granite face when he cracked his wrists. It should have broken the man. But it hadn't. The Stranger still had fire in his eyes. An anger. A thirst.

Watching Venir crawl up the steps, he shook his head. Tuuth unslung the man's backpack from his shoulders and pulled out the sack. He'd already been into the woods and back again, searching for the man's armament. Opening the neck of the sack for what might as well have been the hundredth time, he reached inside and found nothing. Stuffing the sack inside the backpack, he hoisted it back over his shoulders. There was something going on. There had to be. Magic had to be the answer; he'd keep the stranger's clothes.

Grabbing the cloth bag that hung on the stockade, he caught up to the stranger and stuffed it over his head.

"What'd you do that for?" Flaggon said. "It's bad enough he crawls on all fours, and now you've blinded the man too. At least let him enjoy the sights before he gets there. Heh-heh."

The torchlight flickered over Venir's haggard form that kept crawling inch by inch up the steps. Tuuth wasn't the only one that grimaced a little as Venir dragged his mangled legs over the steps.

"It'll take him hours to get there at this rate," Tuuth said. He picked Venir up and hoisted him over his shoulder. "Let's get this over with."

"Suit yourself, Tuuth. I've not the interest to carry the big lout," Flaggon said. "Come on, men. Let the friendly orc handle this. Seems he has an interest in big helpless men."

Snickering, they headed up the steps and out of sight.

Several steps up, Tuuth set Venir back down. "Where are your weapons and armor, Stranger?" Tuuth tore off the burlap bag and grabbed him by the head of hair. "Where is it? Is it magic? Can I summon it?"

Venir's eyes fluttered open. He shook his head. "Comes and goes," he said.

Tuuth wrapped his hands around Venir's thigh and squeezed.

Venir groaned and sputtered.

"Do not lie, Stranger. I will have those weapons and armor. Tell me, and maybe I can get you some water."

"Humph," Venir said. He spit out a laugh. "Like the wind, fool orc."

Tuuth squeezed again.

Venir groaned. He stared back in Tuuth's eyes. "Maybe you didn't look hard enough, Orc."

"Perhaps I should break your ankles as well," Tuuth said. He squeezed harder.

"Perhaps," Venir said, "you should take a bath, you filthy or—" Venir's eyes fluttered up into his head, and his body slumped forward.

"Borsch!" Tuuth said. He grabbed Venir by his head of hair and dragged his heavy body up the stairs.

Chapter 8

ENEATH THE CLOUDS ABOVE THE City of Bone, the most beautiful woman on Bish stood, watching the unraveling chaos below. Trinos. Her world. Her rules. Life and death meant nothing. Meant everything.

Running her elegant fingers through her thick locks of platinum hair, she sighed.

"What to do? What to do?"

In the past, she'd been detached from the lives and deaths of all the colorful people, but now, watching them suffer and cry out, she felt something.

"I wonder where Scorch is, and what he's doing."

Scorch had meddled with her creation for his own entertainment. She sought him out, to hold him accountable. It was the most alive she'd felt since she was immortal. She was feeling all kinds of things.

She imagined Scorch was feeling the same, or was he? Shortly after their encounter at the Void, the two infinite beings had agreed that rather than suffer the endless expanse surrounding the tiny world, they would share a fate on the world of Bish. Each had buried the majority of their power in the heart of the world's center and set out on their own. They hadn't seen each other since.

Soaring the sky, the high winds billowed the robes along her perfectly figured body. She stopped. Hovered and touched a cloud.

"I imagine he isn't nearly so attached as I feel. I wonder what he will do?"

Below her, The City of Bone was in turmoil. The Royals that ruled it had made conditions unpleasant enough to begin with, but now the citizens were in deeper straights. The underlings came. A black menace of small people designed to bring nothing but restlessness and terror to the world.

"Humans win; underlings lose. Underlings win; humans lose. I've seen it so many times before. But they come up with the most interesting ways to destroy one another."

Bodies fell. Burned. They were dragged over the cobblestones and torn to bits. It was having an effect on her. The longer she stayed on Bish, the more attached she became. The world itself, a living and breathing thing. She felt it. So many people were dying, screaming, wailing, and begging for life to be over. Some fought. Most ran, and the Royals, the so called protectors, ignored their pleas. The people pounded on the walls of the castles. Their cries were not heard.

Trinos's fists clenched at her sides when a woman and her children were shot down as they tried to force their way through a gate to find safety. She wasn't sure which angered her more: the underlings or The Royals.

"The hearts of men are so unpredictable."

With little thought and a few gestures with her fingers, the Royal soldiers were lifted off their feet and dropped into the street. Two seconds later, a score of underlings appeared and tore into them. She smirked.

"Well, that was entertaining. What else can I do? Should I bring the underlings to men or the men to the underlings?" She closed her eyes. Her mind probed the thoughts of the people within the castle. "Ah, there you are, you catty little sorceress. I've got another surprise for you, Manamis."

With a wave of her hands, a score of underlings were lifted from the street and dropped into one of the courtyards of Castle Kling. Several more were vaulted onto the rooftops and others through the windows.

She heard one voice in particular shriek out. She laughed. Trinos had dropped two underlings into the bedroom of Manamis Kling, the haughty old sorceress who had challenged her at the fountain.

"Surprise!" Trinos said. She clapped her hands together and smiled. "I like it!"

Manamis shrieked. She shouted. White light burst through the window. The shingles crackled. A loud explosion followed that tore the walls down, hurling underlings through the air. Dead. Smoking. Trinos laughed again as the leathery old woman stood in the smoking hole where the wall once stood, looking around. Trinos grinned. Manamis screamed out orders and blasted the underlings with balls of blue fire.

"Bitter, but strong that one is. Crafty, too. I better keep an eye on her."

Trinos moved on from one incident to the other, observing, interfering, while trying to sort it all out in her mind. Below, she heard many of the people crying out for her in the 21st District.

She'd known the underlings were coming, but she hadn't warned the people. She wanted to see what happened and was curious how it would affect her. Corrin, Billip, and Nikkel had survived, while most of her people fell. The fountain was bloody and marred with death. The survivors had dragged the bodies of man and underling from the fountain, and the waters had cleared.

Why did I let this happen to them?

The men were valiant in their efforts, but the price was great. The big black man with a wonderful smile and cavernous voice, Mikkel, had fallen. His son was on his knees, sobbing and drenched in tears. Even Corrin's hard eyes were dampened.

Trinos felt something stir inside her. Sympathy. Worry.

Focusing, she located Georgio. She liked the young man that was full of hope. Determined to find a friend he so admired. There was something special about him, good, honest and pure. He and his friends were in a bind. The underlings had chased them down the streets and cornered them in an alley.

Georgio and another strange large man stood their ground, each of them battling with the ferocity of many warriors in one, but it would not last forever. They would all die. Even the shaggy bellied animal called Quickster.

"I can't save them all, but I can at least save the ones I like."

BLINK!

The colorful eyes of the underlings widened in the alley when the men, women and pony disappeared. Below Trinos, alongside her fountain in the 21st District, the small party re-appeared, dismayed.

"Where in all Bish did you come from?" Corrin cried out.

It was music to Trinos's ears.

Chapter 9

"Mercy!" Joline shouted into the kitchen, "Get out there and take some orders. We're busy, you know."

"I'm coming, Joline, just give me a moment."

The past several days had been the hardest in all Joline's life. Her best friend Kam was gone. The baby girl, Erin whom she adored, was kidnapped, and for all Joline knew they were dead. She'd taken word of the predicament to Kam's family, but they'd made their thoughts perfectly clear. Kam was on her own. Her daughter too. Of course, she hadn't spoken to Kam's mother but some other family member who was supposed to send the word out. *No wonder Kam left.*

Mercy bustled through the door. Her pretty eyes dull. Long hair tied in a knot on her head. She refused to let anyone fix up her appearance with an enhancement spell.

"Look at you, Mercy," Joline said. "You're too pretty to go around looking like that." Joline straightened the young woman's apron and wiped a smudge of batter from her face. "And pull that lip up. The customers want smiles, not pouts. You look like a frog when you make that face—so straighten up."

Mercy's eyes began to water.

"Ah, now don't you start that again, Mercy. Mother of Bish, we can't both be crying, not now. Not right now." Joline stammered. A lump formed in her throat.

There had been a lot of tears since Kam and Erin disappeared, a lifetime's worth if not more.

And everyone else fun was gone, too. Joline had grown fond of Billip in particular. The man was ornery but a protector. And Mikkel, the Big Charmer, she liked to call him, had the gutsiest laughs she'd ever heard. It seemed like she'd had a new family that she'd grown quite fond of. Tears dripped down her cheeks as she thought more about the halflings, Lefty and his wonderful friend Gillem, who brought the most beautiful flowers. What in all of Bish had happened to them? She couldn't shake the dread that overcame her when she thought of them.

"I miss Georgio," Mercy said. She didn't bother to dry her eyes.

"Are you crying again, Mercy? What are you crying for?" one of the other serving girls said, darting towards the kitchen. "We're busy, you over-grown child! Get out there and help!"

"No need to be nasty," Joline shot back, but the girl was gone.

The Magi Roost was almost at capacity and had been every day since the underlings showed up and attacked. The Royals had taken action, and soldiers had been dispatched. The City of Three was ready, and the citizens liked nothing more than to head into a tavern and talk about that.

Mercy was shuddering. "When's he coming back, Joline?"

"Oh, Girl, you are too young to fall for a man!"

"I am not too young. I'm older than him."

"Well, er…" Joline started, but she didn't know what to say. Mercy had teased the younger man from day one, but Joline had figured she was only being ornery. She remembered those days. But when Mercy found out that Georgio had left without saying goodbye, she'd been heart-broken.

"Mercy, all men are the same. You'll meet someone when the time is right. Most of these men are plenty kind to you." Joline rubbed her shoulder. "You know that."

"They aren't like Georgio," Mercy whined. She blew her nose in a rag Joline handed her. "He was sweet and adorable."

True. Joline liked Georgio, and she figured if Billip and Mikkel didn't spoil him, he'd become an excellent young man. Still, she tried to think of something bad to say.

"He ate like a pig."

Mercy's eyes faded to the past. "I loved watching him eat. He really loved it. It was as if every time he ate, it was the first time."

Joline huffed a little. "Well, his hair was always a mess and dirty. And he didn't bathe much either."

"I loved all those curls, and his hair was so soft and thick."

"And his manners were horrible. Just horrible. He couldn't pass from one room to another without farting."

"That always made me giggle."

"You're hopeless," Joline said. She started fixing some drinks at the bar. "Now, wipe those tears away and drink th—"

"What is it?" Mercy said.

"Uh …" Joline stared at the entrance of the Magi Roost. "Nothin but a-a …"

Mercy followed her gaze to the figures at the front door. Her tears and sobbing stopped.

"I'll get him a table!"

"No, I'll …" Joline said, reaching out.

Mercy avoided her grasp and headed over to the two people in the doorway.

One was a man, adorned in a fine looking traveler's tunic. His face was impossibly handsome, every feature perfectly formed from his chin to his teeth to the golden blond hair on his head. When his eyes met hers, he nodded at her, and she was at a loss for breath. The man was striking, mysterious, and incredible all at the same time.

He must be a Royal, maybe a member of Kam's family.

"Shall I find you a table, Sir?" Joline heard Mercy say.

"Something by the bar, little thing," a stocky woman said. She was taller than most women, garbed in outdoor leathers. Had a brassy voice. She was rugged too. A knife strapped to her wide hips and a bow and quiver slung over her shoulder. "And, do you have any pickles? My friend here really likes pickles."

"Uh … well, yes, we have some pickles. Does is like them raw or fried?" Mercy said. She hadn't taken her eyes off the man.

The man, surveying the room, didn't say a word, but the mention of the word pickles brought the slightest smile to his lips.

The outdoorswoman stuck her hand in Mercy's face and snapped her fingers. "Honey, I didn't ask what kind you had. I just asked if you had them." She looked around at the curious faces. "Now where is our table? We need a seat; my feet are aching."

"Certainly," Mercy said, looking at Joline.

Joline nodded at two stools at the end of the bar where Mikkel and Billip used to sit. Joline usually didn't let people sit there unless it was very crowded.

As the two were about to take a seat, an exhausted group of travelers pushed their way inside.

The stocky woman stormed at them and yelled at the closest one. "March your arses out of here! Wait until we come out."

"But we're hungry, Darlene," one man said. He was old. Eyes pleading. "We have some money."

Darlene grabbed the man by his jerkin and pulled him down face to face with her. "I don't care where you eat, as long as it isn't here. Scorch wants to dine alone, and I've already warned you to keep your distance. And you know what can happen if you don't."

The small group of people shook their heads, averting her gaze.

"Idiots, do I have to remind you?" Darlene held out her fist and flicked open her fingers. "Poof! Just like the underlings."

They started backing through the door, their eyes filled with horror.

"Eat somewhere else, and I'll let you know when he needs you."

Darlene walked towards Joline, spun on her heel and whistled. "Nice place you have here. Mmmm-Hmm. So what do you have that's special to drink? I tell you what, Miss. I'm so thirsty, I think I could drink a goblet of goat pee."

Taken aback, Joline said, "We don't have any of that here, but you and your companion might like this." Without thinking, she reached up and grabbed a half-moon bottle of Muckle Sap from the shelf and poured a sample into a tumbler.

What am I doing?

She glanced at the end of the bar, toward the jaw-droppingly handsome man called Scorch. He seemed to be watching everyone in the room at the same time.

They might not even have any means.

She pushed the tumbler to Darlene. "Try this, a, Darlene, is it?"

"You are pretty quick, uh—"

"Joline."

"Yes, Joline. You know, I had a cousin named Coline, but she stopped talking to me when we were children."

"Oh, why is that?"

"I kicked her in the crotch for being ornery. She said she couldn't pee straight after that, but how can you tell?"

Joline tried to hide her laugh but couldn't. The woman, for all her abrasive manners, was likeable.

Darlene took the entire glass, knocked it back, smacked her lips and smiled. "Mmmmm. That is good. Very good! Scorch, you have to try this … uh … what is it?"

"Muckle Sap."

"Muckle Sap, Scorch. It makes Jig taste like goat piss."

Joline briefly looked up, wondering if indeed the woman had ever drank goat piss.

I certainly hope not.

"Would you like the entire bottle, Darlene? That first taste is a courtesy sample, and it is our most expensive."

"Oh, well, I… Scorch, do we have any coins?" She nodded. "He says we can buy all the Muckle Sap we want."

"But he didn't say anything?" She looked over, saw his smiling face and blushed. "Did he?"

Mercy walked past the bar beaming, a large jar of pickles in one hand and a plate of fried pickles in the other. She set them before Scorch.

"Mercy, I didn't hear him ask for that?"

"I didn't either."

Another barmaid crossed Joline's path, a plate of cheese, bread and meats in her hand. She dropped it in front of Scorch, smiled from ear to ear, bowed, and giggled away.

"What in Bish is going on here? The man hasn't said a thing."

Darlene reached over and patted Joline on the shoulder. "Don't you worry about what is going on here, and everything will be fine. You see, my friend Scorch, well, he pretty much does anything he wants. And you don't want to be on the side of what he don't like."

Joline took a long look at Scorch. She couldn't tell if it was a thrill or a chill that went down her spine. But something wasn't right.

"This place is a lot better than Hohm City, isn't it Scorch?" Darlene wiped her sleeve across her mouth and burped. "Did you try this Mu-Mookle Surp? It's something. Like, really good."

It was the best Darlene had felt since she could ever remember, being here, in a wonderful tavern full of all different sorts of people. No doubt the City of Three was the place to be. She was never bothered before by the misty city she called home, but she didn't see herself going back now either. She shook her head, rubbed her red eyes and took another drink. "To the City of Trees!"

At her side, Scorch had been eating one pickle after another, washing them down with Muckle Sap, and he hadn't stopped for hours. His broad smile was all Darlene needed to see to tell that he was having a good time.

"Barmaid, tell me—Joline is it?" Scorch smiled.

Her face lit up as she nodded.

"So, you take the pickles, wrap them in cheese, and dip them in boiling..." he paused.

"Lard," she said, wiping the same spot on the bar she'd been at for over an hour.

"It's one of the most incredible things I've ever experienced in the entire universe!"

"The what?" Joline said, cocking her head.

"Universe!" Darlene blurted out, slapping the bar with her hand. "He talks about it, but I don't get it. I think it's in the Underpants—*Hic*—I mean the Underlands."

"And this Muckle Sap isn't half bad either," Scorch said. "I bet Morley would enjoy this." Scorch looked around as if he was searching for an old friend. "Oh, never mind."

"Who's Morley, Scorch?" Darlene said. "And why are you always talking about him?" Whenever she heard that name, her jealous side came to life. Scorch was her friend and her friend alone.

"Darlene," Scorch said, "I told you not to think like that."

She grabbed his sleeve, started petting it with her dirty hands and said, "I'm sorry, Scorch. *Hic*. Won't happen again. *Hic*."

Hopping off her stool, she'd started teetering away when she heard Joline say, "Is she going to be alright?"

"She'll be alright, Joline," Scorch said. He reached over and patted Joline's hand. "But please, tell me about all your worries."

"I'll be alright!" Darlene said. She knocked a bottle from one table only to excuse herself and knock a bottle from another.

The men laughed behind her back as she sauntered away, ignoring the obvious stares. The place was nice, very nice, but the people she wasn't so sure about. Many of them were impeccable in clothing, even the handful of dwarves that smoked around the tables. But their manners were lacking. *Oh!* The fire was welcoming on her back as she took a seat on the corner of the fireplace hearth.

"Woo!" she said, slapping her knees. "Sure is nice in here." She fanned herself. "Getting really hot, though."

The tavern chatter was about many things, including underlings, but there was something else going on she couldn't put her finger on. A couple of robed men's faces were masks of concentration, staring hard into one another's eyes inside a small group that gathered around and added more coins to the piles on the table.

"Ten seconds," one said, rubbing his chin.

"Twenty."

Sweat beaded on both of the robed men's foreheads.

"Thirty seconds," the man said.

The bigger of the two men locked in a stare jumped from the table, banging his knee and holding his head.

"Fodor wins!"

Darlene applauded along with the rest of the men, even though she didn't have any idea what was happening. "Say, what kind of game is this, anyway? A staring contest?"

A couple of the scholarly robed men chuckled while another man sneered and walked away. The smaller man in a bright green tunic seated at the table smiled and waved her over.

"Please, come over here and have a seat. I'd be happy to explain," he said, smiling.

"Really?" Darlene said, "My, you men sure have a different way about you. And your clothes." She grabbed the sleeves of one man's robes and rubbed them. "They look more like something a woman would wear. By Hohm, that sure is soft. What kind of fabric is this?"

The man named Fodor cleared his throat. "Ahem, Miss, what was your name?"

"Oh, Darlene. I'm from Hohm City. Home of the Mists, and that over there," she pointed, "is Scorch. My friend. He kills underlings."

Fodor made a polite nod. "I see. Well, Darlene, let me tell you about this game we play…"

"Excuse me, but are you Royals?" She grabbed another man's sleeve. "Where can I get a shirt like this? It's so pretty."

He leered at her and pushed her hand away. "This clothing is made for Wizards, not for a grubby sheep herder."

A couple men chuckled. Others gathered around.

Darlene looked them over. "I'm a hunter and a trapper, and a fine shot with a bow. I bet I could out shoot any of you. And you better watch your manners." She slipped a knife underneath the man's privates. "Or for certain you'll be wearing that fancy shirt as a woman."

The man gawped, eyes wide.

"Certainly, Darlene," Fodor said. He lay his hand on her shoulder. "Please, put the knife away. My companions don't have the best manners when it comes to travelers."

Darlene slid her knife back into the sheath and burped.

"You can say that again. So," she drummed her fingers on the table, "tell me about this game again, Fodor. Is it something I can play?"

"Certainly," he said, clasping his hands on the table. "And it's really quite simple. Even for you."

She swayed forward.

"Well, what do you mean by that?"

"I say that because it's your first time, is all. No insult about your intellect intended."

She nodded. "That's what I thought you meant."

Fodder smiled and continued.

"So, it's called a Mind Grumble. It's a game for everyone, but a mage or wizard must link it.

What happens is our minds are linked together and we engage in a mental arm wrestling contest. A test of wills. Do you understand, Darlene?"

"I think I've heard of this before. I had an uncle that was a wizard, or at least my mother said he was, well said he was my uncle, but I'm not so sure why she'd be sleeping around with my uncle." She shrugged. "Maybe it was on account that my father, my uncle's brother, was no longer around. But he said he did something like this and gave a man a bloody nose for it."

Fodor shook his head. "Who said he gave a bloody nose for it?"

"My uncle."

Fodor looked at her for a long moment as if waiting for her to speak.

"Huh ... I see, Darlene. Are you finished?"

She rubbed her nose. "Will this give me a bloody nose?"

"It's unlikely, but it has been known to happen before. See the floor?" He pointed with his eyes and chin.

There was a dark stain on the floor near their table.

"Is that from blood?"

"Aye, for the bloodiest nose I ever saw. Fogle Boon, one of our kind, arrogant and mysterious, locked minds with a stranger, somewhat like yourself. A rugged wilderness warrior whose name I can't recall."

"What happened?"

"To our shock and amazement, the big fellow won and Fogle Boon's nose was broken."

Darlene gulped, covering her nose.

"Darlene, that won't happen to you, I promise. That night, if anything, was an unfortunate accident. Rather unexplainable, it was. But, in the spirit of things," Fodor snapped his fingers, and a pretty waitress in a short white tunic dress strolled over, smiling, "I treat you to a bottle of wine. Are you ready?"

She eyed the men that surrounded her and the table. They had a shifty look about them, but she felt all right. "You promise it won't turn my mind to mush or anything?"

"It's already mush if you ask me," one wizard said. He had a crook in his jaw and a partially bald head. "Shouldn't hurt a thing."

Darlene's hand dropped to her knife.

"I don't like you."

He stepped away.

Fodor continued.

"Don't mind him, Darlene. He never wins. And if you find yourself feeling uncomfortable, you just need to close your eyes, or look away. It's quite simple. And for all I know, you might give more than I can handle." He smiled and chuckled. "Such things have been known to happen before."

She rapped her fist on the table. "I'll try anything once! Let's do this!" She learned forward on her elbows and stared into Fodor's eyes. "You have nice eyes." She licked her lips. "Now what?"

Fodor loosened the top button on his tunic, nodded to one of the other wizards, and then turned his focus on her. The petite man's eyes were like ice blue water, hypnotizing like a snake.

The men around the table quietly talked among themselves in a strange gibberish and gently laid coins on the table.

"Are they betting for me or against me?" she said.

The mage with the crook in his jaw muttered quickly, twirled his fingers, and then touched her forehead with one finger and Fodor's with another. "What's he doooooo ..."

Darlene didn't feel anything, but the man across from her's face turned snake-like, red tongue licking out of its mouth and striking. It was her, watching herself standing in the dark woods facing off a great snake. She didn't scream, just whipped out a knife and cut off its head.

"Is that it? Is it over? Did I win?" Her voice echoed. But the scene changed. A white mist surrounded her, and the sound of rain filled her ears. "Say, where's the rain?"

In the distance, a man stood waving.

The mist turned from clouds to an Outland desert, and she was hot and thirsty. She watched the man drop a canteen. She was trotting towards it when an orc came from out of nowhere. She shot it with her bow. A gnoll popped up behind her, swinging a bastard sword. She ducked and stabbed in in the thigh. It disappeared. The suns beat down on her as she crawled hands and knees towards the canteen. She grabbed it, tipped it up to her mouth and drank a mouthful of sand.

"Ugh! No!" she sputtered.

Nearby, Fodor stood, hands on hips, laughing.

"Have you had enough, Darlene?" he said. There was something mocking about him.

She threw the canteen at him. "No!"

He picked it up and poured water down his throat and all over himself. "Ah!"

"This game is stupid, Fodor," she said. She tried to yell, spitting sand from her mouth. "I quit." She closed her eyes and opened them. Nothing happened.

"Why am I still here?" she said, looking around.

"You half-wit!" he said. He stormed across the sand, sneering. "This game isn't over until I say it is over! And you, such audacity to speak with me and sit at my table. Oh, you shall pay for it. After this, you'll tell no more of your stupid stories to anyone again."

"What are you doing!" Darlene cried out.

"Teaching you a lesson you'll never forget, inbreed!"

Darlene grabbed her head. Her nose was bleeding! The sound of laughing voices was all around her now, jeering and making fun. Her fears overcame her, and darkness closed in.

NO! STOP THIS!

"Ha! Ha! Ha! Look, she peed herself," someone from somewhere said.

Angry and embarrassed, Darlene tried to fight back. Lashing out, her figure struck at Fodor with a knife. He rose above it, laughed, clapped his hands, and the knife was gone.

"Foolish woman, you are not clever enough to beat me!"

An invisible force squeezed her mind, suffocating her.

What is going on?

She felt a sudden loneliness that she'd never felt before. Deep down, painful despair. No one liked her. No one needed her. No one cared for her. Not even her father or mother. Her brothers and sisters even abandoned her. She had no one. She was no one.

"That's right, Darlene, no one cares about you at all. Your life doesn't even matter," Fodor laughed.

Tears were streaming down her cheeks, dripping onto the table.

I'm not so bad. I'm not so terrible.

A giant snake coiled around her and spoke through its fanged mouth.

"But you are!"

It took the breath right from her.

She deserved to die. She had no friends at all she could count on.

Or did she?

SCORCH!

Joline had just spent the last several minutes pouring her heart out to the man named Scorch. He was a wonderful listener and something to look at, too. She'd just finished telling him about what happed to Kam and the baby Erin when he turned his attention away.

"Pardon me," he said. He was looking for his friend, Darlene.

"Oh my, how did she wind up with them?" Joline said. "I'm sorry, I wasn't paying any attention."

Darlene sat in her chair, catatonic, while the men laughed because she'd peed herself.

"I'll take care of this," Joline said. She rushed from behind the bar straight for Darlene's table. "You men cut that out! She's my guest—"

Plerf!

The first man that looked up's head exploded.

"Mother of Bish—"

Plerf!

The man next to the man whose head exploded's head exploded as well.

An arc of red sprayed across the room like a rainbow.

Plerf!

Plerf!

Plerf!

One right after the other, three more men's heads exploded. Five bodies fell. Blood was everywhere. Silence fell.

Joline was shaking. Blood was sprinkled all over her hands and apron. At the table, Darlene wiped the blood from her face, gaping at her.

"Did I do that?" Darlene said.

Joline's tongue clove to the roof of her mouth.

Darlene turned and looked at Fodor. He sat wide-eyed, blood-coated and trembling in his chair.

"Did you do that?" Darlene asked him.

He shook his head.

Plerf!

His head exploded.

"Guess not," Darlene said. She grabbed the bottle of wine, pulled the cork out of the bottle with her teeth and started drinking.

Scorch was laughing. Everyone else screamed.

CHAPTER 10

THE NEST WAS IN CHAOS.

Find Diller! Save Erin!

Lefty picked his way through Palos's blood bath and into the streets, where skirmishes among the thieves had broken out everywhere. Screams, shouts and cries of alarm echoed up and down the alleys and across the docks, where members of the thieves' guild sought escape from one another—and from another predator: the wrath of Zorth's blade.

Two thieves tumbled through a storefront. One collapsed in a heap, begging for his life. The other drove a dagger into his chest. Lefty darted away.

I have no idea who is on whose side. I need to find Jubbler!

Wind rushing past his ears, Lefty made his way to the docks that had become the battleground of the bloody revolt. Somewhere in the throng, a deep eerie voice rang out.

"I am Zorth! Vanquisher of all evil!"

The pleas and cries of men came to an abrupt halt.

"Get that halfling!" someone cried. "He's responsible for this!"

Glancing over his shoulder, he saw two men and one dwarf coming his way. Behind them was the orcen Quarter Master.

The big orc cracked his lash over his head. "Bring that little blond head to me!"

Lefty dashed down into the Quarters, wedged himself between the crates, and began pushing himself to the other side. Booted feet rushed over the planks.

One. Two. Three. He counted as they passed by his spot.

That was close!

"That's a dead end, rogues!" The Quarter Master yelled. His broad back blocked the narrow space between the crates. "Wait a minute. I smell something. *Sniff. Sniff.* I smell fear!" The Quarter Master turned and peeked into the space." Ah, there he is!" He reached inside the space, fingers clutching, catching hold of Lefty's shirt. "I have you now!"

No!

He pulled away, but the grip of the orc was strong.

Come on, Lefty!

He dug his little fingers into the next crate and held on for dear life.

"Hah! Hah! Hah! You aren't going anywhere, little halfling, except into the murk when I'm through torturing you!"

The orc's pimply and pitted face was pale, merciless. Lefty never imagined facing death would be so horrible. Desperate, he bit down on the orc's finger with all his might.

The orc roared, but held tight, yanking him out from between the crates with one powerful tug, skinning his face. The Quarter Master held him up by the scruff of his collar and stuck the long yellow nail of his finger in his face. He bared the canines of his teeth.

"You bit me like a yellow-headed rodent; now I'm going to bite you!"

The three other thieves gathered round.

"Take a hunk off his leg!"

"No, bite his ear off!"

The dwarf pulled out a long knife and said, "Let me cut off his toes."

Lefty kicked and flailed.

The orc laughed.

"What's the matter, rodent? Are you offended that I won't cook you first?"

"No! I'm offended by the smell of sewage in your mouth."

"Hah! Ha—*urk*!"

Lefty drove his foot into the orc's throat.

The orc hoisted him over his head and slammed him into the ground.

He saw bright spots and felt his shoulder pop out of place. His eyes watered.

The orc stood over him, rubbing his greasy neck.

"Ooo, that little fit cost you, didn't it, Halfling? Hah! The little bird cannot fly away with a busted wing. Tie him up. Once this fight is over, we'll put him on a spit!"

"Heeeee!"

"Hooooooo!"

"Huuuuuuuuuuuh!"

Three burly figures leapt from the crates over them, each landing on a different thief.

One was Jubbler. The crusty dwarf drove a short sword into the neck of the dwarf. The other men's bellies were run through with spears.

Huffing, three dwarves stood there, squaring off on the Quarter Master. The orc ripped his swords from his scabbards.

"Come on then," the orc said.

Lefty scooted back behind Jubbler. The dwarf with pig tails in his beard stepped between him and Jubbler.

"The revolt is over, Quarter Master. Palos's reign is done. Drop those blades of yours, if you want mercy! Huh!"

"Huh!" the orc said. "Fool babbler! Think you I'll surrender! Think I want mercy?" He beat his chest. "The only thing I'm going to do is skin the hide from your thick dwarven necks, you loon, Jubbler!"

The Quarter Master sunk his blade in the nearest dwarf's chest.

"Hah! I'm a warrior, not a thief!"

The other dwarf jabbed his spear at the orc's knees. The Quarter Master spun away, knocked the shaft aside, and stuck his other blade into the dwarf's skull. The orc flashed them a nasty grin. "I'm gonna carve you both into troll food. Tiny little bits that are easy to swallow."

Lefty felt like he was going to vomit. Jubbler was dragging him back, but the dock was running out of room.

"I've a confession to make. Huh. Lefty. Huh. I can't swim," Jubbler said. The dwarf eyed the lake and the orc.

"Everybody knows dwarves can't swim. Don't feel bad. I don't think I can now either," he said. He was wincing and holding his shoulder. He could maybe run if he had to. Dash right past the Quarter Master. He couldn't leave Jubbler though. But he needed to find Erin.

What to do!

The orc wrenched his dripping blade from the fallen dwarf's skull.

"I'm going to enjoy this!"

Can life get any worse in this world? I've failed at everything!

"Tis a shame, Lefty. Huh. We have this thing won! Huh. Huh. Palos's rule is over!" Jubbler said. He shuffled back another step. Only a few feet of planks left between them and the water. "Tell you what. Huh. I'll fight. Huh. You run. Huh. Tell them I need help. Huh. They'll run this pile of pig slat through. Huh."

"Bravery, the blood-letter of fools," the orc said. The Quarter Master was within striking distance.

Jubbler stopped, stood up and wrapped both hands around his sword.

"Nice knowing you, Lefty. Huh. And remember. Huh. Master Gillem would be proud. Just make sure you master those absidium chains." He raised his sword. "My hide and skull much thicker than my brother's, Orc!"

The Quarter Master banged his steel together. "We'll see about that!"

Lefty's heart sank. He didn't have many friends left. The last one he'd lost, Gillem, he wasn't close to getting over yet. Something swelled inside his chest. With his magic feet, he might be able to run right past the orc and find safety. After all, he had to find Erin. But the thought of another friend dying tore at him.

NO!

The orc swung.

Jubbler parried.

Slice.

Chop!

Bang!

Clatter!

Jubbler's sword skidded over the deck and plopped into the waters.

"Run, Lefty!" the dwarf said.

Fight or die!

On magic feet he charged. "NOOOOOOOOO!" He slammed into the Quarter Master's chest, barreling him over.

"What!" the orc cried out.

Lefty kicked. It was all he could do. His shoulder was useless.

Jubbler did the same.

Whop!

A steel pommel hit Lefty in the head. Blood oozed over his eyes.

Crack!

Jubbler fell face first onto the deck.

The Quarter Master gathered his feet under him and stood over them.

"Nice try, little people." He snorted and licked his lips. "But now it's time to die. Mmmm. I'm going to be eating good tonight." He raised his swords over his head.

Exhausted, Lefty couldn't move an inch. Beside him, Jubbler lay face first on the deck. Out cold. Lefty spit blood. He'd fought with all he had in him.

It was the right thing to do. Save a friend a little longer. It had to be. Fight or Die.

He closed his eyes.

I'm sorry, Kam and Erin.

"I am Zorth!"

Lefty's weary eyes snapped open.

Thorn's face and haggard figure quickly approached, wielding a gleaming sword as long as a man in his hands.

"Vanquisher of Giants! Dragons and Evil Doers!"

"What! Thorn!"

The Quarter Master roared and charged.

"You'll not be robbing me of my—"

SLICE!

Thorn swung through the big orc, shattering his blades with one stroke. Blood spilled from the slit in his waist. The orc gawped. The great sword sung again, ripping the head from his shoulders. It bounced off the deck and splashed into the waters.

"I am Zorth! The end of all evil is at hand!"

Lefty leered up at the tall and rangy man. His face was charred and pink. His eyes black. The man he'd known as Thorn was gone and wouldn't be missed. But now, whoever had him possessed was a far superior threat. Lefty lost his breath when Zorth looked down on him with burning black eyes. Blood was dripping from the blade.

"I am Zorth! No evil shall remain!"

Am I evil?

Lefty watched the blade go up like it was a mile high in the air.

Or is he insane?

Blue eyes wide as saucers, he watched the blade descend.

Clatch-Zip! Clatch-Zip! Clatch-Zip! Clatch-Zip! Clatch-Zip!

Crossbow bolts ripped into the big man's body.

Thorn turned and faced his agitators. Filled with bolts in his chest, legs and neck, he stormed up the deck.

"I am Zorth! Avenger of Good. Vanquisher of Evil!"

A dozen thieves greeted him. Crossbows rocking.

Clatch-Zip! Clatch-Zip! Clatch-Zip! Clatch-Zip! Clatch-Zip! Clatch-Zip! Clatch-Zip! Clatch-Zip! Clatch-Zip! Clatch-Zip! ...

Zorth crashed into the ones at the top of the bank. A dozen bolts in his chest. The Sword of Zorth rose and fell. Bones were splintered. Cries went out. Many rogues twitched on the bloody deck. Others searched for their limbs.

"I am Zorth! Destroy—

Clatch-Zip!

A bolt went inside his one temple and stuck out the other.

The great sword clattered to the deck. The remaining rogues chopped Thorn into ribbons.

Lefty wiped the blood from his eyes.

Thank Bish!

A strong hand squeezed his bad shoulder. He flinched.

It was Jubbler. "You alright, Huh!"

"Aye!" Lefty said, swallowing.

Erin!

"Jubbler! Do you know where Erin is?"

Chapter 11

THE WORLD OF PALOS WAS dark, sadistic, perverted and dreary. Kam was choking in the
man's darkness with only his laughter echoing inside her ears.

"Kam," he taunted. "I told you that you'd be my whore forever. Now I have you."

Light of a candle flared, illuminating a small wood paneled room with no doors. Tears swelled
up in her eyes as she sat on her knees, now a little girl with all the insecurities in the world. Bugs
the size of her fist scurried over the room. Each with a different facade of Palos for a face. One
crawled up her bound arms and spoke with antennas twitching.

"Are you afraid, little girl? Do you fear the night?" He shape-shifted into a rat. "The rodents.
The creatures that slither across the floor!" He turned into a burning green snake and coiled his tail
around her neck. "Shall I burn your mind the same as you did my belly?" He hissed. "Hmmm…
you lactating witch!"

She couldn't tear her gaze away. She was hypnotized with his power.

"What am I doing here?" she cried out. "Where am I! Where am I!"

The candle went out. Everything was gone. Only the sound of her sobs remained.

What am I doing inside the mind of Palos?

She had to find him. Find something. Find a way out of his maze.

"You never should have come here, Kam!" His voice screamed. "I'll never let you out!"

The sound of a heavy metal door banging closed. She found herself inside a room, her full
adult body bound up in chains. It was freezing. She shivered without control. Her chin quivered.
Her teeth clacked.

Palos appeared before her, dressed in warm white clothes, handsome and captivating. He lifted
her trembling chin into his soft hands and looked her straight in the eye.

"Kam, swear yourself to me. Be my slave, and I'll end this misery," he said.

She tried to look away, but his words, his warmth, were so inviting.

But I hate you.

A tear dropped down her cheek and froze on her chin.

He kissed her forehead.

"You don't hate me, Kam. You desire me. You want me. Give in to me, and all will be well
again," he said.

Why am I here?

She shook her head and looked down at the frosty chains that covered her naked frame. Her
breath was frosty.

"So cold … I can't think," she said.

She was disoriented, lost and frozen. All of her memories, her passions, feeling and anger were
gone. If she had an issue with Palos, she couldn't remember it. Why would she be angry with Palos?
He was such a charming man.

Isn't he my friend?

"Of course I'm your friend," he said. He stroked her hair with the back of his soft hand. "I'm your only friend now. I can save you. Just swear yourself to me. I'll protect you and your daughter."

"What …" she said, fighting against her dream-like state, "daughter?"

The one you are looking for … A dark, powerful voice spoke.

"Who?" she said. She looked around.

"Who are you?" Palos demanded, jumping back from her. "Who is this, Kam? Who are you?"

There was fear in the voice of the Prince of Thieves now. It was an alarming sound. An awakening. The cold chains that bound her faded away into her green mage's gown. She shook her head.

The dark voice spoke again, more demanding this time. *Where is her daughter, Palos?*

"Erin!" Kam screamed.

A dark figure of shadows emerged between Kam and Palos. Its eyes were two burning rubies, and it had a hooked nose. Its gaze sent a chill straight through her.

Palos's face filled with horror. "Get away from me!" He drifted back into the metal door, panic in his eyes. He turned and pulled at the handle. It would not open.

"Where's my daughter, Palos!" Kam shouted. Her strength was returning.

"I'll never tell! I'll never—AYEEEEEEEE!"

The black figure's fingers stretched out like tendrils, filling Palos's nostrils and mouth, burrowing into his ears.

Where is the girl, deceitful one?

Palos shook his head. He ground his teeth.

"No!"

Then I shall dig it out myself!

The black figure reached deeper into Palos's mind.

The Prince of Thieves screamed.

The black figure ripped out his mind.

Kam's eyes popped open. She was gasping. Lying in a pool of her own sweat by the fireplace on Palos's apartment floor. Rubbing her head, she looked up and found the Prince of Thieves still bound to his chair. His eyes were rolled up inside his head. He babbled. Drool spilled from his mouth onto his chest.

"What happened?" Struggling to her feet, she scanned the room, worried. "Where are you? Where is Erin?" She looked down at her hand. It was glowing like fire. The red gems she no longer held. They were now embedded inside her hand.

"No! What madness is this?" She tried to rake them out on the chair. On the table. She screamed. "You said you'd help me find my daughter. Tell me what you found out from Palos!"

His mind did not escape the inquiry. Time to serve, Kam!

Exhausted, Kam fell to her knees, gaping at her hand. What had she done? She'd wanted to live so desperately that she would have done anything to see her daughter again. Now she was bound with a force she couldn't have dreamed of. Only moments ago, she was going to be the slave of Palos, and now she was the slave to something else. And she still didn't have Erin.

Wiping her sweaty locks from her face, she said, "What would you have me do?"

I must return to my home.

She glanced at Palos. He was drooling like an imbecile.

Serves him right.

"And where is that?" she said. "What!" Her body was propelled to the table.

I'll tell you when we get there, but for now, I need to see through your eyes and ears. Ah ... it's good to smell again, even though it's not like my home.

She grabbed a carafe of Palos's wine to her lips and drank.

The voice inside her head, eerie and dark.

This is good, a fine, exquisite taste, but I have no need for more.

Kam forced the carafe away from her lips and set it down. "Can I—or we—at least try to find my daughter on your way home? Please!"

Not likely. I've waited long enough already.

"But—" Kam said. The front door burst open. "Lefty!"

The halfling boy limped inside, holding his shoulder, face bleeding.

"We've got Diller, Kam," he said. He eyed her then looked at the ground. "But no word on Erin ... I-I'm afraid to say."

A dwarf with a strange beard entered along with four other rogues who dragged a chained Diller in and slung him on the floor. Palos's reliable lieutenant Diller's eyes widened when he saw his boss.

"What happened to him?" he said.

"He didn't tell me what I wanted to hear!" Kam said. She stepped forward and stretched out her glowing hand. "And if you think you will get off any easier than him, Diller, you better think again."

Lefty, Jubbler and the rest of the men moved backward. Diller struggled in the absidium chains.

"You might break me, Princess, but you'll always be Palos's whore!"

With a wave of her hand, Kam slammed Diller into the ceiling and back down into the floor face first.

"LAST WARNING, FOOL!" she yelled. The entire room shook.

Lefty trembled.

"Huh-Huh-Huh. Mercy, never seen the likes of that—Huh—before," Jubbler whispered. The other men ducked out of the room without a glance. "You sure she's a friend of yours? Huh."

Kam whirled on the old dwarf, green eyes like blazing emeralds.

"I tire of you tiny people," she said. Her voice was not hers. *"Away with you!"*

Jubbler was lifted from his feet and went sailing out of the room. The door slammed shut behind him. *"Don't move, Halfling!"*

Lefty tried not to shake but couldn't help it.

"Where is my child, Diller?" Kam's words lifted him in the air, slowly spinning him around, upside down.

Nose dripping on the floor, he rolled a bloody toothpick from one side of his mouth to the other and stared at Palos's vacant, babbling face. "Promise you'll not do that to me. Your word. I was going to protect you from that monster, Kam. I swear I was."

There was some truth to his words. Kam could feel it, but he was a liar. They all were.

"That's the risk you'll have to take, Diller, but the longer you delay, the more dire your future will become." She slapped him so hard he spun in a complete circle. Two gemstone scorch marks were on his cheek. She was losing control.

I'm losing my patience, Kam.

"TELL ME NOW, DILLER!"

"She's here!" He stammered.

"Where!"

"Below. In the tunnels. I'll show you! Oh Kam, I don't want to die. I'll take you right there. I swear it! My word!" He eyeballed Palos, who was vomiting on himself. "Anything at all!"

Diller's body fell hard on the floor. Groaning, he rose to his feet.

"Do you know about these tunnels, Lefty?"

He started to move his neck.

"SPEAK!"

"No Ma'am!" he said. "Never been or heard of there."

She released her spell. Diller fell to the floor and slowly got up to his feet. He rubbed his head.

"Lead, Diller, and if you do anything stupid, you'll be eating your drool with a spoon."

"Certainly. Certainly, Kam!" he said. He headed out the door and shuffled down the steps.

"Come," she said to Lefty. "Shoulder hurt?"

"Yes."

"Good."

The once lively tavern was occupied only by Jubbler, a few other rogues, and the dead. All the living eyes were wary as Kam passed. She could feel their fear. Clutching her hand open and closed, she felt great power—and liked it.

Diller made his way into the kitchen, put his shoulder into a cupboard, and shoved it across the floor, revealing a set of stairs.

"It's Diller," he yelled. "And I'm coming down, with company." He turned towards Kam with a worried look in his eyes. "She's not alone down there, but I can't speak to her condition. Not seen her in a while."

"Go!" she said.

A torch was lit at the bottom of a tunnel that burrowed straight through the ground. Wooden rafters held it up like a mine tunnel. A series of chambers and tunnels greeted them at the bottom.

"This is where Palos keeps his hoard," Diller said. "Josh! Are you back there?"

A man in chainmail lumbered forward from the gloom with a longsword ready. He had a hard face, but was stout with a neck full of muscles.

"Where is Palos? And who are these two?"

Time to serve, Kam. I grow impatient!

"Not without my child," she said.

"Who is she talking to?" Josh said. The guard eyed her. "Is this the mother of the baby? The baby is not well."

"Shut up, you fool!" Diller said.

A charge of fire shot from Kam's hand. Josh was incinerated.

"Erin! Erin!"

Somewhere, a baby cried out.

"Erin!

She ran through the ashes and into the darkness.

"Kam, wait!" Diller shouted. "There's more men in there. This is Palos's—"

A grown man screamed. Another followed, echoing in the chambers. It was a horrifying sound. Lefty pulled out his dagger. Even though Diller's arms were chained behind his back, he was still dangerous, and it had only been minutes since they tried to kill one another. But the man didn't move. He didn't move a muscle.

Lefty looked at his sweaty feet. They'd been like that ever since he entered Kam's room. The beautiful woman he so admired was no longer herself. She was something else. Something dark and powerful had overtaken her. He thought of those gems. He'd given them to her, so her possession was his fault as well.

Can I do nothing right?

"Do you think she's going to kill me?" Diller said. His eyes were fixed on the dark tunnel.

"I think she's going to kill both of us if her Erin isn't alright."

Diller shook his head. "If I live through this, I swear to Bish I'll never do bad things anymore. That Palos, I was scared of him, but nothing like this angry mother."

Diller was spooked. Lefty was astounded. The man had been nothing but cold and cruel since the moment they met, but now there was something different about him. If Diller could change, perhaps he could change too.

Kam's eyes were glowing as she stormed up the tunnel, a baby swaddled in her arms. The baby cried and coughed, a wrenching sound. It was Erin; Lefty could feel it inside his bones. She was alive, but not well.

"Kam, anything to help, I will," Diller said. His eyes were pleading. His arms open. "I'm so sorry for all of this."

She clenched her fist and twisted.

Crack!

Diller's neck snapped. He fell to the ground.

Lefty gulped.

She's going to kill me.

She glared at him, shook her fist, and stomped up the stairs. "Don't ever lose my baby again, Lefty! Now find my father's sword! Whatever might bring Erin comfort, and meet me at those docks."

Tears dropped from Lefty's eyes. His tongue clove to the roof of his mouth. He wanted to say thank you out loud but could not.

Oh mercy! Thank you!

"And quit crying! You've shed enough tears already!"

Time to serve, Kam!

She didn't care who she served now that she had her baby. Erin nuzzled her chest as Lefty shoved the gondola off and waved good bye to Jubbler and his ilk.

"We better not wind up here again, rogues, else I'll kill you all!" Kam shouted.

"Huh! No worries, Crazy Lady. Huh! None at all!" Jubbler waved.

Irritated, Kam summoned a flaming snake onto their deck, bringing fire to everything in their paths. "Piss on them and you." She eyed Lefty. "Row, blast it!"

"My shoulder. I-I can't."

"Is it broken?"

"N-No. Just dislocated."

She held out her hand and spread her fingers.

Lefty's eyes widened like saucers. His head beaded with sweat.

"That hurt?" she said.

He shook his head.

Pop!

"Better now?"

He nodded and rubbed his shoulder.

"Don't thank me," she said. "Just be quiet. Be still."

Time to serve, Kam! I'm losing patience.

"We are leaving, fiend!"

She snapped her fingers.

The oars came to life, whisking them over the dead waters and away.

Time to serve! Time to serve! Time to serve!

CHAPTER 12

CASS HELD ON TO CHONGO for dear life. She was exhausted. The big dog was fast, but not tireless. She could feel him laboring for breath. For over an hour they'd run, chased down by underlings that rode on the backs of spiders as big as horses. It sent a chill through her.

"Run, Chongo! Run!"

Thirty minutes into the chase, she was certain she'd lost them, but that's when more spider riders appeared. Not just a couple either. An entire patrol. Their riders had weapons raised. The spiders' fangs were bared. They scurried right after them.

Sheesh! Those are sick looking things!

Animals were one thing with Cass, but bugs were another. Many druids like the bugs, but they weren't part of her nature. It was fine when the blue bees made honey, but spider webs and slimy toads grossed her out. As a girl, she was fed crunchy bugs once, and she'd never gotten over it.

Chongo dashed into a large grove, paws ripping into the ground beneath him, stirring up dust. Cass hunched down. The branches whipped over her face and legs, stinging her and drawing thin lines of blood on her pale skin.

What have I done?

Digging her nails into the thick mane on Chongo's neck, her free thoughts turned to regrets. She'd left Fogle Boon to blindly chase a two headed dog she now shared a bond with, much further than she ever imagined. Chongo, tongues hanging from his mouth, was going after his master. He'd made it clear he wouldn't stop for anything until he got there. Now she was lost.

"I hope you know where you're going!"

All she could see were glimpses of the sky as they ran under the trees. They needed to hide, outdistance themselves or do something. Behind her, she could hear the spiders crashing through the trees, getting closer.

Don't look back!

She did.

A spider and rider were so close she could see the red in all their eyes.

I've got to do something!

She couldn't think of anything.

Something!

Wind whipping through her hair, Cass struggled to hang on. Chongo raced full speed through the grove and into a ravine. His feet were trampling through a wide creek, bend after bend, when he came to an abrupt stop at the edge of a drop off. It was unlike anything Cass had ever seen before. The creek dropped over one hundred feet, waters crashing into a pool below. She gasped. The underlings and the spiders had caught up with them.

Chongo turned, lowered his heads, and growled.

There were five spiders in all, hairy legs creeping over the creek waters while the underlings chittered and hooted. Cass summoned every ounce of magic she had left.

Bish, give me strength!

Chongo's barks echoed up the ravine. The hairy black spiders hitched up on their hind legs and spewed webs, covering the ground and sticking to Chongo's legs. He let out a howl, trying to tear free.

"No, Chongo! You'll make it worse."

Cords of webbing caught her by the waist. They tugged at her.

"Never Insects!" Magic swelled inside her chest. Fire burst from her hands. She stroked the big dog and moaned. In an instant, both she and Chongo were consumed by flame. The webbing burned away. Chongo charged the nearest spider, jaws tearing off its legs and chomping the underling rider. Everything Chongo touched caught fire. The brush, the spiders, the underling soldiers. The beast tore into them with ferocious fury.

Hold on!

Her strength was already waning.

Two spiders and riders twitched and burned in the creek. Chongo pounced on the third, slinging Cass to the ground. She hit her head on a stone.

"Ugh!"

The flames left Chongo, surrounding her and her alone. She regained her feet.

Focus Cass! Focus!

Thickt!

Thickt!

Thickt!

Cords of web shot all over the big dog, sticking him to the ground. Chongo's jaws remained locked on an underling. The two heads tore the screaming underling in two parts.

Two underlings on spiders closed in on the beast. They launched black lances into his side.

"NOOOO!" Cass yelled. She dove onto one spider's legs, spreading her fire all over it.

It pitched upward, bucking its rider and sending the underling to the ground. She dove on top of it, wrapped her hands around its throat, and watched its flesh burn to the bone.

Too-wah! Too-wah! Too-wah!

Arching her back, hands out, she felt sharp things lodge deep inside her back and shoulders. Her flames went out. She couldn't move.

What's happened?

A forceful hand grabbed her by the hair and pulled her around. A pale blue-eyed underling in dark mail armor, holding a blow gun, stood over her, flashing a row of sharp teeth. He laughed and stepped away, clearing a view of Chongo.

Chongo was coated in webs so thick she could barely see him.

What have I done?

And the ravine, where they'd fled, was filled with the speckled eyes of underlings as far as she could see.

This can't be happening!

There was nothing she could do. The underling reached down, fondled her hair, and wrapped a rope around her neck. Chittering an order, another hulking albino underling, the likes of which she never imagined, grabbed the rope, jerked her stiff body to the ground and dragged her up the ravine through the creek.

She could feel everything.

Chapter 13

"Just tell me," Boon said.

They were doubled up on the horse's saddle, and Fogle had gotten tired of telling Boon no. It did feel good however to have his grandfather by the short hairs of his beard for a change. Still, he wasn't going to tell his secret about how to find the underlings.

"No!"

It felt good saying it.

Ahead, Barton led the way with great strides, swinging his heavy arms that almost dragged on the landscape. Fogle still had a difficult time wrapping his head around people being so big. It didn't seem natural or possible, yet in the City of Three, there were three giant statues in the park he remembered seeing as a boy. The stone-faced figures seemed so real at the time, but as he got older he gave them little thought.

And all this time they said the city was named after the great waterfalls. How many other lies have I been led to believe were true?

Boon hopped off the saddle, scowling. "I'm tired of riding."

"Good," Fogle said.

It was dark, overcast above, the clouds giving off a dull light from the moons.

"'Tis a good way to travel, with the clouds out. The moons cast too many shadows, making it easier for things to hide," Boon remarked.

"Well, what are you up to now?"

Boon was floating along his side, arms crossed over his chest, smiling.

"Are you using magic? I thought you told me to save my power for battles. In the book it says, and you wrote it yourself, 'Not for frivolous use'." Fogle's brows were knitted.

"I didn't write that for myself, but for you. Besides, I have a great deal more power than you."

"What?" Fogle began to object.

But Boon floated high in the air, stretching his arms out exclaiming, 'Weeeeeeeeeeeee'."

Fogle huffed.

Madman!

As he watched his grandfather swoop up and down in the sky, he couldn't help but be a little jealous. He wished he could be carefree and dangerous at the same time. He wished he had Boon's fearless edge.

How did he get like that?

Barton stopped, eyeballing the floating wizard. He pointed his log of a finger at the man, looked back at Fogle, and giggled. "Barton wants to float like birdie too, Wizard. Can you send me up there? Hee hee!"

I'd love to send you both sailing away. Nothing would delight me more.

Fogle rode his horse alongside the giant, stared into Barton's good eye, and smiled. "No."

"Aw." Barton kicked up a chunk of dirt. "I've never flown before. If I could fly, I could beat that dragon!" He punched his fist into his hand. "Hate that dragon!"

Dragon?

"Barton?"

The giant was staring into the sky, looking for Boon, who'd disappeared.

"Barton!"

"Hmmm?" Barton still eyed the sky.

"What dragon are you talking about?"

"Blackie." His fingers clutched in and out.

Whatever Blackie is, Barton really doesn't like it.

"Eh … can you tell me more about Blackie?"

Barton yawned and started walking away, watching the sky and craning his neck as he did so. "I can tell you about Blackie. Barton hate Blackie. Barton hides and Blackie always finds him. Picks him up and flies him home."

"Picks you up? All of you?"

"Blackie's big. Strong wings. Picks Barton up like a hawk and rodent. Hate Blackie. Hate him."

Oh great. Giants, underlings, and dragons are after us. And all I have is this horse to ride on. Bish! I wish Mood were here! What else is there in this world?

"Barton, tell me more about where you come from. Are there many giants and dragons?"

"Oh yes. Many of both, but more giants." He scratched his head. "I think so. Barton likes to hide in the Mist. Many things do."

"Is this dragon, Blackie, coming after you now, you think?"

"Hmmmm … well, little man with axe said he chopped Blackie's wings. Maybe, maybe not, but you'll know. 'Whump. Whump. Whump.' You'll know. Hate that sound. 'Whump. Whump. Whump.'"

All of his life, Fogle had seen many things named after dragons. Taverns. Streets. And so on. But he never knew anyone that admitted to seeing one until now.

I wonder if Mood has seen one? I wonder if it's true.

Fogle dug his heels into his horse. It lurched forward and caught back up with Barton.

"What else can you tell me about where you're from? Is it just like this, but bigger?"

"I guess so. But, I've only seen little of this place. More water though. Much more water. Splash. Splash. I like the water. I like to drown Blackie in water. Yes! Yes! Drown Blackie!"

He's demented.

"Are there people my size?"

"Yes. Many."

"Are there underlings?"

"Those little black peoples that try to kill Barton?"

"Yes."

"No."

Feeling a little foolish, Fogle realized that if he ever got the time, perhaps it would do him some good to ask his grandfather more about where he'd been and what he'd seen. And to remember that Venir had been there too.

Barton stopped.

Fogle pulled on his reins. An eerie feeling fell over him as he watched the backs of Barton's ears bend up and down with a life of their own. Thoughts of a giant black dragon dropping through the clouds raced through his mind.

"Woof. Woof."

"Blackie?" Fogle said. He crouched down, eyeing the sky.

"No. Woof. Woof. Like dog. Big one."

"Like Chongo?" Fogle said, sitting up, excited.

Barton nodded and pointed.

"That way! Uh oh." His ears wiggled.

"What!"

Barton looked back at him, scratching his shoulder, sniffing the air. "I hear many of those little black things too."

"How far?"

"Pretty far for you, not so far for me," Barton said. He turned and jogged off.

Fogle snapped the reins. Inky, his ebony hawk, swooped down from the clouds and soared above him. Focusing, his eyes and Inky's became one.

Scout ahead.

Inky darted through the air, a black streak in the night, soaring by Barton's head and out of sight.

Cass! Is she close?

"Slow down!" Boon said. He dropped from the sky. "I can only float so fast!"

Fogle wasn't listening. He was galloping.

Come on! Come on! Cass, where are you?

Inky's vision was different than a man's. Where a man saw shadows and the dark shapes in the night, Inky saw pale illuminating lines that separated one object from another. Ahead, rocks and brush, typical of what they saw, but they weren't heading south anymore. They were heading west, or so Fogle thought.

"Barton! Slow down!"

The giant kept going. One mile became two, then three.

How far can he hear, anyway?

Inky, flying ahead, didn't pick up anything extraordinary, but a series of jagged cliffs was ahead. Fogle whipped the reins. He was right on Barton's heels.

The giant labored for breath, clutched his side, and slowed. He waded into a pool of water. He pointed towards the top of some cliffs, where a small stream of water gushed like a waterfall.

Fogle's horse clomped into the water, bent its neck and began to drink.

"Hold on, Barton," he said. He closed his eyes.

Inky soared along the edge of the cliff, and Fogle could see everything.

Trees. Trees. Bushes. Creek. Is that a giant spider? "Mother of Bish—Underlings!"

Speckled eyes were like bright dots in the forest as Inky sailed by. A series of crossbow bolts assailed the bird.

Fogle lurched in his saddle and toppled into the water.

"What happened? Barton said. He helped him up.

"Slat happened! That's what! They're up there, Barton." Fogle pointed. "I can feel it."

Barton dug his hands into the ravine rock and began climbing up. "I know."

Fogle sent Inky into the fray above.

"I'll be ready this time," he said, wringing the water out of his robes.

Inky sailed above the top of the grove, dove down and landed high in the branches. He could see the pale figures of the underlings heading back up the creek, dozens of them. And clumps of black hairy flesh on the ground were burning.

What is that?

Bringing up the rear, they were dragging something, something shaped like a—

Woman! Cass!

Grabbing the vines at the base of the cliff, he climbed. Ten feet up he went. Ten feet down he came.

Splash!

Wiping the water from his face, he yelled, "Come back and get me, Barton!"

But the giant was already halfway up a hundred foot scale.

"Save Cass!" he said. "Bone! I have to get up there qui—*ulp!*"

Two strong arms hoisted him for the pool and took him upward.

"You need a lift, I see," Boon said. "Prepare a chain of energy, Fogle."

"No! That will kill Cass! This is a rescue, not a battle!"

"How many, Fogle?"

"Dozens at least." They floated alongside Barton. "And giant spiders too."

Barton laughed. "Many fun. Wizards make many fun."

"Hurry up, Boon," Fogle said.

The thought of Cass being dead rattled him. He could still see her limp form being dragged away.

"We need a plan," Boon said. "Barton, when you crest that edge, get after them. Fogle, you and I will grab the woman, but you need to focus. They'll have darts, poison, paralyzation at their disposal. We'll need thicker skin to drag her out of there. Much thicker."

Fogle knew immediately what Boon was talking about and summoned his power. He'd readied the spell in his mind earlier. His skin toughened like hide leather. Boon dipped under his added weight.

"Well done. Now, when you get her, grab her and get out of there. I'll handle the rest," Boon said. He stopped just below the crest. Barton hung on the rock at their side. "Can you make that jump if you have to, Barton?"

His big face leered down. He said, "Barton will make big splash!"

"And don't forget about the dog," Boon said. "Now listen to me, Fogle, don't come back for me. Get to safety. I'll catch up if I have to. Ah, and one more thing."

Boon led them over the edge and set Fogle down. Barton cleared the lip and rolled to his feet. Fogle could see the underlings and spiders heading back up the path less than thirty yards away.

Boon held out his hands.

"Barton, give me your finger."

Barton extended his hand.

"You going to make me fly?"

Boon wrapped his hands around the giant's finger and smiled. "No. I'm going to make you fast. Very fast! But it won't last long, so make the most of it."

Barton's face brightened like the suns.

"Go! Go! GOOOOOO!" Barton said. He smashed his fist in his palm. "This is gonna be fun!"

Fogle could see every underling stop and turn. Like black coyotes, they dashed down the ravine. Angry. Chittering. Two spiders the size of horses scurried over the waters at full charge.

Barton met them all head on. His fists drummed like giant flails. "Barton hate bugs!"

The first spider and rider were turned into piles of goo. More underlings and spiders piled on the giant. Barton was a hurricane of flesh in their midst. Snatching, stomping, tearing and rending them like bugs.

"I see the dog." Boon pointed. "Move now, Fogle. I'll try to cover you."

Without thinking, Fogle ran up the wall of the ravine. Through the ebony hawk's eyes, he could see Cass's form still being dragged along. He pushed his way through the branches and caught one in the face. *Blasted trees!* His chest was heaving when he emerged in the clearing. He cut into the underling's path.

The underling stopped. Pale blue eyes leering at him. It pulled a short jagged sword from its belt and charged.

Fogle summoned a word of power, shattering its blade.

The underling kept coming. Slammed into him full force, driving him into the ground. In an instant it wrapped its claws around Fogle's throat.

He couldn't breathe. It was strong as a man, but Fogle was stronger. The iron skin he'd summoned saw to that. He grabbed the underling by the wrists and started pulling them away.

"Must! Save! Cass!" he said. He gave it a heave, tearing its arms away.

It hissed, sinking its teeth into his shoulder.

Fogle didn't feel a thing.

It bit again. Its claws ripped at his robes.

"These are my only robes, you fiend! The Bish with you!"

Grabbing a round rock from the stream bed, he clocked it in the head.

The underling held on, determined, like a hungry badger.

Fogle muttered a word of power, ignited his rock-filled hand, and smote the underling again in the skull.

Crack!

Its head busted open like an egg. Its jaw slackened.

Fogle shoved its dead body off him, gasping for breath.

"Cass!"

Pitching the rock, Fogle scurried alongside her. Removing the rope from around her neck, he lifted her limp form up in his arms and backtracked.

Ahead, the battle raged on. Barton's bellows echoed up the ravine like thunder, and bright bursts of energy sizzled and crackled into the underlings from all directions. Even the barks of two angry hound heads could be heard. But the woman in his arms was not moving.

"Hang on, Cass." He was shoving his way through the thicket. Inky, in the branches above, shrieked. Fogle stopped. Something else was moving their way, and moving fast. He surged through the forest.

"Boon! Boon!" he said. Finally, He emerged where he'd started.

Barton and Chongo were finishing off the underlings. Boon's hands were smoking.

"I see you got her!"

"Boon, you know that spell for the portal?"

"Yes, why?"

"We could use it now." Fogle tried to contain his panic. "Underlings are coming. I can see them. Hundreds are close and beyond them, thousands!"

"Go then! Continue your quest, Grandson! I'll slow them down. Use the spellbook!" He looked over the falls. "Make it count!"

Fogle could see Barton and Chongo's work was finished. Both were bleeding, but the underlings and spiders were pulverized.

"We'll all flee together, Boon! You gave your word."

"To save the girl and the dog, not the man!"

"But, he has all the power, you said." Still holding Cass's limp body, Fogle muttered, summoning a cushion of air along the falls. "Barton, Chongo, come!"

Obeying, they came, stepping off the drop into mid-air where they slowly lowered.

"Come on, Boon! They're close! You can't take them all!"

Boon stared back at him with a grim smile on his face. "They're so much more fun to kill in bunches!"

Drifting down past the lip, he lost sight of Boon. He shook his head until they landed at the pool in the bottom.

Barton rinsed the blood from his hands. "That was fun. We do that again soon, right Wizard?"

Fogle draped Cass over the saddle and swung himself up onto the horse.

"Sure, Barton." He dug his heels into his horse.

Barton and Chongo followed.

Inky soared above the grove, showing Fogle swarm after swarm of underlings piling inside. They coated the landscape like black moss.

One moment, the grove was calm and quiet. In the next was a series of explosions and bright colorful spots.

"Enjoy, Grandfather." Fogle didn't look back. He couldn't fight the feeling he'd never see his grandfather again. *No one could survive that. Not even The Darkslayer. Come, Inky.*

CHAPTER 14

T*OOWHIP.*
    Toowhip.
    Toowhip.

Venir opened the heavy lids of his eyes, squinting in the brightness. It was daytime. It was pain time. Everything from head to toe throbbed.

Toowhip.

Toowhip.

Toowhip.

Something struck his face again and again, like tiny stinging insects. His arms rattled, and his wrists ached. From the corner of his eye, he saw a long metal needle jutting from his face.

What?

There were needles in his arms, dozens of them, each leaving a red swelling mark. His head felt like it weighed a ton. He lifted his chin and locked eyes with a ruby eyed underling. One of many. His arm trembled in his bonds. *This can't be!*

It was Outpost Thirty One, but filled with a different ilk, underlings. Hundreds of them were at work within the walls of the huge fort, pushing carts over the courtyard, hammering steel by forges, and ordering motley assortments of men, orcs and kobolds about. Remnants of the Brigand Queen's army. It was a vision of Venir's world turned inside out. A nightmare.

Toowhip.

Toowhip.

Three underling soldiers, little more than five feet tall, adorned in black leather armor, had Venir surrounded. Each reloaded a small blowgun and spat a needle at him. One chittered, pointed at his face with the long nail of his finger, and spat.

Toowhip.

Struck him on the tip of his nose.

"Come closer, Underling, and I'll shove that up your arse," he said. But it was unintelligible. His tongue was thick as wool.

Ignoring the throbbing, Venir scanned his conditions. He was on a set of scaffolding two stories tall and shackled to the wooden blood-stained deck. On the corner of the deck, a bucket sat, with moisture on its lip. He thirsted. Below him, underlings were at work, some staring up with gemstone eyes to catch a look at him. They chittered and gestured. Some laughed before looking away. He'd never heard an underling laugh before. It was a disturbing sound. Shrill and creepy.

One of the underling guards made his way down a ladder, hopped to the ground, and disappeared into one of the buildings below the massive catwalks. It seemed Venir's awakening required the attention of somebody.

Dying of thirst, Venir eyed the other two underlings. He fought the urge to ask them for water. He'd never ask an underling for anything. He'd die first. Despite the ache and stiffness in his wrists, he plucked out a dart and flicked it away.

Toowhip.

Toowhip.

For every dart he picked, a half dozen more replaced it. His arms, legs and torso were covered with a hundred little stings. He kept plucking. Watching. Fighting the pain and ignoring the mocking chitters of the underlings.

Two underlings were whipping an orcen man in the stockades. Other humans pulled carts with weapons and armor, while underlings clad in black armor trained. The underlings moved about the confines of the fort like parts in a well-oiled machine, running drill after drill. Their sharp blades moved fast, glinting in the light of the two suns.

Venir's thoughts drifted to Slim and Commander Jans. Did the underlings know they were near? "Ugh!"

A dart caught him in the lid of his eye.

He reached to pluck it away.

The underling grabbed his wrist.

"Get your claws off me, Fiend." Venir said.

One underling clocked him in the head with a long stick while the other kicked him in the thigh.

Venir yelped. "Bone!" He reversed his grip, snatched the underling's wrist, and jerked it to the ground. Wrapping the underling's neck in the nook of his arm, he squeezed, ignoring all the needles being driven farther into his arm.

The other underling guard beat on his head with fury.

Whack! Whack! Whack!

Venir held on. He'd kill one more underling before the day was done. He heaved. The underling's tongue writhed out of its mouth. Claws stretched out for its last grasp of life. It shuddered and convulsed. Venir crushed its throat. The sound of steel being ripped from a sheath caught his ears. He whipped around. The underling guard's arm coiled back to strike his throat.

A commanding voice shouted out in underling.

The underling sentry stayed his hand, chest heaving. Nostrils flaring.

The platform groaned as a figure made its way up the ladder.

A burly underling warrior, the size of two in one, appeared.

Venir had never seen such an underling before. Dark plate covered its chest, and its arms and chest were as thick as an ape's. Dark ruby eyes glowered at him as it walked over and struck him in the face with its mailed gauntlet.

Venir saw spots. Tuuth's big pale frame appeared behind the underling commander, holding the canister he had carried to signal for the Royal Riders.

A moment of awful clarity. Venir realized his plan was not such a good plan after all. He'd never considered the consequences of the canister falling into underling hands.

Bish, I'm a fool!

All he could do was hope the underlings wouldn't figure out what it was there for.

The burly underling commander grabbed Venir by the hair and pounded the tiny needles deeper into his chest, one blow after the other.

The excruciating pain was blinding. He cried out.

Tuuth was wincing.

"Big human. You should have known better than to kill underlings. Now tell us, why are you here?"

Clutching his chest, he replied, "Hunting red-eyed arseholes."

The underling commander looked up at Tuuth and asked, "What is *arsehole?*"

Grimacing, Tuuth pointed at his butt.

Chittering with anger, the underling grabbed Venir's hair by both hands, dragged him over the planks and slung him off the platform.

He landed flat on his back. "Oooooph!" All the fight he'd had left in him was gone.

Above, the underlings and Tuuth peered down at him.

The underling commander snatched the canister from Tuuth and waved it in the air. "I know about your Royal army. I know what this is. We are ready. Very ready to slaughter them all." The underling ripped the top off the canister, pointed it skyward and whacked it on the bottom.

A ball of energy shot high in the air, darting over the giant logs of the fort and out of sight.

The sound of the Southern gate being opened caught his ears. The underling tossed down the canister, and it clocked him in the head.

"Get a rope, Orc!" He pointed down at Venir. "And drag this *arsehole* back up here by the neck. I want him to see the devastation we shall inflict on his people."

Chapter 15

I

T WAS HOT AND HUMID. Just another day on Bish. The Royal Riders had just about finished breaking down their camp when a myriad of bright spots sparkled and sizzled above them. Every Royal Rider in the area stopped and stared.

Slim was among them.

Commander Jans held his hand over his visor and exclaimed. "Ready your horses, men!"

New energy spread over the spirits of the hard-driven men.

"Seems your friend hasn't perished after all, Healer. Look!"

"I'll be. He did it," Slim said. A surge of energy coursed through him. "Jans! What do you say now?"

All eyes in the camp were on the commander as he pulled himself up into the saddle. The Royal Rider stroked his long mustache, watching above as the twinkling lights from the signal fizzled out. When he raised his sword above his head, the rustling armor of all the hardened men fell silent as Jans opened his mouth to speak. Jan's voice was like a canyon filled with thunder when he spoke.

"Today, men … We ride!"

A chorus of cheers rang out, steel gleaming in the air.

"Ride! Ride! Ride! …"

Jans's war horse reared up on its hind legs as he cried out.

"RELEASE THE HOOVES OF CHAOS!"

It was a moment. One of those moments when the will of men convinced them they could do anything.

Slim, still weary from the sand spiders that almost took his life, teetered over to Jans.

"Shields ready! Spears! Leave the lances on the bottom!" Jans ordered the nearby Lieutenant. "I want two columns going up, a tight formation. I want them ready."

The man saluted. "Yes, Commander!"

"What is it, Healer?" Jan's said. There was nothing but fire in the exhausted commander's eyes. He and his troops were as weary as men could be, but the thought of battle gave them new energy. "Are you riding? If you are, you'll need heavier armor." He smiled. "Can you poke a spear or swing steel?"

"Neither, Commander, but I've been known to play the lute on occasion. Do you think that might help?"

"Not without a lute it won't, and I don't see one." He looked around. "So what worries you, Healer?"

Slim's long frame standing was almost eye to eye with Jans on horseback. "Trap, Jans."

"Aye, Healer." Jans shoved his sword back into his sheath. "We've been trapped for days, if not weeks."

"No—and call me Slim at least once before you die."

"Certainly, Slim, but elaborate your meaning."

"Maybe it wasn't Venir who released the signal. Maybe he's fallen. Maybe the underlings fired it off."

"So?" Jans stroked his mustache, eyeing the hill.

Slim felt silly. Clearly, Commander Jans had considered everything.

"Healer… er… Slim, keep these worries between us. I don't need my men's heads filled with doubt." He spat out some brown juice and wiped his jaw. "We've got the black fiends all around us now. Our best chance of survival is within the walls of that fort. So we are going to ride up that hill and trample every fiend we can find into a spot of greasy slat." He spit again. "And I wouldn't worry yourself about healing my men. You need to be worried about killing underlings, if you can." He reached over and put his hand on Slim's shoulder. "See you at the top of the hill, Slim. And if that gate's closed, we'll try to ride through it. Hope you make it."

They're crazy!

Slim had to admit: the sense of foreboding that had overcome him was alleviated by the energy of the men. The Royal Riders had survived this long, and any fear they had before going into battle had now fled. Still, how was Venir going to open the gate without the underlings finding out? It was a bad plan, a silly plan to begin with. But, anything was possible on Bish.

If I only had more strength.

Slim wanted to shape shift, fly into the sky and scout from above, but he didn't have the strength. He'd patched up several men and sealed some bleeding wounds. He was spent.

Over the next several minutes, all the men in camp got on horseback, their energy flowing and nervousness settling in their eyes as they headed up the dark hill of the forest.

Slim felt useless as he stood in his sandals and watched them trot by.

"You, Healer!" A soldier in a full suit of chainmail was riding his way. "Get on."

Slim extended his arm, and the stout soldier pulled him up into the saddle.

"Commander Jans charged your protection with me. My, I don't see how I can protect a man so tall, but I'll do what I can."

"I'll be careful of the low branches," Slim said. He reached down and grabbed the shield on the saddle hitch. "And, can I use this?"

"It should cover your neck, but I don't know about the rest of you."

Slim chuckled. *Might be the last laugh I ever have.*

Column by column, up the hill they went, leaving nothing but thunder and hoof prints.

Chapter 16

"Easy, Corrin," a stout dark-headed man said, "it's Georgio."

The man, shifty and lean, whirled his blades back into his belt. "I can see that, Billip, but I've no idea about the rest of them. Where did they all come from?" He peered into the sky. "Out of nowhere. Meaning," he rubbed his chin, "maybe Trinos is afoot."

Brak didn't know any of these people, aside from the skinny man named Melegal, slumped over the saddle.

Beside him, Jubilee hugged his leg, blinking, whispering. "How did we get here, Brak?"

He shook his head and slung the dark blood from his cudgel. They'd been running through the streets, dashing from corner to corner, avoiding the underlings, when fortune ran out and they were cornered. He and Georgio had fought like wolves, stomping and hacking at every moving underling in sight, but it wasn't going to be enough. They'd been a moment from being hacked up and forgotten. His stomach groaned.

"Who are you?" the one called Billip asked. "And where do you come from?"

As Brak opened his mouth to speak, Melegal slid from the saddle and collapsed into the street.

"Slat, Georgio!" Billip grabbed Melegal and dragged him over to the fountain. "What happened to him?"

"I don't know. He was like this when I found him at the stables. He had been fighting an imp or something."

"Nikkel," Billip ordered, "Fetch that pail and fill it with water."

The young black man frowned, slumping his shoulders as he did so.

Brak heard Billip speak to Georgio under his breath. "Mikkel has fallen, Georgio. Tread Nikkel with caution."

Georgio fell onto his haunches, holding his head. Brak could see sadness in the young man.

Eyeing the streets, Brak lumbered over to the fountain and took a long drink. It was cool and refreshing.

"You're not a horse," the one name Corrin said, "get a pitcher or use your hands."

Brak kept drinking. He also soaked his blood-stained fingers in the water, only to see the blood quickly wash away.

"Did you see that, Brak?" Jubilee said. "I've never seen water do that." Pale eyed and haired like her grandfather, Jubilee scooped her hand in and drank. "This must be water from the Everwell, but they remain below. How did it get here? How did we get here? Ew!"

For the first time, Brak noticed the scores of dead bodies scattered everywhere. Men, women, children and underlings were dead. Many mutilated. But the most disturbing figure was the black hairy bulk of a long legged monster that lay in the street, some of its barbed tendrils still twitching.

"What is that thing?" Jubilee pinched her nose. "Is that what stinks?"

A sad looking young black man with pale blue eyes walked over with a pitcher of water and handed it to Jubilee. "That's the thing that killed my father." He nodded over to the corpse of a large black man laid out on the cobblestone road. "Who killed that beast to save me. Trying to save us all."

"Doesn't look like there's many of you left," Jubilee said.

Brak nudged her in the back.

"What? We're all going to go sooner than later if we don't get out of Bone. Besides, it's not like you didn't just about die less than second ago, Brak." She took a drink from the pitcher and offered Nikkel her hand.

Nikkel pulled her up.

"I'm Jubilee, and I'm sorry about your father. It seems families don't last very long around here. My grandfather…"

Brak didn't pay her any more attention. Instead, he made his way over to the woman named Haze, who lay alone on the blood-smeared cobblestone road. She was light as a pile of rags when he lifted her up in his arms and poured a swallow of water from the pitcher down her throat.

She sputtered and flailed, eyes blinking.

"Get that thing off me!"

He held her tight.

"It's gone," he said.

Her scrawny neck whipped around, left, right, high and low.

"Where in Bone are we?"

Brak shrugged. By the looks of things, they were still in the city, but where exactly, he had no idea. He was lost again. And it bothered him. All he wanted to do was find his father. The Bone with the rest of these people.

"Can I have some more of that water, uh… what's your name again?"

He set her down. "Brak. And sure."

She took another drink.

A commotion started by the fountain.

"Where's my hat, Georgio? And where's Quickster?"

"He's right over there, Me." Georgio was pointing, and he looked angry.

Quickster lay on his back, facing the suns, legs up, knees bent downward.

"I'll kick your fat arse if he's dead, Georgio."

"I just saved your arse, Me. And you better watch what you say to me."

"Get my hat!"

"Son of a…" Georgio stormed away. "Jubilee! Get over here and bring me that hat."

"Ah, the skinny man lives," Jubilee said. "Drat! I like this hat. Makes me feel smarter." She tossed it to Georgio. "But if he dies, I've got dibs on it, got it?"

"Gladly!" Georgio threw it at Melegal.

The Rat of Bone snatched his hat from the air and scowled as he placed it on his head.

"Where's that case of mine?"

"It's on Quickster's saddle. Now will you—"

"Be quiet," said a voice as smooth as polished silver and as strong as hammered iron.

Brak felt his limbs go numb.

A magnificent woman with platinum hair had taken a seat by the fountain. The edgy man named Corrin stepped to her side, eyeing them, guarding her. No one else moved or said a word.

Trinos found the group before her both interesting and colorful, bonded together for one reason or another. Like the rest of the men and women on Bish, they were survivors, but with something in common. All had been in contact in one way or another with the equalizer, a powerful force Trinos had put in place to keep the scales of good and evil in balance. Something that she had almost forgotten about. Something that whispered in the burst of hot air called The Darkslayer.

Gracefully, she walked over to Georgio and tussled the curly hair on his head.

"You seem disappointed, young man. Don't you realize I just saved your life and the lives of your friends?" She gestured towards the rest of them. "I saved you from certain peril." She folded her hands over her chest, waiting. "Well?"

No one moved.

The skinny man who'd complained about his hat was eyeing her with suspicion.

Billip wiped drool from his mouth.

Corrin's fingers twitched over the pommels of the daggers on his belt.

Even the girl with a penchant for talking was mute.

"Oh... I see." Trinos dipped her chin and waved her hand past her face.

Corrin sighed. "I hate it when she does that."

Blinking their eyes and shaking their heads, the rest of the people took a closer study of her rich brown hair, sun browned skin, common though somewhat exquisite garb, and softer Bish-born features.

The question now was, would they still listen to her.

"As you can see, Bone, your home and my home, has been invaded by the underlings. There are now hundreds of them taking over the streets, and thousands more below and all around us..."

Melegal raised his nose at her. "And who might you be, a Royal? A do-gooder mage from the castles coming here to what, help us?"

"Shut your vile tongue!" Corrin edged between Melegal and Trinos.

"Or what, you saggy jawed bastard?"

"I'll poke a dozen holes in you!"

Billip stepped between them. "Corrin, stay yourself. Melegal's not known for his manners." He dipped his head at Trinos. "Please forgive him and continue, Trinos."

"Forgive? Forgive what, you sawed off slackard!" Melegal said.

Billip grabbed Melegal's sleeve. "That's it, Melegal. Everything was fine until you showed up. Show some respect for our friend over there, will you? She saved your life, you know."

Melegal pulled his sleeve loose. "Oh, pardon me, pretty lady with impossibly perfect teeth. Thank you for saving my life." He bowed slightly. "Without my permission, I might add."

"Fool!" A blade appeared in Corrin's hands.

Haze gathered herself alongside Melegal, a long knife in her hand.

Words and expressions the likes of which Trinos never experienced before came forth.

"Slat sucker!"

"Orcen whore!"

"Sweat from an ogre crotch!"

"Your father bites the heads off chickens!"

"Vomitus Pisswiller!"

Trinos didn't know whether to be amused or offended. "Enough!" she said.

They kept arguing. As if she wasn't even there.

She put a little more power behind it. "SILENCE!"

Everyone stopped and turned to face her.

"First, I am not a Royal. Second, I do command magic, much of it. Third, you don't owe me any 'Thank you' that you don't want to give. But, as surely as my suns rise and fall, you," she pointed at Melegal, "would have perished without me."

Nikkel stepped forward. "Couldn't you have saved us from that monster? Saved my father?" The young man's eyes watered. "Where were you then, Trinos? One moment you were here, and then you left—and the underlings came!"

"Mind your tongue, Boy." Corrin said, "She doesn't owe anyone here anything."

But Nikkel was right. She could have stopped it if she wanted. She couldn't be there for everyone all the time, but in this case, she'd offered these people protection and then abandoned them, all just to see if she could let it happen. People were dying on Bish all the time. Some in the most horrible and violent of ways. Was that indeed how she wanted it? It was, wasn't it? *How cruel. I wonder how Scorch is doing.*

Melegal looked up into the bright lights of the sky.

'My suns'? What a loon! Very pretty. Even smells nice despite the decay, but I've got things to do.

As Trinos continued to enamor the crowd by the fountain, Melegal made his way into the shade behind the walls.

What in Bish is going on?

The last thing he remembered was fighting the imp. Ordering it to stop killing Haze, who now sat slack-jawed by the fountain, hanging on Trinos's every word.

She's a scrappy one. I'll give her that.

Alone with his thoughts, he slid his back down along the wall and checked his pockets.

One. Two. Three. Four. Five. Six. Seven. Excellent.

The imp wanted the Keys for the underlings. The vile little monster was by far the most terrifying thing he'd ever faced. He wiggled his fingers and toes.

All there.

He took the hat off and rubbed his head. It still ached, but wasn't anything so sore as before he blacked out. And he'd been blinded too.

Slat. I've used it too much. Can I use it again?

He placed it on his head.

We'll see.

So much had happened over the past few days, he didn't know where to start. Rayal, what happened to her? She wanted him to find Tonio. Lorda wanted him to find Tonio. Lord Almen, he didn't know if that man was still alive or dead. But what had Rayal said on the matter?

Nothing. I can only assume Lord Almen is alive.

The image of the half-naked cleric emerged inside his mind.

Kill Sefron!

He'd almost pulled it off once already in Castle Almen's arena, but the cleric still lived. He rubbed his dart launchers on his wrists.

Perhaps it's time I used poison.

Closing off the sights and sounds of the other people, Melegal closed his eyes and mediated.

Put it all together, Melegal. What to do next?

The City of Bone was his home. He had no intentions of leaving it again, underlings or not. He had no desire to fight those nasty little creatures or that imp, but they were coming for him.

Perhaps it's time I slid out of here. I'm sure the City of Three would be nice.

Rayal wanted him to find Tonio.

Slat on that.

But she might be his only protection if Castle Almen came after him.

All Royals are the same.

He fingered the Key that had taken him from the chamber below Almen's study to the place he and Haze called home.

Now that's power.

And where would all the other Keys lead? What could they do?

I must know.

He looked around the wall, watching the group still gathered around Trinos. Brak stood tallest of them all, thick arms folded over his chest. Melegal shook his head, ducking back behind the wall.

Things were so much simpler with the big lout around. All I had to do was bail him out. Of course, he's probably the reason I'm in this mess to begin with. But with all the underlings, you'd think he'd be here in the thick of it.

Melegal contemplated many things: Haze. Brak. Trinos. The Almens. Rayal. Mikkel. Quickster. Georgio. The imp and the underlings. Hours later, he concluded his thoughts. Out of all those people, only one promise came to mind.

Get on with it, Melegal. Kill Sefron. The Bone with everything else!

The detail was horrifying. Trinos, despite her elegance, didn't sugar coat what was going on in the world of Bish. Instead, she made it perfectly clear that everyone's nightmare was coming to life. The underlings were taking over.

It was the least of his worries, however. All Georgio wanted to do was find Venir.

"Georgio, where are you going?" Billip took him by the nook of the elbow.

Georgio jerked his arm away. "I'm going out. After my family. After Venir."

"Me too." Brak stood behind Georgio.

Over the past hour, everyone had come clean, thanks to Jubilee who'd blabbed to everybody about everything.

"This is Melegal's sister, Haze, *wink, wink,* and droopy face over here is Venir's son."

Georgio, startled as he was by the statement, felt a connection. Brak had disclosed how he'd come to the city to begin with and lost his mother, Vorla, in the process. The big man who turned out to be no older than him had asked Georgio questions about his father, which Georgio had been more than happy to answer.

Billip put his hands on his hips. "And where exactly do you two fools plan on going?"

"South," Brak said.

Georgio nodded.

"Did you not hear Trinos?" Billip motioned at the woman, who was busy assisting the wounded with Haze and Jubilee. "The south is covered with underlings. The west is too. You wouldn't make it from here to the Red Clay Forest. If you're smart, you'll go north to The City of Three, Georgio. At least up there, Kam will look after you."

Georgio scowled. "I don't need looking after, Billip."

"Ah, you're still mad at Lefty, aren't you? Why else would you not go there?"

"Lefty who?"

"Hah! 'Lefty who' my eyeballs. Sheesh, you haven't been the same without him." Billip thumbed through the feathered shafts in his quiver. "As for you, eh, Brak is it? Let me tell you something about your father. Venir, that is. He can take care of himself. And it might do you some good to go north and meet with your sister, or half-sister. Erin, that is. I'm sure Kam wouldn't mind the help."

"What?" Brak scrunched up his face.

Georgio hit Brak in the arm. "That's right, you've got a little sister. Congratulations. Bone, Billip. How many urchins—"

Brak walloped in in the shoulder.

Georgio's jaw dropped wide.

"Ooooooow! I felt that!"

Brak glared at Georgio. His father's fire was in his eyes.

"I'm not an urchin."

"Er ... Sorry, Brak. But how many Venirs are scattered across Bish, do you think?" Georgio rubbed his arm and looked at Billip. "Are you a father too, Billip?"

"I don't think that's something we need to concern ourselves with now, seeing how the entire city is coming down around us." Billip rolled his shoulder. "Feels great. Strong. That woman Trinos did something to me. I feel ten years younger." He grinned. "So, what will it be, boys? And make it quick, before the City Watch comes back with the Royals to recruit you."

The City Watch, henchmen of the Royals, had made their demands known. Any able bodied man was to be drafted into the ranks to battle the underlings. They'd be given weapons, possibly armor, and the great honor of defending their city.

Billip and Corrin laughed out loud.

"We'll send the Royal soldiers back to get you," one of the two Watchmen had warned. "And see to it you make it to the front of the ranks."

It wasn't a laughing matter. No one, formidable as they might be, could overcome the Royals when they came for you. 'Either fight the underlings, or fight the underlings and the Royals.' Both Corrin and Billip had seemed torn, but after many minutes of heated deliberation, they had agreed that the Royals were still the lesser evil of the two. They had even spit on it.

"North or South, Nikkel?" Georgio asked. "Or are you staying?"

He shrugged and looked over at Billip.

"He's sticking with me, I guess."

"What do you think, Brak?"

Jubilee jumped in. "He wants to go north, to the City of Three! Right, Brak?"

Slowly, he nodded his head.

"Aw, is everyone going?" Georgio whined.

Billip slung his bow over his shoulder. "Before long, no one will be going anywhere, by what Trinos says. There's enough underlings out there to surround this entire city. Georgio, get out now, while you can, else you might not ever be leaving."

Georgio rubbed his rumbling stomach. "Well, a bowl of Joline's stew sounds awful good."

Brak's stomach growled so loud that Jubilee jumped.

"Whoa, and I thought my stomach was loud." Georgio eyed Brak. "I bet you can't out eat me."

A grim smile formed on the corner of Brak's thin lips. "We'll see."

"And what about you?" Georgio asked Billip.

Tugging at his goatee, he smiled as Trinos approached, followed by Corrin.

"I'll be fighting alongside her."

"That's sweet, Billip," Trinos said, brushing her arm along his. "But I cannot guarantee your safety. The underlings are many, and they could overtake these walls any day now."

"They say no force can take this city. We have the walls. We have the Everwells. We just need to vanquish the scourge that is among us."

"Every city falls eventually, Brave Billip."

"Yes, Trinos," Corrin agreed, "but no other place in Bish is as comforting to a wretch like me. I live here; I'll die here." His blades blinked in and out of his scabbards. "Just give me all the help you can give."

As Trinos, Billip, Nikkel and Corrin stood before him, an itch to fight overcame Georgio.

"I'm staying as well."

Someone laughed.

"Who's laughing?" Georgio said.

It was Melegal, leading Quickster his way and handing him the reins.

"Get your fat arse out of here, Georgio," the thief said, sliding a slender box from the saddle.

KAAA-VOOOOSH!

A burning building collapsed in the nearest district, sending up a tower of flames and grey smoke.

"Go, find Venir," Melegal continued, "and tell him when you see him, he's doing a lousy arse job killing underlings."

As Georgio, Brak and Jubilee headed south towards the stables, Melegal felt some wetness in his eyes. *I'll probably never see Quickster again. Fat Arse better feed him.*

Haze wrapped her slender arm around his bony shoulders. "How are you?"

"I'd be better if you went with them, Haze. You too, Billip. You need to take your knuckle cracking self with them as well. That boy can't handle the Outlands on his own. You know that."

"I'm staying here, you thin-necked copper snatcher!"

"Alright fine, Billip. I'll let you win, just this once."

Go with Georgio.

"You say you want to go with Georgio, fine. But he'd be much better off with me, and you know it."

Go with Georgio.

"And don't you forget it!" Billip blinked and stared at Melegal.

Go ... with ... Georgio.

Billip grabbed his gear and trotted after Georgio.

Melegal pinched the bridge of his nose.

Bone, that hurts!

"What just happened?" Haze said.

A confused looking Nikkel was chasing after Billip, strapping on his pack.

"Interesting." Trinos touched Melegal's cheek.

A tingling revitalization raced through his body. It felt wonderful. His headache was gone.

"Are you shaking?" Haze scowled at Trinos. "What did you do to him?"

Trinos grabbed Haze's hand. The woman's lithe frame gently collapsed to the ground.

"Take her away, Corrin, and see to it she's well cared for."

Melegal stretched his limbs. He felt better than he ever remembered feeling before.

"How did you…"

Trinos put her fingers to his lips. "What is it you want, Melegal?"

He cocked an eyebrow at her.

"Besides that."

"Can you get me inside Castle Almen? I have unfinished business."

His vest clanked when she patted it.

"You already have a way in. Just find a door and go."

You smell so incredible.

"I know." She grabbed hold of his hand. "Be careful. The Keys go many places. Many people seek them. Seek you."

"Sounds dangerous. Perhaps I should destroy them."

"Perhaps."

KAAA-VOOOOSH!

Another building crumbled and fell.

A squadron of soldiers on horses could be heard galloping their way. Like a deer, Melegal took off running in long bouncing strides.

Kill Sefron!

The Royal soldiers on horseback thundered past Trinos, Corrin, and all of the other 21st District survivors, but none of them saw a living thing.

"Did you do that?" Corrin said.

"Certainly."

"So, what are we to do now, wage war on the underlings? If so, we could use more people."

Trinos took her seat on the bench by the fountain.

"No. We'll do what we have to when we have to, but I think I've done enough for now." She stretched her arms out and dipped her toes in the water. An image of the lives on Bish formed.

Corrin's narrow eyes widened. "Is this what I think it is?"

"I would not deceive you. Besides, sometimes all you can do is sit back, watch, and hope for the best. You never know what is going to happen on a world like this."

CHAPTER 17

B ATTLE CRIES AND HOWLS OF pain filled the air. Steel punched through bone and metal. Standing on the balcony of Castle Almen's keep, Lorda Almen's eyes were transfixed downward, in awe.

"Kill them, you worthless curs! Kill them all!"

The underlings had laid siege on Castle Almen, and Sefron, standing off to her side, could barely contain his glee.

Oh, you'll be mine soon, Lorda Almen.

He licked his lips, gazing over her hips and legs.

All mine and mine alone.

Her sharp words interrupted his thoughts.

"How many of those fiends are there, Sefron? It looks like hundreds at the wall!" She pointed. "What in Bish are those things?"

"Spiders, and those pale little things, I've no idea."

"Insects!" She recoiled back into his arms.

Oh my, so vibrant, alive ... Delicious!

His hands drifted down on her hips.

Smack!

"I should remove your hands, Sefron! You pervert!" She clasped the plunging neckline of her elaborate dress. "Throw him over!"

"Apologies, Lorda, I only meant to comf—*urk!*"

One Shadow Sentry seized him by the arms, the other by the legs, lifting him over the edge of the balcony.

She means it!

"Lorda, your husband, Lord Almen, needs me!"

"Hold," she said. "Hmmm ... hang him over by the legs."

Sefron clung to the Shadow Sentry's arm with desperation.

The sentry whipped out a knife and jammed it in his hand.

"Ow!" Sefron let go of the sentry's arm and dangled over the edge, held by his feet. "Lorda, please, have mercy! You need me. Lord Almen needs me."

He tried to pull himself up, but he barely managed to lift his head.

Lorda Almen wasn't even looking at him. Instead, her cat-eyes were focused on the raging battle below.

Every soldier of Castle Almen was fighting along the wall, ramming their blades into the faces of every underling that tried to climb over the parapets. Spiders climbed over the walls and into the gardens, carrying small albino underlings with thick shoulders. The heavy crossbows from the towers rocked out, filling the spider and underling creatures with giant splinters.

Sefron flinched.

A dying creature's maw opened and closed stories beneath him.

The men shouted orders and screamed for help. It didn't seem possible that the underlings could take over, not with one thousand, not with ten thousand, for Castle Almen was well defended. Between the towers, turrets and massive keep, the outer wall of the Castle could be defended from every angle. Archers and bowmen manned the towers and turrets, raining down death with deadly accuracy.

Half a dozen underlings cleared the wall, only to be feathered with many shafts.

"Lorda, let me up please. I'm sorry!"

Outside the Castle walls, underlings came from all directions, filling the streets as far as the eye could see.

Surely someone is doing something, Sefron thought.

The blood rushing to his head had turned it purple. Gazing around, he noticed the bordering Castles firing into the hordes of underlings as well, but they weren't falling, not as fast as they should be.

Slat, this Castle will never fall if I don't help the underlings.

The arms of the sentry started to tremble.

"Lorda, he's going to drop me! Please," he whined. "You need all the help you can get. At least let me check Lord Almen once again!"

"Pull him up," she said, not looking. "And punish him."

Sefron felt his body lifted through the air like a baby and slammed into the ground like a stone.

"Oof," he said.

He felt a punch in the gut. In the face. Then nothing but pain. He heard his blood dripping from his nose.

"One more transgression," Lorda said, "and it's over the parapet for you. My word on that, you grotesque fiend."

Through his one good eye, he watched the sway of her hips as she departed.

Mine, all mine.

Pushing himself up, he swallowed the taste of blood in his mouth.

We'll see who begs for mercy next time.

Rubbing her neck, Lorda moved across the stone floor and took a seat by her husband's cot. The strong visage of the man she knew was gone, replaced by a paler, weaker shadow of himself. Pulling the cloth from his head, she dipped it in a bowl of water and replaced it.

"Lorda," Sefron wheezed, limping over, "I should handle those dressings. It is my honor. Please, rest yourself."

"Get this toad out of my sight," she said.

The sentries grabbed him under his arms, lifting him up, toes dangling from the floor.

It was hard to look at the flabby man, with his bulbous belly and spindly legs. But she needed him, for now.

"Sent him to the bottom of the keep. If he causes a stir, send him out."

Sefron gulped.

"And keep him away from my servants. Send a couple up."

"As you wish, Lorda," a sentry said.

The cleric wheezed and grumbled, but Lorda found relief when the door closed, leaving her alone with the sentries. She was safe. She knew it, but her thoughts were troubled.

What do these underlings want with us?

Underlings had invaded her castle before, and now they were back again, forcing their way from outside and from within. And the other Castles along the great wall, they weren't drawing near the amount of attention that Castle Almen was.

"What have you done?" she whispered to Lord Almen.

He had many secrets. He always had, and she was more privy to them than she let on. But, the biggest mystery was what had happened to Tonio. He was still out there, somewhere, deranged and mad. And Detective Melegal, he knew more as well, but she liked him for some reason. Maybe it was because Sefron clearly hated him. And because Lord Almen shared information with Melegal that he did not share with her.

"Hmmmmm," she smiled. She liked men with secrets. She liked to find out what was inside them.

She was stroking her husband's cheek when two servant girls entered the room, fell to their knees, and bowed. Their pretty faces were worried, their hair and clothing unkempt.

She sat up. "What happened to the two of you? You look like urchins."

"Apologies, Lorda. We're cut off from our means."

The younger of the two clutched at her growling stomach.

"Humph, well you better keep your little tummy quiet while you rub my feet, else I'll feed you both to the under—Aaaaaaa!"

A pair of dog sized spiders climbed over the parapet and onto the balcony.

Thwipp! Thwipp!

Spider silk shot out from beneath them and snatched the girls. They kicked and screamed.

The Shadow Sentries burst into action. One caught his blade on the web. The other charged onto the balcony. Another spider scurried through the window and scrambled toward Lorda, its mouth full of dripping fangs.

"Eeeeyaaaah!"

Chapter 18

DISTRICT THREE IN THE CITY of Bone was overrun. Underlings by the hundreds filled the streets, alleys, and storefronts—slaughtering everything in sight. One building burned, another one fell, all to the bewilderment of the Royals on the other side of Castle Almen's walls. Not a single man or woman remained alive. The humans who weren't killed instantly were burned alive. Smoldering corpses lined the streets, and their heads were tossed over the walls. It should have demoralized the Royals, but it did not.

Verbard hovered alongside his brother, silver eyes glinting in frustration.

"Jottenhiem, why haven't we penetrated the wall yet!"

Jottenhiem wiped the blood from his shaven head. "It will take hours if not days at this rate. We need siege weapons. The walls are ten feet thick. And they hold superior position from the turret and towers. These castles are made to hold through all-out war."

Catten chuckled, rubbing his chin over his lip.

Verbard sneered at him.

Chuckling now are we, you stiff?

He recalled the days he might have laughed the slightest in situations like this, to Catten's irritation. Carefree he was then, unlike his brother, who'd been all too serious about all things. But now, things were different. They had changed. He eyed the nearest turret.

"If it was aid you needed, Jottenhiem, all you had to do was ask."

Taking a deep breath, he summoned energy. Tendrils of lightning lit up his robes, coiled around his arms. His hands then struck out. A bolt of energy streaked over the wall, slamming into the turret, scattering chunks of rock and flesh through the air.

The underling army howled with glee.

"Excellent, Brother! I like how you are thinking now!" Catten said. He summoned his own blast of light.

Ka-Chow!

Another Turret filled with archers was gone, leaving a smoking hole in the castle wall.

This is more like it!

Verbard's black blood was like rushing waters. He let another scintillating bolt fly, striking one of the taller towers. Bodies of screaming men plummeted toward the ground, disappearing behind the castle's wall.

"What is that, Brother?" Catten said.

Several robed men appeared at the top of the keep, shouting and pointing their fingers. Purple and green lights glowed from the towers and turrets, covering them like a mushroom with a shimmering cloud of energy.

"NO!" Verbard said. He fired another bolt at the tower.

Ka-Fizzzzz …

"And there be wizards," Catten said. "I suspected as much." He turned to Verbard. "Seems they've drawn us out, Brother. I say we take it to them. Just us. They can't be nearly as powerful as we."

Verbard looked hard into his brother's eyes.

Are you mad?

"Our shields won't hold forever, and we have plenty of magi that can take them. For now, let's try something else."

He's been put into the body of a fool! I liked you better when you were dead.

Catten flashed his teeth. "Well said, Brother. I couldn't agree more."

Catten's smile didn't seem natural. His resurrected brother had smiled more today than in the past three centuries. It unnerved him.

Who is this underling?

Verbard sent a mental signal to the underling magi.

Hold your energy! Send more spiders over the walls! Onto those towers now!

One by one, the robed underling magi's arms went up, lifting dozens of spiders with their albino urchling riders over the wall, sending them off quickly towards the towers.

Let's see if these shields can stop livin—

Verbard jerked his arm up, shielding his eyes from a brilliant light that burst forth from the top of the keep.

BAA-ROOOOM!

The force of the blast sent him drifting back, slamming him hard into a wall.

At his side, Catten was dusting the debris from his robes and Jottenhiem was knocked from his feet. A smoldering hole replaced the spot on the street where over a dozen underling soldiers stood with one mage. The burnt scent of underling flesh was overwhelming.

Verbard grabbed his brother by the collar of his robes. "Did you know they had such power, Catten!"

"Of course I did!" Catten said, trying to push him away, but Verbard held him tight. "Only a fool wouldn't suspect it, Brother! This is war, you know! And their magic, like their rations, won't last forever."

Verbard clenched his fist and socked his brother in the gut. "You are a fool!"

Catten fell to the ground, grimacing, breathless, trying to speak.

"This is only one castle of many!" Verbard said. "And they have power! They have people! If this city organizes, then they'll gallop right through us! Go! Find Kierway, and see to it he penetrates from below. If he does not, we are doomed!"

Catten floated up from his feet, eyes like golden lava. "As you wish, Brother. As you wish!"

With a clap of his hands, a black door appeared. Catten stepped through and vanished along with the door, leaving Verbard floating there, uncomfortable.

Jottenhiem stood, staring at him with an odd look in his ruby eyes.

Verbard rubbed his fist. "I've always wanted to do that."

"Me too," Jottenhiem said. He formed the closest thing he had to a smile.

"Check in with your scouts, Commander, and report back to me quickly. We can't have the Royal forces rallying the city. Keep pressing the wall. We've got to find a way to bring those towers down."

"Yes," Jottenhiem saluted, "Lord Verbard."

Eyeing the top of the keep, Verbard's stomach started to churn.

This is a suicide mission. I know it!

CHAPTER 19

"**N**OT YET!" KAM SAID.

Lefty tied the gondola off on the dock. He'd seen Kam broken and busted up but not beaten. However, now she was something else. Her red hair frizzed all over her head. Her robes were disheveled over her body. Heading towards the stairs that led up to the city, her sultry movements were gone, replaced by the gait of a man.

"Wait up, Kam. You'll need a lantern to navigate those steps." Lefty snatched a lantern from the post and blew on the wick inside. An eerie green illumination came forth.

Kam turned, her face contorted, her features almost unrecognizable.

"Quiet, Little Halfling," she said. The voice was not hers. "Put that light out. I don't need it."

Lefty gasped, shuffling backward.

What is going on with her!

Earlier, he'd seen her kill Diller, snapping his neck with the flick of her wrist. She'd left Palos in a pile of his own drool. And as they rowed across the dark lake beneath the City of Three, he'd found no relief in his liberation, only fear at Kam's muttering and arguments with herself.

He stayed back. She strolled up the stairs, the twinkling of the red gems embedded in her hand giving off the faintest of light. He didn't know what to make of it.

Is she possessed? By what?

The step groaned. She stopped and looked back at him, her eyes glowing with green fire.

"Did you say something, Halfling?" she said.

He shook his head. "No. No, Kam, nothing at all."

Turning, she growled in her throat and headed back up the steps, clutching Baby Erin in her arm like a loaf of bread.

Lefty followed, feet splashing over the dock and up the steps. They were soaked in his sweat all the way up to the ankles.

What is going on? I should be celebrating my freedom right now. How did it get even worse for me?

He wanted to flee as soon as he got topside, but what about Erin? She had to be in danger. But in the hands of her mother?

This is madness!

Staying back a flight of steps, Lefty fell in step behind her. At the top, Kam pushed the door open. The dim light of the alley gave Lefty new life. He had doubted he'd ever see the world above again, and now he was only steps away. Kam stepped over the threshold, through the doorway.

Don't lose her, Lefty. Don't lose Erin.

Reaching the top step, the door slammed shut in his face.

"What?"

Jiggling the handle, nothing gave. It was locked.

Nooooooooooooooooo!

"Kam!" he pounded his tiny hands on the door. "Kam!"

Suddenly, the door shoved inward, the edge cracking on his head, knocking him down to the landing. He rolled up to his feet.

The silhouette of Kam stood atop the doorway. "Get the sword, Little Fool!"

The door slammed shut again.

Downcast, down the steps he went, rubbing the knot on his head.

HURRY! A voice yelled down inside his head, watering his eyes.

Lefty's heart was pounding like a tap hammer when he reached the bottom.

The great sword lay in the gondola, completely wrapped in burlap. He reached in, wrapped his hands where the hilt should have been, put his back into it, and heaved.

How can anyone wield such a long and heavy thing?

He towed the Great Sword of Zorth behind him up the stair. The door swung open at the top. Chest heaving, he stepped out into the alley that guarded the secret entrance to the Nest.

Somebody should be out here.

The alley always had eyes and ears open.

A signal would get an unrecognized thief through. Palos kept strict control on things, and someone should be there to ask questions. It was odd that there was nothing. A stiff breeze whipped down the alley, bringing the foul odors of rotting food and excrement to full splendor. There was something else as well.

Squinting, he saw three forms slumped against the wall, the faint steam from the warmth of their bodies turning thin. At the end of the alley, Kam stood, back to him, chin up, observing passersby. Swallowing, Lefty dragged the sword past the three dead thieves. Their tongues hung from their mouths, and their throats were crushed in. He quickened his pace.

Oh my! Oh my! Oh my! Kam shouldn't be killing people. What is wrong with her? I wish Billip and Mikkel were still here. And Georgio! I've been a fool.

Kam strode down the street, startling the passing folks who came too close. They murmured and whispered while they scurried away.

Behind her, Lefty struggled to keep up, lugging the sword behind him. He wanted to scream at her, "Where are you going?" but the thought of doing so only tightened his neck. So he followed her, past the storefronts, past the high towers, to the edge of the city, where she came to a stop.

"No!" she muttered angrily to herself. The red gems in her hand flared with new life.

Baby Erin began to cry.

"I'll not do this with my baby!" Her body shuddered and convulsed. "Get out of me!" Her knees wobbled beneath her.

Lefty let loose the sword and rushed to her side just in time.

Kam's eyes rolled up inside her head.

Lefty got Erin just as Kam fell. The baby girl was wailing.

Kam lay sprawled out on the ground, bleeding from the nose, her once vibrant form harrowed.

"Easy, Erin," he patted her and bounced her in his arms. "I'll get your mother help. I promise."

There were faces. Some she recognized, others she did not.

"Kam, are you in there?" one voice said. It was Lefty; she was sure of it, but he sounded like he was miles away.

You will do as you promised. You will serve!

The voice inside her was angry, hateful, controlling. But there was something else. Desperation.

It needed her; she didn't need it. That much she'd figured out. So she fought. She fought for herself, for Erin, to regain her life again on this world.

"I'll not serve. I'll not fulfill your evil will." Her mind thrashed against the unseen force.

You will!

Something grabbed the inside of her chest and squeezed it.

"Kam!" Lefty wailed.

"Mother of Bish! What has happened to this woman? She is sick!"

A crowd had gathered.

"Possessed!"

"Bewitched!"

"I'm not anything of the sort!"

But none heard a thing she said. Unknown to her, they whisked her frame through the streets of the dark and dropped her on the porch of the Magi Roost.

"You're on your own, Halfling," one said.

"Don't give up, Kam. We're home!"

You will serve me! You will obey!

Kam had agreed to serve in order to save Erin. Palos had almost killed her before she rescued Erin, but she had made a deal with the force inside the gems. It had assured her the safety of her baby. And now, men were dying. She'd even almost killed Lefty, and more death was coming.

"No!"

She would not bring more death into the world. She was not a killer! Was she?

"I'll die first!"

Yes, yes you will!

Her heart pumped slower and slower and slower. A dark force squeezed it. Burned it. Suffocated her with power.

Kam stretched her arms out.

"Erin, where are you? Erin? I will hold you. See you one last time!"

You'll see nothing ever again!

"Lefty!" an excited voice cried out. "Where have you... KAM!"

"Jo—line?" she said.

The pressure on her chest eased.

What is this?

The force inside her retreated.

She lurched up, gasping for breath, clutching baby Erin in her arms.

"Get some water, Lefty!" Joline ordered. "Mercy! Prepare some clothing. Kam! Lords! My dear, where have you been?"

As the darkness that clouded her eyes lifted, Joline's sweet face took shape. The woman was as distressed as she had ever seen her before. She smelled nice, like flowers. Tears formed in Kam's eyes. She hadn't hoped to ever smell flowers again before.

"You don't want to know," she said, coughing.

"You can tell me later," Joline said. Her friend helped her to her feet and led her to a comfortable chair by the fire.

"No," Kam said, eyeing the flames. "I'd rather sit somewhere... *else?*"

Her word froze on her tongue. The Magi Roost was not what it once was. Flies buzzed in the air, and the scent of blood was strong. Four men lay on or near a table with their heads blown off. She puked.

"Oh dear! Get a bucket too, Lefty!" Joline kept her strong arm around Kam's back and led her to the bar. "You look like you could use some Muckle Sap."

A bottle slid across the bar and refilled a goblet on its own.

"Who…" Kam's voice drifted off. An incredibly handsome man, blond headed and blue-eyed, smiled from the other end of the bar. Beside him stood a rough cut woman that looked like she made a living splitting logs.

"Joline?" the man said. His voice was purposed and poetic. "Can I be of further assistance?"

Lefty returned with a pitcher of water and a bucket.

The bucket clonked off the floor, and he began to shiver.

Kam followed his stare to the headless men at the table. She'd never seen so much blood before. Not even when Fogle mind-grumbled Venir. She retched again.

"Look at that! Just look at that, Scorch!" the rough cut woman said. "I've never seen such an adorable halfling before. Can I keep him?" She waved her arm. "Get over here, Little Fella!"

"That's Darlene, and the man's name is Scorch," Joline said. "And you better drink this and drink it fast. The pair of them have almost finished off the entire stash."

Lefty crept behind the bar and disappeared.

Kam sat up, clasped the neck of her robe, pulled her shoulders back, and shot down her Muckle Sap. There was nothing normal about these people. And where were all her patrons?

"My name is Kam. And this is my tavern. And I'd like to know what in Bish you strangers have done to it!"

"Easy, Kam." Joline patted her arm. "They did that."

"Is that your baby?" The rough cut woman, Darlene, reached out towards Erin. "Can I hold her? We've heard so much about her!"

The woman reminded Kam of a feisty raccoon.

"No. But what you can do," Kam said, "is stop answering my question with a question and give me the answers I seek." She tried to summon her powers, but nothing came forth. She was empty, the force inside her silent, hiding and waiting.

"Easy now, Kam." The handsome man, Scorch, formed the words on his lips in an engrossing manner. "We had an incident. The men over there sought to make sport of my friend, so I taught them a lesson."

"I just love the way his mouth moves when he speaks," Joline said. "Isn't it fascinating?"

It was, but not enough to overcome Kam's anger. All she'd been through. She was home now! She wanted answers.

"So you blew their heads off!" She chucked the bottle at his face.

It stopped an inch from his nose and settled quietly on the bar.

Darlene hopped on the bar and ripped out her knife.

Scorch snatched her by the ankle and dragged her down.

She landed hard, her cheek bouncing off the bar.

"Settle yourself, Darlene. This is her establishment, not ours." Scorch twirled his finger. Darlene rolled over the bar onto the hardwood floor.

"Oooch!" Darlene bounced up, rubbing her cheek and hindquarters. "I'm sorry, Kam. I'm not known for my manners." She took another seat at the nearest table, groaning as she sat down. "It won't happen again."

"Here," Joline said, "let me take baby Erin, Kam. You need to rest yourself."

"No!" Kam said. She held Erin tight to her chest. "She won't be leaving my sight for quite some time, not after all I've been through." She eyed Darlene. The woman didn't come across as dangerous. If anything, she seemed bright and friendly, but there was something that just didn't sit right. "Especially a stranger. But, her bassinet will do. Fetch it, will you?"

"Certainly, Kam, certainly," Joline said.

Darlene started whistling and clapping her hands like she was calling a puppy.

"Here, little halfling fella! Come to Darlene!"

Lefty didn't appear. He could have been anywhere.

Returning her attention to the man, Scorch, Kam caught a glimpse of herself in the mirror behind the bar. The locks of her auburn hair were matted and frayed. Her eyes were sunken, and her cheek was swollen. She rubbed her lip that was split in two places. To top it all off, her robe barely covered her cleavage—or the rest of her.

"I wish I had a figure like yours," Darlene said. "My mother always said I had part dwarf in me on account of these stocky parts. But I didn't think dwarves could breed—*hic*—with other peoples." She closed one eye looking at Kam, shaking her head. "Ain't no dwarf in you, though."

Scorch chuckled. "Forgive Darlene. It seems she's over indulged in your Muckle Sap, which I must admit, is quite delightful."

"So, was it *you* who killed all those men?"

"With a single thought," he said. His teeth were white. Perfect. "And I'm sorry for the mess. I just don't understand why Trinos picked such leaky people. But I have to admit, it does offer a more profound effect."

"You should have seen all those people—*hic*— running out of here like their arses were on fire," Darlene said. "I don't know what was funnier. That or all those heads exploding. It was like blowing up pumpkins with whicker wonkers when I was a girl, 'cept there weren't any seeds in their heads."

That's when Kam got a closer look at all the dark stains on Darlene's clothes. She was covered in them from the waist up. She turned away as Darlene started swatting at flies again and calling for Lefty. "Here little …"

"When did this happen? Haven't the City Watch come to ask questions? There will be a trial for this! And who is Trinos?"

"The City Watch?" Scorch posed in thought. "Oh, I see. The men in the black billed hats that came to conduct an investigation. Simply put, they showed up and didn't see a thing." He waved his hand over at the men at the table. "See?"

Glancing over her shoulder, the main floor of the Magi Roost was in perfect order. The tables were cleaned, the fire crackled, and there was no proof of another living thing other than themselves. A chill went through her.

Bish, he's powerful!

"And I told a convincing tale about how the cause of the rumors and speculation most likely was those dreaded little underlings people have been talking about. I even procured several wild goose chases to keep the Watch of this fine city busy. It'll be days if not weeks before they figure it out."

"Goodness," Joline said. She was coming back down the steps with Erin's bassinet in her arms. "Where did all of those horrid bodies…"

Scorch's illusion dissipated. The bodies, flies and blood returned.

"… Oh." She shook her head and set the bassinet down on the bar.

Kam held onto Erin, keeping an eye on Scorch, fear creeping over her. The man wrapped a slice of cheese around a pickle and stuffed it in his mouth. It only made her situation all the more disconcerting.

Time to serve. Leave now.

"Can I at least change my clothes?" Kam said.

"Of course you can," Joline said. "Mercy, poor thing, as terrified as she is, laid some out on your bed. And is fixing you a bath. All the others left."

Scorch had finished his pickle. His eyes narrowed. "Who are you talking to, Kam?"

Leave now!

Slowly, Kam placed Erin in the bassinet and took a step towards the door. She fought it. Sweat burst on her brow. Her knees trembled.

Scorch rose from his seat, stepping into her path.

"Who said that?" he said, looking around. "I can feel it, hear it, smell it."

"Maybe that little halfling is playing—*hic*—tricks. What's its—*Buuurrp*—name, anyway?" Darlene clapped her hands and cooed again.

Kam was exhausted, and as much as she wanted to fight, she could not hold the force back any longer. It had dug in deep. It was taking over.

"You should move, Scorch," she said. She looked back at Erin. Joline was rocking and singing gently to her. She headed for the door.

"Eh," Joline said, "Where do you think you're going, Kam? You get back here. You get back here right now!"

Tears streamed down Kam's cheek. "I can't. I must go. I must pay my debt."

Leave now!

Compelled, she stepped left.

Scorch was there.

She stepped to the right.

He was there.

"Who are you speaking with, Kam? Show me."

"Lords, help me." She tried to lift her hand, but it would not move. Her lips sealed. Her body lifted up off the floor.

Whatever was inside her had complete control over her now. Its magic melded with her mind, summoning magic and sending her over.

"What is that light from?" Darlene turned around. "Uh! Look! Her hand! It's as red as the suns!"

Kam rose higher in the air, her toes floating above Scorch's chin, her head almost touching the rafters.

He snatched her feet, pulled her back to the floor, and shoved her in a chair.

Get away from him! Get away from him now!

The jewels in her hand flared with life. Her elbow cocked back.

Whack!

Power coursed through her arm. She punched Scorch in the face with all her might. His head rocked back. His nose broke. She waited for him to fall. It should have killed him. At least knocked him out. It didn't. His nose didn't even bleed.

"Darlene!" Scorch said.

He snatched Kam's arm and pinned her glowing hand to the table.

The wilderness woman yanked her shortsword from her sheath.

Shing!

"NO! What are you doing! STOP!" Kam said in a voice that was not hers.

CHOP!

Her jewel-embedded hand was severed from her slender wrist.

Joline screamed.

Lefty screamed.

"Is all that blood…" Kam's eyes rolled up in her head.

Mine?

CHAPTER 20

OUTPOST 31 WAS A HIVE of activity. Underlings, more than Venir had ever seen before, scurried over the complex, preparing for a full scale assault. Some were decked head to toe in armor; others' chests were bare. They all checked weapons and buckles and stuffed small knives into their boots. All he could do was watch. Above, they readied the ballistas on the towers and pulled large vats filled with burning pitch onto the massive catwalks. The smell of battle tickled his nose, raising the hairs on his neck.

"Hurk!"

The underling commander jerked the rope around his neck.

"Arsehole," it said. "Soon your people shall die. Soon you will follow."

Face beet red, Venir's fingers fumbled at the coarse cord of rope around his neck that burned like fire.

The underling jerked it.

Venir fell to his knees. He groaned.

"Is it too tight, man with holes in his leg? Arsehole."

If he got the chance to kill one more underling, it would be him. He hated that one. He'd never heard one talk so much before. He was going to rip its beady ruby eyes from its skull. "I'm going to kill you, Bastard," he said, wiping the spit and blood from his mouth.

The underling commander jerked the rope again. "Orc, what did this man say?"

Tuuth shrugged his big shoulders. "Something about killing bastards, I think." Tuuth glanced at Venir and turned away.

"Bastard? What is a bastard? Hmmm… arsehole." The underling paced around him. "A mighty tongue this one has." It chittered, glared at Venir, shook its gauntlet in his face. It pointed to one of its bulging biceps, then the other. "Power, Arsehole. Which one has more power?"

Crack!

The underling struck him across the jaw.

"No more words from you, Arsehole." It drew back the other arm.

Crack!

Venir's nose caved in. Blood spurted down his chin and over his chest.

"So which one is it, Arsehole Bastard? The one on the left?" It flexed. "Or the one on the right? I'll point, you nod."

Venir balled up his better hand. Punched at the underling's crotch.

It knocked the sluggish blow away with ease with its boot and chittered. A form of cruel laughter. The underling gave Tuuth another order.

"Put him in the stockade. We'll whip what's left of him when it's over." It eyed Venir, a smile forming on its jagged teeth. "Arsehole Bastard. Almost funny if it wasn't coming from you." It jerked the rope hard once more, lifting Venir from his knees and sprawling him onto the deck.

He'd jammed his aching wrists again, and he was choking.

Bone!

His face felt purple. A pair of rugged hands loosened the rope on his neck, slightly, and pulled him up by the hair.

Venir moaned.

"You should be dead, Stranger. I've never seen a man survive so many wounds." Tuuth eased him into the stockade. "What is your name? It should at least be remembered if I ever make it out of this fort. Heh, never seen a man call an underling an arsehole or bastard and live to tell about it."

Venir couldn't speak. He was beaten from head to toe. The stockade Tuuth shackled him to only added to the agony. Within moments, his back stiffened and burned. The rest of his body shuddered.

How in Bish did I get into this?

Nose dripping blood, he watched through swollen eyes everything and anything going on. Bish's ultimate survivor had to find a way out of this jam, but in his bones he knew his chances were grim.

Tuuth took his spot against the rail, leaning against it, facing him, grinning.

Turning his head from Tuuth, Venir tried to find anything helpful. A familiar face. An unguarded exit. He could barely think. Everything hurt too much. His head ached, and his eyes were swollen. His hands were almost useless.

I could still strangle an underling if I got the chance.

The platform was over two stories tall. His view was as good as from anywhere but the towers, and there were dozens of those. The ballista alone would be more than enough to skewer a man to his horse.

Coughing, he noticed the South Gate beginning to rise. It was a massive mouth of wood and steel, almost three stories tall and half as wide. It almost rivaled the main gate of the City of Bone. One by one, well organized underling soldiers spilled outside, armed with spears and small crossbows, disappearing into the green foliage of the woods.

"Won't be long, Stranger. Won't be long at all. It should be a good fight for the Royal Riders, but it'll be their last one. And it won't last long after that." Tuuth pointed at the catwalks. "Once they charge in here, they're through."

Hundreds of underlings manned the catwalks, peering down, waiting. No force would be able to penetrate their superior position. But the underlings had, five years ago. Deceived by their own, the Royals had opened the gates, and the overwhelming numbers of the underlings, combined with the Brigand Army, had overtaken the fort. The battle had lasted longer than it should have, thanks to Venir, Billip and Mikkel's arrival, but in the end, it hadn't been enough. The powerful dark magic of the underlings had confused the well-trained soldiers, and they'd fallen.

Over five hundred men fell that day inside the fort, their bones ground into dust. Now, such men, a small force, only a few hundred at best, were being baited into a return. And it was his idea, not that the Royal Riders had much of a choice. They'd survived in the Outland as long as they could. It was time for one last ride into glory.

Venir shuddered a sigh. He wished he could join them, but all he could do was watch. So long as he didn't pass out.

The minutes passed like hours while the entire fort fell gradually silent.

Venir lifted his head.

Hooves. In the distance, like a machine, they pounded the ground.

The underling soldiers stirred. Every weapon was in place. Every sharp object gleamed.

"They come." Tuuth gripped his weapon, an orcen Fang. "Stranger, let your last day be a long day. At least you'll see more underlings trampled this day. But what they do to the men that survive?" He shook his head. "You won't be ready for that. But if you want mercy, ask for mercy." He held his blade's tip under Venir's chin. "Perhaps I'll cut your head off before the underlings peel your living skin from you."

Venir didn't hear a thing. Just the thunder of hooves coming his way. His heavy head wanted to sag. His fingers stretched and crackled. His heart pumped a little more blood. But his eyelids were heavy.

Stay awake, blast it! Stay awake!

Chapter 21

CHITTERS AND SHORT SIGNALS ECHOED through the spreading fog that was as thick as Boon's beard. He didn't need to see the underlings to kill them, but they needed to see him. He squatted in the crooked arm of a moss-covered tree. Waiting. Biding his time to strike.

Come on, black rodents. Your date with death is at hand.

An entire battalion scoured the grove now. Fogle Boon and company had departed while Boon held the underlings off at the edge of the cliff. Clapping his hands together and screaming up a mighty force, he'd sent a shockwave through the creatures, blasting them into the foliage. Now he waited for them to come looking for him.

Below him, a giant spider crawled, unhindered by the fog. Boon could almost make out the riders on its back. They still sensed he was near. He formed an O with is bearded lips and cast forth a soft popping sound. Somewhere, far away, a commotion stirred, sending the underlings away from his direction.

That should keep them busy.

He should have gone, left, fled while he had the chance, but he wouldn't. He wanted to kill them. Kill as many as he could. Trick them. Trap them. Slaughter them. They were many, but he was one.

Blast, I wish that staff still had its extra oomph. Just get on with it, Boon!

He muttered a spell.

On cat's feet, he drifted through the woodland. Up the creek away from the wary eyes of the underlings. His robes blended in perfectly with the fog as he did so. He stopped, heart pounding in his chest, as three underling soldiers chittered past him. With further caution, up and away he went.

This should do.

He pressed his palm into a tree, scorching the bark. One by one, he did the same to many trees in a row, staying parallel to the search line of underlings, all the while maintaining the sound commotion illusion to keep them away. It was tedious work, but the results would be divine. Over a hundred trees later, he sat down, rested his back against the tree, and closed his eyes. He could hear the chitters of the underlings. The sounds repulsed him.

Ah, what is this?

A breeze started to dissipate and lift the fog. Above, a pair of robed underling magi hung in the air nearby.

As I suspected. Perfect timing.

The wind pushed the fog down through the grove, down the ravine towards the falls.

Boon summoned a word of power.

The last tree he touched burst into flame, igniting the next one, and so on. The chain reaction was quick and devastating. The underling magi's spell to rid the ravine of the fog only hastened the affect. The wind sent the flames jumping from tree to tree. In moments, the grove was a crackling bonfire of smoke, sealing off escape for the battalion of underlings.

Laughing under his breath, Boon crept out of the grove. He could picture the underlings now, burning by fire or leaping from the ledge and plunging to their deaths.

It's a good start.

Zzrcak! Zzrack!

Two red balls of energy struck him in the chest, knocking him down. He rolled to his feet. Spit dirt from his mouth. The two underling magi stood before him. Yellow gem eyes boring into him.

He grimaced, rubbed his chest, and coughed. "Is that all you have for me?"

They flung their arms forward. Balls of bright energy shot out towards him.

Boon caught one ball in one hand, one in the other, and shoved them together. "Amateurs!" He hurled the orb of energy into the nearest underling, catching it full in the chest.

Boom!

Flesh and robes scattered.

"Perfect!" Boon said.

Vines burst from the ground, entwining his legs, pulling him down.

"Don't you have anything new to offer?"

The remaining underling let out a shrill whistle.

"Calling for help won't save you from me!"

Boon shot a green dart of energy from the tip of his finger.

Zing!

It punched through its throat. The underling clutched at its neck and collapsed.

"Blasted vines!" He reached down and ripped them away. "You'd think they'd have gotten more creative by now."

The grove was an inferno. Its smoke a black tower. There was no need for the one remaining underling mage to send a signal; the blaze would attract every underling for miles.

What to do?

Ahead, the barren landscape of the Outlands awaited. If he was smart, he'd try to catch up with Fogle and his friends, but something told him he needed to stick around. See what was going on. He had plenty of spells and energy left.

One more strike, Boon. If you can take one battalion, you can take two, maybe three.

It was his way. Trap and ambush. Trick and destroy. He'd drowned underlings in riverbeds. He'd suffocated them in their sleep. He'd burned them alive in fires. With magic, illusions and a crafty mind, he baited them. Fishing for underlings he enjoyed; killing them he relished.

Boon narrowed his eyes, scanning the horizon. He had no place to hide. He was exposed, but over a mile in the distance, another large grove of trees waited. Could he get there before the underlings saw him? And how much longer could he last on his own?

"I swore if I ever got out of the Under-Bish, I'd take the fight back to the underlings again. Let's go, old man, while your bones and muscles still bend."

Running, he headed straight for the grove, sandaled feet digging into the ground. Ahead, the trees weren't tall, but they'd offer sanctuary, a place to burrow in and hide maybe. Rest. Recharge. Renew the fight on the morrow. He didn't want to use all his spells either. He didn't have the spellbook to renew them. The ones he'd memorized for a lifetime were few.

A blur of black sped his way. Faster than the fleetest deer, it stopped twenty feet away. An underling hunter, armed in leathers, clawed fingers wrapped around the jagged blades of a dagger, barred his path.

Boon sent a green missile its way. A foot from its face, it ricocheted away when two more underling magi appeared in the sky. Another underling sped into his path, followed by another, and another. The shock troops had arrived.

Face grim, jaw set, Boon ground his feet into the dirt.

"So be it then!" Boon muttered a spell.

Arcs of light shot his way. The underling hunters closed in.

Rocks exploded beneath his feet. He dove away and rolled up on one knee.

"This is more like it!"

His beard bristled in and out of a see-through suit of mystic armor, which shimmered bluely around him. A shield wavered in one hand, a black sword of energy in the other.

They came at him. Fury and murder in their eyes. Armed and armored, they were the superior force. Experienced fighters. Killers one and all.

Boon's scintillating blade sheared through one's leg at the knee, dropping it. He gutted the belly of another.

Another stabbed its dagger at his chest, skipping off his chest plate.

Boon caught it in the jaw with a back swing. He was a trained soldier, had been part of the old programs in the City of Bone, before he took to wizardry. He liked fighting, but it couldn't destroy things as fast as he could with wizardry.

Zzrcak! Zzrack! Zzrcak! Zzrack!

Bursts of energy careened off his shield, his chest, his mystic helmet, chipping fragments of energy from it all.

The underlings' weapons gouged and cut. They were useless against his magic. Angry, they slung their weapons to the ground and jumped on top of him.

Boon staggered back under the weight and crashed to the ground. His black sword was too long to stab. *I'll try this!* Concentrating, he shrunk it into the size of a dagger and jammed it into an underling's skull.

An underling jumped on his arm, pinning it to the ground, while the other wrapped its arms around his legs.

Zzrcak! Zzrack! Zzrcak! Zzrack!

He jerked his shield up. Energy exploded out of it, cracking it apart. He kicked and flailed at his underling grapplers.

"I'll try this then, roaches!"

His shield transformed into a dagger, his dagger a shield.

He sunk the mystic blade into the underling's skull and ripped it out.

"No more chittering for you!"

Reversing his grip, he slid it between the other underling's ribs, drawing forth a howl. He extended the blade, shooting out the other side of the underling, cutting its breath short, jaws locking in the air.

Vines exploded from the ground, entwining his legs.

"Not again!" He cut them away. Huffing for breath, he rose back to his feet, ready. "Who's ... eh ... next?"

Gem speckled eyes, on the ground and off, had him surrounded. Rows and rows of them.

He banged his mystic sword into his shield.

"So be it then!"

Bolts of lightning struck from all over, shattering his armor, pounding him into the ground. Everything tasted like metal, and his beard was smoking. Flat on his back, his eyes fluttered open just in time to see an iron net drop from the sky.

CHAPTER 22

MILES AWAY, FOGLE BOON COULD no longer see the smoke in the distance. All signs of his grandfather were faded and gone. In front of him, Cass's limp figure was slumped against him in the saddle. His arm held her tight around the waist.

"Cass," he whispered in her ear, "can you hear me?"

She hadn't moved, but she breathed. Fogle felt a great deal of anger when he got a closer look at her face. It was scraped up, bruised and swollen. She looked awful. *They'll pay for this.*

"Where did Puppy go?" Barton said. Scratching his head, his arms were like tree trunks as he ambled forward. "I like the puppy. He has two heads. Hee. Hee."

It was a good question, but the answer was obvious.

"He's going after Venir," Fogle said. He shifted in his saddle. His back was in knots already.

Barton smashed his fist in his hand

"The man with Barton's toys! Get him, Puppy. Get him!" Barton stopped and leered back with his one good eye. "Wizard, how are we going to find the doggy again?"

Fogle pointed upward. Inky, his ebony hawk was circling in the sky.

"Oh … that's right. Good thinking."

It was good thinking, especially this time around. Taking no chances, Fogle had cut off a lock of Chongo's mane while the beast was licking Cass, then fed it to the bird. The familiar should have no problem tracking Chongo, but he wasn't so sure that the sliver of horn from Venir's long hunting knife would allow Inky to find the man.

We'll just have to wait and see what happens.

Cass pressed her back into his chest. He could hear her smacking her lips. Reaching around, he put a canteen to her mouth and felt her delicate hands wrap around his wrists. A fire went through him as she sighed, drank, gulped and sighed.

"Is that you, Fogle?" She reached back, nails gently scratching the stiff hairs on his cheek. "Did you save me?"

Despite the weariness, he felt his chest swell.

"You could say that," he said in her ear, "but I wasn't without any help."

Without looking back, she gulped down more water from the canteen.

"How did you find me?"

"Barton heard Chongo barking, I believe."

Cass straightened her shoulder and leaned forward.

"He's gone, isn't he?"

"Yes, but I'm tracking him, see?" He pointed into the sky. "We're going right after him."

"Hmmm… I'm impressed, Fogle Vir—, oh, sorry, Fogle Hero. Seems you're getting a knack for this adventuring after all…" Her voice trailed off.

"What? What is it, Cass?"

"Where's Boon?"

Good question. Dead most likely.

"He held the underlings off while we escaped."

"And you left him?" she said.

"No, he could have come, Cass. But he didn't want to, and I couldn't make him, not with a hundred men."

It was the truth. The pair of them had prepared more than enough spells to bail them out in a pinch if need be, but Boon had made it clear. He'd rather save his energy to kill underlings.

Cass turned her hips in the saddle and draped her sensuous legs over his. Her long-lashed pink eyes bore into his. "He's a crazy old man, isn't he?" She brought a smile to her battered lips.

She understands. Thank goodness for that.

He couldn't help but smile back. Despite the bumps and bruises, she was still the most beautiful thing he ever saw. A sparkle was in her eye.

"That might be a mild way of putting it." He cleared his throat. "Cass, I'm glad you're—*mmrph!*"

Cass grabbed him by his thick locks of hair and kissed him. The long, hot wet kiss was beyond words.

She gasped and sunk into his chest. "I'm glad you're well too."

Fogle wanted to jump off the horse and have her right then and there. He pulled her in for another kiss.

She pushed his chest back.

"Control yourself," she said, "We won't have time for that until the danger is over. And that won't be any time soon. So, do you have any idea where we are? I lost track leagues ago."

There had been a time when Fogle took a great deal of pride in knowing everything. He knew all about the City of Three and its histories, its people, its place, the names of all the Royals and the wizards in the towers … But now, stranded in the Outland, he realized that he knew next to nothing. Torn, he didn't know whether to be ashamed or fulfilled. It was as if he'd been reborn over the past several weeks, and he was uncertain whether he liked it or not. But, judging by the legs that hugged his hips, he was getting used to it.

She still smells amazing.

"Fogle," she said, shaking his chin. "I asked you a question. Are you fantasizing about me?"

"No," he said, matter-of-factly.

She folded her arms under her splendid breasts, pushing them up a little.

"Oh really, so you are fantasizing about someone else?"

"Uh … no, never!"

Cass wrapped her arms around his neck, giggled and kissed him on the cheek.

"You're always so serious, Fogle, aren't you?"

One second Cass was expressing her concerns about the danger, in the next she was teasing him. He didn't know what to think.

She might be crazy.

He squeezed her thigh.

She squeaked.

But I can get used to that.

"I'm serious about you," he said.

She ran her finger under his chin.

"Oh, I like that, Fogle. I like that a lot." She turned in the saddle. "But, I am concerned where we are headed. Do you have any idea?"

I'm not a Blood Ranger, you know.

He wanted to say it, but held back. He was in charge now, and at worst, he needed to act like he knew something.

"My familiar is in the air, and whatever it can see, I can. If there's any danger, I'll know, but at the moment, things are clear."

Clear as mud.

The terrain was virtually all the same, miles in every direction. Rocky. Sandy. Sparsely vegetated. He didn't let Inky scout too far ahead, for fear he'd lose him. Instead, he focused on the more immediate threats, particularly the underlings. In the back of his mind, something Barton had said worried him. What about the giants and the dragon?

"What can you see now, Fogle? Are there any forests or streams near? I need to rest somewhere that thrives with life." She shielded her face from the suns. "This is not good on my body. I need water. Natural water." She slumped back into him. "I tire again."

The suns above seemed to be beating down on him all of a sudden, sucking his life through his tattered robes. Above, Inky was soaring west at a gentle southern angle. Soaring above the land, he saw only bone trees and cacti scattered about, with little hope for water or natural vegetation in sight. For all Fogle knew, it might take over a week to traverse the Outlands to get where they were going. His stomach growled, and he thirsted.

She's right. I need to find better shelter. We'll never survive out here if it's too long.

"Follow the birdie," Barton began to sing, eyeing the sky. "Go where the birdie goes and find the puppy. A two headed puppy. And find the man that stole Barton's toys. And smash him."

Cass's head flopped over. Exhausted, she slept.

It worried Fogle. What would happen if he didn't find water or shelter? What would happen if the underlings caught up with them? He sent Inky back for a look.

Barton stopped and turned. "Say, where is the birdie going?"

"He's just making sure no one is following us."

Barton sat his big body on the ground and began rubbing his feet. "Tired of walking, Wizard. Barton wants to fly now."

Inky was almost a mile away when he noticed something. The landscape hadn't changed any, and none of their known pursuers were in sight, but something was coming, something dreadful. It was a swarm of some sort. Inky flew right into it. Whatever they were, they buzzed. Had tails, stingers and teeth.

Fogle turned his horse around.

"Get on your feet, Barton—it's time to run!"

"Why?" he groaned.

Fogle was already galloping away.

"Run, blast you! Run!"

A wall of insect creatures was coming after them like a heavy rain.

CHAPTER 23

THE SPIRE. IT HAD AS good a bird's eye view of the City of Bone as one could get, at least within the district Melegal frequented. He climbed the worn stone steps to the top, scattering the pigeons as he did so. Brushing the cobwebs away, Melegal stepped inside the room and made his way to the opening, where the remnants of a window were still intact.

It seemed like a lifetime had passed since the last time he stood here, a place he came to often, for seclusion and fantasy. He envisioned a magnificent castle and family, relatives of his long past, towering over the streets. When he was young, he'd convinced himself he was a Royal and played his own version of Royal games here. He'd commanded the street urchins from this roost for a while, but as time passed he'd grown out of it.

The wind bristled his clothes. He crawled through the frame and gripped the lip of the tower top above him. Whatever that woman, Trinos, had done, he'd never felt better in years. Fingernails digging into the terracotta tiles, he inched his way another twenty feet upward.

Bish, I haven't considered this since I was an urchin.

Tiles slipped under his boots.

Slat!

His fingers gripped the edges of the tile, holding on for dear life. Three tiles skittered off the roof and shattered on the decayed stone walls below.

There are far worse ways to go, I suppose.

The high winds tearing at his clothes, he continued his ascent at an agonizing pace. Near the top, he stretched out his skinny fingers. A long metal pole, once a place for a castle banner, jutted from the highest point of the tower.

Stretch, you skinny bastard, stretch!

His fingers licked at the metal. His boots scraped, sending more tiles careening off the tower and crashing on the ground.

Almost there, Rat. He stretched. *Almost.* His fingers slid around the pole. *Got it!*

He pulled himself up and coiled himself around the pole. The first time he'd done that, long ago, he'd told himself he could do anything at all. But all he'd learned from it was that he could make an awfully hard climb to an awfully old pole. Still, he kissed it.

I'd like to see anyone else do this.

The viewpoint was unlike any other in the City of Bone. He could see the tops of the buildings and all the way from one massive City wall to the other. None of the intact Royal Castles lined up against the Wall of Bone had as high a spire. How this one stood here so long as it had, while the old castle and everything else around it fell, he'd never know. His keen eyes scanned the chaos.

Smoke from the burning buildings rolled past and beneath him. The massive gates in the four walls of the city were crowded with throngs of thousands of people. Soldiers patrolled the streets on foot and horseback, while squads of underlings darted in and out of the alleys and attacked. The entire city groaned in horror, despair and disbelief.

This place is going to the slatter.

He turned his keen eyes to Castle Almen. His jaw dropped open. Underlings, hundreds of them, surged the main wall. Every tower was lit with mystic illumination, and spiders the size of dogs and ponies scurried over the parapets, up the walls and towers. A chill raced down Melegal's spine. How long could the Royals hold out? And why were the underlings attacking there? His hand drifted to the Keys.

Sefron wanted them. The underlings wanted them. A picture of the imp invaded his mind. *What if that thing shows up here?*

Something was not right.

Think, Melegal. Think!

He squatted down, flattened himself on his belly, and crept back down the steep tower, thinking all the way.

Sefron works for the underlings. Underlings want inside the castle. Sefron is in the castle. Kill Sefron. Stop the underlings. Ridiculous.

As much as Melegal despised the Royals and all their cruel and twisted games, he knew the underlings were a far greater threat. Venir had shown him at least that much. Catching the lip of the tower's edge like a spider, Melegal crawled headfirst back inside.

Whew!

Alone in the tower, his thoughts went to his friends. He hadn't seen Venir since that last time he was here, and despite his anger towards the man, he'd like to be with him now. If anyone knew how to deal with underlings, it was Venir.

I wonder how Lefty's doing as well.

So far as he was concerned, ever since they all left, his life had been far from normal. If anything, it had gotten worse. He smoothed his cap over his head.

"Well, I suppose if no one else is going to defend my home, I'll just have to do it my—"

A small black blur jumped through the outside window over the top of him. Melegal ducked and rolled, the sisters out and ready. A pair of pearl white eyes greeted him.

"Octopus!"

The big cat circled his ankles, lay down and rumbled. Melegal couldn't have been gladder to see his most reliable friend. He reached over and stroked the cat's back.

"And to think, I actually worried you might be underling food."

Octopus stretched out his eight claws that twinkled in the night.

"I should have known better," Melegal said, rubbing behind his ears, "because you have plenty of lives, don't you?"

After the short reunion, thoughts heavy on his task ahead, Melegal made his way down the deteriorating steps. Octopus darted away when he reached the bottom.

Must be a big juicy rat somewhere. Besides me.

Aside from all the distant shouts of alarm and screams, the streets in this quadrant were barren for the most part. Even the urchins and thugs that frequented the remains of the abandoned castle had become ghosts.

Maybe the underlings aren't so bad after all. They're keeping the stink out.

Down the street he went, tugging and knocking on doors as he did so. Reaching inside his vest, he produced a Key. It was the same one he'd used before.

Hmmm. What did the woman at the fountain say? Just find a door and go?

From building to building he went, searching for a key hole, but none were found.

Drat it.

With all the pickpockets, urchins and thieves about in Bone, using keys to secure common doors and entrances wasn't always the securest way to go. Many shop keepers barred their doors from the inside because they lived there. Melegal imagined most were holed up inside right now. Of course, whenever a door was barred from the inside, it only meant someone must be home. Most citizens of Bone never, ever left their home or store empty.

Never cared to rob the places filled with the living.

He made his way farther up the street.

There must be a keyhole somewhere.

He stopped at the next block and stood in front of an entrance to a corner store, where a big black keyhole forged with brass greeted him. Melegal bounced the ancient Key on his chin.

It's not going to fit in there, is it?

Lowering the Key towards the hole, he froze. His neck hair rose. He sniffed.

Smells like a wet dog.

Wapush!

A tail of black leather encircled his wrist and jerked the Key out of his hand.

Melegal twisted his wrist free. *Who in Bone?*

Wapush!

The tail of the whip caught him by the leg and pulled him down.

Bark! Bark! Bark!

An oversized Rottweiler was snapping at his neck.

"Bloody Watchmen!" Melegal cried out. "Back off! I'm a Royal—"

Wapush!

Another whip wrapped around his throat.

"Watchmen! Ha! Hear that, men? This one thinks we're part of the local brute squad." A tall, limber man stepped into view. He was no Watchman. He was savvy. Buckled. Clean. A different breed.

The other two were stout. Menacing. "Ha! Watchmen, and you were about to say you were a Royal! Eh, Melegal?"

He couldn't answer. The whip choked his neck.

Bark! Bark! Bark!

"Heel!"

The dog quieted, but still loomed over him, growling.

That's when Melegal saw it. The insignia on the man's hand. His blood ran cold.

Bone! The Royal Bloodhounds are after me too!

Melegal had heard plenty of stories of the most vicious bounty hunters of all.

The speaking man squatted down beside him, long fingers stroking the finely groomed auburn hair on his chin. His eyes steely flecks of brown and green. Hair brownish red. Intelligent. Cocky. A good manner about him.

"So, a Royal Detective, as I understand. Pretty crafty I'd say, to be serving Lord Almen." He pulled a long dagger from his sheath. "Roll him over, men. Unfortunately, I need to cut those thews behind his skinny knees. Can't have you running off now, can we?"

Melegal started to speak.

Whop!

The Bloodhound leader slugged him in the face.

"No talking," the man said. Almost polite. "Now get him rolled over."

Chapter 24

Lorda Almen cowered behind a chair, trembling.

"All clear!"

It was a man's voice. Strong. Labored. She peeked.

A few feet away, a dog-sized spider twitched, webbing spewed from its mouth and stuck to the floor.

Glitch!

The shadow sentry rammed his sword through its brain, bringing its convulsions to a stop. The sentry wore a helmet of black mesh armor that covered his face. The rest of him was splattered in spider gore. He extended his hand.

"Are you alright, Lorda?"

She shook her head, trying to stand, too weak to speak. Sprawled out on the floor, her servant girls were dead. A Shadow Sentry sat in the corner, coated in webbing, a nasty wound on his face. It appeared the acid from the spider's fangs had burnt straight through his mesh helmet.

You are in command, Lorda. Act like it!

Reaching out, the sentry caught her under the elbow and lifted her forward. He was strong. His girth reminded her of her former high guard, Gordin. She missed him. Her son Tonio had killed him, and Melegal had saved her, so she was convinced. She shook her head.

"Remember these words, Sentry: from this day forward, Spiders are banned from the Castle." She tossed her hair over her shoulder, pulled her shoulders back, and straightened her bodice. Outside, the battle was raging. Explosions, screams and the disturbing chitters of the underlings could be heard from all around.

"Secure the openings, men. See to it nothing again ever enters this room!"

A half dozen soldiers made their way into the room, followed by two more Shadow Sentries.

Making her way to her husband, Lorda lost her shoe. It stuck to the floor. She clenched her fists by her side.

"BONE!"

One of the soldiers grabbed a torch from the wall and burned the webbing. Lorda covered her nose.

Must all evil things stink?

She picked up a small bottle of perfume that lay near a table that had been knocked over, dabbed it on, and stepped in something that splashed.

"What?"

At her feet, water from Lord Almen's bowl had spilled, and the wash cloth from his head now lay on the ground with spider guts on it. Reaching over to grab it, she withdrew her hand.

"Disgusting."

"I'll take care of that, Lorda," the Shadow Sentry said. "Shall I send for the cleric?"

She glanced at Lord Almen.

"Eeeeeek!"

His bloodshot eyes were wide open.

Chapter 25

"**N**EVER SEND AN IMP TO do an underling's job," Master Kierway said, flatly.

It was dark, aside from the glow of the small underling lanterns that cast shadows through the caves.

"What is that, Kierway?" Catten rubbed his gut. His thoughts were still heavy from his brother, Verbard, punching him there. Verbard had changed, changed much. He couldn't decide whether he should admire or hate him.

I'll get him back when the time comes.

"The Keys," Kierway said. "If we had the Keys, we'd have overrun this Castle already. They can get into anything, anything at all, even that door."

Catten remained silent. Master Kierway had a small army at his disposal, filling the caves alongside the Current beneath Castle Almen as far as he could see. All he had to do was get them in there. Time was running out.

Kierway chopped the top off a stalagmite. "Well, Mage? Did you come here to help overtake this castle or to conspire against your brother?" Kierway chopped another top off. "Or both?"

Catten lifted his chin.

"What are you talking about?"

Kierway flashed the sharp grey teeth in his mouth.

"Oh come now. Do you really think I believe you're on your brother's side? You? Then you wouldn't be the Catten I know. And besides, I already know my father can't stand him. Why else would he bring you back to life?" Showing off with his sword, he split a drop of water falling from above. "To see Verbard dead, of course."

"I'm sure there is nothing you'd rather believe, now that my brother has taken over your charge. The one you've spent years on and failed. The Keys. You dare mention them? You should have secured them, but you failed. And my brother, he's not a disappointment to your father, quite the contrary. But you are." Catten's gold eyes locked on Kierway's copper. "Sinway put you at my brother's will and pleasure, and I am here on his behalf. Now, tell me, why isn't this door open?"

Kierway's eyes narrowed. He slid his swords into their sheaths on his back. The master underling had a way of squeezing out of things, but at the moment, both Verbard and Catten had the upper hand on him. It only figured that Kierway would seek an alliance so he could get out from underneath the will and pleasure of Verbard. Kierway made his way to the door. Two robed underling magi were on their knees chittering an incantation, while another made arcane markings along the door's edges.

"It was only wood before when we destroyed it," Kierway said, "but it's been replaced with iron and stone, sealed by magic. There isn't even any key hole."

"So, how would those precious Keys have worked then?"

Kierway shrugged.

"Nothing to say, eh, Kierway?" Catten floated closer to the door. Over eight feet in height, it was more of a slab than a door. "Have you even tried to crack it?"

Kierway motioned to the battering ram propped up by the stalagmites. It was a six foot metal tube with handles

"I was confident the magi could get us in, like the last time," Kierway said. He picked up the small battering ram with a groan and tossed it at Catten's feet. "Perhaps you should give it a try?"

"Perhaps I should... Fool."

With a flick of his wrist, the battering ram lifted from the ground.

"Magi, finish your spell. Kierway, ready your warriors."

"They're ready." He folded his arms over the bandoliers on his chest. "For what, I can't imagine."

Focusing, Catten grabbed the handles on the ram and filled it with energy. It glowed red and hummed with new life, hovering over the cave floor. The symbols drawn on the door flared with life. The underling magi floated backward. The slab door groaned. The light of the battering ram became brighter and brighter as Catten filled it with more power.

No mortal man is more powerful than I!

The giant missile shot forward, striking the door with mind-jarring force.

KA-CHOW!

Stone cracked. Metal groaned. Parts of the door exploded.

A human cry of alarm went up from the other side.

Catten was about to say, "Get in there, Kierway," but the man and his soldiers were already on their way. Juegen in plate mail, Badoon warriors of all sorts, and albino urchlings stormed through the black hole, led by the Son of Sinway.

"Go!" Catten ordered two magi through the opening.

Yes! He clutched his fist.

The underling force jammed at the entrance.

He blew at the wispy fibers of energy that lingered on his fingers. He never would have imagined it possible, but in moments, he was going to be taking up residence inside the walls of the City of Bone.

Perhaps Sinway isn't losing it after all.

An army of underlings with access to the Current could hold that castle forever. It was brilliant.

We'll take them one castle at a time.

Finally, he would have one victory where his brother had failed. He'd penetrated the castle, and in minutes, it would be his.

Elation had filled him, but the underlings up front cried out in disappointment.

"Impossible!" he cried out.

The door he just destroyed had returned. He and the majority of his underling army were trapped outside. Kierway and his men were trapped within.

Chapter 26

ALLIES AND ENEMIES. JARLA THE former Brigand Queen had been on both sides of the war against the underlings. Unlike the Royals who had betrayed her, defiled her, humiliated her and destroyed her trust in all men, good and bad, she wasn't heartbroken to see the City of Bone under siege. Instead, she was thirsty.

Dragging her shoulder along an alley wall, carrying an empty bottle in her hand, she was making her way back to the stables. She just needed to find Nightmare and ride out of here. But there was a problem. She was lost.

"Bastards," she moaned. She stepped over one bloodied corpse after another. "Probably had it com-*hic*-coming."

Dried out and tired, she was rubbing her short locks of braided black hair when she found herself staring at a large road known as the Royal Roadway. A team of soldiers trotted down the street, away from her. She tried to get her bearings.

I know where this is. Hic.

Sauntering along the store fronts where the Royals used to shop, her mind wandered back to her life long ago. Her mother, a seamstress, had been the mistress of a Royal. As a little girl, Jarla watched the proud women come and go, but never desired to be one. She was cut from a different cloth, always fancying the work down in the smithy shops. Down there, as she grew older, she helped in a forge, along with her father who was also a soldier.

She recalled the last day she saw him. Taller than her, eyes blue, black hair long, he'd said, "Jarla, if I don't return, be sure to help your mother." He rode off on a horse and was gone. No word ever came of what happened to him, and her unfaithful mother moved within the walls of the castles. She had never spoken to her mother since. Instead, she enlisted. She had the right through her father, and she passed. Her steel was quick, her determination unrivaled, and after years of training and field experience, she carved her way up the ranks. Then, they betrayed her. She'd been the Brigand Queen ever since.

All the doors she passed by were boarded up or locked, and few of the stores had windows. That would be too dangerous. A pair of long-faced urchins shuffled by.

"Can you help us?" one said. He was pitiful, dirty, scraped up and trembling. "Our parents are dead."

She laughed, handed the boy her bottle, patted him on the head and walked away. "And soon you will be too," she said. She crossed the nearest alley, booted feet clopping over the storefront porch, and stopped. Something rustled inside the store. She pressed her ear to the door. A pair of bottles clinked and rolled. She jerked her head back. Someone inside busted a bottle on the door. Looking up at the sign that hung above her, she licked her lips. It read: Wine Blossoms.

"Where there's glass, there's wine."

Stepping back, she noticed the windows were boarded up and the door had no handle. She cast a glance over her shoulder, noting the streets were empty but distant sounds of battle and destruction could be heard. If anything, there should be widespread looting, but it seemed the underlings had spooked even the looters. The entire city was not itself.

Why not? Someone is in there.

She knocked on the door.

The rustling stopped.

She tried to decide if it would be best to be a member of the City Watch or a person in need. *Besides, I don't think underlings would knock.* She tried again, harder this time.

Knock! Knock! Knock!

She considered speaking. Saying hello. Sounding polite and customary, but such manners weren't in her anymore. Over the years, she'd grown accustomed to taking what she wanted.

"Blasted cowards," she murmured. She pressed her ear to the door again, closed her eyes and listened. Nothing. She was thinking maybe there was another way in when she heard more chittering. Closer this time. Coming her way. Her hand fell to her blade.

Now the little fiends show up.

Jarla didn't fear the underlings as most people did. She didn't fear anything. Besides, she'd seen them bleed the same as anything else. She'd battled them by the dozens when she was a Royal Soldier and found out that their skulls split just as easily as men's. She pressed her back against the doorway. The underlings, so far as she could hear, would be upon her any moment. And by the sounds of things, there were many of them, at least a dozen. If she only had her axes and the armament, she could have handled them.

Slat! I hate running!

Thump.

She heard a heavy footstep on the other side of the door, followed by the sound of a bolt scraping over metal.

She turned just as the door swung open. She took a sharp breath.

"Welcome," a man said. "Won't you come in?"

The man that filled the doorway spoke like his throat was full of broken glass. He looked and sounded like nothing she ever noted before. A hole dotted the center of his forehead. It was unnatural. She blinked and took a step back, hand still on her sword.

Neck cracking, the man bent his ear. "Seems company is coming, huh, Little Lady."

Her eyes drifted to the jug of wine in his grip, then back to his face. His eyes were dark, almost black, and a thick scar parted the brown hair on his head and went down past his neck, stopping at the armor that covered his broad shoulders. Jarla felt something in her bones that she hadn't felt in years. Fear.

"Shall you stay or shall you go?"

She fanned her hand in front of her face. His breath was foul and unimaginable. Everything about him defied reason. Her keen eyes noted the fresh blood stains all over his armor. Swords and long knives hung from his belt and behind his shoulders. His rotting smile turned her blood cold.

He shook his jug of wine. "It's been a long time since I drank with such a lovely lady."

She pulled back her shoulders. "And it's been a long time since I drank with such a fine man." She snatched the jug from his hand and stepped inside.

He closed the door behind her and slid the bolt back in place.

Taking a seat at the bar, the first thing she noticed was what was left of the dead people on the floor. "I'm Jarla." She tipped the bottle her lips.

The man bowed. "And I'm Tonio."

She almost spit all over herself. Something about the half-dead man's name was awfully familiar.

"Bad wine?" He smirked.

Her eyes flittered towards the door. Tonio stepped in the way, a haunting glimmer in his eye. *Slat! I should have snatched the jug and ran.*

Staring at the woman, Tonio felt a degree of fascination. Her scarred face gave him comfort and solace. She wasn't like the rest of the people in this world. He grabbed the jug of wine she'd snatched and drank from it.

"Jarla," he said. It had a ring to it. There was something in a portion of his mind that clicked. "Jarla."

Her eyes narrowed, and her sword inched out of its sheath.

He chuckled. Even though his thinking had begun to clear, his memories were still scattered. "You can leave that where it is, Jarla. I have no reason to harm you."

Scowling, she looked over at the people on the floor. "Is that what you told them?"

"Heh, heh, heh… no, they would have died anyway. They were weak, but you," he eyed her athletic frame up and down. It stirred something in him, "are strong."

"You have better judgment than most men I know," she said. She pulled out a dagger and stuck it in the bar. "Just don't get too close."

Tonio grabbed another bottle and poured it down his throat. It warmed his bones, made him feel alive. But in the back of his mind, the nagging continued.

Kill the Vee-Man.

The image of Venir was still as clear as a bell in his mind. The man had mocked him in the jail cell, in front of his comrades. He could still see the man splitting him in half with that axe. The whistle of the blade woke him up whenever he drifted off. Only vengeance would give him rest.

"Kill the Vee-Man," he growled.

Jarla looked at him and said, "What?"

He slammed his fist into the bar. "Kill Vee-Man!"

Jarla jumped back, ripping her sword from her sheath. "Keep silent, you three-eyed fool! There are underlings out there!"

Underlings, they meant nothing to Tonio. Or did they? A memory came forth, the memory of the underling named Oran. Violet eyed. That underling had saved him after the giant dog's chewing almost killed him. That underling had found the Vee-Man before. Maybe underling help was what he needed after all.

He headed toward the door.

"What are you doing?" Jarla jumped into his path and stuck her sword at his belly.

"The underlings will help me find the Vee-Man," he said, coldly.

"Oh no they won't!" She shoved her sword through his belly.

Tonio didn't feel a thing. He shook his finger at the wide-eyed woman. "You shouldn't have done that, Jarla."

Smack!

He back-handed her across the face, sending her sprawling to the floor. He pulled the sword from his belly and tossed it clattering by his side. Outside, he could hear the chittering of underlings gathering at the door.

Jarla dove after her sword. A second later she was ready. "I can't let you do that, you split-faced bastard!"

"I must find the Vee-Man, and you can't stop me." He pulled a blade from the sheath.

Clang!

Metal crashed into metal. He knocked her swings away, parrying one after the other. With his other hand, he reached the bolt and started to pull it free.

"No!" Jarla said. She poked at his eyes.

Tonio flinched.

"Almost got me, Beautiful."

Jarla gasped and turned away.

Angry churts erupted. Bright underling eyes, teeth bared, poured into the room, surrounding them.

"Didn't you secure the door in the back? You idiot!"

Tonio shrugged at her and turned to the underlings. "Take me to the Vee-Man."

One underling chittered a series of orders; the rest bared their teeth, raised their weapons and charged.

CHAPTER 27

OUTPOST THIRTY ONE WAS UNDER attack. Rider after rider stormed through the gate: three horses wide, twenty horses deep. Their banners streamed in the air, bright and colorful, a symbol of hope among the despair.

His fires stoked inside. Venir fought against the stockade.

The big orc said, "Say anything, and I'll cut your tongue out," then turned his eyes on the burgeoning battle below.

At the front of the riders, Venir could see Commander Jans. His long auburn mustache whipped in the wind as he thundered in.

"Let the Havoc begin!" Jans cried.

Perched on the catwalks and in the towers, the underlings fired. Crossbow bolts, spears, lances and ballista bolts ripped into the men. Hot pitch poured down on them.

Venir wanted to scream, "Turn back!" but he didn't have the throat or the breath for it.

The Riders kept charging, thundering through the giant courtyard, looking for an enemy to strike. One barrage after the next punched into the flesh of men, while other bolts were deflected by their heavy armor.

Venir grimaced. Many men caught ballista bolts in the face. Tuuth pointed and laughed.

Ride out, Jans! Ride out!

Venir's mind was racing. More Royal Riders stormed through the gate and inside. It was just what the underlings wanted. The riders thundered straight into the next assault. Crossbow bolts, heavy and small, ripped into them, separating horse and rider. One rider caught a bolt in the neck. Another was pinned to his horse. Pitch burned horses and riders alike. A dozen horses went down in an instant, and still the riders kept pouring in.

The well-organized ranks of the riders turned to chaos. The underlings splintered the groups, sending them in all directions. Over a hundred warriors rode purposefully around the fort, looking for something to strike. Something to trample. Something to kill. Another volley cut them down.

Blast their black hides!

Venir's fists clenched beneath his broken wrists. He'd cut off his arm to get down to them. They needed help. They needed to get on those catwalks.

Men yelled. Cried out. Horses whined and buckled. The Royal Riders' organized ranks had become chaos. Some circled the courtyard, while others tried to hide. But there was nowhere to go. The underlings fired from every angle, every corner. Venir felt helpless. Miserable. Standing there watching good men get slaughtered.

Run, blast you, Run!

A dark cloud rolled overhead, blotting out the sun as the southern gate was lowered and sealed shut. The Royal Riders were trapped.

"Won't be long now, Stranger. And once they're all dead, it won't be long for you either."

Venir would have stabbed him in in the throat if he could have. But he couldn't do anything right now. He couldn't even hold a weapon. He could barely walk or keep his eyes open. Through his hazy eyes, he caught something. Massive stone towers jutted up from every corner. Smaller towers lined the inner wall every thirty yards, linking catwalk to catwalk. At the bottom of each corner tower was a huge wooden door. The underlings cried out as one of these doors exploded.

A tall lanky man appeared, waving the riders inside.

Slim!

Commander Jans and his steed disappeared inside, appearing moments later on the catwalk.

"What's this?" Tuuth's jaw dropped in astonishment.

Spears lowered, the Royal Riders galloped into the sea of underlings on the catwalk. Jans caught two on one spear with his first pass.

Venir wanted to jump for joy. *Yes, by Bish!*

Underlings were trampled and gored. Men were pulled from their saddles. Underlings were hurled off the catwalks.

Boom!

Somewhere, another door exploded. Men surged into the tower and up onto the western catwalks.

The underlings were caught off guard. Flatfooted, they scrambled for weapons, only to have their brains dashed into the wood. The Royal Riders cheered and charged, tearing into the underlings with everything they had. Somewhere someone shouted, "Take the towers!"

One by one, the underlings on the catwalks fell under the heavy steel of the Royal Riders. The underling rout was over, but the battle had only just begun. The underlings were many. The Riders were already reduced to half the force they rode in with. The underlings, despite their losses, were somehow still at full strength.

Commander Jans was at the other end of the Catwalk, beside the South Gate entrance, throwing an underling over the railing. He was shouting, but Venir couldn't make out what he said. Were there still more Riders to come? Had Royal reinforcements finally arrived?

KA-CHOW!

An arc of energy struck Jans full in the chest, blasting him into the main wall. Above, a host of underling magi had appeared. Arms spread wide, fingertips aglow, they let the Royal Riders have it.

KA-CHOW!

KA-CHOW!

KA-CHOW!

"Nooooo!" Venir's hoarse voice cried out.

Tuuth back-handed him in the face. "Quiet, Fool!"

Men were knocked from their horses. Bodies of animal and man exploded. The triumph of the Riders took a sharp turn into a dark tunnel. Venir turned just in time to catch Commander Jans rising back his feet. Blood coated his mustache. He kept shouting. Pointing at the towers.

Two ballistas swung in his direction. An underling mage hung in the sky, guiding them. Venir's heart sank. The underling pointed at Jans. The big warrior saw them and beat his chest, yelling.

Clatch-zip! Clatch-zip!

Two long bolts ripped through the sky, striking Jans square in the chest. He was pinned to the wood. He shouted once more, hand rising in the air, pointing towards Venir and died.

"Ew... that must have hurt," Tuuth said. "But there are far worse ways to go. You'll find out soon, I bet."

The Royal Riders fought long and hard, but they were no match for the underling numbers and mystic forces. A wall of fire encircled dozens of horsemen on the ground. The horses bucked and whined. Riders were tossed from their saddles into the fires. More missiles from the crossbows and ballistas came, skewering the men and scattering others. Minute after agonizing minute, Venir watched the brave men get picked off. The underling magi cleared the catwalks, and the dead underlings and men were piled up in heaps of torn flesh and metal. The hot fort air wreaked of death.

Slim!

Venir didn't see any sign of him.

An hour later, the men of the Royal Riders could swing no more. The last twelve of them surrendered.

"Not bad, Stranger. Not bad at all, for Royal soldiers. But I think a host of orcs would have fared much better." He slapped Venir on his back. "At least you'll have some company. And who knows, they might have you peel the skin from them before they peel the skin from you." He snorted a laugh. "Now wouldn't that be something?"

For the first time in his life, Venir had nothing to say.

CHAPTER 28

Lefty dashed from behind the bar, shaking his head, tears streaming from his eyes. Everything happened so fast. *What do I do?*

Everyone was screaming at Scorch, but he paid them little mind. Instead, he pushed his broken nose back into place.

"What have you done!" Joline screamed.

Kam's jaw dropped just before her eyes rolled up inside her head.

Joline caught her on the way down.

But Scorch wasn't paying attention to that. It was the hand that held his eyes. It twitched on the table. "Fascinating." Picking it up, he resumed his seat at the bar. "I've never experienced a talking hand before."

"Lefty! Lefty!" Joline cried.

Lefty stood there next to Joline, but still was unsure what to do. There was blood everywhere.

"Scorch!" Joline shouted. "Why, Scorch? Why!" Joline's tone was delirious.

Lefty trembled.

"Oh, put a sock in it, or whatever you people say." Scorch shook his head. "I'll never understand why Trinos picked such leaky beings." He wiped Kam's blood splatter from his forehead. "I can only presume it gives the dramatic more flare."

"Is there anything I can do?" Darlene said. "I can make a fine tourniquet."

"You could've not cut her hand off, you imbecile woman!" Joline said. Tears streamed from her face as she held Kam in her arms. "What possessed you to do such a thing?"

"He told me to. I do what he tells me," Darlene said. The husky woman handed Joline a rag.

"Would you cut your own hand off if he told you?"

"Probably."

The woman defied reason. Scorch defied reason. Everything Lefty had been through seemed to defy reason. But right now, Kam's bleeding had to stop. And Joline needed to stop screaming.

Lefty leapt onto the bar and kicked Scorch in the jaw. "Fix this, you—"

Blink!

Darleen stood by the table, dumbfounded.

Kam, Joline, the Halfling, and the baby were all gone. She wiped the sweat from her brow and swallowed. "What happened to them?" she said. She started looking under the tables.

"Could you bring me your knife?" Scorch said.

Darlene wiped the blood off her trousers and asked, "Sure, what for?"

Without looking at her, he snapped his fingers, popping her ears.

She hurried over, ears ringing, and handed the blade to him, handle first.

He showed her the hand, the gems embedded in it. "Is it customary to wear gems in this manner, Darlene?"

"No." She took a closer look. "I have to say, I've never seen anything like that before." She grimaced. "Looks painful, but you know, there are bugs that'll crawl right inside you and lay eggs. It's the vilest thing. One time this fella was drinking some jig back in Hohm when these eensy weensy bugs came crawling out if his nose and earholes. Huh! He screamed, I screamed, we all screamed for lice cream!" She popped her lips. "I got my chubby arse out of there after that."

Scorch, so far as she could tell, was ignoring her. He always did, but whenever she thought he wasn't paying attention, he'd say something to her. She'd been trying to figure it out, but she'd come to the conclusion that she just wasn't smart enough. Two minds were better than one anyway, she figured.

Scorch dug the knife under the gem inside Kam's palm.

"It seems my little red friends are determined to stay put, Darlene. Any suggestions?"

She propped her elbow on the bar and chin on her fist. "Maybe we should burn it. I can stoke the fireplace up over there, but let me warn you: it'll smell something awful."

The hand twisted away from Scorch's grip. Like a spider, it scrambled away.

Darlene jumped out of her stool. "Great Guzan!" Look at that thing go!" Heart thumping, she chased after it. She knocked over tables and chairs, diving on top of it as it reached the exit door. She held it up with both hands. "I got it, Scorch! I got it!" It felt like a dry wiggling fish in her hands. "Should I throw it in the fire?"

"Hmmm…" Scorch took a bite out of a pickle. "I have a feeling it doesn't want that. Bring it back over here."

"Certainly." Her arms wiggled. The hand was strong. Unnatural to hold. "Maybe you should cut the fingers off. I've got another knife, you know." *Thunk.* She pinned the knife to the table and handed him the hand. "This is the strangest thing I ever saw, Scorch. What are you going to do with it?"

His eyes lit up like infernos. He looked straight at the gems and said, "Time is short." His other hand became a brilliant blue fire. "What will it be?"

The hand clutched and writhed.

"I grow impatient," Scorch said.

The red gemstones popped out of Kam's hand and clattered on the floor.

"Whoa!" Darlene leaned in closer. "You know what, Scorch? Those things kinda look like eyeballs."

Dangling Kam's hand by one finger, he said, "A shame to see such a functional appendage go to waste." *Plop.* He dropped it in the pickle jar.

Darlene let out a snort, watching it float down, but a sinking feeling fell upon her.

Where did those people go?

"Don't worry about that, Darlene," Scorch said. The gems floated up to his fingers.

And that's when things became odd.

Scorch talked to himself, ate pickles and cheese, and sipped Muckle Sap for the next hour. He laughed. Scoffed. Mocked. His handsome features changed from one expression to another. Grim. Scary. Bold. Enlightened. But for the most part, he giggled and used the word 'fascinating.'

Bored, she began to clean up, whistling a lullaby as she picked up the chairs and tables she'd knocked over. She stopped at the dead bodies and smashed a few flies between her hands.

"How am I going to dispose of these guys?"

She had an idea.

"Uh, Scorch?"

He sat there, eyes transfixed on the red stones he'd set back on the bar.

"Scorch, could you?"

Slowly, he turned, a dark look in his eye.

Walking over to him, she tossed a rag over the gemstones.

He blinked at her, eyes regaining their luster. "What is it?"

She jutted her thumb at the headless bodies.

"Oh," he sighed. "Just find some sand and sprinkle it on them."

"Sand?"

"Never mind," he said. He snatched the rag off the gemstones.

Puff! Puff! Puff! Puff! Puff!

"Whoa!" she said.

The dead men had turned to statues of sand. Walking over, she poked the nearest one and watched it implode over the planks on the floor.

"Whoa. Thanks, Scorch."

But he wasn't paying her any mind. Instead, he rolled the gemstones in between his fingers. "I've got to see this." He said more, but that was all she understood.

She tried to ignore the butterflies in her stomach. She'd never had those before, but Scorch had never acted this way before either.

The door to the entry way cracked open, and one of their followers peeped his gray-haired head through.

"Darlene, er ... well, any needs?"

She placed her hands on her hips. "Drag in two more of you, and find me a mop and broom."

Glancing over at Scorch, she almost peed herself. Only the hand and the pickle jar remained. Scorch was gone with the red gems.

"I got a bad feeling about this."

Chapter 29

"What in Bish are those things?" Fogle yelled. But Cass wasn't listening. She wasn't even moving. "Cass!" Nothing.

Ahead, Barton's giant feet shook the ground. Running full stride, his arms swung like giant hammers at his sides.

Fogle whipped the reins on his horse. "Eeyah!"

Behind him, the angry buzz of the insects got louder, like a hunger. Fogle had heard about swarms before. He recalled the stories of insects that picked the flesh clean from the bone. Inky's vision of the insects, each as long as Fogle's finger, was a chilling site. Sharp rows of snapping teeth, black bug eyes, wings and a stinger like a scorpion for a tail. He glanced over his shoulder.

"They're getting closer! Eeyah!"

They'd made it over a mile when his horse began to labor for breath. Ahead, Barton began to clutch at his side. *No! Think of something, Fogle!*

No spells came to mind that could put a stop to thousands of insects, and anything from the spellbook would take too much time.

Looking over his shoulder, he screamed again. "Cass!" The insects were getting closer. His horse was slowing, and ahead, Barton's feet stumbled. "Come on, Druid! I need you! You're the one that's supposed be able to talk to things in this world."

The buzzing became louder, not so much a buzz, but more like the sound of thousands of tiny metal scissors opening and closing. Fogle fought the image of his flesh being ripped from his skin one tiny chunk at a time, a thousand times over.

Do something, Wizard! What had Mood said? *You can die doing something or nothing. It's your life. Make it count.*

Fogle flung his arm back, flinging tendrils of energy from his fingertips. The energy punched into the grey swarm, creating a hole. An eruption of tiny explosions in the sky followed. A second later, the hole closed. Fogle shook his head. He was angry. Every time he overcame one obstacle, he found himself faced with another that he was even less prepared for.

You can't be ready for everything. Boon had said. *Just be ready to act.*

"I'll be ready to act, all right. Act dead!" He whipped the reins. "Barton! Think of something. We're about to have company!"

He couldn't tell if Barton could hear him on not, but the giant slowed and turned.

"Keep moving, Giant!"

Barton just leered at him, clutching at his sides, huffing for breath.

"What are you doing?" Fogle said, riding up to him, stopping.

"No more running, Wizard. No more. Wooooo. Barton tired." His hands fell to his knees.

Fogle tried to summon his energy but couldn't think of anything to cast. It was too late. The swarm was only seconds away. He pulled Cass tight and looked up at Barton.

"I guess this is good-bye, Barton."

Barton scooped out two massive handfuls of dirt from the ground and reached for him.

"What are you doi—ingggg!"

Barton picked them both up off the horse, set them in a large divot in the ground, and huddled over them.

Fogle tried to squirm away, but an infant could have done better. "Get off—mrph!"

Everything went black. Fogle and Cass were trapped beneath the hot sweaty mass of Barton's belly flesh.

I'm going to suffocate in sweaty lard!

Barton's body groaned and twitched over top of him and Cass. He could hear the muffled cries of the deformed giant's moans of pain. All he could imagine was the insects eating Barton alive. How long would Barton hold them off until they got to him? Would he suffocate first?

"Cass." He caught a drop of Barton's sweat in his mouth. "Yecht!"

He tried to think of something. Anything that might help. He needed air. Barton needed help. He grabbed Cass's face and stroked it tenderly. He held her tight. Above him, Barton's big body shuddered. He didn't know who to feel worse for, the giant or himself. Inside him, he wanted to fight, but there was nothing he could do.

This is pathetic.

A minute passed, then two. Barton's moans and cries subsided slowly.

He's dying! The bugs will be through any moment.

Barton's body stopped shuddering. The only thing Fogle could feel or hear was his own heartbeat. He pushed up on Barton. "Let us out!" He drove his knee into his belly. What if Barton died and they were trapped? "No! Blast it, Barton, get up!"

He summoned his energy. His fist lit up and he drove it into Barton's belly.

Sssrack!

Barton's body lurched upward and rolled over. Fogle gasped, basking in the white daylight that greeted him. He could breathe again! One last breath of sweet air before the bugs got him. He crawled out of the hole that Barton had dug and scanned the sky. It was empty aside from a few clouds. The humming of bugs was gone.

"Where did they go?" he said, spinning around.

Barton groaned. The big giant lay flat on his back with hundreds, if not thousands, of red welts all over his body. "Oooooh," he moaned. "My belly hurts."

Fogle stood over his side and patted his belly. "Uh… looks like you've had too much bug poison. I'm sure it will go away."

Barton rolled his big neck his way, staring at him with his one good eye. "You alright, Wizard? Barton helped you, right?"

"Indeed, Barton. I'd be dead without you."

"Pretty lady alright too?"

"She just needs something better to drink than your sweat, but she should be fine. Can you get up?"

Slowly, Barton rose to a sitting position.

"Belly hurts," he said, rubbing it. "Like I got whopped by a giant. Did you do that?"

Fogle turned away. "Have you seen the horse?"

Barton pointed east.

"Ah," Fogle said. Making his way over to the mount that stood basking in the haze of the hot day. "Oh." When he got close, a chill ran through him. The horse still stood with the saddle and his bags intact, but every ounce of flesh and skin had been picked clean. Only the bones remained.

He glanced back at the giant. Barton's thick skin had saved them all. All but the horse, anyway. He grabbed what gear he needed, headed back, and tried to make Cass as comfortable as he could.

"How are you feeling, Barton?"

"Dizzy. Little bugs stung me and bit me, but Barton too tough. Too strong. Belly still hurts though. They didn't bite my belly. I don't understand why it hurts." Barton scratched his head. "Was something else underneath me with you? Huh, Wizard?"

Feeling guilty, Fogle was ready to confess.

"Barton, I—"

The giant's eye closed, and he fell backward.

Thoom!

"Great! Just great!" Fogle put his hand on Barton's chest. It still rose and fell. "I guess he's alive." He kicked the dirt.

Now what, Wizard? Now what?

Cass had curled up like a baby, and Barton began to snore, leaving him as alone as he ever felt before. He found a place beside Cass in Barton's ditch and took a seat. *Inky!*

Closing his eyes, he tried to summon the familiar. The last thing he remembered was the bird flying into the swarm, and he'd completely forgotten about the bird after that. He gave it a minute or two and gave up. He pulled at the locks of his hair with both hands.

What have I done? What have I done? What have I done?

Little more than an hour ago, he had things under complete control. Cass was fine, Barton cheerful and his horse reliable transportation under his legs. They were going after Venir, the Darkslayer. Following the dog Chongo. His ebony hawk would lead straight to them.

Now, all of his plans were crushed. Inky was gone. Barton and Cass were almost comatose, and his horse was dead. He could only think of one thing. Well, two things.

Go east. Or sleep—and wake up dead.

Going east should have been simple, but it wasn't. The suns and moons didn't always rise in the same places, not than anyone ever thought about using them as a compass. Mood had always complained that getting around Bish would be easier if the suns and moons rose in the same places. Instead, you had to know the terrain.

Look for the signs.

A keen eye could see for miles in any direction, and the layout of Bish was simple. All you had to know was where places were and how to get there. Just don't be too forgetful. To make matters worse, some days, especially in the Outlands, were longer than others.

Probably have our bones picked clean out here.

He noted a bird of some sort circling above.

Great. Probably man-eating condors. Let's hope I can handle them.

Fogle pulled his spellbook from his pack. It fit on his hand at first, then, opening and closing, it got bigger and bigger, until he had to set it on his lap. He thumbed through the pages.

There ought to be something in here.

Meanwhile, Barton's snoring made the ground rumble.

Page by page, Fogle scanned his book, finding nothing immediately useful. He'd need more time and rest to learn anything new, and he had other spells in mind he had to keep until he used them. He nudged Cass. Her pale pink lips were cracked and dried. He poured a little water from his canteen on her lips, bringing forth a sigh. *Poor thing.* The feisty woman seemed so vulnerable right now, leaving him uncomfortable.

He stuck his nose back inside his book and read through more of Boon's spells. A bad feeling crawled through him. Was Boon still alive or not? The old man was crazy enough to fight an entire army of underlings and willing to die for it.

Bish, don't' let me get that crazy.

Spell after spell he read, not recalling hardly any of them. He felt ashamed now at his reluctance. Boon's written pages were a treasure that never should have been ignored. He giggled at one of them. *Breast replenishment.* With a special note. *For aging wife.* Fogle shook his head. Much of the magic in the City of Three was used to upkeep images, a practice which Fogle, unlike most, found detestable. He wondered if Boon was one of those who created such a spell to begin with. Page after page he went. Transfigurations. Polymorph. Elementals. Enchantments. Transmutations. Conjurations. A dozen forms of evocations and illusions, and so on. The ones that were most effective on underlings were highlighted. But there wasn't anything he could find that would give him directions. Fogle marked a few pages and closed the book.

"Now what, Cass? Now what?"

She didn't stir.

If only Mood or Eethum were here.

He sat for a while, before he got back up. Nightfall would be coming soon.

"Don't worry, I'll take the first watch." He stretched out his arms and yawned. "No, no, you two go ahead and rest. I'll take the second one too." Instinctively, he started to gather sticks and pile them up together. "What am I doing? I can't build a fire now, can I?" He shook his head. "Am I talking out loud to myself? Am I?"

I can't be. I can't be. I can't be.

He poked one of the nasty red stings on Barton's arm with a stick. Nothing. Barton kept snoring. "Well, I won't fall asleep with you around, that's for sure. And we can't have you drawing any underlings, giants, nasty bugs or dragons straight to us either." With both hands, he tried to pinch Barton's nose shut.

Barton snorted and started to roll over.

"Not on top of me!" he said, jumping to the side.

Barton lay on his stomach now, no longer snoring.

"Sheesh!" Fogle got up and dusted his tattered robes off. "Aw, what's the point?" He snatched up the spellbook. "I need something else to keep watch in case I fall asleep," he said, yawning.

Every scrape, bump, and bruise began to settle in on him, and he wondered if the Outland was making him tougher or deteriorating him faster.

I'm no dwarf. That's for sure.

Instead, he was a man. A lost man. A lamb in the Outland waiting to be devoured by Bish.

"There's always tomorrow if we live that long," he said to Cass. Something strange howled in the wind. He eyed the sky. "I really hope you wake back up by then, because, even though you're small, I can't carry you too far."

Barton stirred and farted.

"Ah!" Fogle held his nose. "Hmmm... I think I have an idea. Did a fart inspire that?"

Stop talking to yourself!

Over the next hour, he dove into the spellbook, eyes pouring over and committing to memory what he could. He muttered a cantrip after his final yawn. A Wizard's Alarm should wake him if anything got too close. He needed rest. He had to risk it. Besides, he couldn't wake them up anyway. "Forgive me, Cass." After kissing her forehead, he closed his eyes and drifted off to sleep, oblivious to a unique sound in the distance.

Whump. Whump. Whump...

CHAPTER 30

MELEGAL SQUIRMED. HE WAS ONLY a few seconds from being a cripple if he didn't twist away.

"My, you're a shifty one. I'll give you that," the leader said. "Like a big fish in man's clothing."

Think of something, Thief!

Melegal had been captured before, sometimes willing, sometimes not. But when being pinned down by a superior force there were a couple of ways you could play it. Fight with everything you had, or panic.

"Help!" he screamed.

Or at least act like you were panicking.

One of the Blood Hounds slugged him in the gut.

"Ooof!" Melegal groaned.

The one that hit him said, "His stomach's harder than old leather, Creed."

"Is that so?" Creed drew back and also socked him in the gut. "That ought to soften it some. Sorry, nothing personal. Just business, squirmy one." He pinched Melegal's face in his hand, grabbed his hat, and stuffed it in his mouth. "Any more of that, and your gonads will be dog food. Understand, Detective?"

Melegal blinked twice.

"Good. Now, be peaceful about this, or we'll be forced to kill you."

Melegal's eyes widened.

"That's right, but you're wanted alive rather than dead. Good thing for you."

One of the dogs snapped in his face. He resisted less and began to turn over. He forced a hardy cough, spit out his hat, and screamed.

"Blast it! Just knock the man out," Creed said. His voice was refined. Confident. Patient. "Hand me your black jack. We've enough fooling with this. Underlings might be crawling all over us if we're not more careful."

Melegal coughed again, dodging.

He felt Creed's hand rise up with the black jack.

Now or die!

Slick as a snake, Melegal twisted free of all of them and took aim.

Zing! Zing! Zing!

"Aarggh!"

The dart launchers caught one man holding him in the face and Creed in the chin.

He rolled beneath another man's fist.

Zing! Zing! Zing!

The man wailed out, clutching at his eyes.

Zing!

One dog yelped.

Zing!

Another dog fled, dart protruding from its neck.

"Yer gonna pay for that," one said, ripping a heavy sword from his scabbard.

Melegal slid out his swords, the Sisters, and faced off the goon.

"Nice trick, Detective," Creed said, plucking the dart from his beard, watching. "But hardly effective."

Melegal shrugged. "What the dart won't do, the poison will?"

Creed drew his longsword and smiled.

"Then you'll be going down with us."

Run!

It was the preferred resolution for his survival, but there was a problem. His hat and case were on the ground, and he wasn't willing to part with them yet.

'Greedy gets you killed,' they say.

Melegal shifted his footing, gently bending his knees.

Creed nodded to his man. "Let's see what the Detective is made of. Take him!"

The man took three quick steps and lunged.

Melegal sidestepped and stabbed.

Glitch!

The man's sword clattered to the ground, and he clutched at his chest. Melegal ripped his sword from the man's heart. His own heart was pounding.

I did it!

He shifted his focus to Creed. The tall man gawped while Melegal slung the blood off his sword.

"Impressive, Detective, I must admit. I didn't think you had that kind of fight in you. But I don't think you'll have the same fortune with me." Creed smiled. It wasn't an evil smile. Just a confident one. A dangerous one. A 'cat about to eat the rat' kind of one. He drew forth another blade that shone brighter than the other.

Oh slat!

Melegal could tell by Creed's stance, his posture, he was …

"I'm a swordsman. My comrade, not so much. Besides, I didn't like him anyway. Slow and stupid, but a good grappler." He sliced his blade through the air and twirled it with his wrist. "Hmmm… I'm feeling spry this day, and well, I don't think that dart was poisoned after all." He lifted his brow and smiled. "And, I think I can disarm you in six seconds. I can maim you in ten. But, it's nothing personal. Just business."

Melegal stood his ground.

Still time to run if you don't think of something.

He renewed his stance: blades up, elbows down.

"Tell you what, Detective: come along quietly, and I won't turn you into my dog's dinner. Not all of you, anyway."

Swish!

The sword flashed like a stroke of lightening.

Slat, he's good. Melegal narrowed his eyes.

He immediately recalled his battle with Teku in the alley months ago. It had taken everything he had not to die then, and Teku had been just an assassin, not a master swordsman.

"So, you're taking me to the Almens, eh…"

"Creed, Royal Bloodhound Knight."

"Oh please, you're no Royal or Knight, but a scavenger."

"Like you," he smiled.

Melegal shrugged.

"Like me, indeed then."

Creed scoffed. "I hardly think so. Sefron's message was abundantly clear. You are little more than an overachieving urchin. I, however, am of Royal blood."

Creed could pass for a Royal, in some circles, but Melegal knew better. The Bloodhounds claimed to be a Royal house, but instead they were little more than a house of mercenaries and bounty hunters of the true Royal houses. But, because of their unique position and the secrets they kept, the Royals ignored their overstated positions.

It was Melegal's turn to laugh.

"Sefron? You took a charge from Sefron? Ha! You might as well be taking charges from the urchins that scrub pots in the kitchen and clean the slat from the bird cages. Hah! Are you even sure I'm the one he really wants?"

Creed's eyes shifted, sword tips dipping a hair.

Melegal kept pressing.

"Creed, you are a fool. Have you not noticed that the underlings are storming Castle Almen? How do you suppose to get me in there? Collect your reward? It wouldn't surprise me if Sefron was dead right now. Can you imagine him fighting an underling? Have you ever fought an underling? This City's doomed, Creed. A smart man would save himself. Not carry out the charge of a fool when total destruction is about."

Creed was thinking. Melegal could see it, the hardness in his eyes weakening.

"What are you thinking, Creed?"

"I'm thinking that a Bloodhound never gives up on a charge until he gets his man."

"Is that so, then?"

Creed raised his blades, flashing a thin row of white teeth.

"So it is, and taking into account all you've said and done so far, I think it's best for me if I take you in dead."

Melegal raised his blades.

I'm dead if I don't run. Think, Melegal. What did McKnight say long ago? 'The mind is faster than the sword.' He glanced at his hat on the ground. *If I can just squirm my way to it.*

"Creed" The man Melegal had shot in the eyes stumbled along the storefronts. "I can't see, Creed, what do I do?"

"Silence, Dolt! I'll tend to you in a moment."

Melegal started left and Creed started right, both men circling.

Good.

Creed stopped, lunged and chopped.

Clang!

The sound of clashing steel echoed through the alley and down the street. Melegal held back his grimace. Creed struck again. *Clang!* Again. *Clang!* Again. *Clang! Clang! Clang!*

Creed pressed, Melegal parried. The man was a true swordsman. His moves perfect. His swing quick and powerful. Melegal's hands were numb seconds into it.

"Not much of an offense, I see," Creed said, backing away, cutting his swords through air. "But, you've an excellent defense; I'll give you that, Detective. I underestimated you. Problem is, how long can those bony arms of yours hold out?"

Not long!

"Long enough to wear you down," Melegal said.

Creed darted in, blades stabbing like striking snakes. "I don't think so."

Melegal battled one blade away, only to shift and catch another.

Creed kept stabbing at his legs, a hungry grin behind his lips.

Slice!

Creed caught Melegal in the inner thigh. He felt every bit of it.

"Hah!" Creed said, jumping away. "First blood to me. Oh, that's already staining your clothes."

Run, Melegal! It's not worth it!

Behind him, the hat and slender case lay unmolested on the ground, but he had no chance of getting them. Creed would pin him to the ground if he tried.

"My, your shoulders are already dipping," Creed said, cutting his longsword over the ground. "More of a fencer than a soldier, clearly. But, I think I've summed you up enough." Creed sheathed one sword, left the other one that gleamed like the sun out, and shrugged. "I feel the need to challenge myself." He motioned Melegal closer with his hand. "Come on, Detective. Attack."

Melegal remained wary. Creed might be cocky, but he wasn't a fool either. Even though the odds had shifted more in his favor, he knew better. Creed had something up his sleeve.

"I'll fight my way; you fight yours. Come on then, Hound. I'm curious to see what you can do with a single sword to my two."

Creed leapt and swung.

Melegal parried and struck.

Pour it on, Rat!

Clang! Clang! Clang! Clang!

Creed parried, dodged and ducked.

Clang! Clang! Clang! Clang!

Melegal stabbed, chopped and cut, but Creed anticipated everything he did. Focused. Determined. Waiting for a weakness.

Move, Melegal!

Out of nowhere, Creed's blade licked out like a rod of lightning. Melegal squatted down. Creed kicked him in the face.

Bang!

Melegal felt his sword ripped from his hand.

Bang!

The other skipped over the cobblestones. The next thing he felt was the tip of a sword under his chin.

SLAT!

"Heh, heh, heh—woot!" Creed wiped the sweat from his brow. "I can't believe you still have your head, Detective. Ah! I missed it! You are fast. I'll give you that."

Melegal started to raise his arms up.

"Ah, ah, ah, keep those wrists down. I can't have you shooting anymore holes in me. I must admit: I'm surprised you didn't try something earlier. But, eh, I figured you were out."

Melegal could feel the sword cut his neck as he swallowed.

I should have run! Idiot!

"EEEYAH!"

A block down the street, someone screamed.

"Eh?" Creed grabbed Melegal by his head of hair and pulled him up from the ground, stepping behind him and keeping the sword at his throat.

That's when Melegal saw them. *Underlings!*

"What in Bish is that thing crawling on the ground?" Creed said, unable to hide his alarm.

Both ends of the road were blocked off. Speckled eyes and spider legs were coming.

"I can get us out of here, Creed. But your word you won't kill me."

"I know better than that."

"There's no time, Creed. You can kill me and die. Or you can trust me and live. And I don't want to die. I've no issues with you."

The chitters became louder, the small bodies closer.

"Cut my throat then, Creed! I'd rather die at your hands than the underlings'!"

Creed's rapid breath was in his ear.

"My word I won't kill you. Your word you won't kill or betray me."

"My word," Melegal said.

Hurry up, Imbecile.

"Done!"

Melegal was a blur of motion, swooping over to snatch his cap and case and darting for the door he'd tried to get in earlier. "Come on, Creed!"

The underlings let out evil howls and charged.

Melegal pulled out a Key.

"What in Bone?" Creed said, looking at the lock. "That won't fit!"

Melegal jammed it inside the lock and turned.

"Sweet Mother of Bish! It wo—*urked*!"

Clatch-zip! Clatch-zip! Clatch-zip!

Creed's face contorted as he stumbled forward. The sound of the underlings was overwhelming.

Melegal shoved his shoulder into the door and pulled the man behind him through.

Bolts zipped past his head. He fought to pull the door closed.

Something slipped in past his legs.

What was that! Hmm—I'll have to live with it.

He kept pulling on the door, catching a pair of hands in the process.

The underlings were pulling it back open.

Melegal grabbed the handle and pulled on the door with all his might.

"No!"

He was sliding forward.

A flash of light ripped through the air.

Slice!

Underlings howled and hissed in fury. The tips of their fingers disappeared, shooting black-red blood everywhere.

Melegal flew backward and felt the door close with a bang.

Creed was huffing at his side, wiping black blood off his blade.

"That was close," Melegal said. "And you better hang onto your stomach."

"Why-yeeeeeeeeeee…"

Melegal remembered hearing that and something else that growled as his body and mind were turned inside out.

CHAPTER 31

"**A**SHUR!" LORDA ALMEN SAID. "You have awakened!"

The face was hazy, but the voice familiar as Lord Almen tried to rise.

"Ugh!" he said, clutching at his side. The area was tender, painful.

"Easy, Darling," Lorda said, gently pushing him back down. "You don't need to tear the wound." She sobbed. "Ashur, I'm so happy to see you."

She nuzzled him. Gently. Wet tears dripping on his cheeks.

"My darling," he said, "I'm quite alright."

Still, she held on, trembling.

It was a good feeling, the scent of his wife and the curves of her body against his, but despite his awakening, something was wrong. He sniffed.

"What is that smell?" Blinking, the haze from his eyes began to clear. Two Shadow Sentries stood at his bedside with gore of some sort on their armor. "And what is that sound?"

Somewhere, a battle raged. His heart ignited.

"Help me up, Sentry," he said, pushing Lorda aside.

Sitting up, his head began to spin. He collected his thoughts. The last thing he remembered was being inside the arena. The haggard face of Leezir the Slerg was there, and a big man. A very big man that went berserk, chopping up people like wood.

"Dearest, lie down, please," Lorda said.

He slid onto the floor and with assistance from the sentry stumbled towards the balcony.

"Why are there underlings at my walls?"

It was insanity. Castle Almen was under a full-scale attack. Black armored underlings and oversized spiders filled the streets and alleys.

"How long, Lorda? How long have I been down?"

"Many days, Lord Almen. Sefron saved you. It was the underlings that infiltrated and stabbed you. I thought you were to perish."

A flood of memories washed over him. Everything that happened in the arena became crystal clear up to the point where he could feel the dagger sliding between his ribs.

The scowl on his vulture-like visage returned.

"Melegal."

"Pardon, my Lord? I ordered Sefron to send the Bloodhounds for him—"

He cracked her across the face, dropping her to her knees.

"You hired those Gormandizing Bastards? And Melegal! He's not here? He lives?"

Lorda's eyes were narrow, dangerous.

She started to rise.

"What is the meaning of this that you would dare strike me, Ashur? I'm guilty of no wrong—"

He drew back again, causing her to flinch.

"It was Melegal that slid the dagger in my ribs. Not the underlings. Not any other!"

Lorda shook her head.

"No, Sefron said it was the underlings."

"Pah! Sefron! Where is he, anyway?" He grabbed a Shadow Sentry by the collar of his armor. "You, go and fetch him yourself, and do not fail me. And see to it word spreads that Lord Almen lives!"

Melegal. The man had gotten him, and he had to admit it was impressive of the man. He would have admired it if he'd not been the victim… But now his entire castle was under siege! And he knew why. The chamber room. The underlings wanted it.

"How long has this siege been going on?" he demanded.

"Several hours, Lord Almen," a sentry replied.

"And the Keep is secure?"

"Yes, Lord Almen."

"And the castle?"

"Casualties along the wall, Lord Almen. Nothing else to report."

Lord Almen folded his arms behind his back, stepped past Lorda, and began to pace. He wondered if his neighbors would come to his aid. Or would they see him perish first? After all, that's what he would do.

"Hmmm."

He reached down and lifted Lorda up. She slapped him in the face.

"I'm—"

She slapped him again.

"I'm—"

She swung, but he caught her by the wrist. "I'm going to throw you off the balcony if you do that again."

"You wouldn't dare!" She was almost smiling.

He did smile. "Oh, of course not." He lifted her chin and kissed her cheek. "I'm sorry, my dearest."

"I'm glad you're back, Ashur." She hugged him. Then she looked him in the eye. "I'm sorry. I never would have suspected Melegal. But we'll find him, and when we do, we'll throw him off this balcony together. "

"Oh, we'll do much worse than that."

Lorda took the next few minutes explaining to Lord Almen everything that had been going on, but he was confident the Castle would hold for days. At some point, the other Royals would have to arrive.

Minutes later, the sentry that left to find Sefron returned.

"Where is Sefron?" Lord Almen demanded.

The sentry bowed. "Lord Almen, I have grave news. The underlings have penetrated the bottoms of the Castle."

"What!" He wanted to strangle the man. Ignoring the pain in his side, he dashed out of the room. He had to get to his study, secure the chamber and the Keys before it was too late.

CHAPTER 32

IN ONE OF THE BOTTOM quarters of the Keep, Sefron stared in a mirror, dressing his wounds.

"She'll be mine," he said, stitching the side of a nasty cut on his cheek, "all mine."

"What's that, Cleric?" It was one of the sentries posted outside his door.

Fool! "Eh … nothing, just trying a cheerful tune. Oh, how it soothes the wounds." Sefron crept over towards the man, letting the needle and thread hang from his face. "My, you are a fine specimen of a soldier. I bet you have a steady hand." With a shaky hand, he reached towards the man, who jerked away. "I need some assistance with this."

Another sentry appeared and shoved Sefron back.

"Keep your hands to yourself, Toad, or I'll slit your throat. We know plenty about what you do around here." His hand fell to his dagger. "And it'd be my pleasure to cut your throat."

Sefron fell back, hands up. "Easy now. You don't want rumors leading you to something foolish, do you? After all, I am Lord Almen's trusted servant."

"As trustworthy as a slimy weasel in a hen house. Now leave my men alone!" He shut Sefron inside the room.

Sefron resumed his position in front of the mirror.

"My, I'll never understand why people aren't more taken by my charm." He smiled in the mirror, noticing how his eyes bulged outside his dark sockets and folds of flabby skin dangled under his chin. He was a sickly shade of pale, and his belly jiggled over his scrawny legs.

"Never a finer specimen of a man on Bish," he said, wheezing. He licked the blood from his purple lips. Then started sewing the gash in his face again. "That should do it." He took a seat in a nearby chair, crossed his dirty feet and lounged. "Hmmmm…"

He rubbed the eye that Kierway had stuck with a dart. The underlings waged war from the outside. Perhaps they'd found Melegal. Perhaps they just needed a little help to penetrate the wall of the Castle. He could sense the power beginning to shift. He was an agent for the underlings, and now was his time to move.

And then I'll have Lorda Almen and her servants all to myself!

He sat up.

"Time to get out of this Keep."

Reaching inside a pouch that hung from a string belt, he withdrew grains of an unusual sort. Rubbing one between his fingers, he murmured to himself. Seconds later, the mystic energies he tapped from Bish filled him, rejuvenated him. *Yes!* So long it had been since he last harnessed his energies, waiting, plotting, and scheming for the right time to recall them. He had hidden them long, oh so long. His skin tightened. His muscles flexed and stretched. His haggard body replenished, his crooked spine crackled as he rose to his feet. Smoke streamed from his mouth and nostrils, slowly filling the room.

"What's that smell?" A sentry threw open the door.

Sefron blew the grains of dust into the air.

The smoke in the room poured out into the next. The sound of men choking and gagging was music to his ears.

"Not so talkative now, are we?" He crossed the threshold, upright on a solid six-foot frame. He pulled the dagger from the gagging sentry's sheath and stabbed him in the spine. "I've been meaning to do that for quite some time."

Two more sentries remained, hacking and spitting, blinded to his presence.

Sefron stabbed one in the neck and left the dagger in the other's heart. He cracked his knuckles, went back into his room, and took another look at himself.

His countenance wasn't handsome, but strong and dark, his skin no longer pale nor sagging. His stomach was tight and his legs firm. His damaged eye was still gone, but better. He felt good. He'd been saving up decades for this, and now his time had come. "Let the powers of Bish last as long as they can last."

He focused on his personal quarters in the castle, closed his eyes, and drew in more power. A portal appeared. He stepped through it, back into his room.

"Ah yes."

It felt good, being back inside his place. Very good. Incredibly good. He grabbed his robes from the wall and tied another belt with pouch around his waist. From the corner of the small disheveled room—littered with vials, jugs and old bits of food—he grabbed a crooked staff.

"It's been a long time," he said, kissing it before exiting his door.

Despite the battle raging outside, the massive hallways were quiet. Everyone in the Castle was either fighting somewhere or dead. No longer shuffling, Sefron strolled, whistling rather than wheezing, on the legs of a twenty-year-old man. Making his way through one of the living rooms, he pressed a panel on one of the decorative shelves. A hidden door popped open behind it, and inside he went.

The spaces between the walls of the rooms were a set of catacombs that Sefron had discovered years ago. Even most of the Almens had no knowledge of them. They'd been used by servants at one time, short cuts through the castle, but Sefron had seen to it over time that no servant recollected them. They were where he did his spying, and they traversed through most of the castle's main rooms, except for the keep.

He hopped his way down a narrow set of steps, a smile on his face. It had been a long time since he moved so gracefully.

If I see Melegal, I'll kill him first.

Stopping, he pushed aside a peephole door and looked through. A dining room greeted him, undisturbed, still shiny in silver and crystal. No longer would he have to watch behind the walls after this. No longer would he be a servant to Lord Almen. No, he would be the Lord of this Castle. He pictured himself and Lorda sitting side by side. "Yes, she'll be—eh?"

Somewhere not too far distant, steel banged against steel. He trotted through the narrow passageway two dozen yards, the sounds becoming more distinct and profound. He lifted another peephole door open and got an eyeful.

Underlings were in mortal combat with sentries and Royal magi. Two Royal soldiers in plate mail armor swung their broad swords into a mass of well-armed underlings. Barrages of green and red missiles of light were shooting back and forth. Men were howling; underlings were screeching.

Sefron made his way down another short level of steps to a dead end. Opening a peephole on the final battle, he saw a group of underlings being forced down the steps that led down to the Current. *Yes!* It was everything he hoped for. The underlings had invaded from below as well as above, but there seemed to be a problem. The underlings were trapped. They were losing.

CHAPTER 33

TRIUMPH! MASTER KIERWAY FELT NOTHING but triumph when the door shattered and he and his brethren blasted through. Leading the way, he bounded up the stairs and greeted a pair of Royal soldiers with his whirling blades.

He drove his steel through the plate covering one man's heart and cut the mailed neck of the other out. Blood, the only shade of red that he liked, dripped from his blades.

"Inward! Inward!" he ordered his underlings. "Nothing human lives! Everything human dies!"

Juegen soldiers, coated from head to toe in black metal armor, surged past, followed by Badoon warriors with crude knives and hatchets, albino urchlings with claws that could rip metal, and underling magi whose fingertips crackled with energy. Their faces told it all. Hungry. Fearsome. Vengeful. Hate filled. One by one they went. Bright colored eyes narrowed. Soldiers of war that meant business. And Kierway had hundreds of them at his disposal.

"Yes, brethren! Go! Slaughter!"

Everything was working. Within hours, Castle Almen would be theirs.

Up the stairs the underlings went. The last one, bringing up the rear, was an albino urchling, all four nostrils flaring.

"What is this?" Kierway said to himself, bounding down the steps. He hissed. The doorway was sealed. "No!" He looked for a handle, a bar, a lock, but there was nothing. "NO! CATTEN!"

Was this a ruse? Had Catten betrayed him and all his underlings? He didn't have time to worry about that now. Trapped or not, he could still pull this off. He had enough underlings, so he thought. Dashing up the stairs, he was halfway to the top when the wind and the screeches came. Mystic power flowed everywhere. At the top, underlings were knocked head over heels by an unseen force. Fire licked over them. Burning them.

"No! This cannot be!"

A blast of hot air came. One, two, three underlings tumbled backward over the stairs, landing at his feet. At the top, an underling's head was taken from its shoulders, green eyes bouncing off the steps all the way to the bottom. Kierway hesitated. How many Royals were at the top? But there was nowhere else to go. Taking six steps at a time, he charged, confronting a big warrior. A heavy blade came down at his head. Kierway sidestepped and cut the man's wrist from his arm. The man howled long enough to catch a blast of underling energy inside his mouth.

Kierway ducked under a blast of lightning that struck an underling mage full force. He rolled alongside a wall and got a better look at things. All of his brethren underlings that made it up the steps were gone.

Where did they go?

On the far side of the dining room, two robed humans were guarded by three soldiers, and the air shimmered before them.

Hmmmm.

Several feet away, an underling Badoon and one albino urchling were in mortal combat with the Royal Soldiers. Kierway chittered at an urchling that had sunk its teeth into the neck of a dead soldier and pointed at the magi at the other end of the room. Blood dripping from its fangs, it tore itself away and charged across the room. *Blink!* The urchling was gone.

Furious, Kierway sprang into action, assisting his brethren, hewing into one Royal soldier after the other. The battle raged for another minute and then the last Royal soldier fell, leaving himself, one Juegen, one Badoon and one mage left standing. He shook the blood from his blades and faced the Royals on the other side of the room. The faces of the men showed no concern, but rather, supreme confidence.

Kierway banged his blades together, calling a Royal soldier out. None of them moved, except the magi behind them. One gyrated his hands while the other one spoke in tones. Kierway slung two knives.

Sssz!

Sssz!

They disappeared midflight

The underling mage hurled a ball of fire, lighting up the room, shaking the chandeliers. It stopped, hovered in the air, and returned. He jumped out of the way just before it exploded. Tiny fires licked over his clothing while the underling mage burst into flame, screaming.

Whatever barrier the humans had put up, he knew they could not pass. It was a mystic dimension spell of sorts, and for all he knew the underlings that passed through were on the outside of Bone. Possibly imprisoned in a wall somewhere. But the spell wouldn't last forever. It couldn't. He banged his swords together.

The Royal Magi acted. A missile of mystic energy burst from the hands of one, then another, careening towards him.

He flicked his blades up. The missile smacked into them with a shower of sparks, knocking him from his feet. One by one, he and his men backed towards the stairwell. One bright missile soared after the other. Behind the human magi, another man appeared, dark and mysterious. Reaching out, the strange man grabbed the two magi by the shoulders. They choked, mouths popping open. Their skin tightened and shriveled. Their faces sunk in and dried. The space between them buckled, images contorting before returning to normal.

The dimension spell was gone. Kierway could feel it.

"Kill them!" Kierway said.

The two remaining soldiers readied themselves.

The urchling, Badoon warrior, and Juegen sped across the room. Kierway followed close behind.

The Royal soldiers braced themselves, chins down, swords up.

The heavy sword of one Royal chopped downward, burying itself in the Badoon's shoulder, drawing a howl. The Juegen and Badoon pounced on the man, knocking him off balance and to the floor. Focusing on the other soldier, Kierway sidestepped one swing, followed by the other, staying wary of the man who had assisted him moments earlier. The man, holding a crooked staff, was laughing.

Clang!

Kierway batted away the soldier's heavy swings, one after the other, hissing and taunting. The eyes behind the soldier's metal helmet were determined but became weary. Each swing came more sluggish than the last.

Rip!

Kierway struck the man's knee, sending flesh, blood and steel across the room. The man stumbled forward.

"Urk!"

Kierway drove his sword through the man's heart. Yanking his blade out, he turned on the man who laughed. He and the remaining underlings surrounded him.

The man kneeled and said, "Master Kierway, it is I, your servant, Sefron."

Kierway could see it now. The man's good eye bulged a little in his socket, and his disturbing expression, though more vital, remained unchanged.

"Do you have the Keys?"

"No," Sefron said, flatly.

Kierway nodded to his men.

"Kill him."

Sefron's arm shot out.

"Wait! Master Kierway, I may not have the Keys you seek, but I can open the door at the bottom of the stairwell." Sefron's eye glanced over the dripping blades of Kierway's two men. "I am your humble servant, Master Kierway, now and forever."

Kierway held out his arm. The underling drew back.

"Do it then," he said, sheathing his blades behind his back. "But make it quick if you don't want underling steel fileting your back."

Sefron rose, led them across the room and down the stairwell, and stopped at the oversized door.

"Hurry!" Kierway said.

Sefron leaned his staff against the wall, pressed his hands on the door and chanted. One syllable after the other, faster, slower, lower, higher. Sweat dripped from his bald head, and his knees buckled a little. Panting, he turned.

"It's over," he said, stepping aside. "Shall I open it?"

"Of course, you fool!"

Sefron pushed it open.

A sea of underlings greeted him.

Sefron stood aside. Several feet away, floating across the great Dining Hall, Kierway was in a heated conversation with an underling whose likes he'd never seen before. His golden eyes radiated with power, and a mere glance in his direction ran his blood cold. Even Lord Almen didn't command such authority. Still, Sefron managed to pull back his shoulders and keep his chin up.

Show no fear. No fear at all.

His knuckles were white on his staff as a squad of underling fighters dashed by. They spread like a swarm of bees through the castle and into the main courtyard. Their numbers were overwhelming. Sefron knew that within hours, minutes possibly, the Castle would be taken over. He began to have doubts as to whether this was a good alliance or not.

It was inevitable. The Lorda and this castle or another shall be mine.

Keeping his head down, Sefron kneeled. Kierway and Catten approached.

"How many are in the keep?"

"A few dozen, if that." Sefron said. He kept his head down, eyes up a little. He could feel heat from Lord Catten's eyes boring into him.

"Master Kierway," Catten said, "do we have further need of this man?"

Sefron's eyes shot over to Kierway, heart pounding in his chest. Kierway rubbed his chin.

"Masters!" Sefron fell on his face. "I've betrayed my castle for your glory! I know many of its secrets I can share. And I am still assisting with the one that has the Keys. Spare me!" He looked at Kierway. "You promised me, Master Kierway!" His voice echoed in the large chamber.

"I made promises for the Keys, which you did not deliver." Kierway said. "And we have an imp that can find the man you speak of, and the Keys, whenever we want."

"But, certainly, you won't kill all of us? Underlings and men have held many alliances before. Outpost Thirty-One and Castle Almen were united on that endeavor." He wiped the sweat from his brow with his robes. "Certainly we can be united on this endeavor as well. I killed off two Royal magi who held a pivotal location." He crawled towards the two husks on the floor and lifted one up. "I am not loyal?"

Catten snapped his fingers. The entire room shook, knocking Sefron over and turning what remained of the corpses into dust.

"Kierway," Catten said, "You say this one is a life drainer?"

"It seems he has that craft," Kierway said, checking the bandolier of knives on his chest. "What of it?"

"Give him your hand," Catten ordered.

"Give him your own hand!" Kierway fired back.

"You'll do as I say, Kierway!" Catten's voice shook the chandeliers.

Sefron came forward, his limbs stiffening. The power he got from draining people didn't last forever, but the magi he'd drained would hold him for hours. He extended his hand.

Kierway sneered at Lord Catten, who sneered back.

"You're such a fool, Kierway. Stupid and cowardly." Catten snatched Sefron's wrist with a grip of iron and said, "Drain me, Human!"

Fearful, Sefron hesitated.

"Do it, else I'll have Kierway skewer and skin you like a rodent."

Sefron summoned his power. The dust stirred on the floor, mystic powers flowing through him, giving him more enriching vitality.

"You like that, do you Human?" Catten ran his tongue along his teeth. "A taste of centuries of tempered energy, something your kind cannot comprehend." He pulled Sefron in face to face. "Well, I'll share a secret with you. I'm feeding you my power, Weakling. You are not taking it."

Catten closed his eyes, holding Sefron fast.

An urge to pull away overcame Sefron.

But Catten held him in a supernatural grip.

Something was wrong. He wasn't draining the underling. Instead, the underling was feeding him dark, exhilarating energy.

"Human," Catten said, "certainly you knew that you are only capable of draining your own kind. I, however, can do both, and what I give, I can take away."

Sefron choked. His breath was gone. All of his vibrancy was being sucked dry. He shrunk. He shriveled. He wheezed, fought to stand, and teetered to the floor. He pleaded with his eyes. Catten released him. He fell down and clutched his chest.

"You really should consort with a better class of human, Kierway. But I should expect so much."

Sefron looked down at his flabby belly, and the skin jiggled under his chin. Wheezing, he pushed himself up on his staff.

Just need another fresh body and I'll be fine, thank you.

"Now, Kierway, take your flabby ally away. Take some of your men and secure the Chamber of

Keys. Certainly, someone will show up eventually. As for me, I'll see to it the demise of the Castle is completed."

Sefron's shaky legs struggled to move. He was in worse condition than before. His good eye caught Lord Catten's hard stare once more. He turned away. It wasn't likely Lord Catten would keep him around if he didn't think of something.

Kierway shoved him forward, "Lead the way, you saggy piece of meat."

Chapter 34

"**D**IE, FIENDS! DIE!"

Jarla's inner fires ignited with every stroke. Underlings, one after the other, fell under the precise patterns of her blade.

Chop!

Glitch!

Zurk!

She rammed a dagger into the last one's throat. Beside her, Tonio hewed the underlings down with powerful blows. A tireless machine among the chaos. The underlings, as well prepared as they might be, couldn't have been prepared for this; two skilled fighters with an unrivaled passion for killing.

Body splattered with red-black blood and gore, Jarla churned out one death after the other.

Toowah!

Toowah!

Toowah!

The darts struck her arms and legs.

"Cowards!" she said.

Whack!

She split one amber-eyed underling's skull.

Toowah!

Toowah!

Toowah!

Tonio laughed, half a dozen darts in his face, and yelled in his garbled voice, "There is no escape from me, underlings!"

They chopped at the man, jumped on top of him, tried to drag him down, but Tonio shook them off like a dog sheds water.

Jarla stayed close. Her lungs were burning behind her heaving chest. Her sword became heavy, sluggish. Still, she hacked. She chopped. Cognizant of the pounding on the door behind her. The underlings would chop through that door at any moment.

"We're going to have company!" she rasped. "I hope you can hold them all, because I can't."

"Let them come!" Tonio said, ramming his sword through one's skull.

Claws and fangs bared, an underling charged, leaping towards her from the bar. Engaged with another one of the underlings, she caught it in the corner of her eye, but couldn't turn in time.

Slice!

Tonio cleaved through it in mid-air, sending a shower of dark blood everywhere.

Over a dozen underling bodies were piled up, some twitching on the floor, behind them another dozen or so, when they backed off.

Jarla wiped the blood from her eyes, trying to catch her breath. They needed an escape route, but the only way was to carve through them.

"Think you can cut a path to the back through them?" she asked Tonio.

"Certainly, but I haven't the same need as you. I can fight them all day and all night if I have to," he said. "But you won't last that long, will you, Woman?"

Chop! Chop! Chop!

The underlings were still hewing at the door behind them, jostling Jarla's indomitable shroud. She'd never quit a fight before, but at the moment, there wasn't much fight left in her. She was exhausted, out of shape, and disappointed.

How did I let myself get like this? Lazy over-drinking bitch!

A twinkle caught her eye. She wiped the blood from the ring on her finger. It glowed a bright green color.

"What is that?" Tonio said.

Fool! How could I have forgotten!

"A way out of here, maybe." She darted for the front door, sliding over the blood-slicked floor. "Hold them off!"

Tonio's big frame stepped between her and the underlings, beckoning the underlings forward. "Come on, rodents. My blade thirsts for your blood!"

Where's the Key! Where's the Key!

Chop!

The blade of an axe emerged through the door. A sparkling eye peeked inside.

Glitch!

She jammed a dagger in its eye, let go and grabbed the Key. She jammed it inside the lock.

Chop!

The Key popped out and fell to the ground. She fumbled for it, grabbing it in her sticky hands.

Chop!

The underlings on the other side kept hacking at the lock. Chunks of wood fell.

Clatch-zip!

Clatch-zip!

Clatch-zip!

Small bolts ripped across the room, burying themselves in the door.

Tonio groaned. "Whatever you're doing, Witch, you better hurry. Looks like the rodents are just getting started."

Thunk!

A javelin juttered in the door frame.

Jarla tried to force the Key into the deteriorating lock. It wouldn't go.

"Blast my eyes! Get! In! There!"

The Key transformed, its head matching the lock. She shoved it in and turned.

Clatch-zip!

Clatch-zip!

Clatch-zip!

Bolts and spears filled the doorway. Over her shoulder, she could see Tonio was filled with them, still standing, snarling and chopping. She shoved the door forward and found herself in a black room. She stepped inside, huffing, then pushed the door shut.

Almost.

Fingers emerged on the door's edge, pulling it open. Tonio's blood-splattered face leered at her.

"Not leaving the party without me, are you?"

"Just get your dead arse in here and shut the blasted door!"

"My pleasure." He closed it on the small fingers of the underlings, crushing them in the frame.

Jarla heard their angry screeches and howls cut short. Everything spun. She wanted to vomit. Her world twisted bloody and black.

I hate this part.

Chapter 35

EVERYTHING IN HER LIFE HAD been turned upside down. And now, she was home, back inside her own room, and once more a prisoner. Kam lowered her shoulder and pounded at the door.

Wham!

"Will you stop doing that, Kam?" Joline said. She was rocking baby Erin in her arms. "Can't you just be thankful you are home, safe for the moment?"

"That troll cut my hand off, Joline!"

Wham!

"And when I get a hold of her, I'm gonna shove my foot up her—"

"KAM! Enough!" Joline said, setting Erin in her bassinette.

The bassinette started to rock itself, and soothing music came forth, keeping Erin in a peaceful slumber.

Kam rubbed her shoulder with her lone hand and fought the tears coming to her eyes. What in Bish was going on? She'd just escaped the unbearable, only to find herself at home, confronted with the inconceivable. She looked at her stump, stupefied. Less than an hour ago, she'd awoken in her bed, the wound dressed and cleaned. Joline had done that for her, saying the bleeding had stopped on its own and the flesh had mended itself.

Who in Bish is Scorch?

She gritted her teeth.

Wham!

Joline grabbed her by the arm, dragged her over to the sofa, and pulled her down. Softly, the woman said, "Dear, I don't know what you've been through, and I can't explain what we are going through now, but you are home." Joline looked around and shrugged. "And safe as far as I know. You, me and Erin." She patted her knee. "A family."

Her tears flowed like raindrops. Her body shuddered with every breath. Kam's voice was a high pitched squeak. "I don't know what's happening to me. I don't understand. I just don't understand. I was so happy to be home, and n-n-now I'm a handless prisoner. Where's my hand, Joline? Why'd that woman do that?"

Joline handed her a handkerchief and rubbed her back.

She blew her nose and wiped her tears away.

"The truth is, Kam, you look better now than when you first walked in here. You looked possessed. You weren't yourself."

Serve and live.

That voice. It would haunt her forever. It had possessed her, controlled her. Empowered her. What was it? Who was it?

Kam had made a deal.

It had saved her. The power in the stones. A being was in the stones, like one was in the sword, the great sword of Zorth, the Everblade. It was her father's sword, and she was going to return it.

Her father would have to answer to her about his dealings with Palos. She shivered. The thought of that man having his way with her. Pawing at her. Humiliating her. Almost killing her. What had happened to him? She'd left him mumbling in his own drool.

I should have killed him!

Joline squeezed her hand. "What is it, Kam? What are you thinking? There's murder in those eyes! You didn't kill anyone, did you?"

The question was like a slap in the face. Diller. Indeed, she had killed a man. Snapped his neck like a twig. And there had been others. In the alley. Broken. Lifeless. Had she killed them too? She looked at the hand that was no longer there. She swore she could still see it, feel it. And the dark energy from it still lingered within her.

She shook her head, sucked in her breath, looked Joline in the eye, and said, "I did what I had to do to save Erin, Joline." She blew her nose again. "And let me tell you, those bastards down below will think a hundred times before they ever come up here again."

Joline's eyes widened.

Kam got up, scooped her baby out of her bassinette with her one good arm and held her tight. "Nobody messes with me or my baby."

"Uh," Joline stammered, "how about some hot tea?"

"Got any Muckle Sap?"

"No." Joline pulled her shoulders back. "And I wouldn't give you any if we did. You need to settle yourself, Woman. I don't know what all you've been through, and you can tell me when you like, but now's no time for drinking. Just rock your baby."

Kam strolled over to the window. The glass was clear, but she couldn't see out. A busted three legged stool lay on the ground beside it. That window, whatever it was, was hard as stone. Kam couldn't help but wonder if it was all an illusion. Was she really here or not? Joline and Erin were real. Of that much, she was certain, but of the rest she wasn't so sure.

Erin yawned and stretched, letting out a little squeak. For the first time in as long as she remembered, Kam felt herself smile on the inside and out. She had the most important thing in the world, Erin. She kissed her forehead and took a seat in a rocking chair nearby.

"That's better." Joline worked the kettle on the stove. "You've got your whole world now, Kam. Erin's all that matters."

Tight as a drum, Kam yawned. Reflecting on everything she'd been through, she realized life would never be the same. Tortured and manipulated, she'd somehow survived. She was sore. Her face was swollen, and her gut hurt from where she'd been stabbed, but she lived. Erin lived. And even though they were prisoners, at least they were together. She rocked and rocked and rocked.

Joline walked over, eyes tired, and handed her a mug of steaming coffee.

"There you go. I put some Allybass in it. It always helps me relax. Are you hungry, Kam?"

Kam nodded.

"I'll fix you something to eat, and how about I run you a tub?"

"No tubs!"

Joline jumped.

"Sorry, just, I'll wash myself off later." Kam shuddered a sigh. "Hopefully, I can still cast a cantrip for it."

"Whatever you say, Kam." Joline fixed herself a cup of coffee and took a seat on the couch, playing with her greying locks of hair. "I might need you to use a cantrip on me, too. I feel like I've been rolled in sow waller."

Kam let out a short giggle.

It was followed by a long silence.

Kam felt safe in her heart. Restless, but safe. And the loss of her hand had been a small price to pay for Erin's life and her freedom. Perhaps Scorch, at least it would seem, had done her a favor. Shown her compassion, though a bit harsh, and merciless. Still, the image of that rough-cut woman chopping off her hand disturbed her. *She's a maniac.*

"Kam, I'm sorry to ask, but was Master Gillem a part of all this?"

Kam closed her eyes. So much had happened that she hadn't had time to take in. She blew a lock of hair from her face.

"You could say that," she said. "He poisoned the well. He seduced Lefty. But, I don't think he had a choice. At least, it was either that or death."

"Oh." Joline sat back. "I, I just really liked his company and the flowers he'd bring. He said the nicest things and told the most amazing stories. One time he told me…"

Kam let her talk, but she wasn't listening. There wasn't any sense in spoiling Joline's memories. 'There's good in everyone,' her mother always said, 'but it's often harder to find in some than others.' Of course, Kam used to believe that, but not anymore. There was no good in Palos. He was rotten to the core.

"Joline?"

"… and those fragrances he made. So… oh, sorry. Did you say something?"

"What happened to Lefty?"

"Well…" Joline looked around. "I, I don't know. I just assumed he was… oh my."

"Oh my?" Kam leaned forward. "What do you mean, oh my?"

"The last I saw him, he was kicking Scorch in the nose." Joline clutched her chest. "You don't think they cut his hand off too, do you?"

"Why'd he kick him in the nose?"

"He was mad. He was telling Scorch to fix your hand I think, then poof," Joline fanned her fingers out, "here we were!"

Kam's chest tightened. What in Bish had happened to Lefty? An image of him stuffed in a pickle jar popped in her mind.

Knock. Knock. Knock.

Kam and Joline lurched up, looking at each other.

Knock. Knock. Knock.

"Uh… er… Do you want me to get that?"

Kam handed her Erin. "No, I better do that." She walked over to the door, grabbed the handle and looked back at Joline.

The older woman mouthed the words, "Answer it."

Slowly, to her surprise, it pulled open. A familiar figure stood in the doorway.

"You!"

It was Darlene.

"Look, Lady." Darlene looked down into Kam's eyes. "I'm sure you're still upset about your hand and all, but I didn't have a choice in the matter."

"Huh!" Kam was baffled.

"But what Scorch says, I does."

"You are a Maniac!"

"A what?" Darlene rubbed her sweaty neck.

"Maniac! A crazy person! Out of your mind! Do you understand that, you featherless turkey!"

Darlene put her hands up. "Easy now, Lady. I'm not a Mannyack or a Turkey. *Hic.* 'Scuse me.

Must be that last bottle of Muckle Sap. Anyhow, I'm a hunter, trapper, and a proud underling slayer. And, I'll warn you once: don't cross Scorch again. He did you a favor, and you know it."

Speechless, Kam tried to measure the woman's words. Darlene still seemed amiable, though taller and formidable.

"So," Kam said, "what is it you want?"

"First, sorry about your hand," Darlene said. "I guess you'll just have to learn to wipe with the other." She winked, pushing her way inside. "Say, this is nice. Better than I imagined it."

"What do you want?"

"Well." Darlene grabbed Kam's cup of coffee from the table and took a sip. "Mmmm... that's fine coffee. Did you make that, uh..."

"Joline," Kam said.

The rocker groaned when Darleen sat down.

"Joline. Like Darlene. I like it." She slurped another mouthful. "Mmmm, that's good. Not like that Muckle Sap, but still plenty good." She kicked her legs on the table.

"What do you want, Darlene?"

She scratched her brown hair, stirring the little flakes that fell out. "Things are getting busy downstairs. I need some help."

"Help with what?"

"Serving the people."

"Customers?" Kam said.

"Yes. You see, I don't have much experience running a tavern. I've always wanted to, but I never had the money. But thanks to Scorch, I now own this one."

"This is my tavern!"

Darlene got up and looked down at Kam. "Nope. It's my tavern now. And you're going to help me ruin it … *hic.* I mean, run it."

Chapter 36

B*LINK!*

"Say!" A dwarf, black-haired and mangy, couldn't hide his surprise. "Where'd ye come from?"

Lefty tumbled onto his butt, shaking his head. "I-I don't know."

The dwarf slammed his fist on the table.

Lefty jumped.

The surrounding men and dwarves erupted in laughter.

Lefty shook his head.

What has happened? Where am I?

He was in a tavern. That much was clear by the layout, the drinking and eating that surrounded him. A fireplace sat cold at his back, and suspicious eyes drifted over him and onto the next patron. There was something else, something weird about where he was. It was misty.

Gathering his thoughts, he looked to the dwarf, who now had his nose buried in a tankard of ale. "I'm from the City of Three, I think."

The dwarf eyed him from behind his tankard, gulping it down.

Clonk!

"Bring another and one more for my out-of-the-city friend here. Say!" The dwarf rubbed his beard. "You're pretty small, even for a halfling. Humph. The City of Three, ye say. Well, that might explain your appearance. Are you one of those magi or wizards I hear about there? I didn't think halflings could take to magic with such fashion."

Lefty crawled up on the chair and sat down. He wasn't certain what to say or think at the moment. The last hours of his life had been incomprehensible enough.

"Dwarf, uh, my name is Lefty Lightfoot, and I really have no idea where I am. Can you tell me?"

The dwarf guffawed as the barmaid, heavyset but not uncomely, set down their tankards, laughing as well.

"Can't ye tell?"

Lefty scanned the room. It wasn't the City of Bone; there were no dwarves there. And it couldn't be the City of Three; the distant roar of the falls didn't catch his ears. And other than the few other places he'd been in his life, he didn't really have any idea at all. It wasn't a village or a logged outpost. He shook his head.

"Have a drink, Halfling," the dwarf said, reaching over and squeezing his shoulder. "Hmm. Hmm. Hmm."

Being polite, Lefty took a sip, glancing around as he did so.

There were women, some dressed in thick but scant clothing, and the men were of a dour but rugged sort. A pair of full orcs sat in the corner, quiet and unusual. At the next table over was a man that might have been half-gnoll with a heavy sword on his belt. Somewhere he couldn't see, someone played a flute, another strings. A sad tune, a slow tune that settled over the room.

"Are you going to make me guess … Apologies, but may I have your name?"

"No, you might just ferget it. Dwarf will do, and no, I'm not telling you where you are."

"I could ask someone else, I suppose."

The dwarf's bushy brown brows buckled, and his calloused hand reached under the table. Lefty heard a dagger or knife slip from his belt. The dwarf leaned inward.

"Ye could, but I'd consider that rude. And I don't like rude people. You aren't rude, are you?"

I might as well be. After all, I'm a thief, a liar, a disappointment, a failure, a lousy friend, and a wretched urchin. Why not be rude too?

The dwarf, who appeared as rugged as they come, reminded him a little of Jubbler, just thicker. Besides, it didn't look like Lefty had any friends in the world anymore. Maybe it was time he made a new one.

"I'm sorry, Dwarf. The truth is, I'm not rude, just really confused. I don't know how I got here. I don't know where I am. I-I—Sheesh, I guess it's for the better!"

"Ho-ho!" the Dwarf said, "Little one, yer frustration will do ye little good. Take a breath, a drink, and tell me a little about yerself, and if I'm satisfied with your tale, I'll tell ye where ye is." The dwarf winked.

Over the planks of the room, Lefty noticed a creeping fog that swirled as the men and women passed through it.

That's odd.

"Where should I start?" Lefty's feet were sweating.

"Wherever ye want, Lefty. Wherever ye want. I've got all the time in the world." The dwarf lit up a cigar, leaned back, and kicked his heels up. "And just so you know, yer a long, long way from whence you come."

A few more solemn faces joined them at the table, each one less friendly than the next. Lefty's feet were as damp as they'd ever been before.

Drip. Drip. Drip.

CHAPTER 37

"CAN YOU HOLD A SHOVEL?"

Venir hesitated, thinking of his aching wrists, then nodded. He was disgraced. Humiliated. Defeated. He reached out with his busted wrists.

Tuuth shoved it in his chest. "Better off digging than dying, for now anyway, Stranger."

Grimacing, Venir wrapped his hands around it and shuffled away, half dragging his feet. He could barely walk. He was dizzy. Thirsty. Hours ago he'd barley had the strength to watch the masses of the Royal Riders be slaughtered, but he'd held on through the bitter end. Watching the underlings chop brave men into bits and pieces was hard. Watching them burn in a pyre was even worse. The stench of burning flesh stung his eyes. It was suffocating.

"Stranger." Tuuth blocked his way with his big body. "What does that tattoo on your back mean, 'V'?"

Venir said nothing. He wasn't even sure himself, so long it had been since he'd even thought about it. Slowly, he trudged forward, joining the surviving Royal Riders, all twelve of them. All busted and broken in one way or the other.

"Stranger, does it stand for Vanquished?"

He looked up at Tuuth through his swollen eyes and said nothing.

"Villain? Vile? Vulgar? Vain? Victorious? Ha! Ha! Ha!"

It happened long ago. Venir couldn't remember if he was drunk when he'd done it or if someone had done did it to him when he was drunk. Melegal used to say it meant Vociferous and claim that he'd done it, but in truth, even Melegal didn't know when he got it. It was almost as if it just happened.

"Start digging, Stranger."

Wuhpash!

"You three, dig as well."

Venir sank the nose of his shovel into the dirt, thinking of all the bodies that would be stuck in the ground. For all he knew, he'd be buried alive again, and suffocated. His thoughts were interrupted when the underling commander showed up.

"Arsehole Bastard can't dig, you stupid orc!" The commander extended his hand towards Tuuth.

Wuhpash!

The underling cracked Tuuth across the arms, watering the orc's eyes.

"Next time you do something so stupid, you'll be digging a hole for yourself. We don't have any need for you, Orc, or any of those men. I'm tired of looking at humans. I'm tired of you all." He held his nose. "And you stink so bad when you burn!" The underling spat on Venir's chest then slugged him in the gut, dropping him to his knees. "I don't like this one, but I like to see him suffer."

Head downcast, Venir listened to the sound of shovels digging into the ground. He hated that sound. It made him think of the day the underlings overtook his village. Groaning, he rose back to his feet.

"Strong, stupid and stubborn, this man is," the underling commander said. "Like an orc." He hissed and chittered to himself. "Let him watch these men shovel until they die. Let him watch us strip the armor from their dead bodies. Let this stubborn man watch it all while you whip him." The underling reached up, grabbed Venir's chin and looked him in the eye. "And if he passes out, wake him up and whip him some more." The underling shoved the whip in Tuuth's chest. "Maybe he'll die before your arm gets too tired, Orc."

"Yes, Commander," Tuuth said.

Venir locked eyes with Tuuth when the commander walked off.

"Men," Tuuth said to some of the brigand army soldiers, "hitch him to the lashing post." He cracked the whip. "Normally, I'd enjoy this, Stranger. But, in your case, I feel a bit sorry for you and your stupid tattoo."

Wuhpash!

Chapter 38

*T*HREEP! *THREEP! THREEP! THREEP!*

Fogle's eyes snapped open.

Threep! Threep! Threep! Threep!

Sluggish, he rolled onto his knees, yawning.

Threep! Threep! Thr—

With a simple thought, he shut off the Wizard's Alarm he'd set it in his mind. It was an awareness, like a familiar, a piece of him outside himself. *Careful, Fogle.* He scanned the harsh Outland. Anything could be coming, be it flesh-eating bugs, giants or underlings. Squinting his eyes, he didn't see anything, but the sore muscles between his shoulders told him something was wrong. *Never felt that before.*

Dust Devils swirled over the landscape. Nearby, covered in a thin layer of dust, Barton snored, flat on his face.

"Am I the only real adventurer left around here?" Fogle said to himself, brushing off his robes. "Ah! Why do I continue to bother with that?" He took a deep breath, scanning in every direction. "There has to be something; why else would my alarm go off?"

He nudged Cass's curled-up form. She looked innocent, at peace. He pushed her white hair back over her ear and whispered into it.

"Cass."

She stirred.

"Cass?" he said, shaking her some more. He was getting tired of being the only one awake. "Cass!"

Her eyes fluttered open. "What? Who are you yelling at? Not me, are you?"

Elated, he couldn't' help but hug her.

Feebly, she hugged him back. "Fogle, where are we?"

He helped her up to her feet.

"And is Barton dead?"

Disappointed with what he had to share, Fogle caught her up, explaining to her what little had happened since she fell asleep. Well, little aside from the swarm of flesh-eating bugs killing their horse and weakening Barton.

She made a shivering face when she saw the remains of the horse. "So, you protected me, did you?" She smiled a little and grabbed his hand. "My big-headed hero." She kissed him on the cheek. "But, if you had some water, now, that I'd be more than willing to give you a kiss for. Oh, and my lips would be so much moister."

Fogle felt his dry mouth begin to water as she turned away, hips swaying as she walked up to Barton. He could make water if he wanted to, but she'd made it clear before that his kind would not help. "I'm sure there is some nearby, but Cass, I've lost my familiar, and the truth is, I'm not the best at determining the direction in the Outlands. But, we were headed that way, east, I believe."

Cass fingered one of the red welts on Barton. "Stingers and teeth?" She continued her inspection, eyes wide with fascination. "Even I've never seen such a thing. Strange."

"How are you feeling, Cass?" He wasn't certain how long they'd slept, but it must have been a few hours at least. He felt a bit better than before, anyway.

"Mmm... not so bad, just stiff." She rolled her neck. "How are feeling, Fogle the Brave?"

"Never better now that I know you're well." He was unable to contain his grin.

"Oh, is that so?" Cass came closer, her busted lip and bruised face all smiles. "And how well am I, exactly?"

Drat! I had one good remark. I wasn't expecting to need two! "As well as a soldier in a tavern full of whores?"

"What!"

"Er ... Better than a dwarf on stilts?"

She folded her arms over her chest.

"Like a cat in a room full of rats?"

She shook her head. "You need to know when to be silent, Fogle Fool. Now—"

Suddenly, Barton jerked up into a sitting position, eye alert, craning his neck.

Fogle could see the muscles tense in the giant's back. Something was amiss.

"What is it?" Cass said.

Barton's hand covered her chest and face.

"Hear that?" Barton said, his voice a low rumble.

"Only the wind in my ears," Fogle said.

Barton's head turned towards the cloudy sky. His jaw jutted out, and he grinded his teeth. "We must go," Barton said. He reached for Cass.

"What are you doing?" she said.

"We must hide," Barton said. "Can you not hear that? Can you not hear that, Wizard?"

Fogle, eyeing the sky, shook his head. "I don't hear anything." Still, he grabbed Cass and held her tight. "Barton, what is it? Giants?"

Barton took a stiff breath through his nose and shook his head. "Not giants. Blackie. Barton hate Blackie."

That's when Fogle heard it. Distant. Foreboding. Massive.

Whump. Whump. Whump.

"A net," Boon grumbled to himself. "Of all things, I fell to a net."

Mile after mile Boon was marched, barefoot on the hot land. His bleeding and blistered feet burned like fire with every step.

Surrounding him, underling soldiers marched at his side, one holding a rope around his neck, jerking it hard from time to time.

Boon glanced over at it. Its red eyes glared back like beacons of death.

"I'll kill you first, you black roach," Boon spat. He looked at another. "Then you." And another. "And you." He was certain they didn't understand a word he said, but he understood them.

They hadn't killed him, but he was fairly certain he wished they had. No, they would torture him. Mutilate him. Cut his tongue off and feed it to him maybe. Of all the races on Bish, it was the underlings that delighted abnormally in peeling the flesh from the bones. The single thought of it disgusted Boon. Everything they did, he despised. He remembered the first time he saw them kill a man, a friend of his. They took pleasure in it. It stirred Boon. It made him sick.

"Oooof."

Underlings shoved him to the ground, chittering with diabolical laugher.

His body wanted to stay down, but he wouldn't let it. He wouldn't give them the satisfaction. "Kill me now, fiends, before it's too late," he said. Rising, his legs trembled beneath him.

Still, they laughed in their own sick way, his threats as meaningless as the ants that scurried beneath his toes. Chests out, sharp teeth bared, the soldiers marched him over the dusty ground, pushing, pulling and jerking him by the neck mile after mile, one agonizing step after the other. *Walk or die, Old Man. Walk or Die.*

Before Fogle realized what was happening, Barton had snatched him and Cass up and started running.

"We must hide! Barton must hide! I won't let Blackie take me again. I won't!"

Over Barton's shoulder, Cass was screaming in the giant's ear. "Put me down!"

Fogle wanted to scream, but couldn't find the breath. Barton had him pressed over his shoulder too tight. *The dragon might want you,* he thought, *but I don't think he wants us!* Reassuring himself, he patted the spellbook in the pocket of his robe.

Barton's feet sounded like giant mallets pounding over the landscape, clattering Fogle's teeth and jostling his senses.

A dragon.

A black one.

Watching the clouds above, Fogle tried to imagine what to expect. There was a wizard's tower in the City of Three with a great hall filled with the most wondrous and colorful pictures. Battles. Cities. Ancient people of Long Ago. Men and dwarves battled orcs, ogres, gnolls and minotaurs. Wizards fought harpies, chimera, dark sorcerers. So many monsters roamed Bish, yet so few were ever seen, but one picture came to mind. A dragon: beastly, monstrous, little bigger than a horse attacking a host of men. It was a terrifying creature, scales a deep red, but other than that, it looked to only be a big lizard.

"Barton!" he said, "you don't even know where you're going!"

"I don't hear any dragons!" Cass screamed over at him, then looked to the air.

Whump! Whump! Whump!

Their eyes locked on one another's. Cass's widened with uncertainty.

Barton picked up the pace. "NOOOOOO!"

Fogle craned his neck, searching in all directions. Above him, a massive black shadow darted through the clouds.

Whump! Whump! Whump!

A powerful gust of air sent a chill right through him

Barton's running came to a sudden stop.

WHUMP!

Ahead, the sound of something heavy hit the dirt, followed by a roar so long Fogle felt his ears splitting. He stuck his fingers in them. *This is it!* Another roar followed, louder than the last. *I'm going to die.*

Barton lowered both him and Cass to the ground, setting them behind him.

"BARTON HATE YOU, BLACKIE! YOU WON'T TAKE BARTON HOME TODAY!"

There was a loud snort and a blast of furnace-hot air.

Fogle could smell sulfur and brimstone. He opened his eyes and looked. *Oh slat!* His knees warbled. His stomach recoiled. His warm blood went cold.

Blackie wasn't only taller than a horse; he was taller than five horses, maybe ten. His scales were black as coal. Hard as iron. His citrine eyes burned with life. Intelligent. Crafty. Teeth tall as a dwarf and sharper than spears. A great tail swiping back and forth like a preying cat. His giant claws dug into the hardened ground like it was mud.

"RAAAH-OOOOOOOOOOOOOOOR!"

The sound was maddening. Without realizing it, Fogle found Cass's arms wrapped around him, eyes shut, trembling.

"Please don't roar again," she said. "Please don't roar again."

Fogle could barely hear her words. Even Barton's bellowing shouts seemed muffled compared to the dragon's terrifying sounds.

"BARTON KILL YOU, BLACKIE! BARTON KILL YOU NOW!"

Fogle was shaking his head. *You aren't going to kill that thing.*

The dragon's wings seemed impossibly long as it spread them and roared once more.

Cass was screaming, tears appearing in the corners of her eyes. They huddled on the ground like two babes in a storm. *This is happening!*

Fogle could feel the hot coals of the dragon's breath getting hotter. Then Barton said the unthinkable.

"BARTON HAVE WIZARD TO HELP HIM NOW. ATTACK HIM, WIZARD!"

The dragon's long neck moved his head from Barton down on the ground facing him.

That thing can understand Barton. Stupid giant! What can I do? Think, Fogle, think!

"HA! HA! HA! BLACKIE GOING TO GET IT NOW!"

The giants were terrifying enough, and he'd had help with them. The dragon was something entirely different. It wasn't shaped like a man. It was shaped like a monster.

The dragon snorted and sniffed. A strange cackling erupted in his long neck.

"WHAT ARE YOU WAITING FOR, WIZARD? KILL BLACKIE!"

"He doesn't want me. He wants you, Barton!" Fogle yelled.

That's when Cass looked up at him with weak eyes and said, "Do whatever you have to, Fogle. I'll fight with you."

From behind Barton's monstrous leg, he touched foreheads with Cass and said, "Fight or Die, my sweet. Fight or die!"

"WHAT?" Barton said, leering down at him with his good eye.

Do something or die, Wizard. A spell came to mind. *Huh! Am I ready this time? For a dragon?* He wrapped his arm around Barton's ankle and yelled upward. "Barton!"

"WHAT?"

"How much to you hate that dragon?"

"A LOT!"

"Get ready then! Help's coming!"

Closing his eyes, he summoned his power. Words of magic filled his head. Rolled from his tongue. Churned from his lips like hummingbird wings. Seconds later, he sagged, Cass holding him up.

"HAMMER!" he said.

A glowing hammer, with a head like an anvil, materialized at Barton's feet. It was longer than

Fogle was tall, radiating with energy. Barton snatched it up and slung it at Blackie, striking him full in the chest.

KAROOM!

The dragon let out an angry screech, flapping backward and away.

Barton charged over the landscape, snatching the hammer up in his mighty arms, swinging.

WHAM! WHAM! WHAM!

Fogle felt the air shake with every blow. Blackie screeched and clawed, angry, hateful.

"BARTON KILL BLACKIE!"

WHAM!

"FEEL THAT, BLACKIE!"

WHAM!

"BARTON HATE BLACKIE!!"

The two titans fought and clawed over the ground, but Blackie was still bigger, quicker, and deadlier. Barton was a man fighting a giant-sized lizard.

Like a snake, Blackie struck, biting Barton's hammer-swinging arm.

"AARGH!"

The hammer fell from his grasp.

Barton cocked his elbow back and socked Blackie in the eye.

The pair thrashed and rolled through the dirt.

Barton was flailing and screaming.

Blackie clawing and biting.

It was an awful sight. Fogle grabbed Cass, pulling her as far away from the Chaos as he could.

"NOOO!" Barton squeezed.

Blackie pinned Barton under his weight, an adult atop a large child.

The giant's fingers clawed at the dirt, clutching for the hammer.

Blackie swatted the hammer away with his tail and hissed in Barton's face.

Fogle could see the giant's futile squirms under Blackie's power and weight. Barton, a giant, yet still a boy, couldn't overcome his adversary, his oppressor. It was a sad thing when the fire in Barton's eye went out, defeated.

"Help me, Wizard?" Barton said, exhausted, fingers feebly clutching at the dirt.

Fogle did nothing. The dragon didn't want him or Cass. It only wanted Barton. Keeping Cass behind him, he watched Blackie dig his black claws into Barton's shoulders.

"OW!" Barton cried. "Wizard, help!"

Whump! Whump! Whump!

Stirring the air like a small tornado, Blackie was up and off, with Barton in his grasp.

The betrayed look on Barton's face would haunt him forever, but he had to protect Cass.

Behind him, Cass cleared her throat.

"What?" he said, watching Blackie and Barton slowly sail away.

"Do something, Fogle Idiot! Shoot that dragon down!" Cass ordered.

The power of a dragon was one thing. The power of a beautiful angry woman was another. Without thinking, Fogle's body charged with power. Flashes of lightning shot from his fingers across the sky, striking Blackie full force.

Blackie roared, this time with pain, not pleasure.

Barton slipped from the dragon's grasp and plummeted a hundred feet to the ground with a thud.

"That's better," Cass said.

Blackie hung in the sky, hovering, flapping his great wings, struggling to stay afloat.

"Whatever you did, I don't think that dragon liked it. Do it again?"

Fogle shook his head. "I don't have enough power to kill it. I'd better protect us."

The dragon's citrine eyes leered at him like burning suns. He'd hurt it. He'd made it mad. Now it was coming for him.

It flapped over towards them, long great neck swaying back and forth.

Fogle grabbed Cass, pulled her close, and summoned a spell.

Hanging like a black cloud over them, Blackie opened his mouth and breathed.

The blast of a thousand furnaces came out.

Fogle stood tall, a mystic bubble protecting them, scattering the flames around them.

The heat was intense, like standing at the mouth of a blacksmith's forge.

The magic shield kept them away from instant incineration. Sweat poured from Fogle's face. The shield would only hold up as long as he could.

How long can this thing breathe! He felt his air begin to thin, his lungs labor, his concentration waver.

"Hold on, Fogle!" Cass encouraged him, her face as red as a beet, "Hold on!"

He couldn't. He fought with all his will, but his will was out.

"I'm sorry, Cass!" He shook his head. "I can't. Cass … I—"

The fire stopped.

Blackie reared up, screeching. Barton was on the dragon's back, holding onto its wing with one hand and pounding it in the back of the head with the hammer in the other.

Fogle took Cass by the hand and tried to run away.

SWAT!

Blackie's tail licked out, knocking them from their feet.

Fogle gathered his knees beneath him and summoned more lighting in his grasp.

In front of him, Blackie slung Barton from his back. Wary, Blackie's eyes focused on Fogle's glowing hands.

"You don't like that, do you?" Fogle rose to his feet. "Stings, doesn't it, Lizard?"

A growl rumbled in the dragon's throat. The creature was intelligent, thinking, planning.

"Leave us be, Dragon," Fogle yelled. "Else I'll unleash all of my fury!"

Twenty feet from his nose, the Dragons' red tongue licked out over its fangs. There must have been a thousand of them.

"AAAIIEEEH!" Cass screamed.

The tip of Blackie's tail encircled her waist and dragged her away.

"NO!" Fogle yelled after her.

The dragon tucked her into his chest, playing with her in the palm of his hand like a tiny doll. Fogle could swear it smiled.

Whump! Whump! Whump!

Up it went, Cass stunned in its grasp, leaving Fogle devastated on the cracked terrain as they disappeared into the clouds.

"CAAAAASSS!!!"

Chapter 39

CASTLE ALMEN, A CHARACTER IN its own right, had many secrets. Many lost over the centuries, others found. It was spotless; no cobwebs or dust coated the dark wood and velvety furniture. Every piece of metal was polished. Every crystal gleamed.

Lord Almen closed the drapes to a large bay window and sealed the balcony door shut. This was once the bedroom of his father. He and his best Shadow Sentry, a long limbed man, fled the Keep and traversed the castle utilizing the secret corridors, avoiding the commotion caused by the underlings.

Still weak, Lord Almen rummaged through the drawers of a black walnut desk until he placed his hand around a dagger and stuffed it into his belt. Quickly, he made his way over to the fire place and stood on the hearth.

"Come, stand with me," he ordered.

The sentry obliged, stepping onto the mosaic hearth, fingering the pommels of his swords.

"Tell no one of this," Lord Almen warned, shoving back a marble block on the fire place mantle. The colorful tiles shifted beneath their feet, then disappeared, leaving a black hole. The lanky warrior in the black ghost armor cocked his head. Rapidly, they were sinking.

"You may want to close your eyes, Virgil."

A quick rush of air followed, the feeling of one flying, the weightlessness of a feather, and an abrupt halt that bobbled his stomach. Opening his eyes, the first thing Lord Almen saw was his office beneath the kitchen, and the front door was still closed.

Beside him, Virgil's knees wobbled, his long arms stretching out for support. Lord Almen didn't bother. Instead, he searched his office. No one would have suspected a single thing was out of place, but he knew. It angered him. Whoever had been here had some idea what to look for and what they were taking. Tonio's sword was gone. The shelf that concealed the small secret door was out of place, and the door was open. A variety of footprints had disturbed the dust. *Melegal* was the first thought that came to mind. *Sefron* was the second. But, more than that, something lingered in the air. The scent of underlings.

"Virgil, see to it that door is secure," he said, opening a small case full of vials. "You be keeping post and sending warning if anything comes through there."

"I hope it's underlings," Virgil said. He cracked his neck side to side and eased his sword from the scabbard. "Or any arsehole, for that matter."

Lord Almen couldn't see the man's face behind his cloth mask, but Virgil was one of his best soldiers. A survivor of the Warfield. A friend of danger. Lord Almen favored men like that. Cold blooded killers.

Lord Almen drank down one of the vials, followed by the other. He tossed one filled with a pale red liquid to Virgil.

"Take that," Lord Almen said. He rolled his shoulders. He was feeling better and stronger already. "It will give you stamina. Improve your focus."

Virgil pulled up his mask—exposing his rugged chin, split lip and rotting teeth—before he swallowed it down.

Lord Almen took a deep breath through his nose, filling his lungs to capacity and slowly releasing.

Virgil thumbed his blade. "This sword is the finest blade I've ever owned, Lord Almen, and I'll put it to good use in your defense." He pulled his mask back down. "I feel like killing."

"So do I."

Disappointed that Tonio's sword was gone, Lord Almen grabbed another blade, a poniard with an ivory hilt, and set it on his desk table. Opening a wardrobe, he grabbed his own suit of ghost armor and slipped it on. It fit like a glove, coating him like a thick flexible skin. A smile came to the corner of his lips. *It's been too long.*

"Sir, you look dangerous, but I plan on killing them all before they make it to you."

Almen put his hand on Virgil's shoulder. "You do that, and I'll give you your own room in this castle and a personal servant girl, too."

Black masked, Virgil saluted with his sword. "My life for my Lord. Their life with my sword."

With that, Lord Almen stepped through the small door's opening and headed down the stairs on cat's feet. Stopping, he closed his eyes and slowed his breath. He heard nothing. Not a shuffle, nor a scuffle, nor a scratch. Breathing through his nose, nothing caught his potion-heightened senses. As they passed the bottom of the stairwell, the torches came to life. The large chamber cast his shadow. All six doors were closed.

Where is she?

Making his way back to the alcove where all the Keys usually hung, he noticed the empty pegs on the wall. How in all of Bish had they escaped his grasp? *Melegal.* It had to be. Or had they been taken by the underlings?

He chuckled, remembering the first time he and his father found the chamber. There'd been more doors. More pegs. More Keys. And rings. Many came, many went. He tried his best to understand it. It seemed the chamber had a will of its own. It would serve him, so he thought, so long as he fed it. A mystery. An advantage he didn't hesitate to press. No wonder the underlings wanted it. But how did they know about it? Who made it? *Seven Keys last I counted. Eight with the one I gave to Jarla. I hope she still has it.* He looked at the floor. The slightest sucking licked at his boots.

Lord Almen paced around the circle of the great chamber. His castle was under siege. The underlings had penetrated for the second time in days. He could have held out in the keep, but the Keys were what he was certain they wanted. He had no plans to part with them. They gave him power. Control. To go whenever and however he wanted to go. And until several days ago, only few knew about his secret. Now that secret had been compromised.

Standing in the center of the room facing the alcove and the ancient doors, Lord Almen stood, watching and listening. *Where is that Brigand Queen?* He twisted the finger ring that he used to summon her. She never appeared at the same duration, but always she came. Minutes, an hour maybe, but never a day. He frowned.

Perhaps she's dead.

She had a Key and a ring. Her Key would open the doors and give him access and freedom if the underlings took over. And if the underlings had the other seven Keys, the Keys that they knew about, what would they do? They could strike day or night all over Bish if they wanted to. Just like he had. He couldn't fight the smile on his lips.

The minutes passed, leaving Lord Almen alone in his thoughts, his memories.

For years Lord Almen had used the Keys, slipping into rival bedrooms and parlors, strangling or cutting their throats while they slept. Already a Master Assassin, the Keys had made his job all too easy. Castle Almen had moved up the ranks quickly on account of it. The ancient chamber was a recent discovery, come upon by accident by his father. Slowly over the years, they had abused the power of the ancient chamber, never truly understanding it. But he knew, he'd always known, someone would come after the power one day or another. And now it seemed that day had come.

He froze. Up the stairwell echoed the sound of wood exploding into splinters. He shifted his stance. Readied his sword. Chitters and the clash of steel followed. A human cry of alarm went out. Silence fell. The room went cold.

Something clopped down the stairs, rolling to a stop at the bottom. It was Virgil's head. A clean cut through the neck. Blood spilled into the mosaic. A sucking sound followed. Lord Almen sheathed his sword.

The first past the torches was an underling, copper eyed with a bandolier of knives around his chest. He was tall, over six feet, the tallest underling Lord Almen had ever seen. Blood dripped from the tip of his sword, and a fierce grin parted his lips. Behind him, others came: two, then four, then six. Some were in black plate armor that didn't clank or rattle; the others wore little more than leather or a cloak. Blades of many kinds hung loose in their grips, and their eyes were bright with color.

Lord Almen rubbed the sweat from his hands. So many adversaries were to be expected, but everyone else in the castle flooded his thoughts. It was entirely possible that his family were being wiped out one by one. *I hope they made the Keep at least.*

Still, he stood tall, a statue by comparison. "I am Royal Lord Almen, Liege of this castle, and I request a parlay."

Coming closer, the copper eyes of the first underling narrowed to slits, a sinister chuckle erupting in his throat. "Parlay," he said, slipping his sword in the sheath in a wink of an eye. "I don't see any need for a parlay, Human Lord. After all, we've seized your castle, within your city. I think there is little you can do to help us."

About then, a wheezing sound caught his ear. Sefron the Cleric was huffing down the stairs, oversized robes hanging from his body, his gnarled staff clacking on the steps. Lord Almen's usual frown expanded when they locked eyes. *Traitor!* Lord Almen didn't hide his rage as the underlings formed a tight circle around him.

"Sefron, you sickening slaggard! It was you that gave up the castle! I'll cut open that fat belly of yours!"

Sefron groaned, straightening the bend in his back with a chuckle. He rubbed his saggy chin and blinked his bulging eye. "Master Kierway, may I have this one?"

"Fool," Kierway said, "this man will prove to be a better resource than you, certainly."

Sefron came closer, trying to push past the underlings, his hand reaching out.

Lord Almen recoiled back the ever slightest. He knew Sefron's secret and what the man was capable of. It was why he recruited him in the first place.

"Don't you dare, Servant," Almen said.

"Stay back, Sefron, you disgusting fool." Kierway shook his head. "You bother me, but this man, he doesn't bother me so much, other than being a human." He scratched his cheek with his long black nails. "Tell me about this *parlay*, Lord Almen. I'm curious."

Tearing his eyes away from Sefron, Lord Almen cleared his throat. "I've a history with your kind, Master Kierway. It was I who aligned myself with you at Outpost Thirty-One."

"So you are a traitor?"

"A survivor." Lord Almen nodded. "A master planner. My family and my castle are what mean the most in life to me. I dare not guess what the underlings have in mind with my castle or this city, but I will assist you. I'm a man of many secrets. Tell me what you want, and I assure you that I can help."

Kierway moved with the ease of a cat, sauntering through the chamber, tugging on one door handle after the other. Standing in the alcove near the key posts, he said, "This architecture is strange, but similar to many chambers in the Underland. Hmmm, so, Lord Almen, tell me, where are the Keys?"

Lord Almen kept his relief concealed. He'd lost track of much while he'd been down for several days. He eyed Sefron briefly. He could tell the cleric must have had something to do with that, or had he? The wound between his ribs should have been fatal, and he vaguely remembered Sefron coming to his aid, only to betray him now.

"Stolen," Lord Almen said.

Kierway crossed his arms and leaned his shoulder over one of the doors. "So, you are waiting for the thief to return with them? Certainly that wouldn't happen in the middle of a siege. Not unless the person with the Keys would have a reason to come back, and into that question you might have more insight than I." He raised his eyebrows. "Of course, perhaps you are down here because you are expecting someone else. Seven pegs. Seven Keys. Six doors. Interesting opportunities."

One of the most frustrating things that Lord Almen had encountered about underlings was that they weren't stupid. Every one he'd dealt with had a calculating mind and cunning demeanor. He admired that about them. And something else. Unlike men, they weren't greedy, at least not in terms of material things. Instead, they thirsted for something else without distraction. Power.

"I can't readily say, and I cannot refute the possibility either."

There was a long pause. Surrounding him, standing like statues poised to strike, the breathing of the underlings was barely audible. Lord Almen glanced over at Sefron, who now sat wheezing on the stairs. He should have rid himself of the slaggard long ago, but Sefron was so resourceful when it came to digging information from his enemies. And there was another thing. Perhaps Sefron was still his ally. The man gave no sign of it.

One by one, Kierway slid three throwing knives from his bandolier. He juggled them with one hand. The blades flashing in the air, hand moving in a blur. Kierway's expression was lax and bored. "We wait, if need be, Lord Almen, but it might be a very long time. Of course, through our sources, we know where the Keys are. They are with a man, one of your own. What is his name, Sefron?"

"Melegal."

Feigning surprise, Lord Almen said to Sefron, "And how do you know this?"

Sefron sat with his legs crossed and sighed. "He's the last one we saw with them in here." He pointed at his ruined eye. "Thanks to him I have this."

Kierway snapped his wrist.

Thunk!

A knife jutted in the support beam by Sefron's head, causing him to jump.

"No." Kierway's eyes narrowed at Sefron. "Thanks to me you have that." He turned to Almen. "This man, Melegal, created the ultimate dilemma. Acts like an underling, that one. Cool and cunning." He resumed his juggling.

Inside of himself, Lord Almen was astounded. Melegal had found the Keys! But how? And why? *Hmmm… I see. The underlings recruited Sefron to find the Keys, meaning they must have known they were here. But why now? Why after all these years? It seems they have even darker secrets than I.*

"What's this?" Putting away his knives, Kierway drew a sword.

By the stairs, Sefron rose to his feet.

A faint yellow glow outlined the door where Kierway was leaning. "Chit! Chit!" he said. Underlings moved into the shadows. Some in full armor, some little, others none. "You, stay with Lord Almen!" He pointed to one then to another. "You, stay with the other one."

Lord Almen was pushed back into the alcove, where on tenterhooks, he and two of the underlings waited. *Finally,* he thought. *For what little good it will do.*

The yellow light disappeared, and the ancient door swung open.

Chapter 40

"**W**HAT IS THIS PLACE?" CREED fumbled through the dark.

"Silence, Creed." Melegal held his stomach.

You'd think I'd be used to this miserable feeling by now.

Creed moaned. "Slat, I feel like I'm hung over. What just happened?"

"You'll see." Melegal searched the darkness for a handle or a knob. "Listen to me, Creed. When I open this door, we're going to be in a chamber. People might be there, and underlings for all I know, so get your guts in order, and be ready for anything."

Creed scoffed. "I'm always ready for anything; just give me a moment."

Melegal pressed his ear to the door. If anything was moving on the other side, he wouldn't know. The door was as thick and hard as stone—and magical, for all he knew. Still, he worried. He assumed the Key took him back to the chamber beneath Castle Almen, but maybe it didn't. Maybe it took him somewhere else.

"What's that?" Creed huffed. "Did you feel something? Something's in here."

Melegal, still frozen, felt a gentle brush between his legs. Looking down, he saw two pale white eyes. "Octopus," he murmured.

"What's that?"

"Don't worry about it, Creed. Now listen to me. Do you want to go in hard and fast or quick and easy?"

Truth was, Melegal had to wonder what would happen if others were in there. Could he slip back in and seal the door? He hadn't thought long enough about it; he'd had no choice. And what if the underlings were inside? He straightened his cap. *Be ready for a nose bleed.*

"I don't suppose there really is a fast and easy way, is there?"

"I don't think we've much choice. Just be ready to fight…" Melegal found the handle and started to pull.

"…or Die," Creed finished.

Quick. Quick. Quick.

Melegal pressed the latch downward and shoved the door open. He darted straight forward, rolled, and rose to his knees, swords ready.

Creed spun along the wall, blades whirling.

The massive chamber was silent, torches flickering, forcing a wavering light.

Narrowing his eyes, Melegal noted the figures lined against the walls in the shadows. Their eyes were glimmering. *Bish! It's underlings!*

Whamp. The door they came through shut.

Leaning against the wall with two swords crossed over his back was an underling as tall as him. His copper eyes glowered at him.

"Ah… you must be the one called Melegal."

The other underlings emerged from the shadows.

The tall underling continued. "I just missed you the last time, it seems. You are the one Sefron calls The Rat."

Stupid! Stupid! Stupid! I should have taken my chances in the streets! One. Two. Three... Seven underlings. No crossbows. No darts. Two torches. Where to go? Where to go?

That's when he caught the heavy stare of Royal Lord Almen. A sword was pressed into the Vulture-like man's back. Wary, Melegal turned in his spot. Sefron's eyes were on him as well.

The cleric shuffled, wheezed, and squirmed at the side of an underling that held a blade to his belly.

Melegal allowed a grin and returned his focus to the copper-eyed underling.

"I am that rat. And who might you be?"

"Master Kierway." The underling pushed himself off the wall.

"Oh, so you are the one that Sefron wanted me to get the Keys for?"

Lord Almen shot Sefron a look, but the cleric remained silent.

"Indeed, and I assume you have those Keys?"

Slowly, Melegal nodded his head. There was no reason to lie now. All they would do was kill him and take them. He searched Lord Almen's face and saw nothing of help. It seemed the Castle was at a loss. But even if the underlings didn't kill him, he was certain Lord Almen would. After all, he'd tried to kill Lord Almen and failed.

How will you squeeze out of this one, Rat?

He glanced at Creed. The man stood tall, eyes darting from one underling to another, ready to fight anything and everything.

"I do have the Keys." Melegal sheathed his swords. "And they are yours to have."

Lord Almen's face turned pale.

Melegal reached inside his pockets.

Creed harrumphed. "Let them take those Keys from your dead body. Don't make a deal with the underlings, Detective. There are only a few of them."

"Mind your tongue, Bloodhound," Lord Almen said. "It's not your back that's dancing with a sword."

"Huh," Creed said. "At least I'll die with one in my hand, not in my back."

"As much as I'd rather not admit it," Kierway said, "I agree with this man over here. I'd rather die than make deals with the enemy. That's the kind of fighter I am. But at the moment, that's not my mission. The Keys are. Let me see them!"

"Certainly." Melegal fumbled through his clothes. *No rush. Not too fast. Not too slow.* Producing the 1st Key, Amethyst, he placed it on the floor.

Every eye in the chamber widened.

"And, Master Kierway," Melegal said, "considering my inevitable death, I would like you to consider another request." He set the 2nd Key, a diamond set in a brass setting, down on the floor. Out of the corner of his eye, he saw Lord Almen fidget the slightest.

Sefron's wheezing picked up.

"Say whatever you like, Human," Kierway said, "as you are intelligent to realize that your death is inevitable."

Melegal stood up and pointed.

"Let me sink my blades into that bug-eyed bastard, Sefron. He's the reason I came back. To cut his throat. I can't imagine you have any practical use for him. He failed to get the Keys. I didn't. And now I lay them at your feet with that one tiny request."

Sefron managed a fearsome snarl.

Melegal jumped. Still, he set the 3rd Key down.

"Let's just fight them, Man!" Creed urged. "I've killed underlings before." He eyed Kierway. "Dozens."

"Perhaps you'll get your chance, Human," Kierway said, still focusing on Melegal. "But first, let me see another Key. And maybe, assuming you do have all seven, I'll grant your request."

It made sense, what Creed was suggesting. If they fought and made it to the doors, they could escape. And so far as he understood it, he could go wherever he wanted, if he used the same door. *Two-Ten City might be nice right now.* As for the other doors, where did they go and which Key fit which door?

Of all the things to forget, he hadn't noted which Key was on which peg next to which door. It had been dark when he took them. *Clumsy fool!* For now, all he could do was buy a little more time and see what happened.

He set the 4th Key down. Its gem burned like orange fire.

As for overpowering the underlings in the room, it didn't seem likely. The ones in plate armor were of the likes he'd never seen before. He ventured any of them would be a match for Creed, who was certainly a superior fighter to himself. And Master Kierway wasn't at all worried. The underling and his brood made the men look wholly inadequate. *He didn't even ask us to disarm ourselves.*

"You'd made a fine Bloodhound," Creed said, "on account of you wanting to kill that Cleric and all."

Melegal ignored him, his shoulders and back tightening as he laid the 5th Key down. So much had happened since Lord Almen had acquired his service and made him a detective. He remembered those days in the man's office, the pressure, the fear the man put into him. He could feel Lord Almen's eyes heavy upon him, but he no longer felt that fear. *I wonder what he has in mind. He must have some plan.* Reaching inside his vest, he felt the long case he had tucked away. *Might not ever get a chance to use this. A shame.*

"Here is the 6th Key, Master Kierway." He knelt and rubbed his hands on his pants. "Can I cut that cur's throat now? Before I hand over the 7th? Just let me take his life, and I'll freely give you mine."

Kierway came closer. "You've made it interesting; I'll grant you that. Perhaps, I'll make you prisoners and lock you in a cage together instead. I think we underlings would find that entertaining."

"Would you want to be put in a cage with him?" Melegal said, unable to help himself.

"Well spoken!" Creed said, shifting on his heels.

Kierway showed him his sharp teeth. "Sorry, Human Called Melegal, but I see no reason to make such a deal." He paused and gestured. "I wouldn't be what I am, giving such consideration to a human. Now," he held out his clawed hand, "the 7th Key, please."

Shing!

In a blink, Kierway had pulled out his blade and put it at Melegal's throat.

For the first time in recent memory, Melegal felt beads of sweat on his forehead.

"You worry me, Human Called Melegal."

Melegal swallowed. "And why is that?"

"It seems foolish that you keep all the Keys on you, understanding their value. If it were me, I'd keep them hidden in many places. A bargaining chip if my life depended on it. A smart man would have hidden them all, would he not?"

I can't be that stupid. Of course I should have hidden them. Am I really going to die a fool?

Melegal's memories flashed to his friends: Venir, Georgio, Lefty, Billip and Mikkel.

I can't be as stupid as them.

But he had thought briefly about hiding the Keys and concluded that so long as they thought he had even one Key, they'd hunt him—the Royals and the underlings—forever and ever. *A clean slate or a clean death is what I'm going for. Let the rest of Bish plot and scheme all they want.*

"I did think of that, Master Kierway, but why risk the torture? They say, 'A quick beheading has no sting.'" Clasping his hands around the final Key, he summoned power from the hat that rested on his head. His mind cleared. Blood and mystic energy mixed in his veins. *Faster. Quicker. One step ahead.*

Everything around him slowed: Sefron's breath. Creed's blinking. The flickering of the torches. The clutching of Kierway's fingers.

Ahead of Melegal, behind Lord Almen, the outline of the ancient door glowed with new life and started to open.

Kierway's sword arm flicked backward.

Move or die! Melegal. Move!

Kierway's arm came forward.

Chapter 41

Catching her breath, Jarla fumbled for the latch on the door. In the darkness, she was alone with Tonio's ragged breathing.

"Don't do anything foolish," she said, brushing against him and pulling away.

"Where are we?" he said, heavy feet shuffling around.

At the moment, Jarla wasn't so sure whether or not it would be a good idea to tell him. It didn't really matter either way. Lord Almen would be waiting, and what other surprises he had in store she couldn't imagine, but he must have needed her.

"Just be ready, you bloodless goon, because you're going first."

She pushed the door open.

Over Tonio's shoulder, the torches were bright beacons. It took a couple of seconds for Jarla's eyes to adjust to the figures in the room. Lord Almen, a few other men, surrounded by underlings.

"Father?" Tonio's body tensed in front of her.

Lord Almen had a look on his face she'd never seen there before. Surprise.

Behind him, an underling had a blade pointed at Lord Almen's back.

It stirred Jarla, her energy renewing, her senses firing a warning.

"Father!" Tonio's garbled voice echoed in the chamber.

Jarla stepped forward.

Another underling stepped between them and Lord Almen. Two long knives were gripped in his hands, ruby eyes glinting, bare muscular chest stuck out.

Across the chamber, two more underling soldiers armed with barbed spears filed inside as well. Other than that, no one moved.

"The odds aren't going to get any better than this!" an unfamiliar voice shouted.

Clang!

Bang!

Lord Almen moved. Fast as a cat, he spun behind his underling oppressor and drove a dagger in its throat.

The bare-chested underling closed in, cutting out a portion of Tonio's chest armor.

The big man rammed his sword through its belly, lifted it from its feet, and slung it into another wall.

"Jarla!" Lord Almen screamed.

When she turned to his voice, an underling in black plate armor stepped in her path, swords moving like striking snakes.

Clang! Clang! Clang!

Parrying with two hands, she found her back against the wall.

Fast and fluid it came. Jarla parried and countered, stabbing its chest, her sword glancing off the armor.

"What in Bish are you?" the underling yelled at Tonio.

Krang!

Tonio hit it so hard he knocked it from its feet.

A split second later, Lord Almen kneeled down and jammed his dagger under its chin, piercing its skull.

Huffing, Jarla found Lord Almen's eyes.

"Get the Keys!" He ordered.

"What Keys?" she said.

"On the floor! Don't let the underlings have them." Ducking under an underling's arm, Lord Almen ripped out a long poniard and started swinging.

"Keys!" Tonio was pounding his way through his underling assailants. "Get for Father!"

Another underling adorned in black leathers surged at her, two short swords in its hands, sharp teeth bared.

Slice!

It howled and jumped back, clutching its split and bleeding chin.

"Don't you chitter at me, you little fiend."

When Tonio emerged through the door, Melegal swore he heard his heart stop. The Yellow-Haired Butcher had arrived. Behind him, the insufferable woman, Jarla. He was uncertain whether to be glad to see either one of them. They both deserved horrifying deaths so far as he was concerned. *Perhaps they'll get them.*

Tonio's face showed an ounce of humanity as he called for his father.

Jarla's scowling face, riddled with scars, showed creases of concern.

Behind Melegal, Sefron wheezed.

Kill Sefron.

The footfalls of more underlings came down the stairs.

Creed took in a deep breath. "The odds aren't going to get any better than this!"

Kierway hissed through his teeth, glowered at Melegal, and cut at his neck.

Everything in the room moved slowly except the underling's blade.

Melegal jerked his head down and jumped away.

Swish!

He touched the thin red line dripping on his neck.

Slat, that was fast!

With a brush of his foot, Melegal scattered 6 of the Keys in all directions.

Clang!

Whew! Keep him busy, Creed. Keep him busy.

Kierway caught Creed's swords in a crossed sword parry.

"Sefron," Kierway ordered, "get those Keys while I cut this man to ribbons! Brethren, help him!"

Man and underling squared off, lightning fast strokes ringing off each other like bells.

But Melegal had his own problems to worry about. He tucked the 7th Key back inside his clothes. *Slat on the Keys! Kill Sefron! Save yourself!*

The battle was furious.

Underlings swarmed, jumping out from all directions at the human attackers.

Tonio stood in the middle, a one-man army.

Jarla's sword darted at underling throats, her eyes darting after the Keys.

Lord Almen. *Slat! Where is he?*

Melegal let his heightened awareness take over. *Ah, there he is.* The haunting form of a man hung like a shadow near the wall, striking down an unsuspecting underling that crossed his path. *Interesting!*

A dozen yards away, Sefron slowly shuffled over the floor, bending over to grab one of the Keys.

Melegal extended his dart bracers and let Sefron have it.

Clatch-zip! Clatch-zip!

Sefron whined like a dying sheep, falling over, clutching at his legs.

Melegal crossed the room—deftly avoiding the melee—and kept shooting.

Clatch-zip! Click! Click!

Melegal overpowered Sefron and straddled his belly, pressing a knife to his throat.

"Remember my friend, the servant girl? You know, the one you almost whipped to death?"

Sefron's bulging eyes were merciless. "Hard to say. There's been so many." He licked his lips. "And there'll be many more to come, I assure you, long after you're dead."

Melegal felt Sefron's clammy hand wrap around his wrist. It was cold, ice cold.

"No, slug, it's you who'll be dead. And if I had the time, I'd whip you to death myself."

Melegal pushed his dagger into Sefron's throat, but no blood came forth, just Sefron's cackle.

"Fool, do you really think I'm so weak that a rodent such as yourself could take me?"

A wave of nausea overcame Melegal. *What's happening!*

Sefron's grip became as solid as iron, squeezing his wrist to the point of breaking it.

His dagger fell from his numb wrist.

Before his eyes, Sefron changed. His hair thickened. His teeth straighten. His body firmed like a fighter's beneath him.

No! What is this!

Melegal watched his hand curl and shrivel. It horrified him.

"No!" he groaned, trying to pull his rawboned body away.

Sefron cackled and sucked his teeth.

"Ah, such succulent life from such a scrawny man. Surprising."

Creed's father had told him that the first time he picked up a blade and swung, he was three. He'd cut into a leg of mutton and saved the butcher some trouble. He'd been swinging steel ever since.

Bang! Chang! Clang! Swish. Swish. Chang!

His opponent: an underling that weaved steel with skill he'd never seen. He thought he'd seen everything. He'd thought he knew everything.

Creed parried, dodged, ducked, and jumped backward. Forward and followed up with a chop-chop-chop.

Always attacking at the same time, the copper-eyed underling batted every blow away.

Not possible! Creed backed away.

The underling's blades were of the finest craftsmanship, archaic and curved at the very end. They moved like black flashes of lightning. Quick as a blink of an eye.

Creed had trained all his life, defeated every man he faced in fence or battle. The ones that would fight him, that is. Many Royals never gave him the honor. It bothered him. And now, entering his prime, for the first time in his life, he was worried.

"I never believed an underling could be so fast," he stalled. "Quite remarkable."

Kierway showed his sharp teeth. "Remarkable is my lowest level of skill, Human. Whatever it is you've done, I've already done a hundred times a year over a hundred years. You should know: this battle is over."

Creed wiped the sweat from his forehead with the back of his hand.

"Then I suppose this is what I've been training all my life for. Ee-Yah!"

In a flash, his gleaming blade leapt at the underling's throat.

Kierway deftly shifted his body a foot out of the way and swatted into the backs of Creed's legs with the back of his sword.

"Ugh! Blast it!" Creed cried out. He could feel the blood dripping down over his thighs already.

The floor made an eerie sucking sound.

Creed's face showed horror. "What in Bish is going on?"

"Interesting," Kierway replied. "It seems the floor hungers. I think I shall feed it."

Creed banged his blades together. One blade the finest of steel, the other enchanted by a mystic forge master. Until today, he'd always felt himself invincible with them and his skill, but it seemed for the first time in his life he'd met his match. He banged his blades again and muttered angrily to himself. "Come on, Creed! Draw his blood at least!"

Use your reach. You're longer!

Steel scraped against steel. Sweat mixed with blood.

They say, 'When your final battle comes, you'll know.'

His father had told him that, years ago, hours before he died at the Warfield. He'd always wondered who killed his father. A great sword. A great hound. Now he'd never know.

He charged. One sword high, the other low, he swung.

Kierway caught both blades on the outside with a smirk.

Creed's booted toe lashed out into Kierway's chin, clattering his teeth and splitting his lip.

Shocked, the underling hissed.

Creed kept swinging hard and fast.

Bang! Clang! Chang! Chang! Bang!

Back and forth the pair went. One master. One ancient master.

The underling's arms were strong like steel, but tireless and flexible as snakes.

For seconds, Creed pressed the advantage.

Slice.

Kierway ended it with a lightning fast stroke across Creed's thigh.

Slice.

Followed by another one across his belly.

Slice.

A hunk of flesh fell to the floor. It was Creed's.

"Hear that, Human? It's the sound of your death getting closer."

Parry, Fool! Parry!

Blue sparks showered the air.

Kierway pounded at his blades. Knocked Creed's steel down, numbing his hands.

That was Creed's plan. To beat his opponent's arms down until they felt like lead. But now his own arms felt like lead. Laboring for breath, he struggled to keep up with the blinding speed of Kierway's blades. Below, something sucked at his feet on the floor.

"You tire, Human." Kierway swatted Creed's blades away like toys. "Drop your blades, and I'll give you a merciful death."

"No. I'm going to cut you just once, Black Fiend. I can't go down like this. I can't."

Bang!

Kierway ripped one of Creed's swords from his hand and paused.

Creed's lone sword arm trembled. He grabbed his wrist with the other to support it.

"You are a fine swordsman, Human. But I've faced many better. All dead now, of course. So take note that you'll die at the hand of the finest swordsman this world has ever known."

Creed labored for breath.

Kierway was barely winded, his eyes darting around, looking for something.

"So be it then, Underling." Head down, Creed took a knee and set down his sword. "Vanquish me."

"With pleasure."

Catching a glimpse of Kierway's nearest knee, Creed lunged forward with everything he had, stabbing with a dagger concealed in his bracer. The blade sank into flesh and hit bone.

Kierway howled.

"I swore I'd cut you!"

Kierway's blade came for his head.

Chapter 42

C ORRIN RUBBED HIS EYES. FOR hours he'd sat watching the images in the fountain, mesmerized. Trinos had shown him the world outside the City of Bone, the home he'd never left. It was all fascinating and horrifying at the same time.

"What do you think?" Trinos said.

Corrin stretched out his stiff arms and shook his head. "It's a horrible, horrible world out there." He cleared his throat. "And just as bad in here."

Trinos lifted her brows without making a crease in her perfect forehead.

"How so?"

Corrin wasn't sure how to respond at first. After all, he was a murderer and cutthroat, even though he was pretty certain that was all behind him now. Watching all he'd seen—people dying of thirst or getting lost in the Outlands, battling for honor in a place she said was called the Warfield—it seemed as if someone was always fighting something else somewhere in this world. All his years, he'd assumed Bone was the worst the world had to offer, but it clearly wasn't. The entire world was in a struggle, and the driving force behind it all was the underlings. Or was it? He wasn't so sure.

He took an apple from a wicker basket, started peeling it with his knife, and looked into her eyes.

"I always figured there was solitude somewhere in this world. But if there is, I've never seen it. And I've never experienced it. At least not until you came around."

"Well, Corrin, you've only seen what I've shown you. Don't you find it entertaining?"

"I can't tear my eyes away from it, if that's what you mean by entertaining, but I have to ask, is all of this real?" He stuck a piece of apple in his mouth and chewed. "Or is it an illusion? Are these places you've been to?"

Trinos's smile was warm and radiant, creating a soothing vibration in his chest. He almost felt ashamed just for looking at her, and even when he tore his eyes away from her, he glanced at her perfect figure constantly. Trinos was a mystery. Powerful. Unlike anything he could imagine in this world, but real. He didn't know what to make of her, but he'd do anything she said.

"Do you want to keep watching, Corrin?"

He shrugged, staring back into the waters where a new image started to form. This time it was different. His jaw dropped. This time it was people he knew, and they were in danger. He felt his heart speed up inside his chest, eyes transfixed.

"Perhaps you'd rather see something," she stuck out her hand and the waters wavered, "more pleasant?"

"No-No!" he said, shoving his hands over the water. "I want to see how this ends."

The waters steadied, and the image cleared. Trinos leaned towards the fountain and said, "Me too."

CHAPTER 43

MELEGAL FELT HIS STOMACH TIGHTEN into knots.

The cleric's hair grew and thickened. His sagging jawline toughened. Sefron's disturbing features transformed into the countenance of a man full of strength and vitality. It was unlike anything Melegal had ever seen before. In seconds, Sefron went from a hapless weakling to a formidable foe that was about to kill him.

"Oh yes, Rat." Sefron's teeth were straight and strong. "You thought you would take me. Avenge the honor of a worthless little slut, but now, just imagine what I'll have in store for her the next time I see her. She'll think I'm handsome, will she not, you fool? She'll be having me instead of you."

Melegal wanted to scream for help, but his tongue shriveled in his mouth, and his throat was dry. The chaos surrounding him was in full force where men and underlings battled. The Keys skittered over the mosaic floor. In his mind, he could hear them, count them all. *One-Two-Three-Four-Five... Forget the Keys! Save yourself!*

"Oh, this feels so good." Saliva dripped from Sefron's mouth.

In horror, Melegal watched his own age spots and crooked fingers form. It felt like Sefron had the grip of an ogre. *Am I to die like this? A rotting old man?* His doubts overwhelmed him. His anger and surprise turned to shock and confusion. *What do I do?*

"Heh-heh-heh." Sefron gloated, licking his lips. "It's time to die, Melegal."

Die? He let out a feeble cough. The air in his lungs felt thin. For the first time in his life, he wheezed. He was confused.

"Ha! Painful, isn't it?"

Melegal shook his head. *Can't let this happen! What do I do?* His mind was drifting. The pain was growing. His focus deteriorating.

"I think I might have what's left of you for soup. Melegal stew, stirred with your own bones and sautéed with your eyeballs."

Now, Melegal's eyes looked at Sefron like a complete stranger. He tried to withdraw. Fear overwhelmed his feeble mind. *Let go! Let go! Let go!*

The hat on his head ignited.

Sefron's grip popped open, eyes blinking, shaking his head.

"Why—why did I let you go?" Sefron reached over, grabbed his staff and raised it over his head. "No matter, I'll just bash your sock ridden he—"

Glitch!

Melegal stabbed him in the heart, plunging his blade hilt-deep in the chest.

"No!" Sefron coughed up blood, groaned, and gurgled before falling over, dead.

Melegal pulled out his dagger and stabbed him once more.

Sefron's stare was glassy, and the cleric's body reverted back to normal.

Filthy Bastard.

Melegal fell flat on his back, sucking for air. Rolling onto his belly, he groaned. "Slat, I feel like I'm a hundred years old." He crawled over the floor, aching from head to toe.

Nearby, Creed was about to die.

So much for him.

He turned his attention elsewhere. *Get to one of the doors!* He had a Key; he could still feel it, but at the rate he was moving the nearest door might as well have been a mile away. Going up the stairs looked impossible. Everyone was fighting everything everywhere.

Bone, I'm not going anywhere! I might as well die right here.

Clang!

The sound of clashing steel was music to Creed's ears. He rolled away and sprang to his feet, limping. The underling, Kierway, was tangled with a big, ugly menace of a man he would not have known had he not called Lord Almen Father. Tonio had changed.

"I like these odds!"

Rejuvenated, Creed jumped into the fray, stabbing his gleaming sword.

On the other side of Kierway, the big ugly brute hammered away with fast, heavy blows.

Kierway parried, the man on one side, the monster on the other, with speed and expertise Creed never before imagined. Still, Kierway was hobbled, blood dripping from his thigh onto the blood-sucking floor. *Wear him down!*

Bang! Bang! Bang!

Creed pounded at the underling's steel. Now, Kierway's chest began to heave, and sweat dripped from his nose.

Stab!

Kierway poked straight through the monster's belly and ripped it out.

The monster grinned.

"You're no man!" Kierway exclaimed, side stepping a heavy swing and chopping into its leg.

"Nay, underling. I'm a monster the likes you've never seen!"

It chopped high.

Creed sliced low.

Kierway howled, tumbling to the floor.

The Bloodhound swordsman felt his sword hit bone.

Kierway's sword clattered over the stones; with the other one, he still parried. In the next instant, Kierway stuck a small whistle in his mouth and blew.

Creed smacked the whistle from Kierway's lips with his blade.

Two more underlings emerged, but Tonio was already assaulting them.

"Time to finish this!"

"Hah, Human! You think you've defeated me. I still have one sword," Kierway said, rising.

"And a really bad limp." Creed huffed. He didn't have much left in him, if anything at all.

"Tell you what, Human. Let's settle this with a draw." Kierway lifted his eyes and made the motion to sheath his sword.

"You first." Creed panted, wiping the sweat from his brow.

Kierway slid his steel over his back and extended his hands. "Now you?"

Creed did the same, over his hip.

"First one out gets the first swing." A wicked smile formed on Kierway's lips.

Creed swallowed the little spit he had left. He'd never been beaten in a draw, but this underling was quick. At least it was an honorable way to go. At least he'd bought more time to live. *Come on, Creed! Think of all those years of training. All those Royals snubbing you. Fight or die.*

"On my wink, Underling."

"Perfect." Kierway casually dropped his hand over his head.

Creed took a half breath, cleared his mind and focused. *One. Two. Three.* He blinked one eye and drew.

Kierway's blade was already out.

Impossible!

Chapter 44

MELEGAL INCHED HIS WAY OVER the floor towards the nearest door in sight. *Look away! Look away!* So far, his plan seemed to be working, either from his hat, or the confusion that was going on around him. *Not my kind of party. Look Away! Look away!* He had to go at least two dozen feet more, every movement in his joints stiff and painful. Still, he was aware of everything.

Jarla cut an underling down with a stroke to its throat.

Lord Almen buried a nasty-looking dagger in the spine of another.

Tonio and Creed battled the one called Kierway with flashes of lightning and the resounding sound of steel meeting steel.

No, it wasn't his kind of party at all. *Vee! I need you. Come through that door any second now.* Grumbling, he slid over the floor: one foot closer, then two.

Down the stairs the underlings kept coming: one to a man, then two.

All the while, the floor seemed to wriggle, draining the life of the fallen, turning their bodies to husks.

They'll never make it out of this.

Everything was happening so fast, but he was moving so slow. *What did that Cleric do to me?* He clutched at the Key inside his clothes and touched something else. *What is that?* Curious, he produced the black rectangular case he'd take from Lord Almen's study above. Opening it, he found a wand-shaped rod made of dark wood with ornate carvings.

Out of nowhere, Lord Almen came and snatched it from his hand. "You just gave your worthless life a few more precious moments, Detective. Enjoy them while they last." Lord Almen snapped his wrist. The rod flared with life, a glowing purple tendril of energy extending from it.

Melegal shielded his tired eyes.

WUHPAZZ!

Two underlings whirled on Lord Almen, ruby eyes wide.

"Taste this, underfiends!" Lord Almen stroked the mystic whip of energy.

WUHPAZZ!

It sheered the arm off one, shooting blood over the room.

WUHPAZZ!

It coiled around the other one's neck. Its skin sizzled. Its eyes rolled up under its head.

Lord Almen popped its head from its shoulders with a yank, and then methodically made his way around the chamber.

The underlings, even the armored ones, were cut up with the whip, like butter with a hot knife.

WUHPAZZ! WUHPAZZ! WUHPAZZ!

Melegal, keeping his eye on Almen, continued towards the door. *I'm going to steal that... again.* Less than ten feet away. *I'm going to make it out of this slat hole!* Five feet away.

WUHPAZZ! WUHPAZZ!

Good for you, Lord Arsehole! He reached inside his shirt and wrapped his hand around the Key. He was all alone. Out of the corner of his eye, he caught someone else.

A golden-eyed underling floated in. Surveying the room, it shook its head, sneered, and opened its mouth.

Melegal's hat pulsated on his head. *Move!* Mustering all the strength he had, he lunged for the door.

A single word burst forth from the golden-eyed underling, turning the chamber asunder.

A wave of energy slammed into Melegal, jarring every bone, every fiber. The Key fell from his grasp, but he didn't hear it land. All he wanted to do was cover his head. Instead, he collapsed, unable to move, hands twitching. He'd never felt anything so painful before. *Please don't do that again. Kill me first instead.*

In the center of the room, Lord Almen, Jarla, Creed and all the underlings aside from Kierway were sprawled out over the floor. Alive or dead, he did not know.

Tonio still stood, listlessly dragging a gore-dripping sword around the room.

Melegal's Key twinkled nearby.

He stretched out his fingers. *So close.*

Kierway stepped on his hand and picked up the Key.

Melegal's vision faded. The last thing he saw was Kierway's dripping blade.

Will death be as painful as life on Bish?

Chapter 45

"**I**'m hungry." Brak moaned.

"You aren't as hungry as me," Georgio shot back, pushing back his sweaty brown locks. "Nobody gets as hungry as me!"

"Am too, hungrier!"

"Please stop it! Both of you," Jubilee shouted from Quickster's saddle. "You two idiots ate all our food!"

Billip wanted to kill both the young men. They'd all departed the City of Bone in a rush, but were amply supplied, a couple of weeks' worth anyway. But three days into it, the food was almost gone, with maybe a day left, maybe two, and it was still at least another week to make the City of Three.

"I didn't eat it all; he did," Georgio said.

Brak, whose big feet shoved the dirt like a plow, chucked a rock at Georgio, smacking him hard in the back. "I'm going to cram the next one in your biscuit hole, so you'll be swallowing your teeth."

Good, Billip thought, stopping to look. *I hope they beat each other to death.*

Georgio picked up a rock as big as his hand and slung it back. "Eat this!"

Brak jerked his forearm up.

The rock skipped off his wrist and clocked him in the head, drawing blood.

Brak's eyes widened then buckled, his big face drawing up. "You're going to die for that!"

Georgio widened his arms and slapped his chest. "I'd like to see you try, you droopy face bastard!"

"You shut up, Georgio!" Jubilee shouted. "Go beat the crap out of him, Brak!"

Closing the distance in two long strides, Brak took the first swing.

Georgio raised his arms up, blocking the blow and laughing. "You're too slow for me, Goon. I'm going to pummel you—*oof!*"

Brak upper-cutted him in the belly, lifting him from his feet.

Billip winced.

Jubilee gasped.

Face reddened, Georgio scrambled to his feet and charged. Slamming into Brak, he lifted the bigger young man from his feet and drove him into the ground. Georgio's fists hammered into Brak, hitting ribs, face and gut. "You're gonna pay for that! I'm gonna beat you to death!"

Brak, the bigger and much older-looking of the two, had his hands full.

Georgio, a big young man himself, was the quicker of the two, sneaking in punches through Brak's blocking forearms.

Billip yawned. He'd seen old three legged dogs fight better.

"Get him, Brak!" Jubilee yelled, shadow boxing in the air. "Bust his jaw so he can't eat any more."

Over the dirt they tussled, kicking up dust, yelling and growling at eat other.

"I'm going to kill you!"

"I hate you!"

"You skinny ogre!"

"Potbellied urchin!"

Billip took a small sip from his canteen, which was getting light. They'd run out of water soon. The past day had worried him. Normally, hunting game of some sort, be it a pheasant or an Outland fox, wasn't much of a problem, but thanks to the mass exodus from the south, game was harder to come by. And Billip had led them on a more difficult path as well, fearing that other weary travelers would be after them or the meat of Quickster.

He shook his head.

Only days ago, he'd been dead set on staying in the City of Bone, helping Trinos to fight and battle the underlings. The next thing he knew, he was leading the young men and Jubilee north towards the City of Three. Did Melegal talk him into it, or was it something Trinos had done? *I'm going to get that thief one of these days.*

Turning his attention away from the mirages that littered the barren landscape in the distance and back to the boys, he shook his head.

Georgio had his meaty fingers around Brak's neck, and Brak had his around Georgio's.

"Stop them, Billip!" Jubilee said.

He waved her off.

Crack!

"Ow!" Brak exclaimed.

Crack!

"Ow!" Georgio moaned.

Nikkel stood over them, his father's club in his hand.

Both young men panted for breath. Brak wiped the dust and blood from his nose, and Georgio popped his dislocated finger back into place, grimacing.

Something tugged at Billip's heart as he saw Nikkel standing there with Mikkel's club in his hand. The strapping young man would be a spitting image of his father in a few more years.

Rubbing his head, Georgio said, "What did you do that for, Nikkel? I was winning."

"Were not," Brak said. "I'm so hungry."

"I'm hungrier," said Georgio.

Nikkel, who'd been glum and quiet ever since they left, showed the slightest smile.

"Well, Nikkel," Billip said, "You found something, didn't you?"

Nikkel shrugged his muscular shoulder. "I think so. Come on."

Following Nikkel and Billip, Georgio glanced over his shoulder from time to time. Jubilee sat on Quickster's back, frowning and holding her stomach. The girl looked like she hadn't eaten in days, and her hazel eyes were sagging. Beside her and Quickster, Brak walked in long slow strides, but he was able to keep up, eyes forward, chin up and casting a scowl at Georgio before looking away.

Georgio clenched his fingers in and out of a fist. Even though he healed quickly, they were still sore. Hitting Brak was like hitting rock. The man, or young man, whatever he was, was tough. Unnaturally so, but so was Georgio.

"What are you looking at?" Jubilee said. "You're fortunate, you know. Brak could have killed you. He was holding back."

Georgio turned and stopped.

"You want to walk or ride?"

"I'm a Royal, you should know," she said, folding her arms across her scrawny chest.

Georgio rolled his eyes. Jubilee had made it a point to mention that at least a dozen times since they left, and he was getting sick of it. And if she was a Royal, how'd she wind up with them? *Venir's right: all Royals are a pain in the arse.*

"Quickster is mine, little girl, and if you don't mind your mouth, I'll have him buck you from the saddle." He glared at her and put his fingers to his mouth, ready to whistle.

Jubilee looked away and mumbled something under her breath.

"What was that?"

She tightened the cloak around her body and said nothing.

He glared at Brak.

The big man stood at Jubilee's side like a watchdog.

"You three quit boogering around, else we'll leave you!" Billip said. "And don't tempt us! We'd all have been much better off if we left you to begin with!"

Georgio didn't even bother to run and catch up. He didn't have the energy, and it didn't seem that Jubilee or Brak did either. Instead, they followed the men up ahead, one ravenous step after the other under the blistering heat.

As for Brak, Georgio still hadn't sorted out all of his thoughts on him. He hadn't even seen the big man smile as of yet, and that disturbed him. Brak's face was familiar. Like Venir's but different. If it weren't for the man's blue eyes, he'd have little resemblance at all. Brak was quiet, whereas Venir was loud. It just didn't sit well. Other than that, when they weren't fighting over food, Brak was alright.

He put his canteen to his lips. Nothing came out. "Ah..."

And of all things, the two of them could only talk about food, and that's what got them in trouble to begin with. Staying on watch one night, while the others slept, they got caught up with themselves, talking about food and eating most of it the same night. When Billip woke them up the next day, he was furious. Not only had they fallen asleep, but almost all the rations were gone. It seemed one had been blaming the other ever since, and they were taking their guilt and hunger out on one another.

Ahead, Billip and Nikkel stood on top of a ridge, talking to each other and pointing downward. Georgio climbed the rocky hill and stood between them.

"What is it?" Georgio said, looking over the ridge.

A field of cacti lay below: some tall, others round, some three times bigger than a man.

Georgio held his rumbling stomach. "So, Nikkel found some cactus. I don't see how that's of much help to us. Maybe the round ones would help, but there's no way to get to them. What are we supposed to do, Nikkel? Feed on Cactus needles?"

Billip shot him a look. "There's game in those needles, Boy. All we have to do is roust it out."

"And how do you suppose we do that?" Jubilee said with a smug look on her face. "And what kind of game are we talking about?"

"Pheasant, antler rabbits, and foxes to start," Nikkel said. "Not to mention the water in the round husks."

"There's no way to get to them!" Georgio said. "It's impossible. Let's just keep moving north. All we've done now is waste time by moving east."

All of them were hungry and weary. Eyes were tired and full of grit. Their clothes and armor coated with Outland dust so thick you couldn't tell what color they were. They'd have been better off staying with the caravan, but Billip had talked them away from that. Now they stood, baking in the sun with nothing to eat or drink but sand and needles.

"Get your bows ready." Brak lowered himself over the ridge like a giant-sized sloth.

Jubilee jumped from her saddle. "Brak! What are you doing? Get back up here, Brak! Get back up here!"

"You fool, get up here!" Billip shouted. "We don't even have a plan yet! There're snakes down there, vipers and such. Step in a nest of those and you're in for! Slat, he's still going in."

Brak ambled down the incline another thirty feet before he stumbled and rolled into a wall of needles at the bottom. Groaning, he got up and started to growl.

"Hungry." He pulled Tonio's sword from its sheath. "Tired of being hungry."

Georgio looked at Jubilee and the others, swallowing. "What's wrong with him?"

There was a wild look to the man. An inferno erupting within. The man Georgio had wrestled with moments ago was gone, replaced by something else, something savage.

"Oooooh," Jubilee said. She took her place beside Billip. "I've seen this before."

In a clap of thunder, Brak turned from man to monster, hacking furiously through the impassable wall of needles.

"He's gone mad," Billip exclaimed, readying his bow.

"No, he's gone berserk!" Nikkel said.

"RAWR!"

Georgio hopped back. The maddened sound of Brak's voice rose the hair on his arms.

Brak hewed through the green cacti and needles like tall grass. A wild man.

"That fool's bound to get snake bit in there!" Billip said, drawing his bow string alongside his cheek. "Look!"

Three antlered rabbits, bigger than cats, darted across the valley of cacti.

Twang!

Clatch-Zip!

One rabbit tumbled into the dust with two holes in it.

"You got him!" Jubilee shouted.

"Nikkel, you shot mine!" Billip said. "You take the rear; I take the front." He nocked another arrow. "That's how Mikkel and I used to go."

Nikkel cranked back the line on his crossbow.

"Got it!"

A silence fell. They all watched the rustling of the towering cacti swaying back and forth, many falling down under the sub-human roars of Brak the Berserker.

"What kind of man fights cactus?" Nikkel exclaimed, eyeing Jubilee.

"A hungry one. A very hungry one."

"Georgio," Billip said, "Get down there and fetch that rabbit before a fox gets it."

"But…" He looked toward the path Brak had created. "What about—"

"Get your hungry arse down there! Run back up here if you're scared!"

A bloom of pheasant burst out of the cacti and into the air.

Clatch-zip!

"Hold your shot, Nikkel!" Billip said, "You have to wait till they clear the grove. Slat. Do I have to do it all myself?"

Twang!

Twang!

Two rock pheasants spiraled out of the sky, falling along the jagged rim.

"Get down there!" Billip ordered, nocking his bow and searching the grove.

"RAWR!"

Georgio's boots slid over the slope, over the loose rocks and dirt, until he hit bottom and fell on his back. "Blast it!" He plucked needles eight inches long from his arms.

A dozen feet away, the rabbit lay just outside the cacti, an arrow and bolt in its belly and thigh.

He glanced down the path that Brak had hewn down. Cacti lay fallen and torn, leaving an ugly path behind, but there was room, just very little. He plucked another needle from his thigh. *I must look like a porcupine by now.* He grimaced.

"Toss up the rabbit," Nikkel yelled, his black face glistening with sweat.

"I will!" Aggravated, Georgio snatched it up off the ground and slung it up the hill. "Happy now?"

Nikkel disappeared, but he could see Jubilee's eyes peeping down at him over the lip of the ridge.

"Go get Brak," she ordered.

Georgio yelled back up, "You go get him!"

"You're already down there, Stupid! Besides, you ate all the food too! So go fetch it!"

"Aw, I'm going!" He stomped off into the cacti.

She was right, but he wasn't very comfortable going after Brak, not after the last look he'd seen in the man's eyes. It wasn't human. It was something else. Something that rent flesh from bones with its teeth or bare hands. *He can't kill me. He can't kill me. Could he eat me?* He shook his head. *He would have to be hungrier than I am, to eat me.*

Tip-toeing his way down the path, he was twenty yards in before he heard Brak's mad snarling and mutterings again. It tickled his spine.

"Brak," he said, barely audible.

White-knuckled hand on hilt, he took a deep breath and forged ahead, painful needles biting into him time and time again. He could hear Billip calling out for him. *If they want me, they can come and find me themselves.*

"Blasted needles!" he cursed, wiping the sweat from his eyes. There was no avoiding them, no matter how much he tried, and they burned too.

Twenty feet deeper, he twisted and turned.

Ahead, a small clearing opened up, with Brak standing in the middle, plucking a yellow fruit from a plant Georgio had never seen before. Two at a time, Brak was stuffing them in his mouth, chomping and squirting the pulp down his chin and jaw. The man had more needles in him than Georgio could ever count. They were in his face, his arms, thighs… Tiny droplets of blood ran over his face and down his clothes. It was painful to look at. How Brak ate only fruit and no needles, he didn't know.

"Alright Brak, you win; you're hungrier than I am." Georgio sheathed his sword. "What kind of fruit is that anyway?" He got closer. "I've never seen it before. It might be poisonous, you know."

Turning, Brak snarled, raising his sword.

Georgio froze.

"Easy now! Go ahead, eat all you want. I can wait." Georgio plucked some small needles from his meaty forearms. "But save some for everyone else."

Brak kept eating, grunting and swinging his sword.

"That used to be my sword, you know. Venir gave it to me."

Brak didn't understand. His face was still sub-human, a wild animal ready to strike at any moment. Georgio didn't care. He was too hungry. Too tired. He sat down.

As ten more fruit disappeared down Brak's throat, the sword in his arm lowered, and the growling stopped. Stuffing another fruit in his mouth, Brak blinked at Georgio and held his hand out. "Hungry?"

Georgio nodded, extending his hand.

"Good," Brak said, tossing it over. A smile riddled in needles crossed his lips.

A long shadow rose up behind Brak. It was a snake. Big, thick and hooded. Eyes like emeralds and a red flicking tongue.

"Brak, look out!"

Brak turned, but too late. The snake sank its fangs into the back of the big man's shoulder.

Georgio jumped to his feet and ripped his sword out.

Two more snakes slithered from beneath the cacti, rearing up and blocking his path.

Georgio struck first, clipping one's pale yellow underbelly.

Something like a hot knife sank deep into his thigh, numbing his leg.

Instantly, the bright light of the suns swirled.

CHAPTER 46

THE GIANT'S FEET MADE A cloud of dust with every step.

Listless and weary, robes dragging on the ground, Fogle Boon followed Barton. His sunburnt face peered into the clouds. Cass was gone again, and the suns of Bish had already set twice since then. He was miserable. Sick.

"Hold up." He fell to his knees.

Barton stopped and turned, scratching his head. "What are you stopping for, Wizard? We're almost there."

Fogle scanned the area. There was nothing aside from the bone trees and tiny lizards that scurried across the ground. Still, he'd been following Barton, wandering aimlessly, empty, with no idea where they were going. He hadn't had any luck finding the remnants of his ebony hawk, Inky. If he ever did, he could summon it again. He wiped his cracked lips on his dusty sleeve and spat.

"Barton getting thirsty. Make water, Wizard. Make water now." Opening a mouth that was big enough to swallow Fogle whole, the giant stuck his enormous tongue out, pointing at it. "Dry. Need water. Make water, Wizard."

He could make water, but he didn't want to. Instead, he wanted to suffer. He deserved that much. *I failed, Cass. I deserve to die. Right here. I'll just wither away into the rock and stone.* He pulled his knees to his chest and dipped his head between them.

"Just go on without me, Barton."

"What?"

Shaking his head, he said it again, louder. "Just go on without me!" He could hear Barton scratching his head.

Barton took a seat beside him. "Ah. Wizard still sad that Blackie take his woman?"

He felt a big hand patting his back. It knocked the breath from him. "Will you just go away!"

"Sheesh, Wizard getting grumpy. Make water, Wizard, so we can be happy. Barton is thirsty."

He looked up at Barton. The reddened dot inside the giant's disfigured eye stared back at him, unable to blink. The good eye shifted back and forth.

"Barton, what makes you think I can make water?"

"You're a Wizard. You can do anything, right?"

"No, if I could do anything, we wouldn't be lost out here. I'd have killed that dragon too. And Cass would be with me."

"Hmmm." Barton stretched out his arms. "But you can make water, can't you?"

No sense in him suffering. I guess I can make myself not drink it. And I only hope the spell works.

"Maybe." Fogle dusted off his hands and got back up. "But, I need to know something, Barton."

"What?"

"Do you think Cass is dead or alive?"

Barton shrugged.

Fogle felt his face redden. He'd been asking questions on and off, but the giant was reluctant to help with anything. All Barton wanted to do was find Venir and get his toys. And for some odd reason, the giant seemed to know where he was going, which left Fogle feeling more lost than he already was. *I wish Boon were here. He'd know something about that dragon. Why didn't that old fool come with us? Why!*

"Tell me something, Barton. Give me some hope at least." He kicked Barton in the toe.

"Ow!" Barton grabbed his toe and hopped up and down, big eye blinking. "What did you do that for?"

Fogle limped away, clutching his head. He wanted to pull his hair out. *What am I doing? Can I not outwit a giant now?* He looked up at the clouds. "Pull it together!"

Barton got up, looked up into the sky and said, "Pull what?"

"Tell you what, Barton: I'll make barrels of water, more than we could use in a month, but you have to help me find Cass."

"Blackie took her; she's gone."

"That's not going to get you any water, Barton. You'll have to do better than that."

Barton folded his arms over his chest. "Make the water first, Wizard."

The shadow the giant cast when he looked up at him gave Fogle little comfort. It made him feel insignificant. He had once been the cockiest mage in the City of Three, and now he was a rattled mess. It made him angry. He summoned his energy, filling his lungs with power.

"ANSWER ME, GIANT! OR DRINK YOU WILL NOT!"

Barton took a step back, covering his face. Peeking through his forearms, disfigured face bunched up, he said, "Yes! Yes! I will tell! I will tell!"

That felt good!

Fogle hadn't often used the Wizards Voice before, always feeling it was more show than effect. *I'm going to have to use that more often.*

"OUT WITH IT!"

Barton's lips tightened.

"BARTON…"

"Ah, Blackie will take her to the giants' castle." He lowered his voice. "Or to his lair. Many bones there. Many bones of the dead."

The way Barton said it didn't seem genuine.

"ARE YOU LYING, GIANT? I DON'T LIKE LIARS!"

Barton covered his face again. "No bones! No bones! Just the castle. Blackie takes people to the castle, and they never leave there. Impossible."

"You will take me there then." The power in his voice was gone.

"No! Barton will not go back there. You'll go yourself. Now make my water. My throat hurts."

Fogle rubbed his throat. It felt like he'd swallowed a mouthful of dirt now. "Hold out your hands and make a cup," he managed in a dry voice.

Waving his hand over his water skin, he summoned the spell. "Decanterous! Everless! Fill!" He tipped the water skin over. Clear liquid poured out like a rushing spring.

Barton sucked up a dozen handfuls, and Fogle, head riddled with guilt, thoughts only on Cass, drank until his throat no longer burned. He capped the water skin.

"Feel better now?"

"Much." Barton patted his stomach. It rumbled like a giant bullfrog. "Now make food."

Fogle laughed. "Water will have to do for now. Plenty of that. If you want food, you'll have to hunt it yourself."

"Alright." Barton wandered off.

"Barton!"

The giant didn't slow.

"Barton, where are you going?"

Barton stopped and turned. "To find the doggie and get my toys."

"What about Cass? You need to help me go and find Cass!"

"She isn't going anywhere. Barton not going back there, but you help Barton find the doggy and the toys, I'll take you there." His smile was wide and creepy. "I promise."

They walked, suns down to suns up, resting little in between.

Fogle, even with all the water, was exhausted, his legs shaking with every step. He'd given up on trying to convince Barton to go back. The little giant wouldn't listen. And Fogle didn't believe all of what Barton said about the castle and Cass being there and safe. He remembered those citrine eyes of the dragon. They had a murderous intent. *Is she dead?*

He stumbled and fell to his knees.

"Get up, Wizard."

Fogle didn't move. Instead, he lay staring into the sky, hoping to see a black dragon pass by. *I deserve to die here. Bake my flesh, Bish. I'll make a fine meal for the buzzards of this lousy world.*

Barton kept on walking.

Chapter 47

P AIN. IT WAS ALL THAT remained of Venir's life. His burning skin looked like raw meat on his back, and there was little left to be seen of his tattoo. Tuuth had whipped him until the rawhide was soaked with blood. Venir had fought the first few hours, making derogatory comments about the orc and his kind.

"That's a nice lash. Did you borrow it from your mother?"

Wupash!

"What's it like being an orc? Stinking and stupid all the time?"

Wupash!

"Is your arm getting tired yet? My back's just getting warmed up!"

Wupash!

"Bone! That's feels good!

Wupash!

"Say, Tuuth, don't they think you can do anything harder than this?"

Wupash!

"If I survive this, I'm going to skin your hide and make a whip out of you!"

Wupash!

It had gone on like that, back and forth, until Venir couldn't say a word, or remember his name. Unable to wake him after the first day, they had dragged him off to his cell, only to drag him back out again and hitch him to the post. That was three days ago.

Wupash!

He remembered watching the Royal Riders stripped of their armor, mutilated, tortured, buried and burning. He saw how the underlings celebrated their handiwork. They'd strolled inside the fort, arm in arm, mugs raised high and chanting strange sounds that would make hound dogs cry. It all made Venir sick. What he could remember of it.

Still, some men survived. Chained and cuffed from the neck to ankles, they served, performing one menial task after the other. Venir caught glimpses of it here and there, but his memories faded until he worked again to suffer another tortuous day.

Now, lying face down in the slime of his cell, he stirred. It was dark, but a pool of yellow light shone through the door. He tried to sit up. Something was on his back, picking at it.

"Wha—?" he mumbled, forcing himself up.

He heard a buzz.

A sharp stabbing pain shot through his back to his chest.

He slammed his mangled back into the moldy wall.

Something crunched and squished.

A sliver of fear raced through him. His blood coursed behind his ears. Something was feeding on him. Something had chewed up his legs, now it felt like bugs were making a nest in his back.

"Nnn—"

He slammed his back into the wall again. Bright spots of light burst in his eyes, leaving him woozy. He sagged down, slumping to the floor.

"Venir."

His eyes popped open, searching.

"Venir."

Somewhere, a tiny voice was speaking to him.

"Lie still, you idiot, and stop squishing the bugs. They're healing you."

"Slim?"

"Quiet."

He felt tiny insect legs crawling over his shoulder to his ear.

"Yes, it's Slim, and I'm getting you patched up... again."

Something crawled off his shoulder and stood before him. It was an insect, like a mantis, but mostly had Slim's face, except brownish green and bug-eyed.

"Uh..."

"Just be still, you big fool!" Slim put his insect arm to his face. "This wouldn't be so bad if you weren't so stubborn. As soon as that white orc whips you, pretend to pass out. Stop running your mouth. Bish, you've got a lot of nerve calling him stupid and stubborn. You should be dead already, you fool, but I've been having the bugs patch you up. You heal fast. Very fast."

A bug the size of Venir's finger that looked like part cricket, part spider scurried up to Slim's mantis-like form. Its antenna twitched back and forth in short furious motions, then it scurried away.

"Listen, you big lout: you smash any more of them, they're leaving, so just lie there and be still. I can't keep you alive forever, you know."

"Water."

Motioning to a stone bowl that was tipped over, Slim shook his head. "You already drank it. You don't remember, do you?"

"Just get out of here, Slim. Escape, tell others. There's nothing more you can do here. If I die here, then I die here. Enough have died here already. You don't need to die too."

"That's a great idea, but the safest place right now is here, under the enemy's nose. I've been keeping a look out. More underlings have come since we rode in here, and they talk as if the City of Bone has fallen. They talk as if they've conquered the world, Venir." Slim blinked his glowing bug eyes. "I've seen it pretty bad on Bish before, but this? I've never seen it this bad, but something's got to happen. It just can't keep going like this. It can't."

Venir never figured Slim's age, but for all he knew, he was as old as Mood. As for the underlings, he'd never seen them with such an upper hand before either. Usually, he'd been able to face them with the mystic armament when things got bad, but now it was gone. Perhaps the underlings had it. *If I could wrap my paws around Brool's handle one last time! Bone!*

"Just do what you can and go, Slim. It's like you said, 'Bish Happens.'"

"I did say that, didn't I? Huh, that's a good one." He scurried over Venir's shoulder and spoke in his ear. "Now you just be still while I have the bugs stitch you up. And remember, keep your mouth closed tomorrow. You're better off dying digging holes than being whipped to death, I'd figure. Of course, I'm a lot smarter than you."

"Thanks, Slim—Yeouch!"

It felt like something crawled into his spine.

"Be still, I say! It's going to hurt, you know. Yesterday you slept right through it, leaving me wondering if you were getting better or worse."

"Worse." Venir bit his lip. Helpless, he lay there listening to Slim guiding the creatures all over his back. "Don't you have any of that blue ointment?"

"Heh, the underlings would sniff me out in a second if I used that. I've got it hidden. Besides, I'm saving the good stuff for me."

"Great…" Venir said just before dozing off.

Slim the Healer kept his astonishment to himself. Venir should have been dead. The man's back was a grotesque mat of blood and skin. The first time he saw it, he felt his own skin turn inside out. Yet somehow, Venir had prevailed.

The bugs scurried over Venir's back, attacking the puss that seeped through the pores. *If he gets the fever, he will be dead.* If he did, there was no way of helping the man, no way at all. Still, it was a mystery. What kept Venir together this long? One by one, the bugs pushed the flaps of skin back into place and sealed them up with a thick gummy spit.

"Aside from all the blood, you don't look half bad," he said, dusting his insect hands off. "I can even see the tattoo. 'V'. Hmmm, what did that drunken fool put it on there for? What was her name? Vorla? Ah, time to crawl back into my hole. Sleep well, Venir, and don't run your mouth tomorrow."

Venir snored.

"That might be a good thing."

On his six insect legs, he made his way from Venir's cell and followed the other bugs into a small hole they had bored into the interior of the fort's wall. Squeezing through the dark and narrow path, he popped into a hollowed-out room inside the massive log from the Great Forest of Bish, big enough for several men. Exhausted, he reverted back to his normal form and stretched out in the dim green light provided by the Elga Bugs from the glowing sacks on their bellies.

Resting the best he could, he couldn't help but worry—as he had on all the previous nights—that Venir would not return alive.

"How much will the underlings put up with, and how much more can he take?" Closing his eyes, he whisked his hand, and the Elga bug lights went dim.

If Venir's no longer The Darkslayer, then who is?

Chapter 48

C ASTLE ALMEN WAS NO LONGER under siege. It was overtaken. Lord Almen sat on the marbled tile floor, arms shackled behind his back, and sighed. A corpse of one of his prized Shadow Sentries lay dead at his side, his mesh mask melted to his face. The rest of the room, his throne room, was in good order. But now, where there had been one high-backed chair of mahogany wood trimmed in the finest metal and jewels sat two. Both were empty at the moment.

His stomach rumbled as he shifted on the floor. He'd been fed, but very little, and he was stripped down to his shirt and trousers. All of his rings and baubles were gone. Closing his eyes and leaning back, the same thought raced through his mind.

How could I let this happen?

He rolled his shoulder and cracked his neck side to side. Something scurried out of the corner of the room. A spider, big as a dog and quick as a cat, on silent legs crawled over towards him. Another nearly his size dropped from the ceiling, jaws opening and closing. They were the underlings' watch dogs. Creepy things. Hairy black creatures with white stripes and venomous teeth that he'd seen suck the marrow from his own nephew's bones two days hence. The revolting sound still rang inside his head. The sucking. The screaming. The anguish. For the most part, Lord Almen delivered quick and silent deaths, but the underlings enjoyed the torment at another level. They delighted in the suffering of others.

He remained still, beads of sweat dripping from his nose onto the floor. A minute passed, then two before the spiders backed away and curled up out of sight.

How did I let this happen?

Until now, there had never been a day when Lord Almen hadn't felt in control, but other things had led to his fall. Melegal had undone him. Sefron had betrayed him. Most men dared not look him in the eye, nor did they have the courage to attack him. But Melegal had. As for Sefron, the man's own lust and fear of the underlings clearly led to his betrayal. However, Lord Almen could not imagine why Melegal had tried to kill him. He raced through that day. What had happened before Melegal stabbed him? Had Melegal done it on his own? Certainly he'd wanted to. Or had Leezir the Slerg pulled off a suggestion? *Hmmm…*

Lord Almen thought through it until his lids became heavy and he drifted into sleep.

Clap!

His head snapped up.

"Almen," a silver-eyed underling named Verbard said, "rise up."

He nodded.

The underling sat on one of the thrones, his golden-eyed brother, Catten, at his side. Between them stood another creature, a hulking black humanoid that reminded him of a panther. The underlings' eyes pierced him as he rose up to stand tall. With a single word, he felt one or the other could destroy him. He'd dealt with underlings before, but not like this. The cleric Oran had been formidable, but the might of these two? Another scale. No, these two had made his finest magi look like carnival enchanters: leaving one in a pile of ashes, the other with a gaping hole in his chest.

"The time has come to negotiate," Verbard said.

"With?" Almen replied.

Catten tapped his fingernails on the arm rest, a callous look on his face.

Verbard took a deep draw through his nose.

"Do you smell that, Almen? The delicious scent, so pungent, so sweet? A dead child? A dead wife, perhaps?" Verbard rubbed the rat-like fur under his chin.

It wasn't what Lord Almen smelled that bothered him so much as what he didn't smell. His castle had always been filled with fresh flowers and the burning of scented candles, oils and such. Now, the beauty of his Castle—that he and Lorda took so much pride in—was gone. The gardens trampled and smeared in blood. Many of his men buried in them. As for Lorda, he had no idea if she lived or was dead, but the Keep had fallen a day later, after the rest of the castle fell. He could only presume she was dead. It was the best way to avoid manipulation.

"I smell death. Decay. What else is there?"

"More, much, much more." Verbard floated off his chair and right past him. "Come. I'll show you."

Lord Almen glanced at Catten and the Vicious. The underling filled his goblet with a bottle of wine, and the Vicious fell a half-step behind him and shoved him forward. He limped but kept up as Verbard made his way through Castle Almen as if it were his. Underlings were posted throughout the castle, their countenances evil and alert.

Grimacing, he followed Verbard into the keep, taking the stairs that led onto the roof. He was panting when he reached the top, rubbing the bandage on his leg where he'd been stabbed at the battle in the chamber.

Verbard floated still higher in the air, robes billowing, turning towards him. *Can you see it? Can you smell it?*

He heard it in his mind.

He did see it and smell it. Black smoke was rolling up over the great wall of the City of Bone, not on the inside but on the outside. Eyes watering, he covered his nose.

Play along, Almen. Play along.

Walking across the top of the keep and stepping into a small tower that led to its highest point, he got his first glimpse over the wall in years.

Underlings. Legions of them.

They were everywhere. It wasn't just underlings either, but giant spiders and strange creatures he'd never seen before, tossing one dead human onto one flaming pyre after the other. His fingertips went numb.

He looked Lord Verbard in the eye. "Would you have me negotiate the terms of surrender for the City of Bone?"

"Serve us well, Lord Almen. You and a select few of your choosing can be our liaisons."

Lord Almen had made deals with the underlings before. He'd supplied Oran with people for various poisons, potions and such. He'd even conspired with others to see the fall of Outpost Thirty-One. It had led to his rise from the 6th house in the City of Bone to the 3rd. But now, in hindsight, it seemed that move might also have led to this.

"I welcome the opportunity." He bowed. "How may I assist?"

"We just need to know which Castles need to fall first. You see, with the Keys, we can infiltrate any of them and slaughter them all. But 'Which falls first?' is the question."

Lord Almen wanted to laugh. *I can send the underlings to do my bidding for me! But to what end?*

"After that, you can negotiate with the weaker houses and on down. Once we control them, then we control everything."

"I see, Lord Verbard. And once they surrender, what are your plans for them? Slaughter? Slavery? A mass exodus into the Outland?"

"Those are excellent suggestions and most likely a great deal for them all, but you shouldn't worry about that. Not for your own sake."

Verbard pointed at Almen's chest and hissed.

"No, you should just worry about yourself."

Chapter 49

THE DUNGEONS BENEATH CASTLE ALMEN hadn't changed any over the past few months, but the guards had. Now, they were underlings. Wiry with gem-speckled eyes that didn't hesitate to punish if you so much as snored.

Melegal sat with his head between his bony knees, contemplating. Contemplating his next move. He'd been doing it for days, but he didn't have a next move.

Keys. Keys. The Keys. Wretched things got me into this mess. The wretched things could get me out.

Two underling guards in dark leather armor dragged a tall man in and shackled him inside an adjacent cell. Stripped down to his trousers, the man's chest was bruised and knotted with painful lumps.

Melegal could feel the man's green eyes on him, but he kept his head down.

The underlings didn't whip the quiet ones, but Creed, he couldn't help himself. You'd think someone of his ilk would know better.

"Ooof!"

An underling kicked Creed in the gut, locked the cell and walked away.

Don't speak. Don't speak. Don't speak.

Nearby were the rest of the survivors.

Jarla lay in her cell, facing the wall in the back. The Brigand Queen hadn't acknowledged any of them since they'd been there. Instead she, despite her condition, maintained her air of superiority somehow. Melegal wouldn't be surprised if she was there as more than a prisoner, but a spy. After all, she had assisted the underlings in getting into Outpost Thirty One.

What are you going to do, Rat? What?

Stripped down to his own trousers, Melegal might as well have been naked. His hat was gone. Worry gnawed at his stomach: that an underling had discovered its powers, powers that he himself had only recently begun to unlock. It had been long ago when he acquired it, and it had become a companion of sorts. He wasn't comfortable without it. Not at all.

Get the hat, get the Keys. Get the Keys, get the hat.

Hiding his yawn, he couldn't stop his stomach from rumbling.

One of the underling guards stepped over and banged on his cage.

He kept his head down, but was unable to contain the next loud sound his stomach made.

The ruby-eyed underling, brandishing a black club, opened the door to his cage, stepped inside, and cracked him in the head, drawing bright spots in his eyes. The underling drew back again.

Slat on this!

In a single motion, Melegal swept its legs out from under it, snatched its keys, scurried out, and slammed the door shut, locking the underling guard in his cell. He tossed the keys to Creed's outstretched arm.

Slice!

The jagged teeth of the other underling's sword ripped over his head.

Melegal leapt over a torment table, snapped up a spear from the wall, and braced himself. The creature, swift as a cat, batted the weapon away and lunged inside. Melegal twisted away, the underling's blade slicing the skin on his back.

What am I doing? What am I doing!

He knew he couldn't overpower the underling. They might be small and lithe, but their bodies were hardened like animals. He'd seen them rip overconfident men to pieces a time or two. The underling came at him, hard and fast. Melegal sidestepped again, pinned its sword arm on the table, and drove a long metal torture needle through its hand.

It screeched, ruby eyes widening, and then back-handed Melegal in the jaw.

His knees swayed.

The underling pounced on him. Its clawed fingers wrapped around his neck and dug into his skin.

Melegal's eyes bulged. *At least I killed Sefron. I'd kill him again if I could.*

Glitch!

The bloody tip of a sword burst through the underling's chest.

It fell over dead.

Creed stood tall, eyes cold and dangerous.

"Now this is more like it. Just what I've been saying all along." He grabbed Melegal's arm and pulled him up like a doll. "What's the plan now?"

"Yes, what is the plan, Fool?" Jarla pressed her angry face against the bars. "To get us all killed?"

"'Die doing something, or die doing nothing.' That's how I saw it." Melegal hunched over, catching his breath. "And I don't recall making you part of any plan. Any of you, for that matter."

Creed gave him a look.

"No offense. I needed you to kill that underling, but I didn't figure it'd take you so long to operate a keyhole."

"Why you sneaky little scarecrow," Creed was smiling. "I like it. But, I took a moment to kill that other underling first." He pointed to Melegal's cell.

The other underling lay back against the wall, a large gash in his head.

"At that point, I wasn't certain I needed you either." He winked. "But you won't be going anywhere without me." He wagged the dripping sword in Melegal face. "At least not without my sword sticking through you."

"Hah, hah, hah." Jarla was still sneering. "You don't have any plan. Do you, Fool?"

Actually, I do. Just not a very good one.

Melegal had learned many secrets about Castle Almen in his stay here, many thanks to Sefron. He knew of the secret rooms and corridors, not all, but some. He figured that should be enough to save himself.

"No, no I don't, but right about now, you're in the cage, not me."

Creed grabbed his shoulder and squeezed it. "We'll need all the strong arms we have if we're to carve our way out of here."

"Let out! Let out!"

It was Tonio's voice, crying out from behind a wooden door with a closed-off portal.

Melegal hadn't forgotten about the man, but he wished he had. The deranged man rattled even the underlings, who seemed to avoid him.

"We're going to need that big fellow too, you know." Creed was making his way around the room, gathering up weapons. "I don't know what he is, but he swings a heavy piece of steel like a needle. Let the monster out." Creed gazed at Jarla up and down. "Perhaps this raven-headed princess can control him."

"You dare! You, a misfit from the Royal hounds of the sewers?"

Creed forced a laugh, shoulders dipping.

"You have the cell keys, Creed. Do what you want." Melegal made his way over to the iron door. It didn't appear to be locked. He pressed his ear against it.

"Let out!" *Wham!*

Melegal shook his head. So far as he could tell, the way past the iron door was clear, for now, but they needed to move fast.

Just lead them out, Melegal. Once they start swinging, you'll disappear and be fleeing. Heh. Heh. Crafty as a serpent, I am.

"Let the monster out then," he said, looking at Jarla, "and Tonio too."

I hope she dies first.

Sword ready, Creed unlocked Jarla's cage.

"Idiot." She made her way across the room and sorted through the weapons on the table.

Melegal kept his eyes on her.

Tall, dark and arrogant. A Queen of Brigands indeed. Other than those hips and legs of hers, I'll never understand what Venir saw in the evil hag.

"Your word: you won't be stabbing any of us in the back, Jarla."

Her smile looked as dangerous as a viper. "Unlike you? No, I'll not be giving you my word, you little ghoul of a man. As a matter of fact, I see no reason to follow you." She came closer, sword ready. "For all I know, you'll lead us into a trap."

Creed stepped between them. "The underlings are the enemy now, Jarla. Survive their invasion. We can settle our differences later. Now, I'll give my word. You give yours, Jarla, and Detective, yours as well."

Bang! "Let out! Give Word! Let out!"

"The word of a liar is as useless as the slat of pigs." Jarla stuffed a dagger in the waistband of what was left of her clothes. "All men are liars. All men are filth. But I'll give you both my word—and my word is 'Slat on you both.'"

Melegal huffed a laugh.

That's good enough for me." Creed eyed her up and down again. "And if we do indeed survive this, I'll like to share some drinks."

"Pig!" She slung a pair of shackles at Creed.

He caught them against his chest and winked. "Just lighting a fire in you, Man-hater. Now, let's get on with this." He tossed the cuffs to the ground. "You've got some ornery ideas for such a fine woman."

Jarla's face reddened. "I'll clip your—"

"That's enough!" Melegal stepped around Jarla and strapped on a sword. "Creed, get the door."

Creed unlocked Tonio's door.

The tall half-dead man stepped outside, morbid and scary, rubbing the hole in his head.

Melegal's spine tingled.

Hate that man.

Even Jarla's breath hastened.

Creed's eyes were wary. "Grab some metal, Tonio. Detective, lead the way."

Swinging the dungeon door inward, Melegal felt something crawling in his stomach.

Why haven't they killed us already? What do they need with us, anyway?

He remembered what he'd seen and what he'd been told. The underlings would mutilate some and send them out to spread fear in the world.

Shouldn't we be dead or crippled?

Up the stairs he went, followed by Jarla, Creed and Tonio's heavy steps.

He'll get us all caught.

The dungeons beneath Castle Almen weren't deep, but more or less a sublevel of the basement with a lone entrance at the top. In this case, Melegal knew where he was, but there were places in the Castle he'd never explored. A lone door awaited them at the top. He knew it led into one of the main basement corridors. It was perfect. All they needed to do was overpower any guards, and Melegal knew a few secret corridors with hiding spots down there.

Alright, Rat. They fight. You run.

Running his fingers through his salt and pepper hair, he felt naked without his hat.

Forget it. Just run, Rat. Run!

He mouthed the next words to his followers.

"Ready?"

Creed nodded.

"One."

"Two."

He grabbed the door handle.

"Threeeeeeeeeee...."

The door transformed into a black mirage and enveloped them.

Suddenly, Melegal was free falling.

Creed was yelling.

Jarla was screaming.

In the next instant, he felt himself land hard on the ground. Spitting the dirt from his mouth, he sat up only to face the heads of many spears lowered in his face.

I know this place. All too well.

They were inside Castle Almen's arena.

"What kind of bloody magic was tha—ulp!"

Creed bit his tongue thanks to the barbed spear at his throat.

"Well, finally, some new opponents come." It was Master Kierway. "And just when I was beginning to wonder whether or not you would show."

Kierway wasn't alone. He was accompanied by several underlings, warriors one and all, being served by men and women, barely clothed, and shackled at the neck. One was kneeling by his side, holding up a plate of fruit. It was Lorda.

"Ah," Kierway rose up, "these will be much better opponents for my Juegen to spar with. The others," he gestured toward the wall of the arena, "didn't last so long."

At least a dozen human heads on spikes encircled the inner wall.

So this is what they were saving us for. Games. Underling games.

Melegal's head felt heavy, and he couldn't stop his chin from dipping. His stomach rumbled. All he could think about was Brak here in the arena. His wailing. His moaning.

How in Bish did I get here?

It was pretty clear that nothing was going to save him now. Not Brak, not Venir and not himself. All those years he fought to escape the horrors of the Castle, and he still wound up here. He locked his eyes on Lorda. She was still captivating despite the scrapes and bruises on her face, and he'd never seen her voluptuous body in such revealing clothing before.

"Who's that?" Creed whispered in his ear.

An underling jabbed the butt of a spear in the back of the Bloodhound's head.

"I hope they let me fight you first," Creed said, "Black fiend!"

Whack!

Creed hit the ground.

"Secure them all, except the skinny one," Kierway ordered, copper eyes on Melegal. "We'll whittle what little is left of him down first."

Melegal raised his brows and allowed himself a smile.

Lorda showed a grim smile back.

Well, it's over. Nothing like a little flirting before you're dead.

Chapter 50

"Watcha layin' there fer?" a gruff voice said. "That ain't what I had in mind when I taught you about adventurin'."

Fogle didn't move. He couldn't. Instead, he lay in the sun, baking like a biscuit in a roasting oven. Still, he forced his eyes open, trying to blink the hallucination away from his mind, his thoughts.

"Go away, Mood. I'm done for," he said with a dry throat.

"What's the matter? Did ye lose your little druid friend? And now yer tender heart is broken, so you quit? This is Bish. You quit, you die. Now get up!"

Fogle didn't. Instead, he closed his eyes, but the scent of Mood's cigar drifted into his nose.

This is one powerful hallucination.

For hours, maybe days, he'd lain there, letting his inner self fight it out. He'd failed. He wanted to go home. Crawl under a rock and bury himself.

He'd been here before. Back when Venir beat him. Busted his mind and his nose. A broken man, he'd left the Magi Roost. It had taken him years to understand his failures. His fears.

Now, those fears returned with a vengeance. The Outlands. The sweltering heat, the chronic battle to survive, and the threat of the unknown had rattled his brilliant mind.

I can't do this anymore. I can't.

"Just leave me alone," he said, rolling over.

"Get up, Wizard!" the gruff voice prodded. "Get up, else I'll kill you myself."

He curled up, covering his face.

"Go ahead," Fogle said. "If my hallucination doesn't kill me, I'm sure something else will. Perhaps a giant will step on me, or some bugs will eat my flesh," he cackled, "or a dragon will roast me like a log." He cackled again. "Or the underlings will cut my throat. So many ways to go. Getting killed by my imagination seems more soothing than the rest. So Mood, my long gone friend, I'm prepared for the worst."

A silence fell. Even the hot winds slowed. The scent of Mood's cigar drifted to his nose again. Fogle sighed. "That's much better." He curled up and pulled his robes tighter. "Sorry, Cass. I failed you."

A minute passed, maybe two.

"GET UP, I TELL YA!"

Fogle's eyes popped open. In the next moment, water was pouring over his head. Down it came, second after second, soaking his hair, his robes.

"GET UP!"

Spluttering a mouthful from his lips, he forced himself to an upright position. Water was still being poured over his head by the figure of a large stout man. When the water finally stopped, he wiped his eyes.

Two emerald eyes under bushy red brows were staring right at him.

"Mood? Are you real?"

"As real as a mole on an ogre's fanny." Mood puffed on a cigar stuck between his two meaty fingers. "Are you finished belly aching now?"

Fogle stretched out his arms and hugged him.

"But how? You were, well, in such bad shape." He patted the rocky muscles in Mood's thick shoulders.

"True, but I was still breathing. And I'm King of the Dwarves. Soon as I fell, the lady dwarves came running. They patched me up leagues away, where Eethum caught up with me."

That's when Fogle noticed Eethum, the big black dwarf, arms crossed over his long blood red beard, standing like a mighty oak. He wasn't alone either. More Black Beards, each just under five feet tall, but stout as keg barrels, sat on the back of dwarven horses.

Fogle couldn't hold his tongue from catching Mood and Eethum up on everything that had gone on.

"A dragon, ye say? Woot! It's been a long time since I've seen one of those," Mood said, taking a knee, wincing.

"Mood, you aren't fully well, are you?"

The ancient dwarf shot him a look. "Ye need to mind what you say, Wizard." He grabbed Fogle by the forearm and squeezed. "I'm well enough to snap you in two."

Biting his lip, Fogle tried to pull away. "No need to be so cranky. I was just concerned."

Mood squeezed harder. "You were what?"

The fingers on his hand went numb. "Nothing! Nothing!"

Mood released him and blew a puff of smoke in his face.

"Mind yer manners." Mood reached into a pouch on his trousers and tossed him something in a cloth.

Fogle unfolded it and found the remnants of Inky.

"Thanks," he said, fanning the smoke. "How'd you find me?"

Mood rolled his thick neck towards Eethum, who said, "We're Blood Rangers. Once we got yer scent, we could track you anywhere, but we did lose you for a bit." He glanced at Mood.

"I hate to admit. You disappeared into thin air."

Fogle knew what he was talking about. It was the spell Boon had cast that got them out of the jam when they fled a wave of underlings.

"Still, why can't you follow Chongo?"

"He doesn't have a scent."

Fogle raised an eyebrow. "I guess not."

Mood handed him his water skin. "Yer gonna need this. We've a ways to go." He grunted as he swung his leg up on his horse. "Get on."

Mood looked like a giant atop his dwarven Clydesdale, large axes strapped across his back.

"Where are we going? What about Cass?"

"We're going after that giant," Mood said, "Find him, most likely we'll find her. Now get on. Time's a wasting, and I suggest you find ye some good spells."

"Why's that?" Fogle said, getting on.

"'Member them giants that socked it to me?"

"Yes," Fogle said, looking over his shoulder as the horse lurched forward.

"Well, they ain't done. YAH!"

As the first dusk settled, Fogle got his first glimpse of green tree tops in the distance, but it brought him little relief. When he wasn't focusing on his spells, he was thinking about Cass and those piercing eyes of the Dragon that Barton called Blackie.

I'll get you back, Cass. I swear it. Even if I have to find a way to the Under-Bish all by myself.

Eethum led the way, followed by the Black Beards, then Mood and himself. The King of the Blood Rangers had little to say, however, unlike before. He seemed grim and angry for some reason. Fogle was about to ask him if something else was wrong when Eethum brought them to a halt less than a mile from the lush branches of the jungle.

Mood rode forward.

"You want two ranks or one?" Eethum asked, bushy red brows raising up and down.

"Two. But no more than thirty yards between us. It's as thick as my beard in there."

"Well, I'm certain the giant left a noticeable trail," Fogle said, dropping from the saddle and stretching his limbs.

Mood huffed.

"Wouldn't he?" Fogle said, gulping down some water, looking around. None of the dwarves had taken a single drink, now that he noticed, and now that he'd gotten used to it, he'd been sipping every hour. He held it out to Eethum. "Drink?"

The dwarf showed his teeth and shook his head.

"Trusting the giants are ye now, Little Wizard?"

"Well, no, just following him. But he's helped me, and I've helped him. I see no harm in it." He plugged his ever-flowing water skin. "Besides, he seems to know where Venir or Chongo is. Where else would he be going?"

Mood and Eethum just looked at him.

Fogle shrugged. "What? I'm not a dwarf, you know."

"A good thing fer us you ain't, Wizard. Now hush your mouth and get back on. We've got a ways to go."

Fogle pulled at his sweat-soaked robes. Hoping for relief in the shade of the jungle, as opposed to the dry Outland heat, he instead found himself overwhelmed by the chronic dampness of the humidity.

"Like walking through water," he muttered.

"Aye," Mood agreed, "but don't worry: you'll never get used to it."

They'd traveled through night, the jungle as black as a cave, before the dawn of a new light. Fogle found little comfort in it, swatting at mosquitos as big as his hand and smashing them on Mood's back.

"Ye want something?"

"Uh…" Fogle wiped his hand on his robes. "No… But, shouldn't we have caught up with Barton by now?"

"Barton? Is that what ye call yer friend?"

"Never mind."

Mood had been plenty clear on his hatred for the giants. He'd even shared a horrible tale of another one called Horace. The insane giant had slaughtered more than a hundred dwarves. Some of Mood's sires. One of his wives. But, how Mood captured the giant, tethered and killed him was another thing. It seemed the giants had a mystic way to come and go as they pleased. Fogle was curious about that.

"Look." Mood pointed his sausage-thick finger toward an opening in the trees.

Squinting, Fogle shook his head. "What?"

"Not thata way." Mood grabbed Fogle's chin and turned his head. "Thata way."

A stark log-made structure like a giant's home sat atop a mountainous hill.

"What is that?"

"Men call it Outpost Thirty-One or somethin'."

"Are you serious?" Fogle knew the history of the fallen outpost that gave the underlings the upper hand in the southern lands. 'Nothing on Bish has been the same since the fall of Outpost Thirty One,' the travelers from the south said.

It was rumored that whoever controlled Outpost Thirty-One controlled the South and would gain a foothold on the North. Now, it sat there alone, abandoned so far as he could tell. The logs that made up its framework were five times as thick as the surrounding forest trees. That was the other odd thing. The fort, a safe-haven for men, had been built by giants, they said. It reminded him of the City of Three, where a few structures still stood that marveled the others in size.

"Mood, you're a giant dwarf. Who built that? The giants?"

"It don't matter who built it. It only matters who's in it."

"Then who's in it?"

Mood shook his bushy bearded head and snorted the air.

"Well, I'll be slat on a stick. I think Venir is in there."

"Alive?"

"Don't know, but there's only one way to find out." Mood dug his boots into his horse and lead the Black Beards towards the mountain.

"I thought the fort was run by an army of underlings."

"So?"

"Well, there's only fifteen of us. Can I assume the King of the Dwarves has a plan?"

"I'll let ye know before we get there. It's still a bit of a ride ahead."

"That's not a plan."

"It's better than whatever you got."

CHAPTER 51

"ORDER UP! ORDER UP! ORDER UP!" Darlene clamored. "Move your boots, ladies! There's hungry fellows out there!"

"I heard you, Darlene!" Mercy said, grabbing a tray of food from the kitchen and rushing it over to a loud and eager table.

Kam had been rubbing the black polish on the bar for over an hour, trying to ignore the rough cut woman. Now, her elbow was sore, and her cheeks burned.

I'm going to kill her!

Over the past few days, the Magi Roost had been turned upside down and inside out. No longer the quaint establishment it once was, it was now a seedy den for travelers from all over the land. It hadn't ever been this bad before, not even when Venir was here. Not by a long shot. And all of Kam's patrons, many of whom she adored, were gone, replaced by anything from an orc to a halfling. The City of Three had become a harbor for Southern refugees, and it was a problem.

"I hope you aren't planning on going through with that."

Taking the dust rag off the stump of her hand and slinging it over her back, she turned and faced Scorch. The man's comely looks were startling. He'd been sitting in the same spot at the end of the bar for days. He never left, and she couldn't get used to it. But, she'd gotten used to it enough.

Eyeing her hand in the pickle jar and blowing her red locks from her face, she said, "And if I am? Are you going to cut off my other hand?"

"Certainly not. It was Darlene who did that, not I. But Kam, I must warn you: I'm not comfortable with murderous thoughts." He refilled his goblet. "I want this to be a happy place. A place of celebration. A place of fun."

She could feel her missing fist clenching. Through gritted teeth, she said, "A place I cannot flee, because you will not permit me to. No, Scorch. If you want this place to celebrate—then leave!"

His blond brows creased a little.

She felt her breath thinning.

"Kam!" Darlene said. "We're shorthanded. Get over to that table of half-orcs. I like those guys. They tell the filthiest jokes. Here," she held a pitcher out, "they need replenished!"

Cheeks flushed, Kam shot her a dangerous look. "You do it!"

Go! Scorch's voice rattled her head.

More on his will than her own, she grabbed the pitcher of ale and started over.

"And show more cleavage," Darlene shouted after her, "they'll pay extra for that. And hide that stump of yours. I don't want the patrons uncomfortable."

Chapter 52

"How's he doing?" Billip asked.

Shaking his head, Nikkel wiped the sweat from Brak's head with his sleeve.

"He's still burning up. I could fry an egg on his big head."

Brak lay still, his big swollen face creased in a frown. His back was red and purple where the snake had bitten him, leaving the man bloated.

Georgio groaned on Quickster's saddle. He was swollen a little himself, and his stomach still hurt. He didn't remember anything after the snakes struck. Instead, he'd awoken on a stretcher of sorts, being dragged by Quickster. That was two days ago. All he could figure was his body's special gift for healing itself had saved him. But Brak, he wasn't so sure about.

"He's still chewing," Nikkel said, widening his blue eyes. "I've never seen a man who could eat in his sleep before." He shrugged. "At least he isn't dead. But it doesn't look like he's going to get up for a while."

Brak's body convulsed, and thick saliva dripped out of his mouth.

"Yech," Nikkel said, tossing Jubilee a rag. "You can wipe that up; he's your friend."

Jubilee lifted her chin up and strutted over to Brak. "I'd be happy to."

Georgio felt miserable. Part poison, part other things. Brak hadn't done anything wrong aside from being hungry, and in all truth, it had been Brak's berserker's fit that saved them, all of them. The man-boy had scared up plenty of food, and Brak's clearing in the cactus pit had revealed many round cacti filled with water. He had filled them all up, but Georgio didn't feel like eating any more.

He pulled at the locks of his curly hair. *It's not my fault.*

"This is all your fault, you know," Jubilee said at him. "If you hadn't gotten him all riled up, he wouldn't have gone berserk, Fatboy Idiot!"

"That's enough, Jubilee!" Billip intervened. "It's not anyone's fault. Things like this happen in the Outlands. You *children* just aren't used to it."

"But—"

"But!" Billip turned on Jubilee, nostrils flaring, knuckles cracking, "I'll tell you about *butt*, Little Girl. I'm going to bust yours from two halves to ten if you don't close that big mouth of yours."

She folded her arms across her chest and stuck her tongue out. "No one's ever whipped me, and no one ever will."

"Don't tempt me," Billip said, taking out an arrow and smacking it into his palm.

"You'd enjoy that, wouldn't you, Rogue?"

He smacked it into his hand with a loud whap. "I certainly would."

"Pervert."

Georgio thought Billip's face was going to crack.

But Nikkel, calm as well water, stepped between them. "Let's not kill each other. Because if we do, who'll take care of Brak?" His smile, which hadn't been seen in days, was beginning to show more.

"Quickster, I guess," Georgio said, starting to chuckle.

"Well, I hope Quickster doesn't understand what she's saying," Billip added, "else he'd kick her in the teeth."

The men started laughing.

"I wish I'd thought of that," Nikkel said, smiling. "Let's give her some rawhide to chew on. That might keep her quiet."

"Stop laughing at me!" Jubilee whined.

They ignored her.

"Stop it, I said! Stop it!"

Georgio felt a little better, and it was good to see Nikkel smile again. He looked even more like his father when he did that. He even noticed a little moisture in Billip's eye.

"How much longer, Billip?" Georgio asked. "This is taking twice as long as it did when we came down here. We aren't lost, are we?"

"No. But we've got a ways yet. I'm certain we'll make it, but I don't' know about Brak. I'm afraid if we can't get him some healing soon… Just keep feeding him bits of the green snake meat."

Everyone looked at Brak again. It was a sad sight. Somehow, he'd managed to save them, but they had no way of saving him.

Georgio fought back the tears in his eyes. He missed Venir. He missed Mikkel and even Lefty. He pinched the tear ducts in his eyes.

"You alright?" Nikkel asked, patting his shoulder.

Georgio pushed his hand away. "It's just dust in my eyes."

"Sure, Georgio, sure. I got some of that too."

CHAPTER 53

"**K**EEP MOVING," TUUTH SAID.

Wupash!

It was early. The suns hadn't crested the fort's high walls yet, but all Venir could think about was the long day ahead. Everything but his fingernails ached. Every step was full of lead, and his back felt like it was on fire all the time. It was misery, but knee deep in an underling slat hole, he kept shoveling muck from one pit to the other.

"Smells good, doesn't it, Stranger?"

Venir kept his head down. His mouth shut. Tuuth had been taunting him day and night, but he wouldn't take the bait. He had to hold out. He dipped his shovel in the muck and slung it over his sagging shoulders.

"You don't look well, but you haven't died." Tuuth spat a snot ball in the muck. "Even the underlings are talking about it. Funny thing, Stranger, the underlings aren't so different than men. Believe it or not, they're betting on you. How much longer you'll live." He spat again. "I'll tell you this much: I lost my wager days ago. So I don't have any motivation to see you live any longer, so die already, will you?"

Tuuth spat again and took a long drink from his flask before he continued.

"One of my comrades, Flaggon, will win if you don't make it through the night. That's a nice bit of script he'd get with the underlings, and he promised the rest of us enough wine to drink all night." He stuffed a large wad of tobacco in his mouth. "So plan on a few whippings and more digging. They won't be stopping at all today unless your heart gives."

It didn't even stir him. He dug. Busted wrists and all. His once taut muscles now sagging on his arms. The thought of men consorting with underlings had infuriated him once, but now it didn't seem to matter. Now, the only thing that mattered was digging from one day to the other.

"Huh," Tuuth said, walking away, "I think I liked you better when you talked more."

Venir kept shoveling, glancing around from time to time.

Watch. Listen. Learn.

The remnants of the Brigand Army and the renegades from other orders were fewer than one hundred, including Flaggon and Tuuth. But the underlings were a different story. Venir had never seen so many different colored eyes before. He hadn't realized there were so many underlings in the world. He'd managed to count over a thousand of them one day, but the next day when he woke there'd been almost two thousand. They weren't all coming in through the gates either. Instead, squads of them came from inside the Outpost walls, out of a building that was once the Royal Headquarters.

And Venir knew there was no way that building could hold them all. Dread filled him.

Have they taken over the entire world?

Digging, he tried to make sense of what was happening, but he could barely think.

Brool.

His war-axe entered his mind. It seemed his days of devastation were over. What a fool he'd been, to remove the armament and leave it behind. And for what? His pride!

Am I a fool?

He couldn't shake the feeling he'd seen Brool and the rest of the armament for the last time. He'd do anything to be reunited with it again.

Curse me for a buffoon.

He slung more muck over his shoulder. One shovelful. Two. Fifty. A hundred. Two hundred.

Steam rose from the muck. The big flies and mosquitos swarmed.

A tall man walked over with a jug of water. It was Flaggon.

"You seem to attract the rottenest things." He fanned the bugs away. "Here, drink."

Venir took a swallow and made an ugly face.

"What did you put in that?" Venir tried to hand it back.

"Keep drinking, Stranger, and make it quick. That's vinegar added to it. You need it."

Venir eyed him.

"I thought you'd win the bet if I died today."

"Ah." Flaggon's brows lifted. "Tuuth told you about that, did he? Well, the truth is, Tuuth doesn't know what's going on. I already have plenty of wine, and there's no such thing as money here. We barter a little with the underlings." He winked. "But Tuuth's not very good at bartering. Besides, now that you've survived this long, I hate to see you die. Ye've defied the odds, ya have." He scratched his head. "And something's to be said for that."

Venir took another drink, finishing it off, and tossed Flaggon the canteen.

"How long do you think they'll keep you around?"

Flaggon shrugged. "I don't have any choice in the matter. No more than you. But I'll tell you this: the underlings are running the show on Bish now. They aren't going to kill everyone, but they will be killing everyone who opposes them. And I figure I'm better off with 'em than against 'em."

Venir scowled. "You make me sick."

"Ha!" Walking away, Flaggon waved at him. "I see they haven't broken your spirit yet, Stranger. See you tomorrow. Dead or alive. I've a bottle of underling port to crack."

Digging and simmering, Venir filled the other hole, crawled over the ridge between the pits, and stepped in it. Rolling his shoulder, he realized no one, not man or underling, even noticed. Instead, they all went about their business. A digging corpse, he was already forgotten.

They were Chittering back and forth with one another, even smiling, some of them.

Could it be true? Had the underlings taken over? He even saw one playing an instrument, similar to a lute. But the thing that disturbed him most was—he was getting used to it. Their smell. Their gray faces and their faint fur-like pelts.

Another hour passed, then two.

"Dig, Arsehole Bastard. Dig!"

It was the underling commander.

Venir ventured a look at him.

His bulging arms were crossed over his barrel chest. A razor-edged sword hung by his side.

"On your knees, Arsehole Bastard," the underling said. "You are now a servant of the underlings."

It felt like all the eyes of the fort were on him. Those of both underling and man. Dying of thirst, tongue swollen, Venir kept shoveling.

"Orc," the commander said, "is this man deaf? I told him to bow, not to shovel. Make him bow, Orc. Make him bow!"

"On your knees, Stranger," Tuuth said.

Venir kept shoveling.

"He looks like he can't hear." The commander slid a sharp dagger from his belt. "So he doesn't need those ears." He extended it towards Tuuth.

Hesitating, Tuuth said, "You want me to cut them off?"

"No, I want you to carve him a new arsehole, Stupid Orc."

Tuuth snatched the blade. "Fine then. Stranger, get out of that puddle."

"No!" The underling pointed. "You get in the puddle, Orc. What's the difference? You always smell like dung."

The surrounding underlings chittered in agreement.

"Last chance to bow down, Stranger," Tuuth warned, an angry look growing in his eyes. "If I step in the mire, I'm going to do more than cut your ears off. I'll cut your tongue out as well."

Venir glared at them. "What are you waiting for?" He slung a shovel full of muck on the both of them.

Ruby eyes flashing, the underling let out a hiss.

Tuuth roared, jumping in, splashing muck all over.

"You couldn't keep your mouth shut, could you?"

Crack!

Venir's head rocked back, falling into the sludge.

The underlings and men let out cheers.

"That'll shut him up, Tuuth!"

"Bust him again, good!"

"Make him eat that slat he's diggin'!"

Even the underlings chittered words of encouragement.

"He'll not talk after that punch!"

His legs felt like anvils, his arms like sandbags, but Venir got up and raised his hands on his busted wrists, squeezing them into fists. Dripping in muck, he eyed Tuuth.

"Fight or die."

Tuuth walloped him in the belly.

He sagged to his knees.

"He's bowing now, ain't he!" a brigand said.

Venir rose again.

"Cut his ears off, Orc!" The underling commander said as two other underlings wiped the muck from his armor. "I want them for a necklace. I might have you add some fingers and toes as well." He spat and wiped his mouth. "I want the tongue too."

Tuuth grabbed Venir by the hair, yanked him up to his feet, and put him in a head lock.

Struggling, Venir's face was beet red, but a ten-year-old boy would have fared better. His strength, what little he had left, was not enough.

Venir grinded his teeth and tried to pulled away.

"You!" Tuuth ordered to one of the brigands. "Get in here and grab his feet."

"Slat on me," the heavyset man said, stepping in and rolling up his sleeves. "Just make it quick, will you? It smells worse than an ogre's outhouse."

"Try not to scream, Stranger," Tuuth growled in his ear.

Slice!

His ear dropped into the muck.

"Did you hear that, Arsehole Bastard?" the underling commander said.

Every eye from the underling camp was watching now. From the towers, the catwalks, sitting on the parapets. If you were within eye shot, you could see.

Fight, blast you! Fight!

Venir's struggles were in vain.

Slice!

His last ear fell in front of his eyes, floating atop the grime.

"Good, Orc, good," the underling rubbed his chin. "And I like your idea. Cut his tongue out as well. No more talk, Human. Instead, you will scream so we can't hear."

"You two, get in here," Tuuth ordered.

One man rolled his eyes; the other one groaned.

"Get in there, idiots," Flaggon said, shoving them forward.

They sloshed through the muck, one holding his nose.

"Get his arms," Tuuth said, and then looked down on Venir. "Any last words, Stranger?"

"You're all orc, Tuuth. And it smelled better before you got here."

Ptui!

A gob of spit hit Tuuth square in the eye.

Tuuth rose his dagger high.

"Just the tongue Orc! Do not kill him!"

THROOM!

Everyone in the fort flinched, eyes searching the southern gate.

THROOM!

All the men murmured.

The underlings chittered, scrambling to their stations.

The wooden portcullis cracked and buckled.

THROOM!

The alarm was sounded, high pitched.

"Move it, men," Flaggon ordered. "Tuuth, leave him. He's not going anywhere."

"Not until I have his tongue first." He rested the knife on Venir's chin. "Hold him."

Chapter 54

S HACKLED TO A STAKE WITH mystic purple bands, gagged, arms behind his back, Boon sighed. *The fight is over.*

All his life he'd been in control. Dominant. A powerful force. Even when the giants had custody of him, as powerful as they were, he'd had a say in his destiny. But now, his say had run out.

Surrounding him, in an underling camp in the Outland, were more of the fiends than he cared to count. Thousands, and they were still arriving. He'd never seen such a large force. He hadn't even imagined one so large.

Nearby, a brood of underling magi watched over him. Their light blue and green eyes in study.

He wondered why they kept him alive.

"Water," he said, licking his lips.

They said nothing to him, chittering to themselves from time to time and inspecting his robes. The only stitch he had left on him was a pair of cut-off trousers. Even his sandals were gone. The suns gave a nice red layer to his back.

He tried to stand, but his knees wouldn't bend.

He never thought he'd ever ask an underling for anything, but he asked again, "Water."

Nothing. But it would come. It had come yesterday and the day before. A humpback urchling had fed him some food that was horrible but digestible. And so it had been. Day in. Day out. Hour after hour.

"I always imagined I'd die battling you fiends. Never a prisoner. Now look at me. An underling's beggar." Again he sighed. "I can't even insult you."

After dozing off, for how long he didn't know, he was rustled. Two underling warriors picked him up, leading him on trembling legs through the camp. The black grey smoke burned his eyes. He closed them until they stopped. An underling chittered at him with an angry tone. He knew what it meant.

Open your eyes, Human.

He knew what to expect. He didn't mean to open them, but he did.

They led him to the edge of camp, where a graveyard of the living and the dead waited.

Trains of people—men, women and children—fell under the lash and spade. They screamed, cried and wailed. Mercy was asked, but none was given. They dug graves. And were buried in them by their own.

A tear fell onto Boon's wispy white beard.

One underling pointed. The other one laughed.

It gnawed at his gut.

"To take such pleasure in it is sick."

They led him through the graveyard until his legs failed.

How could this happen? The armament must be gone. Or the underlings must have it.

CHAPTER 55

A
S QUICK AS HE MIGHT be, Melegal was no fighter. He was a thief. A cutpurse. Shadow. Survivor. Rat. The swords in his hands were heavier than those he was accustomed to, his blades, the Sisters.

"Just get in a quick jab between the ribs, Detective," Creed said. "You have it in you."

Tonio and Jarla stood nearby, surrounded by underlings with long spears, leaving Melegal in the center of the arena, all alone.

Still, Lorda's long-lashed eyes intent upon him gave him a bit of a charge.

Master Kierway chittered to one of his men.

An underling with dark ruby eyes stepped forward, a razor sharp sword in each hand. The steel flickered around his body in a lightning quick display of skill and speed.

Great.

"That's all show! Go for the ribs," Creed said. "Like you did to my man. That was a good jab." Creed muttered to Jarla something under his breath. "He doesn't have a chance."

Melegal glared back at Creed, who shrugged.

"Let's get this started, shall we?" Kierway said, raising up his hand.

Melegal swallowed hard and squared off with the underling. *If I only had my hat.* But it was gone. Everything was gone. The Keys. The hat. His friends. *Maybe they'll survive this. But at least Sefron is dead. Was vengeance worth it?* He thought about Sefron. The man had been much more than he appeared to be. Was anything in Bish what he thought it was? He'd seen so many things the past several years.

Melegal glanced at Lorda one last time.

She blew him a subtle kiss.

I'll be.

Kierway dropped his hand.

The underling sprang, swords chopping high and low.

Melegal backpedaled and parried the snake quick strokes.

Clang. Clang. Clang. Clang. Bang.

"Keep 'em up, Detective!" Creed said.

Drained and starving, Melegal didn't have the strength to fight. *Fight or die.* It rattled in his head, but he didn't have it. He didn't have anything. *Die.* He broke it off and threw down his swords.

The underling paused and looked over at Master Kierway.

"Don't go out like that. Pick the blade up and finish like a man!" Creed said.

Skinny chest heaving, Melegal clutched at his sides and dropped to his knees.

Creed frowned. "He's got nothing left in him. Coward."

No, Melegal wouldn't die fighting. He sucked up all the air he could and fixed his gaze on Lorda. *If I go out. I'll go out doing what I want to.* He winked at her and mouthed good-bye.

She clutched her painted fingers at him, eyes watering.

"Finish him," Kierway ordered, dropping his thumb. "And get the woman ready next. Sad, but I bet there's more fight in the woman than the man. Pathetic humans, letting their women fight with them and against them. Weak."

The underling warrior raised his blade, sharp teeth showing a savage grin.

Melegal kept his chin up, eyes on Lorda.

"CEASE!"

The entire room shook.

The underling warrior froze.

Lord Verbard, silver eyes sparkling, floated down the stairs with Lord Almen and a hulking Vicious right behind him.

"How dare you?" Kierway said, jumping up from his chair. "This is no concern of yours, Verbard, you insolent underling! My father—"

"Your father agrees! You can ask him yourself," Verbard said. "He's coming soon, and no doubt he'll want to evaluate your failures."

Kierway's hard jaw slackened. His ascent up the steps stopped.

"Lord Almen, are these the humans you want?" Verbard said, pointing down into the arena at them.

"Just three of them: Lorda, Jarla, Tonio, Come!"

"Tonio!" Lorda shot Almen a look. "Our son?" She looked at her son. Total shock on her face. She didn't know him.

"Aye, now get moving, Dearest Lorda," Almen said. "I'm out of parlays."

"And that woman, the black-haired witch? Are you bringing your mangy whore along?"

"What about me, Lord Almen?" Creed said. "I'm a loyal Hound at your service! You know that."

Lord Almen shook his head. "A hound, yes. No more, no less. I've plenty of curs at my disposal." He grabbed Lorda by the wrist.

Creed scowled at Almen, muttering to himself.

Lorda twisted away and continued her ascent, giving Melegal one final glance. "If you get her, then I want him."

Lord Almen's jaw tightened. "Be grateful you live, Woman. You can stay with me, or you can stay with Master Kierway."

Lorda called him a bastard, called out for Tonio, and moved away.

CRASH!

A boulder as big as a pony burst through the glass dome, crushing two underlings into the arena stairs.

The castle shook. Shouts of alarm when up.

"We're under attack!" Lord Almen said. "It seems my neighbors have awakened." He looked for Verbard, but the underling Lord was already moving.

"Get your men ready, Kierway," Verbard said. "The next battle has begun."

A large white-yellow ball of energy floated through the broken glass and hovered over the arena.

Kierway chittered a command.

Melegal balled up, covering his ears, closing his eyes.

Ka-Chow!

Something fell on top of him. It was the underling he'd been fighting. He shoved it off.

What in Bish!

Its red eyes were blinking and its limbs were loose. Melegal, despite his weakness, could still move. He grabbed a sword and stuck the underling.

Glitch!

Creed was on the move. Snatching up a sword, he tore a stunned underling's head from its shoulders.

Escape, Fool! Run!

Chaos unfolded. The dazed underlings were gathering their wits, heading for the doors. Kierway and Verbard were moving, ordering, unfazed.

The Vicious, a hulking predator, pounced into the arena and darted towards Creed.

Clank!

Melegal and Jarla froze.

A large leather sack had landed along the arena wall in front of Master Kierway's chair.

Slat on me! Venir?

Long legs churning, Jarla dashed over and dove on the sack. With a ravenous look in her eyes, she opened the sack and reached in.

Tonio was confused. His father was there, calling for him. His mother didn't seem to know him, and then she called for him too. And the underlings were in charge. Deep in the recesses of his mind, he knew he should be able to put it all together, but he couldn't. It was frustrating.

"Mother?" he said.

A rock fell from the sky, and a brilliant white flash followed. He grunted. Clutched his head and shook it. "Mother!"

A creature with a cat-like face shoved his mother down. Down the steps it bounded. He didn't know what it was, but he was going to kill it.

"Tonio kill!"

A pair of underling warriors stepped in his path.

"I'm getting used to this underling steel!"

Stab!

Creed yanked the blade from the underling's neck. Black-red blood gurgled from the hole and seeped into the ground.

The underling, though stunned, recovered quickly.

Creed, Master Swordsman from the House of Bloodhounds, pressed his advantage.

Slice!

He disemboweled one.

Chop!

He chopped another's neck open.

"Who do I have to kill to get some food and ale around here?" Creed shook the dripping blood from his blades. "I'm so hungry I could eat one of you fiends! Where's the kitchen?"

He caught a shadow in the corner of his eye and whirled.

"What in Bone are you?" he exclaimed.

The Vicious. Wicked rows of teeth. Claws like razors.

"I see you're missing some fingers," Creed said. "Let's see if I can even you out and remove a few more."

Creed lunged.

The Vicious sprung away and hunched down like an ape.

Creed felt something crawling in his belly. He'd never seen anyone that big move that fast.

"Yer not born of this world, are you? No matter. I'm still going to gut you with my blades." He banged the swords together. "Give it a go again. I'm ready for you."

The Vicious pounced, arms sprawled out, chest bared.

Slice!

He cut it across the belly and rolled out of the way and back to his feet.

"Let's see how you fight with your guts hanging out."

The monster turned, showed its fangs, and smiled. There wasn't a mark on it.

Creed felt his skin turn pale. "I'm in for."

The Vicious lunged.

Creed chopped with all his might. The blade shattered on its forearm.

The Vicious ripped a hunk of meat from Creed's chest.

"Urk!"

The Vicious snapped him up by the neck and squeezed his neck like a fresh fruit.

Eyes bulging from the sockets, Creed flailed and kicked.

At least I took some more of them with me.

"Mine!" Jarla said, licking her lips, eyes wild.

It was her salvation. Her liberation. The sack, after all these years, was back in her grasp, and nothing would ever stop her again, ever. It would fill her. Restore her. Any kind of enemy Jarla faced, even be they Royal or underling, she would prevail.

Reaching inside, her fingertips tingled in anticipation. The shafts of her axes. The power surging through her bracers. The awesome awareness from her helmet. Down to her shoulder she reached, fingers outstretched as far as they could go.

"Where are they?" She reached deeper. "Where are they!"

Her heart emptied. Nothing was there.

"No," she sobbed.

A shadow fell over her. She looked up. It was the rawboned detective. He held a heavy club with both hands. She sneered.

"That's not yours," he said. "It's Venir's."

"What? Are you mad? I'll never let that lou—"

Whack!

Melegal clubbed her across the jaw.

She tried to speak, but no words came. Only pain. Then darkness.

"That felt good," Melegal said, gathering the sack, "and I haven't forgotten that Lorda wants you dead. But I'll let the two of you fight that out."

Explosions were still erupting all over the castle, so the concerns of Lord Almen and the underling leaders were elsewhere right now.

Hidden along the arena wall, no one had sight of him.

The stunned underlings that were coming out of the mystic blast were focused on the fighting in the middle.

Now I just have to hide until I find Venir. I knew that fool must have caused this.

It was simple. All he had to do was find a place between the walls until he figured out where Venir was. Then he could free him and let him deal with this mess. And he just might be able to get his cap and Keys back. *Just the cap. The cap would be good.*

A doorway, up the steps on the other side of the arena, was open with no one to bar his path. *Move or die.*

He was darting along the arena wall, concealed for the first twenty steps, when he heard a familiar voice shout out.

"Seize him!"

It was Lord Almen pointing and shouting, his face filled with rage.

Melegal jumped up, grabbed the lip of the wall, and slung himself up.

Two underlings bolted towards the door, cutting off his path, weapons ready.

He was too late.

Bone!

Two more were closing in from behind. All he had was a club and a sack. Expecting Venir to appear any second, he shook his head.

Where is that brute?

Dropping the club, he sat down, laying the sack on his lap.

CHAPTER 56

"MMMPH!"

Tuuth tried to pry his mouth open, but Venir wouldn't give. Teeth clenched, he fought on.

"Hold him still!" Tuuth ordered.

The brigands, stout as they might be, struggled. Each slipping into the mud from his efforts.

"Blast you, Tuuth! You hold him! I'm not swimming in slat on account of this wretch's tongue! He's done for!"

"Aye!" the other agreed, letting go and crawling out of the slime.

"You'll both be in the stockade for a week, maybe longer!"

"Pah!"

Still in a headlock, Venir's nostrils flared.

Tuuth cranked up the pressure.

"This isn't over," Tuuth said, looking around.

All the brigands and underlings had abandoned the pit, shouting orders and gathering gear, leaving the two of them all by themselves.

Tuuth shoved him down in the muck and held him under, waited several seconds, and jerked him back out.

Venir coughed and spat.

"Enough of this," Tuuth said, trolling out of the muck and slinging it from his fingers. "Let the underlings kill you themselves, like everyone else."

The ground shook.

"What?" Tuuth stopped in place, arms out.

Venir felt it too, but it was of little notice. Sitting in the muck, he was in agony. Reaching down, he plucked one of his dirty and bloody ears from the muck, tossed it aside, and grabbed his shovel. He pushed himself up with it, legs shaking. Wiping the filth from his eyes, he was watching the southern gate, which was rising, when another clamor went up.

"It's a giant!"

Tuuth tucked the underling's dagger into his belt and looked back. "Don't go anywhere!"

He wasn't. He couldn't. Even if he could, where would he go? Though tempted to at least climb up out of the muck, he remained in what little cover the pit provided, keeping his eyes transfixed on the slow rise of the southern gate. Hundreds of underling soldiers, dark armor and helms gleaming in the sun, stood ready.

A moment later, a collective gasp followed.

There he was.

Tethered by thick ropes and chains, towering more than three times the height of the underlings, a giant stood. They pulled, poked and prodded him. He was angry and confused, each footstep shaking the ground. Bolts and javelins jutted from his body like briars.

Venir's eyes widened.

It was Barton.

The young giant growled and yelled. Slung his weight against his captors to no avail. They had him chained by the neck, the arms, and the ankles. Enough chains to forge an armory.

Venir felt pity. Barton's expression was tormented. A confused child. Miserable.

Barton stomped. Rocked and reeled.

"LET BARTON GO! LET BARTON GO!"

But the underlings had him under control. They chittered. They laughed.

Sitting down on the edge of the muck pit, he watched the underlings bind the giant further. Venir recalled his time in the Mist. It had been Barton who freed him. It had been Barton he tricked, and it had been Barton who said he'd come for him—and he had.

Of all people, he remembered me.

Of course, it wasn't Venir he wanted, it was the armament. The toys. Venir wanted them too, but he was certain the armament was gone.

Barton's going to be disappointed, if he lives to find out.

Barton was bound to the exterior wall, a mere ten yards away, but under heavy guard. He yelled and whined, but after several minutes, he fell silent.

Venir resumed his shoveling. *Nothing I can do. Sorry, Barton.* Whatever happened was going to happen, and there was nothing he could do. Two more hours he dug. He was dying of thirst.

"Dwarves!" One of the brigands shouted from the catwalks. "Dwarves!"

Venir lifted his head up. Stout black-bearded men, shackled, were herded inside like cattle. Some limped. All bled. Hard looks on their grim faces.

"Who's in command of this place?" a commanding voice said.

Mood? He cupped his hand behind his missing ear, peering forward.

"Come on, rodents! Bring yer leader out!"

Venir shielded his eyes from the blazing suns with his hand. Mood, bushy and broad, stood over the rest, a green glimmer under his brows.

The underling commander strutted forward, chest out.

"Blood Ranger, you have no business here. Not on my mountain. The penalty is death."

"Ye'll release us all, Underling," Mood said. "We hunt giants, all over Bish, and where they go, we go. Underlings or no. It's our right. You best let us go, or the entire dwarven world will come for you. Not to mention more giants."

An underling cracked a spear over Mood's head.

The Blood Ranger didn't flinch. All he said was, "I'm warning you."

"Say all you want, Blood Ranger. You'll be dead soon, so it doesn't matter. Bish is ruled by the underlings now, so your threats are of no matter." The underling commander started to walk away. "Flay them. Flay them all. But save the giant for last."

"It's easier to flay a stone than a dwarf, you fool!" Mood said. "We'll dull your knives after the first cut."

Venir shook his head and resumed his shoveling.

"Stay here."

Those were the last words Mood had said to Fogle Boon before he'd departed with the Black Beards and headed towards Outpost Thirty One, leaving him alone with Eethum. That had been several hours ago, and at the bottom of the massive hill they waited. He'd been clutching at handfuls of his hair ever since.

"Eethum, what's the plan?"

Solemn as always, the black Blood Ranger replied, "I don't know."

That was the same answer he'd given five times already, and Fogle was tired of it. He had to know, and even though Fogle didn't question dwarven integrity, he had his doubts.

"So, am I to understand that we are to *stay here* forever? And you're comfortable with that?"

Eethum eyed the long branch he'd been whittling for hours.

"He's the King. I do as he says." He stuck his knife in a tree stump and admired his work. "Look at that. Straight as a dwarven bolt." He smiled at Fogle. "I can make a fine spear with it." He tossed it to Fogle. "Or a Wizard's walking stick. Ha! Ha!"

Fogle wanted to crack it over Eethum's head. He slung it to the ground.

"We can't wait here forever, Eethum."

"We won't," Eethum said, grabbing his knife along with another branch and whittling again.

Pacing around him, Fogle said, "I'm not a dwarf. I can't stand here for a hundred years and do nothing, like you."

"I'm not doing nothing; I'm carving wood. Just find yourself something to do. Study your spellbook. Always be ready for something."

It was easier said than done. Fogle didn't know what was going on. So he turned his attention back to Inky. His ebony hawk familiar stretched out its black metallic wings. It was ready.

He glanced over his shoulder at Eethum. The Blood Ranger didn't pay him any attention.

"Alright, I might have to stay here, but that doesn't mean I can't try and figure out what's happening."

Grabbing Inky, he placed Venir's hunting knife in its talons. "Give this to Venir if you see him. It will be some time before I can connect with you again." He tossed the bird in the air. Black wings flapping, it soared into the sky, disappearing into the tree line.

He turned and faced Eethum.

The Blood Ranger's arms were crossed over his chest.

"What?" Fogle shrugged. "I'm staying here."

Eethum shook his head. "There's at least a thousand underlings out there. Your little bird's done for."

"Why do you think that?"

Eethum batted an eye at him. "Wizard, have you seen a single bird since we've been here?"

Fogle tucked his chin into his neck. "No."

"There's a reason for that." Eethum put a finger to his lips, then pointed upward. "Hear that?"

Fogle cupped his ear. Something hummed in the sky. "I can always bring him back to us."

"Don't do that. You'll just lead them right to us."

"Them?"

"Stirges. Flocks of them. They destroy every flying creature in sight."

"But Inky doesn't have any blood."

"Maybe so, but they don't know that."

Chapter 57

"**Y**ou should eat something, Corrin."

"What?" he said, blinking.

"Eat," Haze said, motioning to her mouth. "I heard your stomach growling from over there. You've been staring in the fountain for hours. Take a drink already. Or a bath even. Just do something other than sit there."

Corrin gaped at the skinny woman. "Don't you see them?"

She leaned over and peered in. "What? Fish? Spooks? I don't see anything except water."

He looked back in the fountain. The living images were gone.

"No!" he said, reaching in the water, shaking his hand. "Where are they?"

"You've lost your wits," she said, walking away, "but I'll still get you something to eat. Get some shade at least. The suns probably cooked your noodles."

"Aw!" he said, smacking the water. "I'm going to miss it. Trinos!" He looked everywhere. She was nowhere to be found. "Hate it when she does that!"

Trinos had told him strange things. She spoke of Bish as if it were her own child and the things that worried him would take care of themselves. There was order among the chaos, she'd said. Sanity with the madness. Good where there was evil.

But, he disagreed. There wasn't any good in the underlings. He was a hired killer. A murderer. But he took no pleasure in it. The underlings did, and he made it clear to her that despite the Royals' lust for power and control, the world would be better off without the underlings.

"No one is ever in control," she had said. "I have planted many seeds to see to that. But nothing will last forever. I tire. When it ends, it ends."

Corrin didn't understand it one bit. All he knew was people were dying and underlings were living. When it came to the battle for Bish, he wanted in. He buckled on his sword.

"First, I'm going to fill my belly with food, and then I'm going to fill gray bellies with steel."

Trinos sighed.

Her world was everything she'd imagined it to be, but worse. It drained her. The people were strong, full of life, bold—but always shadowed in darkness. Peace had come in the past. Only to go and come again.

Scorch had changed that. Now, peace was a lonely cry from the highest mountain top.

She walked, her toes drifting over the sand in the Warfield. Of all the places in Bish, it was the one most at peace right now. Hot and barren, both underlings and men had avoided it among the turmoil that had broken out everywhere else.

Shall I stay? Can I go? Is this what I want?

She knew she couldn't go. Not without Scorch. They had both buried most of their power deep in Bish when they arrived. One could not tap it without the other.

In the meantime, her own power, vast as it might be, had weakened. Bish was feeding on her.

Her powers waned. What had been effortless required effort now. She filled her chest with hot air and slowly let it out. Despite the change, she felt as alive as she ever remembered. Emotions, long forgotten, went up and came down.

Does Scorch feel this as well?

Should I track him?

So she walked, toes sinking into the sand, becoming another part of the world she'd created.

Behind her, two disfigured people followed, covered head to toe in Outland robes, swords hanging from their hips, sandaled but no longer insane.

CHAPTER 58

REED KICKED THE VICIOUS IN the face. It was a last ditch effort.

It head-butted him.

Crack!

He saw bright spots and stars. He was choking. Sharp claws dug into his neck. His own blood trickled down his chest. He always figured he'd die before he was gray. A match of steel against a younger, stronger opponent like himself. Where he held on with skill and cleverness to the end. But this, to fall in the brutal hands of a monster, was unbearable.

If I only had my sword again.

The brute held him by the neck, pushed him up with its long arm like a child, and shook him like a doll.

Purple-faced, he gulped for air.

Such a cowardly way to go!

He kicked at the Vicious again and again, but there was laughter in its evil eyes.

"Blast you, fiend!" Bloody saliva flew from his mouth.

Creed felt his body closing down. The light dimmed. The pain subsided.

This is it, Bish.

The Vicious released him.

Creed fell to the ground, coughing and choking.

Tonio was there. Arms latched around the creature's neck in a headlock of some sort.

Crawling through the dirt, Creed searched for a blade—a knife, anything.

"Perhaps I'll get in one last swing."

"Mother!" Tonio growled. "You hurt my mother!"

Strength versus strength. Power versus power. Two titans thrashed with one another. The Vicious, an underling abomination of magic brought to life in humanoid form. Tonio, a dead man revived, raging within like a forest fire.

He didn't know what he was or how he came to be. He knew he should be dead but he lived, stitched up by the spiderish arachna-men. Magic gave him life, and nothing could give him death. So he fought. His vengeance unfilled against the yellow-haired Vee-Man.

The Vicious twisted out of his choking grip and socked him in the face.

He staggered back.

The creature pounced on him. It punched and clawed at him, one blow as quick as the other.

His skin shredded. His bone exposed. Tonio didn't feel a thing.

The creature let out an angry howl.

Tonio punched his fist inside its mouth.

Its eyes widened. It pushed away.

Tonio shook the spit from his hand and flashed a split-faced grin. "You can't hurt me!" He pounded his chest. "Nothing can!"

The Vicious leapt. Kicked him in the chest. Knocked him to the ground.

Tonio laughed and rose to his feet. The underling was quick. He matched it blow for blow. He slammed it into the wall.

It bit off a part of his leg.

Tonio hoisted it over his head. Slammed it into the ground. Stomped on its chest. It's head.

Back and forth they went. Two monsters. Evil. Tireless. No quarter given. No hatred spared.

Underlings closed in.

Melegal's instincts took over. He reached into the sack, clutching for a weapon. Something. Anything. Bony fingertips stretching. Tingling. He felt something. Cold. Living.

What is that?

Smack!

An underling cracked him over the head with the pommel of its sword, splitting his vision from two to four.

Spine like jelly, he slumped over the benches, the sack slipping from his grasp.

The one underling grabbed him by the leg and dragged him. The other tossed the sack over the rail, into the arena.

Head bouncing off the benches, Melegal stared at the broken glass dome above. The suns gleamed on the broken glass edges.

Venir, you lout, where are you?

Creed crawled. Huffing. Bleeding. Busted inside and out. A rack of weapons awaited him against the way. And that wasn't all.

"I'll be," he said.

His sword lay on the rack. Steel glimmering under the dust. Tonio and the other monster thrashed behind him. *Move, Creed!* He gathered his feet and stumbled over.

"I bet Pearl can poke a hole in that thing."

He stretched out his fingers and grabbed the hilt.

"Bone! Ah!" The sharp stabbing pain of broken ribs bit into him. Something fell over his head, blocking his sight.

What in Bish?

He tore it off his face and beheld a worn, stitched-up sack of leather.

Where did this come from?

His stomach rumbled. He hadn't eaten in days. A savage instinct overcame him.

Maybe there's a loaf or some cheese. I don't fight well when hungry.

Ravenous and wild-eyed, he set down his sword and reached inside.

Lorda Almen squatted along the wall at the top of the arena, hiding in a doorway, trembling. A boulder the size of a sofa had almost smashed her, and a creature as dark as night had shoved her down. Her home, her castle, had become a den of madness, and it had only just begun.

"Lorda, get out of there," Lord Almen cried out, his long arm waving her over.

Underling soldiers were whisking him away, and two more were coming for her. She shook her head.

Down on one side of the arena, her son Tonio smashed two underlings together. He attacked the hulking beast that had shoved her, and he was about to break the neck of another. On the other side, Melegal, a man she'd become fond of for some reason, was pinned in by the underlings, awaiting a certain death.

She tried to catch his eye, but a strong armed underling jerked her off the ground and hissed.

"Come with me, Woman. I can't have my pets running loose, now can I?" It was Kierway. He looked over his shoulder. "I've got more pressing matters than watching humans die."

"Unhand me!" she said.

He backhanded her.

Her legs swayed.

"Speak to me like that, and you'll never speak again."

CHAPTER 59

OULD HE BE DEAD?

Slim the Healer crawled out of his hiding spot and scurried outside. Being king of the Elga bugs was getting old. He needed to stretch his legs. Not the six he had now, but the two he preferred to walk on as a man.

This is tiresome.

Still, he would do whatever he had to do to keep his friend alive. Something had to happen. Something always did. But this time things didn't seem right. His friend, Venir, was being whittled away, one chunk at a time.

Crawling up one of the Outpost walls, he found a good spot, away from the soldiers.

Oh my!

A man the size of three men was inside the camp, talking like a loud child and fighting against his bonds.

A giant!

A dwarf was whipping his blood red hair in the air, screaming and yelling at an underling like an angry bugbear.

Mood! And Black Beards? Captured? What in Bish is going on?

Bug eyes shifting back and forth, he glossed over a man shoveling in the muck.

Ew! But that's what Brigands should be doing.

Still searching, he couldn't find Venir, so he looked for the orc called Tuuth. The big orc was watching over the dwarves, arms crossed over his chest. Fluttering his wings, Slim found another spot and started searching faces all around.

Venir? Where is that brute?

The man was nowhere to be found. Turning back to the man in the muck pit, he took a closer look. Earlier, he'd been looking for blond hair and muscles. But the markings of a 'V' tattoo still shown through the muck. *Venir!*

A sinking feeling started inside his insect belly. Doubt flooded his mind. Over the centuries, he'd seen many things, but he'd never witnessed such a dire scene before.

The underlings singled out one dwarf and chained him to the wall. Above, in one of the fort's turrets, a pair of underlings grabbed the winch and cranked back the draw string on a ballista. Then loaded a bolt as long as a man. The black beard looked up at the underling, set his chin and raised it high.

Slim closed his eyes.

Ballista bolt sticking out of his chest, the Black Beard let out his final gasp, "For the King!" His head dipped. His helmet fell to the ground.

The underlings let out a loud raucous cheer. Venir had never witnessed underlings celebrating so. They danced and jumped. Loaded another ballista. Replaced the dead dwarf with a live one.

"Yer gonna pay for that!" Mood bellowed, fighting against his bonds.

Venir's heart dipped. Mood's rescue attempt was going to cost the lives of all his men, and then that of Mood, himself. This wasn't how the giant dwarves were supposed to end. They should have known by now that his friendship only brought death.

"King of the Dwarves," the underling commander said, flexing his arms and pumping up his soldiers, "what is it like to see your subjects die? It is customary that we kill the leader first, but I like to watch your eyes. I want to make them water. Making a dwarf cry will be a first." He pointed up at the fort tower and dropped his arm. "Fire!"

THWACK!

Another Black Beard fell. The bolt sticking out of his skull.

"That probably stung," the commander said, "but not for very long."

The crowd chittered, sharp teeth gnashing in agreement.

"Two down, many more to go."

Venir was used to people dying, but not when they weren't in battle. Not without a fight. Watching the dwarves fall ate at him. It wasn't right. It wasn't natural. Hands white-knuckled on the shovel, he thought of Brool. The white hot power surging through his hands. A hollow feeling overcame him. An old friend lost. Lost forever. He had lived this long without it, but could he live anymore? He was broken. What there anything else he could do to help this savage world?

"You?"

Barton's hanging head tilted up and looked right at him. The giant sniffed the air.

"Ah-hah, you are hiding in the stink, Venir?"

Tuuth faced the giant. "What did you say, Giant?" He pointed at Venir. "Are you talking to him? Is he *Venir?*"

"Go away, Orc! I do not like your stink!" Barton's eye rolled back over to Venir. "Give me my toys!"

"Gag that giant!" Tuuth ordered his men.

"What's going on?" the Brigand Flaggon said.

"This man, Commander, has a bounty on his head. A big one. This is Venir the Outlander, the one who destroyed the Brigand Army."

Flaggon rubbed his chin. "I thought there was something familiar about him." He kneeled alongside the pit. "Your bounty is big, and the penalty is death. Get his shovel, men. Tuuth, clean him up a little before you cut off his head. We'll want to bring it as a trophy, if we ever make it back to the Brigand City."

Throughout the fort, everyone's heads snapped up.

The sound of trees snapping like twigs echoed in the distance.

"What now?" Flaggon said.

Tuuth kept his eyes intent on Venir. "Get him out of there."

The ground shook. Not like before, but worse.

Thoom!

It shook again. More trees snapped and cracked. Branches sounded as if they were being crushed into the ground.

Thoom!

Above, Venir glimpsed several robed underlings soaring above the walls, clawed hands filling with color.

Wumpf!

An uprooted tree soared over the wall, smacking into an underling mage and crashing them both into the ground.

"Oh No!" Barton said. "They've come!"

The underling magi fired balls of energy over the wall.

The soldiers in the towers fired their ballistas.

Rocks bigger than men flew over the wall.

Men and underlings scrambled.

A rock smashed into a turret. Underlings fell to their deaths.

"They're after the dwarves!" The underling commander cried out. "Prepare for parlay! We'll hand them over!"

"Hah!" Venir heard Mood say. "If there's anything giants hate more than dwarves, it's the underlings!" Mood snapped his chains and punched the wide-eyed underling commander in the face. "But none hates more than I do, Fiend." Mood let out a gusty word. "*SHARLABOTZ!*"

The leather and metal that bound the Black Beards withered and snapped. The dwarves burst into action. In seconds, they were an armed force. Hacking and slashing into the off-guard underlings.

Venir stirred. A fire ignited within. He raised his shovel and brought it down on the back of Tuuth's head.

Snarling, the orc turned, grabbed Venir by the hair, and slung him to the ground. The orc pinned him down. Wrapped his fingers around his neck and squeezed.

Venir couldn't breathe.

"You're done for now, Venir!" Tuuth pushed him towards the muck pit. "And your grave's even ready. Your bones will be right where they belong, Outland Scum."

CHAPTER 60

THUMP.

Thump. Thump.

Boon's heart still beat. His nose still breathed. But that was all he could to. Beat and breathe. Barely. *Is this all I have left?* The mystic cuffs tightened with every move. Biting into his wrists and burning at the same time. Inside, his own mystic fires still burned, but he could not summon them. His mouth was bound tight as well. Eyelids heavy, heart skipping and slowing, it was his magic that kept his fiber together. Without it, he would have died long ago.

Oh, to wield the armament one last time! I'd give these fiends a show.

Sagging on the ground, he was oblivious to the commotion that stirred the camp. His mind was somewhere else, fighting to keep his body on this side of the threshold between life and death.

Fire fell from the sky.

"Eh…" He opened his eyes.

Smoke began.

The hairs on his arms and beard curled and singed.

Hot smoky air filled his nose and lungs.

A cry of Chaos went up.

A clamor spread through the underling camp. Underlings barked orders. Flames spread from tent to tent.

Someone grabbed hold of him. Pulled him to his feet. Cut his bonds and yanked the gag from his mouth.

"Eat this!" his rescuer said. A fruit of some sort was stuffed in his mouth.

He sunk his teeth right in. Juice dripped down his beard.

"Come with me!"

He followed, blinking the dark smoke from his eyes. Flames surrounded them. Underlings screamed out. They burned. They burned alive. The sound of underlings suffering was music to his ears.

Is this real? Or am I dead?

"Grab this and get on!" the voice ordered, placing his hands on a rope.

"What?" he started to say, but was cut off.

Something huge lurched beneath him, stirring up a cloud of dust and fire. Off the ground they rose. Boon fought to hold on. He slipped, but a strong arm grabbed him and held him tight.

"Am I on what I think I'm on?"

"Keep silent, and hold tight!"

CHAPTER 61

CREED'S FINGERTIPS TOUCHED LEATHER. He dumped out the contents of the sack. A sword belt. Different. Two pommels with a dull gray finish were shoved in short scabbards on it. Compelled, he strapped it on. *Two short blades are better than none.*

"Food! There must be something." He reached back inside.

Behind him, Tonio and the Vicious were still having it out, but it didn't matter to him if either one died, so long as it wasn't him. "Just a morsel, eh? Or maybe a skin of wine? Please?"

Instead, the sack served up soft fabric.

"What's this?" Creed held a dark, intricately woven cowl, big enough to cover his head and shoulders.

The cowl throbbed with a life of its own, telling him something.

He traced the tiny swirling rows of stitches with his fingers. "Bish, what kind of garment is this?" Creed's keen eye understood fine craftsmanship. He'd crafted his own blades with intricate designs. But what he now beheld was nothing short of marvelous in his eyes.

"Huh, a bit much for keeping the rain off," he said. He put it on. And forgot his hunger.

The Cowl filled him with great awareness.

He jumped from the ground. "Mother of Bone!"

The Vicious caught Tonio in the nose, rocking the half-dead man, flattening him. It turned on Creed, jaws snapping, claws bared.

Tonio moved, but slowly.

Creed didn't have a stitch of armor on him aside from The Cowl. He wasn't worried. He felt thick. Tough. He sized up the monster.

Its arms were long like an ape's. Its skin tough, like black steel. The claws on its fingers were ten blades to his two.

Creed's hands fell to the steel pommels at his hips. *Maybe they can cut this thing.* He jerked them out. Steel. Dark. Razor sharp.

"Great Bish!"

The blades were long! And heavy, but light in his hands.

The Vicious charged.

Quick as it was, Creed was quicker. Like a cobra he struck.

Slice!

Slice!

One monster hand fell, then the other.

The Vicious howled, fangs dripping with saliva.

Glitch!

The tip of one blade punctured its eye.

Glitch!

The other its throat.

The Vicious sagged to the ground, dead.

Creed looked at his blades. "I'll be." Spun them around. "I could get used to this."

His head throbbed. Underlings were coming. His eyes glimmered. Two underlings surged down the steps and leapt into the arena. Behind them, Detective Melegal's scrawny body was sprawled out on the benches, unmoving.

Creed smiled. He twirled one sword in his hand. Held the other behind his back.

Flanking him, one underling came in low, the other high, curved swords licking out like serpent tongues.

Creed swatted their blades away.

They pressed.

He pressed back, laughing. *If the Royals could see me now! Hah. They'd never face me.*

All his life, he'd been training to fight. We wanted to be respected. Fight the Royals in their arenas. Be their champion. But they wouldn't let him. He wasn't their blood. They claimed he wasn't worthy. Still, he continually perfected his skill and craft. Designing his own steel and other weapons. Now he wielded two as easily as sticks. He felt like he could swing forever.

"Hah!"

His steel flashed.

He clipped through the nose of one.

Zitch!

He tore the lip from the other.

Bleeding, the underling's eyes were focused. Ready.

Creed folded his swords behind his back, stuck his chin out and shook his head.

Chittering, they came at him.

Creed lunged. Stabbed both through the chest.

Their swords fell. Their bodies right after.

"If only my hounds could see this."

He slung underling blood from his swords and scanned the arena. Only one underling was left. Its eyes furrowed beneath its brow.

Creed waved him down.

"Time for a rematch, you copper-eyed roach."

Tonio pushed himself off the ground, shaking his head. The black creature was fast. It confused him. Still, he would make it pay.

Turning to face his predator, he saw something he didn't expect. The Vicious was face first in the dirt, hands missing and dead. He had a sinking feeling when he looked over and saw the next thing.

A faceless man battled the underlings. His swords were fast. Strokes of lightning.

A chill went through Tonio. He looked at the scars on his arms and ran his hand down the split in his face. Something about that man distraught him. He had to get away.

"No," he said, recoiling. The black forest came to mind, the webs. He noticed a gleaming sword near the arena wall and took it. Then, he headed to the nearest door and ripped it open. His mother, Lorda, was screaming after him, but he didn't hear her. He had to hide. He had to plan.

"Detective."

Melegal groaned.

"Detective." It was the soft voice of a woman. Her lips brushed his ear. "We must hurry."

Melegal found himself gazing up into the beautiful eyes of Lorda Almen. His heart thumped in his chest. He reached out and grasped her hand, feeling her breasts brush against his chin as she held him. He savored the moment.

"We must go," she said, lifting his chin to face her.

A moment ago, he'd been ready to let his suffering in Bish end. He'd had enough of facing one bad day followed by another. But for now, he had a new purpose. He fought the pain and discomfort and wrapped his hand around her sensuous waist. *Fight and fondle.* He was going to help the Lorda.

"How many underlings?" he said, coughing a little.

"Hundreds. They come and go. From where, I don't know. It's an army." She pushed her black hair from her eyes. "It's madness, is what it is. We have to get out of here." She pushed him. "Let's go."

Melegal started to go, then froze.

"Venir?"

In the arena, a man in a dark cowl was squared off against the underling, Kierway.

The sight sent chills through Melegal.

The man under the cowl was tall and muscular, but not savage and brawny like Venir. His face was obscured a little. The man moved like a predator, dark blades whirling at the underlings like storms at small boats out at sea.

Melegal then noticed the pants. Well-trimmed auburn hair around the mouth.

Creed?

Sadness fell over him. Despair filled his belly. If his friend was no longer The Darkslayer, then was his friend no more?

"Fool!" Lorda said, pulling him along. "You're supposed to be saving me; I'm not supposed to be saving you."

They made their way to the door Melegal had tried to approach earlier. He passed through it before her.

A corridor led around the arena toward many other exits. There was a clamor everywhere. Chandeliers fell. Vases were busted. Footsteps scrambled over the marble. Castle Almen was under attack, but the usurped were fighting back.

"C'mon," Melegal said. He took her hand. One corridor was blocked off by rubble. Another was overrun with underlings. "There should be more options in a castle so large." Jogging back down the corridor by the arena, they took another path. Melegal had spent considerable time following Sefron and learning many secrets. Others, he'd discovered on his own. He eyed the framework of the wall. "Aw, where is it?"

"What?" Lorda said.

Chitter. Chitter. Chitter.

Underling soldiers were prowling the halls, coming from both directions.

Dripping with sweat, chest heaving, Lorda's eyes locked with his.

Melegal caught her voluptuous form in his arms and kissed her on the mouth.

She dug her nails into his back. Kissing him back. Her soft lips were hungry. Passionate.

They finished, gasping.

"You know," Lorda said, "death is the penalty for that."

Underlings cut them off at both ends.

"Obviously," Melegal answered, pushing her behind him, "but it was worth it."

CHAPTER 62

THE CASTLES IN THE CITY of Bone were all lined up against the great wall: some looking over, some not as tall. On both sides of Castle Almen, the other two attacked. Small catapults hurled heavy stones, and piles of logs and ballista bolts crisscrossed.

Standing on top of the keep, Lord Catten laughed.

"It seems the Royals have decided to engage," he said to his brother, "but it's a bit too late."

Verbard knocked debris from his shoulders. "Or, perhaps it's their way of taking down an enemy. Putting an end to the Almen house, which has betrayed so many."

Lord Almen stood tall and stone-faced. Nails digging into his palms. He would have done the same thing, but seeing it happen to himself and his people and family was a hard thing. "Spare your people, Lord Catten and Lord Verbard," Almen said. "This isn't a full assault, but rather a test of strength."

"And how long will this test go on?" Catten said.

"Several minutes at most," Almen said, giving a quick nod. "Perhaps after that I can begin a parlay with them. Certainly their eyes are on me." He gestured at one of the other castle's towers. "They'll be expecting something."

Floating inches above the roof of the Keep and staying half a head taller than Almen, the molten eyes of the underlings bore into him.

"Mind your place, Human," Verbard said. "Your suggestions are annoying."

"And your Castle is boring," Catten added.

Out of the corner of his eye, Lord Almen glimpsed a missile coming his way. He ducked. The ballista bolt splintered on an invisible shield of magic.

"Such a fool, Brother," Verbard said. "Did you pick him out?"

"Nay, Brother," Catten said. "I believe it was you who suggested we keep him around, but I see little need for a man who flinches at such a feeble attack."

Lord Almen regained his feet. Eyed the attacking castle turret next door. They were reloading. He caught the glimmer of a spy glass turned on him.

"Interesting, Brother," Verbard said. "I don't even think that attack was meant for us, but rather meant for him."

"I agree, but there is only one way to find out." Catten floated to Almen's left.

Verbard nodded and took a place on his right.

"Stay right where you are, Lord Almen. My brother and I have a wager of sorts."

It was hot. Sweat dripped off Lord Almen's brow and nose. In all truth, the underlings didn't have any need for him. They had his Castle. Key sections of the City.

It would take a unified Royal force to prevail against the underlings. *Not likely.* His only sanctuary was knowledge, but he was certain the underlings would risk losing that. They could just learn it for themselves.

Rocks and pitch-coated burning logs sailed overhead, slamming into the castle. Soldiers in the turret were winding the ballista winch back. The one with the spy glass had pointed right at him; he was certain.

"Any last words, Lord Almen?" Catten asked, arms folded over his chest.

Lord Almen took a silent draw through his nose.

"If I die, kill all those bastards."

"They'll die anyway," Catten said, "but if it makes you feel better, you can believe we did it that way."

Don't blink. Don't flinch. Don't move.

Lord Almen didn't have any idea if they kept their shield up or not, but certainly they'd protect themselves now, wouldn't they?

Twack!

The bolt sailed. Lord Almen's quick mind watched in slow motion. Closer. Closer.

Rip!

It tore straight though his leg. He spun to the ground. Three feet of wood jutted through his thigh.

"Hmmm… Brother," Verbard began, "it seems their aim isn't very good. Not good at all. I can't really say if they were aiming for him or us. It was such a bad shot."

"Agreed, Brother," Catten said, turning away, "but I can't fool around here all day. And I don't think our enemies are interested in this human's parlay. No, let us leave him up here and we'll check back and see if they spared him or not."

"Fair enough. Besides," Verbard said, "I think we need a better eye on our neighbors. I think our imp would be a much better ambassador."

"Agreed."

Lord Almen watched them walk away, a hard grimace on his face. Through the door they went, closing it behind them. Lord Almen and his Royal enemies were all alone.

The spy glass reflected in the suns.

He stood up, bit his lip, and searched for cover. *Get to the ledge.* He hopped as fast as he could. Another bolt ripped through his shoulder.

Chapter 63

Tuuth applied pressure to Venir's throat. "I'm going to enjoy this, Outlander." Saliva dripped off the orc's canine teeth. "I want a clean-cut earless trophy."

Venir's kicks glanced off the big orc's sides. He tried to speak. Tuuth squeezed harder.

"No more words from your loud mouth," Tuuth said. "Perhaps it's another challenge you want? Perhaps another insult towards my kind? If I had your ears, I'd stick them in your mouth."

Venir's eyes rolled up in his head. Sound faded.

"NOOO!"

WHAP!

An oversized hand sent Tuuth spinning away. There stood Barton. Fists clenched at his sides. Chest heaving.

"Get my toys first!"

Venir gulped for air. Gasped. "I... I don't have them."

Barton slammed his fists into the ground.

"NO!"

"Giant!" Tuuth beckoned with his finger, one hand still behind his back. "I know the toys you're looking for. Stoop down, and I'll tell you where they are."

Barton grunted, leaned downward, cocking his head.

"Where are they, Orc?"

Tuuth's gauntlets flashed.

WHAM!

He struck Barton in the jaw.

Barton quavered. His eye rolled up into his head. He collapsed.

Tuuth thumped his chest.

"I just broke a giant's jaw." He looked down on Venir. "Imagine what I'll do to you."

The ground shook.

Three giants jumped off the walls, crushing a dozen underlings.

"Can you knock them out too?" Venir said.

"I'm not worried about them." Tuuth swung.

Venir blocked the punch. His bones clattered. He fell in a heap.

"I can't die like this," he said, looking up. "Not to an orc."

Tuuth glowered at him. "You can, and you will." He kicked Venir in the gut.

Everywhere, underlings by the hundreds swarmed the giants. Cutting, Stabbing, and screaming. They crawled over them like angry black ants.

There was another explosion.

The southern gate was shattered. A giant bigger than the other three, with brown hair tied in knots, stormed inside. He swung a hammer as big as an ogre. Dozens of underlings were crushed and swept aside. Their bones powdered on impact.

Tuuth snorted and gawped.

"Where in Bish did they come from?"

Something from the sky fell at Venir's feet. It was a long knife in a scabbard.

"Huh?" Tuuth said.

Venir dove for it.

Tuuth kicked it away.

"Nice try, Venir!"

The orc grabbed him by the hair and pounded his face and chest. Ribs cracked.

Venir lost his breath and collapsed.

Tuuth readied the underling's knife and thumbed its edge.

"This is it for you."

Venir groaned, struggling to rise. He couldn't even open his eyes.

Tuuth pushed him down with his boot.

"No, you won't die on your feet. You'll die in the muck."

Something growled.

Venir's eye popped open.

Tuuth turned.

There stood a giant a two-headed dog. Fangs bared. Hair raised on its necks.

"What the..."

Chongo pounced. Sank one head's teeth into Tuuth's arm.

Tuuth punched the giant dog's other face.

Chongo held on. Growling. Snarling. Shaking his heads.

"Let go of me!" Tuuth screamed, still punching, his gauntlets charged with energy.

Venir crawled over to his knife. A new fire in his belly. He closed his fingers around it.

Chongo's massive jaws crunched the bone in Tuuth's arm.

Still, the orc kept swinging.

Pow!

One head yelped. The other let go. Shaking, Chongo backed away. Sluggish, Growling. Teetering.

Arm limp on one side, Tuuth shook his glowing fist.

"I'm going to kill you, dog."

Venir stepped between them, knife behind his back, swaying.

"You have to kill me first," he said, "and you haven't done that yet, orc."

"I'm going to rip your head from your shoulders, Venir." Tuuth came at him.

Venir braced his feet.

Quick. Quick. Quick.

Tuuth drew back. Gauntlet glowing. Everything was in his swing. The big fist came.

Like a panther, Venir leapt up out of the muck pit and struck. Venir cut through armor. Muscle. Bone.

"Urk!"

The orc's yellow eyes widened. Blood filled his mouth. Tuuth punched.

Venir held on. Driving the knife deeper, he drove Tuuth to the ground. Twisting the blade one last time.

"I hate you, Out—"

Tuuth died.

Shaking, Chongo came by his side and lay down. Both heads licked the muck off of him.

Venir grabbed his mane. "You're too good to me, Boy."

A black bearded dwarf sailed high overhead, slamming into one of the ballista on the towers.

"No time to rest now," Slim said.

"What?"

Slim appeared from behind a wall of cornmeal barrels. "This party just started. They'll need your help. Ew, Chongo! Oh well. Now grab some weapons and gear, Venir. You've got underlings to slay."

"I've got a knife, Slim. I can barely lift it. The armament is gone, Slim. It's gone."

Snap!

With two underlings on his back, Mood continued to pummel the underling commander into submission.

Crack!

"Ye little underlings think yer a match for a Blood Ranger? Their king at that? I'll make a greasy smear of all of you."

Face broken, the underling commander jammed a dagger in Mood's side.

"Ho! Poking me with a tooth pick, now that's just insulting, stabbing me with anything smaller than a sword."

He brought his ham-sized fist down like a mallet into the underling commander's face, knocking it out cold. He tore the other two underlings off his shoulders and threw them to the ground.

Black Beards hacked them down.

Mood yanked the dagger from his shoulder and sunk it in the underling commander's heart.

A Black Beard, grisly from beard to toe, handed him his axes.

"By the bearded goats," he said, assessing the chaos, "we've got work to do!"

Underlings swarmed from all directions, their focus on the giants—the dwarves an afterthought. All the Black Beards huddled in a battle circle, striking with planning and precision, but they weren't here to roust the underlings. They were here to save Venir. The giants were just a distraction. A good one. But Mood had led them here.

They might be big, but they ain't so smart. They'll be after us soon enough.

One giant, with black hair down to his back, was scooping up underlings and throwing them over the wall. Another, heavyset as an ogre, stuffed the black fiends in his mouth like roaches, crunching bone and metal like canes of sugar.

"Get along the walls! Away from the giants!" Mood commanded. He swung, splitting an underling's face in half.

It was a battle. It was war.

I should've brought more dwarves.

A giant swinging an axe stepped into the fort through the southern gate. He was chopping up the catwalks like kindling when a blast of magic caught him in the face, sending him reeling into a store house. The giant's twin followed, helping his brother up before jumping up and destroying a fort tower with a lethal strike.

Underlings were dying. By dozens now. It was a great thing.

"Black Beards! Find my friend!" Mood said. "We need to get our wrinkled hides out of here!"

Days earlier, Mood and the Black Beards had tracked down a lone giant and killed it. That was what they did. Now, the giants were not only after their kin, Barton, but they had vengeance on their minds as well. Mood would deal with them when he had to. He never imagined Barton would lead them to Outpost Thirty One. They'd let themselves be captured. It couldn't have worked out better. The giants caught right up with them. He couldn't have asked for a bigger distraction.

"Hurry, Dwarves!"

A shadow fell over them. A giant with a gore-splatted club in his hand attacked. The first swing crushed two dwarves.

Fogle sat on the back of Eethum's horse, grinding his teeth.

The jungle erupted. Trees snapped, and footsteps shook the ground.

"Giants?" he asked.

Eethum shook his head yes.

"Aye, let's just hope they're not too late. Come."

"Late?"

"Hold tight, Wizard, and have your craft ready. Ee-Yah!"

Less than a mile away, they galloped up the mountainous slope. Fogle readied a pair of spells on his lips, squeezed his eyes shut, and summoned his powers. He was used to fighting underlings now. For a change, he'd be prepared.

"What are we supposed to do when we get there?" he shouted in Eethum's ear.

The big dwarf was silent, long red beard whipping in the wind.

Bloody dwarves are nothing but secrets.

Something big crashed into the branches above them and fell to the ground. Two underlings lay dead, one with a broken branch stuck in his eye. Fogle smiled.

Good. But what in Bish did that?

The horse burst through the trees and onto the road, hooves thundering over the path.

"Yah!" Eethum whipped the reins. A giant wearing a one horned helmet stepped in their path. Fogle's neck stretched upward.

The giant was as tall as the oaks. Three underlings floated in the sky, surrounding it, shooting lighting from their hands.

Zzzraam!

Zzzraam!

Zzzraam!

The giant roared, swinging blindly, covering its eyes with its arms.

The underling magi pressed their attack, shooting out the lightning that coiled up and down their arms.

"I'll show them," Fogle said.

He pointed and shot a bright green missile from the tip of his finger.

Zing!

It pierced one underling skull and entered another before blowing out the other side and into the third one's mouth. It gagged, hissed and swallowed a moment before it exploded. All three forms fell from the sky and thudded to the ground. The giant stomped each and every one of them, grinding them into the ground before moving onward.

Eethum stopped the horse, turned and eyed him.

"Don't do that again."

"What, kill underlings?"

"We're not here to kill underlings. We're here to save your friend—and my king, if need be. Protect yourself and your friend. When the time comes, you'll know."

"Killing underlings does protect us," Fogle said. "Killing giants does too, for that matter. And since when do you dwarves decide when killing is and isn't allowed? I say we go in there, kill them all, and sort it out later."

Eethum flashed his teeth and harrumphed.

"Aw, I like the way you think, Wizard Warrior," the Blood Ranger said.

Did I just say what I thought I said? I must be going mad.

Fogle thought of the image of his grandfather's blazing eyes and wispy white beard. The man enjoyed killing underlings more than anything else. *I'm not like that.* He glanced back at the giant footprints of underling goo and laughed. *Well, maybe I am a little.* He jumped off the horse.

"What are you doing?" Eethum growled, grabbing him by the cloak.

Fogle twisted away.

"Why wait to kill the evil bastards later when you can kill them now? I'm going in."

Eethum jumped off his horse and slapped it on the rear. Whipping out his axes, he said, "Mood was right, as always."

"About what?"

"The best wizards are the crazy ones."

CHAPTER 64

Master Kierway entered the arena, head high. The underling's eyes were more curious than they were fearful.

Creed's confidence dipped.

The Cowl on his head urged him forward.

Blood charging through him like a rushing river, Creed faced Kierway for the second time. Chill bumps ran down his arms.

"Fool, no man nor underling can best me, no matter the steel he swings." Kierway eased his swords from the sheaths on his back. "Your death was only delayed by circumstance." He shifted his stance. Circling.

The underling grandmaster of the sword was the fastest he'd ever seen. When they battled in the chamber, it had taken all of Creed's skill just to parry. *I'm faster now. Better now. Aren't I?*

The Cowl assured him he was. The swords in his hands said they were parts of him now. Like a snake's head and tail.

"I beg to differ," Creed said, "It was your death that was delayed."

Creed lunged.

Kierway spun out of reach.

Stabbing a fly would have been just as easy.

"Blast!"

"So, you grumble already, Human. Good."

Eyes flashing, Kierway attacked.

Ching! Ching! Ching!

Creed was on the defensive. Parrying the lightning fast blows. He'd never seen anyone move so fast before. It was astounding.

Rolling his wrists like a human windmill, he batted the attacks away.

The underling's blades were unrelenting.

Rip!

Kierway clipped him under the ribs.

Rip!

Across the thigh.

"Bone! You can't be so fast," Creed said, jumping away.

Kierway twirled his blades and laughed.

"Maybe you should stop talking and start fighting. You've swung once to my twenty," Kierway said. "Still, it's entertaining." He pressed forward.

Creed backed away. It was embarrassing. He'd been taught everything there was to know about the sword. Offense. Defense. Counters and strokes. But in seconds, the underling had negated all of it with superior speed and power.

'Loosen up, Bloodhound,' his mentor once said. 'Being too stiff will kill you. All the skill in the world won't save you when your instincts fail. Trust in them.'

Creed always had good instincts. He could size up an opponent quickly. A dipped shoulder. A slouched posture. Too much weight on one leg. Short arms. Long arms. Everyone had a weakness to exploit. Not this one.

Holding one sword behind his back, Kierway swung.

Clang!

"There. I'm making it easy for you. Swing back."

He wanted to swing.

The Cowl on his head wanted him to swing.

But one mistake would be fatal. He almost died the last time. He didn't want to die today.

Clang! Clang!

Kierway swung.

Creed parried. Backward he went. Stepping around dead bodies.

"Are you going to bleed to death?" Kierway said, eyeing his wounds. "I thought you wanted to fight. Give me a challenge, Human. Give me a fight of some sort before you die like the coward you are."

"Coward?" Creed said, his voice a little less mortal. It made him mad. His mind surged. "You—whose kind strikes at women and children in the darkness—are calling me a coward?"

"Yes, a soft one. A coward and a shoddy swordsman."

Torn between caution and rage, Creed had to choose. *Sometimes you have to trust your instincts and let loose.* He lowered his chin. *Swish. Swish.* "Let's finish this."

He attacked.

The Cowl rejoiced.

But Kierway was already spinning away. He'd seen the move before it happened.

Slice!

Creed clipped Kierway's shoulder. Red-black blood was spilled.

Kierway snarled and cut at his belly.

Creed sprung backward ten feet.

"Did you feel that, Underling?"

Kierway's eyes were molten.

Creed noticed something. An awareness. A second sight. *Go with it, Creed. Go with it!*

Steel crashed against steel like an armory caught in a tornado. Back and forth they went. Blood was let. Sweat dripped. Attack. React. Anticipate.

Creed's mind, body, and blades were one. His skill and instincts melded together. He turned. He changed. From a swordsman into a fearless fighting machine.

Slice!

Kierway ducked and countered.

Chop! Slice!

The underling's blade ripped into Creed's shoulder.

He drove his pommel into the underling's chin.

Kierway stuffed his knee in Creed's gut.

Steel flashed again. A pair of tireless storms trying to wipe out one another.

Duck!

Jump!

Parry!

Strike! Strike! Strike!

Creed didn't know if it was him commanding his body or The Cowl, but he was doing things he'd never done before. The underling's strikes came, precise and fatal, but they missed their mark, time and again. He bled. He fought. He learned.

"Such improvement, Human." Kierway said, "Unexpected. Impressive."

Master Kierway's hardened face lathered. His thin coat of fur showed a sheen.

Creed's own chest was heaving. He'd never fought so long. So hard. Pressed. Possessed. He fought on. *Kill the underling!*

Seconds passed that felt like minutes. Sparks of hot metal flew in the air.

Clip!

He caught Kierway below the knee cap.

Clip!

And under his left sword arm. His blades cut armor like bread.

"What manner of man are you that fights like many?" Kierway said, breaking off his attack, wiping the blood from his lips. The underling lowered his blade and stuck one in the ground. "A parlay, perhaps?"

Creed opened his mouth to speak.

Whish! Whish! Whish!

The underling's knives flicked through the air.

Creed battled one away, then two, catching the third in his chest.

"Now that's just dirty! Who's the coward now, Underling?" Creed plucked it out and slung it back.

Kierway ducked under it and laughed.

"Such words have no meaning to our kind. Your time to die has come, Human."

Chest burning, Creed shrugged is broad shoulders and stood tall in the face of his enemy. He might not have much time left to live, but he still felt like fighting. *Make the most of it!*

Kierway's swords came at his neck and thigh.

But Creed had seen them coming two steps ago. Lunging forward, he punched his right sword through Kierway's side.

Bang!

He head butted Kierway in the face, breaking his nose.

Kierway hissed, tearing himself away and clutching at his bloody side, copper eyes wide as saucers.

"Impossible!" he said, eyeing Creed as if he were someone else.

"Nothing's impossible!"

Creed charged. Inspired. He spun. He swung.

Kierway's swords were ready.

Creed shattered both of the underling's blades with his first blow.

Slice!

Kierway's head popped from his shoulders with the second blow. Blood sprayed. The underling fell.

Creed clutched at his chest and fell to his knees, sucking for breath and spitting blood.

"Now that was some glorious fighting. If I can only live to tell the ladies about it."

CHAPTER 65

I<small>T WAS STRANGE, STANDING ALONGSIDE</small> one of the most powerful women in the City of Bone, having her huddle in his arms.

If we had a soft bed and a secure room, I bet I could teach her a thing or two.

In little more than a stitch of clothing and without even a weapon in hand, Melegal prepared for his last stand.

"They won't kill you, Lorda," he said, pushing her between the wall and his back. "But I don't think they'll spare me."

"True," she said, her nails wrapped around his belly "but I may be able to convince them otherwise."

The idea had promise, but sooner or later, the odds of surviving were bound to catch up with him. *Cats have many lives, but perhaps rats have more.*

"I appreciate that," he said, "but you don't need to risk yourself. No one lives forever. Save yourself."

"How noble, Detective. You have a charming tongue. I wish we had more time."

Melegal's ears perked up, and Lorda Almen gasped.

Two underling soldiers came closer, black hair braided and old gold hoops in one's ears. One scraped his hand-axe along the wall, and the other let out an unfriendly chitter.

Melegal's grip tightened over Lorda's hand as the other pair closed in. Dark faced and armored in leather, there was something evil about them. Something sinister. Melegal never meddled in the affairs of underlings; he let Venir The Darkslayer handle that. The stories he heard and the things he had seen were more than enough to keep him away from the twisted breed.

Lorda pressed her soft lips into his back. "Sorry, Detective." She stepped into the clear.

The underlings stopped.

She pointed at Melegal. "I am the Lorda of this castle, and this man is my servant. No harm should come to me or him, Underlings." She had a convincing way of speaking. "Seize him if you must, but don't you dare lay a hand on me."

The nearest underling, red eyes glimmering, lowered his weapon, walked over and back handed her in the face.

"Silence, Human."

Lorda fell to the ground, gaping, rubbing her reddened cheek.

Another underling lowered a spear at Melegal's belly.

Melegal crept back into the wall, the spear tip nicking his exposed belly.

"This man will die, a painful death," the underling said, "but you, Woman, your death will look like an accident."

"You wouldn't dare," she said, shocked. "My husband is in good standing with your Lords. They'll punish you for this."

"No," the underling said. He pinched her face in his hand. "Human life has no meaning to us. No use to us. They'll be rid of you soon enough."

"You overstep your bounds, Black Swine. You've no order to kill or harm me, just him," her eyes flicked to Melegal, "... maybe?"

The longer they talk, the longer I live. His stomach groaned. A shadow darted between the walls. *What was that?*

"Put a hole in the noisy one's stomach."

Chop!

An underling's skull was split open.

Slice!

The head of another underling leapt from its shoulders, freeing Lorda.

Melegal twisted. The spear tip jabbed at his center.

Slice!

The underling spear-wielder lost both hands from forearm to finger.

Melegal turned.

Taller than him the battle-splattered warrior stood, eyes glowing a pale green through a dark cowl. Melegal blinked, thinking of Venir, but his man was different. Agile and swift. Quick and merciless. The face was obscured somehow. But he was certain it was Creed.

The last underling charged Lorda Almen, cutting at her throat.

Melegal dove for her, but he was too far away.

In one long stride, Creed cut the underling off and ripped his sword across its belly, spilling its bowels.

Creed sheathed his swords and clutched his chest. Reaching down, he lifted Lorda back to her feet.

"Who are you?" she said. Her fingers grazed his broad chest. "You're wounded."

"Aye, but it's already getting better." He bowed a little. "I'm Creed the Bloodhound, Lorda."

"No," Melegal said, getting back up, "that's not what you are, not right now." He craned his neck. "And more soldiers are coming." Melegal grabbed her arm. "Anything left in the arena?"

"Just the dead."

"Good," Melegal said. "That'll be our way to sanctuary then. Come on."

Through the entrance, down the steps and over the wall they'd gone when Melegal's keen eye caught something in the rack of weapons.

"I'll be," he said. He rummaged through the rack, strapping his swords, the Sisters, around his waist and finding something else. "Yes!" He grabbed his dart launchers and snapped them on. "Where is it?"

"Where is what?" Lorda said, trying to help.

"My cap."

"I'll buy you all the caps you want," she said, running her finger over his ear.

"No," he said, looking at her. "Have you seen it? Do you remember—"

"Yes, I remember. Last I saw it, well," she picked at her lip and shrugged. "It was in my husband's throne room, under heavy guard."

That bothered Melegal. Had they discovered the secret of his cap? Why else would they guard it? *Must get it back.*

"And the Keys?" he said.

"Same place."

"How many did you see?"

"Five, I think. But Kierway had one."

Finishing the last buckle on his dart-launchers, he searched the headless body of Kierway. Nothing. "Are you sure he had a Key on him?"

"I'm certain."

His neck snapped to the last spot he'd seen Jarla. She was gone.

"Slat! The witch has it!"

"What's so special about those Keys?" Lorda asked, brushing her hair out of her eyes.

The question struck him. There was little reason to believe that Lorda knew anything about the Keys. Lord Almen was a man of many secrets. As for the Keys, the easy way out of this was gone. He had no idea which Key went where, or what they all did. Did they need a door from the chamber or could they be used elsewhere instead?

"Did you notice the gemstone in it?"

Lorda's perfectly plucked eyebrows scrunched down.

"Sapphire, I believe," she said. "I only caught a single glimpse of it."

I didn't matter. It wasn't the one Melegal had used anyway.

Swish. Swish. Swish.

Creed was whirling his blades around his body in a marvelous fashion.

"Astounding," he said, "I cannot tell if it's the blades or me." He extended the keen edges outward, eyeing them. "I don't prefer hand guards." *Swish!* "But these are so flexible."

"And how about that... cowl... on your head?" Melegal started.

Creed slipped his blades into their sheaths. He didn't move. Instead, he stood still, cocking his head back and forth.

"Are you coming?" Melegal said. "Or are you waiting for more underlings to arrive?"

"There are so many," Creed said. "I can feel them running through the halls. Their hearts beat in my ears." He cast a dark foreboding glance at Melegal, and his voice changed a little. "I can kill them." His body tensed. "I can kill them all."

"No," Melegal said, "if you could do that, they'd be dead already."

"What makes you say that?"

"I know. Now..." He tossed Creed the sack. "You'll need that." He jammed two fingers down his throat.

"Ew, Detective, what are you doing?" Lorda asked. "Are you ill?"

Melegal spit a metal gob into his palm and rubbed the spit off. He flashed the light of his coin in their eyes and grinned.

"Follow me."

"You're resourceful, Detective. I'll give you that," Creed said. The man was chewing on jerky and flipping his coin of light. "This is the best jerky I've ever tasted."

"You don't have to call me detective, Creed. Melegal will do." He was sifting through a trunk in what used to be one of Sefron's hidden rooms. "Or not."

If Castle Almen didn't have so many secrets, we'd be dead already.

Of that much, Melegal was certain. And as for Sefron, his pasty nemesis, the cleric had been storing up for something. This room barely held the three of them, but it was filled with provisions, and it was only one room within a sprawling network. *I could spend a year exploring this castle, maybe more. I wonder how many secrets are in this world.* He looked at Creed and crunched into some fruit.

The man had finally pulled his cowl down off his head so it rested on his shoulders, and Melegal could make out his face. *Good.* For the time being, Creed was himself again. An overachieving thug in the ranks of Royals.

At least he doesn't have his loud and smelly dogs with him.

"Melegal," Lorda said, chin down, rubbing her arms. "Do you think all my family are dead?" She sobbed. "I saw them gut my niece and butcher one of my uncles before my eyes. They're monsters, aren't they?"

Just a little more so than your husband.

"There's no time to mourn, Lorda. Just escape."

"But?"

He put one hand on her shoulder, lifted her chin and looked into her eyes. "Be strong."

A tear fell down her cheek. Lorda had family, and they meant something. He was certain they were wiped out. Most all of them anyway. If he understood anything about underlings, he knew they didn't need people for anything, other than amusement. They were like cats that played with mice.

He fondled a small ring he'd found in one of Sefron's chests earlier. It was a flat metal with odd symbols, dust coated, and set with a variety of smooth gemstones. There were other baubles, but he had no pockets to stick them in.

"You're gorgeous," Creed said, staring hard at Lorda.

"What?"

Creed game closer, adjusting the bracers he'd pulled out of the sack and put on his arms earlier.

"You're more gorgeous," he repeated, "than the morning light in the gardens. Captivating."

Lorda pulled tighter around her form a gown Melegal had scrounged up for her.

"Mind yourself, Bloodhound," she warned. "I'm not some tavern trollop who'll swoon at your clever phrase of words. The finest troubadours in the land haven't swayed me, so how could a smelly hound like you?"

"Pardon, Lorda." He bowed with a grin. "It's a sincere compliment. But I'd be lying if I didn't admit that I'd cut my own arm off just for a—"

"Don't you dare, Heathen!"

"Shhhh! The both of you," Melegal said. "There's a hundred underlings out there looking for us."

"A taste of those sweet lips," Creed said, "was all I was going to say. What did you think I was going to say, anyway? I'm a Royal too, you know."

Lorda scooted farther away.

The last thing Melegal needed was a conflict with Creed. The man wasn't a brute, but he was all fighter. They needed him. They might have to carve their way out to escape.

Creed resumed his seat and tore back into his jerky. "What's the plan, Melegal?"

Melegal envisioned the last thing he'd seen from his spire before he came in here. Underlings were everywhere. The only safe way out was the same way he'd come in. With a Key.

Slat! And to think: I had seven of them, along with my freedom, and I came right back into this infernal Castle. What a vengeful fool I am!

"We need a Key, Creed. I think one Key is all it will take to get us free and clear. It's either that, or we're going to have to lay low in here, and it won't be long before the food runs out or they find us."

Eyeing Creed, Lorda said, "I'm ready to get out of here. I don't think this man can be trusted with me in these close quarters."

Creed perched his eyebrows. "My intentions are nothing but honorable. You'll need protection, Lorda. You can't expect me to believe you'd prefer the company of underlings to me?" He shrugged and looked at Melegal. "Then again, maybe you prefer the small gruesome kind. No offense."

"None taken."

Creed slipped The Cowl back over his head. "Let's be about our business." He held a finger up. "Wait, something comes."

Melegal stepped in front of Lorda, pushing her behind him. He hadn't heard a thing when a dark shadow slipped into the room.

Creed drew his sword.

"Wait," Melegal said.

"What is that?" Lorda said.

"It's my cat. Octopus."

Lorda let out a sigh.

Creed flipped him his coin. "That's the ugliest cat I ever saw. And those eyes. What is it, blind as a bat?"

"Blind as a bat and meaner than ten of your dogs."

"Huh."

Octopus rumbled, the hairs raising on his back.

Creed froze. "They're close."

"How close?"

Dust and debris fell from the ceiling above.

Wham!

Something pounded the floor above.

"Is that close enough for you?"

Bone! They're onto us.

Chapter 66

Slim dangled the pink flesh of Venir's missing ear in his face. "Hold still. This is going to sting. I can put it back on, but, I'm sorry, I couldn't find the other one."

"That's alright," Venir said. "I never listened much anyway. I don't think putting my ear on is going to do me much good eith—*urk!*"

Grabbing both sides of his head with extra-long fingers, Slim's hands glowed.

"Argh!"

Venir's bones crackled. His skin felt like it was on fire. It wasn't pain, not like all the other torments he'd faced the past few days, but it was uncomfortable. Disturbing. Unnatural.

"Bone! What are you doing, Slim?"

A storm raged between his temples. His bones moved. His skin crawled. His arms and legs thickened.

Slim's long, youthful face changed. His hair thinned. His eyes sunk back in their sockets.

Venir blinked hard.

Slim's red lips turned gray, and the skin on his body became mummified and dry.

"No, Slim! No!"

He tried to push his friend away, but Slim's lanky arms didn't budge.

Finally, Slim let out a ragged sigh, released him, stepped back, and fell to the ground. His long frame little more than a husk of skin and bone.

"Slim! Slim!" Venir said.

The cleric's teeth were cracked when he smiled.

"Don't worry about me, Vee. I'll be fine. Go get you some underlings."

One of Chongo's big heads licked the man.

Then Slim's eyes rolled up in his head.

Venir's head dipped to his chest, and his hand was white-knuckled on his knife. He was whole. So far as he could tell, he was as whole as he'd ever been. He'd been living in such pain.

Grabbing Chongo by the mane on his neck, he swung himself into the saddle. "Let's find me an axe and shatter some bones!"

Chongo surged forward.

Outpost Thirty One was in total disarray. A hundred underlings or more dragged one giant to the ground. A dozen underlings at a time were being stomped, leaving black smears in the dust. A wagon cart was tossed into one of the towers, and a giant bigger than all the rest beat his chest and roared, slamming his weapon across the ground, sweeping underlings away like bugs.

"Now that's an axe!" Venir yelled.

Chongo barreled through the sea of underlings, biting some and trampling others. Venir's eyes locked on the battle axe of a fallen brigand who'd been smashed into a bloody mud hole. Riding by, he snatched it off the ground. A second later, he gored an underling's head.

"It's sharp! It's metal! It ain't Brool. Yah! But it'll do!"

He brought the heavy axe down, busting armor and splitting through a clavicle. He was free.

Unfettered by his helm, he had clarity. Sweeping the battle axe from one side to the other. In seconds, gore coated his arms and chest.

The distracted underlings didn't see him and Chongo coming.

Crush!

Crumble!

Chomp!

"Over there, Chongo!"

Venir had spied an ailing Black Beard surrounded by a thicket of underlings. Chongo pounced on them. Venir dove into the ones he missed. Swinging left and right with all his might, opening chests and crushing in skulls. *Who needs the armament!*

Two strokes later, his corded arms turned to lead. His lungs caught fire. Out of the corner of his eye, he saw another pack of underlings closing in on him.

"Seems fear of the giants has rerouted their attack," he said, raising his axe over his head. "Come on, get them!"

Eethum led. Fogle followed. The Blood Ranger's axes sang to the underlings. A tune of death and destruction. Fogle tasted their oily blood in his mouth and spit it out. Above, the towering giants had failed to take over. Scores of underlings kept coming. Overwhelming the giants with sheer numbers. They crawled all over.

Fogle was torn. *Whose side should I be fighting for?* Even if they defeated the underlings, wouldn't the giants turn on him and the dwarves?

Thump!

Thump!

The entire fort shook. One of the giants, eyes close together, was slamming himself into one of the corner towers. Underlings spilled out, screeching on their way to the ground.

"Help the dwarves, Fogle!" Eethum said. "Keep your eyes out for Venir!"

Find Venir! And get out of here!

Wading through underlings and dodging oversized feet and weapons, Eethum led them up the stair onto the catwalks.

"See anything?" Fogle said.

"No!" Eethum said. The Blood Ranger was holding them off.

"There!" Fogle pointed.

Two Black Beards were fighting for their lives in the corner. Fogle unleashed his power. A bolt of lightning leapt from his fingers.

Sssram!

The chain of lightning ripped through one underling, then another. Piles of ash were scattered in the air.

A giant, bald and cock-eyed, leered down at him, raised his axe and swung. Eethum shoved Fogle out of the way. The catwalk shattered. They tumbled hard to the ground.

Breathless, Fogle got back to his feet just as the giant reached down for him.

Wham!

The ugly giant roared.

Somebody swung a club the size of a tree into its knee. It was Barton.

"Leave my Wizard friend alone, Haddad!"

Whack!

Haddad struck Barton across the face, knocking him from his feet, and turned back to Fogle.

"I'LL EAT YOU, WIZARD!" He patted his belly. "YOUR MAGIC MAKE HADDAD STRONG!"

Eethum burst into action, chopping into the bone below the giant's knee.

"ARGH! BLOOD RANGER! YOU SHALL PAY!" The giant was quick. It snatched Eethum off the ground and squeezed him.

Fogle drew his arms back, summoned his words, and started to cast.

Clonk!

A sling stone ricocheted off his head. Blood trickled in his eyes. The next thing he saw was Eethum flying through the air and the giant reaching for him.

I don't want to fly like that.

Fighting to lift his arms to swing, Venir's knees buckled when an underling's shield clipped the back of his chin. Trying to shake it off, he was too late. The underlings piled on top of him, clawing and tearing at his throat.

"Heeyah!" a familiar voice rang out, scattering the underlings like bloody moths.

Mood's arms pumped those axes into one underling after another, rekindling Venir's fire.

Venir caught his breath and burst into motion.

"Ain't so savvy without that helmet on, are ye?"

Venir, arms high, sunk his axe down into an underling's chest, shooting black and red blood up everywhere.

"No!"

Two more black beards joined in, the five of them forming a circle, keeping the underlings at bay.

"Where in Bish are all these roaches pouring out from, anyway!" Mood shouted, deflecting a chop at his neck on the blade of his axe.

"Northside War Room! There must be a tunnel in there!"

Hundreds of underlings lay dead, but where one fell, two more were coming. So far as Venir knew, the underlings never had a tunnel to the Outpost, but they could have dug one over the past few years. Chopping away, he watched another giant fall, leaving only three.

"What was your plan, Mood?"

"Carve a way in and rescue you! Carve a way out to freedom!"

That wasn't going to happen. The underlings covered the gates, and many were watching the giants fall. Ropes, grappling hooks, and magic cords wrapped the giants' legs and pinned their arms. Another giant pitched and stumbled, his head slamming into the wall. He roared while the underlings cut and stabbed at his back.

Thwack!

One of the Black Beards caught another ballista bolt in his back.

"Bone!"

"Tis a shame," Mood said, still swinging.

"What!"

"We could have made it, if not for all the extra underlings."

Fogle's plan had unraveled. He'd had on his lips the same spell he'd used to fight Tundoor and his breed. It was lost. Now, mind addled, he tried to recall another spell before he was crushed, then eaten.

One foot from his nose, the giant's fingers stopped. An enormous black shadow fell from the sky, shaking the ground.

WHUMP! WHUMP! SNORT!

Fogle's heart skipped. Two citrine eyes bore into him.

Blackie!

A tide of flames ripped through the underlings.

Ka-Chow!

Ka-Chow!

Ka-Chow!

Bolts of lightning fell from the sky, blasting underlings off the ground. Every portion of the battlefield was either lit up in a spectacular array of fireworks or consumed by flame.

Venir's attackers paused. Their hesitation was fatal.

Chop! Hack!

Two underlings fell.

"Head for the North Gate," Venir said. "The south is on fire!"

In front of them, the giants waded through the flames like they were water, stomping and chopping at every underling in sight. The black bodies were burning and dying by the dozens now, the others trying to flee.

Venir led Mood and the remaining Black Beards north under the catwalks, picking their way through the dead.

"We can take the drainage tunnel, if we can get to it."

"MOOD!"

The loud voice shook his bones. The biggest giant of all, hefting a battle axe over its shoulder, was coming after them.

"I'VE GOT YOU NOW!"

The Black Dragon was the last thing Fogle expected to see, until he saw Cass, sitting on its back.

"Cass!" he yelled, but nothing cut through the chaos.

Inspired, Fogle launched a magic missile into the hesitating giant's eye.

"ARGH!" it roared, stumbling backward.

He sent another one past Cass's face.

She jerked back, pink eyes hot with anger before she caught his gaze.

He waved and ran toward her at full speed.

Blackie whipped his serpentine neck in front of him, opening his mouth that was full of flames.

"No, Blackie!" Cass cried. "He's on my side."

One spell. One spell. One spell.

Boon soared off Blackie's back and floated into the sky.

Above Outpost Thirty One, five underling magi hovered, attacking the giants. He let them have it.

Ka-Chow! Ka-Chow! Ka-Chow! Ka-Chow! Ka-Chow!

Lightening ripped out of the clouds and through their robes, sending them twirling and smoking to the ground. Below him, Blackie, flames shooting from his mouth, landed on the ground.

"Burn them! Burn them all, Blackie!"

The smoke was black and thick, and the smell of burning flesh foul, but Venir and Mood waded through it, trying to avoid the giant.

"I CAN SMELL YOU, MOOD!"

CRASH!

The giant was destroying everything in its path, trying to get at them.

"GIANTS! SECURE... THE... GATES! THE... KING OF THE DWARVES... IS HERE! KILL HIM... AND... HIS KIN!"

Ka-Chow!

The giant's face was lit up by a lightning strike.

Venir stopped and took a look.

"Are ye mad?" Mood said. "Keep moving."

Venir gazed up at the man floating in the air. It was the old wizard, Boon, scraggly hairs whipping in the wind, eyes filled with power.

Where'd he come from?

"PARLEY!" Boon said in a voice that was loud like thunder.

The giant, Haddad, rubbed his temples. "WHAT, WIZARD? HAH, YOU... CANNOT... PARLEY... WITH US. WE... HAVE... YOU. ALL... OF...YOU."

Venir tugged at Mood's shoulder. "Let's move."

Mood rose his hand up. "Nay, let them parley, Venir. It buys us time, if nothing else."

Behind Haddad the giant, another one had Barton slung over his shoulders. The deformed giant was kicking and screaming.

"TOYS! VENIR, GIVE ME MY TOYS! BARTON WON'T GO BACK WITH YOU, HADDAD! BARTON HATES YOU ALL! AND BLACKIE, TOO!"

"THE TOYS ARE GONE, BARTON!" Boon said.

"LYING WIZARD TRICK BARTON JUST LIKE VENIR DID BEFORE! BARTON WILL SMASH VENIR. CRUNCH HIS BONES. HE IS A LIAR!"

Haddad the giant reached back and walloped Barton in the head.

"NO MORE... TROUBLE FROM YOU... TEASER OF DRAGONS!"

Barton's hand went to his eye. He started to cry.

"HE STARTED IT!"

"SIIIIILENCE!" Haddad said, shaking everything on the ground. "WIZARD, I OFFER THIS! I TAKE PRISONER THE BLOOD RANGER KING, MOOD. BLACKIE THE DRAGON AND THE TINY GIANT," He pointed at Barton, "MUST COME HOME." He spat a giant gob onto the ground. "THE REST CAN LEAVE."

Another giant stepped forward, squeezing a black beard between his fingers.

Venir swore the black-faced dwarf was purple.

Giants are liars. But are they good liars?

Remaining still, Fogle's eyes were transfixed on his grandfather, who was negotiating with the giants. Out of nowhere, a pair of warm pale arms wrapped around his waist.

"Miss me?" Cass said. She kissed him on the cheek.

He struggled to choke out the words. "I thought I'd lost you, Cass. I'm so—"

She put her finger to his lips.

"Shush, Fogle, I'm alright." She gave him a reassuring embrace. "And Blackie, believe it or not, has been quite good to me."

He glanced over at the dragon. There was jealousy in those yellow eyes.

"But, how?"

"I'm a druid, remember. I can communicate with all living things. And Blackie and I," she said, nodding at the dragon with great admiration in her pink eyes, "we understand one another."

Fogle chewed on his lip. He'd seen that look in the eyes of women before. Her arms around his waist had already slackened. *No. This can't be happening.* What had Venir told him on the trail before? *'Bish is full of surprises. And women even more. Get used to it.'*

"You're going with the dragon, aren't you? Over me—A man!"

She caressed his face, looked up into his eyes, and said, "Oh Fogle, you knew it could never last, me and you."

It tugged at his chest, but he knew she was right. The two of them couldn't be any more different, but what they had shared had been wonderful. He didn't want to let that go.

"I never really thought about it. I was too worried whether you were alive or dead." He stepped away from her a little. "And now," he glared at Blackie, "you choose a beast over me?"

"Don't be that way, Fogle."

"What way? Sane?"

"No," she said. Her cheeks reddened. "A grown man acting like spoiled child who lost his favorite toy. Shame on you, Fogle. I'm not yours to claim. I never was."

"I risked my life for you! I fought that dragon! And this is the thanks I get? Come on, Cass!"

"Oh Fogle, don't be so dramatic," she said, walking away and onto Blackie's back. "It's not manly. An adventurer should know that." She sighed. "At least you'll know what to do with the next pretty woman you meet."

Fogle turned away.

Of all the ridiculous things.

"Here," Mood said to Venir, handing over his axes.

"For what?" Venir said, feeling a little foolish for some reason.

"Cause you'll be needin' them, I'm certain. I'll not where I'm going."

"You can't be serious, Mood?" Venir said. He looked at the giant that talked with Boon. He couldn't understand it. He turned back to Mood. "You're the King of the Dwarves. You can't leave your people."

"It's better to be a live King than a dead one." He winked. "And don't worry; they can't hold me forever. I'll outlive them first."

Venir took the axes. Mood walked out to the giant. "Alright, Haddad! I'll come with you, but all my dwarves and people stay!"

Chongo stammered his paws on the ground. Black tails flicked back and forth like whips. His big jaws snapped.

Venir got in between both heads and hugged Chongo's necks. The dog would do anything for him. He'd do anything for the dog. But things had changed. He could feel it in his bones. Without the armament, the underlings would catch up with him sooner or later. They would catch Chongo too, if he stayed with Venir.

He couldn't protect his dog. The dog couldn't protect him.

"I've got to let you go, Boy." He rubbed his forehead on Chongo's big chest. "Go with Mood." He pointed at the dwarf.

Mood stood, shoulders stooped, holding his side a little.

"Mood needs you, Boy. He's getting old."

Both of Chongo's heads licked Venir one last time.

Venir rubbed his dog behind all four ears. "Take care of him, Chongo. If anyone can lead the old curmudgeon out of there, you can." He hugged the muscular necks once more.

Chongo, with one head looking backward, walked away. Venir wiped the blood from the corner of his eye.

"Dog come with Barton? Good. Barton like that." Barton sighed in the clutches of two other giants, like the child he was. He struggled in vain. His chin dipped. They were bigger and stronger than him.

The other giant set Eethum down, and one by one the giants faded into mist, along with Chongo, Barton, and Mood, whose thick arms crossed his bearded chest.

Whump! Whump! Whump!

Cass and the dragon lifted off the ground and into the sky. Fogle's head was down, but Boon waved goodbye to Cass, a big smile on his face. Only three men, a handful of dwarves, smoke, fire and carnage remained.

"Now what?" Fogle said. "Is it over?"

"Or has it just begun?" Boon cried out, pointing.

The underlings that had fled earlier were coming back now. There were well over a hundred. Venir readied his axes and dug into the ground.

"So be it, men!" He yelled out at the top of his lungs, "RELEASE THE HOUNDS OF CHAOS AND CRY BISH!"

"Wait, Venir. There has to be another way to get out of here," Fogle suggested.

"To the last, Grandson! The time for a final stand has come!" Boon said, lightning racing up his arms.

Eethum the Blood Ranger shouted over all of them.

"Over there! Look!"

One of the Black Beards was waving them over from the entrance to the War Room.

Venir growled. "That's where the underlings came from earlier."

"Well, they're not coming from there now!" Fogle started running.

"Slat! Let's go then!"

Dashing across the courtyard, the small party barreled through the doors, stepping over dead underlings, ignoring the ones that still burned.

The Black Beard led them through a panel in the wall that Venir had never noticed before and down a wide set of carved out steps. At the bottom, a long corridor ten feet tall and just as wide led to another door, which was open.

"Fool! What does this do, lead to the Underland? I'm not going in." Fogle turned away.

Behind them, the underlings were coming. Chittering and screeching as they entered the War Room.

"We either fight them out here, or in there, but having that big door between us will buy us some time to prepare, at least," Boon said. "I say we go in."

"Well, time's a wasting," Venir said, watching the underlings tear up the corridor. "It's now or never, Wizard."

"Fine!" Fogle said, being the first to enter.

Boon was next, followed by the Black Beards, Eethum and Venir, who pulled on the door handle, trying to close it.

"See any underlings yet?" Venir said between clenched teeth.

No one said anything.

Venir and Eethum kept pulling, but the underlings fought them on the other side.

"Heave!" he yelled.

Eethum grunted.

Venir pulled with all his might, pinching underling fingers around the edges.

"Hurk!"

The door sealed shut. Eethum slammed the bolt in place.

"Whew!"

Suddenly, Venir's instincts caught fire. He knew he'd made a big mistake. In the distance, something evil chittered and twisted.

Chapter 67

"Dogs," Creed said. "Has to be."

Melegal could hear nails scratching at the ceiling above them.

"It's your cat that led them to us, Melegal," Creed said, "but I can handle them if they catch up. Just lead us."

With Lorda hanging onto his hand, Melegal led the way through the winding secret passage until the clawing above them came to a stop.

"See? They're stuck in one room, and we're beneath another, so it's not my cat." Shining a tiny beam of light forward, he realized Octopus was no longer around. *Good.* He wasn't going to admit it, but Creed was probably right.

"They're still going to catch up with us," Creed said, eyes glowing in the dark through The Cowl.

Melegal shook his head. Something about the man disturbed him. Creed was eerie. Unpredictable. And to make matters worse, he was a Bloodhound. Part of a notorious bunch of chaotic goons. *Keep your back in the front and front in the back.* There was no telling what the man would do, and he had the armament now. Melegal remembered Jarla, who had it before. She was the most evil woman Venir ever knew.

"Just keep your swords ready, Creed. We've still got a shot at getting out of here yet."

"Are we going to the Throne Room?"

"Aye. We're going to steal a Key." *Or as many as I can get my hands on.*

Melegal's eyes glared through a peep hole.

The Throne Room was empty. No guards. No underlings. No Keys. No hat.

Where in Bone could they be?

"What is it, Melegal?" Lorda clung to him. "What do you see?"

"Nothing," he said, "see for yourself. It seems they've moved the bloody things."

"If I were a Key, where would I be?" Creed said, oddly.

On the one hand, Melegal was relieved he didn't have to face the underlings. On the other hand, he'd have to start all over again, with the underlings already looking for them.

"Perhaps I can find out, Melegal," Lorda suggested. "Lords Catten and Verbard are working with my husband. If I can get to them…"

"No! They tried to kill you once already. Besides, I can only assume they are either in the Keep or the Chamber."

"Perhaps the Chamber is where we should go. The Keys will be there at some point, won't they?" she said, pressing up against him. "We could hide and wait them out."

"I've already thought of that," he said, rubbing his aching neck. He brushed up against Lorda who brushed back. *So amazing. Even in perilous times.* "But they probably have more guards there than anywhere."

"Then I'll have to kill them all," Creed said.

The madness never ends.

All Melegal wanted was his hat, at least one of the Keys, and his own castle. He was pretty sure his own castle was the most attainable of the three.

"Move or die, Detective," Creed said. "Move or die."

"I'll be," Lord Verbard said. "He's butchered."

Lord Catten was holding up Master Kierway's head, unable to hide the shock in his golden eyes.

"Do you think Master Sinway will be angered or pleased?" Catten said, handing the head to one of his Juegen.

Verbard gawped at the mutilated Vicious on the ground. "Probably more angered about the Vicious than his son." He shook his head. "What do you make of this, Jottenhiem?"

"A swordsman," the red-eyed commander said. "An outstanding one at that. Master Kierway was one of the finest swordsmen in the Underland, after me and a few others, of course."

"You boast, Commander," Catten said. "Much as I hate to admit it, Kierway's skill was without rival."

Jottenhiem glowered at him. "If you say so, Lord Catten."

"Stay close, Commander," Verbard said. "Whoever did this... well..."

"Might be The Darkslayer, Brother? Is that what you're thinking?"

It was exactly what Verbard was thinking. It worried him. It more than worried him.

"Eep!"

The bat-winged imp buzzed up to him out of nowhere, rubbing its taloned fingers together.

"Yess, Lordsss. Is it time to kill?"

"It's always time to kill," Verbard said, "but the hunt must go on first. Find who did this, imp, and report back to me, immediately."

"As you wish, Lordsss Verbard," Eep hissed and looked at his brother, "and Catten."

Blink.

With Eep gone, Verbard and Jottenhiem were continuing their brief investigation when he discovered something else.

"We've another problem," Verbard said.

"Oh, and what is that?" Catten replied.

"Master Kierway's Key is gone."

"Well, Master Sinway won't be happy about that either, but he said we only needed one Key. We still have seven. Kierway's Key didn't do much of anything."

"It did enough to help anyone escape."

Catten twirled a dark gray cap on his fingertip. "Are you suggesting The Darkslayer fled?"

"We don't know that it was The Darkslayer." Verbard's nails dug into his palms. "And what is that on your finger?"

"A mystical item."

"What does it do?" Verbard's hand slid inside his pocket over his Orb of Imbibing.

"I don't know yet, but I will soon."

"It's ugly."

"It's charming."

"Well, I wouldn't be wearing it when Master Sinway arrives."

Catten slid it into his pocket. "I suppose the time has come to greet him." He pulled a Key from his pocket. "Shall I let him enter, or shall you? I could lead him to your Throne Room, if you like."

"Or I could lead him to yours, Brother. But we'd better be rid of this scourge first."

Verbard tossed Lord Almen's whip to Jottenhiem.

"Soon you might get your chance to prove who is better: Kierway or you, Commander."

CHAPTER 68

V ENIR FELT LIKE ONE SIDE of his body was going out the other.

"Bish! What is happeninggggg?"

He felt the wind whoosh through his hair. A split second later he stopped.

"Fight, Man! Fight!"

It was the old wizard, Boon, yelling. Yellow strands of light licked from his fingertips, striking at the hive of underlings surrounding them.

Choking down the queasiness, Venir lashed out.

Slash!

An underling warrior fell dead with its neck open.

"You fight well, Warrior." Eethum banged one attack away and countered another. "But can you fight long?"

Glitch!

The Blood Ranger gored the underling's chest.

Venir, brow buckled, did what he did best. He swung and swung, giving no thought to where he was or what he did.

"Fight and die!" he cried

Fogle's first question wasn't 'Where am I?' but 'How much longer am I going to live?'

He blasted the first underling he saw in the face, knocking a hole in it and barreling two more over. In the dim light, he caught glimpses of a large chamber that was rows deep in underlings.

I can't be in the Underland! I can't be!

He summoned a mystical shield and glanced over his shoulder. The door they'd come in was sealed.

There must be another away out of here.

Two underlings converged on him, mouths wide, curved swords low. The first struck hard, its edge glancing off his shield, cracking it. The other slammed into him with its full weight, pushing him backward. They kept swinging, chipping away shards of magic one piece at a time. Something ignited in Fogle.

No!

The underlings. They'd caused so much anguish. So much pain. He'd lost Cass because of them!

NO!

He shoved his arms forward. His attackers were flung backward, clearing a hole at the bottom of a wide torch-lit stairwell that was otherwise filled with more underlings coming down.

"Hahahaha," he heard his grandfather laughing, "Brilliant, Fogle! Brilliant!"

Boon flung a ball of smoke up the stairwell. It exploded in a puff of air, leaving behind it a wall of stone. Those underlings were sealed outside the chamber.

"Have at them, warriors!" Boon cried, eyeing the hoard of underlings that still surrounded the party. "Let's route these fiends once and for all! Hahahaha!"

Like two Juggernauts, Venir and Eethum gored every black thing breathing.

"Bish!" Fogle lifted his feet from the suction of the floor. The fallen were being sucked dry. Dry husks in an instant. A nasty chill went through him. "What is this place?"

"Eight!"

Chop!

"Nine!"

Slice!

Arms heavy, chest filled with fire, Venir kept swinging. Mood's well-crafted axes could cut metal, but they weren't as light and balanced as Brool's keen edge that he'd grown so accustomed to over the years.

Gashed from chin to toe, he fought on and on, mindless of anything else. He'd gotten his wish. He'd sent more underlings to the grave. He could die complete. Happy. He buried one axe in the next underling's chest.

Large drops of dark blood showered the odd mosaic floor, which sucked every bit up.

"Venir!"

Eyes blazing, he whirled.

"They're all dead," Boon said. "Look around."

Twenty underlings, maybe thirty, were being sucked dry by the floor, their flesh withering.

"Aw." Eethum knelt down at the armored shell of a Black Beard. The dwarf was one of only three that now remained.

Venir's wounds dripped like sweat, feeding the yearning floor. His skin crawled. "We need out of this cursed place." He walked over and tugged on the handles of many doors. "Hurk! Get over here, Eethum, and help me!"

The dwarves remained kneeled, holding hands, heads bowed over their fallen comrade.

Venir tried the next. Then another after that.

"You need a Key, Venir," Boon said, with Fogle standing by his side, panting.

"I've got my own Key." Venir swung Mood's axe into the wood, juttering his arms. "Son of a Bish! It's harder than stone."

"It's magic," Boon said, taking a stroll around the room. "Hmmm... six doors." He peeked into the alcove, where seven lonely pegs remained. "I'll be. Strange. Tricky."

"What?" Fogle's face was drawn up as he shook underling guts from his robes.

"This room," Boon said, his voice filled with wonder, "I believe is an ancient device I've read about before. It's a Chamber of Transportation. As I understand, it can take you anywhere in the world. Very mysterious magic this is. Ancient. Dark. Dangerous." He ran his hand over one of the doors. "If the underlings have the Keys... my... well, that would explain a lot of things."

"Any idea where we are now?" Fogle asked.

"If you still have a map in that spellbook, we can certainly find out."

"And what of that barrier you created, Boon?" Fogle said. "How long will that hold?"

"Hours, unless they bust through it or have a mage to dispel it, and I don't think they do."

Venir made his way around the room, testing the doors anyway while he gathered his thoughts.

Fogle had changed a great deal. The lines on his face were hardened, and his skin was darkened and tough. The wizard even had a ragged beard covering his face, giving him a dwarfish look.

Fogle caught him staring. "I'm glad we found you, Venir. And I'm sorry about your dog—and Mood. I spent a great deal of time with the both of them, looking for you."

Venir nodded and turned away. So much had happened. He didn't know what to think. His friends, the best ones he'd ever known, were all gone on account of him. The armament was gone as well. He felt naked without it. Still he lived. And Slim, what had happened to him? Had that man given Venir his very life?

"Aw, give me that book, Fogle," Boon grumbled, taking it away. "You're got mintuar hooves for fingers. It's a wonder you managed to write down anything."

"At least I don't waste what I've written."

"Pah, here it is," Boon said, fingering the book. "Just give me a few minutes."

Leaning against one of the doors, Venir squatted down, took a deep breath, and closed his eyes. He was tired, and his bones were aching.

Boon and Fogle stretched out a mystic map on the mosaic floor and gawped. Then one said to the other, "We're in Bone!"

"What?"

"Venir," Boon said, waving him over. "Look at this."

Venir raised his big frame off the floor and sauntered over. Boon's aged and crooked finger was pointing down on a map that shrunk and grew with a wave of his hand. Venir could see everything. He pointed at a red dot that was located on a drawing of a castle.

"I can see the entire city," Venir said, wiping his brow with his forearm. "I can even see the alleys. Huh, that's Castle Almen."

"Are you certain?" Boon asked, perching one eyebrow.

Venir glared at him. "I'm certain."

Boon rose to his feet and tugged at his white beard. "Hmmm… They've taken over a Castle. Possibly many of them."

"Or the entire city," Fogle said.

"Then that means they'll be coming right back for us," Boon said, eyeing the stone wall that protected them. "Any minute now. We're at the very heart of the battle now. Hah! We may have just squandered their plans after all. But I sense something. Someone familiar."

"I sense something too, Grandfather," Fogle said. "Are you thinking what I'm thinking?"

Venir didn't know nor care what either one of them was thinking. He just watched. They clasped hands.

But knowing that they were back in Bone? A place he thought he'd never see again? That sent a charge right through him! He was ready now. Ready to tear the wall down and carve a bloody path back to the Drunken Octopus. He warmed his hands on the glow of one of the torches.

Boon and Fogle cried out. The pair, fingers locked, were shaking. Eyes rolled up in their heads.

Venir tried to separate them, but Eethum stayed his hand.

"No," he said in a stern voice, "there's nothing we can do now. They're in a battle they must fight on their own."

Crack.

Boon's wall of stone cracked and began to crumble.

Eethum and the two other dwarves surrounded the interlocked wizards. "We'll protect them as long as we can."

Venir took his place at the bottom of the steps. "I'll kill underlings as long as I can."

Chapter 69

"**L**ead the way, Detective," Creed stepped aside.

Still holding Lorda's hand, he brushed past Creed's chest.

"Beg Pardon," the man said. "But that's worth risking your life for."

"You incorrigible, Piiii—"

Two clawed hands burst through the wall. Lorda was yanked through the wood and plaster, leaving a gaping hole.

"What in Bish was that thing?" Creed said.

Melegal darted through the hole and found himself facing his worst nightmare. It was Eep the imp, hovering in the air, holding Lorda Almen by the neck in his clawed fingers.

"We meetsss again, Skinny One," the imp said. Its long tongue licked up and down Lorda's dangling body, which kicked and flailed.

Melegal only had one dart in his launcher. He took aim.

Better make it count.

"Drop the woman!" Creed said, stepping into the clear, swords ready. "Slat, you're an ugly thing. What in Bish are you?" He looked at Melegal.

"An imp."

Creed shrugged. "Drop her, Imp, or taste my steel."

Eep laughed, rose twenty feet high into the throne room, and dropped her.

I've found them, Mastersss.

Found who? Verbard replied.

The Skinny Man who had the Keys, a woman, and the murdering swordsman you seek.

Where?

In the Throne Room.

"That was fast," Catten said. "Even for an imp."

Suddenly, Verbard's and Catten's eyes locked.

It cannot be, Brother, Verbard thought.

"But it is," Catten hissed through curled lips.

Someone was searching for them. An old enemy. A great foe. An enemy they'd fought decades ago.

"Boon! And his grandson, Fogle!"

"How did they get here? Where did they come from?"

"They must be in the chamber."

Verbard fingered the Keys in his pocket, as did Catten. They were all there except the one Kierway had lost, the one that led to Outpost Thirty-One.

"So they were the source of all the commotion? They're here? How did they make it through an entire army?" Catten was outraged. The surrounding castles were still attacking, and he'd sent all their reserves to Outpost Thirty One for reinforcements. How many giants had arrived down there?

"What do you want to do, Brother?" Verbard said.

Catten slipped the cap on his head. "Boon is not what he was; I can sense it. And his grandson is still green." Catten rubbed at his side where Fogle had zinged him months before. "I think I can hold them."

"Then I'm after that swordsman, whoever he is," Verbard said. "Jottenhiem, come with me and bring every soldier you can spare. We'll wipe this out quickly."

CHAPTER 70

FOGLE'S KNEES KNOCKED. HIS CHIN rattled. His mind rocked and reeled. The image of the golden eyed underling Catten snickered in his head. He and Grandfather were somewhere else. A battlefield in the inner mind, inescapable and chaotic.

"Grandfather! Grandfather!" he sputtered out, fingers knotted around Boon's.

The old man's body withered and sagged to the ground, making a feeble gasping sound.

Fogle remembered the last time he'd locked minds with Catten. It had almost killed him, and now, the underling was prepared. Enlightened. More powerful.

"You will die, Human. You and the old man both."

Biting into his lip, Fogle felt his mind collapsing on itself, turning dark and filling with despair.

Hold on, Fogle. Hold on.

The voice was weak and distant.

The underling was slowly ripping Fogle's mind from his grandfather's. A great gaping maw filled with razor sharp teeth was ready to devour them. Swallow them into an abyss forever. A long yellow knotty tongue lashed out around his grandfather's waist and reeled the old man in. Boon's face was sagging and withered, his grip, once strong as iron, struggled to hang on.

I won't let him go! Fogle's feet anchored themselves to the warbling floor. *I beat you once! I can beat you again!*

Catten chuckled and spiked a shard of power in his head.

"Aargh!"

The pain stabbed between his eyes. Excruciating. His entire body felt like it was melting into a gooey drop, ready to be swallowed whole.

Think, Fogle! Think!

His fingers slipped from his grandfather's.

On the other side of things, Catten was laughing and dusting his long nails on his robes.

"This cap is amazing," he said to himself, making his way out of the arena. He thought of his brother and Master Sinway. "It gives me that edge I've been seeking."

The stone wall crumbled. The first underling rushed through. Its head was splattered all over the walls.

"Ten!" Venir roared.

But the stairwell was three beasts wide, and the ranks of underlings deeper than a well.

Hack! A clawed hand was lost.

"Elven!"

Crunch! A chest caved in.

"Twelve!" Blood spurted from an underling's neck.

Glitch!

Venir took a punch to the shoulder, lost his footing and stumbled backward.

"Blast yer hides!" he screamed, swinging wildly, keeping them at bay.

"Get over there, Black Beards!" Eethum yelled and ran at the same time.

Three dwarves in heavy armor rushed forward, plugging the stairwell. Steel clashed on steel. Axes splintered bone. Long knives sifted through weak points on armor. Slowly, the dwarves, busted and bleeding, were being pushed backward.

Venir took a quick glance over his shoulder. The wizards had collapsed on the floor. Like their bones were missing. They twitched. He growled. The underlings had taken his friends, and now they had taken his city. He was tired of losing. A raging storm ignited inside him.

"Rrrrrah!"

Charging, he leapt over the dwarves into the underlings.

Yes, Fogle. Yes! Boon said to him, his withering voice stronger than before. *Do it! Do it quick!*

Fogle hung on. Struggling for his sanity, bearing every cruel twist and turn, searching for a weakness in the underling's probing mind. He summoned The Darkslayer. The underling laughed. One door slammed closed. *Find another.* Fogle found something. *Yes.* The green amulet that he'd given to Venir to track him. *Yes.* He'd put it in Catten's robes when he exchanged them for his spellbook. It was a little something he'd planned on sharing with Boon when the time was right.

The time is right now! Boon said. The old wizard's eyes were opened wide. He grappled with the tongue that held him. Grabbing the lip of the beast that tried to swallow him, his arm now held a pick-axe, which he sunk into its lip and held on. *I can hold on! Let me go and strike!*

"NO!" Fogle said, "I can't risk it!"

You've no choice now. The iron in Boon's eyes had returned. *Do something. Quick! Before he finds out!*

"I can't get out of here." Fogle said.

Do it!

Boon, geared up in his mystic armor and sword, dove into the belly of the beast and disappeared.

"Noooooooooo!"

CHAPTER 71

MELEGAL AND CREED ARRIVED AT the same time, catching Lorda, who'd fainted.

"Nice catch," Creed said, looking upward.

Eep's wings buzzed. He was laughing. *Blink!*

"Watch out!" Melegal said.

Eep popped up behind Creed. *Slash! Slash!* Tore into his back.

Blink!

"Argh!" Creed said. "Bish!"

Melegal's head swiveled on his shoulders. He'd seen the imp tear men into dog food in seconds. *Run! Get Lorda and get out of here!*

Creed turned his back to him and said, "How bad is it?"

Two bloody gashes formed a nasty X beneath his shoulders.

Eyes intent, Melegal took a quick glance.

"Just a scratch."

He moved away. *Where is that thing?* His eyes drifted towards the only exit. "No," he said, shoulders sagging.

"What?" Creed said, looking around.

Several underlings entered the room.

Eep buzzed alongside a floating underling with bright silver eyes. Accompanying him was a burly underling soldier with a shaven head and dark ruby eyes. Lord Almen's whip glowed in his grip. Four other underlings in dark chain armor escorted them. The floating underling hesitated in midair a moment, pointing at Creed as it spoke.

"Jottenhiem, Eep, kill him. Leave the skinny one to me."

Creed could feel them. Sense them. They were going to kill him.

"Let's give it a go then. Shall we?"

One by one, the four underlings, brandishing a variety of sharp blades, surrounded him. He glanced at Eep, his keen ears keeping track of the buzzing. *Not going to let that happen again.*

The bald underling with the whip chittered out a command. The well-trained team of underlings struck in unison.

Creed was already moving. He stepped into one underling. *Stab!* Piercing its heart in a lightning fast strike. *Swish!* He ducked under the next cutting blade.

Clang! Slit!

He ripped the sword out of one's hand and took its throat.

Gulch!

Gored the face of another.

Slice!

Tore the innards from the third.

Chop! Chop! Chop! Chop!

And butchered the fourth's head like a melon.

He took a bow.

"Next."

The imp and the whip-wielding underling circled him.

Blink!

The imp was gone.

The bald underling uncoiled the mystic whip and grinned.

Wupash!

"Oh, Great."

He backed towards the thrones. He had no sense of where the imp was. He needed a barrier on his backside. *You won't be getting to my back again.*

Blink!

Eep re-appeared right in front of his face and latched onto his chest.

"NOOOO!" Creed yelled. He dropped his swords. Grabbed the imp by the throat. The creature was solid. Muscle. Hard knotty skin and bone. He was no wrestler. "Get off me!"

Eep was merciless. Talons dug deep into his flesh. Its oversized jaws bit hard into his shoulder.

Creed punched the imp. It was like hitting a rock. He'd been in hundreds of fights, but he'd never faced anything supernatural like this. He punched and punched.

Wupash!

Eep blinked away, reappearing alongside Jottenhiem.

Creed sagged to his knees, fingers searching for his swords.

Wupash!

The whip coiled around his neck and jerked him to the ground.

Creed's head was burning hot. He clutched at the air.

Melegal's feet were lifted from the ground. He sailed right into Lord Verbard's powerful grasp. The underling squeezed his neck.

"Interesting for a human, you are. A survivor. I might have a use for you yet."

The words registered, but the meaning was lost. *I'm choking to death.* He twitched and recoiled from the depth of evil in those silver eyes.

A long shiver went through him when Verbard said, "Of course, it all depends on how long your breath can last. Can it last longer than my grip, Little Rat?"

Chapter 72

"Eh..." Catten mumbled, his golden eyes flaring.

Boon, a forgotten nemesis, had become a great fish hooked and struggling on his line.

"So be it, Enemy! I'll kill you first and take your grandson next."

He released his grip on Fogle Boon's mind, blasted every stitch of armor from Boon's body with a single thought, and started shoving Boon's broken form into a deep, dark, grave.

Fogle gasped. Breathing again, recollecting his senses, he crawled over to his spellbook and thumbed through the pages. Blinking hard and trying to block out the sounds of battle that echoed in the chamber, he found the page he needed.

He pressed his finger on the first word.

"I never thought I'd do this." He touched his grandfather's unmoving form. Boon was ashen and cold. Knowing it would erase the spell, Fogle read straight from the book.

The first word was soft, like a drink of sweet wine. The next syllable exploded in his mind, taking it yonder and back in a split second. His face lit up. His back straightened when the last syllable fell. "Eethum, get ready!" The page of the spellbook faded into smoke.

The air sizzled, shimmered and crackled.

Underling Lord Catten materialized before them, his wizened face gaping.

"What!" he said, outraged. Bewildered. "You shall pay for—"

Slice!

Eethum's stroke took his head from his shoulders. Its bright golden eyes rolled over the ground.

"I did it," he said, looking at Eethum. "He's dead. He's really de—"

Clang! Bang! Crunch!

Fogle whipped his aching head around. *Venir!* Buried in underlings, the big man was in for.

The underlings. Their hatred was deep. Venir's was deeper.

Chop!

Rage. They ignited it. He hated them. The smell of them. The sight of them. The oily stink of them. And he was going to kill them. Kill them all.

Hack!

He was a hurricane. Dwarven steel gone wild.

He launched a fatal blow into a bright blue-eyed underling's chest.

Sixteen!

Venir was no longer a man, but now a savage animal. Hungry. Starving. Battling for survival. For supremacy!

He brought both axe-blades down hard on a helmeted underling's head, splitting its skull to the teeth. Wrenched his blades free.

Two underlings jumped on top of him, pinning down his arms.

Slice!

A curved blade lashed out across his leg.

Down he went with five underlings on top of him. He fought like a tiger. He fought like a beast. He lost his blades. Something hard, heavy, struck his head. He could not feel. His vision blurred. He swallowed blood. He spit blood. He saw blood.

Small blades rose and fell.

He was going to die. He was certain. He booted one in the nose.

"Remember," he said. "I killed a thousand of you, and you only killed one of me!"

Crack! Stab Slash!

Venir didn't feel a thing. *Fight and die.* Everything faded. Fuzzy. Black.

Chop! Chop! Chop!

What was that?

Something was stuffed in his mouth. He tried to spit it out.

"Chew!" the Blood Ranger ordered. The Black Beards, the two that were left, kneeled along his side, beards dripping wet.

It hurt to swallow, but he did. Then he glanced at his burning belly. It was open, in more places than one.

"Got any Elga bugs?" Venir looked over a Black Beard's shoulder. "Say, what happened to that underling?"

The stone wall was back. A breathing underling was stuck inside it.

Eethum tore a piece of string off his sleeve with his teeth, threaded a fine needle, and started sewing Venir's belly up.

"Hold on," Venir said to Eethum.

Rising to his feet and holding his innards in, Venir limped over, grimacing, and jammed his axe in the trapped underling's head. Sat and lay down again.

"Here," Fogle said, holding a canteen to his lips. "Drink."

Venir pushed it away. "I'm not an infant, and I'll have no part of a bearded nanny."

Boon forced himself up into sitting position and put his throbbing head between his knees.

"Did you get him?" Boon said, holding his stomach.

"One of them," Fogle said, holding Catten's head up by the hair.

Boon blanched.

"You cut his head off! With a sword!"

Fogle smiled. "Eathum did. With an axe as big as my head."

"Well, that's a big axe alright, but," Boon paused, "the other one, Silver Eye?"

"Haven't gotten him yet."

Boon sighed. "How much have you got left?"

"About as much as you, I'd guess."

Boon rubbed his forehead and held his trembling hand out. The fire was back in his eyes. "Give me that spellbook."

Chapter 73

JOTTENHIEM YANKED ON THE WHIP, jerking Creed from his feet and slinging him across the room into the hard wall behind a tapestry.

Creed felt every bit of it.

Wupash!

The dark purple light of the mystic whip ripped the skin from his arm.

Wupash!

It coiled around his other arm, burning like fire. Jottenhiem pulled him across the floor.

Creed screamed. The pain was maddening. It shocked every inch of his body.

"Let me eatss him!" The imp said, wringing its taloned hands and gnashing its over-sized jaws. They opened so wide, Creed could see his entire body fitting inside the imp's mouth.

He grabbed at the whip and cried out.

Jottenhiem slung him into another wall.

Wupash!

He cracked the whip into Creed's blood-seared back again and again.

Wupash!

The whip coiled around his neck with only The Cowl protecting him.

"Go ahead, Imp," Jottenhiem said, flashing his sharp teeth, "I'll hold him still. You eat."

Eep smacked his thin lips and slowly buzzed over.

Creed tried to scream, but he couldn't. All he could do was scream in his mind.

NOOOOO!

Rage mixed with helplessness. The urgings from his cowl now shrouded by the pain. Creed outstretched his arms and flexed his fingers.

I'm not going to die like this!

The imp was fifteen feet away. Ten. Five.

No! Not like this! Where are my swords?

Two sharp objects shot across the room into his hands.

My blades!

Eep paused and blinked.

Creed sunk one blade through its eye before the lid could open.

Slice!

He cut the whip away. The imp twitched and howled, sporadically flying all around.

Slice! Slice!

He clipped one buzzing wing, then the other.

Blink! The imp vanished.

Creed took a deep breath. *That was close.* His arms were shredded. He dripped blood. He hobbled when he moved. He wanted to rest. Heal.

The Cowl wouldn't allow it.

Suck it up, Creed.

Jottenhiem tossed the broken whip away and came running with his swords. They collided at the center of the room, sword hilts locked together. Shoving back and forth, Jottenhiem held his ground. The underling, though smaller, was far stronger than he looked.

Jottenhiem cracked Creed in the jaw with his head, bringing painful spots and slicing right at him.

Clang!

He deflected a blow.

Clang!

Then another.

Jottenhiem sneered, reversed his grips, and came after him slicing, stabbing and spinning. The bald underling was almost as fast as Kierway, but a different skill of fighter. Hours ago, Jottenhiem would have been far better, but that was hours ago. Much had changed in the past few hours.

Creed whipped his blades under Jottenhiem's nose in a flurry.

"Smell that, Underling?"

Jottenhiem's lips twisted.

"Smells of death, doesn't it?"

The underling tore into him. Blades clashed. Showers of sparks went everywhere. Creed felt his hatred growing. His skill increasing. The battle led out of the Throne Room and into another.

Clip! Slit! Clip!

Jottenhiem bled from three separate wounds.

Slit! Clip! Slit!

One ear dangled, and an X on Jottenhiem's forehead dripped blood into his eyes. He broke off.

"Thinking about running, aren't you, Underling?" Creed shrugged, gasping. "But there's no honor in being a coward, is there? Come on, then." He waved him over. "At least you don't have a whip around your throat."

Something propelled him forward, attacking the underling with unrelenting fury.

Bang! Bang! Bang!

Jottenhiem's corded arms started to give, snapping back up slower and slower. It was fatal.

"Enough of this!"

Creed ripped at Jottenhiem with all his might, tearing one sword from his hand.

Jottenhiem gasped.

Flash!

Creed tore the other one out.

Jottenhiem's ruby red eyes were full of hatred. Anguish.

He shook his head, took a knee and bowed.

Creed's next stroke was lights out.

"No!" Verbard moaned. "No!" His silver eyes darted around. Looking for a ghost.

Clutching Melegal with both hands now, the underling's silver eyes filled with anger and dismay. Whatever happened had been bad for the underling. Whenever bad things happen to underlings, worse things happen to people.

Melegal clutched at the underling's wrists and tried to kick at its guts.

Let go!

The ring from Sefron's chamber glimmered on Melegal's finger, and a charge of energy coursed through him.

Zzzzt!

Verbard's brows lifted. His face contorted. His jaw dropped open. "Argh!" The underling yelled, releasing Melegal and clutching his head.

Coughing, Melegal hit the floor, legs moving towards Lorda. The woman had sat up and was rubbing her head, blinking. "Get up, Lorda. Head for that door!" He glanced back.

Verbard spun in the air, shaking his head, arms coiling with mystic energy.

Here it comes!

Zzzzram!

Tendrils of lightning leapt from Verbard's finger, striking Melegal full in the back.

He skittered across the floor, reeling in pain, mouth tasting like metal and stone. Teeth screaming. He couldn't move, but he twitched, fingers curled, stomach knotting, his nose filling with the stench of his seared skin and hair.

Verbard floated over, gloating, and raised his arms.

This is it, Melegal. He found Lorda's eyes once more and mouthed the words, *So long.*

She reached for him.

Melegal crossed is arms over his face.

Zzzzram!

Boom!

Creed didn't stop with Jottenhiem. He didn't stop with the imp. He kept going. Limping. Hunting. Sliding from one room to another like a shadow, he slaughtered every underling he honed in on.

I know where you are.

Most of them didn't see him coming. For those who did, it was too late. One dead underling became two. Two became four. Four became eight. It was a glorious thing.

Melegal's shaking slender fingers patted over his body. *I'm still intact!* He wasn't alone either.

Two robed men stood in front of him, coated with transparent swords and shields. One's hair was long white and wispy, the other looked like he'd just crawled out of the woods. They were accompanied by a blood-bearded giant dwarf and two smaller black beards.

Melegal didn't stick around to thank them. Instead, he scooped Lorda up and headed for the door.

"Heh…" he breathed, stretching his aching fingers into his clothes and grabbing one of three Keys he'd pilfered from the underling Verbard's robes. He shoved the Key in the nearest door and turned. The door opened. "Let's get out of here. Shall we?" He'd hesitated, starting to turn back, when the room shook in its entirety. Shards of marble careened through the air.

A powerful figure shoved him inside and closed the door behind them. His mind and body started to spin. *Creed!*

Chapter 74

"You first," Boon said after opening up a black dimension door.

Fogle gave him a look.

"I cast the spell, and I'm your elder. If it makes you feel any better, take the dwarves with you."

Fogle summoned his power, coating his body in a transparent layer of blue energy and a shield. Armor, mystical or not, wasn't something he was at all accustomed to. As a matter of fact, he'd never worn so much as a bracer before.

"Let's go," he said to Eethum.

Holding his stomach, Venir said, "I'll go too."

"No, we'll need you to pull us out if things go wrong," Boon said, handing him the end of a rope tied to his waist. "If you hear us scream, tug it."

"Let the dwarf tug it," Venir growled. "I'm going in… oof!" Clutching his stomach he took a knee.

"Go, Fogle," Boon said, "I'll be right behind."

Stepping through, they found themselves in the Throne Room facing the back of a robed underling that hovered over a man and woman he did not recognize.

Fogle flicked a green missile into its back. *Zip!*

The underling's arms sprawled out.

Zzzzram!

Boom!

The underling's energy, meant for the man and woman, shot up into the ceiling.

Eethum and the Black Beards charged.

The underling, Verbard, whirled around, silver eyes flashing. With a wave of his hand, he knocked the dwarves around the room, slamming them into the wall.

"Let him have it, Grandson!" Boon yelled, energy erupting from his hands.

A bolt of power slammed into the underling's chest and dissipated. Fogle fired his own charge, which careened towards the underling and disappeared into the underling's robes.

The underling reached into his robes and pulled out a glowing orb of power.

Fogle started to fire again, but Boon stayed his hand.

"This is not good for us."

Verbard laughed.

A burst of energy blinded them.

Fogle heard his grandfather scream.

Facing the black doorway, Venir tugged at the rope. Nothing happened.

"I better get in there," he said, staggering towards the black door.

Srrit!

It disappeared.

"Slat!" He rubbed the back of his head. "Stupid mages! I knew I should have gone with them."

He could see it now, the two of them fighting the underling mage with the silver eyes. He knew it was him. They had said so. Now, he was trapped inside the blood hungry chamber with nowhere to go.

Fogle's wall of stone cracked again.

Venir picked up Mood's axes.

"It's just you and me, underlings."

Creak…

Behind him, one of the six doors opened.

Venir's jaw dropped.

Out came Melegal, whose eyes were as wide as his.

"Vee?"

"Me?"

"I knew you were behind all this!" Melegal said.

"Uh!"

A beautiful black-haired woman was shoved to the floor behind Melegal. The skinny thief jumped away and whirled.

"Creed, what are you doing?" Melegal said, backing away.

A tall rangy form stepped from beyond the threshold. He pointed a gleaming sword at Melegal's scrawny chest with one hand and held a jug of wine with the other.

Venir wiped the sweat and red grime from his eyes with his forearm and locked eyes with the man he'd all but forgotten about months ago.

"Tonio!"

"Vee-Man!"

Nullified.

That's what happened to the plan.

Boon had planned on overwhelming Verbard with his grandson, spell after spell, while the dwarves wove in and out, attacking. It might have worked if it weren't for something Boon hadn't foreseen. The Orb of Imbibing.

"Defend yourself, Fogle!"

Zzzram!

Zzzram!

Verbard launched one blast into them after the other, shattering their mystic armor and skipping them across the floor.

Boon tried to summon the dimension door again, but could not.

Verbard pressed the assault. Not letting him get a word out. The underling hovered over them now, draining their powers.

"Which one of you killed my brother?"

"I did," Boon lied, "and it was quite satisfying. Like a tender piece of veal cooked just right." Boon licked his lips. "The death of underlings is an excellent dessert."

One Black Beard had been crushed inside his armor. The other was out cold. Eethum lay on the floor bound up by yellow magic cords. Fogle's grandfather was a horrible negotiator.

Be silent, Fogle wanted to say, but his tongue was made of wool. Fogle had thought he was ready for anything by now, but he wasn't ready to not be able to use magic.

He gazed at the orb that pulsated in Verbard's hand like a beating heart. *Bish is just one excruciating surprise after another.* He tried to lock minds with Verbard.

"You dare!" the underling Lord hissed, squeezing his telekinetic fingers around his neck. Fogle was choking. Beside him, Boon clutched at the invisible fingers wrapped around his own neck, face turning purple. Verbard was getting stronger as he got weaker. There was nothing, nothing at all he could do. Was there? Searching the deepest recesses of his mind, he had to find the answer. He had to find the key. He heard his neck crack. Or was it Boon's?

"Finally," Tonio said, shattering his wine jug against the wall, "I'll have your head."

Shoulders lowered, axes bared, Venir charged in. "No! I'll have yours!"

Krang!

Tonio's gleaming sword tore Venir's axe from his wrist. The half-dead man was powerful and fast.

Venir ducked under a decapitating cut and tore a gash across Tonio's belly.

Tonio laughed. "You already killed me, Vee-man! You can't kill me again. Sorry yet?"

Whack!

Venir cut across his leg, but Tonio countered, punching Venir's bullish form in the face, cracking his nose open. Spitting blood from his mouth, Venir squared off again, shoulders dipping, belly aching. Whatever Tonio was, it wasn't mortal.

"I've been searching for you a long time, Vee-Man." He ran his fingers down his gash. "I'm going to split you in half as well. Show you how bad it feels. You ruined my life. You ruined everything!"

Venir forced a laugh at him. "Especially your face!"

Tonio grunted and stuck his sword into the stone. "Come on then," he said, walking over, "see what you can do with that little axe of yours."

"I'll be glad to show you, Tonio!"

Slic—

Tonio caught his arms and wrenched the axe free from Venir's hands.

Venir dug in, punching at the monster's ribs with his hardened fists.

Tonio didn't feel a thing.

Whop! Whop!

Venir's head snapped back. His knees buckled.

Melegal had seen Venir brawl with anything from underlings to half-ogres, but he'd never seen him fight something that couldn't be hurt or broken.

Tonio's speed and strength were Venir's match. Toe to toe, blow for blow, they fought and wrestled over the mosaic floor.

Come on, Vee!

Venir hammered away, an angry juggernaut, but his strength was fading.

A lightning fast strike caught Venir in the chin, wobbling him.

"Your head is mine, Vee-Man!"

Tonio wrapped his arms around Venir's head and squeezed. It turned red, then purple, his blazing blue eyes rolling up.

Move, Melegal!

Fogle thought of Cass. Dying, he still found himself angry with her for abandoning him—for a dragon of all things—and now, leagues from his home that smelled of flowers and sweet wine, he was going to die.

Verbard's fading face was gloating from above, sneering at him and his grandfather.

"I'm disappointed. I thought the pair of you would have more power that I could store in my orb. But the power I have should be enough to bring my brother back, once more, if I must."

Glitch!

A dark bloody sword burst into Verbard's chest and disappeared.

Glitch!

Another blade followed. In and out.

"No," Verbard said, incredulous, turning on his captor. "Where did you come from?"

The man in the cowl with the glowing eyes stood tall, swords held in his thick wrists.

"Are you The Darkslayer?" Verbard said, splitting up blood and sagging to the floor.

Creed swung both swords at once.

Slice!

Verbard's head slid from his shoulders.

"I guess I am, Underling."

Fogle clutched at his chest, gasping.

Boon was doing the same. The old man, coughing, reached over and grabbed the Orb of Imbibing.

"Grab my hand, Fogle, so I can restore you. Quickly!"

Melegal whipped out the Sisters and struck Tonio in the back of the knee, tearing out tendon and flesh.

"What? You skinny flea!" Tonio teetered, losing his balance.

Venir bull rushed the man onto the floor and started to 'ground and pound' him, one blow after the other.

Tonio swatted the blows off and clutched at Venir's throat.

Stab!

Melegal pinned one of his swords through Tonio's shoulder.

Tonio caught him by the ankle and jerked him down.

Melegal tried to twist away from Tonio's grasp.

Snap.

His ankle cracked.

"You break like a twig!"

Venir was drunk with battle. He punched, kicked and clawed, almost oblivious to his opponent, but the arrogant tone in Tonio's voice kept him going.

"Ahhh!"

Melegal, his best friend and confident, cried out.

Tonio had the man's leg and still hung onto Venir's throat, holding them both in his vise-like grip.

Venir's instincts took over. He fumbled for a weapon. Found his long knife strapped to his leg. With both hands, he raised it over his head and drove it straight into Tonio's heart.

Crunch!

"That won't work, Vee-Man!" Tonio said. His grip was getting stronger. "I have no heart!"

Venir twisted the knife inside Tonio's chest.

Tonio's eyes widened. "Urk!"

Tonio's body shuddered.

"Grab an axe, Melegal!" Venir said, wrapping his arms around the monster, holding him to the ground.

Melegal hopped over towards the axe. "And do what?"

"Chop his head off!"

Melegal caught something in the corner of his eye.

I have a better idea.

Tonio slung Venir off and ripped the knife from his chest. "You already killed me! I'll make you sorry!"

Venir, huffing for breath, was too slow.

Tonio closed in, stabbing at him.

Melegal! What are you doing!

The thief was fooling with the underling on the blood-sucking floor.

Venir tried to dodge. Tried to block.

Glitch!

His own hunting knife caught him in the leg.

Twisting away, Tonio ripped a hunk out of Venir's back.

Slash!

Getting cut to pieces but still standing on his feet, Venir watched Tonio's final blow start down. The monster's split face had a cruel smile on it. "Time to die, Vee-Man."

Tonio stopped, not moving a muscle, the bloody blade no longer coming down, a surprised look on his face.

"Venir," Melegal yelled, "catch!" The thief tossed him Mood's axe. "Be quick about it!"

Venir snatched it out of the air and whirled full force into Tonio's neck.

Slice!

Tonio's head bounced off the floor and rolled. His big body collapsed on the ground.

Venir collapsed as well. He snorted for air. Tried to shake the spots from his eyes. He reached over and pulled his knife from Tonio's grip.

"I knew I should have killed that Royal brat in the first place."

Pinching his nose, Melegal adjusted the dark cap on his head with the other hand, admiring Tonio's' corpse. He wiped the blood that dripped from his nose. *That was close.*

On the floor, Venir looked as bad as he'd ever seen him. It tugged at his heart a little. *Big lout.*

He helped Venir back to his feet.

"You know, you should have listened to me—"

"Don't start, Me."

CHAPTER 75

"So we all agree then," Boon said, standing in the alcove, eyeing the Keys on the pegs. They were all there except one, which Melegal believed Jarla had.

Fogle didn't care much either way. The only thing that mattered was that the underlings didn't have the Keys. He looked back over at the Stone Wall he'd produced. It was still holding. Behind it were—he had no idea how many underlings.

The party all knew now that despite their victory today, the underlings were penetrating the City. The battle for Bone had just begun.

"Shouldn't we destroy the Keys and the chamber?" Fogle suggested.

Boon rubbed his brow. "That's up to you, Fogle. Take a Key and do with it what you like, but remember, it always leads back here. And as I understand it, the room is here now, but it might be elsewhere later."

"You mean it moves?" Melegal said, leaning against the wall, arms folded across his chest.

"That's how I understand it. But, I could be wrong. It might just stay here forever."

"And the big Key," Melegal said, eyeing the Key on the center peg, "who gets that? Does it work all the doors? Or just one?"

"I don't think we have time for that now," Boon said, twisting his beard. "The goal is to get the Keys out of the chamber and away from the underlings. Once we are free of this, you can do what you wish. Keep them or destroy them."

"Will you destroy yours?" Melegal said.

"Well, er," Boon added, "that's my concern. I think it might come in handy if I get stuck back in the Under-Bish." He looked at Venir. "It could increase our chance of freeing Mood from down there."

Melegal had already told them what his Key did. It would take him wherever he wanted to go, but it always led back to the chamber, where he would have to start all over again. Certainly the underlings would soon have a heavy guard on the chamber. He looked at Venir.

"What do you think?"

"Let's take them to the furnace and destroy them." Venir nodded over at the bodies of Tonio, Catten and Verbard. The underlings were eyeless now. "Or," he said, eyeing the sack that hung over Creed's shoulder, "we can drop them in there?"

"Hmmm…" Boon rubbed his chin. "I have another idea. Creed, would you oblige me and open the sack?"

Creed, cowl down, tossed the sack over to Boon. "Open it yourself."

Boon's eyes widened.

So did Venir's.

"Fogle, let me have the staff."

Taking it out of his backpack, Fogle tossed the staff to Boon, who dropped it into the sack.

"What did you do that for?" Creed said.

Boon stuck his arm inside, down to the elbow, and withdrew nothing.

"Care to try?" Boon held the sack out to Venir.

He took a breath and a step forward. He longed to have the armament back, but he longed for his own freedom too. "I'll pass."

Boon handed the sack back to Creed. "Try not to get too used to it, whoever you are."

Creed couldn't keep his gaze off Venir. The big man looked like he'd been chewed up by a dragon and spit out, but was used to it. Still, the dark circles under the man's bright eyes concerned him. He had the look of a man who'd faced every horror and form of death hundreds of times. He was elemental. Forged in iron.

"So, you used to have this?" Creed said as the others squabbled over the Keys.

"Aye, but it was different, as different as you and me."

"You like women?" Creed said, his voice deep and rugged.

Venir eyed him.

"You like wine?"

"Grog."

"You like fighting?"

"You just described every soldier in Bish."

"We're not so different, you and I."

Venir turned and faced him. Looked him up and down.

"I don't think so."

Creed, bigger than most men, felt small in that moment.

"Maybe one day we'll share our tales together," Creed said, smiling at Lorda. "Chat with some ladies. Share some wine … er … grog."

"No doubt you'll be hearing tales about me," Venir looked down at him, patting his shoulder. "That much is certain." Venir coughed a laugh. "And you'll need more than a goblet of wine to deal with that mantle."

Creed nodded, extending his hand. Venir took it in his. Hard as a rock. Like a vice. Creed grimaced a little.

"We've come to a decision," Boon said, snagging the Keys from the pegs. Keeping the big one for himself, he handed Keys to Eethum, Melegal, Fogle, Venir, Creed and Lorda. "Just give us a few minutes."

Fogle sat down and started reading from the spellbook while Boon held the glowing Orb of Imbibing in his hand. It pulsated with mystic life.

Minutes later, Boon said, "We're ready."

Fogle said, "Melegal, lead the way."

"Where are we going, Me?" Venir said.

"The furnace."

Venir walked over and pulled Tonio's shriveled head up off the sucking floor. "Good idea. We better burn this."

Melegal opened the door with the Key he was accustomed to.

"Everybody inside," Boon said.

One by one they entered, leaving the throbbing orb behind.

"And what is that for?" Eethum asked, pulling the door closed.

"It should destroy the chamber," Fogle answered.

"And possibly the castle," Boon added.

Lorda gasped as the door closed.

The stone wall Fogle Bone had created finally evaporated, to the glee of a stairwell full of underlings. Each of them watched the orb spinning in the room, getting bigger and bigger and bigger. Spinning faster, it started to whine and crackle. The underlings' gem-speckled eyes flittered back and forth at one another, gaping in confusion.

Finally, one said in underling, "Flee!"

Lord Almen was tattooed with long bolts sticking out of his legs and chest by the dozen. He kissed his mystic ring. The assault on him had stopped, and he crawled over to the door on top of the keep. Shaking and bleeding, he pulled it open.

I'll live! I'll avenge!

KA-BOOM!

The entire keep shook and then collapsed. Lord Almen fell through the roof that opened up, landing at the bottom in time to watch the rest of the keep collapse on top of him.

One by one, they tossed their Keys into the furnaces that fired beneath the busy streets of Bone. Hot and fiery flames reflected all over their shadow-cast and oily faces.

Boon pitched two pair of underling eyes in as well. One pair silver, the other pair gold.

Venir took one last look at Tonio's face, his mind eating at him. Had one isolated incident been the start of it all? What would have happened if he never fought Tonio to begin with?

"You aren't thinking, are you?" Melegal said.

Tonio's grey eyes popped open.

"Vee-Man!"

Lorda jumped, but the others remained still. "Tonio," she said, extending her hand and touching her son's face. An odd silence fell.

"Mother," Tonio said, black eyes returning to normal.

"Good-bye, Son," she sobbed, turning to walk away.

"But Mother," he said. His eyes turned black. Brows buckled. Lips curled. "You can't kill me, Vee-Man."

Venir held Tonio's head out over the vat of fire. "Maybe you can't be killed, but I bet you'll burn, Brat." He pitched him over the rim.

"Noooooooooo!"

"The city holds for now," Corrin said, taking a good look at the present company. "The Royals finally got off their arses and stirred a fight. I think the collapse of Castle Almen lit a fire under them."

Lorda Almen was crying on the bench by the fountain.

Melegal caressed her head. The woman had lost her home. Her entire family. He felt bad.

"Where to now, Melegal?" Venir said, drinking from the fountain. "You want to stay and fight, or do you want to go? You should have left for the City of Three last time, you know."

"Just a moment," Melegal said in Lorda's ear, releasing her petal-soft hands.

He limped his way over to Venir.

"Itching to see your family are you, Vee?" he said, smiling.

Venir stopped drinking and said, "What family?"

Splash! Splash! Splash! "Help!" Lorda Almen sounded like she was drowning. "Detective!" *Splash!* "Help!"

Turning, he saw Haze had Lorda's head stuffed down in the water. He hobbled over. Pulled her away.

Haze ripped a long blade across Melegal's chest.

"Are you mad?" he exclaimed, twisting the dagger from her hand.

She slapped his face. "I'm a one-man woman, and you're a one-woman man. Got that?"

He snickered. "Absolutely, my Lorda."

"Good," Haze said, "and I want to go to the City of Three. You promised me."

"No, I did—"

She glared at him.

"I suppose I did."

Corrin then said, "You aren't going anywhere. The city's under siege out there."

"You ever been out of the city before, Corrin?"

"No."

"You want to leave?"

"No, I'm going to stay and fight."

Creed stepped alongside Corrin. "This is where I'll be, as well."

"This is where you're supposed to be," Venir said.

"And what about me?" Lorda said, slinging her dripping wet hair over her shoulder.

Creed put his arm around her. "You're coming with me. The Bloodhounds can always use another queen."

The wizards approached.

"Get all the gear you can handle, men," Boon said. And then he noticed Haze's glare, "and woman. The underlings aren't going to let us congregate here forever. I can teleport you miles from the city, but you're on your own after that."

"I said I would never leave Bone again," Melegal said, shaking his head. "And I'm still certain you're the root cause of all this, Venir."

Limping towards the black dimension doors, Venir said, "Well, at least you have someone to blame. And what family are you talking about?"

Somewhere far away, the Elga bugs came. Slim's body went.

Master Sinway waited on his throne. Catten, Verbard and Kierway never arrived. He petted one of the Cave Dogs at his side and said, "This isn't over. It's just begun."

EPILOGUE

Brak's oversized body held tight on the reins of Quickster as they rode into the City of Three. The poison had passed. He lived, but was far from back to himself again yet.

"Don't worry, Brak. We're almost there. We can get you a bed, healing and a comfortable room. And the stew you'll eat! As soon as you smell it, your mouth will water," Georgio said.

Georgio had been nicer to him since he almost died. But that probably had more to do with the City of Three than actual concern.

He wiped from his face the mist that blew in from the massive waterfalls he could see in the distance.

"Isn't that beautiful, Brak!" Jubilee said. "I've never even imagined anything like it. Billip, can we go there?"

"Yes," Nikkel said, "can we go there?"

"Soon enough. But I'm getting a gullet full at the Magi Roost first!" Billip said, smiling underneath the grit and sand that covered his face.

"I'm filling both my gullets!" Georgio said.

"You don't even know what a gullet is," Nikkel said, laughing.

"I do too."

"What is it, then?" Jubilee said.

"Uh… it's your belly."

Jubilee and Nikkel looked at each other and laughed.

"Isn't it?"

Everyone's mood lightened when they saw the city. Even Brak, who still felt as feeble as a kitten, felt better for it. He looked once up and down at the tall towers whose spires seemed to reach the clouds, but he wasn't impressed. He just wanted to rest. He was wondering about his father, Venir. He hadn't had any dreams about him lately. *Maybe he's dead.*

"This is it," Billip said, stopping in front of a building where a sign hung that read in bright letters, **THE MAGI ROOST.** Billip started dusting himself off. "Joline will kill me for going in there like this."

Georgio took off his boots, poured the rocks out and banged them together. He took a deep draw through his nose. "I can taste the stew already." He sniffed again and made a funny face. "And something else."

One at a time, Billip leading the way, they entered.

"Welcome, Travelers," a tall husky woman said. "Have a seat, and I'll get you some help."

Brak saw Billip and Georgio's hands fall to their sword belts.

"Just who in Bish are you?" Billip said, "And what have you done to this tavern?"

The Magi Roost was darker and filled with a seedier sort of characters. All the long robes and noses were gone. The smell of cheap wine and ale was in the air.

"And how did such an unattractive woman get in here? Where's Kam?" Billip demanded.

"Oh," the woman leaned over Billip with her hands on her hips. "You're one of her friends, are you?"

"Billip!"

It was Joline. She ran up and threw her arms around him, tears streaming down her face. "You're alive. I'm so glad you're alive." She kissed his cheek, then whispered in his ear. "But you need to get out of here."

"Joline!" a man sitting the bar said in a warning tone.

Billip gawped at him. He'd never seen such presence in a man before. Handsome, refined, distinguished, with eyes as blue as water.

"Don't dally with Darlene's patrons. She's likes to welcome them."

"I'm hungry, Joline," Georgio said, patting Joline on the back.

She shook her head. "You've changed so much, Georgio. You're a full grown man."

"Ah, I haven't been gone that long. Where's Kam?"

"Just grab a table," Joline said, "I'll get her."

"Mercy!" Darlene bellowed, "Get these folks a table!"

Mercy scampered over, chin down, and led them to their table.

"How have you been, Mercy?" Georgio said, hitching his arm over his chair and smiling.

"Georgio?" She seemed to wake up from a daze. "Georgio!" She sat down on his lap and hugged him. "I thought you'd never come back!" She whispered in his ear. "Just stay away from them." Her eyes flittered towards the woman Darlene and the man at the bar.

"Who is that?" he said. "I can handle him."

"No, no," she said, grabbing him by the collar. "Just leave them be, and they'll leave you be." She hopped off his lap. "I'll get you stew, to start." She eyed all of them. "And a big bowl for you, Georgio." She saw Brak. "And one for your friend, too." She patted Billip on the head. "I'm so glad you're back. So glad!"

"There's something spooky going on here," Billip said. "I don't recognize any of these people."

"Seems alright to me," Jubilee said, looking around. "Say, who's the beautiful lady with only one hand up there? That's kinda sad."

"What? There's no one in here with one hand," Georgio said, looking around. "Kam!"

She stood on the balcony in a long green dress, sunken eyed and waving her one-handed arm.

"Do you know her?" Jubilee said.

Billip said in disbelief, "What in Bish is going on here?"

FROM THE AUTHOR

Unfortunately, the ending is never as much fun as the journey.

As for this first series, there is more, I decided to wrap it up with this 6th book. It was time. I think readers wanted some resolution. That's what made it so difficult. I had a bunch of characters spread out all over Bish. That said, I didn't want to end it. Originally, I wanted this to be an ongoing saga, but I spread myself too thin and my writing was suffering for it. This first segment of Venir's life ends. But it feels good for me, finishing a full-length fantasy series.

Fear not, Darkslayer fans, the adventures of The Darkslayer continues in the *Bish and Bone* series. Venir and Melegal's escapades are not over, if anything, it's just beginning, so hang in there. But I'm not spoiling things.

Next. THANK YOU! It has been my pleasure writing for you! Your support is a dream come true to me. My goal is to improve and write even better stories for you, but don't hold me to that. That way you won't be disappointed. ;)

So, will Venir and Brool be reunited? What do you think? But there is only one way to know for sure. Check out the next series, *Bish and Bone*. The first book is free and there are already 5 books out in it as of January 2016.

Again, check in with me at The Darkslayer Report by Craig on Facebook. I want to hear what you thought of this series. And if you have time, I'd appreciate a sincere review.

Fight or Die,
Craig Halloran

About the Author

Craig Halloran resides with his family outside his hometown of Charleston, West Virginia. When he isn't entertaining mankind, he is seeking adventure, working out, or watching sports. To learn more about him, go to: www.thedarkslayer.com.

Check out all of my great stories ...

CLASH OF HEROES: Nath Dragon meets The Darkslayer

The Darkslayer Series 1
Wrath of the Royals (Book 1) Free eBook
Blades in the Night (Book 2)
Underling Revenge (Book 3)
Danger and the Druid (Book 4)
Outrage in the Outlands (Book 5)
Chaos at the Castle (Book 6)

The Darkslayer: Bish and Bone, Series 2
Bish and Bone (Book 1) Free eBook
Black Blood (Book 2)
Red Death (Book 3)
Lethal Liaisons (Book 4)
Torment and Terror (Book 5)

The Chronicles of Dragon Series
The Hero, the Sword and the Dragons (Book 1) Free eBook
Dragon Bones and Tombstones (Book 2)
Terror at the Temple (Book 3)
Clutch of the Cleric (Book 4)
Hunt for the Hero (Book 5)
Siege at the Settlements (Book 6)
Strife in the Sky (Book 7)
Fight and the Fury (Book 8)
War in the Winds (Book 9)
Finale (Book 10)

The Chronicles of Dragon: Series 2, Tail of the Dragon
Tail of the Dragon
Claws of the Dragon
Eye of the Dragon
Scales of the Dragon
Trial of the Dragon
Teeth of the Dragon

The Supernatural Bounty Hunter Files
Smoke Rising (2015) Free ebook
I Smell Smoke (2015)
Where There's Smoke (2015)
Smoke on the Water (2015)
Smoke and Mirrors (2015)
Up in Smoke
Smoke Em'
Holy Smoke
Smoke Out

Zombie Impact Series
Zombie Day Care: Book 1 Free eBook
Zombie Rehab: Book 2
Zombie Warfare: Book 3

You can learn more about the Darkslayer and my other books deals and specials at:
Facebook – The Darkslayer Report by Craig
Twitter – Craig Halloran
www.craighalloran.com

63497981R00397

Made in the USA
San Bernardino, CA
19 December 2017